About the Author

Val Sheppard had never written a poem or even a shopping list prior to her debut novel *Is Anyone Listening?*

The youngest daughter in a family of eight children, Val was raised in Wiltshire, the county struggling for recognition between the glorious Cotswolds and the cheeriness of Somerset.

Married for twenty-five years to Dave and proud to be a grandmother of five and beloved auntie to so many that she has stopped counting. Val works full-time as a PA, enjoys racquet sports, swimming and watching ice hockey in her spare time. She loves to be in a warm climate so is thankful to have friends who live in the Canary Islands.

Dedication

This book is dedicated to all those who encouraged me to send the manuscript off – those who dared and challenged me when I doubted myself.

To Dabe, always by my side when I need him, thank you for believing in me. UFFOO TY
To my darling Rikkik and my wonderful sister Cheeky, for being the first, thank you for being open and honest with me about the book, the characters, what you loved and hated about the story right from page one.
For Mama, for reading it once, then again and again for spotting mistakes, for whom criticism comes naturally, but this time it was constructive, thank you.
For my darling Marie-Claude, for saying it was better than DS.
To Jenny, whose regular text message updates made me laugh out loud.
To Barb, for giving me the sunshine and time alone to just get on with it.
For J for your help and advice.
For my oldest friends who never tired of listening to me going on and on, or if you did, you never let me know. Thank you for looking after me in New York.
To everyone I have the pleasure of being "Aunty Val" to.
And finally to my lunch friends, laughing over coffee with you lifted my spirits enormously, you know who you are.

Is Anyone Listening is dedicated to Joey. With love always xx

Valerie Sheppard

IS ANYONE LISTENING?

AUSTIN MACAULEY
PUBLISHERS LTD.

A CIP catalogue record for this title is available from the British Library.

ISBN 9781785540936 (Paperback)
ISBN 9781785540943 (Hardback)
ISBN 9781785540950 (E-Book)

www.austinmacauley.com

First Published (2016)
Austin Macauley Publishers Ltd.
25 Canada Square
Canary Wharf
London
E14 5LQ

Have you ever found yourself in a situation, where it seems you are the outsider looking in, like you are in a bubble, where all those around you are smiling cheerfully and laughing and no one is aware that you are screaming out for help?

It is almost like you are in a really well insulated soundproof bubble, pounding your fists against the walls of the bubble, screaming so loud your throat is raw, but it is hopeless, no one, it seems, can hear you. There is a man stood in front of you, he is wearing a suit and he is asking "Does anyone know of any lawful impediment?" and you know what is coming next, you know what is about to happen, but you are powerless to stop him, you want to scream, "YES, ME, I KNOW OF A LAWFUL IMPEDIMENT," you can hear your own voice screaming in your head, you look around – there is your family, the people you love, all stood smiling, mum looking very elegant in her lilac suit complete with matching hat and shoes, your dad is looking all proud, his chest puffed out like a penguin and looking ridiculous in a cravat of all things, I mean who wears cravats now, I didn't even know he owned one, but there he is all happy and smiling too, everyone is smiling and nodding, the nightmare goes on.

I look around but the faces are a blur as the man continues speaking, his voice monotone, but as I look up, even he is smiling now, "Will you take this man…" he continues, and you hear a voice coming from your head saying I do, the words come out like a whisper, but it is not you that replies, it was as if the voice was far away, watching from a distance, I want to wake up, I need to wake up, I need to stop this, is this a bad dream? Has the sheet fallen over my head like a veil, please, I send out a scream but it seems no one hears, I am desperately trying to shake myself awake, please oh please I want to wake up…, but this is no bad dream, the scene in front of me is very real, so very real.

Have you ever found yourself in that situation? Do you know what I mean? Do you understand what I am saying? Because that is exactly what happened to me…

So how did I get myself into this position? where a surprise weekend away planned for me by my soon to be ex-partner Jason will give me the opportunity to actually sit down and talk about us, and for me to finally end a boringly painful and predictable relationship, a relationship I know he is happy to continue with, where our small circle of friends are not real friends at all, just seem like mutual acquaintances really, everyone seems to be one big happy family. Except I am not happy, not happy at all, I want changes in my life, I want to go back to being me, a single happy woman, so I have a plan, a huge plan to end the relationship. I found out about the weekend away by chance and have now hatched my escape from Jason and our predictable relationship, if all goes well I will be happily single by the end of the weekend.

So how has it ended up with me holding a small pink posy of flowers and wearing what appears to be, someone else's dress? Worse of all, it is an itchy, outdated, frumpy cream linen dress a size too big for me. I am wearing my favourite but impossibly high gold sandals, which means the dress is floating several inches above my ankles, and looks ridiculous, I am standing in a very old-fashioned, musty smelling room which has over-the-top wedding decorations: hearts and flowers are bad enough but peach and pink, it is like I have landed in a 1970 bad sitcom, everything is so old and unoriginal, there is piped music playing some sort of light concerto. I know that we are in a very posh hotel somewhere near the borders of Scotland and I am, it seems, exchanging vows with the man I do not want to spend another minute with, yet alone a lifetime.

Hi I am Angela Staddon, Angie to my friends, this is my story about what happens when you wish so hard for something, build it up in your head as something truly wonderful, then when you actually get it, you then find out you were not careful enough to be specific about what it was you actually wanted.

Chapter One

12 Months Previous

Sat in the pub garden with my two best friends, Ruth and Helen, sun streaming through the brolly, not a breath of wind to clear the humidity, just glorious sunshine, and a whole two days off, doing nothing in particular, what can be better than that?

One bottle of wine has already been consumed with a lovely light lunch another chilling in the cooler. Anyway, Helen had this great idea, some of her friends have their tarot cards read and were amazed at how correct the lady was, so this afternoon that is what we are doing, having our Tarot cards read, we are all pretty excited about it, all three of us are in great moods we are young free and single. Helen knows the woman, well she knows of her, she is a friend of a friend who reads the Tarot cards, *cards* that are used to predict your future happiness. Well okay, Ruth and I are sceptical but we thought, why not, it is a harmless bit of fun, so we agreed we would give it a go, it would be a laugh, who knows she might predict our future partners, and we can all meet the man of our dreams and have 2.4 children, have a picture perfect house with a picket fence, and our wonderful husbands would mow the lawn on Sundays and wash the car, we will be the perfect wife with our aprons on, gazing adoringly at our husbands and it will all be pretty and picture perfect, you know what I mean. I would be the envy of everyone as my husband would not be able to keep his hands off me. We laugh out loud as we describe our perfect lives.

Helen Judd is one of my best friends that I work with, we both work for the local constabulary, that is how we met; I am a controller in the main control room and she is an officer on the beat, so she is WPC Judd, we are both on different shifts so we get together as often as our shifts allow. Apparently big changes are happening at work but we have only heard this through the grapevine, there has been nothing definite, so at the moment, we are not worrying about it, we love our jobs we love our lives, we are single, life is perfect.

Helen is 27 years old, so a bit younger than me, she is 5ft 6 with striking long blonde hair and a body that makes men love her and women hate her, apart from her size 8 feet she is perfect. She has a lovely outgoing personality, a soft caring nature but for reasons unknown to both her and me, she is single. Oh, there is one chink in her perfection, she smokes, not a lot, but mainly when she is out socially. She has been in the force for two years now, I have been there just a few years more, after getting made redundant from my finance job. It seemed something I might enjoy, there were not that many opportunities in the town and I was so bored of reconciling spreadsheets for a living so for me it was a godsend. Helen and I clicked as soon as we met, she sat with me for some training and we didn't stop laughing, we have been friends ever since, we tell each other most things, we double date sometimes, but it seems she has dates but nothing ever comes from them.

I am 29 years old, 5ft 4, I like to think I have a good figure, I am not stick thin, a nice healthy size 12. My worst features are my dimply thighs and my best is my larger than average chest. I wouldn't say I am a beauty but I don't have two heads or anything off-putting. I just don't seem to go many places to meet guys, except for work and I have no interest in dating anyone from work, so it seems like unless it is with another couple and I am making up the numbers I never really date, not sure why, just too busy I guess, well not strictly true. I am kind of, well you know, okay what a crock, who am I kidding, with me it seems I am a date disaster, something always seems to go wrong. I don't know why but nothing goes simply for me and dates, there always seems to be a problem, like I always seem to be the guys confidante, the one he thinks it okay to spend the whole evening just offloading all his emotional crap about his current relationship, or he needs to sort out his previous relationship. I get to have one evening, maybe two but I never get to be the one who gets taken home to meet parents, actually I wouldn't even mind not meeting the parents but a third date might be nice, but it never happens, the date never develops into a relationship but there is never any real reason or explanation. Generally I get the old 'it's not you it's me', sometimes by text, or they say they are not looking for anything serious, well neither am I on the first date. Sometimes they try it on and I think it is all going well, like the last one, his name was Richard, we got on really well I thought, first date was good, second date we enjoyed a degree of intimacy, didn't go all the way, he told me all the things I guess he thought I wanted to hear, then the third date we went back to his house, cuddled up, got closer and I thought okay, time seems right to go a bit further, again not the whole way but pretty much, then immediately after things seemed strained between us then he came out with the emotional rubbish that he thought it was too soon after his last girlfriend and how he needs time. He left me feeling used, stupid and vulnerable, and on my own, again, several dates after that seemed to follow a pattern of them seeming really interested in me, then I find out they just want to chat to me to get to know Helen. Like I said I don't have two heads or any strange affliction, I guess I am a bit standoffish on first meeting but that is down to being a bit shy. Maybe I seem a bit desperate, a bit needy and I know this, I try hard not to be but deep down I long to be part of something – part of a couple, engaged, married, that is what I want, to be someone's wife. I watch other couples, that is what I want, to be married, I always think when I am at weddings or engagements, when it is going to be my turn to be a wife.

I suppose I had better explain about where my hang-up comes from with regards to relationships and men. In my teens I never really had much to do with boys and boyfriends, several reasons really – I had my friends and sport and never any time for anything else, then everything changed when I developed a huge schoolgirl crush on a boy but he was one year older and so in the other class, he was a bad boy, always in trouble – he smoked, hung around in a rowdy gang, wore a dirty old denim jacket and he seemed to spend most of his time in detention, or hanging round the school gates. I never told anyone that I liked him.

Having two older brothers didn't help, although they would bring friends home, they would either ignore me or fight to get my older sister Judy's attention. The biggest event to happen to me was when I was in my last year of secondary school, I actually got a Valentine's card, I couldn't believe it. Valentines is always an excruciatingly painful time for those at school, they should make it a law that the day should be banned until you are in your twenties, maybe not even then, it is a great day if you are wildly popular and a hit with the boys, but not fair if you are a scruffy secondary student with your teeth in braces and hair that has a mind and personality of its own. But there it was, it was mine, addressed to me, put inside my desk – yes, ours was a very old school so we had the lift up desks complete with dried up ink wells, now used to store old and dried up chewing gum. There it was, resting on top of my jotter pad that I left there, it was mine, in my desk in my form class, it wasn't a mistake, it had my name on it. At first I couldn't believe it, maybe it was a cruel joke, but it definitely had my name on it, in slanting italic letters with my name printed underneath. I placed it carefully in between the pages of my jotter and looked round to see if anyone was watching, but no one had noticed and I swear, I felt a tremble inside of me that I have never felt before.

I couldn't wait to read it properly; I didn't want to show anyone immediately, it was addressed to me, to me, no one else. I was nearly 16 and I had my first valentine. The lesson seemed to drag on all day, I couldn't wait to read it properly, it seemed like forever before I could run into the girls' toilets. I took it out and sitting with the loo seat down I studied it carefully, my heart was hammering. It was the most beautiful card ever. It was pink and cream with glitter on the front, on the front was the words "be my valentine" with a teddy holding a heart, as I opened it to read the words, in printed text it said "be mine" along with written words "most beautiful girl" written inside with a snake like squiggle underneath. I hugged it to my chest, it was the most precious thing I have ever received. I remember how I felt for days after, I was walking on air, I cherished it, I showed my friends but their interest waned after the 100th time of having to see it. My brother Scott found it and tried to tear it up saying I made it myself, but I knew the truth, I still have that card in my box of treasures, really dog-eared now, hardly any glitter left, but you know, I never ever found out who sent it!

I am the type of person that loves all that hearts and flowers when I am on the receiving end but I see it as overrated commercialised nonsense if I am not, I am a hopeless romantic, you see I am holding out for my one true love, I know it will happen one day, I want passion, love and perfection; I have seen it in films, and read it in my mum's paperback books, where I won't be able to resist him and he won't be able to keep his hands off me, we will exchange little looks and touches that will say a thousand word, everyone will look at us and envy the fact we are so much in love, that is what I want, other friends seems to have it and I want it too, the whole 100%.

I have never felt anything like that with anyone, well okay, as I said before I did have the desperate schoolgirl crush on Gary Smithson, Gaz to his mates, he was the bad boy in Secondary High school, but everyone loved him; all the girls fawned over him, myself included but he never even looked my way. I realise now, with acute embarrassment that I pursued him crazily – always being where he was, hanging around where I thought he might be, laughing at his stupid jokes, thinking he was the be all and end all. He was just so casual, with his cigarette sticking out of the corner of his mouth, hanging there when he spoke, I thought that was so cool.

Eventually he noticed me, I am not sure why, but I went from being invisible to being someone he spoke to. Okay it was just a gruff "alright" as he passed but I cherished that communication. Sometimes he would speak to me after school, waiting at the gates leaning against his bike, just the odd comment, nothing conversationally spectacular, but I would giggle and hold on to his every word. After just a few dates, well not exactly dates, I would wait until the end of school rush had gone, just sat on the wall, waiting, then as everyone went their separate ways he would walk by as I walked home. He would walk along smoking, he would chat about cars and motorbikes, I would hardly say a word. We would get to the roundabout where he would go one way and I would head the other. After the second or third time of him walking with me he leaned in and without a word he kissed me, he kind of hit the side of my lip then he moved his mouth it was quick and took me by surprise, his tongue stabbing against mine, his lips totally covering mine, he tasted of stale cigarettes but I felt great, as quickly as he kissed me, he left me, cycling down the road without looking back but I didn't care, he had kissed me, that is all I cared about. The next night after school he said he wanted more, I couldn't speak I just nodded, he kissed me again and I knew it wouldn't be long before I gave him what I held on to for so long, what I was keeping for someone special, I let him take my innocence.

I had built sex up in my mind as this huge occasion, something that would be life changing, friends tried to warn me but I wouldn't listen, I confided in one person, my best friend Ruth who had done the deed months and months before me. She said it was painful the first time but she knew her boyfriend Martin loved her and he was gentle and kind, she said that made all the difference, but I ignored her, thinking I knew better I watched them both as they paraded round the school arm in arm then kissing in the corridor when they thought no one was watching. I looked with jealousy as she showed me her love bites − big ugly purple marks on her neck, I wanted what she had. I had it in my head that Gaz and I would do the same, he would be so proud of me, I would be his girl, it would all be so wonderful, nothing she could say to me could stop me. In the end I didn't tell her that I was going to do it, I told no one. When he stopped at the roundabout he asked me to go to his house, I was too nervous to answer so I just nodded my head, it was our third date, okay, well not officially a date, but our third walking the same way, he said he would meet me at the youth club the following evening. I was excited beyond belief, I couldn't sleep that night, I couldn't eat, the day seemed to drag and there was no sign of him at school. I practically dragged Ruth there over an hour early much to her disgust, as we entered I looked everywhere for him, but there was no sign. I had dressed in my best outfit, my new denim skirt and white cotton blouse. The evening seemed to drag, after the last song had played I looked up, and there he was, waiting outside, leaning against his bike grinning at me, he winked and my stomach did somersaults. I couldn't believe it, he had turned up, admittedly he had waited until after youth club had finished then he had hung around outside watching everyone leave. I skipped over to him happy that he was there, he didn't acknowledge me, didn't say a word, just walked off towards the main road, expecting me to follow, which I did, then he walked me to the crossroads towards home, still he didn't say a word. Admittedly he did hold my hand, pushing his bike with the other, I was so excited, he normally turned left to his estate where I turned right, as we approached the roundabout he finally looked at me, he dropped my hand, lit a cigarette then he turned to me and said his parents were out. I wasn't stupid I knew what he meant, I was excited beyond belief, I was already picturing the scene in my head − he would kiss me gently, then lay me down and tell me I looked amazing, and obviously he would say how much he loved me, it would be a romantic evening full of declarations of love and promises. No one could have changed my mind or prepared me for the reality. My closest friend had tried and failed to warn me that the first time is probably the worst, but I wouldn't have it, I was the last of my friends to actually lose my virginity, and I thought it was going to be the most wonderful event of my life.

The reality was that it was over in a matter of minutes, it was horrendous from start to finish. His house was in total darkness, the entrance hall smelt of wet dog and stale cigarette smoke, although I never actually saw the dog there was an unfriendly growl as we entered the house. Without switching the lights on he pulled me by my hand up the stairs, I followed tripping over items, we went straight up to his room, it was messy, I stumbled over some clothes on the floor, he kicked them out of the way impatiently. The curtains were half drawn making the room in semi darkness, he flicked a lamp on which didn't make much difference but gave just enough light for me to see the place was filthy, clothes were strewn all over the room, he kicked them aside and pulled me to him. There was an assortment of empty drinks cans on the bedside cabinet which also housed an over spilling ashtray. My heart was hammering in my chest, I was scared, but also excited, this was it, finally I thought, this is what it is all about.

He kissed me, he smelt of cigarettes and he had really bad breath, his tongue was hard in my mouth stabbing at my tongue, his lips bruising mine, there was no tenderness. He pushed me back onto the bed, he pawed at me, pushing his chest down hard on mine as he lifted his hips to undo his trousers. He kissed me again, his mouth was wet, too wet, it felt slippery against mine, I wanted to wipe my lips but I couldn't move. I laid there as he fumbled with my clothing, dragging my skirt up to my hips, grabbing my cheeks of my backside then pulling my underwear down roughly to my thighs, before moving to the side for a brief moment I watched as he pulled out a condom and I stared as he pulled it onto his hardness. I was scared; it seemed so big, even in the semi darkness it seemed so massive. I was alarmed but also I was excited too. His hand pawed at my breast outside of my clothing, he pinched hard, too hard, I cried out, I heard him grunt for me to turn around, pushing my face into the pillow, I wanted to gag, it smelt of staleness, cigarettes and body odour, I felt sick. I wanted to be back at home, I wanted to say I made a mistake, I wanted to leave, but it was too late.

Without warning my knickers were pulled down my legs and he thrust around hitting my thigh several times before entering me, I felt a stabbing pain, the only physical touch was his hand as it rested on my shoulder, my body tensed, I let out a scream. To silence me he pushed my head further into the pillow, I wanted to cry, he pushed harder, thrusting into me. I could hardly breath, my face was pushed so hard in the dirty pillow it hurt and I held my breath, I didn't want to breathe in the stench of the pillow. His weight was painful on top of me, I couldn't move, then as he thrust really hard two or three times more, I screamed into the pillow as I felt a huge tearing pain inside of me as if I had been ripped apart. My eyes watered, my tears lost in the pillow, I sobbed out loud, but then just as quickly he moved away, I wasn't sure if it was over or not, as there were no violins in my head, no gestures of love, nothing, I laid there, my face still in the pillow, still half-dressed, my knickers around my ankles and my skirt up around my waist. I laid there for a minute, unsure what to do, not daring to move, feeling cheap and humiliated. To add insult to injury, he stood up, checked his phone and sat across the bed from me pulling up his jeans. Throughout the whole thing he never said a word, then he stood up, grunted something undecipherable then walked out of the bedroom. I sat up quickly, I could hear his departing footsteps, then they stopped, I listened as he was approaching the bedroom again. I sat there unsure what to do, I thought he might come back and make it all better, show me some tenderness, tell me he loved me and how wonderful it had been for him, but he came back to the bed, picked up his cigarettes and disappeared out of the door. I heard the front door slam. My heart was beating so hard in my chest, quickly I pulled my briefs up, I pulled my skirt down, I sat for a while on the dirty duvet on the bed before going downstairs, I just wanted to get out of there, I didn't give the dog a second thought. I tidied myself up and looked hopefully around for Gaz but he wasn't to be seen, I was devastated.

As I opened the front door I heard the growl of the dog, then I heard its paws hitting the wood flooring, I didn't stop to see what sort of dog it was. I wrenched open the door and threw myself out into the night, leaving the door open in my wake, I ran so fast and so far my chest burned, my tears flowed down my cheeks as I sobbed loudly.

So that was it, my virginity gone and I had let him take it, at no point did I tell him to stop, I had just let it happen and I said nothing, I had wanted it to happen so much and had shown him no resistance, I felt cheap, used and stupid. I crept into my house after the long shameful walk home, I cried on my sister's shoulder, then spent ages naively watching my phone for a message. Even after the way he treated me, I was young and inexperienced. I told Judy that he might not have credit on his phone or that something had happened, making so many excuses for his silence. Judy said nothing, there wasn't anything she could say, and so she held me close and wiped my tears. My whole body hurt, there was blood all over my panties, I was so scared my mum would see, but Judy was lovely and helped me clean myself up whilst trying to comfort me, but nothing she could say could make me feel better. I was a fool, I gave myself to him willingly, there was no denying I wanted it to happen, I just expected so much more.

Several hours later, the text message that I wanted so much arrived, it was to say he didn't want to see me anymore, he said the sex wasn't great, he added that he thought I might be frigid, he told me not to tell anyone we had done it, he would deny it, as he already had a girlfriend. For Christ's sake, I didn't even know what the word frigid meant. The only saving grace was at least he had the forethought to use protection. He never spoke to me again. I didn't see him around school for a while – I think he was expelled, maybe even the teachers got fed up with his attitude, but I knew I loved him and I thought naively that he loved me, how wrong and stupid was I?

Judy tried to make it better, she tried to explain that the first time is never good, no matter how much you love someone, but nothing she said could make it any better. Scott knew I was upset as I was quiet for days, he thought I was heartbroken and went after him, I wasn't heartbroken just humiliated. School for the next few weeks was excruciating, I kept thinking I would bump into him or he would tell someone, but thankfully he never did. It was only years later Stuart and Scott admitted they had put a stop to any bragging he might have done, I cringed inwardly not wanting to know any details.

I was 16, nearly 17, for Christ's sake, it was my first time, it hurt, even days later it still hurt, I just wanted to cry. Every time I thought of the whole episode I felt humiliated and so let down. I was such a late starter, I should have listened to my friends but not me, not stupid bloody me, I thought I was different and special.

Chapter Two

Helen, Ruth and I, well the three of us were young, free and living the dream, oh well almost. Okay, scratch the perfect picture because my friend Ruth is not free but she is single, very complicated, well isn't it always? She is seeing, well, not actually being seen in broad daylight with but she is in a relationship with a married man and to make it worse he is her boss, yes, the old cliché I am afraid: his wife doesn't understand him, he is stuck with his wife because of the children and once they are grown up he will leave her and be with Ruth. And the sad thing is, that Ruth being the fool that she is, believes him, but hey, it is what it is.

Historically she always goes for the bad boys, the ones with huge baggage attached to them; even her childhood sweetheart Martin ended up getting a girl pregnant whilst they were still at school. She was devastated for a while, said she would never trust anyone again, but within a few weeks she is madly in love again. This time she met Danny, but he turned out to be just like Martin. They met at bowling, I was with her at the time, I must admit he was handsome in that kind of nineteen-fifties leather jacket look, his chiselled features and slicked back black hair, bit dated but suiting him, he was with a group of friends, he was lovely, so entertaining, they all were. I did feel a little bit jealous when he took her home that night leaving me with his geeky friend Cliff, who was okay, but not as handsome as Danny, but he was kind and saw me to my home.

In the morning Ruth called me, she was on cloud nine, in love again, this time, she told me, she knew he was the one. She had spent the night with him and his was fabulous, I listened as she told me every minute detail about how he made her feel and how he said he felt he had known her all his life. She said they told each other everything but what he failed to tell her was that his girlfriend was heavily pregnant. She lived in a world of Danny for two weeks, despite only being able to see him late at night, apparently before he went on the night shift, she was smitten.

It was only when I was at the hospital having my appendix out that she found out. She was visiting me, she saw him playing happy families, he was embarrassed, his partner was livid, there was a huge scene where everyone seemed to be shouting, poor Ruth, she was devastated. Then, after sitting on my hospital bed weeping and decrying all men as liars, sniffing loudly and declaring she was never going to trust another man.

Before I was out of hospital she was having a romance with her brother's friend Robin, unbeknown to her he was due to be married in just a few weeks and she only found out when her brother mentioned the stag night; turns out he wanted a final fling. Once again Ruth thought he was the one, finally she thought she had met the man for her. Again, it was a terrible situation, the bride-to-be found out and there was a terrible scene. She was devastated, but I supported her and listened as she cried her heart out. A part of me felt sorry for her and a part of me didn't understand her not challenging his absences or sudden disappearances, or at the very least asking her brother what he thought of him, but then hindsight is wonderful and I guess we can all play judge and jury. But she is our friend and so we do what all good friends do... nothing – we mop up tears when we need to, we try very hard not to get angry at last minute dropped plans, we meet up and listen to each other's woes, but we never judge.

I don't blame men for wanting her, Ruth is the same age as me, a few weeks older, she is totally gorgeous, beautiful brown eyes and dark complexion. Her dad is Jamaican and is very dark, but her mum is white, so she has lovely olive colour skin, her hair is jet black, very long and curly and very uncontrollable, her lips are beautiful with a perfect cupids bow, she wears scarlet lipstick which emphasises their fullness, she has beautiful dark brown eyes that shine when she is excited about something. As I said before, we were at school together and the only time we actually got together was when we were in the hockey and netball team but we didn't really spend much time with each other until the sixth form, then we were inseparable. She is very serious and works in a legal office, something to do with investments, wills and things like that, I should know what she does, I think she is a secretary. She is lovely-looking, slightly overweight, she has a huge chest which doesn't help and she is forever on a diet, but I think her weight suits her, she lives at home, her mum is an excellent cook so she is always going to lose any fight with her weight. She has a huge family but is very insecure. She always wears black trousers and long tops, rarely anything different. She has a huge loud, infectious laugh which makes everyone else smile. She is great fun.

As I said before, now I am happily single, I have a few dates occasionally, which after my first sexual encounter I am surprised I just didn't book myself into the nearest convent as it put me off blokes and intimacy for a long while. I left school and got a job in an office that dealt with personal finance, it wasn't what I wanted to do, but as I never had an idea of what I want to do career wise and my dad knew someone who was looking for a young administrator, and bang, there I was, working in an office with a nice friendly group of people. They were always talking about dates and boyfriends and I never joined in really. I did have a date with a nice lad called Luke a short while after I joined, set up by one of the older lads in the office. We went for a drink, he was kind, we chatted, it was normal, nice and normal. He didn't throw himself at me and I relaxed in his company, this led on to a lot more dates He was fun and entertaining, but although I enjoyed the time I spent with him nothing came of it, he moved to another job and although we had a few more dates it fizzled out, he kissed me and we did have a degree of intimacy but didn't go all the way, I didn't want to. Besides, he lived at home and so did I, so whatever we did was in his car, I wasn't in any hurry for anything else, still I had not been intimate with anyone since my first time.

I was just happy to be working and earning money, going out with Ruth when she has the time and the girls at work would sometimes go for pizza. My life was bumping along quite happily. Judy my sister has met a new man and although I don't like him, she seems happy, she has been seeing him for a month and now he has moved in with her and the children, which I think is a bit soon but I don't say anything. Mum and Dad are looking at buying a property abroad they are really excited, not much else going on really. Life is just ticking away nicely. Then an opportunity arose that I couldn't turn down, I was off work, in hospital having my appendix out, the same time as Ruth was going through her Danny phase. Normally I would be in for just a day or so but just my luck it was a complicated procedure as I got an infection, not nice, but the upside is I had lots of visitors.

Judy moaning about her new man, who although perfect in the bedroom was not perfect anywhere else it seemed, I was a captured audience, even when I closed my eyes she didn't stop moaning about him. He was lazy and got the sack from his job and spent all his time at home watching the television, she went on and on about him. Then when she left Ruth took over, crying, complaining that all men were the same, and then mum with the agent's details on houses in the sun, I was exhausted. The wonderful opportunity arose when one of the girls came to visit, as I laid in my post anaesthetic state she talked excitedly about her upcoming holiday, I secretly wished I could be going with them, sat in my hospital bed I just felt more and more sorry for myself. Then when I returned to work I had to listen all over again, them all chatting about it, I had been spared listening to them organising every minor detail whilst I was off so I had not heard all the plans going ahead. When I returned there was a lot of fuss about the girls' holiday and I must admit, I was envious, really envious, two of them in the office were pouring over the brochure and talking about their outfits they had bought. At lunch time they would bring in their latest purchase – a small red bikini or a mini dress, I was so envious. Every conversation that happened eventually worked its way round to be about the holiday, it was driving me nuts. Then just one month before they were due to go, one of the other girls I didn't know dropped out as she couldn't bear to leave her new boyfriend.

There was a huge upset at work as they all discussed it, how could she do this, how could she be so selfish, what was they going to do at such short notice?. When they asked me, I couldn't believe it at first, I was half excited half nervous. Everyone in the office thought it was a great idea, the perfect solution. I couldn't wait to get home to discuss it with my family, my parents thought it was a great idea, and so after thinking it over for just the shortest time I thought why not; I knew two of the girls already, we met up with the other girl for a few drinks a week or so beforehand, I seemed to get on okay with her, she was a bit quiet like me, I knew we would get along. Mum and Judy enjoyed the shopping trip to get me all kitted out with new clothes, my hair was styled and tamed, I had just a few weeks to go and I couldn't wait.

As soon as I got there and saw the apartment in the hotel and saw the beach, I knew I would love it, everything looks so much better when the sun shines, we all got on so well immediately, we had a ball, I feel I need to take a bit of time out to tell you more about it. There was just us four girls together, all young, crazy and excited to be on holiday we partied at Ayia Napa at night. There must have been about thirty different clubs belting out the latest club hits. We danced, we drank and partied not getting in till the very early hours, then we lazed on the beach or by the pool all day, we danced until our feet hurt and we chatted, flirted, danced, kissed and canoodled with different lads every night, nothing too intense on my part, just good fun.

The weather was perfect, we had wonderful tans, I loved the attention we got from the various lads on holiday. After my first experience of sex I was not in a huge hurry to try again, but it felt good to kiss and cuddle, maybe fumble outside of my clothes a bit, just as I did with Luke, but that was as far as I wanted to go, although the others went a bit further there was nothing really serious for me. I wasn't disappointed, everything about the holiday was perfect for me, I really came out of my shell and enjoyed myself, I was just enjoying relaxing, and sex was the last thing on my mind really. Then when it happened, it was when I least expected it, and with a partner that ordinarily I would have never chosen, never would have even looked at him twice. He was totally different and it all happened so quickly, it blew me away. It was a perfect beautifully hot, sunny day, towards the very end of the holiday, just two days to go, I was nicely tanned, I was having a day on my own at the pool as the other girls were off deep sea diving (I hate putting my face in water), and the thought of putting a mask over my face and diving under the sea fills me with dread, so I declined and as it was an all-day excursion they left me at the hotel. I knew I would be plenty happy enough to stay behind, I read my book for a while, listened to music, sunbathed, then went for a swim. The pool was almost deserted, just a few occupied beds on the other side of the pool and well away from me. The water was deliciously refreshing, I swam for a while but I didn't take much notice of anyone until

22

an older chap swum up near me, he remarked how quiet it was, then he leaned on the side of the pool and we soon we got chatting. I had seen him around the hotel with his wife, they were both very friendly, I didn't see her about today. After swimming and chatting for a while about nothing in particular, I got out the pool, sat on my sunbed and looked around. As I dried off I noticed he was watching me, then I looked up and he caught my eye and smiled, he then wandered over to my sunbed; it was nearly lunchtime so the pool area was now deserted as most people that had not gone to the beach had headed to the restaurant. He sat on the end of the empty sunbed next to me, we just chatted a bit more about the hotel and the resort for a while longer. He had been to this hotel many times, he told me his wife was on an all-day excursion too, only not diving, she had gone to look at the ruins somewhere. Well he sat with me, he was funny and entertaining, he was old, older than my dad, and I knew that he fancied me, I could tell the way he kept looking up and down at my body. I was only wearing my tiny wet bikini which clung to my body. We flirted and I giggled, I am not the best flirt in the world, but he made me feel good, I wasn't embarrassed to be chatting to him, he had a nice strong body with a great tan. I pulled my sarong around me and he made a comment that he was enjoying the view, this made me giggle again. He asked me if I wanted a drink and said he would choose something appropriate, I watched as he walked towards the bar, I looked appreciatively at his broad shoulders and lean body bronzed from the sun, I ignored the sagging skin and the wrinkles on his face. I watched him as he walked back towards me, he had a smattering of grey hairs on his chest, he came back with a cocktail called slow comfortable screw, we both laughed out loud, how original I told him, but it still made me smile, we chatted for ages, he had a knack of making me feel at ease and of making me laugh. He was so laid back and interesting, he kept making remarks about my chest, I have quite a large chest and the wet tiny bikini wasn't hiding much of it, but I didn't feel embarrassed, he made me feel good about myself, telling me silly stories and making me giggle, it all seems a bit cheesy now looking back, but it was fun. The cocktail was delicious, icy cold and it was quite strong but wonderful in the heat of the sun, we sat for a long while drinking a few more of the cocktails. My head was buzzing with the alcohol, I should have had something to eat but I felt okay, I wasn't drunk, I told him I felt lightheaded, we both laughed, I felt wonderful, so when he asked me if I would like to go to his room, I didn't say no.

I pulled my sarong around me, and just abandoning my things on the sunbed I followed him as he headed into the hotel. We didn't speak in the lift, just looked at each other, then when the lift door opened he took my hand and we skipped like children to his room. As he closed the door he pulled me close to him I looked quickly down at his trunks and his intentions were very clear. When he asked me if I was okay I murmured yes. He asked if I wanted some fun I smiled encouragingly. He pulled me close to him, his kisses drowned me, he certainly knew how to kiss. I didn't take any notice of his greying hair, his slightly sagging body, I forgot all that as I closed my eyes and felt his hands stroking my body gently. Then his lips replaced his hands as he kissed my neck and my breasts, he was so slow and deliberate, he whispered to me what he was going to do to me, and I didn't say a word, hearing what he was going to do to me sent my senses racing. I raised no objection as he pulled my body to his, his body warmed by the sun, his lips pressing gentle kisses on my shoulders He told me how beautiful I was and I melted. Whilst his wife looked at the ruins in Cyprus, that man made my holiday one I will never forget and he erased any memory of my first time. I had no illusions of what it was, he was just a one- off; he was definitely too old for me and obviously married.

Whilst we spent the afternoon and early evening together I didn't give his wife a thought and neither did he, he restored my confidence in myself, he stripped me naked, which took seconds as I just had my bikini and sarong on, then just looked at my body all over. I was self-conscious but he wouldn't allow me to cover myself, he made me stand in front of the full-length mirror totally naked as he showed me all the pleasure zones on my body, stroking me slowly, he made me feel tremendous, kissing, stroking me. Then licking my body everywhere, ensuring I was pleasured before he took any pleasure from me, he was incredible. Looks didn't play a part for me, it wasn't important, he made me feel incredible, he kissed me in places I could only dream, there was no embarrassment with him, I felt wonderful, I had my very first orgasm and he left me begging for more. We were together for the best part of five hours, he showed me how to return the favour and make a man feel incredible, he was a patient and expert lover, exactly as I wanted it to be. We showered together, I felt no embarrassment with him, as he soaped my body clean and then pulled me back into the bedroom and made love some more. I laid in his arms, naked and happy, I didn't want to but eventually I left his room, I was exhausted, sore but very content, it was just what I needed, a perfect end to the holiday. I never told anyone, not one of my holiday friends knew at the time, although I did confess several months later and they said they knew, but I am sure they didn't. My body glowed with the effects of the sun and my whole insides glowed just remembering how he held me and made me feel as he made love to me.

At the breakfast buffet the next morning he passed me a note to ask if I would meet him again that afternoon, he added his telephone number back at home, but although I was tempted, I never had any intentions of continuing anything with him. Well, there was no point, I saw it for what it was, we had fun, it was good for both of us, he restored my faith in men. I knew now exactly what it was to be made love to with complete abandonment, I knew what being made love to felt like and I never wanted to have anything else, I wanted more of the same. We went home the next day. I didn't want it to be anything more. I had a smile on my face that lasted a long time. I knew then that any man I was intimate with had a lot to live up to. As we boarded the coach to take us to the airport he came out to wave goodbye, I kissed the piece of paper he had written his number on. As I climbed the steps to the coach I handed it back to him, I just added the words thank you.

Anyway back to the present, I am not seeing anyone, well I am kind of, but, again it is a bit complicated. I know people don't understand and I have to admit, even to me it is a bit weird, I am kind of seeing a chap called Jason, Jason Freedman. Although we don't actually acknowledge we are in a relationship, we get together in a group of about eight of us that do a weekly quiz at the local pub, again, when my shifts allow, and sometimes we go out for a meal if it is someone's birthday, nothing special just a curry maybe, but we have never actually had a date together on our own, the quiz is about it really as far as regular meetings go. I like him, he is a lovely man I have known him for years.

I don't brag about being that smart or clever, but I do have a good knowledge of trivia, and current music, sometimes I surprise myself when I know the answer to some random question, with seven other brains we do quite well.

Jason is a loveable nerd, he is very analytical, he is an inventor or creator for want of a better word, he says he is an applications designer, which means nothing to me and I am sure that is not what it says on his contract, he is a gadget man and has several patents pending on his products. He works for a very large, well-known company which produce household appliances, and he is very heavily involved in the development side. Hey, would you know it, I have impressed myself with my knowledge there. He tries to interest me in what he does, but even he knows I am bored so I cannot even begin to pretend to be interested or to tell you. He doesn't pay any attention to my job either, which can be exciting, but most of the time events are happening in our town so we cannot speak about them anyway. We have a good enough relationship.

Since my parents have moved away Jason always comes to my house and looks after any small maintenance jobs that need doing. He has a key and lets himself in, not sure how that first come about, I think I must have been working and he needed to get in, there is no problem, I am comfortable with that, it makes sense, I don't have a problem as I know I can trust him. Sometimes I get home from a shift to find he has mown the lawn and little jobs I think it is so sweet of him, but sometimes it aggravates me that he doesn't check first. I guess I would moan if he didn't do it so there is really no pleasing me.

Anyway, back to the quiz night, the team is made up of myself, Jason, Jason's younger brother Sean and his mate Phil and Phil's girlfriend Gemma – she is fab, super clever when it comes to historical dates and anything to do with the royal family and who married who? She knew who was sat on the throne at any given time. She loves trivia, reads all the glossy women's magazines so she knows who is dating who, and she is so definite in her knowledge that no one argues with her and she is normally bang on the nail. She is a bit ditsy in life in general, but she makes me laugh. Firstly, her appearance is so individual – she used to be a Goth, and still wears her hair jet black and dark make up, but she finishes the look with extraordinary bright clothes and huge boots, I like her, I like her a lot. She is funny, sexy and doesn't take herself too seriously, once whilst we were discussing a dubbed film – I think it was *Moulin Rouge*, she said, and she was serious, oh I didn't know Nicole Kidman spoke French, I tell you, I nearly wet myself laughing, and she joined in, as did everyone else. She is so sweet and she drinks martini and diet coke, which even the bar tender shudders at. She is the same height as me, which is 5 foot 4 on a good day and she wears huge doctor martin boots which swamp her feet, she is precious and she loves Phil to bits, not sure why as he is a complete bastard to her, I am sure he is not as faithful as he should be, and the reason I think this, is because I have known Phil for years, he is older than me by two years, he lived in my street.

Phil, Phil Foster he knows all about me and my family, in fact it seems he knows everyone, as an only child his parents adored him, they used to run the small shop on our estate so he knows everyone, and because he is an only child he was very spoiled, but so loveable, everyone likes him, we have always had a good relationship. We flirt with each other but we both know there is nothing in it, he flirts with everyone, even Judy. He teases us both all the time, he is lovely but so totally annoying, I really like Phil because he is down to earth, he brightens up the room when he enters, he is hilariously funny, but there is a serious side to him too and he is a good listener. We go back a very long way, but then he is one of those chaps that seems to know everyone – he knows my mum and dad and all the extended family, my two brothers and my sister.

My eldest brother Stuart lives in Dubai, he is head of department for an export business and has been there for a few years, Skype and email means we get to contact him loads, I know he keeps in touch with Phil and Sean.

My other brother Scott is a journalist and lives in London – alone, he has had a whole load of girlfriends but never commits to anyone for any length of time, he says it is because he travels so much.

Then there is Judy my older sister she is divorced with two children: Harry and Juliet. She lives locally. She has always had a crush on Phil but thinks nobody knows it. Her husband left her for another woman while she was carrying Juliet four years ago, she was devastated, she just managed to hold everything together. Then she met a right wrong un, the one I never liked, the one I got to hear so much about when I was in hospital. Apparently he was on drugs but she didn't know it, he hid it well, until she noticed that he was behaving really unpredictably. Eventually she found out that he stole her money, he sold her jewellery and furniture, he was really heavily into drugs. She couldn't help him, whatever she tried didn't work. Eventually she got rid of him, now she is alone, just the two children and she finds it hard to trust men.

Mum and Dad have retired to live in a lovely villa in Menorca. Mum is a semi-retired accountant; she occasionally has work sent over to her, which keeps her busy. Dad is a retired watchmaker, he had his own jewellery shop which they sold when they moved overseas, it was when the property boom happened so they were very fortunate. They do have a lovely apartment in a retirement block in our town so sometimes they come home for a month or so in the summer, but most times they just leave it for when it is needed. They are very lucky – they are very financially secure and both in relatively good health. They finally moved when Mum's arthritis got really bad. We were all really pleased when they finally decided it was time after speaking about it and having the villa for a year or so. My mum despairs of her two daughters ever actually settling down and making her proud. Mum always asks after "the boys" she means Jason, Phil and Sean. I think she maybe hopes Phil and I will get together and he will make me happy, I don't think she knows Phil that well and we dare not tell her that it is Judy who is the one that likes him. Okay so that is my family in a nutshell. I realise I was originally talking about Phil and I will get back to him at some point.

Jason and Sean are one year or so apart from each other and they grew up in the street next to ours but are about three years older than me so I was aware of them but didn't really know them growing up. I was the irritating little sister always hanging around or telling tales on the boys when they were up to mischief. They know Judy very well as she was older so stayed out later. Sean went to school in the same year as her. Phil knows both families very well, he used to go over the fields with all of them shooting pigeons and rats, yes lovely isn't it, typical boys the lot of them, and they really have never grown up. Well okay, now they have grown up they have all got good jobs and are fairly responsible, no illegitimate children or criminal records. Sean is a quantity surveyor, he is always really busy at work but always seems to be able to get time off to go to the pub lunchtimes or play golf. As for Phil, well he is a police officer, based at the same station as me, although he is not on the same shift as me. I sometimes see him as I am leaving work but our paths don't cross that often thank goodness – I think he might drive me mad, but he is on the same shift as one of my really good friends Helen Judd. I like Phil, he makes me laugh, I think out of the three boys he is my favourite but I would never let him know that, besides, it is Judy that fancies him.

Anyway, what generally happens is that after the quiz we all go different ways, some walk and some drive, but we live locally so Jason will sometimes, if the weather is okay, he will walk me home as he rents a flat a couple of streets away.

I own my lovely three bedroom house at the top of a quiet road; nearby to where I grew up, I am extremely proud of my home. My parents did help me with the deposit for which I am eternally grateful. They helped Judy and the boys too, which is great, they were all very open about it, we are very lucky, I love my home. Dad did help me choose it and it is my pride and joy. Dad insisted on me buying a three bedroom as he said it was the better investment, as it was his money too, I didn't argue. After his shop sold he gave all his children a lump sum to get us started. Both he and mum helped me chose the furniture and even to decorate it.

Going back to Jason, well, Jason is a really clever man, a genius some would say. He does tend to intimidate me sometimes, not in a nasty way, but he seems to be so learned, so on a higher level educationally than the rest of us, but he is also, well he can come over as emotionally detached. He will correct grammar when people speak, which can be very condescending, although I don't think he realises it when he is doing it, but it makes me uncomfortable. I like his company, but sometimes, just sometimes, he is a bit well, middle class, don't get me wrong, we get on well, I just could never talk to him about my thoughts or feelings though, never, we just don't have that sort of relationship. He is sweet and kind. When he walks me home we talk, not of us, but life in general. I like him, I like him a lot, but for some reason I have never invited him in after a night out, funny really as, as I have said before he has the key, for emergency use but never uses it when I am with him, I am quite happy about that, I am not sure how I would feel if he did. I am confused about our relationship, most times he will wait at the gate as I let myself in, but sometimes he will snuggle and kiss me at the doorstep, generally if the quiz has gone on longer than normal and he has had another pint, but a snuggle and kiss is as far as it goes, it has been like that for a year or more.

I don't know why we don't take it further, he never has pushed it and I kind of don't want him to really, I like him, not sure I would want to have sex with him though, although maybe I could fancy him if I put my mind to it, but why should I have to settle for that, when I see him I don't feel anything really – I don't miss him if he is not there, and although he is attractive in that he has a nice body. I love his cute unkempt strawberry blonde hair which falls over his forehead that he is continually pushing it back. He is 5ft 8 and has a nice smile, but I don't really fancy him at all. Sexually there is nothing, naught, zilch. Sometimes I wish there was, I have this on-going wish that I can settle down and be part of a couple, like most people have, but I know I am different in that I am not sure if I have an unrealistic view of what being a couple means, but I have built up this picture in my head of it all being very loving and intimate, you know, cannot keep our hands off each other intimately. There is definitely nothing like that with Jason.

The best thing I like about Jason is his dress sense – always designer shirts and straight leg jeans, always casual but smart, nice clean, leather shoes. His hands are always clean, nails immaculate, he doesn't bite them which I am glad about, I hate bitten nails, he doesn't seem to have any annoying or irritating habits. He always smells nice, oh and he has lovely kind eyes, almost a slate grey in colour, but that is it, there is nothing heart stopping striking about him. He is not husband material. Would I mind if he met someone else? No I don't think I would. In fact I know I wouldn't, would he care if I did, no definitely not, we are not a couple, not in that way.

Sad really though isn't it? I guess at my age I should have had a few engagements or at least a long relationship, but nothing, nothing at all. As for Jason, well there was a barmaid at the local pub where the quiz is, she has gone now but when she was there she made it so plain that she so obviously liked him. She would always make a fuss and go all out to get his attention, our table was wiped so often we found it quite comical but he never seemed to notice and even when we brought it to his attention he did nothing about it. He has had a girlfriend once, Phil has told me about them, he told me once when he was a bit drunk. Apparently they went out for a long while, over a year I think, in fact I think maybe they were engaged, they didn't live together though and no one really knows what happened to the relationship and as she wasn't a local girl, it is never mentioned. The only other relationship I know about was a holiday exchange he had to Germany, I think it was in sixth form, he exchanged with a girl called Veronica, she stayed with his family and then he went over there for a week but for some reason it got extended for a few months, because of this he speaks fluent German. It has come up in conversation as he was in Dusseldorf, so if ever that country is mentioned someone will inevitably mention he stayed there, but he never elaborates with them and he certainly will not discuss relationships with me.

His brother Sean is always going on about us being the odd couple, and I never bother to correct him as I don't see us as a couple at all. I always hoped that when I met the special someone, I would know instantly, there would be a thumping of my heart and cupid arrows flying everywhere, maybe even fireworks, yes definitely fireworks, but no, nothing yet, I am afraid I feel nothing but brotherly love really for Jason,

Yet, sometimes he kisses me at the doorstep and I respond, but I never take it further, I don't know why not, it would be easy to love Jason, but surely love isn't like that is it? Not just acceptance of a relationship because it is easy, comfortable and reliable, there must be something more.

Anyway, I am doing it again, digressing, so back to the group in general, the final couple who make up the group in the quiz is a married couple who are called Brian and Carol, well that is their proper names, but Jason and I call them Brain and Cruella, because he is super bloody clever, but also super arrogant and even when found wrong will argue until it is embarrassing to all those around. He frequently argues with the quiz master which can get quite heated.

Cruella well she is just so evil and makes barbed comments about everyone in the pub, really sarcastic comments which keeps me amused but are really quite nasty. She pays no attention to the quiz, never gives any input and will sit and roll her eyes at every opportunity, she will speak on her phone whilst the questions are being called despite people giving her cold looks and the quiz master asking her to go outside, she totally ignores him, she is a rule unto herself and I find myself liking her, mainly because she gives a two finger salute to everyone in authority which I just cannot do. She is a smoker and since the smoking ban has been brought in she spends a lot of the time outside huddled under the plastic shelter they laughingly call the smoking shelter, I think she has, at some point had a fling with Sean but I am not certain. Sometimes the innuendo between them is embarrassing and it is sometimes so personal that they have to have known each other intimately, but Brian never says a word, if we do have another player it is generally made up of Sean's current girlfriend, this changes on a very regular basis and sometimes we only see them once and never again. When a new girlfriend is present, Carol sulks, drinks too much and gets louder and louder to get Sean's attention, it never works, he just ignores her and this makes her worse. Sometimes we play one member short because Sean has just finished one relationship and hasn't struck up a new one, we always know because he sits there all moody wanting attention like a child. This is where Carol will sit and crow, she will snuggle up to Brian and try to wind Sean up, but again he just ignores her, everyone is waiting for the big explosion that we know one day will come. Phil just seems to be so laid back he has no idea what is going on with Sean and Carol, everything just floats over his head, he doesn't mind losing the quiz and cares more about his beer and the free sandwiches than anything else, he really is very laid back.

Sean is similar in appearance to Jason but a bit shorter and carries a bit more weight but the main difference is that Sean sulks, he is petulant and moody, and has a chip on his shoulder, I don't see that in Jason. Jason and Sean have been brought up by their Jewish parents, both of them have been adopted, their parents died in an accident when they were very small, they are true brothers, this might explain the chip on his shoulder and his need to be loved by so many different women. They both follow certain aspects of the Jewish religion but not all, they pick and choose, unless their Ma is around then they behave but normally they eat what they want and do not follow kosher rules. Everyone calls their adopted mother Ma, she is a devoted Jew and has some crazy followings and practices about her religion that you won't find in any version of the Tanakh,

She rules her home and everyone in it, she is loved by everyone and is only 4 foot tall but very formidable she is a lovely wrinkled family lady. She

is very difficult to define in age, she must be the same age as my mum —
possibly late fifties but she looks so much older. I have never known her to
be out of her old-fashioned black wraparound apron and she loves the boys
to bits. She bakes cakes and pastries and insists Jason and Sean bring them
along, so we know on quiz night we will get fed well. She will clip her sons
round their heads in front of everyone and rant at them in Hebrew. She is
funny and loving and they love her to bits.

Chapter Three

Anyway I was telling you about the Tarot, firstly. Just to clarify we were not drunk, we were a bit tipsy making us a bit lightheaded, it was a really lovely sunny day, we were having fun. The tarot lady's house was just a short walk from the pub. It was a respectable modern detached house with a small front garden, a light blue Mercedes is parked on the drive. We arrived in time. The lady opened the door and introduces herself as Paula, she was very welcoming to us all. She is an attractive woman, slim and casually dressed in jeans and summer top, she must be in her forties and has short blonde hair pulled up into a pony tail, she wears light make-up. We could see through to her dining room which was light and airy, we only had a quick glance but then as Helen was going first Ruth and I were ushered into the lounge to wait. The lounge was almost completely in contrast to the dining room, and to the rest of the modern house. Immediately on walking in, it had a dark dreary feel to it, there were heavy brocade curtains at the windows, making the room dark, all around was old-fashioned dark wood furniture and every surface seemed to be covered in cat ornaments, funny lace doilies on the tables and arm protectors on the chairs. Some of the cat ornaments were lifesize, it was a bit weird as we felt their eyes staring at us. Ruth and I both said it felt a bit bizarre. I stood up and looked at the pictures, again really old-fashioned faded sepia prints of old buildings. The whole room could have been picked up and put in a nineteen-fifties house and would not be out of place, but here, it seemed really unusual, really out of place in the modern house.

Ruth wasn't happy, she was sat on the edge of the sofa, she said she sensed something was wrong, she felt on edge, she was sweating and kept mopping her forehead with a tissue, she kept saying her gut instinct was telling her to leave, she said she felt ill, the whole room was making her feel creepy, I was worried she was going to throw up, so I made her sit with her head up and taking deep breaths in and out. I persuaded her it was the wine and the sunshine and she would be fine, and not to take it too seriously. She seemed to settle at this and at my insistence she sat back on the sofa and concentrated on looking through a magazine. She did worry me for a while but she seemed to calm down after a short while, I just settled into a comfy chair and played a game on my mobile phone to distract me from the cat's eyes. We could hear the mumble of voices and occasional laughter but could not work out what was being said. Occasionally when I looked at Ruth she was still mopping her head and looking uneasy. I pick up a magazine and leaf through it.

Helen was gone for a good forty-five minutes before the door opened and she came back, Helen almost bounced into the room, she was smiling and clutching a small disc with the recording of the whole thing, so we could all listen later. Ruth went next and Helen and I made small talk, we had promised each other not to talk about what was said until we were altogether. Helen took her time looking around the room.

"Bit freaky in here isn't it." I nodded my head she continued, "The rest of the house is really modern and nice, and Paula is lovely." She looked around. "But this room looks like it is a mausoleum, looks like someone died thirty years ago and nothing has changed since." I nod my head again, Helen sighs she picks up the magazine I was reading and sits down, "and the cats freak me out," she adds, I nod again. "Ruth, was really freaked out, she was really nervous and wanted to leave." Helen nods. "I know, I would be if I was sat in here for any length of time but it is fine, Paula is really lovely, actually" she pauses, "I think it was her mum's house and she inherited it, or her mum lived here with her, something like that."

I nod my head. "That would explain this room," I reply. Helen stands up, looks out of the heavily curtained window.

"You have nothing to worry about, honestly, Paula was lovely, a bit strange maybe in her delivery but very good." Helen picks up a cat ornament.

"I remember now," she says, "it definitely was her parents' house, she couldn't bear to change the lounge so it stayed as it was." I look around, we look again at the pictures and then chatted about non-Tarot things to keep us from discussing her reading. I was quite surprised when the door opened and Ruth came out quite quickly, not even ten minutes had passed, her face seemed ashen, there was sweat on her forehead and upper lip, she looked close to tears, but as I was next I couldn't speak to her, only to ask, "are you okay" and squeeze her hand, which she nodded yes and I watched as she turned away and sat down on the couch. I knew something was wrong but Paula was smiling at me and ushering me into the dining room.

I went in and sat down at the dining table. The dining room was bright and cheery, it was in direct contrast to the lounge. One wall was full of modern family pictures of Paula and her husband and children, the room was amazing, so bright, so modern and sunny. I looked at the pictures and remarked how happy they all looked, and what a lovely family she had, I wasn't nervous at all, Paula never commented or responded to any of my rambling about her family and offered me a glass of water, I nodded yes and I watched her as she popped through to the kitchen to fetch it.

I sat silently just waiting, she came back and was busy resetting the recorder. We went through what she was going to do, she said sometimes thoughts and images came into her head during a reading and she would share them with me, I didn't object, she looked at my hands and then passed me the pack of cards, I shuffled the cards. I was pre-warned by my sister to take everything the tarot lady said with a pinch of salt. I am open-minded, but her first words made me go cold.

"You know your husband." she looked directly at me, then she paused for quite a long time, kept frowning and then she kept referring to her books and then referring back to the cards, frowning all the time, putting me on edge a bit. Then she was asking me to turn another card over and then to pick another from the pack. Out of the blue again she stated again that I knew my husband, she kept looking at my marriage hand as if questioning the absence of a ring, she looked at me for confirmation and when I gave none she said she couldn't change what the cards were telling her or how she felt. She still kept on frowning at me as if I was hiding a great secret from her, she then repeated that I knew my husband, not my husband-to-be, but my husband and that I was true to him. Then she asked if I was recently married and when I said no she said that the cards showed I would be married twice in my life and I would know great love.

Her next words made me go cold, she said, "You will have the one thing you ask for but that is not the thing you need and really want." She looks at me. "You understand what I am saying?" she asks, I shake my head.

She gives a big deep sigh, looks out of the window then back at me, she looks down at the cards. "Your love, when it comes, it will be a deep and committed love but before that you will know great heartache and you will lose a dear friend." She then paused again, for quite some time and said. "I think you know both of the men you will marry."

I frown at her, she asked me again if I was married already or had I been married, when I said no, she said, "Oh dear, oh okay, this isn't making sense, this is the present cards I am looking at." She kept repeating herself, she asked again, "Have you been married?"

I shook my head no, she frowned then shook her head, I think she thought I was telling her lies, she frowned some more.

Then out of the blue she said, "You love to have fresh flowers in your home." I nodded then she said "You should always have them no matter what." I smiled at her.

Then she completely lost me, she took a deep breath. She then said she loved fresh flowers too. "Are you a florist?" she asked. I shook my head, she continued, "I can see lots of flowers, lots of them," then the questions were barked at me, did I have a red car – she could see a brand new red car and she could see travel overseas, an unexpected journey was I training to be a nurse as she could see me caring for someone. Very soon, did I wear a uniform, was I a nurse, she said she could definitely see a uniform but she could see hospitals and doctors and then she asked me did I train to be a nurse? She completely flummoxed me, her questions didn't make sense, she never waited for answers, I nodded or shook my head in response to her rapid fire questions, she exhausted me. She turned over a few cards and the death card came out, I must have registered worry on my face as she quickly reassured me this didn't mean death of me, but death of a situation, she spoke very quickly. Ignoring the cards she took both my hands in hers, my hands were warm but hers were cold, she looked at them for some time, she didn't speak for a while, she turned my hands over and looked at my palms for quite some time. She then looked me straight in the eyes, she told me my job was helping people that I couldn't see, did I understand that, I nodded to her, it was the only thing she had said that actually made any sense.

She held my hands tighter, too tight, she said my heart would feel like it was broken that I would feel despair, but I was not to worry, everything would be as it should be, I was totally lost, I wasn't sure what she was talking about. Then she looked back at the cards, she turned a few over and consulted her book again she spoke about a personal debt that would be paid, but it wasn't my debt, she said the man looking after me would not stop until he considered the debt was paid, and then his job was done. I automatically thought of my dad and the money he loaned me.

As if reading my thoughts she continued, "This debt will not be financial." She frowned then struggling to find words, she went on saying the man would know that he would have failed me but would look after me, this man was not my husband. I nodded my head, confused but acknowledging what she had said. She looked at me, "You are very lucky, you have five or six men here looking out for you, I don't know if they are family members or lovers, but they are all watching out for you." she placed her hands on the table. "Friends are the family we choose for ourselves". I nod my head in agreement; I have seen that written somewhere before she has not just come up with it. "You need to learn to love yourself or how will anyone else love you." She asks it like it is a question and I have no response for her, I just frown.

She looks back at the cards, I was totally bewildered, she rambled on with some dates and did they mean anything to me. She asked me if I had a gentleman's pocket watch and I said no, she said it was antique and worth a lot of money, I told her I thought it might be my dad she was referring to, he mends clocks and watches, she said no, it wasn't that, this is a watch that has been handed down. She told me to think about it, was I sure I didn't know someone with one, it was the key to my future happiness. She didn't wait for an answer she just fired more dates at me – did February and August mean anything to me I said no, because they were just months, and very vague. To be honest the rest was a bit of a haze, something about lies and deceit and justice would prevail. She said my cards and hands showed a good future, she said there was a lot of cash surrounding me and I would not have any money problems, I had two men in my life who put up a wall of protection. She asked me if I had twins, did I know someone with two children – I thought of my sister, but she changed it back to definitely being twins, I thought of my friend Annabelle, she shook her head she said I would have two children, twins she thought, she didn't know the sex of them, she said it was irrelevant, she said she could see the man I would settle down with and spend the rest of my life with. He is very handsome, very tall, and I would only know one true love. She smiled at me and said I was very lucky, she then seemed to smile to herself, she looked down at the cards, she laughed out loud at something then, her whole face lit up, she was still looking at me.

She asked if I had seen a strange bath, or if I had a bath in an odd location, I thought she might have lost the plot totally at that point, but she said she couldn't change the images that came into her head, it had nothing to do with the cards, she just had images that came to her during readings and she had to say what she saw. I shook my head, she paused then picked my hand up, she stroked it gently then whispered to me, "Do you know." She leaned in closer, almost face-to-face with me, she spoke clear and direct to me I could feel her breath on my face as she spoke. "The brightest candle is one where the flame burns with love."

She turned to look out of the window as if collecting her thoughts. When she turned back she dropped my hand gently, she closed the cards. Her whole demeanour changed, she was back to being relaxed she asked if I was okay, did I want some more water. I guess I must have nodded yes as she refilled my glass, I drunk it down in one large gulp, I was hot and sweat was running down my back, I just wanted to get out, I could not remember half of what she had told me. She had returned to being the polite and accommodating hostess – very smiley and chatting away about the weather and her garden.

She flicked the CD player off, pushed my disc into a plastic case, handing it to me she said, "Try to laugh more than you cry." She then walked down the hall and we returned to the lounge.

I noticed immediately that Ruth was missing from the lounge, I did look questioningly at Helen but before I could say anything she had pulled me in the direction of the front door and ushered me out calling over her shoulder and thanking Paula for her time. As Helen dragged me towards the direction of the pub I tried to slow her down and ask what was happening but she didn't stop, I just allowed her to pull me by the hand, within minutes I could see Ruth in the distance sat at the same seat in the pub garden that we had vacated earlier. She was sitting with her back to us and so she didn't see us approaching as she was busy texting someone on her mobile phone, as we got closer she looked up and I could see she had been crying.

I forgot all about my CD with the details of the reading on, I pushed it to the bottom on my handbag and sat to listen to what Ruth had to say. Ruth's reading did not go as she planned, she should have listened to her gut instinct, she explained as soon as she walked into the dining room she immediately saw all the family pictures and her heart sank, for there on the walls of the dining room were pictures of her man posing happily with his wife and children, pride of place in the middle was their wedding picture, both of them smiling at the camera.

Paula had been very calm and cool towards Ruth, not saying anything but sat down and had read the cards. The first things she had said in the reading had clarified a few things – yes, Ruth had a good job and was a professional person who loved travel, things that could have been applicable to anyone. But after just a short time she had placed her hands over the cards and stared straight into Ruth's face, as if reading Ruth's mind Paula had worked out exactly who she was – she wasn't a stupid woman, she knew, she knew her husband was cheating on her, she had her suspicions on who it might be. When she saw the stricken look on Ruth's face she knew who she was and of the full situation, it was a very uncomfortable time for both of them, and Ruth spent most of her time saying how sorry she was, with Paula just listening and being very compassionate. Paula didn't need the cards to tell Ruth that the man she was seeing was a womaniser, a cheat and a liar, she knew first hand. She told Ruth she wasn't the first and she wouldn't be the last. Ruth was devastated and our own readings were forgotten as we offered her our support. None of us were sure how to handle the situation; I offered her to come and stay at my house for a while, not sure what that would achieve but offering anyway, I had nothing else to offer by way of support and Helen had nothing to say. We had a quick chat about my reading and I said it was very vague and a bit rubbish really, I didn't want to go into all the details, I was a bit embarrassed really about the fact she thought I was married and got so much wrong. Helen's seemed to be much better than the rest of ours and we all agreed we would have to wait to see if any of it came true.

Chapter Four

Funny how your life trips along quite happily. In the weeks that followed I was busy at work, my very old car has failed its MOT and so I have decided to change it in for a new one. I am now the owner of a brand new Volkswagen convertible with a pretty girlie flower in the front; there was a choice of two, a lovely blue one and a red one, I wasn't bothered about the colour and I told Phil as much, but we decided on blue, a beautiful sky blue, maybe it was because the tarot lady said I would have a red car that I chose the blue, I don't know, but I wasn't really bothered, which in hindsight was a good thing as when we went to collect it there was an error on the paperwork so my new baby is bright red and has lovely cream leather seats and I love it, I really love it. It is my first brand new car and my mum and dad have paid some towards it, I think they were relieved when my old fiesta finally died a death and so I was forced to get rid of it.

Phil came and helped me negotiate a good deal. Helen was the first person to see it as I arrived at work. "Oh a red car," she said with surprise, "The tarot card reader was right, she said you would have a red car."

I stop in my tracks, she did, I can remember that much, she said a red car, and I chose blue, maybe somewhere in my head I didn't want her to be right, but she was. I dismiss it as coincidence. There are so many posh cars in the car park at work, now I won't feel out of place. There are a few BMWs and Mercedes and even a really posh sports car, I think it is a Masserati, a beautiful blue one, not brand new but still gorgeous, tinted windows, very sleek and classical, not sure who owns it, but I love it. I am not normally a car person but this car screams for you to look at it.

At work lots going on, the new shifts were being announced and I am not overly bothered, whatever changes are made will not really affect me, no matter who I worked with we always seems to bond together like a family. Each shift is headed up by a sergeant and then sometimes an acting sergeant and then a mix of civilian officers and police officers all based permanently in the control room. We work three sets of shifts: early shift which means a 6am start; late shift which is 2pm or 4pm; and then night shift. I don't mind any shift but after night shift we get a nice long break off which is perfect for me to catch up with all my friends and family, even managing to sneak a quick trip to see my parents in Spain. The shift who we allocate the jobs coming in to are based in the parade room and generally follow the same shifts as the control room which means you get to form close bonds with them and they become an extension of your family. We tend to socialise together at the police bar which is closed to non-police personnel and has a function room for social events. Everyone has heard that all the officers' shifts will be changing but that is something that is always being gossiped about, and might not happen. I love my shift, they are great, I am the only full-time woman on my shift and I have to admit I do sometimes use that to my advantage.

The lovely maintenance man Rex seems to think I am his surrogate daughter, he is near to retirement and he fusses around, he insists on moving my car closer to the station for me when I am on late shift so I don't have to walk so far in the dark and there is also another favourite of mine. Martin the lovely chef in the staff restaurant he will always text me to let me know when he is cooking roast lamb as he knows it is my favourite. I am not sure if this service is offered to everyone, but I once went down too late and missed out and he was so upset for me. So he has done this for me ever since, he is lovely and kind. In return I am happy to listen to Rex chatting to me when I am eating lunch, his favourite subject is also his passion. Martin once had a problem where he needed lots of forms filling in for him, I had a spare few minutes so I sat and helped him, and we have been friends ever since. I think he is gay, but not sure, he never mentions a partner, but he is very effeminate, I don't care if he is, I like him and he makes me laugh, and he does make a beautiful roast lamb, so it is swings and roundabouts. They are both lovely and there is no hidden agenda. Some people are unkind about Rex as he is very slow and a bit deaf, but again, if I am sat in the restaurant or walking about the building I will always stop and chat to him, I think he is a sweetie.

We have part-time staff that are allocated to any shift and we call these floaters, yes, I know they have probably heard every joke associated with the word but they are vital for covering when someone is off. My sergeant is called Craig McDonald, he is a very dry humoured dour scot and he makes me laugh sometimes until my ribs ache, normally in the early hours of the morning when it is mid-week and we have to catch up on admin duties he will sit and we will put the world to rights, he is so supportive of everyone, has a huge family and I don't know of anyone who doesn't like and respect him. He is a real hard worker, a fair man who expects a lot from his staff but he will also support us all with all the trials and tribulations life throws at us, he is very protective of his shift which is made up of a mixture of three civilian chaps Gavin, John and Max. Then there is me and two police officers, Steve and Rob, we look out for each other, we know each other's families and friends, we support each other. Part-time people also work in the control room but as I said they are not attached to any specific shift.

Back on shift tomorrow night, so have just this afternoon to spend with Ruth, she should be arriving shortly. Helen has left us to it, she is a bit fed up of the drama of it all, she has enough of it at work, I don't blame her, so am I if I am being honest, I have listened to Ruth over the years and the story never changes, I am not sure what I am going to say that we haven't already said. Her boyfriend Marcus is a heel and a cheat and a liar, his wife is right, but Ruth doesn't want to hear that from me, she is meeting up with him for a chat at a local café and she is sure he is going to finish it with his wife and they will be together at long last. I cannot see it myself after all this time, but I haven't the energy to go through it all again, there is always so much drama, it is like watching one of the soaps on television but when you turn the off switch the screaming continues. My house phone is ringing and I get up to answer it, it is Jason, out of the blue, he says he is coming over; he has to speak to me about something important.

I am not going to get all worried or bothered about it, this is typical of Jason, it will just be something trivial, this is something he does when he wants to chat to me about work or something he doesn't want to bring up at the quiz, not sure what his problem will be and normally I don't have to give him any solutions he just needs to get things clear in his own mind when he has a problem, sometimes he wants my opinion on something he is buying, or he needs me to witness his signature, I never get worried. As I am working tomorrow I want to chill out and relax with a glass of wine and put my feet up ready for the four late shifts I have coming up, I won't get home until well after midnight on those days and I know it is going to be heavy going as it is coming up to the Easter Bank holiday so I know it will be demanding in the control room – just the luck of the draw to get late shift. Bank holidays are always hectic, but on the plus side the time goes quite quickly.

Ruth arrives and the afternoon is as I predicted – she has bought a mountain of food from her mum, who always seems to think I need feeding, fattening up. After I have packed the fridge and freezer with it all we sit, we chat, she asks nothing about how I am, I get up and get the ironing board out as she talks, I plough through my pile of ironing, she hardly notices, she tells me about how unreasonable the wife is being towards Marcus who she manages to portray as the injured party. I iron and she talks, I pack the ironing board away and sit back down, she is so totally wrapped up in her own life, she drops everything when her chap calls and nothing we say will change that. He will never leave his wife, we know that, I think deep down she knows that, she is making me cross as she cannot see that she is the other woman and she is being played as a fool, after nodding in all the right places her phone indicates a message coming in and she hurriedly packs up her bag, I know she has been summoned by him who can give her maybe 30 minutes of his time, but I say nothing. I am annoyed with her and I think she knows it. She has exhausted me, I just want to rest for a while but just literally seeing Ruth to the door and the phone rings, so I shout my goodbye's and let her see herself out, it is my old school friend Annabel calling for a catch up, I do love to hear from her, as her life is so comical and as she runs a riding stables with her husband – she always has amusing stories to tell, she is married to a crazy ex jockey called Frank and she has twin boys Howard and Ralph, but I have to cut her short as Jason is hovering in the lounge he is pacing and running his hands through his hair, I cannot read the expression on his face so not sure if he is bothered about something but Annabel is fine, she is always doing this to me, with the boys and a busy business to run neither one of us takes it personally if one of us has to rush off, we can catch up later.

Jason is looking nice today, he has his light blue shirt on which I have told him is my favourite on many occasions as it brings out the colour in his eyes. I wasn't expecting him so it is a nice surprise I suppose, with him he has a nice bottle of wine, and it is my favourite, a rosé. He walks straight through the lounge and into the kitchen, I guess to open it, none of this twist bottle for him, so he is fighting with the corkscrew when I get to him.

"Well, this is a nice surprise," I say lightly, because it is, I am genuinely pleased to see him as I reach to grab some glasses in the cupboard behind him, he grabs my hand, then he pulls me close to him and kisses me, kisses me, full on the lips, he kisses my chin and my cheeks and then goes back to kissing me full on the lips. This time his tongue sneaks in and we are both kissing full on, it feels warm and pleasant and I don't stop him, not sure why, but I don't. I just allow it to happen, I stand leaned into to him, glasses still in my hand, it feels nice being kissed, I like it, it has been a while for me but this wasn't a desperate frantic kiss, it was slow and sensual.

He is holding me round the waist, not too tight but tight enough to be a hold, and he is continuing to kiss me, my eyes are wide open, but his are closed and he is running his hands up my back. His hand wanders to the front of my blouse but I meet him with my one free hand stopping his route, he stops kissing me and opens his eyes, not sure what my expression says but he must have been concerned as he says, "Are you okay?"

It is all I can do to whisper, "Yes."

My mind is playing hoopla with my brain, this is Jason, this is good old reliable Jason, he has never done this before and it is late afternoon and we haven't even had a drink yet, and he is feeling me up in the middle of my kitchen! I don't know how to react, it has been a while since I have been with someone, it feels good, but that doesn't mean I am going to throw myself at him. My body is screaming yes, but my brain is shouting equally loud no.

"Jason," I catch my breath, "What are you doing, what is all this about?"

His voice comes out all breathless, "Don't you think it is about time?" he says nothing more, as if that is the only explanation I need. He brings his lips back to meet mine, this time I relax and enjoy it, and when his hand reaches my blouse, I don't stop him even when he reaches inside and cups my breast in his hand, I don't stop him, I do think about it for a second, I am not wearing my most flattering underwear, the bra has seen better days and all the white bits have turned grey in the wash, but this doesn't seem to bother him. He reaches down and falters with the zipper on my jeans, okay maybe I should be saying something, this is obviously leading somewhere and although he might not have noticed my grey over washed bra, if this goes further he will definitely notice my huge comfort knickers, again in a lovely shade of grey, not exactly matching the bra but grey nonetheless, but still I offer no resistance. This is Jason, dependable Jason, it feels nice, it feels okay, it has been a long time since I had someone hold me like he is doing, he won't hurt me, he won't call me frigid, there are no thunder crashes or lightning flashes, no fireworks but as he takes my hand, removes the glasses and places them on the kitchen unit and pulls me towards the stairs up to my room I offer no objection as he lays me on my bed and slowly kisses my neck and shoulder then lower to my breasts, the only thought in my head is, this is Jason, and this is nice. It has been too long, my head is saying what the hell do you think you are doing but my body is saying, come on, it has been a long time, my body wins, I relax back into the bed, I really want to feel the closeness of a male.

I watch as he stands up, undresses quickly and pulls the condom from his wallet, he is so prepared, so precise and neat, so analytical, we have hardly spoken but I know we are going to have sex, I should be angry at his arrogance but I am not. He lays his clothes tidily on the end of the bed, unsure what to do I sit up in bed and then he joins me, he pushes me down gently and lays next to me, he strokes my face, he slowly undoes my bra and I raise my hips to remove my underwear. I look at him I am so thankful his eyes are closed, I hope it is with the romance of the situation and not because he has glimpsed the size of my knickers, I lie back on the bed it is early evening and I am lying here being seduced by Jason, I cannot believe it, there is no talking, just silence as he makes love to me, I cannot think of anything to say, so I lay there watching as he kisses my breasts, teasing my nipples with his tongue. I never have thought of Jason as a lover, he is slow and deliberate, I stroke his shoulder gently as he caresses my hips but doesn't move any lower. The lovemaking is slow and gentle, there is not much foreplay but it feels good, he enters me quickly and moans loudly as he climaxes almost immediately, he lays on top of me, there is no change in position, it is all very ordinary, I feel a pang of disappointment and a small part of me just wants to cry. It certainly isn't like Cyprus. We lay afterwards in each other's arms, I look at him, already he has drifted off to sleep, I don't know why people do that, why do they have to sleep immediately afterwards, it wasn't exhausting, there was no effort of any kind really, the whole event has lasted just a few minutes, I am thankful though, as I don't know what I would say if he was awake, not sure if it would be awkward. Oh Christ, what have we done, I look at him, now he is laid next to me now snoring gently and I prop myself up on my elbow, I look up at him, really look at him, he looks very peaceful, he isn't so bad really, okay maybe sex isn't all it is cracked up to be, it wasn't as bad as my first, okay so maybe it wasn't as good as Cyprus, I would have wanted it to have lasted longer, or for my needs to be met, maybe he was nervous, maybe next time it will be different, but for me it was the first time in a long time, it was nice, is nice okay?

I hate that word, it is on a par with the word glad, or fine, both of which I hate too, but that is the only word I can use to describe our lovemaking. It wasn't the worst I have ever had, I had no orgasm, he never touched me below my waist, there was no hip raising intensity to our lovemaking, it wasn't mind numbingly body shaking wonderful as once experienced with a previous lover, but it was gentle and nice?

Chapter Five

We kind of went on from there, when he woke up there were no huge discussions or declarations of love, we laid facing each other I asked him why now and his reply was, "Because it feels right doesn't it?"

I didn't argue, I didn't say anything, I just shrugged, it felt okay to me, just okay – I wasn't unhappy, I wasn't happy, it was that horrible word again, nice. We spent the evening watching a film and ordered a take-away, we drunk the wine, it was nice. He stayed the night although he didn't make any move to make love to me again, I did try, I stroked his chest but he didn't respond I moved my hand to the top of his thigh, but still no reaction, I cuddled up to him, but he turned over so I was facing his back I laid back and listened to his breathing as he slept.

I tried to examine my feelings towards him, what had happened to make him turn up at my door with a bottle of wine and seduction in mind, how do I feel about him – do I love him, I could answer that immediately, no I didn't but I cared for him, can caring turn into love, can it turn into real passion, or does passion have to be there straight away. I cannot sleep, I lay for hours mulling over what is the basis of a good relationship, can you exist without passion in a relationship, can I pretend that sex doesn't matter to me, well good sex, was Cyprus just a one-off, was Cyprus the dream or is what I have just experienced with Jason the reality, do all relationships have an element of bad sex? I go over the same question in my mind over and over again, is this the best it is ever going to get. Eventually I drift off to sleep.

When I wake up Jason is laid next to me, he has pulled his underwear on, I find this really odd, really dismissive, I wonder to myself why he wouldn't want to lie naked next to me. I watch him as he sleeps, he is good-looking, he has a nice body, I have to admit that, but do I feel passion, I shake my head, no I definitely don't.

When he wakes up, he stretches and turns to face me, I can smell his morning breath, this is all new to me and instinctively I turn my head away.

"You okay" he asks. I look back at him and smile weakly and without waiting for my reply he gets up and heads into the en suite. I don't know what to do, do I get up and go downstairs to make tea, do I offer him breakfast, what is the expectation in this situation? If he makes a move to make love to me again, do I really want him to, my body shudders involuntarily as if answering for me. I am still thinking, my mind racing, as I watch the closed door, do I turn him down, and if so, how, what do I say? I don't get to choose as Jason comes out of the en suite and reaches for his clothes, I watch him and give a sigh of relief as he dresses quickly and without a glance in my direction he heads out of the room, I dive into the en suite as he heads downstairs.

He is halfway down he shouts back at me, "I will put the kettle on, cannot stay long as I promised Sean I would help him move some furniture." I just stand there, one hand on the en suite door and I give out a huge sigh of relief.

After that everything seemed to happen very quickly and within weeks Jason gave up his rented flat and moved in, I cannot recall a big discussion, his tenancy was coming to the end as they were selling up and he said it made sense for him to pay me rather than look for somewhere else, I am not sure if I agreed, but I find that when speaking to Jason he assumes his good ideas mean everyone thinks the same, so without any great discussion I come home to find all his things turn up in boxes, it happens one weekend when I am working, much to the surprise of his family and mine too.

Sean helps him carry all the boxes and they both seem happy with the arrangement, when Sean and I are in the kitchen and Jason is grabbing a quick shower he turns to me, "Brilliant timing for Jason wasn't it, I mean where would he have gone, eh." I say nothing and he continues, "I mean, I couldn't see him moving back with Ma, that would drive him nuts, you two getting together officially is the best thing and you have loads of room here."

I said nothing, because there was nothing I could say, it was almost like I was a convenience. I loved my life before, yes, I did want someone to share the evenings with, I did want a partner, and maybe I did send signals to Jason, but well, overnight my home has changed and he has moved in, without any meaningful conversations about our future or our feelings for each other, it seems to me that Jason gets an idea in his head and that is it, it happens, and stupidly I let it.

He has totally taken over my home, his company car is a permanent fixture outside of my house. Before I realise it the weeks turned into months and before I knew it he had been with me for five months. See if we were a proper couple I would have said we were together for five months, but I said he was with me, like a lodger, but we share a bed, well we sleep next to each other, after a few short episodes of intimacy, nothing different than the first time – very quick, very predictable, nothing spontaneous or passionate, my needs are not met, and I lay there feeling frustrated, then we fall asleep next to each other, that is all. My house and my life feels like it has been taken over, there have been two large boxes in my lounge one on top of the other containing paperwork, they haven't moved since he moved in, they drive me mad, every time I hoover I manage to disturb them and the top box falls over spilling the contents on to the carpet, I have picked the stuff up so many times I could scream.

I am glad he had a furnished flat and no furniture has come here, I don't think I could have coped, I like minimalism, I like to be neat and tidy, but nothing of his things has been moved into a logical place, because there isn't a logical place, it is old paperwork and this is a home and not an office, everything has been dumped with a view that he will sort it out one day, but he never does, it drives me nuts.

If my family are shocked about him moving in, none of them comment at all, even my sister Judy says nothing, asks nothing and make no comment on my relationship. She used to visit quite often with the children but I seldom see her at my house, we seem to be distancing ourselves and I am not sure why. Sometimes I wish the family would question me – I wish they would ask me, how am I, am I happy, how is Jason, but there is polite silence. I know they find Jason a bit patronising, if they would only ask me then I could tell them the truth but they all accept it that we have always been a kind of item. How wrong they are.

My home is lovely, well, it was lovely prior to Jason moving in, and I was very proud of it. I have decorated every room in light colours, the kitchen is bright and airy and all the carpets are neutral, there used to be no clutter, just carefully placed sentimental items I have purchased or been given. I like to describe my house as modern, light, bright and feels just right, although now, it doesn't feel that way at all, it feels like a huge archive area for paperwork and boxes, all collecting dust, he has taken over both of my spare rooms and his "stuff" boxes of all shapes and sizes occupy every part of the house. He has so much stuff, he is always intending to have a sort out, get rid of things, but it never happens.

At first I didn't create a huge fuss, in an odd way it is reassuring to see someone else's belongings in the cupboard, to see his clothes in the wardrobe, and his toothbrush in the holder in the bathroom, to me it meant that I was part of a couple, I belonged to someone, I wanted it, I liked that, made me feel a part of something, like I wasn't on the outside looking in anymore, I was finally part of the great couple's mystery.

Sex was okay, a bit routine I guess, never anything different despite my trying. When he does bother, he never touches me intimately, he will stroke my stomach and nothing lower, it feels detached, always the same position – him on the top, I wish maybe it could have lasted longer and still no thunderbolts, but it was okay.

Now we were a couple I thought maybe we could do couple type things, I don't know what couple's things exactly – have dinner parties maybe, go round to other couple's houses, but we didn't, we could do couples things like making plans for holidays and shopping but actually we never did. We don't go anywhere or do anything except for the quiz night; it is like nothing has changed for him except his postcode.

I am not sure if Jason is happy, he seems it, he goes about his life, he plays squash with Phil and Sean on a regular basis and sometimes meets them at the gym or goes for a pint, sometimes even golf, we still go to quiz night together, but only when my shifts allow, if not he will go on his own, I ask who was there and what happened, but he normally gives the same response, "Oh you know the usual."

I push the issue, "Did you win?"

But he either shakes his head or replies, "What do you think."

I push even further, "I don't know, that is why I ask." But his head is in the newspaper or in his laptop, if I push it as sometimes I do, he looks at me, shakes his head and either walks out if he is stood up or ignores me and watches the television, or even more maddening he will put his headphones on and work on his laptop, I think that is just so rude. It seems that we have no conversation, nothing to talk about; I am not sure even now what the reason was for the seduction in my kitchen. We are like strangers sometimes, I generally only get to know his whereabouts by the sports clothes that are in the wash, and yes I have somehow got lumbered doing all the washing, we never really talk, I ask him how Sean is and his standard reply is always the same, "yeah he is okay."

He sometimes invites Phil and Sean over to watch the Rugby, he has upgraded my Sky package to include sports and movies so we have all the top games on our television, I have to say he does pay his way, we halve the bills and halve the mortgage, at his insistence, sometimes I ask him for his contribution towards the food which I hate doing, so I generally forget, but if we have a take-away he usually pays, if I am on late shift, I will come in to find them sprawled out in the lounge, sometimes if I finish early I will join them and we have beer and pizza and it is all very entertaining and easy-going. We are all mates, there are no secret looks between Jason and I like I see with other couples, no intimacy, I miss that, I would love to cuddle up to my man on the sofa to watch a movie, but I always have to sit by Phil as Jason prefers the recliner chair, I want to be able to make love with total abandonment, maybe even sit on the sofa together, but when I ask him to sit with me, he always replies the same, that he prefers the chair. The only intimacy seems to be when I ask Jason for a foot massage, this only happened by accident when I slipped and sprained my ankle, he was so attentive, rubbing it gently, I was almost sad when it recovered. I have given up asking now, but I would love for someone to make love to me spontaneously, without listening to excuses just take me anywhere but the bedroom, I want someone to be demonstrative and even a little bit tactile, maybe perhaps pull me down to sit on his lap and hug me sometimes, even join me in the shower or bath, something to show me I am sexy and beautiful, and something tactile to show everyone we are a proper couple, but I guess it is just the way it is going to be, Jason is not that type of person, not tactile at all, no matter how much I want him to be.

Phil is always jovial, always taking the mickey, finds humour in most situations, and Sean is either very happy or down in the dumps depending on his love life, Phil is very entertaining with stories of his love life, he is the resident philanderer, how he treats women is terrible and I only maybe half believe what he tells us, but I am also envious of his exploits, the one-night stands, the quickie sex with women he will never see again. Part of me envies those women, I could never tell Phil but I relish listening to the details, and he is never shy of telling us what he has been up too and with whom.

The four of us get on really well. We have curry nights but always just the four, never with any other couples, we never think to extend the invitation to those at the quiz night or to anyone else. Jason never asks about or shows any interest in my friends. Phil and I will mess around play fighting and teasing, sometimes Sean will join in, but never Jason, he just watches and laughs. Phil is very physical, he will hug me, his arms pulling me close to him, and I just want to stay there, just to be held, to feel his strong arms around me, or he will kiss my cheek and I long for it to be more than just a peck on the cheek. Every time he sees me he messes with my hair, and I complain loudly but I love the fact someone is touching me, he will tickle me, making me squeal with laughter, I love it; it is not done to make Jason jealous, not at all, but sometimes I wish he would show that he cares, but there is nothing. We were watching a film once, it was just a normal certificate 18 which had fighting and some sexual scenes, Phil teased and kept raising his eyebrows at me whenever the people on the screen were intimate, when we took the dishes to the kitchen Phil pulled me into his arms and said, "Do you want me and Sean to bugger off so you lovebirds can be alone?"

But I just shook my head. "It isn't like that, Phil, it would take more than a film."

Phil just stared at me his face frowning, he tilts my head up then brings his lips to mine, as soon as our lips meet he pulls away. "That is a shame." He kisses me gently on the lips once more then pulls away again. "A real shame."

We go back into the lounge, the credits are rolling and Sean has fallen asleep, Phil kicks his foot. "Come on, you, let's get going."

I watch as they leave, Sean heads to the downstairs toilet, Phil leans over and kisses me again, his body blocking Jason's view as his lips meet mine for the third time that night, Phil's lips are gentle on mine, I look at him, our eyes meet unblinking, then he pulls way and shakes his head slowly, I look at Jason, but he hasn't noticed, he is still watching the screen I am sure if Phil threw me down on the carpet and made love to me, all Jason would do would be to turn the volume up, no matter how much I long for it Jason, , it seems, is totally devoid of any emotion when it comes to me. Sometimes I will tell him about my friends, what they are up to, but I am sure he feigns interest, he couldn't name one of my friends which is a real shame. I know a few of his friends, he mentions them occasionally if he is checking his emails, I make a point of being interested but he never elaborates, no one ever comes to visit. The house phone rarely rings for him so he never answers it, I know that he keeps in touch with his University friends but they don't live locally, so he may go and see them sometimes, but not often. He has one close friend I know of but I have never met as he lives in London, Jason emails him and speaks to him on Skype on a regular basis, he always takes his laptop into the other room and wear headphones so he can talk in peace and leave me to watch television or he will speak when I am on late shift, there is nothing suspicious going on, he tells me he has spoken to whatever friend, he just never goes into details.

If I am being totally honest Jason is okay to live with, a bit like living with your brother really, I thought there would be shared secrets and little intimacies but Jason isn't like that, I thought there might be little gifts, spontaneous shows of affection, but nothing like that either. I do try, I leave his favourite chocolate bar on his briefcase but he never says anything, he doesn't reciprocate in any way. I cook a chilli one night, Phil and Sean are coming over as it is Phil's birthday, the chilli and rice are prepared and I have just put the garlic bread in the oven, everything is done, Jason is upstairs showering when Phil arrives, I let him in and walk into the kitchen.

"Where is Sean?" I ask.

Phil shrugs. "He has popped into the shop to grab some beers, I told him I would walk on ahead."

I smile and walk into the kitchen, I stir the chilli, Phil's arms envelope around my waist his lips nuzzling into my neck. "Now something smells good enough to eat," he murmurs.

I push him away playfully. "That is the chilli," I say brightly.

He sticks his finger in and sucks the sauce. "Mmm lovely, but I wasn't talking about the chilli." He smiles at me and pulls me close. "You smell delicious, happy birthday to me," he murmurs as he kisses me gently on the lips, I want so much to pull away but I don't, my lips respond to his, his hands roam up my body, his tongue pressing to mine, he pulls me close to him, pressing my body against his, we stay like this until we hear Jason's footsteps on the stairs. Phil pulls away and sticks his finger back in the sauce as Jason enters the kitchen he motions to the saucepan.

"Have a taste of that, Jason, bloody lovely, I didn't realise Angie could cook too."

Jason just shrugs and claps Phil on the back. "Happy birthday, mate, I got that film you were going on about, we can watch that tonight if you want."

He looks at me. "Don't bother about the table, we can have it on our laps okay." Without waiting for my reply he looks at Phil. "Where is Sean then?"

I don't hear Phil's reply as they walk into the lounge together, I look up and Phil has looked back and is watching me I shrug and reach over the table to collect the placemats. The evening carries on as usual, we eat on our laps, Phil and Sean both make lovely comments on the chilli but if they notice there is no comment from Jason none of them say anything, I sit on the sofa next to Phil, I have my legs tucked under me and he is stroking my ankle, it is comforting. We have an enjoyable evening, I take a small cake and put candles on and we laugh as Phil blows them out, he looks at me just as he is going to take a bite of his cake.

"You didn't make this did you, Angie?" I sneer at him good naturedly, he takes a huge mouthful, "Bloody lovely, if you did make it, and the chilli, seriously, girl, I would marry you tomorrow." I poke my tongue out at him as we join him laughing.

Later Sean helps me clear everything away and as I go upstairs to change into my pyjamas, I reflect on the night, Phil kissing me and putting his arms around me when I was cooking, stroking my ankle, Sean filling up my wine glass, helping me clear up, and Jason, well Jason doing nothing for me at all, all I want from him is just a little show of affection, some emotion, but there is nothing. I feel guilty that I allowed Phil to kiss me, maybe I shouldn't but I have needs and what is a small kiss. Jason acts more like a houseguest, mmm houseguest, can your lover be a houseguest? Is he your lover if you never make love, a houseguest who shares the other side of the bed? Well, that is how I see him, he isn't too bad in that he was tidy in some respects – he always put the cap on the toothpaste and the toilet seat was always put down, he makes the bed and he keeps his clothes impeccable, at first no real annoying habits, but then it seems once his lease was up on his flat and he moved in properly and, oh my word, it becomes clear to me that his work is totally chaotic, all his gadgets and half built possessions seemed to arrive almost overnight, they drive me mad, all at various stages of development, with paperwork and Post-it notes stuck everywhere. He is heavily involved in Patents and often leaves me forms to sign witnessing his signature, he leaves big pointers showing where I need to sign, like I am stupid, these are to register them as a patent, I did start reading them at first but now I just sign them and leave them for him on the table. The papers can lay there for days, and I tried at first to ignore it, but they were on the dining table and then on the coffee table in the lounge. When I try to move anything, they fall on the floor, it drives me nuts when I complain his standard response is that he was just about to move them, then, in fairness he does, so why can he not do it straight away, why do I have to get all wound up and angry before he does anything about it? I buy some clear storage boxes for him to use but they are still in the carrier bag untouched.

Sometimes when he is working from home and I am on a day off I could scream at the chaos that he has created, but I bite my lip and go to the gym or go for a run, which is my new passion, when I am angry or stressed or upset I will put on my trainers and run, trouble is, I seem to be running an awful lot lately, if I don't go for a run then sometimes if the weather is nice, maybe I just stroll around the shops on my own, that is the downside of shifts, when I have days off, everyone else is working, the upside to shifts is that I don't have to spend every evening with Jason, I think I might just want to kill him. So I get time on my own and we both have time apart to do our own thing and then spend some time at home, the main social event for both of us is still at the quiz together. This is the highlight of my social calendar, I especially love it if both Phil and Sean are there, when we walk home altogether, the four of us, it is Jason and Sean in front and Phil and I walking behind.

Phil is always entertaining, telling me stories about his shift, he gets on well with them all and I know he likes Helen, he just won't admit it, he always holds my hand until we get to the crossroads where he turns off for his house, he shouts a cheery goodbye to the boys then reaches down to kiss my cheek, well he used to, until the exchange in the kitchen, now he kisses me on the lips, I don't object, I know I should do, but I like the softness of his lips on mine it is the only intimacy I have with another man, it is only a matter of seconds but I crave that feeling of intimacy. There is nothing ever said, sometimes he will hold my face as he kisses me; it is not a lover's kiss, it is always on the lips but it is a companionable kiss. Before I know it, it is over and I watch as he walks away and I walk fast to catch the boys up. At the next road turning Sean turns into his road, he kisses my cheek and says goodnight, I link my arm through Jason's, it is the only intimacy we share, as we walk in companionable silence, if Jason has seen Phil kissing me he never mentions it. Am I being unfaithful to Jason, no, I don't see it as that; Phil is just my friend, nothing more.

Chapter Six

If ever I want to moan or complain about anything it was Craig McDonald, my Sergeant who I use as my sounding board, everyone does, we know we can trust him, I especially know I can, I know he will never betray that trust. Sometimes we talk long into the night on shifts when it is quiet and I know I can confide in him things that I would never tell anyone, well, it is normally me that talks and he listens.

One quiet night shift we were in the administration office just updating the system and he asked how everything was going at home, and so I told him, I told him the truth, the words just poured out of me and I couldn't stop them, it was as if he had caught me at my most vulnerable. I told him everything, I said that I didn't know if I loved Jason, well I did love him, but as a brother, not as a lover. The sex was boring and predictable and not very frequent, I asked Craig if the fact that I didn't love him make me a bad person? I just blurted it out, and once I had started I couldn't stop, the words just wouldn't stop, and he listened, Craig just listened. He nodded his head occasionally and he didn't offer any advice, he made tea and we carried on chatting, if someone came in, he waited for them to leave, then encouraged me to carry on, I felt a huge sense of relief that I finally confided in someone. Not that it will make any difference at all.

We are very lucky to have Craig as our Sergeant, he is a fair, loyal and supportive man. It isn't just me, he often takes one of the chaps out into the meeting room for a chat if they need to have some support, or they will go to the end of the room so they cannot be overheard but still be there if we need him, he will never discuss anyone's problem, he can be totally trusted.

He isn't that much older than me, only maybe ten or twelve years, but he has an old head on his shoulders. Craig is happily married with two children, he married very young the first time at just seventeen. He was married for just a year or so, and then divorced. He admits he had a really bad childhood, he also reveals he was a real rebel until he met his new wife and he joined the force, so he has been through a lot himself. His first wife was an alcoholic and he went through hell with her, in the end she took her own life, it must have been hell for him but he is amazing. He never judges anyone, he never tries to tell people what to do, he listens, really listens and as he has been though a bad marriage himself and only now is he very happy, he can appreciate our problems, it is great to hear him talk about his wife and children, he still gets a buzz when he sees her and still loves to be near her and to make love to her, he tells us this, he is not embarrassed, he relishes his time with her, he spends a lot of time and effort on gifts for her – browsing the internet to find unique ways to make her birthday or Christmas special. I used to wonder all the time if she knows how he feels, I used to think about their marriage and wonder if she is as happy, then we all got to see for ourselves just how happy they are, just by the way she speaks to him on the phone and when she has come in to bring something for him, they have the secret looks, the gestures, they look so much in love, we watched them out the window one evening. He had forgotten something and she brought it in then came in to say hello to us all, he walked her back to the car and we watched as he laughed with her then held her close, kissing her goodnight, then running his hand under her chin and holding her like he couldn't bear to be parted from her. We childishly bellowed out of the windows and he just looked up and laughed, he wasn't embarrassed at all, I couldn't help but watch enviously, why can it not be the same for me?

For some reason I felt I couldn't discuss this with my parents. sister or friends, although she has helped me in the past, my poor sister Judy has been through so much emotional stress I cannot burden her with my problems. I know if I told my mum she would just be really upset and come out with quotes like "you look at life through rose-coloured glasses" or "you expect too much." I cannot be doing with that, so when she rings I chat to her as if everything is okay, and I do that to most people, even going to the point of inventing nice things that Jason has done.

I seem to be isolated from everyone – I shut myself into my little world and from the outside everyone would think we were a normal happy couple. Mum and Dad are pleased I have settled down, I chat to Annabelle on the phone and tell her everything is fine, and Helen and Ruth think I am happy but sometimes I wish I could tell someone that sometimes I am a bit scared; scared because Jason has his dark side. I know he would never hurt me physically, he is not like that, but if I thought Sean was bad, Jason is much worse, he is often moody, he can be so patronising and so argumentative but then when I argue back he becomes sulky and withdrawn, we can go days without speaking, I hate it. I know people have to argue, they just do, but my parents would have it out and then get on with life, there were no long silences between them, they said their piece and then moved on, I want the same I just want my home to be a happy place, I want to have fun and laugh and make love, I want so much to have intimacy, I crave intimacy but Jason it seems wants none of that. I make suggestions for nights out for both of us, but he doesn't want to, I wear pretty nightdresses but it has no effect, he stays up late watching television or online to his friends, I don't know what else I can do, it seems that unless I have a patent pending on my forehead Jason just is not interested.

He has quite a few idiosyncrasies: he always wears his shoes for one day only then puts them back in the box and chooses another similar pair; he is fastidious about his clothes, he has to iron them himself which gets no argument from me, although he will sometimes iron my uniform shirts and when he does they are always perfect. He is also obsessed with his company car, it is a lovely Audi but he won't let me use it, the company gave permission but he still won't let me, or anyone else for that matter use it. Another one of his worst traits he has is that he is very mean with money where certain things are concerned. I never knew that about him, I am shocked at just how mean he can be. I don't understand why, he is in a well-paid job, we both are, we are not short or struggling but he just won't spend his money on anything he calls frivolous. I can go on and on and probably write a very boring book about Jason and his horrible habits.

I love fresh flowers in the house, I always have, but Jason complains it affects his sinuses, I know the truth is that he thinks them a waste of money, I have never seen him so much as sneeze in the summer time. His lovely Ma would come around with freshly picked flowers from her garden, spend ages arranging them and he never objected to them. My parents sent a lovely bouquet on my birthday and he thought they were beautiful, they didn't seem to affect his sinuses then but then I guess because they are free. I see a totally different side of him where money is concerned, he will pay his share of the bills without argument, I cannot argue with that. If I buy beers or anything different he will ask how much he owes me, but I hate it, I want to buy something for him because I know he will like it, just little things that I think might make him smile, maybe his favourite aftershave but his comment is always the same "was it on special offer?" or "you should have waited for my birthday." He drives me nuts. On my birthday he told me to buy myself something and he would pay for it, I didn't bother and he didn't notice, he bought a very general card and put best wishes Jason in it. Phil bought me a girlie pack which consisted of a very large pair of knickers, a face pack, some false spots with ugly fake pus on the top and some false eyelashes, we both thought this was hilarious but Jason just pulled a face. Phil's card was funny too – two goldfish in a half filled bowl with one saying to the other, "I think we drank too much last night," I thought it was hilarious and so did Phil, but Jason just smirked.

Jason loves to spend money on nice clothes but doesn't like the heating on claiming it was cheaper to wear another jumper, to be honest, sometimes, I cannot bear to be at home sometimes so I will willingly swap my shifts or work extra to avoid it, or when he really pushes me to the limit I drag my trainers out and go for a run, running is something I do quite often now.

In just a few short months whatever life or hope there was in the relationship has died. He hasn't changed, we never were that tactile, neither did we leap into bed in a frenzy to be together but the sexual side eventually has dwindled to non-existent. My life with him is dreary, I suppose I am to blame as I still have this idea in my head that love will be fireworks and passion but I have none of that with Jason. He is, as I always knew he would be – reliable, steadfast but equally boring Jason. The truth is, I know what I have to do, I just have to pluck up the courage, choose my moment and do it. I wish I had someone to talk to about it, but everyone seems to think he is great, they think I am so lucky to have landed myself such a good catch, I should be so grateful, but no one knows the real truth – I feel suffocated, like this is it, this is my life.

Today I will be working with another shift which is always strange, I won't know their collar numbers, which is their individual Police identity number, they wear it on their shoulder and it is used to call them on the radio, when they are in a vehicle they are allocated a call sign for the people in the vehicle. I will just offer to answer the phones and log the calls as it takes a while to get to know their personalities: who can be relied on, who will let you down, who will respond to a job, who will respond in an emergency. The shift I am working with today will know it off by heart, they will know all the officers individually. When we change shifts it is all something that we will have to learn all over again, with the other shift we all knew each other really well, and over the few years I have worked there I have got to know many officers but not this crowd, I wasn't too bothered as I was just working the one extra shift today and I do know both Helen and Phil on the shift so I will be okay.

I put my name down as the shift was short and to be honest Jason has been particularly difficult lately, I just need to be out of the house, we don't really need the extra money but I have to get out, I just have to, he will drive me nuts if I don't.

I am trying to be extra patient as I know he has something important going on at work, but recent events, well one in particular, really made me angry. I came home from a late shift, just winding down, I had tidied some papers away before going to bed after the shift, I just shuffled them into a neat pile and put them on the desk. I didn't hide them, they were in the same place he left them but tidy, I snuck into bed, without waking him, I try to be considerate when on late or early shift, it isn't fair to interrupt his sleep but I wish he would return the favour. This particular night in question I was exhausted, it had been a busy shift, very demanding, so I fell into bed, what seemed like minutes later I was woken by him standing over me in the bedroom shouting about my uselessness. I had no idea what he was ranting and bellowing about so I turned over and ignored him, he ranted and stamped about for several more minutes then slammed the bedroom door and I heard him stamping his way downstairs, with more stamping, swearing and slamming of doors, it then dawned on me what he was talking about, he was looking for his precious papers, the ones I had tidied, they were right where he left them but in a tidy pile. I wasn't in the mood for another one of his

55

pointless arguments or silences so I quietly went downstairs, got the papers from the desk which he needed and were right on top of the desk so he couldn't have looked that hard, I handed them to him and as he reached to take them I childishly dropped them to the floor then walked back to bed without a word, I didn't even look at him, I couldn't be bothered, this was the last straw, I have had enough, I am not his mother or his secretary, it is over, he has to go.

I woke up several hours later, the sun was streaming in through the window and I couldn't sleep, I laid for a while then tossed and turned in the duvet no more sleep is coming to me, so I thought no point in just lying there, so I showered and then made myself some breakfast, just toast and juice and then I just sat eating at the dining table, one of my favourite places in my home, gives a lovely view of the garden and the sun comes through the large patio window. Well, there used to be a lovely view, some of it is obstructed now by Jason's golf bag which he has dumped against the patio door and his muddy golf shoes are on the floor next to them. I shake my head and already I can feel the irritation growing inside of me, I pull the mail towards me and look with interest at the holiday brochures left half hidden underneath some other paperwork, I frown as I have never seen it before, I gently pull it out, Jason must have picked them up. Intrigued I flick through and immediately saw that Jason had highlighted a Scottish break, there are notes and figures in the column, it has always been my dream to go to Scotland since watching monarch of the glen on television and Jason knows that I have always wanted to go there. On the side of the brochure he had noted some dates, I am even more intrigued now, so I get up to get my calendar, when I check I can see it coincides with my few days off, in just a week or so time, so he was planning a short break was he? I am a bit more than surprised, shocked more like it, he has made an effort, but I also see it as my opportunity, a weekend away with just the two of us, it couldn't be better, this would be the time I could sit with him away from any distractions, and away from the house, we could talk about us, I could speak to him about how I was feeling, I would tell him it just wasn't working – that we were not ideal for each other, that I wanted out, out of this relationship, well it is hardly that, I am sure deep down he feels the same, he must do.

I quickly check on the time – have I got time to make a few phone calls, I hadn't spoken to Gemma or Ruth in a while and I know I have to call my sister and discuss it with her, she has a way of putting things into perspective, she can give me the support and courage I know I am going to need. I dialled her number but there was no reply, I wouldn't leave a message if I couldn't tell her face-to-face then I would at least speak to her directly to tell her that I was finishing with Jason, she would be supportive, I know she would. Suddenly I feel excited, I was going to make changes to my life, I was going to finally be honest and free myself from the monotony of Jason.

I never made that call, still working an extra day with the other shift I got changed and got myself into work, immediately I arrived I could tell the shift was busy. As soon as I got in, it was full on, the calls were non-stop. The motorway running by our town was very busy so I didn't get a break until a few hours later.

I was taught a trick when I joined the force – always keep a packet of cigarettes in your handbag, as smokers get breaks but non- smokers get overlooked, so this is something that only a few people know. I don't actually smoke, never have done, never likely too, but when the sergeant on the shift offers me, I take a cigarette break with everyone else, no one notices or pays any attention, I have never been asked why I am not smoking, I guess they think I have just finished one. Normally I just stand with the other smokers and take in a bit of fresh air, have a chat and chill out before returning to the business of the control room, okay fresh air might be a slight contradiction maybe but I stand and try to clear my mind before going back to the phones ringing and the busy radios. There was no one out there at first, it was nice and peaceful the sun was trying to shine and I held my face up to try and get the warmth, my eyes closed I leaned against the wall and relaxed, it was lovely, a few precious moments of silence was wonderful. I heard someone walk towards me and then felt someone next to me and when I opened my eyes, Phil was mirroring my stance, his eyes were closed and he was smiling, I nudged him and we laugh.

I can always speak to Phil on a one-to-one, but when others are around he reverts to being jack the lad – always teasing me and turning everything into a joke, normally a sex related one that boosts his ego. Today was no different, he asked me how I was coping on his shift and having to really work as opposed to playing at work with the other shift and chided me about my fake smoking, but I give as good as I get, he is a social smoker, he doesn't smoke normally unless there is someone else having one. We chatted about the lovely warm sunshine and then I asked how Gemma was. Surprisingly for Phil he spoke about his on-off relationship with her and how it was on at the moment, they were happy and it was going well, and then for no apparent reason he pushed himself off the wall, facing me directly he looked at me straight in the eye and asked how was it with me and Jason and how were we getting on. This was new territory, we didn't normally speak about our personal relationships and private things, thoughts and feelings are taboo, there is no hilarity to be had by him in discussing those things, and I don't know why but before I could stop myself I burst into tears, how embarrassing, I sobbed and sobbed, the tears would not stop, my shoulders were shaking, a very shocked Phil put his arm round me and drew me close. Someone came out, I heard the door open and then close again so they had obviously thought better of coming out and had gone back in again. I don't know how long I stood there, but he just stroked my head and said, "That good eh."

I couldn't hold back the tears, I let out a huge sob, my nose is running, I look an absolute mess, and when I can finally get my words out I speak through my tears. "Oh, Phil, it is so much worse than that, I am so unhappy with Jason." I sniff back my tears and continue, "I mean I used to look at Sean at the quiz nights and think he was a moody bastard, but Jason, well he wrote the book, he is the master." I look at Phil he doesn't say a word, he just looks at me, his face blank I go on, "I cannot stand it anymore, Phil, really I cannot bear to be with him any more – I am going to finish it, I want my house back and I want my life back."

Phil looks at me. "So what are you going to do?"

I reply immediately, my voice a bit clearer now. "I know he has booked a trip to Scotland, it is supposed to be a surprise but I saw the brochure, it is after my night shift, I saw the confirmation too, so I am going to wait until we are away and then I am going to tell him." I look at Phil, he is now looking down at his boots kicking at the tarmac, I feel really strong now, so I continue, "I know it is for the best, I am not happy, he cannot be happy, I mean we never," I pause, it is too personal, Phil looks at me, I sigh heavily. "Phil, we never have sex, well I say never, I cannot remember the last time we were intimate, and then it was predictable and over all too soon, it's like he doesn't care, we are like an old couple, we never do anything together, we don't even bother fighting, we are not a couple, you know what, Phil, you and I have been more intimate when we play fight than Jason and I are, you certainly kiss me more."

I hiccup loudly and reach in my sleeve for a tissue which I use to blow my nose, I look at Phil his face is blank I continue, "I know what I am about to say is terrible, Phil, but I don't even think I like him anymore, does that make me a bad person?" Phil shakes his head, he doesn't say a word.

"Anyway," I go on, "I have decided, I will wait until we are away and then tell him, it is only fair to both of us, isn't it?" I question, still he says nothing, there is a long awkward silence but eventually I shake my head and continue, "You know, this holiday he has booked, well this trip to Scotland, it is the only thing that he has done in our relationship, the only effort he has made, I don't even know why he has bothered with that, but it is too little too late, what do you think?"

Phil says nothing, still he just stands there, saying nothing but he just looks at me, I look down at my feet, waiting, just waiting, but he says nothing.

I know he is probably embarrassed but I cannot stop, I shrug then continue, "Well, I know he is your friend but we are friends too, Phil, and I am sorry if I have upset you but I have decided anyway, I am finishing it, I am entitled to a life better than this." Suddenly I felt better, more in control. "Thank you, Phil, for listening, I feel so much better now, and I know I am going to be okay, I am doing the right thing."

I kiss Phil's cheek, then I pull him close to me and hug him, almost immediately his arms wrap around me pulling me into a bear hug, he holds me really close, this is what I want to feel a man's arms around me, making me feel better. I want to stay like this forever, but I pull away and look at him for a few seconds.

"That is all I want from Jason, just a hug sometimes, to show me he cares, I don't need huge declarations of love, I am not that needy, but I get nothing, nothing at all, I am not wrong here, am I?"

I look at him – my eyes searching his but I cannot make out his expression, when he doesn't reply I move away, I think I have really embarrassed him. "I had better go back," I say quietly, "thank you for listening."

He nods his head slowly, I leave him leant up against the wall, as I reach the door he calls out, "Angie." I look back and wait for him to say something but he just shakes his head. "Nothing," he says.

I pop to the bathroom to wash my face before I returned to the control room my shoulders a little less heavy, one of the girls asks if I am okay, remarking on my eyes and I easily fob her off telling her I had just had the worst coughing fit, she believed me, that is sometimes the good thing about working with people you don't know very well, they don't know you either.

Chapter Seven

Annabelle has called, she is worried that her husband Frank is being unfaithful, she has found a few receipts that don't check back to anything she has bought and she purchases everything, she is going to confront him tonight. She is blaming herself for being too wrapped up in the boys and the business and she just has no time to take care in her appearance and she has no energy left for sex, so she tells me she would blame herself if he did stray. Part of me wants to confide in her everything going on in my life – tell her what a sham my life is but for some reason I choose not to, she has enough going on and a small part of me feels ashamed that I cannot make Jason love me or want me, and that our relationship has failed, I have failed, I know for certain Jason isn't having an affair, that would be such an easy way out, but I know he never would, so we chat about mundane things, then when the conversation is coming to a close, and when I am least expecting it she asks me directly the one question I don't want to answer: do I think that Frankie would cheat on her with another woman, oh please no, don't ask me that question.

You see I know the answer but it is a secret I will never tell her, I can never tell her,

I don't think I will ever tell anyone, how can I, it is a secret I think I will take to the grave. You see, Annabelle seems to have the perfect life, from the outside she seems to have it all: the looks, the figure, the devoted husband and the successful business and twin boys. I almost used to envy her, but then I saw it from a totally different perspective when Annabelle was taken into hospital, she was having her boys, all through the pregnancy she was very organised, super organised, making sure the fridges were stacked with healthy snacks and ensuring that the freezer was full so Frank wouldn't starve without her. She packed her bag ready with everything she would need, but as it all happened very quickly, she went into labour whilst she was in a supermarket and an ambulance had to be called. Despite given him specific instructions, Frank packed her another bag and met her at the hospital. Everything was very hectic, but when she needed her things the next day she opened it to find the most impractical clothes in there: a dress she last worn to a Christmas Party, tiny underwear, two totally different coloured ridiculously high stiletto shoes and some other items she couldn't even remember having, so when I visited her in the cottage hospital near her home she asked me to pop to her house and pick up the proper bag which had everything she needed, plus a few bits.

She had been continually trying to contact Frank but he wasn't answering the house phone or the mobile phone or text messages, she was genuinely worried for him. I know her house very well, it used to be a rundown farm house but now restored to complete unashamed luxurious splendour with a large brand new stable block attached, it is quite chocolate box pretty and at the end of a country lane. I have been there many times. Unfortunately when I get there I realise that I have a problem, Annabelle has given me the keys to the back door but she has forgotten that there is a huge set of gates which need a remote control to open or a pass code, none of which I had, I think they are normally left open during the day unless horses are moving about, but it is not a huge problem. I left the car in the lane, jumped over the gate and walked up the short gravel drive, I let myself in by the back kitchen door and went up the back stairs to her dressing room where I started looking for the items I needed to pack.

Annabel and Frank have separate rooms for dressing with the bathroom and wardrobes in between, Annabelle has a lovely large bright dressing room and she is very well organised so I could find the case and most other things straight away, I had packed most items and was just looking for a smaller holdall for the cosmetics and things.

When I heard a noise, I didn't think anyone was home, I admit I was bloody scared, my heart was in my mouth, I felt for my mobile phone in my pocket in case I needed to call for assistance. I crouched down and stayed quiet, if it was burglars I wasn't going to confront them, no way, I am not that brave or stupid, so I just hid in the dressing room, I saw through the crack in the door the main bedroom door pushed open with force and I cowered down scared that I would be seen. I held my breath for a second and was shocked to see Frank and a young dark-haired chap stagger in to the room, the door crashed against the wall such was their urgency to get in, they were held in a clinch together and kissing as they entered the bedroom, they didn't notice me as they were far too busy ripping each other's clothes off, within seconds they were naked, and I couldn't move, I didn't know what to do.

I looked at Franks skinny sinewy body, I shuddered, it was not attractive at all, the other chap, he was also short, dark-skinned and jet black hair, I couldn't help it I have never seen two men together, I stood and watched as Frank and the young male who I recognised as Deano their stable hand fell onto the bed, Annabelle and Franks marital bed. I watched as they proceeded to kiss passionately and fondle each other. By the look of things this wasn't the first time this had happened. I couldn't help but stare as their mouths and hands sought each other, they were getting very intimate and I knew I had seen enough, I didn't want to see any more, I am not sure how but, somehow I gathered my wits about me and put items over my arm and sneaked down the back stairs, closing the door quietly I made my way back over the gate and back to my car. I was so quiet I know that they were totally unaware of my presence.

I returned to the hospital in a state of shock, I couldn't believe what I had seen, I certainly could not tell Annabelle that her beloved four foot nothing git of a husband was also bisexual and currently romping with the hired help as she pushed his children into the world. So I said nothing and cooed over the babies. When Frank arrived an hour or so later he didn't remark on the clothes she had on, and as he leaned over to kiss my cheek I am sure I flinched a bit at the memory of where his mouth had recently been but I don't think he noticed.

So when she asks me if I think Frank would cheat on her with another woman, what can I say, I say what anyone would say, "No, of course not," and under my breath I think, a man maybe.

Nights were uneventful, busy but not hectic, still Jason hasn't mentioned about the Scotland trip. I generally leave the house at about eight forty-five to start the night shift at nine-thirty, so we have a few hours in the evening together, but he has made himself scarce. So we leave the normal trail of notes about, that is how our life has progressed, a succession of notes; Post-it notes are our new best friends, none of us even bothering any more to add our names or kisses, not that he ever did. So I read the note and it tells me he is out with Sean and Phil, Phil must have booked a days holiday as I didn't think he was on rest day I am not sure when Jason is going to tell me about the weekend, and then a thought hits me, what if it isn't me he is taking, maybe that is why Phil gave me a strange look, maybe Jason was going to finish with me, that would make everything so much easier for me. I hug myself and dance around but then I think, that cannot be right, this is me, things don't happen like that for me, I am not so lucky, also because I have noticed items missing, like my travel hairdryer and my posh overnight bag, and my high gold shoes that I absolutely love.

I have one more night shift to go, still I haven't told anyone but Phil of my plans to finish with Jason, not even my sister yet. I really should have called her by now, not sure why I haven't confided in anyone, maybe they will think I am a failure, I think that they might try and talk me out of it, saying he is a nice lad and not that bad, and that I should be grateful, and maybe I should, but I want the lightning bolts, I want the fireworks, I am entitled to that surely I am. I want to go to bed feeling loved and wake up the same, isn't that the lyrics in a song, if not it should be, well anyway that is how I want to feel, I want to feel fantastic after making love, I want to look at my man and want him, want him so much it hurts. I want to have the unsaid conversations and private messages you see between couples who are so close they know what the other is thinking without ever being told.

So it is three am on the last night shift, I am inputting duties into the computer in the admin room when Craig comes in with a cup of tea, we chat for a while about the new shifts and he asks how things are going, he puts his arm around my shoulder, he says I seem distracted lately, I am not sure what he says but something hit's a nerve and before I can stop myself there I am once again spilling my problems out to him, tears streaming down my face, choking on my words as I spew out everything I pour my whole heart out to Craig. He is kind and patient as I blow my nose and calm down, the sobbing stops and I am able to speak properly, just the odd sniff, I tell him everything, I am much calmer now. In fact I am now very much more controlled, I tell him everything that I want to tell my sister, my mum and my friends I want.

No, I am determined, I want changes in my life and soon, I want my house to be mine again, all the masses of paperwork and cardboard boxes have to go, I do not want to wake up next to Jason for the rest of my life, I should never have let him make a pass at me, I should not have encouraged him, I am totally to blame, I know it and now I am going to be strong and despite the fact he has been lovely to me all this week, it is too little too late. It is all a lie, we are living a lie, it is now time to face the truth however painful, he is not what I want, he never was. And it is only fair on him and me for me to end the relationship. Craig agrees, although he doesn't say anything he just nods his head and when I finish he hugs me close, which just makes the tears start all over again. As he leaves the room he smiles at me and winks.

"Be strong, Angie, you do what is best for you, babe," he says. I smile at him through my tears; it gives me courage to do what I know I have to do.

Chapter Eight

When I get home in the morning Jason is excited, the bags are packed and although I am tired he is very insistent that I can sleep in the car. I haven't seen him like this ever, he is so animated, that is the only way to describe him, I cannot understand what has gotten into him, I just have time to grab a quick shower, hoping that it will wake me up a bit, but my eyes feel heavy and I am ready for my bed. I just manage to throw some personal items in my handbag before he is ushering me out of the door, he says I don't need anything, he has sorted everything for me, this does concern me as his version of what I like and mine are worlds apart but I go along with it anyway.

I throw my new boots, my jeans and a jumper in a carrier bag in case of emergency then we head to the car. He stops for fuel and I feel so tired, I cannot stop my eyes dropping and the motion of the engine helps me nod off for a few hours' sleep I wake to find we have covered some miles. We are now heading off the motorway and onto county lanes. I have to admit that the car ride is lovely, Jason is in a good mood, I just don't understand it, I want to ask him what is going on, I am scared to upset him and put him in a temper, he is so chirpy. When I ask questions he just taps his nose, smiles and says we are going on a road trip and it is a total surprise, I don't want to ruin it so I keep up the pretence of being happy, and I keep trying to guess.

I have decided that I will do the deed, but the timing has to be right, so I will not spoil the whole weekend, I will have the conversation on Sunday, before we leave, maybe at breakfast. I did initially think it would be a good idea to talk in the car on the journey, but I was not aware we would have company with Sean and his current girlfriend with us, you would hardly know they are there though as she is listening to something on her headphones and he also has headphones on and is playing with his mobile phone. I think it is very rude, extremely rude really but I don't say anything, to be honest I fell asleep almost straight away and they were like that when I fell asleep and are still the same when I wake up, they haven't said a word to us or each other, I have tried to speak to both of them but the headphones ensure the wall of silence is maintained, I am not sure if this is deliberate. Sean spends most of his time looking out of the window or tapping on his phone, I have never seen the girl before, she seems nice and pleasant enough, but it is strange for me to see two people who I think are a couple to appear to be totally unaware of the other person's existence, there is no conversation with them at all.

We are doing well, although the journey is going to be a few hours more, according to Jason we are making good time, the roads are clear and although he will not give the location. Jason is telling me all about the hotel and surroundings and what we can do when we are there. He even has my choice of music on the car stereo. I keep thinking of how different the return journey is going to be, he might not give me a lift home but I wouldn't care if he didn't. Oh how great it will be to be a free woman, to get home and de-clutter my house and become me again. I nod off for another hour or so and when the car stops just after lunch I am feeling refreshed and not tired at all.

The hotel is all that Jason has hyped it up to be; it is a large, modern mansion style house with large windows all up the side of the building. It has been made to look old but is quite a relatively new building. There is a large welcoming sign which says Colford hall, perfect for weddings and conferences, involuntarily I give a shudder. As I look up towards the hotel there is a lovely paved drive that leads up to the main house, Jason parks the car out the front of the hotel and we go in. Immediately on arrival we are greeted in reception with a glass of bucks fizz, I take a sip and look around at the grand reception, Jason checks in and our luggage disappears and he takes my hand, this shocks me, he never holds hands. Sean and the young girl have disappeared, I didn't see them speak as they got out of the car, Sean didn't even look at me, how rude is that, maybe he has fallen out with his new girl already. I am guided up the central curved stairs to our room on the first floor. It is stunning, it really is picture perfect, it is one large room, with a bathroom on the end, the main room is furnished in dark wood, there is a four poster bed with dark burgundy swag effect curtains and lovely rich deep burgundy carpet, there is a lovely floral bouquet stood on the main table, the room is all very dark and cool, cooling in an ice bucket. Jason points out my favourite sparkling rosé wine, he knows I cannot drink Champagne, don't ask me why but it has me throwing up in minutes, I think my stomach cannot cope with the bubbles. He is being very attentive, this is going to be harder than I thought, however, I will enjoy the weekend and let him pamper me, but my mind is set – on Sunday I will have that talk with him.

Jason is running a bubble bath for me, not sure what the hurry is I would have preferred to have had a quick shower and maybe a nice walk round the gardens to relax a bit, but I give in to his demands, he seems so excited, still so animated, he has made more effort today than he has ever made in our relationship to date. I don't know why but I shudder, you know, like someone has put an ice cube down your back, I look at him I really want to protest but I don't have the fight in me, so I get undressed. Jason is fussing about with towels, there is a knock at the door, Jason lets the chap in with the luggage and I am shocked as he hands him a tip, he then says he has to disappear to sort a few things out, he kisses my cheek and leaves me laying back in a luxurious beautifully smelling bubble bath, glass of wine in hand I sink lower into the bubbles and close my eyes, mmmm finishing with him might be more difficult than I thought. Maybe this is a new Jason.

I laze in the bath for twenty or so minutes, the water is going cool and I cannot be bothered to refill so I get out and then wrap myself in the large fluffy hotel towel, and stroll over to the window. As the afternoon approaches it is getting chillier outside but the sun is standing her ground and casting a lovely yellowish colour across the hotel the sun is holding her own against the clouds and there is no rain. I open the window and take a deep breath, the air is crisp and I take long deep breaths of the lovely Scottish air. I close the window, the room is lovely and warm so I just stand and watch people coming and going in the car park, a limousine arrives and collects a very elegant couple, then I watch as it disappears again, the hotel is quite busy, lots of cars coming and going, I am gazing with my head against the cool of the window pane when I think I see someone like Phil in the distance but as he is very average-looking, with shaved head and wearing sunglasses I couldn't be certain, and besides he was miles away back home. Then I think I see Gemma carrying a long dress, that is strange, I think to myself, that they should be here too, maybe there is a large group of us all coming up here together. I don't know why Jason wouldn't have mentioned it. Suddenly I feel a bit better, if Gemma is here, it means I have a way of getting home if Jason abandons me.

I hear the key in the lock and Jason comes back in the room, he seems edgy, his confidence seems to have gone the animated confident Jason is replaced by a pacing nervous one. He has a funny smile pasted on his face, he has on his nice dark suit, with a matching grey shirt and tie, he looks lovely, so smart and even his hair seems to be behaving. I am not sure when or where he changed, but I don't question it.

"Are Phil and Gemma here?" I asked him, "I thought I saw them in the car park just now." Jason looks nervous and laughs, but not his that joke is funny laugh but his nervous gritty laugh.

"Okay, well they might be here, I thought it would be nice, us all together, is it a problem?" he asks.

"No, not at all, the more the merrier I guess," I replied.

Jason is carrying something from the wardrobe, "I have got a dress ready for you, I chose it myself, and I rather hoped you would wear it." Jason's voice is stammering now, I have never heard him stammer, ever, if he seemed nervous before he is very nervy now, on high alert, his hands are shaking.

I look on the bed, he has laid the dress out, it is a long cream linen dress with a V-shaped neckline to the back and the front, and kind of funny-looking pull ties to the shoulders, not something I would choose or even like, it is a bit old style Laura Ashley and quite dated, certainly not my style. In fact it is a bit old-fashioned, well very old-fashioned really, but I see the look on his face, and I think, okay it isn't so bad, two more days and my nightmare will be over, what is one crappy dress to me, so I smile at him and pick it up and go to the bathroom. I don't feel so great, something isn't right, my stomach is churning, I feel really heady, I cannot stop shaking, I have an odd feeling about me, maybe the bath was too hot or the one glass of wine I had was too strong, I only sipped the bubbly I was given in reception so surely it wouldn't be that. I pin my hair back on one side and apply light make-up. I look okay, a bit frumpy, my face looks a bit red still but I lean against the cool mirror trying to calm it down, it helps a bit but it is still pink, but it will have to do, I look in the mirror, it doesn't look like me, the dress is worse on than laid on the bed, it doesn't fit properly, the funny ties at the shoulders hang awkwardly, there is a horrible bow on the back.

I have seen movies where the heroine rips the dress in a few places and voila a beautiful dress appears but no amount of ripping or remodelling is going to make this dress look any better. It is too tight on the bust and too big everywhere else it looks like something from the eighties, but I cannot be bothered to argue now over it. I think longingly about my jeans and jumper in the carrier bag in the boot of the car, then I look at myself in the mirror again, I go all hot and cold, I place my face back against the mirror to cool myself, after a few minutes I feel just a bit better, I slip my gold shoes on which do not go with the dress, most of my ankle and a fair bit of calf is showing, it looks ridiculous, I love the shoes though, and at least they fit and feel good. I spray a light perfume and open the door.

When I come out of the bathroom Jason is waiting for me. "You look nice," he says immediately. I am surprised at his comment, I don't know what to say, I mean there it is again, that word, nice, not lovely or beautiful, but nice, a description you would give to a maiden aunt, not someone you had bought on a romantic weekend away. My head aches, I am too hot, the dress feels constricting around my chest, I can feel sweat running down my back, I don't know what to do or say so I just stand there and shrug.

"Shall we go downstairs?" he asks, he takes my arm and tucks it though his and we walk down the stairs together. I certainly don't feel lovely or beautiful, I don't even feel nice, I feel like a frump, the dress is horrible, I don't even know where he has got it from, it wasn't in my wardrobe, I would never own something like this, it is too big, it gapes at the sleeves, but far too tight across the chest, it is frumpy, I feel really hot and shaky inside.

He, on the other hand, looks casually smart, not overdressed in ridiculous heels, I glance at him, everything he is wearing fits him perfectly, a plain black suit with a lovely pin stripe grey shirt, and matching tie. I walk slowly next to him and oh my god, as we reach the top of the staircase I see her, there, stood within fifteen feet from me, and looking up at me, is my sister, she is stood about four steps from the bottom of the staircase, she is staring straight at me, her face is ashen, she looks nervous and she continually chews her lip, that is something she does when she is worried, she is dressed in a lovely dress with matching jacket. I look over her head and Christ, shit, it feels like someone has punched me in the stomach. What the hell, behind her is my parents, Mum has a lilac suit and a bloody hat on her head, she is smiling, my dad is smiling, Jason's brother and his new girlfriend, now without the headphones, and they are smiling, both are dressed up, Jason's parents are there too, shit shit, everyone is bloody smiling, what the hell is going on, I look to the left as I walk down the stairs, there is Phil and Gemma. Gemma has her hands behind her, she looks beautiful I look at her lovely gown, she looks stunning in a long peacock blue floaty number, the heavy make-up has gone and replaced with light day make-up, yes she is smiling. I look to Phil, stood next to her but he is not smiling, he is not even looking in our direction, he is preoccupied looking out of the window. Suddenly I can hear the strains of some kind of concerto starting up and I don't know what to do, I don't know what the hell is going on. Jason's arm goes very tight on mine, he is crushing me, we are now at the bottom of the staircase and being guided into a room set out with gold and white chairs, and I want to laugh, I want to laugh out loud, everyone is looking so ludicrous, but then I see the bouquet that Gemma is handing to me, and suddenly nothing is funny anymore.

So I ask you dear reader, have you?

Have you ever found yourself in a situation, where it seems you are the outsider looking in, like you are in a bubble, where all those around you are smiling cheerfully and laughing and no one is aware that you are screaming out for help, it is like you are in really in an insulated soundproof bubble, pounding your fists against the walls of the bubble, screaming so loud but no one can hear you – there is a man stood in the suit in front of you and he is asking "does anyone know of any lawful impediment," and you know what is coming next, you know what is about to happen, but you are powerless to stop him, you want to scream, "YES, ME, I KNOW OF A LAWFUL IMPEDIMENT" there is a voice screaming in your head, you look around there is your mum smiling, she is looking very elegant in her lilac suit complete with matching hat and shoes, your dad is looking all proud, and wearing a ridiculous cravat of all things, I mean who wears cravats now, but he is happy and smiling too, everyone is smiling and nodding, the nightmare goes on as then the man continues speaking, his voice monotone, but as I look up, even he is smiling now, "will you take this man…" he continues, and you hear a voice coming from your head saying I do, but it is not you that replies, it was as if I was far away, watching from a distance, I want to wake up, is this a bad dream? Has the sheet fallen over my head like a veil, please, I send out a scream but it seems no one hears, I am desperately trying to shake myself awake, please oh please I want to wake up….

Have you ever found yourself in that situation, do you know what I mean, do you understand what I am saying, because that is exactly what happened to me…

So I ask again, have you ever found yourself in that situation, do you know what I mean, do you understand what I am saying, well that is exactly what happened to me…. On my wedding day.

I am not sure how I got through the ceremony, my mind was blank, but my heart was racing, there was a man and woman smiling and stood in front of me, with a book in their hands and rambling words that all seemed to join together, I am so obviously getting married, but it doesn't feel like me, it feels so surreal, it is like I am looking through the window, observing the stranger with a stricken look on her face, wearing the strange ill-fitting dress, having the world's worst nightmare. I hear words, but I am not sure what is being said, I must have said the correct words at the correct time as I felt the ring being placed on my finger. I see Jason's face coming towards me, his lips touching mine for the first time in a very long time, then I heard the cheer and everyone clapping and Sean slapping Jason on the back and saying well done mate, as we were pronounced man and wife and all I could think of was, what the hell have I done.

I look to my sister, she is crying, my parents are crying, but they are all happy tears and I want to cry but not with happiness. Everyone is crowding around us, people are patting Jason on the back, shaking his hand, congratulating him on his organisation, people are commenting on how lovely I look and didn't Jason do well to keep it a secret, and the person inside the dress is smiling and nodding her head, but it is not me, my heart feels empty, my head is pounding, I am still screaming in the bubble, pounding my fists against the walls, screaming at someone to let me out of this nightmare.

Phil is coming towards us, he cannot meet my eyes. He pats Jason on the shoulder, smiling like all the others, he shakes his hand, I cannot help it I feel such rage inside me, a loathsome anger directed at him, bubbling inside me like a hot cauldron, I want to scream at him, beat him with my fists, he knew, he knew when we spoke at work, how I was feeling, he knew what was planned, the whole thing, he had already made his travel plans with Gemma, booked his room, his time off and when I poured my heart out to him, he listened, but he said nothing. I honestly cannot remember what I said to him but whatever I said must have hurt him deeply, as he visibly shook and then stood back, he shook Jason's hand again, leaned over to kiss my cheek and whispered in my ear, most women may never remember what was said to them by guests on their wedding day, the normal congratulations, well done, you look beautiful, but I will never forget the words he said to me they are ingrained in my head, he whispered, "I will never forgive myself for today, never, sorry doesn't even begin to tell you how I feel, I have let you down so badly, and I swear I will spend the rest of my life trying to make it up to you," and then before I could respond he turned and walked off. I walked to the bathroom and got there just in time before I put my head to the toilet and was sick for so long I thought it was never going to end.

Chapter Nine

So, how stupid am I, I am married to the man I intended to finish with, my parents are overjoyed having Jason as a son-in-law, they are totally unaware how I felt about him, which is totally my fault, I feel very stupid, I wish I could turn back time, I wish I could tell someone, I know deep down that my sister knew, even without me telling her, she knew. She told me later that as she watched me as I walked down the stairs she could tell in my face, she had wanted to confide in me so many times but couldn't bring herself to ruin the secret and what might have been the best and happiest day of my life.

I cannot understand it, apparently Jason had told her I had proposed to him many times and she believed him, why wouldn't she? This is so unlike Jason, he doesn't care about me, I am sure he doesn't, we have been like strangers the last few months, with the last few weeks being unbearable, I felt it, so he must have too, I cannot believe he has put this wall of pretence up for everyone just to be married to me. I can only blame myself, and I do, I hate myself for not confiding in anyone, not least Judy. In fairness I had thrown myself into my work over the last few months doing so many extra shifts to try to forget the nightmare of my home life, so hadn't made as much of an effort to see her as maybe I should have, so it was totally my fault.

Naturally Mum was over the moon, kept saying what a lovely man he was and how lucky I was. Jason's parents were equally overjoyed, Little Ma was crying throughout the service during which she kept calling out Mazel Tov. I think they were happy tears. I was just crying inside, I felt that part of me died as I said my vows, stumbling over the words, people would have mistaken it for nerves. I know that there were two people in the room who didn't feel the happiness, one of them was wearing the frumpy cream ill-fitting dress and carrying the bouquet. And the other didn't stay long enough to see the ink dry on the certificate, I don't know where Phil disappeared to, all I saw was his departing back. The one thing I cannot understand is why, why did Jason want to marry me so much when we live like virtual strangers.

After a lovely meal and I have to admit it was delicious, not too fussy. Just simple. Phil had returned I am not sure when, but I never even looked at him, I cannot speak to him or even look at him, I feel intense anger in the pit of my stomach towards him. I must admit I did glance around the room and saw him and Gemma stood away from everyone else, their heads close together, speaking quietly, by the expression on both their faces it seemed to me they were arguing, but I was past caring, this day was everything I didn't want it to be.

Dad said a few words, I think maybe he made a joke, maybe someone laughed, I don't know, I think I must have smiled, there was a chink of glasses and I watched as Jason took to his feet. I stared at my left hand, turning the gold band, I didn't hear anything, his words were a blur to me, there was laughter around the room as he made some joke, and I smiled, the smile was fixed on my face, I didn't meet anyone's eyes, I didn't lift my head, I have no real idea what he said, again there was laughter, all I could do was look at the plain band choking my third finger on my left hand and think, I am married, I wanted to be married for such a long time and now I am, the ring feels uncomfortable and alien to me.

Then the meal was over and everything seemed to be happening at break neck speed, people kissing my cheek and saying well done, the voice in my head kept saying just smile, so I did, I smiled a lot, but my lips didn't speak to my eyes and I felt dead inside. It was all very quick and very uncomplicated. Afterwards there were photographs to be taken in the hotel grounds, and it was all very bizarre, like watching back a rerun of a film only the main character has been changed to me, I stumbled around in my impossible high inappropriate shoes and tried hard not to look at the gaudy dress, the cake was cut, a small round plain cake, with a plastic ornament of a bride and groom on the top, I signed inwardly, then camera flashed and I smiled appropriately, the same smile remained plastered on my face for the rest of the day. Cameras flashed and if anyone detected that I was unhappy they never said as much. Gemma looked stunning, she should have been the bride, she was doing all the things a bride should do, she was floating around fussing around everyone like it was her own wedding, making people comfortable. I looked at Phil, leaning against a pillar, a bubble of rage still burned inside my stomach, but he wasn't looking at me he was watching Gemma as she worked the room. I watched his face as the photographer called him he went and dutifully stood by Jason for one more photograph, I watched Jason, he appeared to be totally comfortable and his smile seemed genuine, I watched as him and Phil hugged then I watched as Phil walked over to Gemma and they both disappeared out of the room. I never really had time to collect my thoughts, or to have a minute to myself until much later in the ladies bathroom with my sister, I sat on the chair and she came and hugged me, she apologised over and over again, I wanted to cry, but for some reason the tears wouldn't come, I sat there almost in a state of shock, I didn't cry, I couldn't, I just felt numb, totally devoid of any feeling, words were too late now, it was too late for anything, what is done is done. I was married to good safe old Jason. To the whole world I was Mrs Angela Freedman.

There were no bolts of lightning as my new husband kissed me, there were no private looks of love exchanged between us, he didn't say a word to me for most of the day. I had been caught, hung drawn and quartered, isn't that the expression, whatever I thought or felt, we were now a married couple and there was no going back, and I had no one to blame but me, it was my own entire damn fault.

Except for the vows, we didn't actually get to speak to each other before, during or after the ceremony, we were caught up with other people and it was only much later in the privacy of our room that I took my dress off and got into my nightwear. I was very tired and ready just to close my eyes in the hope that sleep would come naturally and that I would have a good night sleep. I really hoped he didn't want sex, I had too much pretence today, my jaw ached with the fake smiling, my head was throbbing with the onset of a headache, the stress and pretence of the day had taken its toll, sex was the last thing on my mind, and after all the pretence of the day I don't think I could fake an orgasm too.

Jason had his back to me most of the time I was undressing, but I could see he had undone his tie and half his buttons on his shirt were undone, he sat on the other side of the bed, he half turned to me and said very quietly, "Do you hate me?" At first I didn't think I heard him properly, but I know I did, a cold shudder went all over my body, I knew what he said, and for a minute I couldn't look at him, what could I say, what would you say?

It was the evening of my wedding, my wedding night, the night most girls dream of, and my husband was asking me that sort of question, I couldn't look at him, couldn't bear to see the hurt in his eyes, I felt sick, I wanted to be anywhere than in that room at that time, part of me wanted to shout that yes I hated him, he had ruined my life, taken away what should have been the happiest day of my life, I wanted to scream so loud that I hated the dress and the whole bloody day, that he was an arse and he had ruined my life and that I felt more than hate for him, there are so many things I wanted to say. I wanted to bellow that he sickened me with his controlling and manipulative way he had handled my family, that I truly hated him, that I was ready to finish the relationship but I never............. and neither dear reader would you. Instead I turned round to face him, I looked into his eyes, and I could see that yes in some strange way, deep down maybe he did love me, maybe in his own detached way, I just didn't feel the same but I couldn't say the words I wanted to say, it would achieve nothing.

I was exhausted and didn't want confrontation, or to upset him so I took the easy way out, I walked around to his side of the bed, I took his face in my hands and whispered, "Never," and kissed him gently on the lips, but I felt nothing as I pulled away from him, his anxious smile told me it was what he wanted to hear.

As we lay side by side he made no attempt to make love to me, if he had I would have probably told him I was tired, but there was no need to, he kissed my cheek and turned over to sleep. I lay there in the darkness, with my arm behind my head thinking of the whole day, he asked if I was okay and I replied yes fine, within minutes he was sleeping. I look across the room, the bouquet of flowers catches my eye, it seems this bouquet didn't affect Jason's sinuses, I give out a huge sigh, I look over at Jason again, my wedding night and my new husband is asleep without any intimacy at all, would I have wanted it, no, but it would have been nice to have had the chance to say no, but I will be fine, I know I will, fine is the word I will use, it was my wedding night and I had just lied to my husband, it was the first of many lies I was to tell to so many people when the subject was brought up about my marriage.

Chapter Ten

Married life, well it wasn't so different from before, after the fuss of a wedding breakfast with the parents and guests, I got through on auto pilot, smiling when I needed to smile. I noticed Phil sat on the furthest end of the table engrossed in a newspaper, even Sean seemed to struggle to speak to me, maybe I imagined it. My mum and sister kept the conversation going, chattering on about nothing in particular. Ma and Pa just smiled a lot, I was so relieved when the breakfast was over and everyone said their goodbyes. Jason and I returned to the room and packed in silence, I looked at the large bed and tears pricked my yes, this was my honeymoon bed, this was supposed to be one of the happiest days of my life. Instead I felt empty inside.

Judy came up to say goodbye and Jason retreated out of the room giving us privacy, she looked at the bed and smiled, "You tired then," she joked, but the smile died on her face as I burst into tears, she pulled me into a hug and held me close. "That bad eh."

Through my snotty tears I replied, "No, worse."

She pulled away and looked at me. "Things will be okay, Angie, Jason is a lovely man, he loves you so much, that is clear to everyone."

I smiled at her, it is what she wanted to see, so I smiled the big happy bride smile. "See, you are better already, it was probably just a shock that is all."

I smiled at her again and headed to the bathroom to wash my face, when I came back out she had gone. I packed the rest of my things in silence, Jason hovering around in the background, he paused by the bed watching me pack. "I thought we might have a honeymoon later on in the year, when things are less hectic at work maybe" he pauses to add "okay,"

I look at him and give a slight shrug, I don't know what he wants me to say, my honeymoon will be delayed because of work, I would have to fit in with his plans, seems to me married life is not going to be any different than how we were before.

And I am right, within days of getting back home Jason has referred back to his normal self, the house is still full of his paperwork, spilling onto the floor, the cardboard boxes haven't moved one inch, driving me nuts as normal the only other difference was my name changed to his on certain things but I kept my maiden name for work, I am not sure why, but for the other things a man and wife share we changed it to his, the house became ours and not mine. He dealt with everything, he insisted and I haven't got the energy to argue, so I just signed where I needed to sign and he sent everything off.

After the first few months we had gone back to our usual routine – Post-it notes are again our new best friends, we communicate via them. Jason in fairness has become very involved in something very hush-hush at work, he is very committed to this new project so we don't see much of each other, I often wish things were so different from the reality that is my life, if anyone was to ask me directly was I happily married? The definite answer would have been no I wasn't. I will be honest with you, sometimes I wished I would have spoken up and said I didn't want to be married, I wish I had drunk lots of champagne so I was too ill to take part in the ceremony.

My sister felt so guilty after I cried in the bridal room, she still does she told me so many times afterwards that she thought about getting me drunk so I couldn't go through with it, but she was so taken in by Jason and his plans for the wedding, and yes she left him to choose the dress, we had a giggle about that. One day when Jason was out, she tried it on, and was dancing around the bedroom with the foul dress on she admitted she let me down, she feels terrible, but she never let me down, I let myself down.

Our wedding is old history now, we have been married over six months, sometimes I crave male company, male intimacy, well sex really, I crave it like I never did before the marriage, it is as if I need to have confirmation that I am attractive and I never get that from Jason. I am not much of a going out clubbing person, preferring a few drinks with friends, so I don't see blokes socially but sometimes when I look at the men at work who flirt and I am tempted to flirt back, to let them know I am interested, just to feel the closeness of a male, but I won't, I know I won't.

From outside looking in, everyone thinks we are all doing fine, a newly married couple who need to be left alone. We never mention the wedding, it is all in the past and hindsight is a wonderful thing, there is just one wedding photo of the two of us on the shelf in the lounge, my face is smiling but my eyes look vacant, almost dead, every wedding picture taken is the same, there is not one of me looking the happy smiling bride, the picture in the lounge is probably the best out of the whole lot, the mail tends to be placed in front of it so I don't see the haunted look of my own face looking back at me.

Work is fine, everything is just fine, fine is a word I use a lot now, when people ask me how I am it is the phrase I use, I plaster a big smile on my face and say I am fine, how is Jason, yes he is fine, everything is fine.

I used to make one wish over and over again, if there is anyone up there listening to me then please, hear my wish, my wish to be a wife, someone's wife, so that I belonged to someone who totally loved me, the word wife, that is what I thought would make me happy, having the title of wife, and now I am, I have that title, I have the gold band on my left hand signalling that I am part of a couple, but it is not what I thought it would be, I ask myself all the time are all those couples I see holding hands and going about their business together as miserable as I am. I watch couples laughing at the supermarket and feel anger, what are they laughing about, what is so funny, if I could turn back time I would turn it back to ask my wish again, I would wish that if anyone was listening to me then it would be to send me someone to love me, love me so totally, so completely, even if there was no ring on my finger, my new wish would be to find complete and fulfilling reciprocated love, a love that is so deep it hurts. Sometimes I want to cry, for the situation I have found myself in, but tears won't change anything, it won't make me feel better, I will dry my tears and still be someone's wife, the thing I thought I wanted the most in my life, is now the invisible constraints that keep me to one person, it is my own fault, I have no one else to blame, I just have to make the best of it.

Of course, people get divorced all the time, is divorce an option? I thought about it many times, but something stops me doing anything about it, no one would understand, I tried once to talk to my mum, but to my parents Jason is a wonderful man and I should be happy and grateful, he isn't a drinker or a gambler, he is just nothing, he is not exciting in any way, he doesn't want to do anything, nothing, not holidays or anything, so I take trips to see my parents in Spain alone because he doesn't like flying or boats or anything, he prefers to stay at home and work on his projects. I give up arguing, I know he has been abroad many times, but it is not worth it, I go on my own or with Judy and her children, it is another part of my life he is not involved in. Trouble is, it is beginning to get difficult to see exactly what part of my life he is involved in.

A funny turn of events at work has now happened, all the gossip that went on for months and months has now stopped, there are emails and memos letting us all know about the many changes happening and how it impacts on us individually. Some of the changes have already happened, changes in all departments, some of the staff have been moved around, a few staff have left, now the main admin room will take a lot of the basic paperwork and assist the enquiry office, nothing that really affects me though, for me. Well, it is all good, I have no complaints, we have known our shifts would be changing and there was lots of speculation, I do like the shift we are attached to, we get on really well and I will be sad to be assigned to another shift, but that is what happens.

On arrival to work one day there was a memo, basically letting us know that as from next week all the shifts will change over, it is sooner than we anticipated, nothing drastic is changing about the actual shifts just a change in the personnel. We are now lined up with group two, the same as us, makes sense really and for me it means that Helen and I are on the same shift now, we are both pleased as it means we get to spend more leisure time together which is great, we intend making lots of plans to spend rest days together – going to the gym and getting fit, it will fill the long days when I am not at work and just at home with Jason, so I am looking forward to working with her, but the downside is that this also means Phil is on the same shift as me, this is a bit more challenging for both of us.

Things have not yet been sorted out properly between us. When I first saw him after the wedding, he was popping in to collect Jason for golf, he stood in the lounge and we exchanged the briefest of hellos. Then I totally ignored him and disappeared upstairs deliberately waiting and leaving them to gather their things and go, I cannot help it, I still cannot forgive him for letting me pour my heart out when he knew the plans Jason had, I know things would be a little strained between us, well more than strained. I pretty much didn't see much of him for a few weeks; if I knew he was coming round I would make sure I wasn't around.

Then one day I came home after a day shift, got home late as I went to the gym, only to find that Jason had invited both Phil and Sean around to watch a film, if I had known I would have stayed out later and maybe met up with Helen or visited my sister, but I didn't, there was no Post-it note telling me, there was that excruciating uncomfortable silence as I walked in the room. Sean thankfully jumped up and gave me a big hug and a kiss on the cheek, Phil just sat there, he was playing with his phone and showing Jason something. I just walked into the kitchen, I didn't know what to do, I wish I had known he was going to be there I would have come home much later or maybe not at all. Anyway I said a kind of hello to the room, and not to anyone in particular and headed into the kitchen closing the door behind me, I looked back when I heard the door opening and there he was, stood watching me, I don't know what he was going to say but whatever it was I stopped him in his tracks. I put my hand up and told him not to say a word, I wasn't interested, he just slumped back to the lounge, I knew I was being unkind, but I couldn't stop myself, it was too raw for me to be speaking about the wedding, and especially not to him. I poured myself a glass of wine and returned to the lounge. I sat as far as I could away from Phil, there we were all sat watching the film and whenever Phil spoke, he spoke to the room and not direct to me, it was uncomfortable but bearable. When he got up to leave he leaned over and kissed my cheek, his lips were warm on my face, but I didn't respond, I didn't move, I didn't say anything I remembered how he used to kiss my lips, I almost craved it now, but I didn't look at him, he stood at the door watching me for a few seconds before shaking his head and walking out. I looked at Jason, but there was no reaction from him or Sean. That seems like such a long time ago now, I know it is my fault and I cannot blame everyone for my situation, I have to be the bigger person here,

I thought maybe Jason would say something but he never, I walked Sean to the door and he held me close, he whispered something to me and I looked up at him frowning, he smiled.

"I said it cannot be as bad as that can it." He smiled again and I smiled back, I watched as he walked away then he turned to me. "Whatever it is Phil has done, Angie, it has been going on for a long while, surely you can cut him some slack now don't you think, it cannot all be his fault." I smiled back at him, a weak smile but a smile nonetheless.

So I decided yes Sean is probably right, it is time I gave Phil less of a hard time, so at work I tried hard to make an effort and although initially it was difficult, and when we found out we were to be on the same shift we kind of skated round each for a few weeks, almost avoiding each other, but we have to speak on a daily basis at work whether it is on the radio or telephone or face-to-face, it was challenging for a while, but I would send him to jobs on the radio and he would come and tell me about them later, it seems we are okay now, he is almost back to being his normal jovial self, he does still poke fun at everyone but I have noticed he is quite protective over me.

Craig and the shift are still a tower of support for me, Craig was initially horrified that my plans went so horribly wrong but he totally understands why I did what I did, and when everyone on my shift kept congratulating me and going on about the bride and groom he was the one who chides them about workload and got the subject onto something more work related – I will always be so grateful to him.

In the early days if I wasn't portraying the role of the happy newly wedded woman, no one ever commented. Whatever Craig has told them, if he has told them anything they know it is personal and not for discussion.

Changing shifts has been good in that it is now only my immediate colleagues in the control room that know of my recent marriage, and of course Helen and Phil. Helen was not invited and she understands it was all a big surprise and although she did ask a lot of questions at first, when she didn't get a response she gave up. she knows I am not happy, she asked to see the photos lots of times and I haven't brought them in, as it has been nearly six month and I still haven't bothered she knows all is not well, I know she does. Sometimes I catch her looking at me but I don't say anything, the rest of the uniform shift think I have been married a while and I am certainly not going to be the one to explain. I don't always wear the wedding band, I wore it for a month or so, then when I was painting I took it off and I sometimes put it on, but it feels alien to me, I took it off a few weeks ago and never put it back on, no one questioned it, not least Jason, he never wears his either. If he put up any protest then that might give me the opportunity to discuss our marriage but he never has. The only thing that has changed in my life is that my house is messier but I am better off financially as he has renegotiated a better mortgage deal and he contributes more now, to be honest I was happier single and poor.

I think I know quite a few people on the new shift, there are several officers that I have worked with before, but it was quite some time ago, one of the older WPCs go to the same exercise classes as I do so they are not strangers, they come in gradually and introduce themselves, they are all good natured, really friendly. Craig attends one of their teams meetings and comes back saying he is happy we will all get along. He joined the same time as their sergeant and he knows he has a very strong work ethic which is important to Craig, we all discuss them as a group and we have some crazy characters like Phil and some quiet ones, but I know we are going to get along well, I am relieved my shift in the control room is staying the same and we are all happy about that. I also think I know the new sergeant on Phil's group, I haven't told anyone but I think, in fact I am sure we were in the same class at secondary school – his name is Michael Simms, I know he won't recognise me, as I have changed at lot since then, but he hasn't changed at all. He is tall, really lovely- looking, if he would only smile more often, he looks so serious, he was one of the tallest of our class, he has really dark brown almost black hair, he wears it short with a short fringe pushed to the side, he is broad-shouldered and solid but is not fat, he has the most amazing dark eyes with black eyebrows that shoot up when he is surprised, he was always really sporty at school, I know it is him, he was in the clever group in the class and from what I remember he played on most of the teams at sports.

I am sure he won't recognise me at all, I have changed so much from the dorky kid at school – the braces have gone and the wild mane of my frizzy hair has now been replaced, much to my Dad's disappointment, he loved both mine and Judy's curls but as soon as I was old enough to know my own mind I went to the hairdressers and within a few snips the untameable dark locks were replaced by a short sleek dark bob that moves back in position when I move, I love it, and I am proud of perfectly straight teeth. My parents didn't put up much of an argument regarding my hair as Judy did exactly the same.

Some of my shift have discussed Phil and Mike and some others whilst we have been on duty, some of them have been discussed at length, both Phil and Mike have had a character assassination as we discuss it at length and most of us all decide that Phil is a bit of a wild child, and I do confirm that, and Mike, well, we all say he is a miserable man, I have seen him and he certainly looks it, he hardly ever smiles, but Craig knows him very well and defends him he says he is a great bloke, they both joined at the same time, they seem to be quite close. Craig says Mike has three loves in his life: his job, his rugby and his car. He goes on to say he is great at rugby plays in two teams and even though he can hold a ball, holding his drink is a bit more challenging.

Craig tells some stories of his own stag night where Mike was left in a bar on his own somewhere in Amsterdam, Craig spent most of the time searching for him, when he finally found him the next morning Mike was fast asleep, still very drunk and under the very table they had left him at. The end result was that Craig nearly never made his own wedding, everyone laughs at this, the character assassination is over, we all agree that Phil will need to be managed by us quite carefully and Mike has got off okay, we figure that if Craig rates him then we will have to give him the benefit of the doubt and give it time I guess, Craig is normally a good judge of character.

I have seen Mike from a distance; he is really nice-looking, he is sporting a really lovely holiday tan and looks a lot better than I remember him being. Helen speaks very highly of him, she knows him well, I have heard her mention him many times when we have talked about work but I never put the name to the chap at school, anyway she says he is good fun and he goes out quite often socially with her group, she reaffirms his love of rugby, says that is all he talks about, some of them have been to watch him play, she says he is very passionate about his game, she says he has a real inability to match the other lads with drink, she says they call him lightweight, this makes me laugh. I am holding back on my judgement as I have yet to formally meet him. Just after lunch Gavin comes in, he remembers Mike from a long time back when they worked together, so they got re-acquainted, then he was invited to join the new shift at lunch, he said everyone is right, Mike is well into his sport, couldn't shut him up, he plays rugby and seems a decent bloke, he is a no nonsense sort of bloke Gavin explains, he overheard him putting one of his chaps right on how he wanted a job done, Gavin was impressed, and if Gavin and Craig both like him he must be okay. Gavin seems happy that the new shift will mix well with ours, he voices his concern about one or two officers but won't name names. Steve, Rob and I are still reserving judgement, and Max doesn't ever talk about anyone, he will not get involved in what he calls idle gossip.

As part of our job we should take it in turns to go down to the CID office to type up some statements, just to help out, this is something I don't mind doing although we are all supposed to take a turn, I am the one on my shift who seems to always have to go. I very rarely complain, it is easy work, just copying from handwritten statements or listening to the tapes and typing with the audio machine, this is sometimes daily but depends on what is going on, all shifts have to do it and I quite like the change, it gives me an opportunity to do something different and chat to the other officers, so hopefully I will be able to get to know them better and suss them all out.

Jason is being very quiet of late, things have really bothered me lately, I have called him a few times when I have been at work and had a spare five minutes, thinking it might be better and easier to chat on the phone as at home we are like strangers, but I get the engaged tone when I call. I try again and again and sometimes it is engaged for up to an hour, I am not prying but when I ask him if anyone called he says no, when I tell him I called and it was engaged he is non- committal. I know he cannot be seeing anyone else as in of the female kind because he never goes anywhere but even the phone bill gives no indication of calls being made out, I once called the phone company to say I thought the phone was left off the hook but when they checked they said it was engaged in conversation.

Later that same evening I asked Jason and he said no one had called, I tried to challenge him but then he got all defensive and stormed up to bed, I don't know what I have done so wrong. Soon it is our one-year anniversary, but nothing really has changed between us, sometimes I sleep in the spare room when I am on nights, just so I don't wake him, well more often than not now I choose to sleep there. But tonight I have made an effort, I don't normally cook, although I used to enjoy it, Jason doesn't generally like what I cook, he prefers to eat at work and just snack at home, but tonight I have made his favourite meal. I pour him his favourite beer, but he eats a few mouthfuls then pushes the food round his plate, he is disinterested, he will not meet my gaze, I ask him questions, just normal questions about work, he won't answer, I try to make small talk, I tell him funny little tales of what Judy's children have been up to, just funny things, stories, things that I think might make him laugh. One example being about what little Juliet said after one of her first days at school, she stood at the school gate at the end of the day and said, "Well I am not going there again so don't ask me to." I fell about laughing when Judy told me, but Jason didn't even break into a grin, nothing, so I try a bit more, I ask about his parents, his brother Sean, but it seems to fall on deaf ears. I am tired of making an effort, I am tired of attempting to make my husband talk to me, so tonight I make the final effort, I look at him, watching him for a while, he is sat at the table with his laptop on his lap.

"Jason," I speak his name, he looks up, he frowns at me, I nearly stop, but I have to know, I have to ask him, I take a deep breath. "Jason, when you married me, did you love me, is that why you wanted to get married?" There I have said it, the question I have asked myself so many times since we married, now I just need to hear his reply, I hold my breath, he looks back down at his laptop, "Jason," I persist, he looks at me, his expression is blank, my heart is beating hard in my chest, part of me doesn't want to know but the needy side does.

When he replies his voice is low, he puts his laptop down onto the table and reaches across to the newspaper and picks it up, he glances at me then says, "Angie, don't be naïve, you sound like a needy child, people marry for lots of reasons, not just love."

His words hit me like an icy sword through my heart, the answer to my question was not what I expected, not what I wanted to hear, I wanted him to say he loves me, even in his strange way he loves me, but I didn't expect that. Trouble is, I am not sure what I have done wrong, if anything, I don't know if I have upset him, we haven't really argued or had words about anything, this is the first time I have spoken about anything personal, I have no idea what is going through his head, he doesn't make any comment or attempt at further conversation just gets up and leaves the table. I look up as he speaks again.

"I am tired, it has been a busy day, I am going to bed." I look at him, his face is impassive, he gets up, as he passes he touches my shoulder, just a light pat. "Don't over analyse things, Angie, we are married, we are a couple that is enough for me, it should be enough for you too," he says quietly.

I listen to his footsteps on the stairs, I place my arms on the table, I cannot believe what he has just said, just being a married couple should be enough, why would he say that, maybe he is just tired too, we both are, I just don't know. I eat a bit more but the food tastes of nothing, I sit with my chin resting on my hands and my elbows resting on the table, I try to work out what went wrong with my life, I wanted to be married so much, to be part of what other couples had, but now, now when I have it, now I am someone's wife, well I feel even lonelier than I did before, now I just feel sad for us both. I want to cry, but the tears won't come, so I sit just looking out of the window, as the night draws darker I see myself in the reflection of the window, I look so unhappy. I give a big sigh, I look at the food now congealed on the plate, I need to clear up but I cannot face it right now, I need to go and speak with him. I go upstairs and he is in the en suite, I can hear him being poorly, now I feel guilty, I didn't know he wasn't feeling well, what sort of a wife am I that he didn't tell me, the sound of him retching makes me feel quite ill, it sounds terrible as he cannot stop being sick, I call out to him that I will get him some water. When I go back upstairs he is in bed, his eyes are closed, he looks pale and tired, I feel his forehead, it feels clammy and so I pull the covers up for him, leave the water at the side of the bed and go downstairs to clear everything away.

I am worried as I have noticed over the next few days that he hardly touches his food, if I have made something in the past I generally leave a note to tell him what it is and where it is, I hate him just snacking, so lately I have taken to making him a proper home cooked meal and leaving it in the oven, but when I come home it is still there, or even in the bin. I have spoken to him but he says he has just lost his appetite, he was poorly the other evening after our meal, and then again tonight, it is difficult to monitor as working shifts mean we don't eat together. I ask him if he has eaten at work, he doesn't actually lie to me, but his answers are vague, I try and cook for him but I have picked up on the fact he now puts the food in the main dustbin maybe he is hoping I won't notice but I know it has been happening quite a bit but he is so stubborn and refuses to go to the doctor.

Over the next few weeks I try to discuss his symptoms, I try to push him on how he is feeling, it is obvious he is still unwell, he looks pale and is tired all the time, despite me asking him over and over he is just vague. When I try to press him he tells me to stop mothering him and leave him alone, he gets angry with me and is very rude, I don't know what more I can do. I take myself off for a run, just to get out of his way, but I come back feeling as bad as I did when I left. I make him a hot drink which he leaves untouched and we sit in silence for a while, I ask him what he thinks it might be, but he shrugs, eventually he says he thinks it might be a bug from something he has eaten, I try to argue and tell him it would be gone by now, I try to instigate a discussion but he won't have it, we don't really argue, he makes a statement I make a statement, there is no real conversation. I offer to get him some medication but he doesn't want anything, I make a mental note to speak to his mum, maybe she can convince him.

He has told me he has to go to London for a few days, he explains that this will be when I am on night shift so I won't be on my own, I am not worried about being alone in the house, I don't know why he even mentions it, he has done this a few times recently but so far he has never stayed overnight. He does have his friend in London he is visiting, he has mentioned a few names but I am not sure which one he is going to visit, I know they went to university together, well at least I think that is the friend he is speaking to. I offer to buy his ticket online for him but he says he prefers to pay by cash and he will get it on the day as he always does, we argue again as the tickets are cheaper in advance but he won't have it, he would rather queue up on the day. I cannot understand the logic of queuing up, it is ridiculous but I don't bother to argue.

I sit and sip at my wine just thinking about how I am going to speak to his mum without her immediately contacting him and demanding to know what is going on. I look up as he enters the lounge, he sits in his favourite chair and then looks at me, he smiles and for some reason it bothers me, he wants something, he must do. He leans back in his chair and then he seems to lighten up a bit, he asks how I am, which shocks me, but he doesn't wait for me to answer instead he says about the train times, then in his next few sentences I know why he is being nice, he mentions something about some patents that he wants to change, again I kind of know what it is about, all this registering patents but I don't really get involved, he asks me to sign some documents he has in his hands. I don't argue or even check them I am happy enough it is just to protect his ideas, he has come up with a new revolutionary system for some household item and needs to protect it, although as his wife I have occasionally to sign some forms relating to his business I don't really pay that much notice. I see my opportunity to use my signature as a bargaining tool and he laughs but he gives in, he has promised if he is not better when he comes home he will make an appointment to get his stomach sorted out. I smile inwardly; it is a small victory for me but a victory nonetheless. I go to bed a bit happier that I won't have to live with a poorly Jason, that would put an even greater strain on our fragile relationship.

CID office is very quiet when I go down, this is not unusual, I quite like it, I know what I have to do, the statements and tapes are always kept in the same place. I set up the laptop and put my IPod on, I need to copy the handwritten statements onto the system first, there is no one around, I lose myself in my music, singing along quite happily, I don't notice anyone coming in so I jump as someone touches my shoulder, I see someone in front of me waggling a mug I acknowledge them with a "yes please, Tea white no sugar" and carry on typing, I continue to pound the keyboard keen to get the statements finished. I type the statements without really thinking about the words, it is all second nature to me. I pull the earphones from my ears, and put the headset on, I need to listen to the recorded statements and type these up too, when there is a break in the dialogue on the tape I look up and notice the tea has been placed on the mat next to me. I didn't even notice so I look up to say thanks and am embarrassed to notice it is Sergeant Mike Simms who has made it for me, I call out thanks but he doesn't respond.

People are right, he does look miserable and moody, with a big dark frown on his face, he doesn't seem to be pleased that he has waited on me. I try to smile at him but he doesn't look impressed, his expression doesn't change, in fact he ignores me. Oh dear I sigh to myself, probably not good for a first impression. I am not overly bothered, I won't have to report to him directly but for the sake of our group we have all to be professional. I just wish our first meeting could have gone a bit better.

Phil comes in, he stands over me as I type, I reach the end of the page and remove my headset. "You okay?" I ask him, he smiles.

"Yes," he replies, "it just looks odd to see you here in uniform, I guess I will have to get used to it, but I prefer your pyjamas," he laughs out loud and I smile back as he wanders down the end of the room towards Mike. I watch as they chat together, whatever it is that Mike says has Phil laughing out loud the radio breaks their chatting, I watch as Phil responds, I know it must be an emergency shout as they both grab their things and race from the room.

I finish the tapes for the next hour in silence and return to the control room, I look at the logs, they are both at a domestic disturbance, one very drunk man has been arrested for assault and he is still kicking off in custody. I look up to see Mike wander into the control room, he is chatting to Craig, so I get to look at him properly, he looks more relaxed, he is actually laughing, he has an infectious laugh, his whole face lights up when he laughs, and yes he was definitely in my class at school, there cannot be that many Mike Simms that look like him, he is really quite handsome, I am not sure if he would recognise me as he was in the clever group that sat at the back of the class.

I look at him, he is really very good-looking, quite tall too, just over six foot with broad shoulders and a really good physique, the tan suits him too. I look to his left hand, there is no ring there, not sure why that matters to me, but the absence of the gold band makes me smile. I look down at my left hand, for some reason I chose to put my wedding ring on today, it still looks and feels alien to me, I twist it round and round as I watch him, he has a habit of running his hands through his hair, it makes it stick up and I smile to myself. He is stood now with his hands balanced on top of his head reading over Craig's shoulder I look at his body, he certainly is very fit.

It is busy in the control room so I don't get to speak to him but when it calms down a bit Phil comes in and has a chat with me, he seems okay, we are working hard at our relationship, it isn't as natural as it used to be, it could be much better so we are both trying. To me it is a bit strained and it is still mostly my fault, but I am making an effort and we are getting there. Jason and I are okay, it is what it is, I am not going to complain, there is no point, we are married by the words on the certificate only, like friends really, so I have resigned myself to living the life I have. Phil still pops in to see Jason and still the three of them go out together. I come home sometimes to find Phil and Sean with Jason, spread across the sofas watching sport with beer in their hands.

Today he sits by me in the control room, his shirt has been torn in the domestic and there is blood all down the front, Mike comes over to him. "You okay?" he asks.

Phil smiles. "Yes, he didn't hit me despite his trying, he hit the wall mostly, I think he looked at you, thought better of it then had a go at me, he wants to make a complaint about me anyway."

Mike frowns. "Do you need to go home and change?" he asks.

Phil shakes his head. "No thanks, Jim has a spare of mine in his locker, I am just waiting for him to get it then I will go and change."

I watch as Mike just stands there, I think he wants to say something but he doesn't, he doesn't move, he continues to just stand watching. There is an awkward silence, he looks at me then Phil and then finally walks out of the control room. Phil watches him leave, he shrugs and pulls a face at me, he leans back in his chair tells me that he and Gemma are having problems – he says he thinks that she wants to finish with him, I am not sure why but he laughs, he doesn't seem to be that downhearted, he tells me he is already looking round for someone else. Also he is hoping to be moving house and buying a new car soon, a lot of it is big talk I know he is just entertaining me by pretending there is loads going on and I am loving the diversion that his silliness is creating.

Phil avoids asking any questions about Jason and I, in fact no one asks me at all, no one in my family or his, it is like the marriage has happened and we are all playing happy families, but the reality is so different than what people think. I scroll through the logs as Phil disappears to change.

Within minutes he is back, he tosses the torn shirt at me. "Do you want to keep that so you know that you always have me near?"

I laugh at him and throw the item in the bin next to me. It is very quiet, everyone is sitting around, Phil is now flicking an elastic band at me, he is bored too, there is little going on now, it has quietened down giving us a chance to catch up. The shift is nearly over, I take the band from him and flick his thigh, harder than I intended, he shouts out as the band hits his skin. I laugh out loud.

I look over at the main control desk and notice Mike is back sitting by Craig. I can see he has the duty sheets so I know they will be there for some time, he is watching us, a frown on his face. I don't think he is impressed by our giggling, but I don't care, I don't report to him and I am still working.

I pull Phil close to me. "You're being watched," I warn him, I nod my head towards the centre console.

Phil looks and smiles. "Nah, Mike is okay, if he had a problem he would say."

I smile. "So he only looks miserable then." Phil looks at me, he hands me a piece of chocolate, I shake my head. "No thanks."

He laughs, "Seriously, Angie, you haven't give him a chance yet, he is okay, a nice bloke, he is a bit of a dark horse though, do you know he taught English in a school in Cambodia, and he was offered a football scholarship but turned it down, he has done quite a lot with his life so far, more than most of us have, don't judge our shift too soon, they are better than the deadbeats on your old shift." He puts the rest of the chocolate in his mouth, speaking with his mouth full. "You will have to come out with us one day, they are a good lot, and he is a decent bloke. We watched him play rugby the other week in a charity match, he was really good, we had a great laugh, then we went for a few pints. I think he said you were at school together, he was in your year, don't you remember him?"

I frown, then I lie, I am not sure why but I shake my head. "No, I don't think so." Phil doesn't question it further, but I am intrigued. "Why was you talking about me then?" I ask.

Phil is rifling through my bag. "Have you got any mints in here?" he asks.

I slap his hand away. "Get out of my bag, yes, I do, come out and I will find them." I look in my bag and I hand them to him. "Now tell me why you were talking about me."

Phil shrugs, "I don't know, he was just asking, that is all, he asked us all what we knew about you lot as we are going to be working together, he knows Craig and Gavin quite well I think, but not the rest of you, oh and he knows Steve from when he first started here." He hands the mints back. "Do you want one?"

I shake my head, "No thanks."

He sniggers, "Seriously I think you should," he laughs out loud at his own joke and I punch his arm, he shouts out, I glance over to the main desk.

Mike is still watching us, but I don't care, if Craig had a problem he would have no hesitation in speaking out, and as it happens I am watching the logs for updates, there are no calls so I can easily work whilst also listening to Phil who is both amusing and entertaining. The time goes quickly towards the end of the shift.

Mike stands up, I watch as he stretches and walks over to Phil. "Come on, skiver, let's go," he says good naturedly, he stands waiting, as he gets up to leave Phil ruffles my hair, kisses my cheek and even though I hate my hair being messed with, I like it – I like the familiarity of it, he shouts a cheery goodbye to everyone and saunters off. I think I am beginning to forgive him just a little bit, well, I don't hate him anymore, in fact he is okay, I like him.

Jason is home tonight, I am making a big effort, he has been away for a few days on his trip to London, then came back for one night then went off again. There is something strange that I cannot put my finger on – some of his clothes are quite damp, I only notice when I am filling the washing machine, it hasn't been raining here so he couldn't have got caught in the rain. It is so frustrating that I am his wife and we are a married couple but I have no idea what is going on with him. It makes me cross that we are more like brother and sister, so tonight I have cooked, his favourite, it is a Jewish dish his mother makes, it is a cholent, which is a slow-cooked stew of meat, potatoes, beans and barley, served with potato filled cigars, all original Jewish recipes from his mum's little book, she is so pleased I am cooking for him. I have made some macaroons to follow.

Everything is ready, the table is set with candles and our wedding napkins and although Jason doesn't drink much wine I have a bottle of sparkling wine in the ice bucket, it looks nice, I am pleased with the end result. I pop upstairs to change into a short shift dress and apply light make-up, then finish with a quick spray of perfume. I am hoping his business has gone well and he will be in a good mood. We seem to be swaying between okay and bad at the moment. Yes, he still frustrates me and one day I fantasise I will meet the man of my dreams, I have no idea how that will happen as I am married and never go anywhere to meet anyone.

Jason keeps hinting about starting a family, not sure how he thinks it happens but sex is hardly ever on the agenda. Anyway, I am not that stupid, I do not want a child with Jason, I might have been stupid enough to get married when I didn't want to marry him – that decision was taken out of my hands but this one won't be. When we got back from Scotland I took matters into my own hands, I had the contraception implant in my arm which will last for two years, I just never told him and he doesn't need to know.

When on the rare occasion he tries to pull me close to him in bed I tell him I am too tired, he doesn't press the issue. I feel sad that we are wasting our lives together when somewhere out there is someone for both of us, someone that will make us happy, fulfil our lives. I am still ever confused about why Jason married me, he made such an effort to get us married and now we are, he makes no effort at all. It is all such a shame, not just for him but for me too. Tonight I know it will be different, well I am hoping so, I set the music going, just low background music.

I hear his key in the lock; I light the candles and wait for him to come in. When he does he doesn't look at me, he looks at the table.

"I cooked for us," I offer, sounding a little bit pathetic I think to myself, oh he looks at me.

"I ate a sandwich on the train, I am not really hungry."

I frown. "Can you not manage something, Jason?" I urge him. "I cooked your favourite, I thought we could spend the evening together." Jason runs his hands through his hair, I can see he is struggling to form the right words. "Maybe just try a little bit," I coax hopefully.

He looks at the table again. "Is someone else coming?" he asks.

I shake my head, "No, the table is set for two, us two." My heart sinks.

Then right then, I know I have lost, he isn't going to sit with me, we are not going to eat together, it was all a waste of time, just like our marriage, I sigh, he looks at me. "Bit of an effort for just us two isn't it, I would sooner have it on my lap watching television, but not now, maybe a bit later, I will help myself though." He runs his hands through his hair again. "Bit tired really," he stops. "Did my mum cook it?" he asks.

I look at him with contempt, I want to punch him, I push my nails into my palm, why does he have to be this way? "No, she didn't," I reply through gritted teeth, "she gave me the recipe, I followed it, because I thought you would like it."

He nods his head, he attempts humour but it is all too late. "Ah, so I guess candles and music were needed to distract my taste buds, eh?"

I think it is a joke, at least I hope it is, but he doesn't smile, nothing to indicate he is joking, no twinkle of the eye. There it is, the patronising condescending part of Jason that I hate, I really hate.

I walk to the table, blow the candles out and without a word to him I go upstairs, I pull my trainers from under the bed and savagely tug off my shift dress, replacing it with my leggings and sweatshirt. I march downstairs, grab my keys and go out the door. As my trainers hit the pavement I let all my anger spill out, the tears spill down my cheeks but I don't care. I cannot believe how stupid I was to make all that effort, all that bloody cooking, all the expensive special ingredients and for nothing, for him to be patronising towards me.

I run so hard and so fast after just a short time I am breathless, I stop and place my hands on my knees bending over to take deep breaths, there is a burning in my chest, but I stand for a short while and I can feel myself calming down. I look at my left hand, I have my wedding band on, I take it off and hold it in my right hand. The large lake is just in front of me, I turn it over and over in my hand, I am so tempted to just throw it as hard and fast as I can, but for some reason I don't, I turn it over and over in my hand, then put it back on my left hand. I am calming down now, I realise my marriage is what it is, whatever I want Jason to be it is never going to happen, I am never going to feel the way I yearn to feel. There is nothing I can do, I have to make the best of it, I bite back the tears and stand up straight.

I look up, I am halfway around the park, the burning in my chest eases a bit so I start off again in a slower pace this time. It is getting a bit dark. I watch as the group of men in front of me are exercising, I sit down at the park bench and watch for a while. There are about fifteen of them being led by a chap through a range of exercises, they are all calling out to each other good naturedly and I smile at their banter. I look around the park, it is unusually busy with dog walkers, runners and people hurrying home. I jog gently for another half an hour then head home.

When I get in Jason is indeed sat in front of the television with the empty tray in front of him, he has eaten some of the food I cooked, I can tell by the gravy on the plate, he looks up as I come in. "Good run," he says. I don't reply, I don't trust myself to speak, I don't know what he expects me to say.

I know he is leaving early in the morning again. I stay upstairs, showering and sorting out clothes for the morning, I hear him moving about but he stays up way after I go to bed just watching television. I think he doesn't want confrontation, well he is lucky as neither do I. Today I have decided that my days of making any sort of effort in this marriage are well and truly over. I drag my wedding ring from my finger and throw it in my jewellery box, a wedding ring is a symbol of love and commitment and I have neither with Jason.

Chapter Eleven

I have a very busy morning, I leave Jason in bed, I don't know if he should still be in bed, but I have bills that need paying, parcels to take to the post office. Then after meeting my sister Judy for a lovely lunch I grab some groceries and stay out of the house for as long as I can.

I don't know what we have to say to each other anymore after last night. We really should talk about us, I cannot live like this, it is not fair to him or to me. I can only stay out so long so in the end I make my way home. Jason's car is still in the drive, he is still home. It is 2:30 in the afternoon, I thought he was meant to catch the morning train from London but he is in bed. I can see the curtains are drawn, I shout up the stairs if he needs anything, there is no reply. His laptop is left on the dining table, still running; this is very unusual for Jason, he is very particular where his laptop is concerned, but I shrug to myself. I turn on the television and leave him for a while but this is very rare for him to be in bed, in the end I give in, I make a drink and take it up to him.

He is laid back in the bed, half sitting up, he is very hot to touch, I think he has a fever. He wakes up when I go in, I ask him what is wrong but he says he just has a cold so I take him some capsules and he says he is going to stay in bed. I ring his mum to ask her advice and she is going to pop and see him later as I have an appointment to have my hair cut she tells me she will make sure he goes to the doctor. When I go downstairs I glance at the laptop, I know I shouldn't but I cannot help myself. His internet browser is open and there is no screen password, I can see he has been looking at trains on the northern line, I frown at the screen and look at his history, it shows different train lines for up north. I try to go into his emails but I don't know the password, I frown at the screen. I thought his recent trips were to London, but it seems he is going up as far as the northern line which actually goes as far as Scotland. I hear him moving about so I leave the laptop as I found it and grab my coat and leave, I cannot stop thinking about his mystery trips.

When I get back home much later he is still asleep. I don't disturb him; I make myself a snack using the leftovers from the stew and finish off the macaroons. I busy myself watching television, as the evening ends I grab a quick shower and look in at him; he is still fast asleep but still very hot. I put a cold flannel on his forehead and he moans gently, I leave a glass of water at the side of the bed for him. I sleep in the spare room again so I don't disturb him.

In the night he wakes me several time as he is restless, I can hear him moaning and groaning, I go into him, he is very hot and his pyjamas are soaking wet. It is 3:00am but I need to make him comfortable, so I make him stand whilst I change him, I notice his skin is all yellow and there appears to be marks like old bruising all on his back, he is shaking but feels very hot. I put the cold flannel over his chest and neck to cool him down, I give him a glass of water and help him back into his fresh pyjamas then back into bed, but he just gets settled back on the pillows and he lurches forward, he is sick again, all over the clean pyjamas, down the front of my nightie and the bedding and carpet.

I am tired and angry, I can really do without this, I fight back the tears. I am not the best nursemaid – I am so intolerant, but he just lays there so helplessly, he has no energy, he just keeps asking me to help him and saying sorry. so I slip my nightdress off and pull on a clean one then dutifully wash his face and neck where he has been sick then change his pyjamas again. I pull the duvet off then drag the spare one from the other bedroom, I sit on the bed and ask where he is hurting, his breath is laboured but he puts his hand across his stomach. He cannot keep his eyes open and seems delirious, he cannot hold his head up so I lay him back on the pillows. I am not sure what to do, he is scaring me, I have never seen him ill, well nothing more than a cold or cough. I tell him I am going to call the ambulance but he says he doesn't want me to, he begs me not to, so I do the next best thing, I call his mum and she is a darling, she is around with his dad in tow within fifteen minutes.

It is now almost 4:00am in the morning and they are not phased at all, none of them mention the time, she goes into overdrive taking his temperature, she fills a bowl with cold water and sits at his side, cooling him with a flannel on his forehead and making him drink the water, she is fabulous, all the while his dad sits and watches her just nodding as she chatters away. I use this time to clean the carpet and put the bedding in to wash. Jason has calmed down a lot and is now asleep but is still very restless and very hot. She has a look at his bruising on his back but she doesn't know what it is either, she sends me to fetch some clean water so she can give him a cooling bed bath. I watch as she cradles his head lovingly, placing kisses on his forehead, she washes his chest and arms and tenderly dries him. He remains with his eyes closed, I am not sure if he is sleeping but he is more restful.

We decide we will see how he is in the morning and then decide our next plan of action. I am relieved when they ask if they can stay, I readily agree and organise bedding for them as they settle in the other spare room and I go back to mine. Several more times we have to get up but this time he is sick into the bowl, she sends me back to bed and I watch as she lies on the bed next to him, the love for her son is evident on her face.

It makes me so much happier that Jason is much brighter this morning. He has had a cup of tea end even eaten some toast, his mum has fussed over him and he doesn't object. He is still very quiet and looks washed out, but his mum is very happy, bustling around him, doing washing and ironing and I think she is enjoying having free reign in our home. Jason's dad is watching the news, he loves the fact we have Sky television, he loves to watch the documentaries, he keeps channel flicking, so I leave him to it.

I feel Jason's forehead, I don't know what I am feeling for, only that hot is not good and he still feels really hot to touch. I have called in work to say I will be late, I want to make sure he goes to the doctor. I shower quickly and when I come out of the bedroom he is coming off the telephone, true to his word he has an appointment with the doctor for a few days' time. I am quite cross that he didn't insist on an emergency appointment but he is meeting with his friend from London again later today and says the sickness and fever will probably be gone. I must admit he seems in much higher spirits or he is a very good actor, whichever it is he is insistent that I go to work as he has things to do, so I go off to work leaving him with his mum and dad chatting in the lounge. I am happy that the worst is over and whatever bug he had he has hopefully got rid of. I may not love him desperately as maybe I should as his wife but I do still care for him very much.

Chapter Twelve

Just a week or so later I get a text from Gemma, telling me that her and Phil have got engaged, quite surprisingly, well actually quite shockingly she texts me to say how happy she is. I thought they were both on a cooling period, so maybe she gave him an ultimatum. Her text says she has a lovely diamond rock on her finger. I haven't had a chance to speak to Phil about it, I am surprised he hasn't mentioned it to me, he is still the biggest flirt and I think maybe this is why they had problems, but this is good news and we are all going out for a meal tonight to celebrate, just a group of friends to the local Italian which is one of Phil's favourite restaurants. Then the real celebration for Phil will be when his colleagues are all meeting him at the police bar after the last day shift tomorrow night so they can all celebrate properly, in true Phil style, which means just get very drunk and behave irresponsibly.

I have got to know nearly all of them on the shift now; they are great, a really nice bunch of people. There is one married couple Julian and Jo and I like them, she is a part-time admin assistant and Julian is a full-time police officer in the enquiry office, they are coming out for the meal with us too. We are picking them up on the way to the Italian restaurant. Sean will be there and Brian and Carol. There are two others but I don't know who they are yet. I was disappointed that Helen isn't coming as she gets on so well with Phil, but she said she has plans but she will be at the bar tomorrow. It should be a good night and we are both looking forward to it. I cannot believe Phil is getting engaged and will be a married man in the near future.

Jason and I get ready together, I watch him as he dresses, his lovely navy shirt and black jeans suits his tall frame. I watch him, I hadn't realised before but he has lost quite a bit of weight, his belt hooks is now put on two holes tighter. I go to say something but change my mind, I don't want a row tonight, I just want a nice night out like normal couples. I dress casually – I choose blue jeans and a pale green shirt, with light make-up. I tell Jason he looks nice but he doesn't return the compliment; I don't know why I expected him to, but it would have been nice. We hardly say a word even though we are both in the bedroom together. I sit and put my jewellery on debating on whether to put my wedding band on, in the end I slip it on my finger then stand up to go downstairs. As I pass him I say excuse me as I would to anyone, he moves out of the way but still not a word between us.

The journey is uneventful, Jo is chatty but Julian like Jason says hardly a word. As I listen to her chattering about the restaurant I just respond with a nod when I am expected to, it is only a short journey for which I am thankful. The Italian restaurant is very busy and lively when we arrive and we are quickly shown to our table. Everyone is there already so after greeting everyone we all take our seats, I am surprised to see the last two guests sat at the very end of the table are Mike Simms and a dark-haired girl. She is quite a knockout, she has very long jet black hair, she is wearing what seems to be very tight, black leather jeans and a jacket to match, and underneath that, just a black bra. She is chewing gum and swigging red wine at the same time, she looks so kind of cheap but not cheap, she looks so, what is the word, sexy, yes sexy. She has one arm draped around Mike's shoulder as if owning him, and she is stroking his hair her long talon like nails painted bright red. He doesn't seem to be taking much notice of her or anyone else.

Phil is telling some sort of lengthy tale and Mike is leaned in listening intently. I don't think he has noticed our arrival his face is turned so he can hear properly and he is looking down to my end of the table but he is not looking at anyone. Phil hasn't noticed our arrival either. I wave casually but it goes unacknowledged, then I cannot help but do a double take, Mike, wow he looks great in casual clothes, he is dressed in a blue striped shirt and jeans and my tummy kind of flips. My face feels flushed and I have to be nudged by Jason for me to listen as Jo is talking to me. I try not to keep looking at his end of the table but I cannot help it, my eyes are drawn to him. I watch as he picks a chunk of bread from the breadbasket, his large hands moving about rapidly as he is explaining something to Phil.

I sit back and look at the menu. "What are you having?" I ask Jason, just because I need to fill the silence at our end of the table. He shrugs. "Not sure what I fancy really," he doesn't elaborate, but he does smile at me. I go back to looking at the menu, the conversation has died our end of the table but luckily Phil eventually notices our attendance at the table. He comes to the end and greets us all vocally, Gemma is stood behind him, we kiss her hello and admire the shiny rock on her hand. Even Jason smiles as she flashes her left hand around, she reaches down to kiss his cheek and he actually pulls her into a hug, this is not like him at all, but she hugs him back and then leans over to kiss me on the cheek.

I admire the ring which is a solitaire diamond and it is beautiful, shown to perfection on her beautifully manicured nails. She leans in to show Jo, and I watch as they both compare jewellery. I have chosen the wrong place to sit – I have Julian next to me and he is just looking down at the table, not attempting to make any conversation at all, Phil is chatting to Jason and I watch them both, there is too much noise for me to hear what they are talking about, but Jason is doing most of the speaking with Phil nodding his head in agreement. I glance down the table, Mike is sat looking down our end, I look at him and he gives a smile then his attention is immediately taken by the strange girl sat next to him as she shows him something on her phone. I watch as he takes the phone, reads something then laughs, he looks down at me and smiles again. I am embarrassed that he has caught me watching him so I look down at the table.

Jason seems to be in a good mood tonight too, he has been all day. I watch him as he chats to Phil, then he turns to Sean and all three of them have a laugh at something. I think he maybe is feeling much better, whatever he has had he must have got out of his system We sit opposite each other and the candlelight flickers across his face, he is studying the menu now, and I notice not for the first time, Jason looks better, more colour in his cheeks, but he looks tired, very tired.

The waiters mill around the table clearing away some of the starters, Jason hasn't eaten much, he chose to share mushrooms with Sean but it is obvious to me that Sean has eaten most of them, Jason sips at his wine.

"You okay?" I ask him, but he doesn't answer, he won't look at me, I kick him under the table. "Jason," I say quietly, "are you okay?"

This time Sean looks at me then at Jason, Jason smiles. "Yes, fine, I am okay, looking forward to the main course."

He looks at me, his voice sounds false to me, I frown but he smiles, but the smile doesn't reach his eyes and I know he is lying, I know because I do the same thing all the time, it is all a charade. He looks like he is hot, there is a film of sweat on his forehead, Jason never normally sweats, maybe the bug hasn't completely gone. He looks at me and I go cold, his expression is totally devoid of anything, his look is hard as stone. I smile back at him, a half-hearted smile, I don't know what is going on in his head, and sometimes he looks at me like he hates me.

The starters have all been cleared now ready for the main meals. There is a nice hum of conversation around the restaurant. The girl with Mike has not been introduced to us and is ignoring everyone and just fixing her eyes on Mike and Phil and no one else, I don't think they have even noticed we are here, it is like they could have had a table for three people for the attention they give the rest of us is non-existent, it is quite rude really but it is clear she only has eyes for Mike and when she does take her eyes away it is only to play with her phone.

I still cannot stop staring at them, they seem so unlikely, Mike and Phil are still talking non-stop, well Phil is talking and Mike is still leaned in listening intently, nodding his head in agreement. Carole and Gemma are chatting and everyone seems to be enjoying themselves. The woman just looks totally bored and just keeps touching Mike all the time, I am not sure why she has to touch him when he is eating, I don't know why it bothers me, she is so unusual in her behaviour, it is as if none of us exists, and no matter how I try I cannot stop looking down that end of the table, no one else notices as Jason and Sean are chatting, Jo is on her phone and Julian is nursing his huge glass of red wine leaving me to just look around. The woman intrigues me, I think her name is Nancy but I am unsure, she makes no effort to speak to anyone. There is a general hubbub of conversation around as everyone else is chatting, but it is like our table is divided into two parties. I attempt to make conversation with Jason, but he isn't interested, he looks anywhere but at me, then engages himself in a conversation with Sean. I watch them both, so alike in so many ways but so different in others. I pick at the breadstick then watch as Jason stands up, excuses himself and disappears. We are still just keeping to our little parties, Jo and Julian seem to be struggling to have a conversation, he hardly ate any of his starter and has already drunk a fair few large glasses of red wine.

The waiter arrives with more drinks. It is quite warm in the restaurant. I look down at Gemma and Phil, she is now busy playing on her phone, why do people do that, it is so rude. Phil is still chatting to Mike, the woman sat next to Mike is now speaking on her phone, chatting away quite happily, her hand still on Mike's shoulder. So much for a party, Sean is chatting to someone he knows on the next table, I could be invisible as I have Carole on one side who is chatting to Brian, then Julian who is drinking, and ignoring everyone. Thankfully, the main course arrives but there is no sign of Jason returning I lean over and interrupt Sean.

"Jason is a long time," I question.

Sean stands up. "I'll just go and check he is okay." He chats for a little while longer then he gets up and disappears.

I pick at my meal, I look up and see Sean speaking with the head waiter and within minutes he is back, he leans over and whispers in my ear not to make a fuss but to get my things and go with him, I stand up immediately pulling my jacket from the back of my chair. Phil looks up at me, he frowns, then straightaway gets up and follows us, telling everyone else to start their meals. Sean stops him.

"Stay here, mate, you have guests." Phil looks back at the table, he shrugs, I think he is going to sit back down but as we walk off he grabs his jacket and follows us. He doesn't say a word to anyone just follows us.

Sean leads me out to the car park, laid on the gravel is Jason, I run over to him, he is breathing, very shallow breaths, but still breathing, there is vomit all around his face, I kneel down.

"Jason," I call his name, "Jason." I pull his face towards me so I can see him, his eyes are closed.

It is raining very lightly, the ground is wet, little puddles forming in the potholes. The waiters have explained they saw him go out, they thought he was going for a cigarette but when they looked out a few minutes later they saw he had collapsed. The waiters had thoughtfully covered him with a tablecloth, there was another cloth supporting under his head. He has vomit all down his shirt, the rain is seeping into his clothes. The head waiter comes out to inform us that the ambulance has been called. Sean pulls me up away from him, then he kneels down, he is crouched in the car park talking to Jason quietly, I watch as he puts him in the recovery position then cradles his head in his arms. I don't know what to do, I feel so helpless, so I just stand there looking at Jason and Sean, holding back my tears, Phil puts his arm around my shoulder and pulls me close to him, we just stand in the light rain. I can hear the sirens of the ambulance approaching, when the medical staff get out of the ambulance they immediately kneel down to him, firing lots of questions at us all. I tell them he has been off his food and has been sick a few times, I choke back tears as I tell them he has had a fever a week or so ago. Sean looks at me in surprise.

As they load him into the ambulance I explain to Sean about the yellow skin and that I had to call his parents to help. As Phil climbs into the ambulance we try to convince him to stay behind with his guests at his engagement party but he is having none of it. We all sit in silence as the ambulance takes us to the hospital. There are no blue lights as Jason is alive and breathing. He has an oxygen mask on his face and his eyes are closed throughout the journey. We don't speak in the ambulance, not a word. As we reach the hospital Phil takes my hand and smiles at me, but it is an empty smile, I cannot smile back or say anything, I feel numb. Phil helps me out of the ambulance, we are told where we need to go, Jason will be taken through the emergency entrance. Sean insists on going with him but they won't allow anyone else, I watch as they leave us stood in the car park as Jason is wheeled in on the trolley into the emergency unit.

"He is going to be okay." Phil puts his arm around me reassuringly; I wish I believed him I think to myself as we watch as Jason is taken through the swing doors and disappears from our sight. I have a funny feeling in the pit of my stomach that something is not okay, it is not going to be okay.

The next few hours pass in a whirl. The hospital staff are efficient, working whilst asking me lots of questions, they are superb, very caring and professional, but no one will confirm what they think it is. He has monitors attached to him. Within a short time Jason is admitted to a private room, he is made comfortable he is linked up to a drip and is now sedated, he is resting, at least he is not being sick anymore. Phil and Sean are with me in the room, so much for his engagement party, Gemma must be so cross, I tell him as much but he just shrugs, he doesn't seem bothered. We are sat waiting for the consultant to respond to his pager, but the nurse warns it could be quite some time. Another nurse comes in and takes blood samples from Jason and does his blood pressure, she makes no comment to us, she makes notes in the file and moves pillows so that Jason is more comfortable in the bed, but he doesn't even move. I think to myself that maybe I should have done that, but I am so tired, I can feel my eyes drooping at the monotonous sound of the machine. I close my eyes and sleep fitfully for a few hours.

When I wake, Sean and Phil are dozing in the visitor's chairs, their legs sprawled out under the bed where Jason is still asleep. I sit quietly watching the monitors that are attached to him, he is very pale and looks so frail and his hair is flopping in his eyes, I lean across and stroke his forehead, he feels clammy and he smells of sick, so I reach for some paper towels and rinse them under warm water. I wash his face first, very gently I wash the vomit off his neck and then I undo his shirt and sponge down his chest, he opens his eyes and smiles at me.

He takes my hand and brings my fingers to his lips, he whispers, "I am sorry," and closes his eyes again. I glance at Phil and Sean, Phil is awake and just watching me, I finish washing Jason then I lay my head gently on his chest listening to the steady beating of his heart, I push my hand into his and hold him. I don't know how long I stayed like that, but it was comforting, I liked the reassurance that his beating heart gave me, it was a strong heartbeat.

I didn't hear the consultant come in until he gives a polite cough. It is now very early morning, I can hear the clanging of the breakfast trolleys being wheeled about, I can smell the cooked breakfast, my stomach growls, I am starving. I lift my head and as I do I disturb Jason's other hand which had been resting on my shoulder, he is stirring too now. Phil and Sean are both awake. Everyone is looking at the consultant.

The consultant Mr Myers does not mince his words, surrounded by about four interns in white coats all stood taking notes, he is very clipped and professional, he looks like he could have walked out of a catalogue, he is in a grey suit, lovely blue shirt with a white collar. I notice immediately he has very nice nails, beautiful hands, I cannot stop looking at them as he explains that Jason is a very poorly man indeed, looking round at us all he asks how long the sickness has gone on for, I don't know what to say. Jason is sat up in the bed now, he is fully alert, I am totally taken aback when Jason answers the questions himself, he tells the consultant it has been quite some time, quite a few months, I am embarrassed, I should have known I thought it was just a week or so and had all cleared up, I was totally unaware that he had been poorly repeatedly since his first episode several months ago. The consultant says he needs to run further tests and organise a MRI scan, which would be later that day but he recognises the symptoms. The blood results are back and early indications which will need to be clarified, but it seems that Jason has got secondary liver cancer.

I don't remember my reaction, but I remember Jason's, he pursues his lips then closes his eyes and nods gently, as if accepting the diagnosis without question. I feel sick, my head is pounding, I need to sit down, I am aware of Sean's arms around mine, I feel myself being guided to a chair. Phil has disappeared out of the room, he comes back, my hands are shaking as a glass of water is placed in my hand and I sip from it gratefully. I look at Jason but he won't meet my eyes, I look up to Sean and he is looking away too. I feel so empty and lost, I want to have answers to so many questions but I cannot get the words to form in my head, so I just sit and sip the water until the glass is empty. Later that day my worst fears are realised, the consultant was right. From this day on our normal lives will change forever.

Chapter Thirteen

Jason has full private medical and nothing is left to chance. Everything happens very quickly, he has the best staff looking after him, his scan took place later on the day he was admitted. Before I know it a whole week has passed. There is a hospital bed in the lounge where Jason now sleeps. The consultant was correct in his diagnosis, Jason has been living with this liver cancer for a long while, longer than any of us knew, he has kept it to himself, but the consultant says he would have struggled, possibly for the last few months, maybe longer. There is a part of me that feels so angry and saddened as I think he knew and never told me, but I never mention this to anyone.

I watch as Jason struggles to make the stairs, trying to hide the pain but I know the ache in his back is just too painful. Eventually he will not be able to get up the stairs. I look at him, I want to cry for him, his skin all over his torso now has a yellow tinge all over it, his face is a washed-out grey colour and he tires very easily. The prognosis is not good; Jason may only have months to live. There is a drip which gives him pain relief and when he is not in pain he sleeps.

Over the next few days he gets worse, I am not sure if it is the medication making him worse but he struggles to eat or drink properly so depends on a drip to prevent him being dehydrated, and also gives him pain relief, he does try very small meals but his appetite has gone. It is clear he is not going to manage on his own, he needs someone at home to care for him. The consultants come and see him and discuss their plan for treatment. Jason is so very fortunate to have excellent private medical, everything is covered for him and he will be supported by them for all his medical needs. Our home has been transformed, after just a week in the hospital Jason is now home, everything seemed to happen very suddenly.

I decided, no I am determined that I want to spend whatever time he has left with him, I feel I owe it to him. I sit with Craig at work and explain to him that I need to be with Jason, I owe it to him, I don't care if I have to leave my job to be with him. Craig says he will make enquiries to find out how he deals with this type of situation. When I get home I have my mind set, I make a drink and then I sit down with Jason I start to try and tell him how I feel, I am sure he is listening to me, but he says nothing and picks up the newspaper and hides his head. I know it is deliberate but I wait patiently, just getting on with jobs around him, then when finally he puts the paper down and I sit opposite him, I take a deep breath and look at him.

"Jason, I need to speak to you about us." But before I get to say another word the doorbell goes and it is Sean and his parents. Little Ma comes in with a large pot of stew and smiles at me, she goes into the kitchen and I can hear her getting plates out. I want to delay the conversation until we are on our own, just so I can tell him how I feel, but I forget that Jason has never really considered my feelings, he is closer to his brother and parents and even Phil than he is to me, so he will not hear of it, he wants to discuss it with everyone there.

The doorbell goes again and it is Phil – I cannot believe it – I am sure Sean or Jason has text him to come round. It all gets very unpleasant. Ma comes into the lounge wiping her hands on her apron as she listens to Jason talking, he tells them what I want to do, that I want to nurse him then he tells them he is against it. It starts out quite civil but before I know it, we have had a very heated argument, it was awful, it started off as a casual enquiry by Sean asking me if I would think about the possibility of carers coming in, then a reply by me that I wanted to care for him, then before I could stop it we were shouting at each other, a very rare family evening where I have all his family round, maybe somehow hoping I could get them to see my point of view and be on my side, but so quickly it all went so wrong. The lovely stew his mother made stays in the kitchen. no one, it seems is on my side, everything goes very wrong very quickly, one minute we are all sat around chatting civilly talking about general things and I heave a sigh of relief that the topic has gone from Jason's health, Ma and Pa are sat with Sean and Phil too, they just sat in the lounge. Then Sean starts everything up again by asking what he thought was an innocent question, he asks if I will continue working shifts or just work days, I respond that day shift is an option for me and then it all kicks off again. I was aware of all of them listening as he shouted at me, making himself exhausted but he still shouts, he wants me, no he is insisting that I carry on working proper shifts, nothing must change. He says that Sean is right, that he wants carers to come in. I cannot believe he is being like this, I scream back at him that I cannot believe that he would prefer strangers to come into our home and nurse him instead of his wife.

We have never raised our voices to each other, never, I am shocked, I am shaking with anger. Everyone sits there just listening to us both, not one of them say a word, he shouts at me and I rant and shout back at him, the words spew from me. I shout that that I recognise ours was never the conventional marriage, but I made my vows and I will keep them – in sickness and in health, I will nurse him and it will be a labour of love. Jason has very different ideas, he shakes his head all the while I am shouting, tears are streaming down my face, nobody moves, then Jason calms right down. Suddenly, the shouting stops, there is a long silence, I stand there with my fists clenched, he breathes deeply until he is calm and collected, I just stand there unable to move, he puts his hand up as if to stop me saying anything, then he speaks very slowly and deliberately.

"Angie, I love you, I know I haven't maybe shown it the way you would have wanted but I need you to know that I love you regardless, I don't care how other people see our marriage." He doesn't look at anyone else, just me, I watch as he struggles for breath then as I go to interrupt he holds his hand up again silencing me, he continues, "Angie, I do respect your feelings but you have to respect mine, I have made the decision, it is mine to make, no one else's, I have signed all the necessary documents, Phil has witnessed the documents." I glance at Phil and this is not lost on Jason, he looks at me. "Do you have a problem with that, Angie?"

I shrug, it seems even if I did, it doesn't matter, no one will listen anyway, so I say nothing, Jason continues, "I am of sound mind and I have decided that my affairs will be handled by my brother, it is out of your hands, Sean is my power of attorney, he will handle all my financial and personal affairs relating to my healthcare and beyond." He looks at me before going on, his voice softens.

"Angie, please understand that I am not doing this out of spite or anything else, it is not that I don't love you or that I don't trust you, it is purely that I think Sean is the best person to be making decisions for me, and furthermore, both my parents, Phil and Sean all agree with my wishes."

As I turn to look at them I am amazed that they are all able to look me straight in the eye, none of them flinch. I am not sure when all these agreements were made but they all seem pretty sure it is in the best interests of Jason. Phil doesn't look at me, he is watching as Little Ma is speaking, although she speaks fluent English she is speaking too quickly, it is in her native tongue and I have no idea what she is saying, Sean is translating, "We know how happy you have made Jason, you were his friend before you were his wife and he respects you."

Sean looks over to Jason, I look over to Jason then back to Sean. "Is this okay, mate, can I continue?" Sean's voice is shaking, Phil has moved across the room, sitting on the arm of the chair he is holding Little Ma is his arms, Jason nods, Sean clears his throat and continues, "Since Jason was young he has always wanted to be part of something special, part of a couple, for whatever reason, being married and having a family was important to him, Angie, you made one of his wishes come true for him, for that, we, the family will always be thankful to you."

I feel very drained, I feel faint, I grab hold of the armchair for support and to steady myself, I sink gratefully into it I look up at Phil, he meets and holds my stare, he gives a half smile, he doesn't break his contact with me visually. I try to read his thoughts, he knows how my marriage was, he knows the truth. It wasn't the special thing that Sean is speaking about, and Phil knows it, if the whole truth be told so does Jason, they all know it was a lie, we lived like brother and sister, surely he must have told the family, they must have known, they have never seen us as much as kiss each other they must know. I should tell them how it really was, they need to know, they are his family, his flesh and blood, they deserve to know, if he was so close to them, but Phil closes his eyes as if reading my mind he shakes his head gently.

Little Ma stands up, she comes to me, she hugs me and is crying, but slowly Pa takes her by the shoulder and leads her out into the kitchen. I watch as he lovingly helps her into the chair and then stands behind her just holding her gently by the shoulders as they both sob quietly. Sean is holding Jason's hand and I watch them both as the brothers share a very tender moment, the world has stopped for a moment, there is no sound in the room.

I clear my throat, I have to know, I have to ask, but I cannot trust my voice, in a small croak, I ask, "And the other wish."

Sean's shoulders tense up, he remains holding Jason's hand and turns to me, he looks back at Jason and again he nods his head as if giving permission, Sean's voice is full of emotion.

"Jason always seemed to know he wouldn't make old bones, he would never speak of retirement and old age, he hated making plans. we always ignored him, but it is, as if he always said it would be, somehow he always knew, he has never been scared but his other wish in life, was to leave this world with dignity and we will make that one come true too, won't we?"

I know the comment is directed at me and me only, my heart is in my mouth, I stood up, I nodded to Sean, I couldn't speak, suddenly I felt something for Jason, not pity, not anger, but love. Okay, maybe not the love that lovers or newly married couples generally have, there are no thunderbolts or lightning flashes, but I know it is love all the same, a kind of brotherly love. On shaky feet I stood up, not sure how my knees coped but I did, I walked over to the bed, I looked at Jason and then to Sean, Sean left the tears unchecked on his face, Phil has joined us at the bed, I reach down grab his hand and kiss Jason very lightly on the lips.

"Yes, my darling, we will." I cannot look at Phil, I am not sure how I feel about him witnessing the documents that make decisions that I should be included in, I know he is Jason's friend but a little bit of me feels he has let down all over again.

I leave them chatting in the lounge, just for the need to get a bit of fresh air I pull the washing from the machine and take it out to the garden, I hear the door open and without looking I know it is Phil stood behind me, I don't turn around, I continue hanging out the items, I reach down to pick up an item and Phil is holding it for me.

"It is not the same thing, Angie, surely you can see that." I nod my head, he hands me another item and I take it from him and pin it up, we stand there in silence as he hands me the items one by one. "Angie," he speaks softly, I look up. "Please tell me you don't think I betrayed you." I nod my head again, he continues, "Can you understand why I did what I did?" I shake my head, I cannot speak, my throat has closed, he continues, "What you are going to have to deal with is enormous, I don't think you will appreciate how difficult things will be for you, well for both of you."

He pauses, he stands there for just a minute unaware he has a pair of my panties in his hand, I take them from him. "I would have coped, Phil, I am not a child, I would have coped."

He stands there just looking at me, I reach down for the next item. "But would you, Angie, be honest, darling, would you. You have a full-time job and you run this home, Jason is a moody bastard at the best of times, can you imagine him being confined to bed too, he just wouldn't cope and neither would you."

I look at him, I know deep down he is right but I still am not happy, I give a big sigh. "I know you are right, Phil, deep down I know that, and I don't hold anything against you, not this time, honestly I don't." he picks up the next item and still holding it in his hands he pulls me into a hug, "Thanks," I say quietly, I hear him snigger and I pull away, he has my brand new white lacy bra in his hands.

"Bloody hell, Angie, this is massive, your tits must be amazing." I snatch the bra from him and he laughs out loud, I look down at the basket there are a few items left, most of which are my underwear.

I look up to him, as he leans down I hold his arm blocking him reaching them. "It's okay, Phil, this is something I think I can cope with on my own." He laughs and takes a few steps back.

"Anytime you need a hand, Angie, you give me a call okay." He walks away then looks back. "No matter what time of the day or night it is, or whatever task, you call me okay." I nod my head and watch as he walks back in.

Later that night after Sean and Phil have gone it is just me and Jason in the house, he is sleeping quietly, he is not restless, we have had a light meal which he has managed to keep down, and I just sit in the silence and look at him, I am not sure how I am feeling. Tonight I am relishing the peace in my home but I know tomorrow the carers and medical visitors will be in and out of the home, so I have prepared myself to be tolerant for Jason's sake.

When it happens it is a real shock, part of me feels relieved and part angry at the intrusion, I know it sounds petty but just things like my magazines are read before I get to them, and my toiletries have been moved out of the downstairs bathroom and put upstairs in the en suite, it is as if I have been evicted, although I do fully understand they need the bathroom for them to use and for Jason, the upstairs bathroom will be kept for me and my visitors to use. I know I am being silly, and it is common sense to have the downstairs bathroom with all Jason's things there for ease and convenience, but it does irritate me sometimes, just sometimes. We have made rules that mean that care staff will not have to go upstairs for anything, this means I retain my privacy, Jason has his clothes which are mainly pyjamas and track suit bottoms, he gets too hot for anything else, so the care staff wash them daily with his bedding which generally needs to be changed daily too.

Jason's work has been good to him, making everything easy for him to contact them when he is feeling well enough to discuss his work, they immediately send someone to him to take notes and go through the open projects with the rule that once he is tired they have to leave. They know the rules and the boundaries. I am angry that they take his car, but Jason is happy with this, he thinks they have been so good to him, he doesn't need the car, he cannot drive it and it is of no use but I feel cross anyway. I get cross very easily, Jason is happy that they come round for just an hour or so every day, this way he gets to tie up all loose ends with the projects and it breaks up his day, if Jason is happy then I am too.

I know that Sean is keeping a close eye to make sure Jason isn't doing too much. To my relief some of the boxes disappear from the lounge, not many, and still there are piles in the two spare bedrooms, but just the stack in the lounge is a bit of a victory. My work have been wonderful too, initially Craig called round to the house, to explain that it had been agreed that I was to be given leave of absence, he looks so different in everyday clothes, I am so used to the uniform, he has just played squash so is in blue sports trousers and some kind of designer sports polo shirt, he looks so casual. He sits down in the lounge and I know he is shocked to see the hospital equipment in the lounge, he shows me some forms to complete but I explain that in order to keep the promise I made to Jason I won't be needing time off, I make it clear to him that I must return to work leaving the caring team to take over.

Jason was asleep when Craig arrived so we took ourselves into the kitchen so we could talk, but he calls out that he is awake, we go back in and he is sitting up, Craig just sat and listened as I explained, then as I made coffee I listened as Jason explained to Craig exactly what his terms were and why they were so important to him, there was a little discussion between them which I didn't catch but when I go back in they are chatting about everyday matters it seems that Jason has got his point across and Craig seems to understand where he is coming from completely. I ask him for just two days leave to sort things out and he agrees, Jason is happy with this too, I disappear to sort out lunch and when I come back into the lounge they are chatting about cars and boys stuff, I leave them to it. It is nice that Jason has someone to chat to about normal things, and for just a short while he is able to concentrate on something else.

When I see Craig to the door almost an hour later he pulls me close. "This must be very difficult for you, Angie, very difficult indeed."

I just nod my head, I cannot speak, I know if he is too nice I will cry and I don't want to cry, I don't want Jason to see me upset, he pulls me close to him into a hug. "You know I am always here for you don't you." I nod I cannot speak as the tears that I am holding back just pour out, he holds me close. "Oh, Angie baby, this is so tough on you, I wish I could make it all better for you both." I nod my head as he lets me go.

I watch as he goes to his car and gives me a cheery wave. I know Craig will make sure everyone understands at work. I am also happy that Sean has told the carers the situation so they understand that this is Jason's wishes not mine. I don't want them thinking I am cold and uncaring. They all know my shift pattern – it is pinned on the notice board in the kitchen with all contact details they need. We have a system that they will arrive half hour before I leave so we get to support him together. Everything seems to happen like clockwork, I feel so supported by those around me, I know that Craig has told them at work because they have been so supportive too, they text and email me on the two days I take off, calling my home is difficult when Jason sleeps quite a lot in the day, I think it is the medication. I feel much better that Craig has now visited and chatted to Jason, they got on really well and surprisingly Jason has asked him to come to visit again.

I am back to work today on evening shift so the carers are due in the next hour. Phil and Sean both been given keys to the house so they can pop in and see Jason when I am not there, he is very happy about this, I am not sure it is needed as the carers are there anyway but I am outvoted. It is very difficult to have strangers in your home, never knowing who is going to be there at any one time, they have tried to promise the same carers but this might not always be possible, so they come in bright and breezy, on time every day. The front door is left on the latch for them, I want to ask them to knock first but it seems so childish, I also want for them to remove their shoes, but I don't know how to broach the subject so I don't say anything, I just smile brightly, but I am struggling with it all, I am trying to be patient.

We have a good set of carers, well the ones I have met which will be the regular ones, the team have been introduced to Jason and he has got to know them, he has a lovely chap who likes the same books and is going to read to Jason regularly. I just know the older ladies will love him and he will love them as they all flirt with him, which he loves, they make bed baths fun and doesn't make it a chore for him, they keep his dignity, but he won't tolerate the young ones who he says witter on at him and drive him nuts. I thank our lucky stars that we have private health and everything seems to happen like clockwork, I have Sean and Phil to thank for that. Sean is sorting out the claim forms and the critical illness cover.

Before I leave for work I answer the door to a chap in a suit. I glance up and see Sean racing down the road, as he walks in the gate he calls the chap by name and he stops and waits for Sean to reach him, they shake hands and walk in together, I stand there silently. As they pass me Sean at least has the decency to explain.

"Jason's solicitor," he says, "come to sort a few legal things out for Jason, I will explain it all later okay." It is getting close to the time I should be leaving so I have no choice – another thing going on which I have no clue about, I feel very cross, but I keep my temper. I go back in and Jason is sat upright. There are two carers today, one is training, they are both in the kitchen, my kitchen, with the door closed. It seems Jason and Sean have private business and although as his wife I would expect to be involved, something tells me if I challenge their business or ask any questions, it will just lead to another unpleasant argument, so I lean over and kiss Jason on the cheek.

"I will leave you chaps to it," I say good-naturedly even though I am feeling anything but. I get into the car and put my favourite music on turning the volume up loud to try and calm my temper.

Chapter Fourteen

When I arrive at work I am relieved to find that the control room is busy, I like to be kept occupied, it stops the guilty thoughts in my head, guilt about carers being there when clearly it should be me. Every shift just before I leave the house the changeover happens, I am quite impressed it is all very fluid, very efficient, no fuss or bother. For the first few days the older lady is here, she is lovely, she brings her slippers which makes me smile, she will stay for the first four hours. I know Jason likes her, she is very approachable, professional and caring and she chats to him all the time she prepares his medication, letting him know what she is doing and why, she is very efficient ensuring she completes the accompanying paperwork.

She ushers me out of the door like a mother hen saying they will be just fine, she will find anything she needs and she will call if any problems. No matter what she says I still feel guilty when I get into my car and drive off, but I have to keep reminding myself, this is not my choice, not my decision so it is out of my hands. As I get in the car selfish thoughts take over, it is my blooming house I say out loud to no one in particular.

At work the changeover happens quickly, there is little time to talk as the calls just keep coming in, everyone keeps their heads down and keeps working, we shout out to each other regarding the different logs, and the new jobs being added, there is no apparent reason for it being busy, nothing major going on, but we all work hard clearing the logs and allocating officers. There is no opportunity to speak to anyone other than on a professional basis and before I know it I am being sent to my break, I am starving, I grabbed two cheese rolls and a chocolate bar before I left the house as the restaurant will be closed. As I approach the rest room I can smell the delicious aroma of chips, my stomach growls, ooh I wish I had known someone was going out for chips, I could just eat a nice portion of fish and chips, but I am out of luck. Phil and a few others have finished theirs, the wrappers screwed up in a ball on the table, there is just one untouched wrapped parcel untouched.

"That smells wonderful, none spare is there?" I enquire hopefully.

"Sorry, hun, you just missed out," one of the chaps replies, "that there is Mikes and he is on his way up here, but he might notice if half are missing, but you never know he might let you have some."

My heart sinks, anyone else, I thought to myself and I would know I will be okay to ask, I would be cheeky enough to get them to share, but I feel a bit shy round Mike. We still haven't spoken to each other properly, the opportunity hasn't presented itself. He sits with Craig as they work on allocations but he always looks so glum all the time, he doesn't seem to be the one for small talk.

The door opens, I look up, it is him, he says a cheery hi to everyone, sits down, opens his chip paper, and starts to eat, whilst watching TV, I say nothing, the aroma is delicious, I sit and unwrap my rolls quietly.

There is an advert break in the programme, Phil and his big mouth, pipes up. "Don't suppose you could throw a few chips to starving Annie over there can you, Mike? You nearly never had any, we had to prise her nose off the chip paper." Phil addresses Mike but indicates me, he laughs out loud.

I could kill him I am so embarrassed, I can feel my cheeks reddening, he stands up, gathers his things then he and the others get up to leave. As Phil leaves he looks back at the two of us and he jokes over his shoulder, "Ah, bless, nice romantic meal for two – all you need is a candle." He blows me a kiss, laughs out loud and departs.

I want to strangle him I am so embarrassed, I can feel my cheeks reddening even more so, but Mike is laughing too as he passes his chip wrapper to me. "Just ignore him," he says chuckling, "here, help yourself there is plenty, far too much for me, and we cannot have you wasting away."

I want to say no but it would seem childish to do so. They smell so delicious so I reach over to take some and his hand touches mine, I feel an electric shock go through me and I pull away, but it seems that he hasn't noticed. I am so close to him I can smell his aftershave, and I can see the hairs on his chest poking out of his shirt where he has taken his tie off. I have to swallow hard, I feel all flushed and hot, but he continues eating, he obviously doesn't realise the effect he is having on me. I move back into my seat, I look at him under my lashes, he is watching television intently, the programme is back on, Mike is listening to the presenter speaking about something to do with cars, but I don't hear or see anything. I feel all light-headed and flustered. I realise that I haven't eaten or drunk anything and I guess that is why I am feeling this way, my stomach growls, so I put the hot chips into my cheese roll, lining them up neatly, I sense Mike is watching me and when I look up from placing my chips in an orderly line in my roll he is smiling.

"New recipe for Master Chef is that, cheese and chip roll?" He indicates my creation, I giggle and relax a little.

"Oh yes," I reply returning his smile, "don't knock it until you try it, here you go, only fair I should share with you."

I pass him a plain cheese roll which he takes, asking, "So what makes this so special?"

110

I watch as he lines up the hot chips into the roll, he looks up. "Is this right?" I laugh then I have to explain to him. "Okay, watch and learn, the roll has to be white and crusty, with real butter and mature cheese, no butter substitutes okay."

He smiles. "Okay, wouldn't dream of it, butter substitutes is a definite no-no." He makes like he is noting it down on his hand.

I ignore him and continue, "Please listen, it is important."

He laughs, "I know it is, I am taking notes." He laughs again, I glance at him and he is pulling a very serious face, still with his hand making make believe notes in his hand.

I laugh then continue. "Then the chips must be hot so they will melt the butter and cheese, delicious but not in any diet books you will read."

He is smiling as he puts the roll to his mouth and takes a huge bite. "Mmmm," he mumbles, speaking with his mouth half full, "absolutely scrumptious, you are a genius, this will be my new food of choice."

I grin back at him. "Not that good for your waistline though," I warn, he doesn't reply but looks at my stomach area and smiles, raising his eyebrows.

His smile makes his dark eyes twinkle and he looks so handsome, he should smile more often. I watch as he wipes the butter from his lips with the back of his hand, my stomach does a little flip. I don't know what to say; obviously he doesn't either, so we eat quietly just watching the television. I glance over to see he has half polished off his chips and his roll has disappeared.

He looks up and smiles. "Care for a few more?" I shake my head, I have had so much now I feel so full. I watch as he crumples the paper up and expertly throws it at the bin.

"That usually never happens when someone is here," he laughs, I smile at him; he is so lovely, so friendly. We say nothing, the restroom telephone interrupts the silence and I answer to hear Steve announce he has the carer on the line, she has been trying my mobile apparently but couldn't get through, I frown at the phone as he puts her through. She has taken over from the lovely carer that was there earlier, she sounds really young, I don't know who she is, but she is complaining that Jason is being argumentative as he wants a beer; she is adamant that it doesn't say he can have alcohol on the sheet and is arguing.

"Okay," I say calmly, "don't worry about the sheet, it is okay, he can have a beer, really it is okay." I glance over at Mike, but he is watching the television, I turn my attention back to the call.

"But it doesn't say on the sheet," she argues, I take a deep breath, this is going to be a challenge, but I try and keep composed but to no avail. Despite my trying to reason with her she will not give in and let him have anything that is not on the list. At first I try to be calm and reasonable I explain it doesn't say he cannot have alcohol, it doesn't say anything about alcohol, so of course he can have it, he is a grown up. Jason knows what he can and cannot have, and he can have a beer, but she keeps on arguing and finally I lose my patience and shout at her.

"My husband has just a few weeks to live, do you really think a bloody beer is going to make that much difference!" Then I hang up, I am shaking with temper, I look around, Mike has left, the door is still closing.

I am alone in the rest room the last fragments of my roll on the table doesn't not look so appetising now. I throw it all in the bin and tidy up, I am not sure when Mike left or how much he heard, but I don't care anyway. I check my mobile, there are no missed calls showing. The signal strength is really good, this makes me even angrier, she lied, she didn't even bother to call the mobile. I make a quick phone call to Sean, but he is not answering, it goes straight to voicemail, I know I could explain to Craig and he would let me go, but I know there would be a scene when I got home and I don't want Jason to be upset. I put a call in to the answering machine of the care supervisor to let her know I am not happy about the situation, then I call Phil, although he is on duty the same as me, he is just going out and about he promises he will go round and sort it out for me. I feel so helpless. I return to the control room and check the logs, I can see he is out and about on enquiries. Then I groan inwardly as I see he has Mike with him. In a short while he sends me a text saying all is okay with Jason and adds a few kisses. I have just an hour or so to go but it makes me feel so much better knowing Jason is okay.

I get home later and the carer is still there, she is young and I didn't expect to see someone so young to be sent to look after Jason, she makes me cross as soon as I see her, and I know I shouldn't judge her on her appearance but I do. I am not happy that she has too much make-up on, a nose piercing and peeling nail varnish. I expect nurses and carers to have a clean and clinical look about them, I know Jason would hate it too, there are certain standards I would expect from private nurses, she certainly does not meet any of them. I can almost see him grimacing as he hears her giggling as she walks back to the kitchen so I know he is not happy with her.

Phil is back there too, still in uniform he must have left work really quickly to get home before me. Jason is sat up in bed and as I take my shoes off I can hear them, they are all laughing and joking together. There are dirty cups and glasses around, I gather them up noisily, with a self-satisfied smile to myself I notice Jason has a beer bottle in his hand.

"I see you got your beer then." I smile at him and he smiles back. As I walk into the kitchen I shoot her a dirty look, she stands and watches me as I put the cups and glasses in the dishwasher.

"Sorry about earlier." I can hear the nervousness in her voice. I look at her, she is very young, blonde and her uniform is far too tight, and she has her shoes on. I glance down at Phil's feet as he wanders into the lounge, he at least is just in his socks. I look at her again, her trousers are far too long and she flaps about when she walks.

I decide immediately that I don't like her at all, she won't be coming again, the sound of her whiny voice grates on me. She continues, "It is just there were no guidelines on alcohol so I didn't know."

I know I should be nice to her and make her feel better but why should I, so I snap back at her, "I suppose there were no guidelines on filling the dishwasher either or putting the washing in the machine." I turn away and continue to load the dishwasher noisily. Phil joins us and there is a silly banter between them, and I can see by their body language that there is a chemistry there, he is openly ogling her and smiling at her and she is gazing up at him, leaning back with her elbows on the kitchen unit pushing her chest out provocatively, her big eyes listening intently to Phil, I see red, I get very cross, very quickly.

"Oh for Christ's sake, there is no area out of bounds for you is there," I address Phil with anger, she is now stood up straight still pushing her chest forward. "Maybe the two of you should bugger off and do what you obviously want to be doing while I finish doing what she should have been doing."

I pick up Jason's dirty pyjamas and push them into the washing machine then ignoring them both I storm back into the lounge, I am tempered, it is very late and I am tired.

Jason pats the side of the bed. "Join me." He smiles, why not I think. So I leave them two in the kitchen giggling, I lay down next to him, I feel myself calming down, we lay like spoons and I cuddle up to him, we lay in silence, my head on his chest, he is stroking my hair and I can hear his heartbeat, we can both hear the muffled voices coming from the kitchen.

After a few minutes the carer, whose name I still do not know comes in, she looks at me and starts to say, "I don't think...."

But I interrupt her, "Fuck off, no one cares what you think, he is my husband, see yourself out, you will not be coming here again." I shock myself as I am not normally rude and it is very rare for me to swear, but the sight of her and Phil flirting and giggling made me cross, I will certainly make sure she doesn't come here again. Jason doesn't say a word, he continues to stroke my hair. She looks over to Phil and he shrugs, he walks the few steps towards us both, he leans over to kiss me, pats Jason on the shoulder, says a cheery "see you soon" then heads for the door. Without a word she gathers her coat and bag and follows Phil. I guess I know what they will be doing soon, I lay down with Jason and that is where I stay all night, still in my uniform.

We both wake up at the same time, we have slept in that tiny bed all night, it is the closest I have ever felt to him, I look at him, he smiles at me and I hug into him, we just lay there in each other's arms, my leg has gone dead but I don't want to move, this is nice, it is calming and comforting, I feel so very close to him. I don't want to break the intimacy I cannot remember us every holding each other all night.

"Do you want breakfast?" I speak gently to Jason.

He shakes his head, "No, I want to stay like this for a while, just me and you, before the military turn up."

He strokes my face and then his hand goes down to my neck and he strokes me gently, his hand moves lower, and I think I need to stop him, I start to say, "Jason I don't…"

But he silences me with a light kiss on my lips, "Please," he whispers gently. I relax back in his arms, his lips are soft and gentle, there is a slight medication smell about him which I ignore, it feels good what he is doing, it has been so long, his fingertips stroke the front of my uniform blouse and he undoes my buttons, he fondles my breasts, pulling them out over the top of the bra, I reach behind and unfasten the bra, pulling it through the sleeve of my blouse and dropping it to the carpet, Jason places a light kiss between my breasts and moves his hand to hold the side of my cheek, he murmurs, "You have such beautiful breasts." He kisses my neck and my chin and then my forehead, I don't know where this is going, he normally has no energy, he certainly won't have enough energy for sex, but I just let him do as he wants, it feels nice, just nice, he lays his head on my bare chest for a few minutes, his tongue grazes my nipple, then he just rests there, his breathing is calm he then raises himself on one elbow and looks directly into my eyes.

"I wanted to tell you something, something that I have had on my mind." I stroke his cheek. "I want to say I am sorry about all this stuff." He lifts his hand with the drip attached, "I am sorry it has taken over your home, I miss you, it seems like forever since we have been alone together, to talk, I worry about you, you look so tired all the time, Angie, tell me are you okay?"

I am shocked, alone together and to talk, we never done that, even before he was poorly, I don't know what he is talking about, maybe he is delirious, maybe it is the medication but I don't argue, I don't say anything, I don't know what to do, or say so I just hold him.

It is clear that this display of affection has exhausted him but I am surprised by Jason's clear voice as he speaks to me, he seems very much in control, I turn to look at him, his eyes look clear and his breathing is not laboured, it is as if he is not ill, it looks like the normal Jason, but then I notice his drip is attached as he has learnt to do, so I know he has probably pushed the release valve by himself and therefore he has had his morning painkilling medication already.

I am not sure how to answer his questions, we never had the relationship where being alone and talking was high on the list of importance. When I wanted to talk he always found something else to be doing, but I don't mention anything, there is no point. I am not sure what he is thinking or where this is leading, what do I do, I don't know, should I lie and tell him it is all okay, I am coping well, but I cannot lie to him I have lied to him about so many things over the time we have been together, bitten my tongue in order to keep the peace, so I decide I will tell him. I move to make myself more comfortable and he sits up, I sit up too, I start to close my blouse, but he stops me and puts his hand back on my breast, caressing me as I speak. I don't stop him, it is nice and comforting. He encourages me to go on, I lie back against him and let him squeeze my breasts, he lies on his side facing me, he kisses my breasts gently one at a time, caressing and kissing them, then sucking gently, I am not about to complain as it feels wonderful, so I talk to him. I tell him that I hate the carers for removing my stuff around and about my magazine being read before I get to see it, even the crossword being half completed. He looks up, taking his lips away from my breast he is smiling at me, it is a nice smile, and I find myself laughing at the pettiness of it all, we are both laughing so we don't hear the key in the front door. Without us hearing them Little Ma comes in with Sean closely followed by Pa, they find both Jason and I laughing and holding each other, looking ridiculous as I am still in my uniform with my blouse undone to the waist, Jason still is holding me, my breasts exposed in his hand, his mouth still on my nipple. I am not sure how long they stood watching before Sean gives a low discreet cough, I look up and jump away turning myself into Jason to cover my exposed chest as soon as I see them. I am absolutely certain they saw what he was doing to me, it would have been hard of them to miss it. I am mortified that Sean and Pa have seen us, and especially where Jason's hands and lips were, but they say nothing, little Ma chats on obliviously, Jason laughs out loud, Pa heads straight for the television remote control totally unaware. At least Sean has the decency to look away as I frantically fight with the buttons on my blouse, covering myself to make me decent. I get off the bed, kiss Jason on the lips and walk into the kitchen, Sean follows, my frilly white bra in his hand, he dangles it from his finger.

"That was nice to see," he says, I snatch the bra from him, he pulls me into his arms, I laugh nervously, and he joins me. "No, not that, I didn't mean that, you know what I mean, you know, you both being so intimate, it is nice to see you both laughing. Trust my brother, he barely has any energy but he can still manage to cop a feel, and judging by what I just saw, who can blame him."

I dig him hard in the ribs but he laughs and kisses my head, I give him a big hug back.

And so the day begins again, I go into autopilot, I pop upstairs and shower quickly, dressing in sweatpants and T-shirt, then I prepare breakfast for everyone, fussing around with jams and marmalades, listening to Sean and Jason chatting. I would normally make bacon sandwiches but I know Little Ma would not approve. They have to be content with toast and cereal, she overlooks a lot of what goes on but will not sit at the table if pork or pork products are there, so we hide it in tin foil or plastic tubs in the fridge so as not to upset her. Jason's dad turns up the television and is engrossed in his favourite documentary, we all sit around reading the papers and eating breakfast, discussing the events of the forthcoming day. I take Pa his breakfast and he holds my hand and kisses it gently. He is so lovely and such a gentleman, as soon as I turn away he is back watching his documentary.

We hear the front door open and Phil walks in, bright and breezy he kisses me and little Ma as if nothing has happened, gives a high-five to Jason and flicks Sean's ear, but I am not happy with him, and I want to speak to him alone. I have to have my say, so when he is refilling his orange juice from the fridge in the kitchen I seize my opportunity and go out to join him. I keep my voice low and calm, which is not how I am feeling, I am still so angry with him.

"Phil, have you totally forgotten that you are engaged to Gemma, what was all that about last night, what the hell are you playing at chatting up the hired help."

Phil is straight on the defence, but he won't look at me, his head remains in the fridge. "Well, if you want to know the truth, Angie, Gemma and I have broken up, I cannot see it going anywhere and so I told her, you see, I don't think I am the person she wants me to be, there is no one else," he pauses, "well, not as yet but it probably didn't help that I have not been entirely faithful in our relationship." I look at him, he takes a drink then replies, "Don't look at me like that, she hasn't been an angel either, she has admitted as much to me, so I guess she is not the one for me either," he pauses, taking a drink of his juice then continues. "Truth be known I don't want her to be, she is sexy and clever and that is it." He looks at me and shrugs and goes back to the fridge, I watch as he helps himself, I am shocked, I thought those two were forever. Yes, I know he is a flirt but a funny comical flirt.

"How long?" I ask.

"How long what?" He looks straight at me.

"How long have you not been together, is it a recent thing?" He shrugs again, concentrating now on buttering his roll.

"Well, we had the engagement meal and we never took it from there, she kept the ring though, as she chose it and paid most of it anyway it seemed only fair; it was all her idea really and I just went along with it." He is so matter of fact I cannot believe it, have I been living in a bubble. As if reading my thoughts, Phil takes a bite of his roll, chews for a while then goes on, "Well, it is not as if anyone would have noticed anyway, you have all pretty much been living in a bubble with what has happened with Jason, and rightly so, I didn't want to burden you all with more, what's done is done – we are both cool with it."

"And last night?" I ask, I have to ask, I have to know, I don't know why.

116

Phil is so matter of fact when he replies. "A pretty diversion, one-night stands are my thing now – no complications, women try to own me, and I don't want to be owned, the one I really want to be with doesn't know I exist, at least not in that sense." He winks. "Still there you go, at least I can have a beer when I want and go to the gym without having to answer to anyone." He drains his glass. "I can play the field, but I am sorry about last night, I had no right to do that and it won't happen again, not in your home." He is being so lovely I have to give in, his face breaks in to a cheeky grin, so I cannot be mad at him for long. "Forgiven?" he asks.

"Forgiven," I reply. He drops a light kiss on my lips and leaves me stood there speechless. What else is there to say.

He returns to the lounge and within minutes I can hear him laughing and joking with Jason. As I go in they all fall silent, I know Sean has told Phil about the incident this morning, Jason smiles at me. "Sorry, love, didn't mean to embarrass you this morning."

I shake my head smiling. "Don't worry, Jason, looks like even you copping a feel is off the cards now." In a small way I am glad they have seen some intimacy between Jason and I, would have preferred for them to just have seen us kissing though.

Chapter Fifteen

I realise I am guilty of letting my friends drop, it has been nearly two months now and I have had hardly any contact with anyone, except Sean and Phil who are my rocks. There have been messages left for me on my mobile and on my email but I have left them all unanswered as I am caught in a busy routine of work and home.

Jason is deteriorating, I can see it in his skin colour and he is losing weight. We now have a good routine of carers that he likes and he has visitors regularly coming in the house. His medication has been increased so he can manage his pain, but he gets tempered with the medication as it gives him a nasty taste in his mouth and puts him off his food, he has to be coaxed to take it and many times it has been thrown across the room in dejection. This week I start early shift so the carers will be here very early so I have time to shower and get ready and then sit and have breakfast with him, today is not a good day, I know he has not slept well as I heard him moaning in the night. In the end I get up and give him more medication and I sleep downstairs on the sofa to be near him. To add to everything else, I have got PMT, my stomach is painful, my breasts heavy, I am tired and I feel very emotional, so we are both a bit fragile this morning.

He is angry from the start and throws his juice and toast across the room, I am so angry at the mess he has made, just a small cup of juice has gone up the walls and over the carpet, I go to him to try and calm him down, but as he flails his arm out it catches my tea and it all goes over my uniform blouse. I am shocked by the heat of the tea and jump up shouting and swearing, before I know what is happening I am shouting and he is shouting back, we scream at each other for what seems like forever, but is just a minute or so, then he is collapsed and breathless and I am crying, it is all just too much today.

I go upstairs to change but I hear a crash and run back down, he is out of bed and trying to clear the spilt tea from the bedding. He has got his drip all tangled and is struggling to breathe, he shouts at me again and I shout back at him, the front door is opened and the carer finds us both sat on the floor in floods of tears. Within minutes she has everything under control. I am back upstairs changing my blouse when she comes into the bedroom, I didn't hear her at first but she tapped on the door and walked in. She is gently spoken and she says she is going to arrange some extra care as I need to have some time out, so this week on Thursday and Friday I will have a few hours in the evening to go out and do something different. She cannot do much more but I am thankful to her, I have to admit it is a relief to me.

I still feel dreadful when I get to work, my head is throbbing, I think I am getting a cold to accompany the cramping pains in my stomach and the pain in my breasts, I just feel so rubbish today.

Craig calls me over. "You okay?" he asks quietly, I shake my head.

"Bad start to the morning," I say quietly.

He pulls me towards the admin room, he closes the door. "Want to tell me about it?" he asks, I shake my head.

I don't want to say anything I look up at him, he is waiting patiently, I cannot help it, I burst into tears.

"It has just been the worst of days so far today." Then I tell him about how rubbish I am feeling with a cold and PMT, the incident with the juice the toast and then the tea, the shouting between us both, he just stands and listens, that is all he does, he doesn't offer any advice or empty platitudes, he lets me get it all out of my system, then he lifts my head up by my chin.

"Better now."

I nod my head, "Thank you."

He leaves me and goes back to the control room, I know he would have told the guys to be gentle with me, he is such a nice man. I blow my nose and wipe my eyes, I know they will be all bloodshot but I don't care. I finish the admin duties and return to the control room. Steve has put a chocolate bar on my keyboard and Gavin has made me a cup of tea, tears prick at my eyelids, they are all so sweet to me.

As I said, I realise I have let my friends slip, I knew it was happening but I could never seem to find the time to keep up with everyone I have been so absorbed with Jason and work and nothing else, it seems I have nothing else to speak about, so I spend my whole rest break sending out emails to those friends who I have ignored, apologising for birthdays I have missed. I return every email and text message and phone call. I am relieved sometimes that I get the answering machine so I can leave a brief message, sometimes it is easier to copy and paste the same email to different people, but some have to have a personal reply. Then I call my sister and mum, they both ask the same questions: how is Jason, how am I coping. I tell them I have Phil and Sean to help me and we are doing fine, both offer their support but I tell them about the carers and they understand how Jason feels but how I feel too.

It is great to catch up but after the hour, I am exhausted but I feel so much better. I think I am doing really well, even though I have had to explain the same situation to lots of people most of them have understood and I have re-established my friendships and smoothed over the cracks in the ones I have upset I have made a few plans to meet with people, to be honest it feels good that my life is restored to being a bit more than just work and

Jason. I still feel over tired and very emotional, my whole body hurts and I just want to get home and have a shower and a sleep. I pop to the ladies, I stand and look in the mirror, a tired washed out woman looks back at me. I try to add a splash of lipstick but it looks too bright and gaudy so I wipe it off again, I don't care how I look, if people don't like it they can look away, that is just how I am feeling today.

Later I am busy photocopying the shift rotas as usual, there is a huge pile to copy, in fairness Steve did offer to do it for me but I fancied the break, but it seems to be not my day today, it is normally fairly straight forward, but not today. I get half way through, pleased that I am making a good job of getting it all sorted ready for the following week, I set the originals in and hit send. Immediately the copier jams, this is normal occurrence and just takes patience and calm to get it working, but today is not going to plan, I feel fractious, my nose keeps running, I am tired and emotional and the damn machine won't play, it is bleeping, red lights flashing on the display telling me there are five paper jams but despite checking every drawer for the paper jam I get more hot and frustrated and angry. I finally clear all the jams, put the original back and hit the button, immediately it jams again to make matters worse it has torn the original paperwork which will create more work. As I pull the bottom drawer out to check it is clear I knock all the other paperwork from the top, it was all stacked in alphabetical order, the newly printed copies scatter over the floor, it all flutters down like a flock of birds, reason says I should walk away but I lose it totally. I grab the rest of the paper and throw it down on the floor, I get myself in such a temper, I go all hot, my face goes red and I slam the drawer, catching my hand I start swearing loudly, I just want to cry. I storm off down the corridor pushing the door with such force I didn't see anyone coming. Mike grabbed the door and held it open and I flew through careering straight into him.

"Hey careful!" he shouts, but it is too late, I crash straight in to the other door coming back at me as it hits me on the shoulder, I cry out with pain and immediately burst into tears.

Mike pulls me into a vacant meeting room and pulls me to his chest in a hug, he wraps his arms around me holding me tight. I offer no resistance, I stand with my hands at the side of me, just leaning against him, he strokes his hand up and down my back and on my bad shoulder, he pulls me to him, I cannot stop myself, I sob and sob. It feels good to have strong arms around me, it feels good to just cry myself out. Mike just strokes my hair and says nothing, his chest is strong and solid and he smells lovely, his breath is regular and calming. I try to speak as my sobs subside, but my throat feels tight so everything comes out jumbled, my nose is running, I must look a sight but I don't care, I just relax into his chest.

When I feel cried out, and so much better, I feel him put his head to mine, I am not sure what he has just done, it felt very intimate, I look up to him I have to know, I sniff loudly and wipe my nose on my sleeve, god I must look a mess, but I clear my throat and ask him, "What did you just do?" I ask. "Did you just smell my hair?" I ask quietly.

"No," his response is equally quiet, "I kissed your head, is that okay."

He strokes my hair back from my face, my hair is usually pinned back neatly, but now it is all coming out of its clip in a mess, I look at him, my heart is racing, I am hot and flustered, my nose is running my face is tearstained, I must look an absolute sight, I don't answer, but yes it is okay. We stand there quietly for several seconds, I place my head back on his chest, his radio crackles into life calling his number, he hugs me close once more before pushing me gently away, he holds my chin up and looks at my face.

"Better now?" he asks.

I sniff. "Yes, thank you and sorry, it was the bloody photocopying machine got the better of me, that's all."

My cheeks are bright red, my nose all runny and the tears that haven't dissolved on his jumper are on my chin, I must look a dreadful sight, he takes a tissue from his pocket and dabs gently at my cheeks as I look up at him. He looks straight into my eyes and strokes my tear-stained cheek with his thumb.

"Don't worry, the copier machine does that to me too. I will go and sort it now, why don't you take a few minutes to go and wash your face okay." I cannot speak so I nod instead.

He disappears off down the corridor speaking into his radio and leaving me to watch his departing back and his strong shoulders as he walks away with long purposeful strides and I return to my papers, I cannot face them, I leave them in a heap, I go back to the admin office. I sit for some time playing back the scene in my head, why did he kiss my head? What does that mean? Phil always kisses my head, is it a gesture of friendship or detachment. I like it when Phil does it, not sure I like it so much when Mike does it.

I wash my face and feel a lot better so I pop down for my cigarette break and catch up with some of the admin girls. Marcia works with them – I have known her for years, she was one of the first people I met when I joined, she is very knowledgeable of the main administration office and we often call on her to help us. The lady Sue who she works with is getting married, she is having her hen night this Friday and she has invited me, she is really sweet as she says she wanted to ask me ages ago but others told her I probably wouldn't want to go, but I tell her I would love to, I take the details and I feel a bit excited, the more I think about it the more I realise I am really looking forward to it.

When I return to the photocopier all has been sorted and all the paperwork is back in order and piled up neatly and is just sat there waiting for me, there is a note left on the top saying "all better now" with a smiley face drawn at the bottom and a small kiss, it makes me smile. The machine behaves and I catch up with all the rotas, when I return to the control room Mike and Craig are sat looking through some paperwork, I sit down and engross myself in the jobs coming in. I cannot help but keep looking at him out of the corner of my eye, he really is lovely-looking. Once he caught me, he looked at me and smiled, I smiled back and he mouthed "you okay" and I nodded back to him. I was okay. Very okay. There is only an hour or so to go to the end of the shift, I am so tired.

Craig gets up and wanders over to me, "You okay now?"

I look up at him. "Yes, I am thanks, just a bad day, sorry about earlier."

He leans on the desk next to me. "You get yourself all packed up and head off home now."

I look at him. "Thanks but honestly I am okay."

He stands up. "Now," he orders, I smile at him, I must admit I cannot wait to lay my head on my pillow and sleep. .

I pack up gratefully and with a cheery wave to the rest of the shift I make my way to the car. As I am crossing the car park Phil catches up with me, I am surprised to see him in his full body armour.

"You okay, Angie?" he asks, he walks beside me, I look up to him and frown. "Gavin said you were a bit upset."

I nod my head, "Yes, I was, Phil, I am just very tired, had a bad start to the day with Jason and it didn't improve when I got to work, I was feeling sorry for myself, the photocopier pushed me over the edge but I am okay now, thanks."

He pulls me close to him, as close as the body armour will let him be. "I am always here for you, Angie, you just call me and I will always be there for you." He looks at me. "You know that don't you."

I nod my head. "I know, Phil, I know and thanks."

Phil pulls me back close to him, he pulls me as close as he can. "Better?" he asks.

"Yes, much thank you." I look at him. "What is with the body armour?" I ask.

"Oh, just some incident we have to attend with CID – nothing exciting." He pulls me back into his arms, then kisses my head and lets me go I get into my car I cannot help thinking how much I liked being in Mike's arms.

Chapter Sixteen

When I get home, Jason is full of apologies, the consultant has been out and he has had his medication increased and seems to be a bit more stable, he is subdued, but I cannot be mad at him, I am not in pain and he is, I am not going through his nightmare and so I give him a hug. He wants to order in Chinese food which I know he won't eat but I go along with it anyway. I am so tired but I open a bottle of wine and we have a small glass each. I tell him all about the hen night and he is excited and pleased for me. He makes suggestions about what I should wear, I am shocked, bloody hell, this is totally new for Jason, he has never commented on my clothes, I didn't realise he knew I actually had any wardrobe so little attention did he pay, and I haven't even given a thought to the actual night and what I will wear. So we have a mini fashion parade and I discover most of my clothes are a bit too big, I have lived in uniform and sweats over the last month or so, mind you, as I looked in the mirror, the weight loss seems to suit me, I don't look scrawny but my hips have appeared again and I am pleased with what I see. Jason chooses a navy short dress with cute pleats to the bottom and high patent shoes and he tells me how he thinks I should get my hair done, he is being very sweet and very attentive, we have a lovely fun evening, he asks me to sit with him into the early hours, I am dead on my feet but as I don't have to get up early in the morning I agree. It is a very pleasant evening. When he finally pulls me towards him he kisses my cheek and says he is tired, he wants to sleep, I squeeze his hand gently, I watch him for a few minutes which is all it takes for him to fall into a restful sleep. I fall into my bed too tired to shower, too tired to do anything but sleep.

Friday evening comes round quickly and I am really excited about going dancing in the local nightclub, something I have not done for ages. Just to get out is new and exciting for me, I am not looking for pity, I just want to have a bit of me time. Sean is over to sit with Jason, he has cancelled the carer, they are having a boys' night in with beer and DVDs. They are having a curry delivered later, not sure how wise that is as Jason is struggling to keep food down, but they are both giggling and being stupid. I take extra time with my make-up and I am pleased with the result. When I come downstairs to show them my outfit, Jason says nothing, he just looks at me, he goes very quiet, I cannot read his expression, he holds his hand out to me and I go to him, he pulls me close to him and strokes my thigh as I stand next to him by the bed, he runs his hand up my thigh and I put my hand there to stop him, but his hand runs over mine, pushing it away, he is stroking the very top of my thigh, his hands move over my dress. I try to push his hand away again this time he puts his hand under my dress and caresses my bottom. I glance quickly to Sean, he is sat very close to the bed, but is being discreet and looking the other way. Jason pulls me down to him and whispers that I look beautiful, he tells me to have fun and I kiss him gently on the lips and then I hug Sean. The taxi toots the horn and I have to go. It is only when I am in the taxi that I think back over the recent shows of affection from Jason, is it because people are there that his displays of affection are happening or something else? I wish he would have showed me the same affection when we were both healthy enough to enjoy it.

The police bar is busy and I catch up with lots of people. I have a few glasses of wine and I am having a great time just relaxing. Helen is out with us and she is looking fabulous in a black slinky mini dress and high silver shoes. Within minutes we are chatting and laughing, we head off to the ladies and catch up with other girls we are going out with who have just arrived. We dress Sue up in a hat and feather boa, we all stand around the mirrors and gossip as we check our make-up, suddenly I feel young and carefree, I want to totally enjoy myself tonight, to totally forget about the hospital bed occupying my lounge or the barrage of carers that come in daily, tonight is all about me, oh and Sue of course.

An hour later I am in my element in the night club, I feel good, I love the music and get straight on the dance floor with Helen, within minutes everyone else is dancing with us, everyone is chilled out, laughing, dancing and enjoying themselves. The drinks are flowing and I am forgetting all my problems at home, just being here being silly, laughing and chilling out. I think I see Phil by the bar, but I am not sure , I just stay dancing, my feet are starting to ache but I love the pounding of the music, my head is going to throb tomorrow but I don't care, we are having a fabulous time.

Helen pulls me from the dance floor and we head outside for some fresh air, ironic really as the first thing Helen does is lights a cigarette. Phil comes out to join us, he and Helen are chatting, he grabs at her cigarette and takes a huge drag, I frown at him, he laughs and pulls me close to him then kisses me on the lips, I push him away.

"That is disgusting." I wipe my mouth, "like kissing an ashtray." I pull a face at both of them.

Helen leans over, before I can stop her she pulls my face towards her and kisses me on the lips, I try to pull away but she holds me close. "Mmm," she murmurs, "nice, Angie, very nice." She moves away and I push her away.

"Eeeuugghh get off me, you crazy woman." They both laugh, Phil looks at Helen.

"I have never kissed an ashtray, do you mind." He leans over and pulls her close. I watch as his lips meet hers, she puts up no resistance, I watch as he kisses her deeply, they seem oblivious to everyone around them. I just stand looking at my drink.

When they part Helen looks at me and smiles. Phil looks at me. "Mmm I quite like kissing ashtrays."

Helen pokes him in the ribs and we all laugh. Sue the hen comes out, she heads over to us, she lights a cigarette and soon is chatting and flirting with Phil, he is lapping up the attention grabbing at her and making suggestive comments, but he is entertaining everyone. Phil is a good-looking bloke and has the gift of the gab, saying things he knows she wants to hear; I can tell that she is loving it. I look at Helen, but she is laughing with them, everyone seems to be having a good time.

I look around the smoking area, I notice Mike stood in the doorway, I have to do a double take, he looks fabulous, he has black jeans and a light blue button down collar shirt, opened at the neckline, hairs are poking out of the top of his shirt and his thick hair is spiked up, he usually wears it flat. I look down at his feet, I normally see him in his boots but tonight he has modern trendy shoes on, he looks so attractive, I have to look twice, I cannot stop staring at him. I don't know if it is the wine having an effect but I think he looks handsome out of uniform and extremely kissable. I can see he is on his own so I push myself off the wall which is doing a great job of supporting me, I wobble a bit as I take one step towards him then I notice he is not actually on his own, there is someone stood at the side of him. I watch as he hands a drink to the girl, she wraps her arm around him I feel something that I haven't felt for a long time – jealousy.

I turn back to Helen and Phil, Sue the hen has disappeared and it is just the two of them chatting, their heads close together. Phil is speaking and Helen is shaking her head disagreeing, they both laugh and I try to listen so I can join in, but I am distracted, I cannot help but watch Mike with the girl, I just stare, he is stood with one hand over her head leaning on the wall behind, she is smoking and sipping her drink through a straw, he is laughing and stooping down occasionally so he can hear her. I cannot stop looking at them, I don't know who the girl is, she is very pretty, quite short with blonde cropped hair, a short leather mini skirt and knee-length boots and a very skimpy top and a very large chest, I have never seen her before, I know she isn't with our group. I watch as she strokes his face then pulls him closer to her and kisses him lightly on the lips before pulling away and laughing out loud. I watch as they laugh together, then he reaches down and they kiss again, this time it is a serious kiss, I cannot stop staring as his lips own hers, he pulls her close and it seems they are totally unaware of anyone else around them – I don't like it, I cannot bear to watch, but I am caught where I am as he is stood in the doorway where, if I am going to leave, I need to pass.

I grab Helen's hand, I cannot watch any longer. "Come on, I need to go, let's dance."

I pull her away and she willingly follows me, I glance towards Mike, he is now snuggling into the neck of the blonde woman, she is giggling and seems to be having a wonderful time.

Helen wobbles her way towards the exit, as she approaches the door she calls a cheery, "Hi, Mike," towards Mike who turns to us both, he is now stood up straight and totally blocking my entrance back into the club.

"Hi, how nice to see you, how are you doing?" He is addressing me directly, he looks me up and down slowly, he is smiling, he doesn't hide the fact he is looking at me either. "Nice dress, we don't often get to see you dressed," he comments, he raises his eyebrows, my stomach flips, he is smiling his whole face lights up. Christ he is so bloody sexy. He looks me up and down again then holds my gaze, he doesn't say anything, just stares at me. It seems to me that the blonde girl has been forgotten, I take a quick glance at her but she doesn't seem to care as she is texting or playing on her phone, I watch as she lights another cigarette, then I turn my attention back to Mike.

"Oh thanks," I stammer then even though he says nothing, I continue babbling, "It's not a new dress, I have had it ages," I babble, unable to stop myself.

He leans forward. "Well it is very lovely." He raises his eyebrows then smiles. "Are you having a good time?"

I blush and can only babble again, "Great thanks, I am having a brilliant time," I gabble away, "I am loving the music, and enjoying the girls' night out; it is Sue's hen night, we are off to the police bar now for a nightcap, you coming?" I am not sure why I said that, I certainly didn't want blondie to come with us.

He just smiles, reaches out for my hand, he lifts it to his lips and kisses the back of it. "Maybe see you later," He winks, then drops my hand.

He turns back to the short blonde, she is now smoking her cigarette and I wrinkle my nose as the smoke wafts over to me, I glance at him and he is watching me, he is frowning again.

Helen grabs my hand and pulls me through the door. "Laters!" she shouts with a cheerful wave.

I take a look back, Mike is watching us leave, my heart thuds in my chest, I don't want to leave, I want to be back there with his lips on my hand, I look back again, he is still watching, I would like to think he was watching me. I kick myself, why did I gabble on like a schoolgirl he must think I am some kind of lunatic, what would he be thinking, why does he care if my dress is new or not.

We move back on to the dance floor, there are a few of us dancing, I pull Helen towards me. "Who is the blonde girl?" I shout over the music, she looks over but shrugs and walks on.

"Might be his girlfriend – I dunno," she says non- committal. I want to know, but all I can do is follow her. I notice Phil being dragged on to join us, he doesn't put up any resistance and is now dancing with the hen, he is a bit drunk, but he is a good dancer and he knows it, he is being very rude, rubbing up against her and making suggestive moves, she is loving it, I cannot believe she is getting married soon, she now is dancing close up to him, we can clearly see his hands on her breasts. I watch as he pulls her close and their mouths meet, I look at Helen, she is staring at him, Phil is stood just a foot or so away snogging the hen, who is loving it and having a great time, her hands all over his body, then he stops, takes her hand and leads her off the dance floor, she puts up no resistance at all, I just watch, my mouth open in shock.

I look at Helen. "What is she playing at?" I ask her.

She shakes her head, "I have no idea what the both of them are playing at." We dance for a short while then she pulls my hand, as we make our way off the dance floor to the exit, we spot Phil in a dark corner, he has his hands all over Sue, caressing her body, his intensions are obvious, she isn't putting up any fight, they are in a world of their own, I am stunned, she is getting married in just a week, I look at Helen and shake my head, I cannot believe what I am seeing. As we walk out I spot the blonde girl getting into a taxi, alone, I don't know why I am suddenly so pleased, I cannot stop smiling. I look around hoping to spot Mike but there is no sign of him.

The police bar is quiet, there were only four of us girls there, the chap behind the bar is ready to go home but he brings over a bottle of wine and we sit down, he locks down the bar and disappears. Helen is intent on getting very drunk, immediately filling her glass and taking a large gulp. I have sobered up a bit, the walk in the fresh air has done me good, but my feet are throbbing, I am not used to killer heels. I pour a small glass of wine and sit back, we get chatting, we laugh about the fact we have lost the hen, the reason we were out in the first place, but no one is overly concerned, we know Phil will look after her. Then we talk, silly girlie nonsense chat about who we would like to be on a desert island with, we start with celebrities, mine is shouted down, but there is nothing wrong with Justin Lee Collins, he is comical and would make the time go quickly. Helen chooses Johnnie Depp which, in my opinion, is just too obvious. Then we have to choose from our shift, this is a bit more difficult, none of us will commit to an answer even though we were just having a laugh, drinking more than we should and it all gets a bit raucous.

One of the girls picks up her drink. "Craig Macdonald," she says, we all go quiet, she shrugs, "he is just so lovely, he is my desert island chap, I love his accent and his body, I love everything about him." She pauses and looks at me. "I hear him speaking to you all on his shift and he seems so caring and his accent well that does it for me." I nod my head in agreement she continues, "But he never notices me." I look at her and frown, I am not sure when she would actually get to see him, but I listen as she carries on talking. "I see him when he is on early shift, I fight with Marcia so I to get to take his post to him, but he never even acknowledges me, doesn't even know I exist."

I smile at her. "You are right, he is lovely," I add, I lean in and stroke her arm.

"But so, unfortunately is his wife and he is besotted with her," she half smiles, "always the way."

She looks at me. "So is it in bad taste to ask you then."

I smile but before I get to answer her friend butts in. "Did you see Mike tonight, wow did he look good, he looked like someone from a Mills and Boon, you know all dark hair, dark eyes, fit body, he is bloody gorgeous, I think I have changed my mind, I think I will add him to my list." Her friends shoots her a look.

"You said he was miserable and you said he was a pig when he had a go at you and called you incompetent for getting all his statements mixed up," the girls shrugs.

"Oh yes, I did didn't I, well he was, Oh well." She takes a swig of her drink and empties her glass, "I will have to go back to my first choice then, Nigel in the enquiry office, now he is gorgeous." She stands up. "Come on, our taxi will be coming soon."

They both stand up and after lots of hugs and promises that we must do this again the two other girls disappear off home and leaves just me and Helen, the bar is empty, it is just the two of us. I half sit and half lay on the comfortable chairs, my shoes off and my feet up on the adjacent chair. It isn't very ladylike but I don't care, I don't want anything else to drink, Helen turns to me with her seriously drunk face just inches from mine, she is so close I think she is going to kiss me, I am seriously worried.

As the wine fumes hit me she says, "You do know don't you," I have no idea what she is talking about, so I just smile, but she remains very close and almost in a whisper she says tearfully, "it's Phil, you know, my desert island choice, I cannot help it, but it is always Phil, always has been and always will be, but he doesn't even know I exist, he laughs and jokes with me and tells me all about his one-night stands, and he has no idea that he is the one," she sniffs loudly and goes on, "and I know he is shagging Jo and she is supposed to be happily married to Julian and Julian told me he hopes they are going to start a family soon, and he has no idea, what is going on. Then there is someone called Carole, apparently they all go out in a group somewhere and he shags her in the pub car park, when everyone has left them, he is terrible, he brags about it all the time, thinking I want to hear, but I don't, I really don't, I mean look at him tonight." She hiccups then continues, "Sue is getting married in just a week's time and tonight she was offering herself on a plate to him, he won't turn her down, I know what he is like, he cannot say no, so no prizes for guessing what they will be doing later. Both the women he is seeing are married and he thinks it is funny, he was shagging one of them when he was with Gemma, she found out, she went mental, she actually caught them together in his flat, you know, he told me all this, he wasn't even bothered, not ashamed at all, if anything he thought it was funny." She stops and takes a swig from her wine glass, hiccups, then she continues.

"And all I did was listen, do you know how hard it is, Angie, to listen as he tells me there is only one woman for him and she doesn't know he feels the way he does, and I have no idea who she is, so he uses the women to get her out of his system, and he tells me and it kills me that the man I want to be with treats women that way. Do you know how hard it is for me, Angie, do you?" She hiccups again, unaware that her voice is getting louder. Before I can stop her she lights a cigarette, I watch her, then as she takes the first puff I take it from her.

"No smoking in here, honey," I say gently, she nods and looks at me with her big eyes. I throw her cigarette in a discarded glass, I look at her she is so upset, her mascara has run, black pools of mascara tears on her cheeks, she cannot stop the tears, she sniffs and wipes her nose, she looks at me, the unchecked tears running down her cheeks. I pull her close to me, I cannot speak but all I can do is nod, I cannot believe what she was saying. Phil does not deserve to have Gemma or Helen liking him let alone loving him. He is a fool and will end up with no one.

"Please don't say anything," Helen begs me, she has recovered a bit now, she wipes her nose and eyes on the back of her hand, she looks at me. "I would be mortified if he found out."

I make my promise and then we discuss poor Julian, he is a lovely man, a bit boring and predictable, but still it is clear he loves Jo and it is terrible that she is treating him this way. Helen takes a swig of her wine, refills her glass then smiles.

"So come on," she coaxes, "who would your desert island man be?"

I smile at her. "Jason of course," I reply, she looks at me, her tear-stained face serious for a moment.

"Angie, I might be drunk, but don't take me for a fool, I am not stupid, even I know that you are lying, there is so much you don't tell me and I wish you would, Angie, I really wish you would." I look at her I give a big sigh as I think of Mike and how he looked tonight. "Well," she prompts me. I shake my head, I never answer the question as her phone bleeps signalling the arrival of the taxi.

Christ my head is pounding and my feet are crying, I couldn't help keep thinking all the way home what Helen had told me. I mean I had my suspicions about Carol, I thought it was just harmless flirting, and I also thought it was Sean she was after, certainly not Phil I am shocked, and a little bit saddened really if I am honest. I think everyone knows about him and Jo, although again, no definite proof, Helen is a darling and I cannot believe Phil acts in such a way, he is such an arse.

I fall into the front door at around two o'clock in the morning, my head is buzzing from too much wine and my feet are throbbing due to the heels. Jason is awake and so is Sean, they think my drunken state is hilarious. I go into the lounge and sit down on the edge of Jason's bed and at his insistence I put my feet up on the hospital bed and he asks if they hurt, I nod yes and he offers to massage them, he does do the most amazing foot massage so I am not about to decline, I spin round putting my legs up and straighten them out and push my toes towards his hands, my short dress has rode up to around my thighs but I don't care, the foot massage is heavenly, painfully pleasurable. I just lay my head back, close my eyes and enjoy it, I couldn't stop even it if I wanted to. When he moves on to the second foot I leave my eyes closed and just give out the occasional murmur of pleasure, I stay that way for some twenty minutes, and when I open my eyes I am aware that Sean is looking at my legs, I giggle and good-naturedly push his head away, but he doesn't stop looking. I cannot keep my eyes open, I need my bed ,when he offers to help me up the stairs I take him up on the offer, I am feeling a bit light-headed, not trusting my judgement on the stairs, I kiss Jason goodnight and take hold of Sean's arm.

As he helps me up the stairs he leads me into my bedroom, he holds me in a tight hug and whispers, "You are very special lady you know, this must be very tough on you."

I cannot answer, my throat is blocked and I clear my throat, he holds me closer, it feels nice to be held, we stand at my bedside his lips meet mine in a gentle non-brother-in-law kiss and he holds his body close to mine, I push myself closer to him, the closeness of another male feels so good, it has been so long, so very long. A long shudder runs through my body, my hand is up stroking the back of his head, I close my eyes, he gives a low moan, his tongue is gently stroking my lip, his hands are on my sides, gently stroking me, his hand goes higher it glides over my breast and I put my arm around his neck. His tongue is mixing with mine in a sweet caress, his hand is now stroking my breast, I show no resistance, his hands getting more urgent. He pushes his groin into me. I moan, I put my hand to his head holding him close to me, I can feel his hardness, I push back into him encouraging him. He undoes the buttons of my dress, his fingers tracing the outline of my bra, it feels so good, I don't want it to stop, his lips are hard against mine. His other hand is on my thigh moving upwards. I push myself closer against him, my dress is off my shoulders now, Sean unclips my bra and grabs my naked breasts, oh my god it feels so good, his hands massage my breasts, as his lips leave mine he moves lower. My hands reach for his zip, I pull it down slowly, my head is spinning, his lips kiss my neck, moving slowly, it feels so wonderful. I let out a moan of contentment, I push my hand into his zipper and feel his hardness, I squeeze gently making him groan, his hand moves lower pushing my dress up over my hips, I want this so much, I want to feel the closeness of a male. I open my eyes as Sean's lips meet my breast, I need him, I want so much more, this is all I need to make me feel better, to make me feel like a woman, a sensual woman. As Sean's lips caress my breasts I give out a low moan, my whole body is crying out for more, then all of a sudden the last drop of alcohol seems to leave my system and I am suddenly completely sober, the realisation of what is about to happen crashes into my mind, he is kissing and licking my breasts, it feels so good but I push him lightly away.

I love the closeness of a male, sometimes I crave it but this is Sean it is Jason's brother, Jason is downstairs dying and we are up here groping each other, I feel sick, quickly I gather my thoughts together, I stammer, "Oh my god, Sean, I am so sorry, I am so sorry, what am I doing, I am so sorry, it must be the drink."

I am stammering, my dress is around my waist, my bra somewhere on the floor, Sean looks shocked at what we have done, he pulls me close covering my nakedness.

"Oh my god, Angie, I am so sorry, what have I done." He moves away slightly as I cover myself. "Christ, it was my fault, I feel such a heel, I took advantage of you, I am so sorry."

I pull my dress up to cover my nakedness, hastily pushing the buttons through the wrong buttonholes, he looks away zipping his trousers up, I put my hand on Sean's face turning him to face me, I plant a kiss on his cheek.

"Let's forget this ever happened, okay, please, Sean." He smiles, it is just a small smile, I open the bedroom door, letting him know he needs to leave. "Thank you so much for looking after Jason for me, I really appreciate it."

At the mention of Jason's name Sean pulls himself together, he stands in the doorway, leans close, kisses my cheek and whispers quietly, "Goodnight, Angie, sleep tight." And he is gone.

I hear the murmur of voices downstairs and then the opening and closing of the front door as Sean leaves and as I lay back on the pillow, my thoughts drift between that of Jason, Mike, Phil and Sean. I am so confused, I am so very lonely, my body craves intimacy I have so many men around me but none that will hold me like I want to be held.

Bloody hell my head is pounding out of my ears now, it is not letting up Thank goodness I have the day off today. The consultant is coming to see Jason at ten, just enough time for me to shower and recover a bit. I prise my head from the pillow to look at the clock, it is eight thirty, I stand in the shower and let the water stream over my face and down my body. I cannot stop thinking about Phil and Carol and Jo and then about Mike and my tummy does a flip, what about the blonde girl, I am so glad they didn't go home together, I wonder if he wanted to but she declined, I wonder if he wanted to hold her, to make love to her, Oh please I hope not, What? Where did that thought come from? What if he did, it is nothing to do with me.

And then I think about Sean and the bedroom, his hands, his lips on my breasts, and the kiss, oh no the kiss, so wrong but felt so right, so wonderful to feel the closeness of a male, it seems I need someone to hold me close, I crave it now more than I ever did, his lips caressing mine, I must admit I was a little more than tipsy but he was sober. I shake my head, the image of his stricken face when he realised what we had done, I groan out loud, what was that all about? Why did I let that happen, how can I face him? Christ what a mess I have got myself into.

Jason is still asleep and I leave him and go into the kitchen, I clean up last night's curry, there is quite a lot left so maybe it was too adventurous for Jason, there are more than just several beer bottles so I guess Sean was a bit tipsy last night, that makes me feel a little bit better, at least he didn't try to seduce me sober. I start preparing toast and tea, I feel very shaky today, I really regret going out, my head hurts, my feet are still sore and every time I think about Sean I feel really guilty, poor Jason, what sort of a wife am I? He is laid downstairs and I was upstairs being seduced by his brother. I vow never to drink like that again, I lose my inhibitions too quickly when drink is involved, I need to be more in control. I need to give Jason my time, all of my time, I cannot be encouraging blokes when he is laying there so poorly, I have a full on mental argument with myself, I know I have behaved appallingly and I resolve to concentrate on Jason's needs in future and nobody else, he comes first from now on.

I fill the kettle I can hear him stirring but when I go in he says he doesn't want breakfast. He is in pain today, I can see in his face, I give him his medication and I hold his hand, he is looking very yellow and just wants to sleep. I stroke his face gently, he closes his eyes and I sit and watch him for a while, it was too much for him last night, the late night the beer and the curry have all taken its toll on him, his face is racked with pain and his body seems to be shaking.

The consultant calls on time and starts to check his blood pressure and temperature, he is very detached and efficient but he is really very thorough, but I wouldn't expect anything less from a private consultant. Sean arrives, lets himself in and as soon as I see him I know I don't have to worry about last night, he comes in, in his normal cheery manner he messes my hair up and leans down and kisses my head and takes the consultants hand in a handshake. Jason is still asleep; the consultant beckons us into the kitchen. He explains that the medication will be increased as from today, we will notice the skin will get more yellow and they will do all they can for the pain, but there is little else they can do for Jason now, it is a waiting game and just a matter of time. Thinking about the curry and beer last night I ask about any limitations Jason has regarding diet but the consultant says there are none, he can eat what he wants but he probably won't have any appetite, slowly the liver will give up and the medication will manage pain, he may not feel like eating or drinking but will continue to receive fluids and pain management through the drip, if he wants to eat or drink we should let him have what he wants, I feel my heart stop as he continues.

"It doesn't really matter now," he says it so matter of fact whilst he is writing his notes, he is so devoid of emotion. We all return into the lounge. Jason is blissfully unaware, he sleeps soundly now, his body has the medication it needs to allow him to sleep pain free. There is no sound from him, just the quiet murmur of the machines in the background.

I am so torn, torn between wanting to do the right thing which is to be by Jason's side in what might be his last weeks or to do what he has asked, and that is to carry on as normal. When I first agreed with his wishes I thought it would be okay, but it is not okay; it is very hard, hard to watch a dear friend losing his battle to live right in front of my eyes. It is okay for everyone else, they get to go home, but every day I have to face him, watch him as I fight to hold back my tears when he is trying to turn over in the bed and it all looks such an effort, then he looks at me and smiles, as if it is all going to be okay and I bite my lip to stop the tears. A nurse has now arrived and is talking them all through Jason's chart, making notes for the carer that is with her to be aware of the new medication. She is very efficient and clipped; she ignores us just sat in the lounge watching them both, so clinical and professional.

The consultant wakes Jason up to continue his checks, the older carer arrives even though she is not scheduled to be there today, she wants to see what the consultant has said, they speak for a while in the kitchen. I watch as she asks him questions and he stands and shakes his head whilst he completes his notes, he shakes our hands and they both leave together, I watch them continue chatting in the street. Jason and I talk a while, I ask how he is feeling and he says he is in no pain, but he is tired, so very tired. My eyes fill with tears as he tells us he is not scared, and then we sit by him and hold his hand until he drifts back off to sleep. Sean says he will stay for lunch and when Jason wakes up we sit with him watching the rugby and eating sandwiches and cake.

There is no sense of embarrassment between Sean and I, I don't need to mention what happened, there doesn't need to be any explanations or apologies, it was a silly moment, I was tipsy and needy and he was there, it was over in just a few minutes and no one else needs to know.

Jason says he wants to sit with us on the couch so with a bit of a struggle and lots of laughing as none of us realise Jason has his pyjama cord undone. As his trousers hit the floor Sean is the one with an eyeful and as he has the drip in his hand and supporting Jason with the other hand as he gets off the bed he has to remain in that position until I can get round to the other side of the bed to restore decency; it is hilarious and it is good to hear Jason laugh. Finally we manage to move Jason and his drip from the bed to the couch, he is much more comfortable, he is in a good mood, he is really pleased when his team wins, both he and Sean rib each other good-naturedly. He has a light beer and after the rugby we sit together and watch the afternoon movie. To any onlooker, seeing Jason in his pyjamas, it would look so normal, he doesn't look that poorly from a distance, but his eyes are sunken, his skin is mostly yellow all over now and he looks exhausted.

After the movie we move him back to bed and he lays there and takes my hand and in barely a whisper he says, "I love you so much, thank you."

I want to cry, so many times I have longed for him to say those precious words to me, and now he is, it is all too late, so very late. I stroke his cheek I tell him to rest but he says he needs to tell me something he wants Sean to hear too. We both move close to him, Sean and I both stand close to the bed, we lean closer to hear him.

He is struggling to catch his breath and he almost whispers, "I will look after you both, it is all sorted out, don't worry, I have sorted everything, you have been the best brother and wife a man can ever wish for and I love you both, I am sorry for all this trouble, promise me you will look after her, Sean, won't you, look after her until she meets someone who can love her like she always wanted, like I never did." He smiles and without waiting for a reply he closes his eyes, he falls asleep almost immediately.

Fear grips my heart, I look at Sean, but he smiles. "It is okay, he has just worn himself out, he is sleeping."

I look at Jason, his breathing gentle and relaxed. I give a big sigh of relief, Sean is leaning with his arm over my shoulder, we both hold his hands as he lies still, the murmur of the machines is again the only sound. Sean takes my other hand in his and we just stand there quietly for several minutes. I cannot hold back the tears. I let them run unchecked down my face, I look at Sean, his eyes are glazed over, it seems he is struggling too.

Chapter Seventeen

Late shift today, I am looking forward to working and getting my head down and concentrating on something else. Jason has been in a good mood, we have a lovely late breakfast and he asks me for a notepad and pen, he wants to write a list of everything he wants done today, he has achieved so much lately, the house is almost transformed back to being a normal house, I am so proud of him.

His favourite the lovely older carer called Martha has turned up and has promised to help him again. She has recently been doing some organising of Jason's paperwork for him, the boxes in the lounge have disappeared to those people who needs them and the ones upstairs have now been brought down and are now spread out over the lounge in logical piles and some of them are beginning to diminish. There are a whole pile of letters she has taken away and has typed out for him, I will post them on my way to work, I have no idea what they are but I am happy that he is happy. I can tell he is really pleased, she is not supposed to be doing all of this but she says it keeps her busy and keeps him happy. There is a huge pile of shredding which I can take to work and all his files are neatly marked up as he wants them to be, some of the boxes are already packed up, so many have already disappeared, he really is on a mission, he is returning anything he has borrowed from people and he seems to have so much energy. Martha has arranged a courier to collect everything later this afternoon and I feel a bit ignored as they discuss the paperwork and the packages and where they have to go and to whom they must be addressed to. Some of them he wants sent to London for some reason. He is very demanding, issuing her orders and she just does it, she doesn't argue, she is a saint, I leave her to it, they obviously do not need me, she clearly understands him and she is clever in that she lets him work for a short time then he sleeps.

She is doing the double shift today so she will be there when I get home. She is really a wonder – so tolerant and organised, she is more like a friend to him, she never gets annoyed when he is in a mood, she doesn't pander to him, she is witty and professional, she is an excellent nurse and even when she has to give him a bed bath she makes him laugh. I know he likes her very much, he makes no secret of the fact that she is his favourite. I make a note to buy her something nice to say thank you.

As I leave Sean arrives, we meet at the front door. "Hi" I greet him, "everything okay?" he shrugs.

"Not sure, really. Jason has asked me to pop in." I smile.

"Well, he is in good form today, very organised and keeping Martha very busy with his paperwork." I walk down the path and call back to him. "Give me a call if there is a problem, won't you," Sean waves and smiles at me.

I don't know why, but I am not in the best of moods today, I have had a nice few days off, Jason is in good form, he called me back to give me a kiss and a cuddle before I left then he called me back again, he pulled me close to him and kissed me gently on the lips. Martha left us alone and I just relaxed into his arms, why couldn't he be like this when we were married or before that I think to myself, as I moved away Jason looked me straight in the face.

"You are a very beautiful woman, Angie, I should have told you that more, and I am sad that I didn't."

My eyes fill with tears as he pulls me close to him, I know he loves me, in his own little way, and I know I love him too, I get up and stand in front of him.

"Don't do too much today, Jason, okay." I smile at him. "Promise me you won't."

He smiles back, a tired smile. "Okay, I promise."

I walk to the door he calls my name and I look back to see him smiling, he says nothing more just smiles at me as I leave. I should be happy but I cannot shake off this mood, I feel so very low, like I want to cry, even my favourite tracks on the system in the car cannot make me smile today, I feel quite down. A sad song comes on the radio and I want to cry, to really sob my heart out, I just don't know why, it cannot be PMT as it is not the right time. I grab myself a bar of chocolate from the vending machine and make my way up the stairs to the control room munching it. I spend an hour or so in the control room and everyone is chatty as normal, it is steady but not overly busy then Craig comes over. As I am finishing my call I can hear he is telling the rest of the shift I have to go down to CID office today, just for an hour or so to catch up with statements. Max is out today but Craig explains they will have to cope as it is not that busy, I am more than happy to do this. He waits a bit longer but the call is going on longer and longer, so he goes and sits back down.

When the call finishes I call over to Craig, "Can I take my break first then go down as I am starving."

He nods his head I gather my handbag and bits together, my mood has lifted a bit, not as happy as I normally feel but a little bit better, I give a cheery wave to the rest of the shift who call out rude comments about me skiving. I laugh and go down the stairs to the rest room, there are a few officers in there, I find a seat in the corner and join in the chatting. Within a few minutes Mike comes in and sits in the seat opposite me, I watch as he gets his lunch out, he is just biting into his sandwich when Helen bursts in, she spots me and steps over the legs of the officers until she reaches Mike.

"Can I sit there?" she asks him, he looks up.

"Why" he asks, she doesn't hesitate in replying.

"Because I want to talk to Angie about our night out and I don't want to have to shout."

Mike sighs and gets up, he moves to the spare chair just two down. Before he sits down he motions to her "this one okay" she smiles at him but he raises his eyes up she looks at me.

"Can you believe someone described him as a Mills and Boon hero?" she asks me.

He looks over. "A what?" His face creases into a frown.

Helen chats on. "You know, we were doing our who would you like to be alone with on a desert island and someone chose you, said you looked dark and mysterious," she laughs, "don't worry," she adds, "it wasn't me." She turns away from him and leans forward to me, "Did you hear about Sue?" I shake my head. "Apparently, so the girls were saying, she didn't get in till three in the morning and she cannot remember anything about it." She leans closer before continuing, "she is really embarrassed – it is hilarious."

I take a sip of my drink and look over to Mike, I can tell he is listening. "Did you have a bad hangover?" I ask her, she shakes her head.

"No not really." She turns to Mike. "Who was that blonde you were with then, Mike?" He shakes his head.

"As if I would be that stupid to be telling you anything, Helen I will not have you adding my name to your gossip," he laughs, "so who thought I was Mills and Boon material then?" he asks, but Helen is too quick for him.

"Spill the beans on blondie and I might tell you," she quips back at him, he laughs and picks up the newspaper shaking his head. Helen leans forward to me whispering, "I think Sue and Phil went home together, what do you think?"

I shrug. "Wouldn't put it past him, but I don't know enough about her really."

I watch as the three officers finish their lunch and get up, they exchange a few words with Mike and leave, there is just the three of us in the rest room. Helen leans back in her chair.

"How is Jason?" she asks, I nod my head.

"He is okay, good days and bad days, he had a nice night with Sean when I went out, and he has been very upbeat today, but then he has his favourite carer in and he is always different when she is there."

Helen looks at her watch then stands up. "I am glad to hear that, Angie, really pleased. I gotta go, slave driver here will be on my case if I stay any longer." Mike doesn't acknowledge her comments and she walks to the door. "If you need to talk give me a call yes?" I nod my head.

"Thanks, Helen."

She stops and speaks to Mike. "I am going to check on that woman in custody okay, can you sign off the arrest papers later for me?" His mouth is full of food so he just nods his head and she leaves.

I check my watch, I have a few minutes left, I pack up my lunchbox, check my phone, I have a text message from Judy: "so are you a Mills and Boon reader". Mike interrupts me reading a text, I shake my head, I stand up, he moves his feet as I pass.

"Shame that," he adds.

I smile at him and I am rewarded with his lovely twinkly eyes looking back at me. My stomach does a somersault, I pop into the ladies, I spend a few minutes replying to Judy's text then I head downstairs to the ground floor where CID are located. I put my phone in my bag hovering just outside the door, it is half open and I can hear Clive, one of the officers talking, he is asking Nick who is typing up the statements today, I am not sure why, but I stop, just stand there listening. I can see them both stood near the desk that I am going to use, they cannot see me. Mike is back downstairs, he is stood with his back to me talking to another officer, he is sorting papers out by the printer which is next to the desk I sit at.

Nick replies, "Angie."

Clive asks questioningly, "Which one is that, have I met her?"

Nick responds, "You know, Angie, pretty girl, quite short, really great typist." I smile at this, then the smile dies on my face as he adds, "And the bonus is she has a great stack, you know, great tits." He puts his hands in front of his chest as if making a pair of breasts, he laughs. "For obvious reason she is one of my favourites and if we are lucky she won't be wearing her jumper," he continues, I am frozen.

I am so angry, so immediately angry, how dare he refer to me like that, I have always liked Nick, I thought we got on well, both socially and professionally, if he had said it to my face I could have come up with an equally demeaning comment, I thought we had a mutual respect, yet here he is belittling me, as if my chest is relevant to my skills, I don't know what to do. I want to stamp in there and punch his stupid face, I want to demand an apology, to tell him what I think of him, but I know I would just burst into tears, none of my words would come out as I wanted them too and I would just make a fool of myself, so I don't, I walk quietly and go to the nearby ladies bathroom. I lay my forehead on the cold mirror trying to calm myself, I am not sure why I have got myself so angry, I hear comments all the time, why is today so different, why am I feeling so emotional? Maybe because I am normally present and therefore able to give as good as I get. I didn't notice Mike's reaction, I wondered whether he joined in and laughed, or would he defend me, but why should he defend Nick's comments, he might think the same, oh no, what if he did? I would hate it if he laughed at my expense; I really hope it is not what he thinks of me too?

I have to go back in there, I know I do, so I check my face to make sure it isn't all red, I always go red when I am angry – two red spots on the top of my cheeks, but a splash of water removes them, I look in the mirror, a determined look on my face, well he is out of luck today, I have got my jumper on, and will wear it all the time now I know. I push open the office door and head for my desk, Mike is now sat at the far desk, his head is down, he is writing, everyone is working as normal. Clive is in the cupboard on his knees sorting through property and Nick is on the phone, he winks and smiles at me as I approach, I don't respond, I just glare at him, not that he would notice I think to myself, he is so bloody full of himself.

I sit down, put my headset on and begin typing, when I sense someone is next to me I assume it is Nick so I don't look up. I haven't completely calmed down yet and he might say the wrong thing which will start me off, I am in such a bad mood today, I cannot shake it off, someone taps my shoulder and I look up to see Mike is waggling an empty mug in my direction he gives a thumbs up signal and I smile weakly and nod yes, as he walks away I call out "thanks" he turns and smiles, he is so sweet, no not sweet but cute. I watch him as he walks away, he has such a great body, broad shoulders and thick strong thighs, no trace of fat on him at all, my mind drifts off as I watch him, I wonder what he kisses like, what it would feel like to stroke his face, to feel his body against mine, I lose myself in a dream where my life is so different, when I look back at my desk Nick is looking at me questioningly. I shoot him what I hope is a very harsh look and get back to my typing.

I work quietly for the next hour or so, there are not that many to type up and I work through them quickly. Nick answers the office phone as I am just completing the last statement, just ten more minutes and I will be finished, I look up as Phil walks in and heads to the end of the office, Nick calls him over, they go back into the corridor and I can see they are joined by someone else, I ignore them and continue typing. I look around quickly to see Craig and Phil come in, they are stood next to my desk, there is no one else in the office, Nick and Mike have both disappeared. The cupboard where Clive was working has been left open, there is a pile of property left on the floor, he will be cross about that I think to myself. Well serve him right for laughing at my expense.

Phil takes my headset from my head and says gently, "Come on, we have to go."

I start to object, "just five minutes and I will be done," I protest, but Craig has my coat and bag in his hand, I don't argue, I don't say a word as he hands them to me and I am led out to my car. As if on autopilot I get in the passenger seat and fasten my seatbelt. Phil gets in and drives, I don't say a word, not one question, I have no idea where I am going or what is going on, I move in autopilot, all I can think of is that I should have finished the last statement, I hate leaving things undone, did I finish my tea, I wonder, and the cupboard is open, that should have been locked. The drive home is silent, there might have been music on the stereo, I cannot remember much about it, I don't ask any questions, I look at Phil but he is staring ahead, I gaze straight ahead, there is not much traffic on the road and it is a very short journey to my home and when we arrive my lounge seems to be full of people.

Martha is there at the side of the bed, Sean, Little Ma, and Pa, Sean takes my hand and leads me over to Jason, he is grey and his breathing is laboured, his skin looks yellow, there seems to be a film of sweat over his face, his eyes are closed, my voice is a whisper, "How long?" I ask no one in particular, Martha strokes my hand.

"Not long now, honey, not long at all, he took a turn for the worse a while ago he asked me to call you." Her voice is choked too, I can see she is trying to keep her composure. Little Ma is sobbing gently into her tissue, Pa is stood unmoving, he is biting on his finger, trying to keep his emotions in check, I watch him as he stands there just staring out of the window.

I am not sure why, but it just seems right, I go to the stereo and put on Jason's favourite music, I turn the volume up to a level that I know he can hear. I leave everyone in the room and go upstairs and reach into the wardrobe and pull out the dress Jason bought for me to wear to our wedding, I don't have an idea why I kept it, the dress I hated so much suddenly it doesn't seem so drab. I know what I want to do, I lay it on the bed and slowly get undressed, I pull my uniform jumper and shirt over my head in one go, and slowly remove my trousers, I stand in just my underwear, as I reach out for the dress I see Phil is in the bedroom with me, he smiles but says nothing. I am still moving on autopilot, I don't care that I am stood half naked, he walks to me, he pulls the dress over my head and turns me round and zips the dress up, it is now so big it practically hangs off me, but I don't care, I turn to face Phil, he holds me close for a while, it feels good to be held, then we walk downstairs. I sit by Jason's side, I stroke his face and he opens his eyes, I know he notices the dress; I am almost positive he does, for he gives a little smile, his finger reaches out and strokes the neckline, and I lean over and kiss him.

My lovely Jason, despite all his pain he smiles at me, and I smile back at him, my dear friend. I don't look at anyone else. I don't know what the protocol is for this situation, and no one objects when I move all the tubes and wires to one side and I lie at the side of him, I lay on my side and pull him close to me, we lay facing each other. I can feel his ragged breath on my face, I close my eyes and hug him gently. I am not sure how long we laid just listening to his music, I am totally unaware of anyone else in the room. Jason's favourite track is now playing on the stereo, I stroke his face, I close my eyes holding him close, I feel his body slump.

After a minute or so, Martha reaches over and strokes my face gently, I open my eyes and she whispers, "He has gone now, honey." I nod to her, but I cannot move, I have gone numb. I reach my hand out to Phil and he takes me in his arms, pulls me up from the bed then leads me into the kitchen, he holds me in his arms, he is stroking my hair. I don't know how I feel, I am numb, I want to cry, but the tears won't come, the music is still playing but it seems too loud now. Sean stands in the doorway, I can see he is trying to hold it together, he runs his hands through his hair, just like Jason does.

"If it's okay with you I will deal with everything from now on?" he chokes the words out. I am not sure what that means so I just nod yes, I glance up at Phil he is trying and failing to hold back the tears, he holds his eyes tight shut for a moment then turns to look out of the window. Sean brings little Ma and Pa into the dining room and sits them down, he pours them both a brandy and hands them the glasses, I watch as their frail hands grasp the fragile glass, I notice Pa's hands are shaking and I look at him the tears slide gently down his cheek. Sean points to the bottle and gives me a thumbs up, I cannot find my voice so I nod yes, and he pours me a glass he fills three glasses, takes one himself and hands the other one to Phil and I. I move away from Phil and he brings it over to me, holds me close for a few seconds. Everything is happening in slow motion, no one seems to be speaking, Sean disappears into the lounge and I hear the music get turned down and I hear him on the phone, I just stand there, I cannot move, I feel so numb, so incredibly numb, I can feel Phil's arm supporting my waist, I just stand there sipping my brandy and welcoming the strong burning in the back of my throat. I remain in the kitchen, Phil moves into the lounge, I hear him on the phone but I don't know who he is speaking to, there is no one I want to talk to, I sit at the dining table with little ma, we hold hands, it seems like forever. Then I hear the doorbell and the front door opens and I hear the sound of voices, but I don't move, Little Ma and me sit in the dining room holding hands until we hear the movement of people in the lounge, I know there are people at the front door, I look up as Sean comes towards us both and pulls ma away from me.

"Come on, Ma, you know what you have to do," he speaks gently, she stands up nodding her head gently, I sit for just a minute or so before Phil comes in and takes my arm and directs me through the lounge.

There are two strangers dressed completely in black stood over Jason, they do not acknowledge me, as I move to go closer Phil pulls me away, he places his finger to his lips to tell me to be silent, then he leads me upstairs, he lays me on the bed fully dressed and pulls the duvet over me.

"It all has to be done their way now, Angie, you know that don't you." I nod my head, my throat feels tight, I reach out and hold his hand tight.

"Stay with me please," I ask, "don't leave me." He nods his head, he sits at the side of me and cradles my head in his arms, I lay there feeling the warmth from him, feeling the scratchy wool of his police jumper, I lay just listening to the subdued voices coming from downstairs, I hear the front door open and close several times and I know they are taking Jason away. I turn my face into the pillow and sob, I feel Phil pulling me closer to him, I need to feel his solid arms holding me tight, I fall to sleep nestled in his arms holding his hand.

Chapter Eighteen

Jewish funerals are very different from normal Christian funerals, and I don't understand much of what is going on, I let Jason's family take over and he is given a very traditional Jewish funeral. Sean tries to explain it to me but I hardly take in a word of what he is saying, it all happens very quickly and with great calmness and dignity, Sean has made all the calls to the Jewish church leaders and Little Ma washes Jason and chooses what he needs to wear. This is a very private thing, I am not to be involved, apparently Sean explains it is not to exclude me, it is just not viewed as my duty to do this, I totally understand, even though it is all happening in my home, Sean makes more calls and lets me know the service is arranged for tomorrow. I spend most of the time either in the kitchen or upstairs, I do not see them take Jason's body away.

So soon, too soon, Phil calls my family and lets me know my parents are arriving on the very early morning flight and the funeral is booked for the following late morning. My brother Scott is coming on the first train from London and Judy has decided the children should not attend so she is meeting Scott and they are going to go together with my parents, they are all staying at Judy's, I am not sure why I didn't offer them to stay with me, I just don't think, I cannot think of anything. I have this vacant look about me whenever anyone asks me anything, so all questions go to Phil and Sean in the end. I do everything on autopilot. Mum and Dad have an apartment in the town which they kept when they moved but they prefer to be with Judy. Flowers and cards have been arriving for me at the house all morning, Jewish funerals do not have flowers but these are personal flowers for me so I put them in vases around the house, it makes me feel better when I look at them.

On the morning of the service Little Ma comes to my house she brings me a crochet black arm band, she has made it herself and the detail is beautiful, it is very light crochet with very intricate stitching, she has one on her arm and asks me to wear it. I am not sure how long for and she tells me I will know when I can take it off, I don't understand, she holds my face in her hands.

"Okay, little one, I will tell you when to take it off but you wear it for me please, for Jason, wear it every day as a sign of remembrance." I kiss her lovely soft face, I will wear it every day until I die if she wants me to. I am not sure if this is a Jewish tradition or one that she has dreamt up herself but I don't want to upset her. I am just letting everything happen as the family want it to,

Little Ma is not happy about the flowers in the house, she walks around tutting to herself, but I explain to her gently that these flowers were sent to me for me, and that no mourners are coming to my house as everything is happening at her home, so no one will see them. She chants a bit in her own little language but I know I have won, after all these are personal. Not sure what her expectations were but they are for me from my friends, from the shift and from my parents, they mean no offence it is what we do in my religion. As I need to be getting ready I point to the time and hurry her out of the house reminding her that people will be waiting for her. Some of the mourners have travelled a long way and the gathering after the funeral will be at Little Ma's house, it should have been at our home but I am grateful to them as they have a large garden and can accommodate everyone. The day is bright and sunny, I am glad, I couldn't bear it to be raining and cold.

I shower and dress carefully, I keep my make-up simple and wear sensible shoes for the churchyard. No cremation for Jason, he has to be buried strictly according to the Jewish faith. I take my heels to change into after the service. Phil comes to collect me, and when we arrive I am touched that a lot of his work colleagues have turned up but there are quite a lot of people I don't know, but Sean seems to know all his work colleagues, and everyone else; I am gratified that Craig and my immediate shift are here too. Steve, Gavin, Rob and Max are stood in their suits looking very sombre, Craig immediately comes over with his wife and pulls me into a hug.

"Be strong," he whispers as he moves away, his wife just squeezes my hand and smiles. I feel comforted that people I know are there, even if I don't get to speak to them before the service which thankfully is quite short. I cannot help but shiver as it is so cold in the chapel.

After the burial and the service we return to Little Ma's house, I manage to catch up with them all then, we all stand around with nothing much to say. We all stand and watch as the Rabbi moves amongst everyone. Sean looks exhausted, he has been the one that has stayed with Jason's body since he died. Observing the Jewish tradition, I found this to be the most difficult to accept and told him so at the time, but Sean had just smiled at me and said he would be honoured to do it for his brother and it was exactly what Jason wanted. I took a while to comprehend how Jason was so set on how he wanted to have his funeral but didn't really follow the Jewish faith when he was alive. Sean shocked me even further by telling me that both he and Jason went regularly to the synagogue, and the Rabbi called to the house several times when Jason was poorly, I just never knew that, how can I not have known something that was obviously so meaningful to my husband, but I say nothing to Sean or his parents, it just confirms what I knew already, our marriage was all built on secrets and lies, it was a sham really, to think I was excluded from something that I think was so important to Jason, he didn't think enough of me to share this part of his life.

At the call of my name I look up, Judy is indicating that people are waiting to show their respect to me, people I don't know, people who I have never met. There seems to be a long procession of people that arrive and greet Sean and his parents and then nod respectfully at me – some kiss me, and others just hug me, some just touch my shoulder as they walk on, I stand back and let it all happen. Over the next few hours so many people arrive, bringing food and drink and most of them I don't know and I am sure Sean doesn't either. Gemma arrives she is looking pale and lost, she stays long enough to hug me and gives me a small book of poems, she offers condolences to Sean and then leaves, she is not here longer than a few minutes. I am appreciative she has took the time to come, I like Gemma very much, I note that she keeps away from Phil and although I see him looking in her direction, she leaves quickly before he gets a chance to come over to her. Helen is looking lost and so I send Phil over to speak to her. Everyone is very quiet, too quiet, speaking in respectfully hushed voices. Helen and Phil move away from the main throng of people and towards the end of the garden, I watch their departing backs and as I look back towards the house I am moved that Martha and a few other carers have taken the time to come today and I can see her bright smile as she approaches me with her arms out as she pulls me into a big hug and guides me away from everyone as I feel the tears start to flow.

She looks around to ensure no one is listening before speaking quietly, "That was so generous of Jason to think of me, I don't know what to say." She pulls me close and hugs me. "You know, he and I talked about so much over the last few weeks and I cannot believe what he has done."

I have no idea what she is talking about, but it doesn't seem right to tell her, so I just smile, I am at a loss for what I need to do, she makes me feel better by telling me that I am doing what is expected of me, just be there to shake hands with people, the rest is all taken care of, Jason had explained everything to her and the mourning period is not relevant to me as I am not a Jew so no one expects me to do anything but to just be there and accept their condolences.

I look around, there are discreet waiters with small items of round food on platters and non-alcoholic drinks milling around between the visitors. I have no idea who organised everything, this is a traditional Jewish funeral, I didn't understand a word of it and neither did Phil really. I think Sean went to the Rabbi when he knew Jason was not going to make it, so he could try and understand what was expected of him, but I know nothing really, the service at the grave was all following the Jewish way and I was just told where I needed to be and what I needed to do with Sean at my elbow most of the time. Everyone related to Jason and Sean was at the service and a lot of people I didn't even know, everything seemed to be going like clockwork and I just let it all happen.

I have to respect the Jewish way and although we were not a typical Jewish couple, this was for his family and for Jason, I was never a typical Jewish wife and Jason was not a devout Jew but he wanted his funeral to be that of a Jewish faith and I was never going to offer any resistance, everything has been done for me, I have not had to think of anything, my outfit was chosen by my sister and she has stood by my side the entire time. When people have approached me she has gone to stand with my parents but immediately coming back when I needed her. Little Ma and Pa have endless energy, continually greeting people and hugging everyone. Those of us who are not Jewish have kind of stood on the side line and watched as the Rabbi and other religious elders went amongst everyone chatting quietly and embracing people. It was gentle and dignified affair and I felt that we had given Jason his last wish. Everyone there may not have understood the Jewish religion but they certainly respected it. My remembrance armband raised a few eyebrows amongst my family but I have decided that obviously it is important for Jason's family for me to wear it and so I will explain its presence quietly to people when they ask and when I am told I can take it off I will do.

It was late evening before people started leaving, Sean comes over, he sits by me. "It is okay, it is now appropriate that you leave if you want to." But I don't know if I do, I don't know if I want to be on my own, Sean continues, "Most of the mourners have left and you must be exhausted." I nod, I am so very tired, I feel drained, but I sit for a while longer listening to the chatter going on around me, we sit in the lounge together until nearly everyone has gone, I look at the clock, it is nearly midnight, I look at Sean, we both look drained and tired.

Sean takes me upstairs to the spare room, I cannot face going home and they all understand that without me saying anything, he sits with me on the bed, he takes my hand. "Are you going to be okay?" he asked.

I shake my head, I cannot speak, my throat is raw and I am so exhausted, so I just shake my head again. I don't know if I am going to be okay, I hope I am, I have lived a lie for such a long time, no one really knew how I was feeling before, no one really ever found out the truth, not really. I don't know how I am feeling, kind of numb, kind of lost really, I have no idea how I will cope now, what do I do, who am I now, everything has changed.

He pulls me close to him. "Shall I ask Phil to come home with you?" he asks, but I shake my head. I don't want to go home, not on my own, or with Phil.

I lay back on the bed, but I know that I don't want to stay here either, I don't belong here, I don't know where I belong but I know I want to be with someone. Sean goes downstairs, I can hear him speaking in the lounge, I know he is wondering what to do with me. I sit up and text Judy, she calls me back immediately, she will arrange for Phil to pick me up and take me to her house. I feel relieved I go downstairs to let Sean know my plans. I think he is relieved that I have somewhere to go, someone to be with. As I get into Phil's car Sean pulls me close and whispers for me to take care and stay in touch.

Chapter Nineteen

I am a bit lost now, my life for the last few months has been work and home and spending time with Jason, my house has been filled with carers and nurses and I haven't done much else, I am not sure what I am going to do. I have bereavement leave from work but everything has been done for me and so I don't know how I will fill the next two weeks.

After staying the initial night at Judy's she invites me to stay a few more days, and I accept, I think a few days there will be just what I need, so I don't bother going home. She pops to my house and picks up a few things I will need, the rest I can get at her house. Her children are a wonderful distraction, they keep me busy and I relish their company, but I feel like such a fraud. Sean calls to ask if I want him with me when I eventually go home but I decline, I think I need to be on my own for a while.

It feels really strange when I let myself in the front door when I return to the house after staying at Judy's, it seems like I have been away forever but it has just been a few days after the funeral. The first thing I notice is that the hospital bed and all the medical paraphernalia that was keeping Jason comfortable has been removed – I am sure I have Sean and Phil to thank for that, I am not sure I would have been very good at dealing with all of that, or have it greet me as I walked in the lounge; the only evidence it was there is the indentations in the carpet.

I wander round the house just looking at the small items of Jason's that are left. I look in the wardrobe and I am relieved that his clothes are still hanging there, he loved his clothes, cared for them so much. I pick out his denim shirt and pull it on over my clothes, it feels comforting, I pull his favourite rugby shirt from the hanger and press it against my face, I breathe in deeply, I am sure I can smell the mustiness of his aftershave. I lay the rugby shirt on the bed, and look around, there are two of his aftershaves on the side, I look at his neatly laid out shoes, so beautifully polished. I close the wardrobe and look around, there are just the two aftershave bottles giving any indication that a male has occupied the room, it seems like a dream that he was ever here. I feel guilty that I used to moan and go on about his muddles around the house, and that I made such a fuss about papers everywhere, but now every surface is clean and tidy, all the boxes have gone, every one of them, there is emptiness about the place.

I walk into the spare room, all the boxes have disappeared there too, it is all so neat and tidy, something I craved for so long and now it seems just empty. I go back downstairs, some of the flowers have been removed and a huge bunch of flowers have thoughtfully been left in a vase on the table, definitely not from Jason, this definitely has Phil or Sean's name on it – flowers that Jason and I used to argue over, the constant barbs from him about his sinuses and the wasted expense of fresh flowers. I push my face into the middle of the bouquet and draw in a big breath taking in the scent of the roses mixed with carnations and my eyes fill with tears. On the table is a single house key, and I know it is Sean's. Suddenly I cannot stop the tears flowing down my cheeks I am not sure why I am crying or who I am crying for, was it for the person I have lost, a friend, not a lover or a husband but a friend, was I crying for the marriage that has gone? Only I know the real truth about the marriage, was it tears of relief? I don't know, I feel so shallow and empty for playing the part of the grieving widow and accepting the condolences when I know the marriage was so empty – a big charade just so that Jason got his wish, to show the people in his life that he was a happy married man with a successful career when he died. A lie because the truth would be too painful for him to deal with, so now I have to play the part of the widow, a young widow, to see the looks of pity on people faces for the woman whose husband was cruelly taken from her, and they will never know that the young woman was tricked into marriage by her own stupidity and ended up living a lie. I know now why I am crying, I am crying for me.

I sit for a long while, my chest hurts, my throat feels sore, I fall into an exhausted sleep on the sofa. When I wake up I sit there for what seems like hours not moving, but I know I have to get up, to do something, so I shower and change, I choose a pair of baggy tracksuit bottoms and a plain cotton T-shirt , I pull the denim shirt over the top then I sit and watch TV. I feel clean and relaxed, the tiredness has gone and I suddenly feel better, I feel back to being me – no one fussing about in the kitchen making meals or measuring doses of medicine, the carers won't come in any more, there is just me, alone, there is no one looking at me with pity, the black dress has been hung up, but the armband is still in place.

I am hungry but not sure what I want to eat, I fix myself a glass of wine, it hits my empty stomach, there is no set procedure for what a widow should do on her first real night alone. There is seven days of mourning in the Jewish tradition, but I didn't want to stay at Jason's mum's house, it was like I was on show, everybody fussing and I just didn't belong there. Everyone keeps asking me if I am alright, did I want anything – I felt smothered, but now I feel lost. However long I had spent at Judy's I knew I had to come home at some point, I didn't expect to be alone so soon, I thought I would be okay, but as soon as the people that were at the service left, I felt a bit lost. It was good for me to stay at Judy's for a while but I have insisted on coming home on my own, so now I sit and look at TV not really noticing what is playing. There are some cards and letters which I really must open, but I haven't got the energy, not today.

The doorbell rings, but I don't get up, I just sit there, I don't care who it is, I don't want to see anyone, I remain with my legs tucked under me and the nature programme on television still playing but going unseen.

I am brought back from my daydream by a knocking at the window, Phil is at the door, I don't move, eventually he lets himself in, he has bought Chinese food, he is so thoughtful. I didn't realise how hungry I was, it smells delicious, my stomach groans, he just looks at me, smiles weakly then he goes into the kitchen and I follow and watch him as he serves out the food onto plates and finds everything he needs in the cupboards. I don't help, I just watch, then we sit with it on trays on our laps, we talk about everything and nothing: the funeral, the guests, the house, work and the future. I am starving, I clear my whole plate as we talk way into the early hours.

At one point I do get very emotional as Phil mentioned the wedding, I don't think I am ready to talk about that yet and I tell him so. Phil pulls me into his arms, he kisses my forehead and pulls me really close to him, it feels wonderful to be held, we lay on the sofa in quiet companionship, I lay my head on his chest and watch the rise and fall of his breathing, we fall asleep and wake up in the morning to find the television playing to itself and the sun streaming through the window. I sit up and look at him, he opens his eyes.

"Thank you," I say, I get up and walk into the kitchen flicking the kettle on, I look up and he is stood watching me.

"Thank you for what?" he asks, I smile.

"For making the first night here bearable, for just being you." I walk over and move into his arms again, it feels safe and warm. As the kettle flicks off I move away. That wasn't so bad, thanks to Phil the first night in my home was over, I had gotten through it, but the second one might be totally different, I cannot ask Phil to stay with me every night, I have to manage on my own.

As it happens it isn't too bad, I keep myself busy during the day. I have just one more day off before going back to work, I shop and get all the uniform sorted for the return, I stand by my ironing board and pull the uniform blouse from the pile, a vision of Jason ironing comes to my mind and I blink back the tears. In the evening I ring Judy and we chat for a while until I am tired, I make myself a hot drink, read my book for a while, when I wake up in the morning my book is open at the side of me, I fell asleep naturally.

Chapter Twenty

My first shift back to work, I could have had the full two weeks off but there was no point. I have been asked to attend a training course so I have said I will come in, it was booked a month or so ago and I am sure it will do me good to be using my brain again and concentrating on something other than me. The course doesn't start until nine thirty so I have a long lay in and shower and dress. I sit at the dining table, I pull the pile of mail towards me. As I slit open the first card I notice, it is a thank you card, not a sympathy one, it is from Martha. I remember her mentioning something at the funeral but I totally forgot to ask Sean what she meant, now I am intrigued, I smile as I read the words. She is thanking me again for the gift that Jason and I sent, she says that she and Jason chatted about travel and how much she would love to visit her sister and we have made her dream come true, she will use the five thousand pounds to go and visit her sister in Australia and how thoughtful it was of us to think of her, she writes a beautiful card, and I have no idea Jason was doing this, it seems, even in death he has made people happy, even if he did totally exclude me.

I drive the short distance to work and park up, I spend a few minutes catching up with Rex and hearing what he has been up to and then I head towards the parade room. Sometimes there is the odd person working but today there is no one there so I make my way to the training room, I push open the door and everyone is already there. All talking stops as everyone looks up, they are all already sat at their desks, it is only nine twenty so I am not late, the lady at the front is speaking and she looks up questioningly at me. She is tall and slim, wearing a plain grey suit, she has her hair pulled back in a severe bun, the only make-up she has on is a splash of vivid red lipstick making her look very austere, she has steel framed glasses on the end of her nose. She peers at me over the top of them.

"And you are?" she asks, her voice shows her annoyance at the interruption.

"Angie Staddon," I reply, I look around the room there are mostly familiar faces; there is Nick and Clive from CID and Paul from custody and my friend Sue from the typing pool.

"Oh right," she says snottily, "you are late."

I look at my watch. "But it is only nine twenty," I challenge her. I don't know why but already I can feel tears pricking my eyelids, I continue, "the course started at nine thirty,"

"No," she replies tartily, "the course started at nine, I sent an email a week ago changing the time, you obviously didn't bother to check." She rolls her eyes at me.

I look to the clock on the wall and my eyes drop down, I cannot help it, I know I am going to cry, my eyes fill up, I will myself not to cry, I bite my lip hard, I glance up and notice Inspector Wallis at the back of the room sat under the clock. I have known him from my childhood, I don't know what to do, I stand half in and half out of the door waiting for her to say something, to take charge of the situation, but suddenly the Inspector makes everything alright by saying gently, "Hello, Angie, nice to see you, go and get yourself a cup of tea and a bottle of water and join us reprobates here at the back, the water is just outside."

The woman looks like she wants to protest but I see him stand up and walk towards the front of the classroom where she is standing. I see him perch on the end of the desk facing her but I don't stop to listen I let the door drop. Grateful to be able to escape, I grab myself a coffee, biscuit and a bottle of water and when I come back in she is waiting for me, she smiles, ever the professional there is a false smile, a smile that she has pasted on her face but a smile nonetheless and indicates with her hand that I should sit down and I look at Inspector Wallis who has now sat back down. I give him a grateful smile and I sink into the only available chair, which just happens to be next to Sergeant Mike Simms.

We have to start again at Inspector Wallis's insistence and after she has gone back over the course details she explains the first thing we will all do is an icebreaker – we have to introduce the person next to us, and to do that we have to ask them a few questions.

Before we start Mike puts his hand over mine, his hand is warm and comforting, he squeezes my hand, he whispers, "I was genuinely sorry to hear about Jason, really I was, must have been a very difficult time for you." I smile at him, I cannot say anything back, as if sensing my discomfort he goes on, "Anyway." He moves his hand and continues, "The icebreaker, you go first."

I relax a bit, I am in a room with people I know, the tears have gone now I am in my comfort zone, if only Mike wasn't sat so close and leaning so close, close so we can chat quietly and not be overheard. I take a drink of my coffee.

"What do you want to know?" I ask.

"Everything," he replies and winks. I cannot believe him, he is so cheeky, but my grey mood has lifted, I am in a better frame of mind now so I will play along.

"Well, I don't have that long so I will tell you the relevant bits okay, I have been here for three years, I love my job and the people I work with, I think I am good at my job, mainly due to my bossiness, oh yes, I forgot, apparently I have a great stack." I tilt my face to look at him I watch his expression, the muscles in his cheek flinch, I can see immediately he knows what I am referring to. I don't know why I said that, I wanted it to come out as light and amusing but it came out all flat and now it is so excruciatingly embarrassing, why did I mention that for god's sake, I cringe inwardly, but he smiles and glances down.

"Yes, I can see that for myself but let's not share that with the group, eh, lets share your other qualities, you love the people you work with, lucky people." He stares at me for a second before adding, "bossy, eh?" He winks at me again and I want to hug him. I will play that stupid conversation back in my head over and over again and kick myself. I turn to him.

"Your turn." He smiles. I drown in his dark eyes.

"Okay, well." He clears his throat. "Sergeant Simms, nearly ten years in the service, love rugby, well, most sports really, love all food and good company, oh and I am a dab hand at photocopier repairing." He looks at me and smiles. "Enough," he adds. I laugh and push him away "Enough".

I have to go first with the introductions, I mimic what he has told me leaving out the bit about the photocopying, it is his turn next, he stands up.

"This is, Angie, she is a controller, has been for three years, admits to being very bossy, and." He stops and looks at me. "She has a great..." he pauses looking down at his notes, "what was it now." He looks at me, his dark eyes twinkle at me, he continues, "Ah yes, great, knowledge of photocopiers." Everyone laughs, and I narrow my eyes at him then smile shaking my head, he is so comical and relaxed.

He sits back down and I scribble on the note pad that he is *so not funny*, he scribbles back, *oh but I am*, I smile at him as he scribbles again, *oh and as I work with you does that mean?* he just adds a question mark, I giggle but it a well-timed giggle as someone else has made a joke so everyone laughs. I look at Mike and he is laughing too his eyes crinkling up, brightening his whole face. I just shake my head at him.

The course goes well, we are all competing against each other in our teams, Mike and I agree that we must beat both Clive and Nick, we make it our mission, we don't mind losing to anyone else, so we look at the different scenarios we are given and pool our knowledge and compete the assignments together, they are not difficult, it is about putting yourself in someone else's situation, to show empathy. The morning goes quickly and in the break I check my text messages, one is from Martin in the restaurant, I smile, he is so thoughtful, he even sent a card to me when Jason died, signed by both him and Rex. I must make sure I go and thank them both.

There is general chit chat around me and I hear someone enquiring if anyone knows what was on the menu for lunch, I pipe up that it is roast lamb, Inspector Wallis challenges this and asks how on earth I would know that as I have not been in, then I have to come clean and explain that I had received a text telling me, I share the text with them which just says "roast lamb", they all think it is hilarious and Nick says they are going to be looking to use Martin as an informer.

We all trudge up to the restaurant and Martin has never been so popular. He comes round the counter, he says it is lovely to see me, I get to thank him for the card, he gives me a big bear hug, his arms totally embracing me, I look up over Martins shoulder and look straight into Mikes face. I cannot read his expression.

We all sit and eat in a large group, it is such a friendly group, I feel more relaxed than I have been in a long time. The course leader comes over to me.

"I must apologise for earlier," she says, her expression looks relaxed now, I smile at her, she continues, "I would like to offer my condolences," she says, and I smile at her.

"Thank you," I reply. There is nothing else I can say to her, I sit down and I eat my food then sit back and listen to the general chit chat. Mike is sat at the other end of the table but he only stays long enough to eat his food then he raises his eyes as his name is called over the PA system for him to report to reception.

The rest of the afternoon passes again very quickly, we come second in the group and we do indeed beat Nick and Clive, Mike pulls me into a hug.

"Well done to us, eh." He lets me go almost immediately and shakes Nick's hand. "Beaten by the best," he comments, Nick accepts defeat with a pat on Mike's back and he touches my shoulder gently.

"Well done there, Angie, I am sure you did most of the work." I smile graciously at him, we pack up our things, Clive is asking who fancies a quick drink, there are a few murmurs about it being a good idea, it has been a good day but I am not sure I want to. As I get my things together Inspector Wallis comes over.

"Hi, Angie." He touches my hand. "How are things with you?" He sits on the edge of the desk, I smile at him.

"Okay thanks, I am getting there, wherever there is." He moves his hand from mine and touches my shoulder gently.

"Take one day at a time, Angie, one day at a time." I smile and nod, Mike is stood next to him checking his phone. "You are coming for a drink with us aren't you?" Inspector Wallis continues, "We have to celebrate our victory over the CID boys, don't we?" I shrug.

"Well, I probably need to get home." It is a pathetic excuse and he knows it, he is having none of it.

"No you don't, you need a drink, you don't need to go home to the empty house, you are staying, I insist. We all deserve a drink too, and better still, I am buying, so you are coming even if it is only for a quick one, Barb will never forgive me if I didn't catch up with you properly." He walks towards the back of the room to fetch his coat, he turns back to face me before adding, "No excuses, see you in ten minutes." He calls out cheery goodbyes then he is gone.

Barbara is his wife of some twenty odd years; she used to babysit for me and Judy apparently. Mike has finished with his phone and looks up to me.

"Looks like you are going then, glad about that, he is right you deserve a drink, see you there." With a cheery smile he pushes the door open and he has gone. I watch as he walks down the corridor.

The police bar is busy when I arrive, there is no room at any table but Rex is at the bar and he insists that he buys me a tonic water. We chat about the funeral for a short while, Nick comes to the bar he buys a bottle of wine and pushes the filled glass towards me, but I shake my head and decline. I have to remember I have my car, so no drinking. Nick smiles, shrugs and walks away carrying the bottle and glass with him.

Rex has just come back from Majorca his first holiday abroad, he is so sweet, he is excitedly telling me about the airport and the flight as if I have never been overseas, he is deaf so tends to shout, and I don't actually get to reply or speak as he is so pleased to have someone listening to him, so I smile, I like him. He stands there in his usual brown work coverall, looking round at the room, just chatting happily, I don't mind being in his company, it is a lovely distraction after the last few weeks.

After ten or so minutes my eyes travel around the room too, I am all listened out but Rex shows no sign of stopping, the police bar is now getting busier, there are still no tables available and people are waiting at the bar. I can see Phil and the rest of his shift stood in one corner, he is chatting away and I try and attract his attention without Rex seeing. I wish I could send a quick text for Phil to rescue me, I need saving now as Rex is describing the coach journey from the airport to the hotel, I am sure he is going to take me through his holiday day by day. I can see a disco is setting up in the corner, so there must be a party on tonight. Rex has indeed started to describe in detail the hotel reception, I am now desperately looking round the bar trying to attract someone, anyone's attention. I see Mike approaching but he is not looking at me, he heads straight for Rex.

"Appreciate you are off-duty, mate, but I have been told there is a problem in the car park and I wonder if you would be available to help out, seems like you are the only person who knows who all the cars belong to." Mike looks directly at Rex who seems to have grown inches with pride.

"Certainly will, sir," he salutes, "sorry duty calls," he says to me and hurries off, I look at Mike.

"Thank you so much for saving me, I do think he is wonderful but I don't think I could stand listening to any more of his holiday stories, I owe you one." I smile at him, he smiles back his eyes just staring into mine.

He moves close to me speaking quietly, "Don't say that." Mike is smiling

"I might just call that in one day," he laughs again then moves away, "there is some sort of problem in the car park genuinely." And with that he turns to the bar and orders a soft drink, "Can I buy you one?" he asks, I shake my head.

"No, I am fine thanks, I am only on tonic water as I am driving." He smiles again, he looks so much nicer when he smiles.

"Tonic water it is then." He places the order and leans up against the bar. "Must be a party here tonight – do you know whose it is?" I just shrug, shaking my head.

He is having a strange effect on me, my heart is thudding so hard I think he might be able to hear. The drinks arrive on the bar and he leans over to pay, his phone goes off and he answers it, he gives me a big smile, winks then answers his phone, he picks up his drink and disappears, I watch him leave, a frown appearing as he is speaking into the phone.

Marcia comes towards me, a big smile on her face. "I think I am going to make your day." I look towards Mikes retreating back, too late for that I think to myself.

Chapter Twenty-One

Marcia says that she has emailed me already but had no reply, she has been away on holiday so missed the funeral. She did send a lovely card though, I have barely had chance to catch up with anyone and I haven't had a chance to check all through my personal emails yet, but she explains that she has one spare ticket to see the boy band Take That, she got the tickets whilst I was away on bereavement leave, someone bought two but only needs one now, she didn't want to contact me when she was buying them as it didn't seem appropriate. The concert is next week. She is stood in front of me now asking me if I want to go, I so want to shout yes I do, yes, I so want to go, but is it appropriate for me to be dancing around at a concert so soon after losing Jason? I might have to ring Sean and ask him what he thinks.

"Well," Marcia breaks into my thoughts.

I reply enthusiastically, "Oh great, sounds brilliant, what date is it and I will let you know?" Marcia writes the date and time.

"There is a mini bus included so all you have to do is turn up." She leans forward and hugs me. "Come on, give yourself a treat, you deserve it."

I nod my head, but before I can stop them my eyes fill with tears, I don't know why, it is just the kindness she has shown or maybe it is because this is what I have wanted for so long, to just enjoy myself, to let myself go and just be me, not nursing a poorly husband, but I am not sure what people will think. I have a mental fight with myself, I turn to Marcia but someone calls her from across the room.

She walks off calling back to me, "You have got till Friday to let me know okay, ring me." She holds her hands up in the telephone gesture and I give her a cheery wave and walk over to where Phil is, I might run it by him and see what he thinks.

Phil thinks it is a great idea, he cannot see any reason I should not go, he is also going, he was taking a girl but that has fallen through and he is now going on his own. Helen has bought his other ticket, he apologises for not offering it to me but Helen was there when he got the text cancelling. The mini bus has been organised, there are twelve of them going in total, I ask him who I need to pay for my ticket and the mini bus but he starts to reply when he is interrupted by another chap leaning over and speaking in his ear,

I cannot hear what he says as the disco is now starting to play so I just stand there waiting. When he has finished listening the man throws his head back, laughs out loud and moves away and is soon whispering in someone else's ear, soon it seems everyone is erupting into laughter.

Phil knocks back his drink, he joins in with the laughter but does not elaborate, so I prompt him, "Problems?" I ask, he laughs again.

"Not for me thank goodness, but Mike is having one hell of a problem downstairs with his girlfriend – she is in the car park creating a right merry hell wanting to be let in. She has parked her car totally blocking the car park and poor old deaf Rex is apparently trying and failing to deal with it."

My heart sinks, I didn't realise he was still with his girlfriend, I try and keep my voice steady and ask casually, "Is that the one from the Italian restaurant, what was her name again?"

Phil is now checking his phone, he is distracted, but he answers without looking at me. "Yes, not sure what her name was but the very same, all I remember is her big chest, big hair, big mouth, I call her big bird," Phil laughs, "it must be on and off with him and her if you get my drift." Everyone laughs again. Phil adds, "There must be something about her that cannot keep him away, wonder what that might be," he laughs again at his own joke, everyone else joins in.

My heart sinks. I sit back and listen as they all give their own additional comments on Mike's love life. I don't want to hear about his conquests, I don't want to think of him with someone else.

Phil leans back in his chair. "He has got a right bunny boiler there I can tell you, I used to bump into her all the time hanging around the station, but now he is living back with his parents I think she hangs about there; he should just have the balls to dump her." He swigs on his beer. Rob who is sitting opposite leans forward.

"I think maybe he likes the attention, you know, she isn't that bad, great body on her." Phil nods his head in agreement.

"Cannot argue with that, mate, great chassis but she is a bit missing in the head department I think." I look at Phil and shake my head.

"Do you not think of anything else?" I ask, he looks at me and smiles.

"Is there anything else worth thinking about, Angie?" He leans towards me and kisses my head. "Come on, have a proper drink."

I shake my head. "No, I am okay, I think I will head off home, catch you later okay." Phil smiles.

"Okay lightweight, see you later, avoid the car park though, there is already one mental woman out there, they don't need two." He laughs at his own joke and turns back towards Rob.

I am no mood now to stay and dance and join in with the party, I think I will go home and catch a bit of television, I might give Sean a call and see what he is up to, I cannot be bothered to seek out Inspector Wallis so I slip out down the back stairs. Immediately I know I am not going to get away with it as I hear him call out my name, so I spend the next half an hour chatting to him in the corridor where it is quieter and I am glad I do stop as I must admit it feels good to have a nice talk with someone who doesn't ask about Jason, but asks about my parents and my family. Finally he lets me go but not without reminding me that his 25th wedding anniversary party is coming up and he expects me to be there. With a big hug I leave him at the top of the stairs. I feel a lot happier now and I will call Sean and see if he wants to grab a take-away, I might text Phil and see if he is interested.

I get to the bottom of the stairs and stop, I am just fishing about in my handbag to find my keys and my phone when I hear hushed voices coming from the dark office on the ground floor by the exit, I am intrigued, there is just ten feet from where I am to the main exit but I don't walk on, for some reason I stop and listen and can hear the carnal sounds of intimacy coming from within, I chuckle to myself, some people have no respect. I then hear Phil's voice and realise it is him and a female in the office, I recognise her voice too, the chuckle dies on my face. I don't know why I am shocked really, I know it goes on, he tells me about his conquests, yet I have never witnessed it for myself, he just refers to his various women, I never know the details I would probably be appalled by his behaviour. I hear a groan and I know who it is, it makes me feel quite angry, how degrading for the woman to be used that way and to make it worse in a grotty old dark office when they could get caught. I didn't realise the noises have finished and if it wasn't for the scrape of furniture I would have been caught listening at the door. I walk quickly to the exit and push the door, I hear Phil calling my name.

"Angie, wait," he calls, he hurries towards me, "I thought you had gone already, where have you been?" Without waiting for me to answer he continues, "Where are you off to then, why don't you stay?" he asks walking towards me.

I can see Jo's shadow in the doorway, she is holding back, not exactly hiding but not showing her face either, I expect she is not certain of what the protocol is for this situation, being caught shagging like a cheap tart by your work colleague, but Phil is as cheery and cocky as ever, he is stood in front of me now.

"I told you – I am going home, I just got caught chatting, but I am going now," I reply, "I thought I would treat Sean to a take-away, I don't fancy a night on my own." I keep my voice light.

"Okay, count me in too."

Phil does not even look back to her, doesn't even acknowledge her existence but follows me out of the door and to the car. I cannot believe he has left her like that, how cheap must she feel? I don't say anything until I am in the car, then I turn to him.

"I cannot believe you have just done that," I say trying to keep my voice casual, Phil is messing with his phone.

"What?" There is protest in Phil's voice, but he doesn't look up from what his is doing.

"You know," I reply immediately, adding, "And with her." I cannot keep the scorn out of my voice. He looks up at me and I shake my head at him. He smiles and holds his hands up in defence.

"What have I done wrong? She wanted it, I wanted it, *no* big deal, no one is hurting."

I reply immediately, "Julian is hurting, Phil, that is what is wrong, *he* is hurting." I am amazed at how calm my voice comes out, I don't like the thought of cheating – fidelity is important to me. Phil seems to view sex so casually and I cannot think like that. "Do you think she is going to leave Julian to be with you?" I enquire.

"Christ, I hope not," Phil laughs, before continuing, "you don't get it do you, Angie, it is just casual, just a bit of fun, no strings, no harm in it and for your information I don't think Julian cares, I am giving his missus what she is obviously missing at home, filling the void as it were." He laughs out loud at his own joke. "Pardon the pun," he adds.

I feel a bit naïve, but I still push on, "No, really, Phil, maybe I don't get it, I expect a bit more from a relationship, I don't want to be pushed over a desk, used and then disregarded, without so much as a goodbye, I want the whole one hundred per cent, I won't settle for anything less, I did once, but never again, I want fireworks."

I am not sure why I said that, it just came out, I didn't mean to sound disrespectful of Jason and our marriage. Phil is looking at me, I can see him as I am driving, but I don't look back at him, I concentrate on moving the car out of the car park.

"I know, Angie, I know all of that about you, but you are not her and she is not you, and don't knock having it over a desk," he laughs, "not until you have tried it." He nudges me with his arm and I cannot help it, I smile at him.

"You are terrible, Phil, really terrible." He looks up and waves to a colleague walking across the car park, I pause as the chap stops by the window.

"Where did you disappear to?" he asks Phil, I raise my eyebrows, waiting to hear his reply, but Phil winds up the window laughing and shaking his head.

"Never you mind, might have had to sort a plumbing problem out," he shouts cheerfully. I pull out onto the main road, Phil looks at me. "Let's not invite Sean tonight," he says quietly, "let's just have a night in together and talk, just the two of us." I nod my head in agreement and watch in frustration as he messes around with the radio station until he finds music he likes.

I park the car at home and we walk to the takeaway together, we chat about nondescript things but I cannot stop thinking that half an hour ago he was having sex with another woman, a married woman who will be sharing her bed tonight with her husband. It is all really rather sad, and a bit desperate, surely Phil could get better. It is a short walk to the takeaway and we wait for our order, I am thinking about what Phil said some time ago about liking someone who doesn't even know he exists, I haven't thought about it until now, who could it be?

I jump as he asks, "Penny for them."

"What?" I reply.

"Your thoughts." He picks up the order from the counter, takes my hand and we walk back together. we hear the toot of a car horn and I recognise the driver as being an officer who lives nearby, I see Mike in the front seat, and a few others in the back of the car, they have the windows down, they shout out of the window but I couldn't make out what they said, they all hoot with laughter and Phil holds up the takeaway bag as in a wave, the other hand is still holding mine.

The moment has gone, we walk back home in quiet companionship, he doesn't ask for my thoughts any more. It is not until much later that I think of it again, we have eaten the takeaway, watched television and drunk a bottle of wine, I am relaxed and chilled out in my comfortable clothes, we are just watching the credits go up on the film we were watching. Phil is half laid on the other end of the sofa, I am at the other end my feet tucked up underneath me. I stare at him for a few minutes taking in his face as he studies the credits, he scratches his chin unaware I am watching, he bites his nail and looks at it casually and then he looks at me.

"What?" he says questioningly.

"Nothing," I reply, "just watching you." He pats his end of the sofa.

"Come up here with me." I swivel round and tuck under his arm and lay my legs the same way as his, we lay like spoons, I watch the adverts on the television. I am feeling all warm and a bit tipsy from the wine, he feels warm and safe, I can smell the mustiness of his aftershave. He tilts my chin up towards him and kisses me gently on the forehead, I close my eyes, he kisses the bridge of my nose.

He whispers, "You okay?" And I can only nod in reply. It seems forever since I felt the warmth of a male body next to mine, I try to block out it is Phil, his lips seek mine and he kisses me gently, I return the kiss and his tongue seeks mine, I can taste the wine on his breath, I hold his face with my hands, I can feel the slight stubble grazing my chin, it feels wonderful to have this closeness again. He is kissing me deeper now, his tongue brushing my lips, his hand is stroking my breast over my sweatshirt. I don't stop him, I close my eyes tighter, I just lay there losing myself in the feeling of being close to someone, his tongue is entwined with mine, his hand reaches under my top and his hand seeks my breast. I run my hand over the front of his jeans and I feel him groan in my mouth. His kisses become more urgent, he pulls me up to him and my sweatshirt is pushed up over my breasts and both his hands are inside my bra and he is pulling at my breasts so hard, almost too hard, but it feels wonderful. We rub against each other, I open my eyes and meet Phil's open eyes, I see the shock in his eyes and immediately we pull away from each other and he removes his hands, we jump apart as if we have been scalded.

"Jesus, Angie." Phil sits up.

"I don't know what happened, I was totally out of order." He scratches his head. "I mean, Christ, I am sorry." He wrings his hands together. "I guess it must be the wine." He rests his elbows on his knees holding his head in his hands, he stays like that for so long I wonder if he has fallen asleep.

"Phil, are you okay?" I ask gently, he looks up, he shakes his head.

"Sorry, Angie, that was bang out of order, that wasn't good." I laugh at him.

"Gee thanks." He shakes his head again.

"No, I didn't mean like that, I mean, well," he pauses as if thinking about his words, before he continues, "I mean, I guess I have sometimes wondered what it would be like to kiss you properly, not the normal way I kiss you, but you know, properly, but I am sorry I crossed the line, all I could see when I opened my eyes and looked at you was Jason." He looks up at our wedding picture on the mantelpiece then he rubs his hands over his head. "I am so sorry, geez, what sort of bloke am I, I mean bloody hell, I even felt you up."

I laugh out loud, I adjust my clothes and pull my sweatshirt down, I stroke his arm but he looks mortified, he won't look at me, so I know it is me that has to make him feel better.

"Phil, honey." I sit up and turn his face to look at me, "Don't blame yourself, it was both of us, you didn't kiss me, we kissed, and if I am truthful even before Jason died and we were not getting on so well I used to wonder what it would be like, then when you used to kiss me after quiz night, I kind of looked forward to it. Don't beat yourself up, even after he died..." I pause, "well, I used to think about it, not with you but with anyone, it seems to have been so long." I stumble a bit on my words. "And if I am honest, it was good, it felt good." I look at him and smile. "You are not a bad kisser, not the best but not bad." I laugh at his pained expression. "Phil, I just closed my eyes and lost myself for a moment, and yes, you did feel me up, and I didn't object, but it was nice, and in another time and another place I think we might have been good together." I pull him close and hug him.

"So did you?" he questions. I shake my head, Phil pushes me away gently.

I know what he is asking, whether I felt the fireworks, I shake my head again. "No sorry, Phil, nothing, no pounding in my heart, no fireworks, not this time." He laughs and stands up.

"You and your fireworks, Angie, you make me laugh." He walks towards the kitchen. "I think I will grab another quick coffee, do you want one?" he asks.

"Yes please." The discomfort between us has gone, we are okay. I follow him to the kitchen and watch him help himself. "Phil," I speak quietly, "I have to know something." He doesn't face me, he puts the coffee and milk into the mugs and stirs. "Phil", I continue, "remember you said once that the girl you want doesn't even know you exist – who were you speaking about?"

We carry the coffee back through to the lounge and sit back on each end of the sofa, I sip mine, but it is so hot I put it on a coaster on the floor, Phil doesn't say anything and part of me is very glad. I think he heard, but now I have asked I am not sure I want to hear the reply to my question, I am nervous as to what he might reply, it might complicate matters, and then it hits me, oh god, what if it is me, what if the person he wants and cannot have is me, what would I do, it would be the Jason thing all over again, I don't know what to say now, I do not want him to reply, I wish I had not said anything, I didn't think it through before I spoke. I don't want to know, and to hear it is me would change everything, and I don't want things to change, I like them just as they are.

It is too late, after a long silence he finally speaks, "What?" he asks questioningly. He is busy flicking through the television listings and not really listening totally oblivious to my discomfort, I chicken out.

"Nothing. Find something humorous to watch will you and then give your favourite person a foot massage." He smiles and puts his legs down. "Come on then, just a quick one."

And as I plant my feet in his lap, he says, "If I had a sister I would want her to be just like you." The discomfort from earlier situation has gone. "I don't just do this to anyone you know." He picks up my foot and begins to rub it through my sock, and then I know, his comment makes everything okay, I don't need to ask him, I know I am not the one, I will beat myself up over the next few weeks wondering who it is though.

Chapter Twenty-Two

I wake up early, very thirsty, Chinese food does that to me, I sit looking out of the patio window drinking a cold orange juice, I go over the events with Phil, we had finished the evening by watching a rerun of a very old comedy, but we sat in companionable silence. When he left I noticed he kissed my cheek and not my lips, I am not sure why, he cheekily grabbed my bottom and I punched his arm, he walked off down the road laughing. I sit at the dining table, looking out on to the garden, watching some birds in the garden, then a little robin flies down and walks about looking for scraps of food. It is getting colder in the mornings and I just sit watching just this one little robin scraping the earth trying to get a stray worm. I hear the arrival of the postman as he drops the letter box with a clatter. There are some small envelopes which are mainly junk but with them is a very official letter and I return to my seat in the dining room and open it. I read the letter several times, it is from the life assurance company regarding my recent claim, I haven't made any claim, I am very puzzled.

When Jason died, Sean handled all the mortgage company and that was all settled very quickly, he notified everyone that needed to be notified of his death, even the pensions people, everything has been changed to my maiden name for me but as I read I realise that this is something completely different, it is asking me to complete further forms on diagnosis dates and the consultants details again. It says that in order to settle the claim they need to have further information as they are not happy with certain statements of the dates etc. I am not sure what that means, again, I haven't completed any before. There is a paragraph which is very worrying, it mentions fraudulent claims and false declarations, and even imprisonment, I have no idea what this refers to. I reach for my phone to call Sean, but I don't, I ring Phil instead. He is with me within half an hour and during this time I read the whole letter again, it is definitely a claim for a life insurance policy in Jason's name with Sean and I showing as the benefactors, I had no idea of its existence, but it is a large amount of money. I explain all this to Phil, he puts it back in the envelope and says he will be back soon, he has a short job he needs to do but whilst he is gone he says I am to say nothing to no one, not even Sean until he is back.

As promised he is back within an hour, he has copies of the whole document, I don't know why the copies are needed but I don't ask any questions, I am so confused but there is a phone number and so we call it together. Phil highlights the copy as the person at the end of the phone gives the details, we put the phone on speaker so we can both listen, my jaw drops as the woman speaks, to tell me that it seems that a month or so before we married, Jason took out a life insurance policy for a six figure sum. He gave them the date of the impending marriage and provided my birth certificate then when it was needed he provided them with a copy of the marriage certificate. I am astounded that I had no idea this was going on, and now they are in receipt of a claim, they have sent forms out which were completed by Sean, I am totally flabbergasted. Phil makes lots of notes as she is speaking, I am not sure why Sean has never mentioned these to me. Then the lady says she need to make an appointment as the record is showing that the Insurance advisor wants to come and see me in my home to discuss the claim further, the woman is quite determined that the appointment must be sooner rather than later. I set the appointment for tomorrow and I am so pleased that Phil has agreed to be there too. When we hang up we both look at each other.

"Don't worry, Angie," Phil says reassuringly, "it will all be okay, Sean will sort it all out, don't worry." But as I reach to fill the kettle I know I will worry, why is it life is never simple. When Phil leaves I busy myself tidying up and pop to do some shopping but I cannot get it out of my head, it seems Jason has made more of an effort in our marriage for me after his death than he ever did when he was alive.

Chapter Twenty-Three

Tonight is the concert, I am so excited, I am meeting the mini bus at the pick-up point which is just a twenty minute walk away. It is cold but not freezing. I have worn jeans and a T-shirt bearing the Take That picture, I have a short but warm jacket on and my comfortable boots. The mini bus is there when I arrive and as I get on the bus I say hello to Helen and Phil and I am surprised to notice Mike is on the bus, I wouldn't have put him down as a boy band fan. Helen and I sit by each other and then Marcia joins us, kneeling up on her seat so she can talk to us, I have still not paid for my ticket, I should have asked Phil earlier but I totally forgot, so I ask her once again, I have the money in my pocket, I just don't know how much, but she shrugs and says, "We can sort it out tomorrow, don't worry."

I push her again, "I have the money here, why wait until tomorrow, just tell me how much and who I am paying and I can sort it out now, please let me." But she won't budge, she turns back around in her seat and chats to her companion. I turn to Helen. "How much was the ticket, do you know?" She bought hers cheap from Phil so cannot help me, Phil is talking to Mike so I lean over interrupting to ask him, he waves his hand to wave me away.

"Just chill out and enjoy yourself," he laughs, "deal with it tomorrow." Oh well I tried, so whoever paid will have to chase me now I tell Helen and we sit chatting to each other and Marcia in the seat in front for the rest of the journey.

The concert is brilliant, my ears are buzzing, my throat hurts for all the screaming and singing I have done and my feet are killing me, but I love it, I have totally let go of my inhibitions, I feel more relaxed than I have felt on a long time, I have not stopped laughing and smiling and it is fabulous. I am on cloud nine, I buy another T- shirt and tug my jacket off to put the new one on immediately. Phil calls my name and as I turn to him the flash of his camera surprises me, he tells the girls to stand together and we pose in our new T- shirts. When he shows us the pictures we all look really happy, our faces are shining bright with our smiles, Phil pulls the group together and gets a stranger to take the picture of all of us together. I have my arm around Marcia and Helen and the boys are stood behind us, they take lots more pictures of them being silly and posing, it is great fun and my jaw is aching with laughing so much, almost too soon the final encore is over and I scream loudly along with everyone else.

I climb on the mini bus with a huge smile on my face the music still ringing in my ears only to find Helen and Phil have taken up spaces together and he is smiling but pretending to be asleep on her shoulder, which leaves me to sit by Mike. I look at Helen but she smiles at me and puts her arms through Phil's, they look so comfortable, I look at Mike, he is texting on his phone and doesn't look up, I didn't see much of him at the concert until the photograph session as I stood by Helen and Marcia, but I knew they were behind us somewhere. Now he is sat in the bus in the seat by the window.

"Looks like you have the short straw and are lumbered with me," I say cheerfully, he puts his phone in his pocket.

"Definitely not the short straw," he replies patting the seat. There is that lovely twinkle in his eyes as his mouth turns up into a smile, making my heart pound a little faster. I ask Phil for his camera and I scroll through the pictures, Mike leans in to have a look and we laugh at the posing ones, there is one where everyone is together and Mike is stood to the side of me, it is obvious in the picture that he is looking at me and I blush. I pass the camera back to Phil then Mike and I chat about the concert for a while. When I cannot stay awake any longer, my eyes drop and I fall asleep my head resting on his shoulder. We stop at the services, everyone gets off but I don't need anything so I stay on, Mike is the first to get back on, I look at the bag on his seat.

"Did you buy a T-shirt too?" I ask, he nods and smiles, but he doesn't respond, I question him further, "I wouldn't have put you down for a Take That fan," I tease him,

But he just smiles as he replies, "It is not that I am a fan, I don't dislike them but I bought the tickets intending to take someone, then they couldn't make it, I thought I would come and see what the fuss was about, it seemed a shame to waste them, and I bought them a T- shirt to make up for the fact they couldn't go."

"Tickets, you bought tickets?" I question him, my mind is racing, who would he have bought a ticket for, my heart sinks, of course the crazy lady, he would have bought the ticket for her, I wonder why she couldn't go.

He interrupts my thoughts, "Yes, I did, and it was the best money I have spent in a long time, I had a really good time, despite the fact my ears are ringing, I quite enjoyed myself and by the looks of it, you did too, it is lovely to see a smile on your face." I don't reply as the others get on the bus and we begin our journey home. Within a few minutes the motion of the mini bus makes my eyes droop and my head falls back on his shoulder.

I have very mixed emotions today, I am sure Mike has paid for my ticket and I have decided I am going to give him the money. I am unsure why it had to be a big mystery he had a ticket and I wanted it, I pay for it, I don't know why there has to be a big drama over it, it is simple.

I am also very nervous as to what the financial investigator is going to tell me, Phil is supposed to be here with me, the appointment is at 10:00 and it is nearly that now, I got up early so I would be ready, I shower and dress, then clean the house to keep myself busy, it looks like a new pin, but no sign of Phil, I can see a chap parking his car in the street, I text Phil quickly but I have already sent two or three text messages but there is no response, I am not sure whether to call Sean or not, but then I decide not to, I am so nervous I am shaking. The doorbell rings, oh well, I take in a few deep breaths and reach for the door – so much for Phil's support.

"So." The investigator places his briefcase on his knees and pulls out a copy of the paperwork. He is short and very plump, with a shiny bald head and silver-framed glasses, he looks very serious, he looks up at me as he speaks. "As you can see we do have to investigate all claims of this value and I appreciate you are still very much grieving for your husband, but the timing of him taking out a large six figure life assurance and then being diagnosed with a terminal illness is so short, we have to ask you the questions and I hope you pardon the intrusion."

"Of course," I reply brightly, "I am happy to answer any questions."

Everything has been made clear to me now, Jason had taken out life assurance a month or so before we were married, he provided them copies of my birth certificate and then the marriage certificate, he was very thorough. The chap is happy with my dates of when he took poorly and when he fainted at the restaurant and then had the MRI scan and it matches up with what Sean has told them, then he asks me a strange question.

"Did your husband go to university?" he questions.

"Yes, he did," I reply. I am not sure why this is relevant but he carries on.

"And can you confirm what was his major?" I am stumped, I should know this, but I don't.

"Oh, I am sorry I am not sure off the top of my head, I do have it all somewhere." I am embarrassed that I don't know this information, he was my husband after all, and if you were to ask if I knew Phil's I could reel them off from memory, how embarrassing. "Shall I go and dig them out for you?" I offer. He nods his head but doesn't look up.

"That will be most helpful, thank you Ms Staddon." I frown at him.

"You do use your maiden name, don't you?" he asks, I nod my head. "You never took your husband's name then?" I shrug.

"Yes, in some things, in official things but for others I kept my maiden name." He nods.

"Ah right, but say for membership of a club, would that be your maiden name or married name?" he asks. I go all hot, I can feel my face reddening.

"Well, we never joined any clubs, I was a member of a gym before I was married and kept my name the same." He notes something down on his page.

"Tell me," he pauses, "don't most brides practice signing their new signature," he smiles, "you know excited brides-to-be." He looks up and smiles at me, but I don't smile back.

"The wedding was a complete surprise to me. Jason booked everything, and this excited bride-to-be had no knowledge until the day that she was getting married, so sorry to disappoint you, there was no practising of the signatures for me." He notes something else down on his pad as I continue. "But Jason was my husband, we exchanged vows and I didn't need my name changed at the local gym to prove it, like it or not, we were married, husband and wife and in the areas that mattered I took his name, now I will go and search for the paperwork you were asking for."

I leave him downstairs and run upstairs trying to think off the top of my head where they might be. I feel so angry that he has challenged my name change. I hear the front door open and close and I am expecting to see Phil but it is Sean who pokes his head round the bedroom door.

"Who is the chap in the lounge?" he enquires brightly. "Financial investigator," I reply and I turn to face him.

"And how the hell did you get in?" I don't wait for a reply. "The chap downstairs, is the investigator, you know the one who is investigating the claim for the six figure life assurance that you failed to mention to me." My voice is a harsh whisper. I look straight at him in his eye, "So why didn't you bloody tell me, what the hell are you hiding from me?" Sean is round the bed and taking my hands.

"Shhh keep your voice down, the front door was open, I just walked in, now tell me what have you told him so far?" he questions,

I reply in a harsh whisper, "Everything he has asked me of course, what do you expect, I have nothing to hide, and now he wants to have Jason's university papers, I don't know why and I cannot bloody find them, and he isn't happy that I use my maiden name." I can hear the stress in my voice.

"Okay, okay." Sean stoops down and picks up the papers I am looking through. "Calm down, don't worry, it is all okay, lets cross the name bit when we come to it." He stands up and scratches his head. "The certificates, if they are not here, they will be in his main blue education file, do you know where that is?"

I shake my head. "I cannot remember, I last saw it ages ago, before the funeral, your mum had it, I have no idea where it is." I stand up and sit on the edge of the bed, I can hear the chap speaking on his phone downstairs, Sean goes around the bed and closes the door.

"Just tell him that you cannot find them but they might be with mum and dad. I remember now maybe they were using it to show after his funeral, I can check for you later and get them for you, tell him that okay, don't tell him I am here. I will wait up here for you until he has gone, don't worry." His voice is still a whisper.

"But I am worried, Sean," I hiss at him, "he has mentioned about fraudulent claims and prison and court, and how strange it was that the wedding was a surprise, and me not taking his name, of course I am worried," Sean runs his hands through his hair, the way that Jason used to do.

"He is bluffing, he knows nothing, it is a genuine claim they just don't want to pay out, go on." He pushes me towards the door. "Go back down there, do as I tell you, it will all be okay." I stand and look at him for a second he looks at me.

"What is wrong, what are you waiting for?" I look at Sean, I look down at his feet.

"You should have taken your shoes off," I say drily to him, then I turn and walk out the door, leaving him stood open-mouthed.

I return downstairs, the chap is looking at our wedding picture on the mantelpiece, he turns to face me as I walk back in. "Nice photo," he comments. I shrug but make no comment, I explain that I thought I had the certificates but they must be at Jason's parents. He seems happy enough that I know he went to Cambridge and the year he graduated, he writes everything down and then hands me a business card. He shakes my hand and leaves. As I close the door I lean against the wall for support, I am shaking so much. Sean comes down almost immediately, I follow him into the lounge and stand there as he sits on the sofa, he runs his hands through his hair, at this point I hear a key in the front door and we both look up as Phil walks in.

"Well, thanks for bloody nothing," I sneer at him, "you are too late, he has been and gone and Mr here." I indicate Sean, "is just about to explain everything." I look directly at Sean, "Aren't you." Phil looks at his watch.

"I thought you said eleven and it is only quarter to now." He looks at me as I shake my head crossly.

"I said ten, you bloody idiot."

Sean to his credit, at least has the decency to look guilty, and has now removed his shoes, he stands up then changes his mind and sits down again, running his hands through his hair.

"Look, I am sorry," he explains, "I wanted the claim all sorted out and to present you with a cheque, but it seems the insurance company are not happy about several things. Firstly, they have a clear procedure for all adopted children, it is to insist on a pre- medical report, and this should have happened as Jason was adopted, he declared everything, gave them the adoption certificate but for some reason they missed it, he should have had a medical but didn't, there is no parent history, but he gave them all the certificates they asked for as in your birth certificate, his adoption one and then the marriage certificate so it is their fault. Also they are questioning the timing of the diagnosis and subsequent death of Jason, this has raised some questions, they think he must have had a private diagnosis but have nothing to substantiate this claim. They have checked with local hospitals and cancer specialists but they have nothing." I sit down, I look at Sean.

"I wish you had told me all of this." I glance at Phil, he shrugs, I look back at Sean then I continue, "Do you think Jason had any idea he was going to die long before he collapsed in the car park of the Italian?"

Sean just shook his head. "If he did he never confided in me," he pauses, "no, I won't believe it, I cannot believe my brother would do that to me." Sean shakes his head.

"So," I ask, "where do we go from here?" Sean says nothing he runs his hands through his hair again.

"I don't know, I guess they will do their investigations and then we have a choice of whether, if they refuse to pay out, we challenge the decision, or accept it." Sean moves over to the sofa where I am sat, he turns to face me. "Look, Angie, there is nothing we can do, please don't worry, we didn't know, and if Jason had some way of knowing, or of finding out he had a terminal illness, it doesn't mean that we knew, they cannot prove we did, worrying about it won't help, we can only answer the questions as asked and leave the rest to them." I nod my head, I have to agree with him, I am not totally happy with Sean or Phil but I guess it is out of my hands.

Then a thought occurs to me, I shake my head. "Something very strange has just crossed my mind and I cannot get it out of my head," I pause, "I don't know if this is relevant but Jason would not ever let me buy his train ticket online or buy it in advance – he always insisted on paying cash on the day." I look at them both. "Do you think that is strange?" Sean shakes his head but Phil shrugs he then looks at both of us.

"Untraceable I guess, that is why." He raises his eyebrows. "So I guess that answers your question." He turns to Sean. "Based on what Angie has just said, yes I think he did know, he must have been covering his tracks."

Sean shakes his head, he stands and walks over the window and looks out. I don't think they both knew in advance, I don't think they would lie to me, but some niggle in the back of my mind won't go away: Jason did go to London to see his friend several times, and sometimes it seems even further afield, but he never told me exactly where and he always paid cash for his ticket, also he had private calls late at night on many occasions. I don't even know which friend though, but surely every hospital with a scanner cannot just scan anyone, there must be a procedure. There are so many thoughts running through my head it is exhausting, I just don't want this hassle, I know everyone will say I should fight it tooth and nail, but money has never motivated me, I would rather just pay my way and be happy, I don't want the stress of this hanging over my head.

Chapter Twenty-Four

Just when things are looking rubbish for me, then I make a decision that makes me very excited. When we were on the minibus going to the concert Marcia asked me if I would like to go on holiday with her to Egypt. We cannot speak much as once we get to the concert venue it is too noisy, when we are walking back to the minibus we whisper for a few minutes excitedly about our one week in the sun, in just six weeks' time. The more she told me about it the more excited I get, I hope I can go.

I just have to clear it at work and then we are going to book it, Marcia is okay there is always plenty of cover in the main admin office and she doesn't work shifts. She knows a lovely small family run hotel that is right on the beach, not near any noisy nightclubs and the more she talks about it the more excited I get, I am so looking forward to it. I might struggle to get it signed off at work as Christmas is just a few weeks away and I am off to see my parents with my sister and her children. I am looking forward to the break, but I know I might be chancing it getting another holiday approved.

I am really excited that when I look at the rota there is no one else off so Craig agrees the leave, he is really pleased for me and confirms the date I am going by adding, "You go the day after Mike's surprise 30th birthday party, perfect timing," he adds, "but I haven't heard of any party, I don't know anything about it." I frown at him and he smiles back. "That's because there are no written invitations, as it is too easy for people to leave them lying about, it is all word of mouth, I will give you the details later, we were told around the time of the funeral, I think his sister is dealing with the invitations, so I guess no one mentioned it as it wasn't a great time for you, but of course you are invited." He walks off whistling and I hug myself. That means in February I have a party to go to then we will be jetting off for a week, lots going on. I cannot wait, but first I have to sort out a small problem, I have the envelope in my handbag with the money for the concert ticket.

I pop down for a short break, there are quite a few people in the office downstairs, I ignore them and walk to the end of the office, I put the envelope on Mike's desk, clearly marked for him. I have included extra for the mini bus, I don't know if it will be enough but I am sure someone will tell me if it isn't. Working it out, it is easy to see it was Mike's spare ticket, everyone else was in pairs, and Phil had sold his to Helen, so what all the secrecy is about I just don't know, but I am happy I have paid my way now.

As I make my way up the stairs I hear the running of footsteps I look behind, my heart sinks, it is, Mike, I really don't want to be seeing him right at this moment, he holds the envelope out to me.

"I don't want this, Angie, please you have it."

We are now right outside the admin office, within a few feet of the control room. I ignore his outstretched hand, my hand is up on the wooden panel ready to push it open, I turn to face him.

"Mike, it is obvious to me that you bought and paid full price for the ticket, I wanted to go and so I bought it, I don't know why there was such a big secret, please take the money, it would make me feel better." I push the door open but he grabs my arm, gently pulling me back.

"Angie, I was so pleased that the ticket went to you, everyone was, you looked like you had a great time, probably just what you needed after what you have been through lately." His face looks so concerned, so genuine, but all I can think of was people discussing me, talking about me behind my back, I cannot bear it, I can almost hear their voices: poor Angie, needs cheering up, been through so much lately, let her have the ticket, she needs it – that is why no one would tell me who I had to pay, it was all decided between them. My fiery temper takes hold and I look at him, shrugging his hand from my arm I lose my temper.

"So because of what I have been through I get to have a free concert ticket, is that it?" I ask, then because I am so cross I continue, "I am not a charity case thank you very much, and poor Angie is fine, you can tell that to the charity commission who decided I should have the ticket, thanks."

I storm through the door without looking back. I stomp to my desk, I sit there fuming, hating Marcia, Helen, Mike and everyone else, no one questions my mood, they have seen me in a temper before and although it doesn't happen very often it is generally known to keep away, for which I am grateful, it doesn't normally take me long to get over any upset, but I know I am more upset because it involves Mike. Now I have paid the money back I am glad, I will be okay, I just need to calm down and I will be fine. Even Phil doesn't come and see me, but chooses to send a text instead, he sends just a kiss.

It is something very minor that has me back in a good mood, I lose myself in the logs on the system, allocating officers, and generally keeping busy, it goes quiet so we take advantage and we take a break and sit just chatting to each other. Max and Gavin are having some kind of debate, I am not sure what about, so I listen for a few minutes.

Gavin calls to me, "You have got Sky TV at home, haven't you, Angie?" I nod my head. "How much is your package a month?" he asks, I frown.

"I honestly don't know, Gavin, honest I have no idea, I pay by direct debit." He looks at his magazine.

"Do you have all the sports channels?" he asks.

I nod my head, "Yes, I think I do, Jason had them all, he changed the package a few times so I am not sure what I pay for, I guess I need to check, why do you ask?" He holds up his magazine.

"There is a special here but it is for new customers only, really good deal, you don't know anyone who wants Sky, if you introduce them you get some store vouchers and they get free installation."

I walk over to him, I read the advert, I hear the door bang behind me but I take no notice. I look at Gavin, an idea is forming in my head, my bad mood totally gone. "You are a bloody genius." I lean forward and kiss his forehead, he looks at me in surprise, Craig laughs.

"What's going on, Angie, free kisses for everyone" he asks laughing, and scrunching his lips up hopefully, I look up to reply and there is Mike stood leaning on the cupboard next to Craig, I walk over to Craig but turn, to face Gavin so they can both hear.

"Jason's dad, my father-in-law, well he adores our television, he used to find any excuse to come around and watch the world news and the discovery channel, I have been thinking what I can get them for a nice gift for Christmas, I wanted to get them something special, a bit different, but all I came up with was a hamper, but this, well, this is brilliant, I know that he will love it. He only has the very basic channels, he will absolutely love it," I pause, "I cannot wait to tell Sean, he will be made up." I turn to Gavin. "You are officially my favourite person and a bloody genius."

I blow him a kiss and return to my seat, my mood has totally changed, I cannot wait to set the wheels in motion. I type out a quick text to Sean. Craig looks over.

"Not using your mobile phone over there are you?" he chastises me good-naturedly.

"As if," I reply. I smile at him, Mike has now sat down beside Craig, they speak in quiet voices, I have no idea what they are talking about, I don't care really. I cannot wait to get Pa's gift sorted. Suddenly everything is right in the world.

Helen comes in whilst Mike is still sat there, she calls out to everyone, "We are having a pizza night on the last day shift if anyone is interested."

I am taking a call but give her a thumbs up, I watch as she moves around the room taking notes of names then wanders over to the main control desk to Craig and Mike, she spends a few minutes chatting, then when I am off the phone she comes over to me.

"Should be a good night, so far there are at least fifteen of us going." she shows me the list, she smiles.

"Where are you going to book?" I ask, I love pizza and any Italian food so I am not bothered where, she holds a menu out.

"Pizza casa on the high street," she replies, my heart sinks, I just knew she was going to say that particular restaurant, I lift my head to call to her but before I can say anything she is distracted by Gavin calling her over, she waves the menu at me. "I will get a pre order before so there is not a huge wait okay." she smiles and walks over to Gavin, but I know I won't be going, it is too soon for me to go. That was the restaurant where Jason was taken poorly and taken away by ambulance, I can still see him laid on the cold tarmac in the car park, the light rain falling on his motionless body. She hasn't realised, maybe she doesn't even know, but I don't want to return there, not now, not in the immediate future.

She leaves the control room and Gavin comes over. "Should be a good night, they have karaoke in there, I fancy myself as a bit of a Tom Jones," he laughs and wiggles his hips, I laugh with him.

Steve chips in, "I have heard the food is good too, I am definitely going, I do a mean Neil Diamond."

I listen to them both as they discuss pizzas and Italian food, Craig and Mike join in the conversation, I ignore them and just flick through the logs, I will make some excuse before I am asked to place my order, but I know that I just don't want to go to that place, it is just too soon for me.

Phil comes in looking for Helen, Steve calls out to him, "You going for the pizza night then, Phil?" I watch as Phil laughs and pats his stomach.

"Oh yes, just need to check with Mike something first, not sure if it clashes with the rugby thing he has roped me in for." I laugh out loud and he looks at me. "What?" he asks, he frowns and comes over.

"You playing rugby, I don't think so," I scoff at him, but he shrugs.

"No, you cheeky mare, I won't be playing, he needs someone to help put all the equipment away with him. It is heavy stuff and the chap that normally does it is on holiday that week, so they need my muscles." He flexes his arms to show me his muscles, I laugh at him he heads to Mike.

"I need to check if I am still needed, then he can pay for my pizza as wages."

He laughs out loud again as Mike replies, "I don't think that was part of the deal." Mike sits on the desk next to Craig. "And I probably couldn't afford the amount of pizza you can put away," he laughs and Phil joins him.

Phil wanders over and sits by me. "You are coming, aren't you?" he asks, I smile at him.

"Maybe." He frowns at me.

"Why only maybe?" he asks.

I shake my head. "I need to check if I am doing something else first, I will let Helen know." Phil stands up.

"You okay?" he asks, I smile brightly at him.

"Yes, I am fine, honestly, I am okay." He frowns again, he leans one arm on the back of the chair.

"No, you are not, there is something on your mind, come on," he chides, "out with it." I look at him, he is leaning right down, I look behind, there is Mike stood waiting for him.

"You have to go." I nod my head in Mike's direction, "But, Phil, I am okay, really I am." He stands up, musses my hair.

"I can tell there is something, regardless of what you say, we will talk later okay." I smile at him.

"Okay."

He follows Mike out of the control room and I give out a huge sigh. Why is everything so complicated? I look at the time, my rest break, I sit in the television lounge, it is empty so I call Judy, I explain about the restaurant and I am relieved when she says she totally understands. "I wouldn't want to go back there so soon," she replies, "don't worry, you can say you are coming to mine for some reason," she pauses, "in fact, I think that is the night I have Harry's parent teachers evening you could come and sit with Juliet for me if you wouldn't mind, that would be great and a good excuse."

I sigh, "Judy, you are a star, that is great, thanks." I note the details in my diary, chat to her a little while longer then say goodbye, I flick the television on and spend the rest of my break just relaxing.

I have my flight details all sorted for Spain already, part of the reason I wanted to go was that I didn't relish the thought of being pulled by different people to spend Christmas with them, this way no one is offended. Jason and I only had one Christmas together and he was a nightmare, he just wanted to watch old films on the television and then disappeared to his parents without even telling me where he was going, I was so upset, then he came back with some gifts for me from his parents and made lame excuses. I was furious for days and so this year it will be totally different, Christmas with my family will be wonderful, a whole week in Spain with my mum fussing will be great, spending time with my dad and my sister and the children will be so easy, we won't have to do much as my mum loves Christmas and she will not allow us to do anything that might sabotage any part of the festivities. We can all be very lazy and chill out by the pool, it might be a bit too cold to go in but we have been lucky in previous years. My brother Scott may join us if he can get the time off and if he can get the flights at a reasonable price, but Stuart will have to make do with a rowdy Skype call on Christmas Day. I have bought all my gifts and have been super organised. I will miss the shift Christmas party but that cannot be helped, I have been to plenty in my time to know that someone will always get drunk and behave inappropriately and I could probably win if I placed bets on who it would be. My last shift will be the day before Christmas Eve and the party is Christmas Eve so well timed. Sean is delighted with the Sky idea for his dad he wants to go halves, which I am not overly happy with but I give in, we go and tell him together, he is made up, so excited and the best news is Sean has managed to wangle early installation as there was a cancellation we have managed to get it installed before Christmas. The icing on the cake is that by reducing my package and taking out all the movie and sports channels that Jason added to my package when he moved in, the bill per month is less for both mine and his dads than what it was for just mine, and I get some kind of vouchers as a reward, I am so pleased.

The pizza night is in just a few days' time, Helen was not overly happy when I told her I was not able to make it, I could tell by the look on her face, but she accepts my excuse without questioning it, and surprisingly so does everyone else. I thought I would get a hard time from Phil, but it is Craig that causes a fuss. I am making a drink for everyone when he walks up the stairs and hovers in the doorway leaning on the door frame.

"What time does the parent teachers thing finish?" he asks, I shrug.

"Not sure really, Judy didn't say." He frowns.

"You could come afterwards couldn't you, the table isn't booked until seven thirty, you could still make it, just come later."

I shake my head. "No it is okay, I am fine, I want to catch up with Judy anyway." I keep my voice light, he shakes his head, I know he suspects something but he just isn't certain what.

"Surely you will have plenty of time to catch with her on holiday," he pauses then continues, "if I know you two you will be sick of the sight of each other by the end of the holiday, and also," he pauses "who has a parents evening just before Christmas." I turn to face him.

"Craig, can you just drop it please, it is not a big deal okay, I cannot go, that is the end of it, I have another commitment, my life doesn't begin and end here okay. I have told Helen, she is cool about it, I told her maybe next time."

He just stands looking at me, I can tell he knows there is something else, but I turn away and busy myself putting the cups on the tray, I do not look at him. Eventually he gets the hint and disappears, I am really not that bothered about missing the night out. As I go back into the control room the conversation stops, I look at Craig and he looks at me guiltily, I know he has been talking about me, I don't know why it means so much to him that I go, I ignore him looking at me, I don't look at him as I place his tea down in front of him and head back to my desk, I am reading through the logs when I look up, Steve and Craig are stood at the main console, they are not really whispering but chatting quietly, Steve looks over to me.

"I can pick you up from Judy's if you want," he calls out, "I am getting there a bit later too."

I clench my fists, why is nothing ever easy, why do I have to justify not going, why don't they accept I am not going. To make matters worse, I look up and there is Mike and Helen walking in, bloody hell I think to myself, have they never got any jobs to attend, why are they always here. The phone rings and I hit the button to accept it, I watch as they both walk over to Craig, Mike stands but leans on the cupboard and listens as Craig is speaking, he looks over quickly and gives the game away. I just know they are talking about me, but I don't care, I am not going to that restaurant, I don't want to. I check the logs, it shows both Mike and Helen as waiting for custody to call them so I cannot even send them to a job, I give out a big sigh. I listen to my caller, it isn't urgent, so I take the details of the call and create a new incident, it needs to be attended tomorrow, so I print off the details and walk the short distance to the admin room to add it to the diary, I am busy entering all the details into the calendar when I look up and Mike is stood there, he smiles.

"Just one question and the subject will be closed, I promise," he says, I look at him and frown.

"Okay," I say. I shrug, I have no idea what he is referring to, he leans on the cabinet, he speaks quietly.

"No one understands why you cannot come to the pizza night after you have finished babysitting, but I think I know."

I look at him, titling my head on one side, he really is very good looking, I could lose myself in his dark eyes, I raise my eyebrows at him but say nothing, I don't need to as he carries on.

"It is because they don't know what happened the last time you were at that restaurant do they, and even Phil hasn't managed to put two and two together has he," he pauses, "I am right aren't I?"

I give him a weak smile, I nod, "Yes, I guess you are, it might seem silly to anyone if they knew, and Mike" I look up at him "I don't want to make a big issue out of it, I really don't, I am just not ready to go back to that place, but I would rather no one else knew the real reason if you don't mind," I pause, "honestly, I really don't need a pizza that much." I look up at him, he smiles.

"But if the venue was to say, change at last minute."

I interrupt him putting my hand up to stop him. "No, honestly, please don't, there really is no need, everyone is creating a fuss and there is no need, I am fine. As I said I can exist without a pizza that night, really I can."

He laughs gently, "I have heard some bad reports about that restaurant," he laughs again, "maybe I might mention it to Helen."

I shake my head. "No, please don't, Mike, it is fine honestly, you will have a good evening, I am sure you will."

He smiles again, that lovely, twinkly eyed smile. "Ah but not a great one."

My stomach does a somersault as he walks off back into the control room. I continue with the admin tasks and head back into the control room, both Helen and Mike have disappeared, I sit back down and shake my head what a lot of fuss about nothing. I look at the logs, there has been an incident with their prisoner and they are both shown as attending custody, I give out a sigh of relief, hopefully the subject will now be closed.

No such luck, it doesn't take long for all the plans to be changed, suddenly it seems everyone has heard bad reports about the service at the restaurant, the poor unknowing proprietor has lost custom through no fault of his own as the venue is changed to another local restaurant, everything is sorted out without me really being involved. Steve is picking me up from Judy's so I can go, it all seems so much of a fuss but no one has managed to associate the change with me except for Mike. Craig is happy – I can tell by the look on his face, he gives me a smile as he listens to Steve making the arrangements to pick me up.

Actually the more I think about it the more I am looking forward to going. I dress casually in jeans and a blue shirt, then I drive over to Judy's. Juliette is very pleased to see me, she brings all her books and toys downstairs, looks like I am going to be kept very busy. Judy and I manage to have a quick catch up before she heads off for the school and I spend a very pleasant hour or so playing with Juliet.

When Steve picks me up we chat light-heartedly all the way, we don't arrive that late but when we do arrive at the restaurant everyone is already there. There are two spare places and I just smile as I see one is between Phil and Mike, deliberately I choose the other seat which is at the end of the table, but I am outsmarted as Phil shouts to me over the noise.

"You have to sit here by me, you are sharing your garlic bread with Mike."

I look at him and shake my head. "Thanks anyway, you can pass it down to me," I call back.

I cannot do it, I cannot sit that close to Mike all evening, I don't know why but he makes my heart thump hard in my chest when he is near to me, and when he looks at me with those beautiful dark eyes I cannot help but want to just drown in them.

I take my seat at the other end, Helen is sat in the middle and we call out to each other, everyone is chilling out, I look around at the smiling faces, we have such a good time, everyone is happy and relaxed, I do glance down the other end of the table and they seem to be having good time too. As the main course arrives I walk to the other end of the table to get my share of the garlic bread. As Mike hands it to me, our hands touch and I look at him, I am so glad that I am not sat by him as he doesn't break my look, we stand there just staring at each other.

"Garlic bread is going cold," Steve laughs and interrupts us, I snatch my hand away and pull a face as both he and Mike laugh out loud. My cheeks burn as I walk back to my seat, I shoot a look at Steve but he is totally unaware of my discomfort. I look at Mike, he winks then smiles at me, my stomach does a flip. I look the other way quickly, that man is far too good-looking and he just doesn't know the effect he has on me.

After a huge fiasco over the bill where we have the usual debate over who owes for what, I look down to Mike, I wave and finally manage to catch his eye.

"I have paid for garlic bread okay," he nods, "looks like I owe you then." He smiles and I cannot help but blush as I shake my head; I wonder if he knows how much I like him.

Eventually the bill is sorted out and paid, the evening comes to an end, I wait for Steve to finish chatting, he is giving me a lift home. As we leave the restaurant I link my arm through his, we walk the short distance to the car park chatting about nothing in particular, Steve looks back as his name is called out there is Gavin and Mike walking towards us.

"Any chance of a lift, the others are going on to a club," Gavin calls.

Steve shouts back, "Yes, no worries, but she stinks of garlic," he adds laughing."

I cringe inwardly, I have managed to keep away from Mike all night except for the garlic bread incident, I have done really well, now I have to sit in a car with him, I don't think my poor heart can cope. I watch as they walk towards us, he is so handsome, wearing a blue round neck jumper and jeans, so casual yet he still seems to have an effect on me. As we all walk to the car, my arm still in Steve's I listen to them chatting about the meal and the night, Steve looks back at them behind us.

"What are you doing on your few days off then, Mike?" he asks.

Mike looks at his watch and groans, "Well, in about six hours' time I am off on a stag break to Amsterdam."

Steve laughs, "Amsterdam." He looks at Gavin, then laughs, "Didn't you have a bad experience in Amsterdam and wasn't that on a stag night?" Mike pulls a face, we are at the car now.

"Don't remind me, it was a nightmare, I got so drunk I slipped under the table in the first bar we went in and they didn't find me until the bar opened up the next lunchtime, the owner had locked up and gone and didn't even know I was there," he pauses, "how did you know that?"

Steve laughs, "It was Craig's stag night, he told us."

Mike laughs, "Ah yes, of course it was, and this time it is one of the rugby guys, those guys can seriously drink, I can barely walk after just a few pints, I am really regretting saying I would go. Luckily my brother is going too so we can look out for each other," he laughs again, "hopefully," the guys all laugh but I don't speak.

I am not sure I trust my voice not to come out in a little squeak, he seems to make me tongue-tied whenever he is around. Gavin and I sit in the back as Mike is so tall. As I stand waiting for Gavin to get in Mike leans on the door.

"Didn't want to sit by me then?" he asks.

I blush and before I can say anything Steve answers for me, "She couldn't trust herself to keep her hands off you could you, Angie," he laughs and Mike looks at me.

"Missed opportunity for me then," he says quietly, then a bit louder he says, "it was okay though as I had Steve's good looks and sparkling company, didn't I Steve," they both laugh.

Mike places his hand on my head guiding me in so I don't knock myself, I sit in the back quietly, taking in his words, I am not sure if he is teasing me or not. Gavin keeps nudging me and nodding his head towards Mike, who is looking at something on his phone, I frown but say nothing. Steve pulls out into the busy traffic, he glances in the mirror at me and smiles.

"So you seeing anyone then, Mike?" he asks. I shake my head at him and roll my eyes, Mike looks at Steve and gives a short laugh.

"Are you chatting me up, Steve?" he asks, they both laugh but Steve is not to be outdone.

"No, I just wondered that is all, I thought there was a rumour going round about you and some blonde bird." He smiles into the mirror again and I feel my cheeks reddening.

Mike laughs again. "And just where would that rumour come from then?" he asks, this time Steve laughs with him but Mike continues, "No, Steve, I am not seeing anyone, but if you know of any interested women tell them they can apply in person," he gives a laugh, "just here will do, mate, thanks," he indicates a cut in by a bus stop, he leans in and kisses my cheek then shakes Gavin's hand. "See you on late shift, have a good few days off." He closes the door, Steve puts the window down.

"Before you cop off with any birds, check for an Adam's apple!" he shouts. Mike looks back and laughs, I look around.

"Where does he live?" I ask casually, Steve points to an alley.

"Just through there, there is a cut through to the new housing estate, very nice, very posh, so I have heard." He pulls off.

Gavin speaks up, "He is a really decent chap you know, never hear a bad word about him." Steve nods. "Surprising he is single really." he continues, Gavin smiles at me, but I make no comment. Within minutes we are outside my house. I kiss them both good night, they both wince and comment on my garlic breath but I kiss them even more, they wait until I am inside before they drive off. I sit with a coffee and think about the night. I like Mike, I really like him, I wonder if he is seeing anyone. I go up to bed, I lay there and cannot get his face out of my head, my mind drifts back to when he held my hand over the garlic bread, my heart beats just a little bit faster.

Back to work and it seems like I have hardly had any time to myself, there are lots of CID incidents going on so lots of statements to be typed up, I am sat in the CID office on my own just typing them up when I notice

Mike walking towards me, I haven't seen him since the pizza night out, I smile as he gets closer.

"Good stag weekend?" I ask him, he smiles.

"I survived, that was the main thing." He stands at the side of me, "And I haven't forgotten I still owe you for the garlic bread," he says tilting his head as he looks at me.

I shake my head. "No you don't it is okay, please don't worry." But he leans down and places an envelope in front of me, I recognise it immediately as the one I gave him with the concert money inside, it has not been opened.

"Oh no," he says narrowing his eyes at me, "I am not a charity case either and I absolutely insist." He places the envelope on the desk next to me and turns to walk off, he calls back to me, "And I won't take no for an answer no matter how cross you get." Then he turns and smiles, winks and walks off. I watch him as he sits at his desk and he looks up and smiles again. This time I smile back at him. He really is far too good-looking. I give a sigh and put the envelope in my bag, it is obvious he considers the subject closed and I have lost that argument.

Christmas is an exhausting time, it is not a great time for the police officers and the control room: the jobs come in thick and fast, the bad weather doesn't help. Every shift the police officers are run off their feet going from job to job, I am on the late shift with just one more to go before I break up for my holiday with my parents. I was very busy getting everything done on my days off so now the case is packed and I am ready to go, we hardly see any officers as they are kept so busy but as normal I have to go down to CID for an hour or so tonight but first I take my break in the rest room. There is little on the television and there are a few of the shift in there, I take the only seat left by the window and listen to the discussion going on, they are watching some kind of documentary about people with ailments they are too embarrassed to go to the GP about, so they go on television in front of an audience of millions to discuss intimate details. The lads are loving it, there is a man with erectile problems and suddenly the subject turns to sex, of course it does, the room is full of male testosterone, firstly they try to give Mike a grilling about Amsterdam, they tease him about drinking under the table but he just smiles and says nothing, no matter how much they try he will not tell them anything about the trip. After a few minutes they change the subject and I listen as they are talking about their own sexual conquests and the age of their first one. I notice Mike is joining in on the laughter and I am shocked to hear that some of them started as young as thirteen. Phil is in a very cheeky mood and asks me what age I was, even though we have discussed this before and he knows the answer, before I realise what I have said the words are out of my mouth.

"You know full well when it was, Phil, and I am not going to be drawn into your childish games, get your cheap thrills somewhere else." I sound cross but I laugh to show there is no hard feelings.

"Okay so you won't tell us that so tell us who your first love was then," Robin another police officer chips in.

"No, I won't, just leave me alone," I say good-naturedly, "my love life can be summed up in one word..."

Simon interrupts me, "And what is that word then – Phil," and he laughs and everyone else joins in.

"Hey enough," Phil speaks up, then a little harsher, "enough." Phil and Simon stare at each other but Simon is not scared or intimidated by Phil.

"No hold on, Phil," Simon continues, "how would you know her first, when and where, if you were not there?" Phil shoots him a look.

"Yeah, yeah, very funny, enough I said." Simon turns his head to the others sat there.

"OOOhhhh," he says sarcastically, "hit a nerve there, guys," he laughs out loud, others join him. I cannot help it, I colour up, I don't like that Phil has defended me, it makes it seem like we are a couple.

I have made it worse by my comment to Phil, I have to make it better, so I pipe up and I don't know what made me say it but before I know it the words are out of my mouth I have said, "well, Simon, thank you for your kind concern but I can sort my own love life out thank you, without Phil's help. Phil was not my first sexual encounter neither was he my first love, so I hope that clarifies that for you, and as for my love life, well as it happens I have a date set up so my love life is getting back on track, thank you for asking." I smile at them all and then open my lunchbox and pull out a sandwich. Whilst picking up my phone with my other hand I send a quick text to Marcia that she needs to set me up with her single vet friend that she has been harping on about for ages, desperate to get the two of us to meet, and she needs to do it soon. I look around the room, Simon is laughing and winks at me as he reaches for the remote control.

"Glad to hear it love, glad to hear it."

Mike is staring at me and Phil looks at me questioning, "Since when?" he asks quietly, I look straight back at him.

"Since Marcia arranged it," I reply.

I hate lying to Phil but I don't want to lose face now, I know it is far too soon for me to be dating, and if it wasn't for his stupid comment I wouldn't have got myself into this mess. My text bleeps and Marcia has responded, tomorrow night, I shake my head, bugger that was quick.

"When is it then?" Phil asks.

"Tomorrow night," I respond, "it is a late drink after I finish." Phil nods his head.

"Where are you going?"

His eyes are staring at me, he has this look on his face, I can see he is trying to keep his temper, he is clenching and unclenching his fists a clear sign he is annoyed. I take a bite of my sandwich and smile at him, chewing slowly before I reply.

"I don't know yet, Phil, don't you worry, I am a big girl, I will be okay." Phil stands and walks towards the door.

"Angie," he motions with his head, "have you got a minute?"

Oh Christ, I think as I stand up, here goes the interrogation. I put my lunch box on the table and my telephone in my handbag, I place my jumper on my chair.

As I walk towards the door Simon cannot resist the final remark, "Oh dear, seems the green-eyed monster is showing its face there, you be careful, Angie." His tone changes to sarcasm. "But hey what am I saying, you should be safe he only goes after married women."

As I walk towards the door I hear the officer sat next to Simon comment, "Below the belt that one, mate, below the belt." I don't hear Simon's reply.

Phil has a face on him and I know he is going to be cross, so before he can start I jump in first. We stand halfway down the corridor, he leans against the wall and looks at me folding his arms, I turn to him.

"Look, Phil, I know you are cross so you can take the look off your face. I have to come clean and tell you that I had made up the date, then I text Marcia quickly as she has been going on about her friend Adam, she text back that he would like to meet me and I have decided that I am going." His brow furrows.

"What the hell does she think she is doing setting you up on a date?" His voice is low and controlled, I can tell he is cross, so I try to placate him I hold out my hand and place it on his arm.

"Phil, I am a big girl I will be okay. He is a vet, a professional man and he knows Marcia and he is single, where is the harm?"

Before he can respond the door of the rest room opens and Simon comes out I snatch my hand away from Phil's arm.

"Oops, sorry to interrupt your domestic, Angie, if you need any help, just shout okay." Then he pushes between us.

"Fuck off," Phil calls after him. Simon stops and turns, his face is set hard, his voice is aggressive.

"You got a problem?" he addresses Phil and moves closer.

"You and your mouth has the problem not me," Phil returns the remark with equal tone. They stand within feet of each other, squaring up to each other, I don't know what to do, I just stand there pathetically, they are both large chaps, they match each other in height and size, the situation would be laughable if both of them didn't look so serious. The door opens and Mike is stood there, he is not smiling, he looks at both of them.

"At ease, boys, on your way now," he says to both of them. "Angie, your phone is ringing in there, you might want to get it," Mike addresses me directly, Phil just stands there, he is now leaning back against the wall and we watch as Simon walks down the corridor, I look at Phil, but he doesn't look at me, I know he is angry and upset with me, I shrug and walk back into the restroom. Mike follows Simon and they both disappear down the corridor.

I know I have not got off lightly, Mike might have diffused the situation but he was just delaying the inevitable. At the end of the shift, I get home and start packing the final items for my holiday and I make myself tea and toast. I sit watching television for a while and I think about the date and in a way I am quite looking forward to it. I pick out an outfit of jeans and a casual light denim shirt and boots, teamed up with a warm jacket and I put them on the bed ready for tomorrow, I am going to shower at work, take my lunch break at the end and meet him for nine o'clock, lots of us do this if we have something going on, and I am pleased that Craig has agreed the change. Marcia calls and we chat for a while, she tells me a bit more about Adam, she says he is adorable and really interesting, then she says Phil had told her he wanted to speak to her but she managed to avoid him until the end of the shift. I warn her what it will be about but she is not afraid of Phil, she says she will be happy to tell him what she thinks, she tells me she will be in the police bar after her shift tomorrow so if I want to pop in and see her after the date she wants to hear all about it. I hear the key in the front door and say a quick goodbye to Marcia, I know who it is going to be, I wish he would ring the doorbell sometimes.

Sean has given his key back but as yet Phil hasn't, I wanted to broach the subject several times but the right time has never arrived. As he comes into the lounge I can see by his face that Phil is not happy, I am not sure what he is more cross about, the squaring up to Simon, the being told off by Mike or my blind date. He comes in, removes his shoes and without saying a word to me he sits on the sofa and flicks through the TV listings using the remote control, he watches the television for a few minutes before saying, "I wish you would tell me these things without me having to hear them with everyone else, you made me look a fool." Phil looks at me, there are so many things I want to say, but I don't want to hurt him, so I clear my throat.

"Phil." He looks at me, I go to speak but he interrupts.

"I think it is too soon, I think you are making a big mistake, you should cancel it." His voice is low and calm, he is cracking his knuckles, I hate it when he does that.

I argue back, "No, I don't agree," I retort back, "it is one date, and then I am off on holiday, and I am quite looking forward to it now."

"Well," Phils says resignedly, he concentrates on the television, "if your mind is made up, I guess there is nothing else I can say." He reaches over and bites half of my toast, speaking with his mouth full he continues, "I just worry about you getting hurt, you know, I don't want you rushing in to things and making the same mistake twice, I want you to marry for love the next time."

I look at him with a start, "Bloody hell, Phil, calm down, this is one date, a one-off, no one is mentioning marriage, and I promise you, if anyone ever mentions to me ever again about a surprise weekend away, you can be one hundred per cent sure I will be travelling in the other direction."

I see a smile on his face and I go and sit by him, he puts his arm around me and we cuddle up and to my surprise he speaks about the wedding, my wedding. "I will never forget the look on your face," he speaks slowly, "or the words you said to me after the ceremony, they cut right through me, Angie, no one has ever hurt me as much as you did that day, and I will never ever settle with anyone until I know you are happily settled, you know, the complete package." His eyes looks straight into mine, I know he is serious.

"Phil, please don't say that," I implore him, "and please don't waste your life with someone else's wife, find that special someone of your own."

Phil's jaw is set. "Never," he says, "until you look me in the eye and tell me you have met the man of your dreams and I am forgiven."

I interrupt, "Please, Phil, don't say that, it is okay, I have forgiven you, truly I have." Phil looks at me, his eyes cold.

"You might have forgiven me, Angie, but I have not forgiven myself, you have yet to meet the man of your dreams, so the debt is still there." The word debt makes my heart freeze, I watch Phil as he takes the last bite of my toast.

"Subject closed." He finishes off my tea and I watch him. "So?" I ask tentatively, "Are you going to vet all potential suitors, no pun intended."

He smiles. "No, just the serious ones, the ones that make it to a second date." He pulls me closer to him and we snuggle up to watch the film that has just started.

The last late shift goes quickly and I am showered and in my car on time, everyone has wished me well for my holiday tomorrow and Marcia has text to say Adam is looking forward to meeting me. I am nervous but excited, despite everyone knowing about the blind date I am not that bothered, in fact I am a bit excited if I am honest, I take all the comments with a smile, I am really looking forward to it. I shout a cheery goodbye to the shift and head out to my car, I turn as I hear my name being called, Craig strides over to me.

"Okay I don't want to come over as big brother or father figure, but be careful and just send me a quick text at eleven to let me know you are okay, yeah?" I look at him and smile.

"Yes, Dad." I smile at him and he puts him arm around my shoulder.

"And have a good holiday too, be good won't you." I smile at him.

"Yes, Dad."

I get into my car and watch as he waves and walks back in, I really like that he cares about me. I hear nothing from Phil I am not sure if I am surprised or not, the shift has not been particularly busy but hardly any of them have been up and even more surprisingly we haven't seen Mike at all. I pull up outside the wine bar and am pleased to see he is waiting outside, I know it is him as he has on a green sports jacket and brown jeans as Marcia told me he would be. He is very polite, he kisses my cheek when I get to him and we go inside, I order a soft drink as I am driving and we head towards the huge leather couches to sit down. I sit and study him as he speaks. He is the same height as me which I find quite amusing as I am only short, his hair is the same dark brown as mine, worn short with a slight fringe, he has a round boyish face with small steel-framed glasses, he is wearing a light brown checked shirt with his dark brown jeans and brown suede shoes, he is casual but smart. He looks older than I know he is, the only surprise is that he has a gold signet ring on his little finger, which he holds aloft when he drinks. I cannot help but watch as he is very demonstrative, using his hands to describe things. He makes his stories come alive.

He makes me laugh with stories of chasing a half anaesthetised cat around the surgery. I look around; it is a new wine bar, very classy, very smart, with waiters serving at the table, no queuing at the bar. Adam is really interesting to listen to, I don't get to speak much as he tells me about an assignment he is working on – he will be going to Africa for a month in January to look at a zoo exchange programme, something he has been looking to be involved in for a long while. He is passionate about his work, he is obviously very excited and I am a genuinely interested audience, so much so that I don't realise the time has gone quite quickly. He asks me what sort of things I like to do when I am not working, I take a drink from my glass but as I am about to reply his mobile phone interrupts the conversation, he says he quickly needs to take the call as it is urgent. He listens for a short while, then confirms it is his practice and he needs to go in to tend to a dog hit in a road traffic accident. As he sits back down, he leans over towards me, I don't know why, but I totally misread the situation, for some reason I think he is going to kiss me, I don't want him to, so stupidly I panic, I want to divert him away, everything seems to happen in slow motion. I reach down very quickly to the table for my drink and as I am coming up I bang my head on his nose very hard. I am mortified, he shouts out in pain, immediately blood streams down his face, I am so embarrassed, there is blood everywhere, he is trying to hold his head back to stop the flow, I beckon the waitress, but she doesn't see me so I have to shout which attracts more attention before she comes over and I am able to ask for ice and napkins. I am blushing crimson red now, I think he is too. There is blood on his shirt, on his face, he grabs the napkins and holds them to his face and holding his head up as high as he can he makes for the door, I follow him apologising profusely.

The waitress calls me and is holding the bill for the drinks, I apologise again, I scrabble around in my handbag, frantically searching amongst all the rubbish in there and after putting most of the contents on the bar top I finally find my purse, I have nothing smaller so I hand her a twenty pound note and when I turn back Adam has totally disappeared. I am mortified, I cannot believe I have headbutted him on the first date, I do not even have his number to check he is okay. I am not sure what car he drives so without waiting for any change I throw everything back in my bag then race towards the door to look around the car park to see if I can see him, there is no sign of a car starting up or moving, no lights, no engine sound, nothing. I am too embarrassed to go back in to get my change so instead I drive the short distance to the police bar, I need Marcia to check he is okay, I cannot believe what has happened, I am mortified, I just hope no one finds out about this, I will be the laughing stock.

No such luck, as I walk into the bar, I immediately look around for Marcia, she is not there, but all the rest of the shift are there, sat around in one big circle, everyone I didn't want to be there is there: Nick, Mike, Phil, Simon, Helen, Steve Craig the whole bloody lot of them and they are all trying to keep a straight face.

"How did the date go?" Steve asks. I hear one of them give a snort of laughter but I ignore it, I slump down in a vacant chair.

Robin pipes up, "Was it busy on the roads, Angie?" he asks, "we heard it was nose to tail traffic," he laughs and this sets everyone else off, I look round at them all.

Steve pipes up again, "Don't be horrible, don't make her the butt of our jokes." Again they set off laughing, I look up as Marcia comes back into the room, she heads straight for me. She has her mobile phone in her hand waggling it at me accusingly.

"Ah, so there you are," she says accusingly, "I have just been speaking to Adam, what have you done," She doesn't wait for me to reply. "I cannot believe you headbutted him, what did he do that was so bad."

I groan out loud, hearing the sniggers around the table, I try to explain how it happened, I try to move the chair to recreate the scene, but this makes everyone roll with laughter. I am mortified, I can feel my cheeks burning with embarrassment.

Helen says, "What if he did want to kiss you, what is wrong with that, after all?" she adds, "I myself think you are extremely kissable." Everyone laughs out loud, Simon immediately picks up on her comment.

"Mm, Helen, do you want to explain how you know Angie is a good kisser," She pokes her tongue out to him.

"That is for us to know and you not to find out," she replies cheekily. Everyone laughs, I am so embarrassed, I look around, Mike is laughing with the others.

"Well," I say slowly I can feel myself going redder and redder. "I got it wrong, but if he was going to then he could have, well he should have warned me, it took me by surprise that's all, we were in the new wine bar there was lots of people about, it was all going well until then, he was a really lovely interesting person."

I look around for someone to back me up, but they are all sniggering, "Yes, he sounds it."

Phil has to put his comments in. "I mean that is generally how you tell someone you like them, you headbutt them, god knows what you would have done if you didn't like him, or worse still, if he wanted sex."

Helen has to join in again. "What does he have to do, make an appointment to kiss you, does he have to carry a placard, send an email, text message and twitter to forewarn you."

She high-fives with Phil and I shoot her a look, but she doesn't care, she laughs out loud with Phil. I look around, there is no one that I can count on to back me up, they are all laughing out loud, I poke my tongue out to them all childishly, then I have no choice, I have to laugh with them. We hear the telltale tone of an incoming text message, Marcia checks her phone and makes things a little better.

"Don't worry, Angie," she says, "he has just text me to say he is okay, nose isn't broken, the dog is going to be okay and he is asking if he can have your number, he wants to call you when he gets back from Africa, he says you are to have a good holiday."

I poke my tongue out again to everyone childishly. "See," I tell them. "My love life is back on track and just fine thank you, I got a second date, and none of you will be invited to the wedding."

Everyone laughs and we spend the next hour chatting about Christmas. There is a good feeling amongst everyone, but I am getting tired so I get up to leave, I have an early flight in the morning, I am feeling very happy and looking forward to the break. The jukebox is playing silly Christmas tunes as I go round giving everyone hugs and kisses, everyone pretends to be scared and tries to dodge my head, but it is all good-natured ribbing and I can take it.

Phil hugs me and says, "Have a great time – give my love to the family, text me to say you arrived safely." He kisses my cheek, I am looking directly at Simon and he raises his eyebrows. I ignore him, I wander out of the bar and head for the stairs. Mike wasn't in the bar when I said my goodbyes, I think he has left already, shame, I didn't get to give him a kiss, I think I might have been brave enough to, but as I turn into the corridor, there he is, at the end of the corridor, stood looking totally gorgeous, a big smile on his face as he looks towards me.

"Merry Christmas," I call out cheerily, "have a great time," I add.

"Hey wait," he calls after me, "don't I get a Christmas kiss?" I laugh out loud and then skip back to him.

"Of course you do."

He scoops me into his arms and kisses me full on the lips, his lips are warm and soft, he moves them gently against mine, his tongue flicking my lip, it is more than just a quick kiss, my heart starts thumping in my chest, but within seconds it is all over. The juke box is playing 'All I want for Christmas is you', *how* apt I think. He lets me go and pulls back still holding me with one arm around my back, we don't move.

"Mmm," he whispers, "I just need to check if Helen was right." He doesn't move away, his lips meet mine again, I close my eyes and lose myself in the kiss, he pulls away and he looks at me we just remain close, then he touches his nose. "Don't worry," he teases, "Helen was right and no broken bones, it's okay it is intact." I smack him playfully and run down the stairs, I am suddenly feeling very joyful.

Chapter Twenty-Five

Nothing can change my mood, the busy roads, the busy airport, the huge queues at check in, nothing, I am happy, I am beaming, I keep playing the kiss back in my memory. He kissed me, not once but twice, his wonderfully soft lips his gently probing tongue stroking my lips, if only for a second it felt wonderful, I wish it could have lasted longer. My heart beats faster when I play the scene back over in my mind time and time again, the way he leaned forward, the delicious smell of his aftershave and in the background the perfect music all I want for Christmas was playing, and it all was over so quickly. My sister just thinks I am excited about the holiday and I am but a warm feeling comes all over me when I think about Mike. It is whilst we are sat on the plane that I think about my friends – I wonder how Ruth is doing, we only send the odd joke email now and I really need to catch up with her, in fact I decide that when I get to Mum's I am going to send an email wishing her a merry Christmas and to arrange to meet up.

Judy is napping on the plane so I fill the time by playing games with the children and before I know it we are beginning our descent. Mum and Dad meet us at the airport. It is sunny, not really hot but enough to not wear a cardigan or coat. It is lovely to be pampered for the week and I do manage to get a bit of a tan. I log on to my emails and send one to Ruth and one to Annabelle, I am surprised to see one from Sean, it is just a two-liner saying have a great holiday and he has heard from the Life Assurance company, nothing to worry about and will catch up when I get back. Christ I had forgotten all about that, I haven't even given Jason a thought, it is as if he was an acquaintance and not my husband, how can I be so callous, so dismissive of him after all he has done to ensure I am provided for. I think about the claim again, I must grab my mum and speak to her about it, she might have come across something like this in her financial career.

Dad looks tired, I forget how old he is and he tries to keep up with the children but retires to his chair quite a lot to have a nap. Scott has come over on his own and spends most of the time on his phone or his iPad, I can tell this makes my sister cross, he lives in his own little world, we don't really know of his friends or partners, but Mum is just happy he is there so doesn't say a word.

She is fussing as normal and I seize my opportunity to get her on her own when the children go for a nap and Judy is having a swim. I walk to the local shops with her. I tell her about the claim and the company's reluctance to pay, she is not happy with the timing either, in her words she said, it was as if Jason knew he was terminally ill before he was told, she tells me the best thing to do is to give them all the details and let them make their own decision, the money, well her advice on that, was what you have never had you never missed, and what would I do with that kind of money. Then the tirade began on how it will attract the wrong sort and how my sister was cheated by a man who lived with her less than twelve months and still she had to pay him fifteen thousand pounds as a settlement, oh no, I thought to myself, not this again, and mum continues, what about Uncle Peter, have I spoke to Uncle Peter.

Uncle Peter is Mum's brother, a lovely man, he works in a solicitors office, he is an office clerk, a fifty something office clerk. He has been there for years and years but he has never progressed from anything more than a clerk. But many years ago, I think Peter was in his twenties, he is in his fifties now, but there he was a young man, there was a famous celebrity couple divorcing, it was a very messy court case and even made it almost daily on the television news, as the lawyer for one party was speaking to the camera crew, Uncle Peter could be seen in the background just inside the shot holding a huge pile of documents, that is all he was doing, he wasn't involved in any way, he didn't speak or even look at the camera, he was stood in shot behind the person being interviewed, but that is all we heard about for so long, it was like he was the celebrity. Now I love my Uncle but my mum basically thinks uncle Peter is the world's authority figure on all things legal: divorce settlements, property, in fact anything remotely linked to the justice system. Though he didn't do my sister any favours, he referred her to a solicitor who charged the earth in fees and then she ended up having to pay a settlement, it is strange the way my mum is so protective over Uncle Peter as she is usually a very intelligent woman.

I wish I had not mentioned anything to mum, all the way home she then goes on about watching out for gold diggers and how her and dad have worked hard to make sure they could help us all financially and how it nearly killed Dad to see what that man did to Judy and if I am not careful I will be caught the same way. She goes on and on about having my head in the clouds and caring too much about love and romance I what I really need is a man who is financially sound and can support me. I argue that I can support myself but the lecture goes on and on, she asks about Phil and when I am non-committal she starts again on how he just needs the right woman to settle him down and why don't I get together with him she asks. I don't bother answering as she gives me no chance she is going on about how she thinks he obviously cares a lot for me and we have a lot in common, she moans on about how him and Judy are never going to get together, on and on it goes, until I start dreaming of the cold and damp of the UK. When we return to the villa, I shake my head at Judy and I sneak off for a bit of peace in my room I make a point of trying to avoid being alone with her for the rest of the time we are there.

The holiday comes to an end and before we know it we are boarding the plane home. Our suitcases are a few kilos heavier and our waistbands a bit tighter, the children have been fabulous fun and I have loved spending time with them. Mum is very emotional at the airport but she has to leave us at the check in and she continues to wave even when we cannot see her any more. It has been a truly lovely time, and despite the lecture from Mum I have enjoyed the rest and relaxation, even better that soon I will be jetting off to Egypt. The flight is once again uneventful; I play with the children and chat with Judy. We have a private taxi which drops Judy off at her house first, I give her a huge hug and promise to ring her before I go. I get home to a huge pile of mail, cards and letters and a lovely wrapped gift from Annabelle, the Christmas tag says 'if you haven't used this by June I want it back', I open it to find the most exquisite cream short lacy negligee with beautiful silk ruffle detail around the top of the low cut neckline and then repeated on the hemline, complete with matching knickers. It is totally gorgeous, I have never owned anything as sexy as this, it is beautiful, I have no idea when I will ever get to wear such a stunning sexy item. It makes my Molton Brown hamper that I sent to her look positively dreary.

Chapter Twenty-Six

The first day back to work in the new year on a day shift is not kind, I am overtired so I end up ignoring the alarm several times. Eventually I get up at 5:00am; I need to be at work for 6:00am so I have a quick shower. I have no real energy or enthusiasm for anything so I look at the pile of mail that keeps calling my name, I really need to plough through it all and get it sorted, so I grab a cup of tea and make a start, sat in my dining room I look out at the frost covering the garden, the lovely cobwebs making patterns across the window, I lose myself for a few minutes in a daze. When I come back from my daydream the mail is still there beckoning me, I pull the paperknife through the envelopes, there are still a few cards addressed to both Jason and I, I should have let people know at the time, but there was so much going on and I know that I really need to reply to them as soon as I can, not sure what the protocol is for that but I am sure a nice letter will be okay, I will ask mum. It is mainly old neighbours of Jason but one of them is his university friend so he will need to be told, I might leave that one to Sean. I write notes on the top of each envelope which should remind me who is going to deal with them. There is no letter from the Assurance Company which surprises me, but the mail has been piled up on my dining table in order of importance so I guess Phil has been in and so Sean might have that one. I must ring him later.

I start writing a list of things I need to do on the back of an old envelope. One of my New Year resolutions is to keep my jobs up-to-date. I plough though the majority of them before I get so fed up that I cannot face anymore, there is still a large pile but I am fast running out of time, I am tired but I finally manage to push myself up the stairs to dress and get ready for work. I cannot get motivated, I sit on the bed putting on my make-up and day dreaming. Eventually I get going and as I drive into work, I am thankful it is quiet and there is not much traffic about.

In a way I am quite looking forward to seeing everyone and also I haven't heard all the stories of what people have got up to. The Christmas party gossip is the best, I received quite a few text messages from various people wishing me happy Christmas but none are telling me anything that is going on, there is nothing exciting, well except that Helen has text me to tell me that Simon and Phil had some kind of altercation where no actual fighting took place but some pushing and shoving did. From what I can make out from her text wording is that Helen pulled Phil away and someone else grabbed Simon, apparently there is no action to be taken as no senior officers were there but I am surprised Phil hasn't text and told me. We are meeting for dinner tonight so I am sure he will fill me in with all the goings on.

As soon as I get in the shift is busy, we each have to take handover from the departing shift as there has been a very busy night shift. Craig is in late today, we listen as Mike explains he will be covering Craig and working between the control room and downstairs, he tells us we need to call him immediately if there are problems or emergencies, he sits and looks at the logs with Steve but although it is busy there is nothing urgent and we work together to clear the logs. It seems strange to see Mike sat in Craig's seat. He comes over to me to challenge why I am sending an officer to a particular job, he kneels down at the side of me and he is so close, I am in controller mode, ready to argue my point, but there is no need, he accepts my reasons, the officer is allocated, he watches me add the details and then stands for a while just at the side of me. I am not sure what he is doing so I just continue working, without a word he walks over to speak to Gavin too about a job, obviously he seems happy we are all working, I watch as he picks up his things, then he calls that he will be back in an hour or so.

It is a good few hours before the staff in the control room actually get to have a chat, by then I am almost bursting with curiosity, but some of them didn't go to the Christmas party. I try to get Max to tell me when we are fixing the printer but he will never engage in gossip, he says it is not his business which makes me even more impatient and curious to know, but he won't budge, he won't say a word. It is Steve I need to wait for, he is involved in an abnormal load which needs to be escorted through our town, he has to concentrate on ensuring the road is kept moving and no traffic builds up, it is an important job and we leave him alone, as it is so busy it is no surprise that no one comes in for a visit as everyone is catching up with jobs.

Craig comes in but gives no indication of why he was late, I don't question him, I am too interested in getting to speak to Steve, and finally he becomes free and immediately he cannot resist teasing me when I ask about the party.

"Ah yes," he smiles, "the party." He looks around making sure everyone is listening before he continues, "You, young lady, have a lot to answer for," he says with a mock stern look on his face, "even when you are not here there are men fighting about you."

"Me," I exclaim, "not guilty, I was not even in the country; I cannot be guilty, besides which it was Phil and Simon fighting wasn't it?"

The others have lost interest, so Steve comes and sits on the desk at the side of me. "It was quite comical to see them both, and yes, they were both pushing each other about, but it was something and nothing really. Simon couldn't resist having a pop at Phil who was being his normal self, it all kicked off because Simon and Nick was speaking about you. Initially he asked where you was, then apparently and I am not sure of the facts so don't quote me but Simon mentioned that he might be interested in asking you out, as you were clearly now available and happy to date, he made some derogatory comment about widows which I will not repeat and I think Phil must have heard and took umbrage at this and had a go, totally provoked I might add," he pauses, raises his eyebrows, "is there something you are not telling us?" Steve asked questioningly.

"No, not at all," I reply quite casually. "Phil is too protective and always has been, I am meeting him tonight so I will hear his side of things I guess."

Craig interrupts, "Come on, Steve, back to it please, those logs won't clear themselves and, Angie, you need to pop to CID for an hour today now might be a good time before it gets too busy okay." I sigh and stand up.

"Catch up later," I say to Steve and call to Craig, "On my way now."

The CID office is empty and so I sit at the desk, there has been nothing left for me to get on but I can see a huge pile of stolen and recovered property that has been labelled up. I sit for a while then I make a cup of tea in the only mug that is clean and sit down to wait for someone to arrive. I pick up a pen and just doodle on the pad, after a few minutes Helen comes in, she calls me down to her end of the office and asks me about my holiday. So I sit down with my mug of tea and brief her a bit, telling her about Mum and Dad and Judy, then we gossip about shift work and everything, everything except the Christmas Party. I try to bring it up but she is deliberately vague, I am not sure why but I do not pursue it. Something has definitely gone on. She mentions Mike's 30th party and I make a note of the date and she explains there is a collection going round, they are getting him a stripper as part of his gift, I hate strippers, I think they are low forms of entertainment and I tell her this, she raises her eyebrows and gives me a look but I don't care, I decide I will get him a gift of my own, and tell her so. I am not sure what, I don't know him very well at all, I might ask Helen for some ideas later but she doesn't seem in the best of moods today, but one thing is sure, I am not wasting money on a stripper. Mike comes in to the office.

"Nice holiday?" he asks casually.

"Yes, lovely thanks, spoilt rotten by my parents and sunshine too, couldn't ask for more." The phone rings and Helen answers it.

"Nick says he will be ten minutes, can you wait?" she asks. I nod yes and she goes back to speaking into the phone, Mike is stood at the side of me, I realise that I have his chair and I go to stand up, but he motions for me to stay where I am.

"No, that is fine, I can see you have already helped yourself to my pen, my chair, my mug, is there anything else of mine you want?"

I can see he is joking, he raises his eyebrows, he looks so sexy, I smile at him, he holds out his hands as if by invitation, his dark eyes are twinkling, my pulse quickens, I struggle to look at him, if only you knew I thought if only you knew. I cannot help it I immediately redden. Mike laughs and wanders out. Helen is off the phone. There is a red velvet pouch on the top of the desk, I stroke the fabric and ask Helen what it is, she shrugs.

"It is Mike's; it is his late uncle's pocket watch, he was left it in the will," she explains. "He died last year and left both the car and the watch to Mike, but the watch doesn't work and he has had so many people look at it and they cannot mend it, it is a shame, he is gutted."

I smile to myself, I know that if that watch can be fixed then there is only one person who can do it, possibly the only person I would trust to fix it. I now know what I am getting him for his birthday. I just need Helen to help me get hold of it for a while. I check to make sure we are still alone and I explain it to her in hushed whispers what my idea is, she thinks it is great and she is really pleased, I only hope he doesn't notice it missing. Helen has a good idea to leave the pouch in place so we just pack the watch up and as I finish at four o'clock I can take it straight to the post office, I feel very excited inside. I sit with Helen for a while longer, she pulls his card out and I sign my name with a few kisses, then she hides it back in the desk, she pulls her chair close to me watching the door.

"It seems everyone is looking forward to the party." she says "nearly everyone I know from here is going, it is just what we all need, a party, a chance to let our hair down and have some fun, all our shift are going, then some from the previous shift, oh and the admin girls are going." I look at her.

"Admin girls?" I challenge, "Do they all know him then?" She smiles.

"Yes, of course they do, he has been here years, he knows most people. In fact, I am sure he went out with one of the admin girls, Dee I think her name is." She pulls her pocket book out and starts writing, I sit trying to digest the information, I look at her.

"Mike went out with someone who works here?" I question, she looks up at me.

"Yes, don't sound so shocked, he is a great-looking bloke, obviously not our type but you cannot deny he is good-looking, he is hardly going to be single for long is he, he is not a monk." I look at her.

"Who is she then, I don't think I know her, are they still going out?" I question, she laughs.

"Mmm you need to be careful there, Angie, sounds like an interrogation to me, one might think you were interested yourself."

I snort at her, "No, I am not, I just thought he was seeing the girl from Phil's engagement that is all, nothing else." She stands up.

"Okay, calm down, I was only joking and yes, I forgot about her, I think Dee was seeing him before her, they only went out on a few dates, not sure why they finished though, maybe he likes to keep his relationships out of work." She drags her bag over her shoulder. "Gotta go, duty calls," she says casually as she walks out.

I sit there for a moment trying to place the girl called Dee, I think she might be the very slim girl, very skinny, but very beautiful with huge eyes, she is very quiet and shy and hardly ever speaks whenever I go in there, but in fairness I always head straight over to speak to Marcia. I cannot believe Mike and Dee would go out together it seems unlikely, I don't know why it would be unlikely, I just don't want to think of him with anyone I feel a pang, and I know it is jealousy.

Day shift finishes and I shower and get ready, Phil is picking me up at seven, I dress casually, jeans and my favourite blue shirt, I look in the mirror and I am happy to see the black lines under my eyes have gone and the tan suits me and I have a healthy look about me. I hear the toot of a car horn signalling he is outside and I grab my handbag and run to the car. Phil looks nice tonight, he has on a blue check shirt and jeans and black boots.

"Twins," he says as I get into the car and we both laugh, I reach over to give him a kiss on the cheek, Judy phones to ask me if she can borrow some of my CDs and I chat with her for a short while, so there is no opportunity to chat to Phil as we drive to a local pub. He goes straight to the bar as I find a table, whilst he orders the drinks I study the menu, I am starving, Phil comes back and sits down, he places both our drinks on the table.

"I ordered our usual." I am about to protest but he interrupts, "I am starving and you take too long, so you have got chicken and I have got a steak, it is what you would have ordered anyway, you would have looked at the menu for ten minutes then had chicken so I thought I would speed up the proceedings."

I nod my head, he is right, it happens every time. He takes his jacket off and places it on the back of his chair then he leans in towards me. "Okay, I know you are dying to know, so here goes, shut up and don't interrupt." I open my mouth and close it again, he takes a swig of his drink and continues, "I am not proud of what happened, so don't give me a hard time." I look at him in surprise but he doesn't look at me, he goes on, "Simon and Nick have had it coming to them for a long time now, they get on my bloody nerves both of them, they were asking for it, they were winding me up and it worked. I am not proud of my behaviour but I had a few beers and they were getting on my case right from the beginning of the night. It was nothing and now everyone has made a big thing of it and I want to just forget it okay?"

"Not really," I reply, "what set it off this time?"

Phil sighs, "Well, everyone thinks it was remarks they made about you but it wasn't, it was," he pauses, "okay well, maybe it was what they said but it was also just a combination of things, they were out of order, you know what it is like. Jo and Julian turned up later than everyone else and she started playing the fool – messing about with me, flirting and she got me going, it didn't help that she was looking really cute and she knew it, but I was a bit drunk, you know how it is." I raise my eyebrows but say nothing he goes on, "Well she is giving it all that." He makes a chattering gesture with his hand. "You know getting me going even more, so I called her bluff, and she called it right back at me, so when Julian was at the bar we nipped out together." He has the grace to look embarrassed at least. "Well there was a patio thing outside, I thought it was private, there was just the two of us but I didn't know everyone could see us in the shadow as the light was on, anyway, she goes straight for me, you know, I wasn't about to complain, I mean, what man would, what I didn't know Julian had got the drinks and then followed us and she was doing the business and he caught us, well he caught her on her knees, her head in my jeans."

"Oh my god," I interrupt him, I clasp my hand to my mouth. "No, really, you wore jeans to the party." I put on my best shocked face, Phil smiles.

"Ha bloody ha, ever the comedian." He takes a swig from his drink, I lean in to him keeping my voice low.

"Seriously what did he do?" Phil shrugs his shoulders.

"Well, he came out and looked at both of us, I didn't see him at first and obviously she didn't either, it took quite a while and the noise of the disco meant we didn't hear the door open, like I said, she didn't realise he was there at first, neither did I. I had my hand on her head you know like you do, just enjoying it, you know encouraging her a bit, you know how it is, then I happened to look up and saw him just stood watching us, I felt sick, honest I did, so I tried to push her head off from me but she didn't notice, she just kept going on, you know," he pauses again, "then he said out loud to her that he wasn't feeling well and was getting a taxi home, he would be out front when she was finished, he walked off slamming the door." Phil takes another swig of his drink, he looks at me. "To be honest I felt like a real heel, she started crying and run after him and I was stood with my pants round my knees on the patio looking a right dickhead."

"Oh, Phil, no." I couldn't help but giggle. "Poor Julian, that poor man, I cannot believe he stood and watched, how he didn't swing for you I will never know," I pause and frown at him. "Hold on." I frown. "How did that make you have a fight with Simon?"

"Well," Phil continued, "as I made myself decent," he laughs, "which took some time, as I pack a mean package, took a while to put the beast away," he laughs at his own joke and I just shake my head. "Well then I walked back in to the main event room; it was obvious that people saw what had happened, they were all stood just staring at me, I didn't know what was going on. Then Nick pointed to the window and I realised they would have seen everything, then Simon made a comment to Nick that I clearly wasn't missing you at all, then he just went on and made some stupid comment about you."

"What comment?" I ask, Phil shakes his head.

"You don't need to know." I lean forward and look him direct in the face.

"I might not need to, Phil, but I want to, please tell me what he said, I am a big girl I can take it."

Phil laughs, "You might have wanted to phrase that differently." I frown at him, Phil gives a huge sigh.

"He said he wondered who was best you or Jo, I just saw red, I don't like him speaking like that about you, not him, not anyone, I am not going to have it, I could have punched him right in the face, but I didn't, I pushed him and he started to have a go but Helen was there and so she pulled me away." He runs his hands over his head. "Good job really as I would have not been able to stop myself, that man really knows how to push my buttons and I would not have been responsible for my actions."

I sigh, "Oh Phil, what a nightmare, Simon is a crude man, you love to wind people up but you are not malicious, I think he is jealous of you, he is not a nice person."

Phil takes a sip of his drink, he pushes the glass away and stares at his drink for a while, I just watch him, I know he wants to say something so I don't say a word, I just give him time, eventually he looks up at me.

"Christ, Angie, I feel such a heel I really do, I mean there was I leaned on a post and my manhood in his wife's mouth, like you said how the fuck he didn't hit me I will never know."

"So," I ask him, "have you learnt your lesson, is it over now between you, are you going to find someone who wants you for you and not someone who scores points against her husband?" Phil at least looks embarrassed, then he smiles, the old Phil smile, he reaches for his pint.

"Hell no I will just have to be more careful in future, she does give good head, really good, honestly, the best." He throws his head back and laughs.

"Phil," I say quietly, "come on, I know you too well, you are too good for cheap second hand wives and quick fumbles in dark offices, you can do better than that I know you can," and I mean it.

Our meals arrive stopping any further conversation, then Phil's phone goes off, it is the batman theme so I know it is Sean calling, he answers it and then mouths, shall I invite him to join us, I nod yes and Phil finishes the conversation.

"He will be here in five minutes, he is looking forward to seeing you."

"Hold on," I say, "you are not getting out of it that easily, tell me why you are being Jack the Lad, why are you behaving this way, it seems ever since Gemma you have flitted from one girl to the next and most of the women you choose belong to someone else, what is going on, come on tell me, I want to know."

Phil puts his knife down and picks up a few chips with his fork, he stops and looks me straight in the face.

"You want to know, you really want to know, then I will tell you, you see the girl I thought I could spend the rest of my life with, well she kind of broke my heart without realising it, I left it too late, she went and got married to my friend, and I never had the chance to tell her how I felt. As I said I left it too late thinking she would always be there, but she wasn't, she was snapped up right under my nose, now I have her as a best friend and wouldn't want it any other way but......" He fills his mouth with chips and chews, he takes a swig of his beer and continues, "I realise now that if we did get together back then maybe it wouldn't have been right, maybe she would have loved me the way she loved her husband, like a brother."

My stomach flips over he looks at me straight in the face, his look is serious. "And I couldn't bear to have a marriage like that, oh and yes, I am talking about you."

My heart is thudding so hard I think it might burst out of my chest, my head was trying to take all the information in. Bloody hell, how can it be that two men who say they loved me have actually no effect on me whatsoever. Two men, who wouldn't hurt me, cheat or lie to me and I feel nothing but friendship towards them. I look at Phil, he is lovely and kind, kind of good-looking in a plain sort of way, humorous and caring, and I feel nothing, but I bet when I do fall headlong into love it will be with a real bad boy who steals my money, sells my belongings and breaks my heart just like they did to Judy. Phil takes another swig of his beer and steals some of my chips.

"You don't mind, do you?" he asks.

"Mind about what?" I reply, still with thoughts racing through my head.

"Both I guess," he says and smiles. "You'll never eat all those chips anyway." He smiles again and helps himself to more from my plate.

"Why did you never say anything to me?" I ask, I fork some chicken to my mouth.

"No point," he replies, "never meant to be, I love you now as I would love a sister and relationships shouldn't be like that, then when you told me at your wedding you would never forgive me. As I have told you before, I decided that until I know you are settled and happy with someone you really love this time, then I would look after you, I will protect you, and I won't settle until I know you are, sad isn't it?"

I feel the tears prick my eyelids, how could I have made him feel so bad, it was my decision to go through with the wedding, no one forced me to say I do, and now he was putting his life on hold for me, it just wasn't fair.

"Oh, Phil," I stroke his cheek, "I was so mean to you wasn't I, I don't know why I said those horrible words to you, you are such a darling sometimes, and a complete git other times, we are a right pair aren't we." And I lean in and gave him a hug, his arms came around me and we stayed in the hug for a few minutes. His solid arms enveloped me and I felt very safe and warm, if only I could love you as a man and not a brother, I think to myself.

"Hey hey, is this a private party or can anyone join in?" Sean arrives at the table, he scoops up some of my chicken into his mouth and before I could object he plants his greasy lips on my forehead and sits down, Phil and I part and sit upright.

"Nah, you can join in," Phil said jovially, "just having a moment with my best girl eh," he smiles at me, then returns to his food, I look down at the remains of mine, good job I wasn't hungry as between the two of them they had nearly polished it off.

Chapter Twenty-Seven

Sean has lots of news to tell us, the Assurance company are still pursuing evidence that will make the claim for life assurance invalid. Sean has given them all the information they need and we are to attend a hearing in few weeks' time, it is all very formal but as we did not know of the existence of the policy before Jason died we should not be called to give any more evidence. Little Ma and Pa have been unable to give any more information than they already had, but the Insurance Company are convinced Jason had a diagnosis by someone several months before he had the episode outside the restaurant. Both Sean and Phil say there is nothing more we can do and we must just sit and wait for the hearing.

Sean is also seeing a new woman, he won't say any details, he has a huge grin on his face, he says they have been out a few times, she is great, wonderful, his whole face lights up when he speaks of her and his text goes off several times and he beams when he reads the messages but doesn't share the content with us. He says he is going to see her tonight and they have so much in common, he is so alive, he says he thinks she went to my school but he won't say her name just says we must know her, we, as in me and Phil, I am intrigued, but no matter how much we push him he won't budge. He says she is everything he wants in a woman and he is besotted, it is lovely to see, and then for some reason Gemma comes into my head, oh no, oh no, what if it is Gemma, what will Phil think.

Very pleased to hear from my dad, he says the watch is an antique and very valuable, he can fix it relatively easy, he was not sure why other watch menders didn't know how to fix it, he goes to explain about the mechanism but it is all lost on me, he passes the phone to mum she says she has not seen him so animated in a long while, she is still sorting out a few customer's accounts so keeps herself busy but Dad has been a bit lost lately, having the watch to fix will give him something to concentrate on and she says he has been locked away in his study all morning. She is now going to see if she can make contact with some of his old customers so he can have an interest like her. I am really pleased, both for my dad and for the watch, only Helen knows about the watch, and I have seen Mike reading John Grisham books and the new one comes out today so I will buy him that and a bottle of red wine and it will be all wrapped up for the party, I am really looking forward to it now. I have a lovely strapless dress in pale grey with soft pleats to the front and a full skirt, I have a matching bolero which will conceal my armband a little bit, I finish this off with silver sandals with a high heel. I still have to wear the remembrance band but I slip that on every day without thinking now. Helen thinks I am silly going late to the party but Marcia is also going later and I am picking her up so it works out great, and I cannot bear strippers, or maybe I cannot bear the thought of seeing Mike with one.

Last day shift tomorrow, and then time off, woohoo, everything is going to plan, the watch has arrived and I have to go and collect it later, and I have lots of girlie things to do at the beautician, then in the evening it is Mike's party, then on the Sunday I am off on holiday. When I finish work today I am going to buy a few last minute purchases and then put everything in my case and get it closed.

The control room is quiet today, there is something going on which we in the control room are not involved in, some of the shift have been taken off the duty so they are not available, we manage to keep up with the jobs coming in but it is now quiet and everyone is talking about the party. Most of those that are going are making an effort and dressing up, everyone gets so sick of uniform, this is a great opportunity to bring out the posh suits and little designer numbers, so it should be a good fun evening. I sit in the CID office typing up statements, I have about an hour to go, the statements are challenging with lots of foreign names so I have to concentrate. Phil comes to sit with me, he is bored and keeps interrupting me, he has not been selected to be involved in the incident so he is sat next to me tapping his pen on the desk, I type the same sentence three times over before I turn to face him.

"Go away," I chide him, "I am busy and you are distracting me." He laughs out loud but doesn't move.

"How much longer do you have to wear this?" he says flicking my remembrance armband. I move my arm out of reach.

"I don't know," I reply, "leave it alone, I forget now that it is even there."

"Well, it is all a bit frayed now and looks a bit sad," he goes on.

"Phil, just let it be will you I will wear it until Little Ma says she wants me to take it off, it is no big problem to me so it shouldn't be to you, have you no work to do?" I question.

"Not really," he replies, "bit bored really. Helen caught a shoplifter earlier, he was a bit of a fighter so I had to give her a hand but she is booking him in and I am waiting to book some property in." He taps his pencil on the desk. "A few of the shift are helping CID out with a search warrant, quite a big job but we weren't selected." He pulls a face.

"What you wearing to the party?" I ask him more to distract him than from me wanting to know, he shrugs.

"Dunno really, shirt and trousers I expect." I smile at him.

"Wow really pushing the boat out, Phil." He hits me with the pencil and I laugh. "Wear the blue, Phil, it brings out the colour in your eyes." I look at him and smile. "Or wear the yellow, it will match your teeth," I laugh and he mimics my laugh then picks up his pencil and hits me on the head with it, I can tell that both of us just want to be out of here and he now says he is coming shopping with me, I might persuade him to come for a pizza too, not that he needs much persuasion for anything food related.

The PA system crackles into life and the voice over the system calls him to custody, he stands up and tucks his shirt into his trousers pulling them up really high on his waist he turns to me, waddling around the room. I giggle out loud and push him away. He is so comical, he always brightens my mood, he slopes off out of the room and mooches off down the corridor.

"Duty calls, see you in an hour out front, don't be late," he calls over his shoulder.

As he walks out, Mike walks in, he has all his body armour on and looks quite formidable, he walks over towards me.

"You got the short straw again?" he asks, I smile at him.

"I don't mind, it is quiet in the control room so it gives us a chance to catch up."

He smiles, I just melt, he is so good-looking and he doesn't know the effect he has on me, he leans over and looks at what I am typing.

"Ah CID statements, you will be kept really busy, and it is going to get busier." I look up at him.

"How did the incident go then?" I ask, but I don't get to hear his reply, Simon walks in, dressed with his stab vest on, he heads for Mike.

"Sorry about that, Mike, are you okay?" he starts, "I thought everyone was out." Mike turns and I look at his face, his smile disappears as he walks up to Simon, pushes his finger to his chest.

"It is no good saying sorry now is it, the damage has been done and you were very lucky."

There is a long pause, I just sit unable to move, I just watch both of them, Mike moves as if to turn away then changes his mind and turns back to Simon, his voice is cold.

"You didn't bloody check did you, you didn't follow the basic rules, you were too full of your own self-importance, you left me and Pete totally exposed in there." They stand face-to-face, Simon is now a beetroot colour, Mike turns away from him again, then turns back. "Let me have a copy of your complete report on my desk by the end of the shift, and make the call to the hospital to check Pete is okay to come out, I don't care how late it is, you can pick him up, it is the least you can do."

Simon nods and walks out, his face still bright red, he hasn't looked at me, I am not sure he has realised I was even sat there. I look back down at my work and type quietly, Mike walks away to the cupboard behind him he turns to face me, his face more relaxed now. "You are off on holiday on Saturday aren't you?" he asks, he is removing his outer clothing whilst speaking to me.

As he pulls his jumper over his head his shirt rises too and I get a glimpse of his back and his lower torso. He is beautifully tanned and very well-toned, his stomach is flat like a washboard and he has dark hair from his navel going down, I cannot help but stare.

I am a bit distracted but manage to look away and reply, "No, Sunday." My voice is bright, "After the..." SHHHHHIIIIIIIIITTTTT I think to myself I have nearly gave the whole surprise away.

"After the what?" he asks, he stops and puts the jacket and jumper in the cupboard, he just has his normal uniform shirt on. I watch as he tucks it into his trousers, I can see the dark hairs on his lower arm, he sits on the desk where Phil has just left, so close, too close. "After the what?" He smiles at me, but I have recovered now, I don't look at him, I look down at the statements I am copying, I cannot trust myself to look at his lovely dark eyes.

"After the concert I am going to on Saturday," I say brightly and a little smugly, pleased that I thought so quickly.

"Ah," he replies nodding his head, "of course, the concert." He leans forward. "What concert is that then?" He leans in closer to me, trying to look in my eyes, but I look the other way, I cannot trust myself not to blurt everything out. My heart is thumping, I can feel my face getting red as I fluster now for an answer, I am not great at lying, especially not on the spot lying.

"My niece's school concert." I glance up at him quickly, he is smiling at me, he is so close I can smell his aftershave, I feel hot and bothered, I know if he asks me any more questions I will blurt something out. He is staring at me, his face gets closer and closer, I put my headset on and move away, he pulls the headset from my head.

"You are typing from written statements, there is no tape to listen to." I go bright red, I feel my face so close to his, why doesn't he move away, I shuffle the papers, and I make my voice bright.

"Must get on." He clears his throat he leans very close, his head is almost touching mine.

"Oh, just one more question before you do, what school is your nephew's concert at?" I am stuck now, I don't know what to say, I cannot remember the school, any school, I cannot think of one quickly enough, I look at him shaking my head.

"I am not sure which one he goes to," I say weakly. I pull the headset back on, then he is laughing at me.

He pulls the earpiece away from my ear he whispers, "You are a rubbish liar, you said it was your niece's concert, I don't think you are going to a concert at all, I think you are going somewhere else," he laughs, "now where might that be?" He stares at me and I look back at him, I cannot think of anything to say, I open and close my mouth, but he continues, "Mmm a Saturday night, now what might I be doing that night," he smiles. "Don't worry, I am just teasing you, I love that I made you blush, but I won't tell anyone, the secret is safe with me, but that means you are in my debt, and you owe me now."

He taps the side of his nose, slides off the desk and walks off laughing, he is just a few feet away when he turns back.

"Hey you never know I might see you at the concert, now wouldn't that be a coincidence," he laughs again.

I watch as he walks down the office shaking his head, he sits at the end desk and looks up catching me looking at him, he winks, I put my head down quickly, my cheeks are burning. He has such an effect on me.

The statements are a blur, I cannot stop thinking about his party, and him, how he sat so close, bloody hell, I cannot believe him. I am now not sure if he knows about his party or not, I am not sure if he was winding me up or not, I don't know whether to say anything to Phil or keep quiet, so I decide on the latter. Phil walks back into the office, he smiles at me but heads for Mike.

"You okay, I have just heard what happened, should you at least get checked out?"

Mike remains seated and Phil sits next to him. I can hear the murmur of them speaking quietly, I cannot hear what they are saying, I guess something serious has happened, I will ask Phil later. I go back up to the control room, Gavin is packing up, Craig has said he can slip off early so I sit and look at what we have left to deal with and listen as the others discuss several incidents none of them mention Mike though. Maybe Phil will tell me later.

Phil and I pop into town, I want to bring up the subject of Mike but I don't want to be too obvious, so I wait, but the opportunity doesn't come up. I have to go and collect the watch from the special delivery office and I cannot wait to have a look, I leave Phil waiting in the car, and I open the box when I am in the mail offices and I am really pleased when I see it as Dad has done an excellent job and it looks beautiful, really bright and clean. I look at my watch, the pocket watch appears to be keeping perfect time and it positively shines in its box. I slip it back into my hand bag, I don't want Phil to know what I have done, I cannot explain it really but he might not like the effort I have made. I am not really sure why I have made so much effort, I like Mike, I like him a lot but it is too soon for me to think of being with anyone else, but that doesn't stop my heart from beating a little bit faster or my stomach doing somersaults whenever he is near.

I think the holiday is perfect timing, I need to have time away, for many reasons the holiday is just what I need. Phil is waiting for me by the car, thankfully he doesn't ask what I was collecting. He pulls out into the main traffic and within minutes we are in the main shopping area. Phil and I wander around the shops, we are like an old married couple, we moan at each other about taking too long and then moan about the queues. He makes a few purchases, we moan and fight as we queue up for me to pay for mine, he thinks pizza is a good idea, there is one in the main shopping precinct so we find a cubicle and sit down. It is quite dark in the pizza restaurant but it is not very busy so we sit and study the menus and wait for the waiter to come over. I lean towards Phil.

"Has it been busy today?" I enquire casually, Phil shrugs.

"We had to cover a few officers that were on a CID incident but nothing we couldn't handle." He studies the menu, I seize my chance.

"Oh right, so the incident was the one that Mike referred to earlier then." I pause and look at the menu, still trying to keep my voice casual. "What happened with Mike earlier then?" I ask him, he pulls a face.

"Bloody Simon, that is what happened, that man is a liability." I go to question him more but I can tell he doesn't want to talk about it. We have sat there just a few minutes when the restaurant door opens, I look up and see Ruth coming in, before I realise what I am doing I am hiding behind my menu, I don't want her to see me. I know it is selfish but I just cannot bear to listen to all of the relationship nonsense, not today, I have only exchanged a few text messages with her over the last few months and a Christmas card joke email and that is about it. I feel mean and know I should make more effort, especially when she is going through a horrible time, but in fairness, I have made as little effort as she has, so I just sit there and peek over the menu. She has her back to me and is with a tall chap who is stood in the shadow so I cannot see him, they both are shown to a table and as the chap sits down his face moves into the light, and the chap facing me is Sean. I gasp out loud, very quickly I pull the menu back up to cover my face, I kick Phil under the table and motion my head in the direction of their table, but he is oblivious, his mind is on his food, so I nod again and indicate their table, he looks over and shrugs and carries on looking at the menu.

"Phil," I hiss at him, he looks up at me. "Do you not recognise who that is over there?" He has no idea, I can see him looking over again. "Don't stare," I hiss at him again.

He frowns at me. "I am not staring, but I cannot see them from here, who is it?" The waiter arrives at our table.

"Sorry, we are not ready yet, can you come back in a few minutes," I say quickly, the waiter shrugs and walks away I continue, "its Sean, with a woman," I say quietly.

The waiter is now stood at their table. When he is blocking our view I grab Phil's arm and drag him out of the booth and push him towards the door, I pull the door open and run out into the street.

"For Christ sake, Angie, what the hell is going on with you, so what Sean has his bird there, he is allowed."

But I continue to drag him away from the restaurant. When we are a fair distance away I stop him and look him straight in the face, I turn to him a bit breathless. "That was Ruth with him, you know my old friend Ruth." I see the light go on in Phil's head.

"Oh what your crazy friend, the one who is shagging a married man, my female equivalent." Bingo he has got it eventually.

"Yes, the very one."

Phil looks puzzled. "Well, does Sean know?" I cannot believe he is being so dense.

"I don't know do I, I haven't spoken to her properly for ages and the last I heard she was still seeing him, but I think the wife found out, I don't know, and Sean wouldn't say who he was seeing, I am not sure he knows Ruth knows me, but I am pretty sure Ruth knows who Sean is related to, she must do, I mean the surname would give it away wouldn't it."

"Wow." Phil eventually catches up with me. "So Sean wouldn't know she was shagging a married man then." I look at him as we are walking along.

"No, I doubt it, it probably isn't the first thing you tell someone when you meet them, what do you think we should do?" I ask questioningly.

"Do," Phil replies, he stops in the street. "Do, what do you mean do, we do nothing, Angie." He runs his hands over his head.

"Listen to me, Sean is a big boy, he will not thank us for interfering, he has had a lot of girlfriends and we have never interfered and the same for this one, it is none of our business, if he wanted us to know he would have told us, if you hadn't been so panicky we could have made sure they saw us in the restaurant and we could have said hello, but no, you had to make a big drama out of it and now you cannot do anything." Phil was right, I know he is right, but I have a plan.

"We could go back there," I say quietly, "and we could let them spot us, maybe as we go in." Phil stops walking.

"You are bloody unbelievable." He grabs my hand. "Right, come on then, hurry up, enough of this nonsense, I am bloody starving, I am going to have the biggest bloody pizza they do and you are paying."

He half drags me along the pavement heading back to the restaurant, my head is spinning. Is this a good idea, what if she is still seeing the other chap, the married man, what if she is playing Sean for a fool? I couldn't bear it if she treated him badly, the other women in his life I never knew but this is different, this is Ruth and I know her. This is Sean, he is my family, and he has always looked out for me. Oh why is life so complicated?

We push open the door of the restaurant and the table we had vacated is still available, so we slip into the booth and immediately the waiter comes over with menus.

"Are you ready now?" he says with just a hint of sarcasm. "Or do you need a few minutes." He doesn't wait for an answer, he just walks off.

We sit for a while but both Sean and Ruth are totally engrossed in each other's conversation, he is holding her hand over the table and she is leaned in listening to him as he is speaking, I feel like a spy, I am intrigued, I cannot help but stare, I watch them until the waiter comes over and blocks my view. Phil reels off his order and mine, I am such a creature of habit, I normally have the same pizza every time and he knows this. When the waiter leaves, Phil grabs hold of my chin across the table.

"Can you concentrate on speaking to me now please." He drops his hand.

"Sorry," I say and say brightly, "what do you want to talk about?"

Phil waits until the waiter puts our drinks down, he takes a sip of his beer before replying, "Well, you as it happens, any more dates lined up at all, or are you waiting for the vet to return," he laughs and I laugh with him.

Being with Phil is so easy, I totally forget about Sean and Ruth. The starters arrive and when the waiter leaves I take a sip of my drink and reply, "No I don't think so, he was nice but I will always be thinking of him with a bloody nose."

Phil interrupts, "Or with his hand up a cow's arse." And he hoots with loud laughter at his own joke.

"Sssshh." I try to quieten him but it is too late, Sean has looked over and seen us both, I smile and raise my glass as by way of saying hello. Ruth doesn't look around, she is eating, Sean slides out of his seat and comes over to us.

"Hi, guys." He is very cheery. "Forgot you two come here, you on days this week then?"

Phil has a mouthful of garlic bread and so I reply, "Yes, last one and then off on holiday on Sunday." He nods.

"Ah right I remember, Egypt isn't it, okay, hope you have a good time."

He leans and gives me a kiss on the cheek. Phil has now emptied his mouth. "You going to introduce us to your friend?" he asks smiling, I shoot him a look but he doesn't look at me, Sean shrugs.

"Well, I wasn't going to," Sean replies, "but you guys will bug me until I do, and I guess you already know her anyway." He calls her name. "Ruth honey, come over here and say hello."

Ruth turns round and I can see on her face the answer to my questions, that Sean has no idea of her last relationship. She walks over, she kisses me, well we kind of clash cheeks, she says hello very brightly, too brightly so it sounds almost false.

"I am sorry," she gushes, "I am terrible, I thought about ringing you so many times, I just got so busy, you know how it is."

And I know I could make it hard for her, but I am equally to blame, I have been caught up in my own life and avoided her because of her situation, what sort of friend am I? So I just smile at her, she shakes Phil's hand and slides in the booth next to me.

"Can we pop to the ladies?" she whispers.

"Yes, of course," I whisper back.

Chapter Twenty-Eight

Oh Christ what have I got myself into, everything was going great and now I am in the middle of a big horrible situation, Ruth has explained to me that she was until very recently still seeing the married man, she kept trying to finish it and he kept begging her to stay with him, even threatening to take his life, she got very frightened and it all got very messy with his wife, then Sean came into her office for an appointment and apparently she just fell headlong in lust with him, she said as soon as she met him she felt something special, and since then seemingly they haven't spent a day without seeing each other, I asked if she knew it was Jason's brother and she said she didn't until she looked in the appointment book and saw his name, she thought about ringing me but thought it might be inappropriate, so she waited until he had concluded his business and then they got chatting outside her offices and he asked her to go for a drink. Something nags in my head, so I ask her if she asked Sean out or did he ask her, she admits that she actually asked him out, then she begged me not to say anything about her having an affair and I am so torn, she was, well she is my friend but Sean is my friend and my family, I am not sure I can do this to him, he deserves to know the truth and make his own mind up, just like I deserved to know about my wedding, that thought just popped into my head, I am not sure why, but he was another one who never told me about my wedding, all keeping the big secret, even sharing the journey with us in the car, so I convince myself in my head that I am doing the same as him by keeping Ruth's secret.

We return to the table, my pizza has arrived and Sean and Ruth return to their table, before I even sit down Phil asks, "She still shagging the married man then?"

"Shut up," I hiss, "he will be able to hear you," I look over to see if they might have heard but they are sat back down, holding hands again and ordering coffees.

"So," Phil says matter of fact, "she is, that much is clear, so you are now wondering what you are going to do, strange situation you find yourself in don't you, so you are turning it over and over in your head, aren't you," he looks directly at me, then he continues, "you are so transparent, asking yourself do you tell him, or have you already promised her you wouldn't." Bloody hell this man knows me so well, I feel the blush on my face. "Thought as much" he continues, "why is that then, what do you owe her, why should you keep her silence, what is it, what are you thinking, don't answer, Angie, because I know, it is something else isn't it," he doesn't stop long enough for me to answer, his eyes stare into mine as he continues, "maybe just maybe," he pauses, "you still angry at him too for not telling you about Jason's wedding plans, is he like me, both forever condemned to hell and never to be forgiven?"

I look at Phil, am I so transparent that he knows what I am thinking, he is right, so totally right, what the hell do I do now? I shake my head, I don't know what to say, Phil leans over he squeezes my hand, "Let's talk about something different, Angie, let's not fall out over this, so what if she is still shagging a married man, she is a big girl, Sean is a big boy, let them sort themselves out, honey, okay ."

I nod my head at him and concentrate on my food, we change the subject and continue to eat our meal chatting about every other topic except Sean and Ruth, as they leave Sean gives us a friendly wave, Phil waves back and turns to me, "Quite a fit bird isn't she."

I kick him under the table. "You are so not funny, Phil."

He laughs out loud, "Hey, what have I said wrong, I mean she is quite fit, Sean obviously thinks so." I poke my tongue out childishly.

As we walk back to the car, he takes my hand, "You looking forward to the party then?" I look at him but he is looking ahead so I make sure my voice is casual.

"Yeah, should be a laugh, good excuse to get dressed up and party, everyone together having a laugh and a dance," Phil takes my hand we walk the short distance to the car park, "it will be a busy night, he is a very popular bloke," he remarks, we arrive at the car, I am really full up and getting tired, thankfully it is only a short drive home. I drop Phil off at his car and head for home.

I cannot sleep, over and over I play the conversations in my head, I try to imagine how I would even broach the subject to Sean, but how would I feel if I was in his position? Does he really need to know, she has finished it now with the married man, well I hope she has, she wouldn't lie to me would she? Is it really the same as when they knew about my wedding and I didn't, how would I have felt if they had told me, would I have done anything about it, I toss and turn over in the bed, sleep will not come, my mind is racing with everything going on, I try to erase the thought of Sean with Ruth but it won't go – I end up thumping my pillow with frustration?

An image of Jason and I on our wedding day comes into my head, the whole day replayed like a video in my mind, everything, the music as we walked down the staircase, the look of my parents, I throw questions at myself not knowing the answer, if I knew in advance would I have had the guts to cancel it, would I? I don't know, I toss and turn and keep looking at the clock, this is ridiculous I am never going to sleep, I might as well get up and go for a long run. It six o'clock in the morning, I must be crazy but I need to get these thoughts out of my head, Sean and Ruth, Ruth and the married man, me knowing about my wedding, what would I have done, does anyone have any lawful impediment, the man and the lady standing in front of Jason and I. I run fast for quite a while, welcoming the quiet of the paths, I slow down, my trainers hit the pavement in a steady beat. I have not run for a long time, my chest is burning, my heart is pounding, and my face is flushed, it hasn't worked, it doesn't make things in my head any better. I am supposed to be at the beauticians in just a few hours, I need to go home, shower and get changed, the run has not helped me at all I am so confused.

Chapter Twenty-Nine

The party is in full swing when Marcia and I arrive, there are just so many people there, I cannot believe it, he has more people at his party than I know in my life, the disco is noisy and there is a loud hub of noise from people in the main room. I have the gift bag all ready and as we walk in we are guided by an elderly chap in an old- fashioned tweed suit, he looks like he could be a grandfather, he points us to the separate room at the back where the food is laid out, there is a separate table that is groaning under the weight of the gifts piled on there, Marcia hands me her bottle bag, "Put mine in there too, honey, please, I will get the drinks."

I walk up to the table, there are mostly bottle bags on the table and several large slabs of beer, then several large wrapped gifts under the table. "Well hey, what a surprise to see you here, how did your concert go then?"

I hear Mike's voice before I see him and it makes me jump, I turn to see him leaned up against the doorway, I smile and reply, "It was good thanks." I don't look at him, he pushes himself from the doorway and walks right up close to me, he looks me up and down, then smiles.

"You are a rubbish liar you know" he says quietly, "but I am glad you made it, I thought you might not be coming and I was disappointed."

I look at him, he looks gorgeous, he has on a blue checked shirt with the top buttons undone, the chest hair is poking at his neckline, I try and resist the urge to kiss it, he is dangerously close to me now.

"No, of course not, always like a party, did you enjoy your surprise?" I try and keep my voice bright, Mike just looks at me confused.

"My surprise?" he raises his eyebrows.

"Yes, I thought they had a stripper planned for you," I put my hand to my head, "oh bloody hell have I put my foot in it again?"

Mike laughs, "Well, those type of entertainment things are a bit dated and really not my thing and I think the lads know that, maybe they were winding you up , unless of course it is your birthday gift to me," he looks me up and down slowly then laughs and raises his eyebrows again.

I cannot help it I go a deep red and suddenly lose my ability to speak, so I stammer, "No, no, here is my gift for you, it is only a small gift, but I hope you like it, everything you need for a perfect night in," I hand him the bag.

"A perfect night in, eh, can you fit in the bag?" he is flirting with me, I know he is, I am not coping very well, my stomach flips, he winks at me and again I go bright red. "Sorry, I am being terrible to you, but you blushing is so lovely to see, I am sure I will love whatever is in here, but really you shouldn't have," he smiles, and my heart flips, "I am intrigued now as to what in your opinion is a perfect night in," he makes as if to open it.

"Oh no," I reach out to stop him, "you need to be on your own when you open it or I will be embarrassed."

He smiles again, "Okay, if you insist," again his eyebrows shoot up as he smiles. "On my own eh, now I am more than intrigued," he places the bag on the table, he leans up close to me, he smells so delicious he speaks very gently, he is so close I can feel his breath on my face, "so as the birthday boy I am sure it is my prerogative to get a birthday kiss from all the pretty girls," he smiles at me, I smile back.

"Of course you do," I lean to the side to kiss his cheek, he turns his head and his mouth reaches mine, our lips meet gently, none of us move, my heart is thudding, his lips are warm and soft, slowly he opens his lips and draws me in closer to him. His breath is warm his lips are gently kissing mine, then his kiss is more urgent, my stomach is doing somersaults, my whole body is on high alert loving the feelings this kiss is giving me. Feelings that have been dormant in me for so long, now are on full alert, somewhere in my head an orchestra has started playing. My eyes are closed and I can smell him, I can taste him it is wonderful, his body is close to mine I can feel his chest pushing against mine and our lips do not stop caressing, his tongue entwines with mine, his hand moves to the small of my back and he holds me very close. The kiss is wonderful, I don't want it to end, I place my hand on the back of his neck and hold him close to me, this is just perfect. The world can end now, and I will be happy, my whole body is melting into his. The door opens, along with the blast of loud music I hear a small cough, then a clearing of the throat, still Mike doesn't let me go, he continues to kiss me, his tongue dominating mine.

"Mike," a woman's voice interrupts us, I pull away quickly, wiping my lips with the back of my hand, I look to the door, there is the woman from the Italian restaurant, the one from Phil's engagement party stood there, she is wearing red leather jeans, impossibly high stilettos and what looks like a red string vest with a black bra underneath, she has an amazing figure and if I am being bitchy I would say she looks cheap, but if I had a figure like that then maybe I would dress like that, who wouldn't. As we both turn to her, she continues, "Mike, honey, come on, you are ignoring the rest of your guests," she purrs at him, she holds her hand out, displaying her perfectly manicured long talon like nails painted blood red, but he doesn't move, his hand is still on the small of my back, his kiss is still lingering on my lips, we all just stand there. "Come on you party pooper," she giggles and then she bounces over in her impossibly high shoes, she takes his hand, and pulls him towards the door. She doesn't look at me or acknowledge my being there.

Mike shows no resistance as she pulls him away, he looks back at me, "Catch you later," he smiles and winks. I watch as they both walk out together, unable to move I just stand there feeling a little cheap and very stupid. I thought he had finished with her, I am sure I recall something about her being in the car park making a scene, I try desperately to remember when it was, but it isn't happening, I cannot remember for the life of me when it was or who told me.

Marcia comes in the room followed by Helen, "What are you doing in here by yourself?" she asks.

"Nothing," I reply quickly, "just leaving my gift, come on let's go and join the party." I leave the room and feel a bit embarrassed and silly.

The music is very loud and already the dance floor is packed, I can see Phil and the others around the bar area so we make our way there. Marcia nudges me and gestures with her head that I should look to the left, standing there is the tall leather clad woman, she is stood on her own with a drink in her hand sipping from a straw. "Who the hell is that?" Marcia says none too quietly.

"That is the birthday boy's girlfriend I think you will find," I reply a little quieter.

Marcia nearly chokes on her drink, "Bloody hell, you are joking," she spits out, I pat her back. Helen and Jo have just joined us.

Jo has overheard us and interrupts, "I think you will find she is not his girlfriend; she is his friend with benefits, if you get my meaning," she raises an eyebrow, Marcia and I both look blankly back at her, "oh for goodness sake, you know, friends who, you know, look after each other's needs, do you get me now?" she asks.

"No way, no way," Marcia is shocked, "no way, not Mike, no way, he wouldn't have that, anyone else I would believe but not Mike no way, I don't believe you, Helen did you know that?"

Helen is not listening, she is staring off over the dance floor, "Hear what?" she asks.

Marcia answers, "Jo says that woman in the red leather is Mike's friend with benefits," Marcia again nods her head towards the girl who is still stood on her own but now has turned her back towards us and is playing with her mobile phone. Helen gives Jo a scathing look.

"Well, some people would know more about that situation than others, but no she definitely is not, don't be stupid," Helen is indignant, Jo doesn't bite at the comment directed at her, Helen continues, "Mike is not like that, he is not seeing anyone, I have not heard him mention her once since Phil got engaged, I think she is a bit of a fruit loop that's all."

217

Jo is not having it, she argues, "Then why is she here then, why would his parents invite her to his party if they didn't know her, answer me that," but Helen shrugs, she cannot give a reason.

I look up as Phil comes over and Helen asks him, "Oh her?"

He laughs, "Simon bumped into her in town and told her about the party, she reckons she has a birthday treat for him that he will never forget," he laughs and leans on the bar. "Wouldn't mind a birthday treat from her myself," he laughs out loud, I watch as he looks directly at Jo, she doesn't look at him, she looks down into her glass. "Whose having a drink then, it's my round?" he asks, my heart sinks, I can guess what the birthday treat she has planned for Mike, I think a drink is a good idea, that is just what I need, Bloody Simon and his big mouth.

I turn to Helen, "What did the shift get him in the end, he didn't have a stripper."

Helen laughs, "No, why would you think that?" she frowns at me, I shake my head.

"You told me they were getting him a stripper, that is why I got my own gift, I hate those types of things," Helen laughs, "I was winding you up, Mike would hate that too, no we got him vouchers, a brand new rugby shirt, a rugby ball which we all signed and some tickets to see England play at Twickenham," she looks at me, "you really believed me about the stripper."

I nod my head, "Yes, obviously, I did, and I didn't contribute to his gift, I feel mean now."

Helens smiles she looks up and says loudly, "I am sure you can make it up to him somehow eh, Mike," I look around he is stood just a few feet away.

"What's that?" he asks, Helen repeats our conversation, but the music is so loud I cannot hear everything she says, he leans in to me, his face close to mine, his lips near to my ear, he puts his hand up covering his lips as if he is going to say something then he kisses me gently on the ear and the side of my face, pressing his soft lips against my face, then he stands up and smiles at me Helen looks at me.

"What did he say?" she asks, I cannot answer I am blushing a deep red, I cannot tell her that at the busy bar he has managed to kiss me so intimately and under their noses too.

The party is now in full swing, there are so many people there, Craig and his wife are there, I look at her, she is stunning, I watch as he is talking to her and she throws back her head and laughs, they are exactly what I have dreamed of, so happy with each other. I watch as they head off to the dance floor and he takes her in his arms, the music is fast but they don't care as he holds her in his arms and pulls her close.

Steve comes up beside me, "They are a great couple, aren't they?" I nod my head, "maybe one day you will meet someone new eh, Angie."

I look at him and smile, "Maybe, Steve, maybe."

He turns to me, "Until them you always have me," he takes my hand and pulls me onto the dance floor guiding me nearer to Craig, as we dance by them Steve expertly swaps partners so I am dancing with Craig. "Sorry," he says, "but I wanted to dance with the pretty one," we laugh out loud and I make to swipe him but miss. Craig holds me in a waltz even though the music is too fast.

"You having a good time, Angie?" he asks, I smile at him.

"I am, Craig, I really am."

He smiles back at me, "It is good to see you laughing and letting your hair down," we dance for a short while until Craig spots his wife circling next to us with excellent footwork he manages to move himself back into her arms leaving Steve facing me.

"Oh god not you again," he laughs drawing me close, I look around.

"I never knew Mike played rugby, I thought he liked rugby."

Steve looks around, "Yes, he does play, for two teams apparently, he is really good, look at all these handsome blokes and you are dancing with sad old me." I look around as Steve and I head off the dance floor, He is right, all his team are there, big strapping fella's and us girls are never off the dance floor, the minute we walk away we are dragged back by another bloke, we are loving it. There is one lad in particular that keeps pulling me on the dance floor, he introduces himself as Dean and drags me to the bar to buy me a drink, he is lovely looking, blonde short hair and an impressive physique, we stand chatting for a long while, he is good-looking, amusing and he keeps stroking my hair and telling me I am beautiful – I could listen to him all night, we dance some more, he makes me laugh all night with his jokes. I catch sight of Mike a few times but he is always in a group and I can tell he is getting merrier and struggling to stand the more the night goes on, maybe he won't be able to have his birthday treat I think spitefully. The DJ slows the music right down and I find myself enveloped in Dean's arms, it feels lovely and safe and warm, I am not drunk, I am happily tipsy, I know exactly what I am doing, I lean in close to him, he is slowly moving me round the dance floor and when he moves his lips to my neck I moan with delight, I push him away playfully but immediately I feel his lips on to mine, I don't resist, it feels good, not as good as Mike's lips felt on mine, but he smells just as great and he is just what I need at this moment. The music finishes but we don't part, we stay close just moving round and round, then all too soon the party is coming to an end, we hear shouts, it is Dean's friends calling him to go as the taxi is on its way, he pulls me towards the door and we go out to the car park.

"Come to the club with me," he whispers.

"No, I can't," I whisper back.

"Come on, I won't tell anyone," he laughs and I push him away.

"You are bad," I scold him.

"I know, let's forget the club and just come home with me let me show you how bad I can be, come on, please," he pulls me to him and kisses me again, he really is a good kisser, the taxi driver toots the horn and as Dean types my number into his phone his friends jeer good-naturedly.

I walk back into the hall smiling to myself, I look up, a very drunk Mike is stood near the door, "Hey, that's not right," he calls grabbing my hand as I go by, "he shouldn't get kisses – he isn't even the birthday boy." I pull my hand away from him and walk on, he calls out but I ignore him and walk back into the hall smiling, I am feeling great. I like Mike, I really like him, but he is attached, and I have no intention of getting involved in anything complicated.

My feet are killing me, but I have had a wonderful time, my head is buzzing with the loud music, I feel great, I am on a real high. The disco is packing up and there is a handful of us sat in the corner by the bar which has now closed. We are trying to decide whether to go on somewhere else or just go home, Marcia is in clinch with a very tall chap in the corner, they are still smooching totally unaware of the fact the disco has finished, packed up and gone home, we watch as his hands wander up and down her body, the boys are taking bets on how far he will try to go and how far she will let him. Mike's parents are clearing up the hall and Mike is still leaning up at the exit door saying final farewells to people leaving, it has been a very good night, everyone behaved and although we are all merry, none of us are drunk, Phil walks over, "Well, you certainly were enjoying yourself weren't you," he doesn't wait for me to reply, "who is the chap that was looking for your tonsils with his tongue, did you tell him he was fifteen years too late?"

I grin at him, "His name is Dean, he plays rugby with Mike and he is very lovely," I explain, I kick my shoes off and put them on the chair in front of me.

"Is that a hint?" Phil smiles at me.

"That would be lovely," I reply and put them in his lap. He takes one in his hand and rubs the ball of my foot I wince in pleasurable pain.

"What is it with you two?" Simon pushes himself off the bar he was leaning on and walks towards us, "you say there is nothing going on, and that you are just friends, but I don't massage my friends' feet, and I don't carry on with my female friends the way you two do, so come on, what is it?"

Phil looks at Simon, "You starting up again mate," he says in a non-too friendly manner.

Simon holds his hands out in a non-aggressive way, "No, I am not starting anything, but you know what, I just want to know, just to clarify, if anyone is interested in taking Angie out, do they have to go through you, I mean the chap tonight, has he been personally vetted by you before she can exchange her number?"

Phil places my foot down and stands up, I stand up too in my bare feet wincing in pain, I look around and notice Helen is stood next to me.

"No," Phil squares up to Simon, "Angie can make her own mind up about who she chooses to date, she doesn't answer to me, she is a grown woman and even though I don't have to answer your questions I will just say one thing just to satisfy your perverse mind," Phil takes a swig from his pint. "Angie means a lot to me, she was married to one of my best friends, I will always look out for her and god help anyone who messes her around, they will have me to answer to," he pauses, "got that? Good?"

Phil sits back down and finishes the last mouthful of beer in his glass. We all just stand there, I don't know what to say, so I just look down at my hands, Marcia is now stood holding hands with her chap, she pulls a face at me and manages a little smile, Helen sits next to Phil, she says nothing.

Mike walks over, well staggers really and breaks the awful silence, "Had a good time then everyone?" he leans on Simon's shoulder for support, "I am a little bit pissed," he adds and nearly falls down, Phil stands up and guides him into a chair.

He looks scathingly at Simon, then turns to Mike, "You are looking at the wrong person depending on him for support," the comment is lost on Mike but Simon goes a deep red and opens his mouth to say something but shuts it again.

"Where we going next then?" Mike slurs and looks round at us all, his shirt has come out of his trousers, he has spilled beer down the front of it, he looks like he is about to keel over, he looks so strange as I normally see him so smart, so meticulous in his appearance, he smiles at me, "hello, Angie," he slurs again, then looks to Helen, "you both look pretty," he smiles a wonky smile before turning back to Phil, "where are we going?" he asks again.

"Home, mate," Phil answers, "that is the only place you are going," Phil looks over to the door, the red leather girl is stood there tapping her foot. "Looks like your birthday treat is waiting," Phil laughs out loud, everyone looks over to her, but she ignores us all, Phil puts his arm under Mikes and motions for Simon to take the other arm and they guide him to the door.

"Happy birthday," we all shout in unison, Mike raises his hand in a wave as he is half dragged and half carried out of the door.

"So," Marcia says sitting down and turning to me, "whoever knew Simon fancied you, I certainly never did." Helen sits down with us. "I thought he was seeing someone though, wasn't he, hasn't he got a small child?" None of us knew, I shake my head I have never thought of him as potential partner, he isn't my type at all. Phil and Simon come back in the room; they seem okay with each other.

"Well, I am off home, who wants to share a taxi?" Simon asks, Phil, Helen and a chap half asleep in a chair say yes and they all head out together.

Phil comes over and kisses my cheek, "Text you tomorrow," he says ruffling my hair, he kisses Marcia and walks out, Helen kisses us both quickly and follows him.

Simon leans over to me, "So what about it then?" he asks.

"About what?" I reply.

"What about you and me going out on a date next week?"

I am tipsy but not that tipsy that I am going to agree to something I will regret, so I stand up. "Well, I am in Egypt for a week and I believe you are seeing someone already aren't you?" I reply.

He winks and laughs out loud, "Yes, I am, but it is nice to know you didn't say no to me immediately," he laughs and kisses my cheek again, "missed opportunity for both of us I guess then," he says as he walks towards the door waves his hand back at us.

"Pratt," I say to his departing back.

As we get into the taxi I look at Marcia, "Have I missed something?" I ask, she looks at me, "you know Simon and Mike, Phil's comment earlier," I look at her questioningly.

"Oh that," she exclaims. "I thought everyone knew about it, Mike and Pete got injured in the search warrant incident the other day, they were expecting a lot of trouble so they were all wearing protective body armour, Simon is supposed to count officers in then count them out before they put the dogs in, Mike was knocked to the ground by one of the dogs, he hurt his shoulder and Pete has quite a bad injury to his arm as the other dog brought him down, there is going to be an inquiry," she looks out of the window. "Didn't Mike look great tonight?" she asks before adding, "Well until he got totally plastered that is," she looks at me. "That is one lucky girl getting to go home with him don't you think," she pauses, "well, maybe not tonight but in the morning," she leaves her words hanging and I smile at her, she raises her eyebrows, I shake my head, I am saying nothing, if I was to confide in anyone of how I feel about Mike, much as I like her, Marcia would be the last person.

Chapter Thirty

Sunday morning, in just a few hours I will be on my way to the airport with Marcia. I have had a lovely text from Dean telling me to have a good holiday and asking if we can catch up when I return, I send back a cheerful text message and even add a few kisses. I am having lunch with Little Ma and Pa and then I will be collected late afternoon. The case is packed and ready and I have phoned my parents and even skype Stuart in Dubai, he is really pleased to hear from me and we catch up with everything: he tells me about his work and that he might be coming home for a business trip in a month or so and if he cannot use Mum and Dad's place he would like to stay with me, I would love that and tell him so, he needs to fine tune all the travel but he will get back to me soon he promises before he logs off. I call Judy but she is out so I leave a message on her machine and Scott is also out, or in his case he might even be still in bed. I dress casually and walk the short distance to Little Ma's.

As soon as I enter I can smell the lovely lunch cooking, after the usual round of kissing we sit down chatting, I relax in the lounge and enjoy being waited on. The lounge is bright and sunny and I close my eyes and enjoy the warmth coming into the room and the noises of Little Ma busy cooking in the background. I hear the front door opening and then the lounge door, I look around without moving from my lying down place on the sofa, in walks Sean, I sit up and wait for him to come in properly. He comes and immediately presses a kiss on my cheek smiling at me, "All ready for the off then?" he asks.

"Oh yes, all packed and ready and very excited," I smile back at him, he looks relaxed and happy, Little Ma calls him from the kitchen.

"Back in a moment," he says and disappears, I look over towards Pa, he is half reading half snoozing in his chair, I decide I won't disturb him, I get up and go towards the kitchen to see if I can help with lunch. Little Ma is speaking very quietly to Sean, I cannot hear what she is saying and Sean is leaning right down to her so she can speak in his ear, obviously something private, I can see he is nodding at her, I turn to go back to the lounge and leave them alone. I grab a magazine and sink into the comfy chair.

We sit around the table in the dining room at lunchtime; it is a pleasant room full of sunlight and photos all round of the family growing up and of

Jason and I together at the wedding. Sean is sat at one end and his dad is smiling happily at the end of the table, they are a very traditional family in that the roast meat has to be carved at the table. There is an empty place laid at the table, I look to Sean questioningly but he just smiles, I am sure if there was someone else they should be here by now or it is just rude, maybe Phil is invited. When Ma goes into the kitchen and I whisper to Sean, "Who is the other place laid out for."

Sean leans over, he checks no one is listening, "In case you have forgotten, and I think you probably have," he whispers, "it would have been Jason's birthday today."

My heart sinks, why didn't he warn me, why didn't he text me to tell me then I could have brought something, flowers, anything, Oh shit I think to myself, I look at him imploringly, "Help me please," I whisper to Sean, "I did forget, and I know I am rubbish but please Sean, please help me, she will know I have forgotten, she will be so upset, please help me," I put my hands to my face I want to hide away.

"Okay, it's okay," he says reassuringly. Little Ma returns to the table with the rest of the vegetables, she pours the wine and takes her seat at the table, no one mentions the spare place. Sean raises his glass. "I think Angie should do the toast," he says. Little Ma nods yes and I look to Pa, he nods too.

I look at Sean gratefully and raise my glass, "To our dearly departed Jason on his birthday, a wonderful son, brother and husband," I take a sip and Little Ma gets out of her chair and comes to mine, she kisses both my cheeks.

"See," she looks around at both of them, then says proudly, "I told you she wouldn't forget, she was probably just upset, she is a good girl, one of the best."

I look at Sean and send him a thousand thank yous. I feel such a fraud, it has meant so much to them both that I remembered and that I am sat with them on this day. Little Ma disappears back into the kitchen, she walks back and stands behind her chair.

"Angie, my Angie, you come here," she beckons me with her hand, I look down at my food, I am famished, but I give in and stand up beside her at the table, her voice shakes as she speaks, "today before you come here we are speaking about you."

Sean moves his chair aside to make room, she pulls me closer to her, she has a huge pair of scissors in her hand and in one fluid movement she snips away my remembrance band from my arm, I immediately put my hand up to stop her, but she smiles at me, "You are a very good girl, a good girl you make us very proud," she pulls me close in a hug, "you were a good wife you make my Jason very happy, thank you, you are a good girl," she holds me so tight and Sean stands up and pulls her away.

"It's okay, Mum, it's okay," he whispers to her as he cradles her head to his chest, I just stand rubbing the space the remembrance band was, it feels weird and empty, I look at Ma, she is crying gently into his shirt. He looks over her shoulder to me "thank you" he mouths. I go to Pa and notice his eyes wet with tears, I give him a huge hug too. I press my lips to his bristly cheek, he places his hand against my face and holds it there for a short while, they are so wonderful to me, and I feel such a heel. They are such a loving family, I am so lucky to be part of it. They didn't deserve to lose their son, and I feel so terrible for forgetting.

At the end of the meal Sean helps me with my jacket, my arm feels very bare without my band and again I rub the space where it was on my arm. "You will get used to it," he says, "come on, we need to go," Sean beckons me to the door, with my goodbyes all said I walk along with him.

"Thank you for back there, I wish I had remembered."

He looks at me, "Angie, don't beat yourself up, I only remembered when I got there and Dad said about it, Mum would never forgive me for forgetting, and I couldn't even text you as she never left me alone."

I smile at him, "Thanks for making everything better and looking out for me, you know," I start to say, and then I make a decision. "Sean, I need to tell you something. I need to get something off my chest and I cannot go on holiday without you knowing this, so here I go," I take a huge breath in, I cannot look at him and he says nothing back to me, we walk on, so I continue, "I am not sure how serious it is with you and Ruth, but before you she was seeing a married man, it went on for a long time, it all got a bit ugly with his wife when she found out, I know she is my friend but we haven't been in touch for a while so I am not sure if it is over with him and her but I know if I don't tell you it will be wrong and now I have told you that might be wrong too, but I love you and you are my brother-in-law and I have to tell you, and if you hate me then that is okay," I run out breath and look at Sean, he is smirking at me, he pulls me into a bear hug.

"Thank you for eventually plucking up the courage," he goes on "but I knew already, Phil told me after you saw us both, but he wasn't so eloquent in his choice of words, but it is okay, I am not actually seeing her at the moment, lots going on, she is a nice girl but I have things I need to be sorting out and she is a complication that I just don't need at the moment." My thoughts are racing, Phil is a horrible pig, he could have told me. "Of course," Sean continues, "Phil could have told you that I know, but I asked him not to, you see I have always wondered if you have forgiven me for not telling you about the wedding and I wanted to see if you would tell me of your own free will, or whether the wedding still means there is this barrier between us, I guess not huh," I push him playfully on the shoulder, "no, I guess not".

We walk on in companionable silence, "Care to share your burdens?" I ask him.

"Maybe, soon, but not yet," he replies. He gives a big sigh, he turns to me, "Angie, I have something to ask you," he doesn't look at me, "this is really difficult for me to ask but Ma has asked me to speak with you, you see," he pauses, "Christ I cannot believe I have to ask you this, but," he pauses again, "well, she wants to know."

I can see he is struggling so I stop him, I hold his arm. "Sean, stop, just tell me please, just ask me what she wants to know," I am so scared, I am frightened she will say she doesn't want me to go round anymore, she might think it is too painful for her, I love those two fragile beautiful people, I couldn't bear not to see them.

Sean looks at me, "Look this isn't easy, but Ma wants to have Jason's things at her house," he falters again, "you know as in his clothes, she wants them back in his wardrobe at home, I know it might sound crazy and I don't think it is a good thing for her, she has kept our rooms exactly as we left, so I know it is going to sound absurd, I just know it is, even as I am saying it, I know it is but."

I hold my hand up to him, "Sean, it is fine, really it is, I am relieved it is only that, I was so worried what it might have been, and I am fine with it, after all, you cleared the boxes and all his project stuff and sorted it out for me with Martha, if you think it's okay and wouldn't upset her more I have no problem with her having his clothes, no problem at all, it is something I should have maybe sorted by now, but it is so difficult, especially when the wardrobe doors are closed I don't give a thought, they just hang there," I stop and look at him. "I know you might think I am sad but I will keep his denim shirt and maybe a rugby shirt if that is okay, they were his favourites and I want to keep them, but she is welcome to have the rest," I rest my hand on his arm. "Sean, it isn't crazy at all, maybe it is her way of coping," I look at him, he looks so nervous. "Sean, shall I leave it to you to sort out, I trust you, you know where everything is, I don't know what I was going to do with everything, I thought I would just leave it all there, but I understand it is probably time for me to let everything go, I hate the thought of bagging it up and donating it somewhere, and I would really like for you to have something, you know how he felt about his clothes, you were always borrowing his shirts, so make sure you have something of his, if you want to, it would make me happy, so please do what you and Ma think is best," he pulls me close. "Seriously, is it all still hanging in the wardrobe and all in the drawers," I nod. "Yes, except for his denim shirt which I wear sometimes, and an old T-shirt of his I wear to bed, as I said, I didn't know what to do with everything, I don't want it thrown away and couldn't bear to pack it all up, so thank you," Sean smiles, "not sure it is going to be easy for me, but it needs doing and as you are going away seems like a good time, I will get Phil to help if that is okay as he has a key," I nod again, "thanks Sean.".

I head towards my house but he pulls me back. "Angie, the remembrance band."

I frown at him, "What about it?"

He takes a deep breath, "Let someone else into your heart now, Angie, the band was a physical reminder but you don't need it, you never really needed it, find a place in your heart for Jason, think about him sometimes, but move on," he pauses, "it is time, Jason would want you to be happy." I nod my head, I can feel tears in my eyes. We are now stood outside my door, he watches me let myself in, I watch as he walks on back up the road.

Chapter Thirty-One

The travel to the airport was uneventful as was the flight, Marcia and I talk about almost everything, she knows everyone at work and keeps me entertained with idle gossip about the different shifts, she has dated a few officers, nothing serious, she is happy just with casual dates, she gets on with most people and I know a lot of people confide in her about personal things, I have spoken to her lots of times about Jason and things, I would never admit to her that I like anyone as I think she might want to push things, so I don't tell her about the party and what happened with Mike as I think of him I feel a glow all over, I remember his kiss, his warm soft lips on mine.

Marcia is speaking to me she nudges me and smiles, "Penny for them."

I smile back at her, "I wasn't really thinking anything," I lie convincingly, I wish I could tell her, tell someone, I am half tempted, as she is an easy person to talk to, but I don't, I keep my thoughts to myself, I close my eyes and remember the kiss, playing it over and over in my mind. I snooze for a while and before we know it we are landing, as we walked out of the aeroplane door the heat hit us, Marcia and I hug each other, one whole week of sunshine, I just cannot wait to lay in the sun and do absolutely nothing. A small white jeep meets us and two chaps jumps out and grab our cases, they both smile and chatter all the way to the hotel. The hotel is small and family owned and run, we watch as they carry our cases to the room as we head for the bar, the owner immediately joins us, kissing us both on the cheek and pulling us into a hug, he is large and loud and bellows out to us as he introduces his wife. The two chaps are now back down and he introduces them as his two sons, within minutes he has practically told us the story of his family, we sit and drink our wonderful cocktail as he introduces Hasani and Caleb, he explains that Hasani is Egyptian and Caleb is not, Caleb is his late sister's son, she died in childbirth. He looks at them both with pride, he goes on to explain that he has brought them both up as brothers, they are a little bit older than us I would say by looking at them. The whole family are very welcoming, little nibbles are brought out until we make our excuses and retire to our room, they are all very lovely and we are both pleased with our choice of hotel. It is quite late when we arrive. We are both tired so after we have spent a polite short time with the family, we head to our room, we unpack quickly and plan to both have a quick doze on the bed. Before we know it we are fast asleep.

As soon as we wake up the heat hits us, we shower quickly then get dressed and head down for breakfast, the dining room is tiny, just six small tables with red checked tablecloths, there is just one couple sat down, we both look around, the room is spotlessly clean, it is just the owner's wife who serves us, she doesn't speak hardly any English but we make ourselves understood by pointing at the menu, we enjoy a delicious breakfast. We plan to just relax by the pool today. We grab our things and settle by the pool, there is no one else around, it is perfect, the pool is beautiful and cool, I don't want to go on any trips, I told Marcia that from the very beginning. She is happy with this, I don't want to do much else but relax by the pool under my umbrella. I nod off for a short while, when I wake up Marcia is sat in the cool of the lounge speaking to the eldest son Hasani, he disappears and we sit and chat whilst we have lunch, she tells me that Hasani is more than happy to take her out and about, he seems a very reliable chap and I cannot see them doing anything to upset his father. I know she likes him, she continually talks about him and her eyes dart around the pool looking for him, he returns with a drink for both of us, he cannot keep his eyes off her too, but I wish he would smile a bit more, his face seems so dark, obviously she doesn't notice as she giggles like a young girl, she seems to be smitten with him, I can see the chemistry between them. I lay back on my sunbed, fair play to her, she is a lovely girl and I am not sure but I think she has recently broken up with someone, so she deserves a bit of relaxation. I text Phil and Sean to let them know I am okay and arrived safely and relax back to read my book.

It is very quiet in the day, we find out that in the hotel there are just three other guests, one is a couple and another is on a short stop over as he is travelling to meet friends, we chat to them all over our meal, which is served again by the owner's wife. We sit back and relax with a drink and we are amazed as the hotel is transformed, it seems to come alive, it is such a small hotel but the family invite friends over, they in turn bring their own friends, there is lots of food and music and noise and then three guys with guitars and flutes turn up, then a singer arrives. Everyone eats and drinks until the early hours, Marcia is enjoying a little romance with Hasani, they keep disappearing, although I am happy for her, to me, he looks mean and moody, he frightens me a little bit, he never seems to smile, just sits glowering and looking intimidating in his long white robes, but she seems okay with him and I am just happy to look on. She is a free agent and like me she enjoys male attention, I remember her smooching with the chap at Mike's party, nothing serious although I think she might have gone home with him, I will have to ask her when I remember, I look around me everyone is relaxed and happy. They do keep trying to push Caleb and I together but we both just smile at their attempts even though I do occasionally get up and dance with

Caleb, I also dance with the owner and his brothers and other various family members, I am not sure why it seems the feeling is mutual as Hasani keeps away from me and I avoid him.

The days go so quickly and I am developing a nice tan, I look and feel very relaxed. I have ate too much and hardly taken any walks or any exercise apart from a cooling dip in the pool. The week goes by so quickly and we are pleased that on the last night of the holiday it is Hasani's birthday. There is a big party planned, more people are invited, they all coming from everywhere, there is a big barbecue being set up on the beach, the main party will be there which is just a short distance from the hotel, everything is decorated with banners, so many people are involved and we just sit and watch all the activity. I know that Marcia and Hasani have had a lovely holiday romance, sometimes I wake up and catch her sneaking in to bed in the morning, I don't say anything, I just smile to myself and pretend I am sleeping.

Later when we both lay on the bed, we chat about nothing and everything, she admits she did go home with John from the party, she also admits it was a one-night stand, "I have had a bit of a nightmare where men are concerned" she admits to me, I watch her put her make up on. "I have made so many mistakes in my life, you name it I have made it," she pulls a face, "one-night stands, marital affairs, yes, all of those, I am not proud of it but I don't judge anyone for any choices they make now, I just want to have fun and enjoy myself and Hasani is certainly helping me to do that," she laughs and looks at me. "Are you shocked?" she asks.

"No," I reply too quickly, "okay, well maybe a little bit, I am a bit naïve when it comes to relationships."

She smiles at me, "Oh I know that, honey," she turns back to the mirror, "I know that."

I frown at her. "What do you mean by that?" I ask her, I sit up on the bed and watch her applying her mascara, in two strokes her make-up is complete.

She turns to me, "You have no idea how attractive you are to the opposite sex, you are totally unaware of the effect you have on them aren't you?" I shrug.

"I guess I am not that confident where males are concerned, I like them, don't get me wrong but I am not that good at flirting."

She laughs, "It wouldn't suit you anyway, Angie, although the chap at Mike's party couldn't take his eyes off you, and he wasn't the only one," she stands up, she looks stunning, "come on, let's go show these people how to party," she pauses, "and yes, I intend to be very naughty again tonight," she laughs and this time I laugh with her, I wish I had her confidence.

I look at her, she is wearing a long red dress, it has a split up to the thigh and has spaghetti straps, she finishes it off with flat black sandals, she looks amazing, I wear my floaty black strapless dress and wear low gold sandals. I pull a pashmina over my shoulders and we head down the stairs. The barbecue is in full swing, the music is very loud, Marcia brings me over a glass of wine and sits down next to me, we sit in quiet observation of everyone around us, within minutes more people arrive and the table which is already groaning under the weight is laden with yet more food. I get up and help myself to some more from the buffet and sit down again to eat, Marcia is sat chatting to the other holidaymaker opposite her, I look around, it is a lovely place, we both look really healthy and are sporting great holiday tans, we sit quietly and watch the dancing, it is too loud for conversation, the music is playing really loudly and the night is warm it would be too hot if there were not a gentle breeze coming off the sea. We watch as the musicians make the music faster and faster, the dancers struggle to keep up, as the music finishes everyone admits defeat, they give out huge cheer and then everyone heads for more drink and food, the music slows to a soft ballad. Caleb comes towards me and holds his hand out to me, I put my plate and glass down on the table next to me. I hold my hand out to him, I stand up slowly as he guides me to the middle of the area marked for dancing. His dad is stood clapping, suddenly everyone is clapping, we find ourselves surrounded by everyone, we are the centre of attention, we dance a strange clapping type dance where he spins me round and round, I look around, others have joined in, I smile at him, I am much more relaxed as I didn't like being the centre of attention but now everyone is just dancing and we are ignored, Caleb takes my hand and guides me to the edge of the party.

"Want to come for a walk?" he says gently to me.

"Yes," I reply, I follow him as he heads away from the party, I look back and his dad is stood watching us as we are walking away, I smile at him, he smiles back, nodding his head, I watch as he leans down to speak to one of the older relatives, they both look over and smile . Caleb is holding my hand, I shrug, let them think what they want, I am happy, his hand feels warm and comforting in mine, it feels nice, I feel very relaxed and happy, I slip off my shoes and carry them. The sand is still warm under my feet. Caleb moves his hand from mine and holds me round the waist drawing me closer to him. We walk quite a long distance, I can see the lights of the hotels, I can hear strains of music coming from different resorts, Caleb stops and turns to face me I hope he isn't going to try anything on, because he is lovely and I do like him, but not in that way, I am just happy to be walking along the beach nothing too complicated. He turns to me, he looks me straight in the face, he pushes my hair back over my bare shoulder his face is serious.

"I do like you, Angie," he says very quietly, he says my name like a caress, I love his accent, I smile at him and he continues, "but I love someone, someone who is very ill, but who I love very much, is that okay," I nod yes to him, I reach for his cheek and stroke it tenderly.

I speak gently back to him, "That is very okay, I think I like someone very much too, but they are not ill, they are just not mine, you understand," he nods his head too.

"We are, how do you say it," he pauses, "stuck then yes."
I nod my head in agreement, "Yes, that is it, we are stuck."

He pulls me to him and holds me in a gently hug then he puts his arm around my waist again and we walk some more, it is pitch dark, I am not worried, I feel safe with Caleb I look back from where we have walked, it is quite a long way, but I can still hear the party music, Caleb pulls me to him, I stand in his warm embrace, we stand and just watch the waves crashing on the shore, it is so beautiful and relaxing, we stand like that for a long while then he pulls me by the hand up the beach towards the breaker, we find a half wrecked rowing boat, he takes my hand and helps me climb into the wreck, he pulls me down onto the soft warm sand, we lay on the wooden bench at the top, Caleb puts his arm around me, I lay in his arms and we look up to the starry sky, sheltered by the carcass of the boat. Caleb explains his love of his life is called Marla, she is in a medical coma in the main Cairo hospital she was in a car accident nearly six weeks ago, she is in a very bad way, the doctors have had to put her in a coma so her body can repair, they were due to be married next summer but the doctors want to switch the machine off if she doesn't show improvement soon. Her parents want to leave it on, they pray she will get better, he loves her so much, his voice chokes with emotion, he is silent for a while before he continues to tell me, that he goes to see her every other week but she is so very far away, it takes almost a day to get there, so he goes and stays for a few days. His father tells him he must give up and find a new wife, he wants grandsons, it is important to him and nothing Caleb says will stop him matchmaking. All the time he keeps looking for a new bride for him but he wants Marla no one else, he won't ever love anyone as much as he loves his Marla, I hold him as he cries gently and I kiss his forehead, we lie in each other's arms, we look up at the stars. We lay in silence for a long while just listening to the waves, then for reasons I don't know I tell him about Mike, I tell him about the hug and then the lovely smile that Mike has and how he smells so gorgeous, I tell him about Christmas and the kiss, then as the night goes on I tell him about Jason and how he never made me feel the way I feel when Mike is near me, I go on and on and I tell him about the woman at the party, I tell him all about the birthday party and I tell him about the birthday kiss, and how Mike kissed my ear in front of everyone but without them seeing a thing. I tell him how I hug myself and think about the kisses all the time. The words flow from me like a fountain, once I start I cannot stop. Caleb is patient and understanding, he listens to me, without interrupting, I tell him things that I have never told anyone else. I lay with my head on his chest as I open my heart to him.

"Sounds like you both have got it bad," he says, I love his accent, I love the stilted way he talks, he goes on, "this man, this Nike, he keeps trying to tell you he likes you, the kisses, they are his way of saying he likes you, he doesn't kiss any other women no."

I look at him, I smile, "No", I pause, "no other women I know of, just me."

Caleb laughs out loud, "Then that is it, he likes you, he likes you a lot, pretty soon he will find his way to make you his woman I am sure of it," he hugs me close, "you will have your Nike and I will have my Marla," he kisses my forehead. "Let us wish upon the stars and our dreams will come true." I snuggle into his warm arms, I really hope so.

We talk for the rest of the evening, the sun goes down bringing a chill into the air, the sand gets blown up by the wind, I pull my pashmina over us and we fall asleep in each other's arms. I feel I know so much about this man, I have laid in his arms all night, we have been so close, we have done nothing more than cuddled, I don't know this Marla but I know I would like her if I met her, I have heard so much about her. I tell Caleb he must keep me informed as to her condition and I watch as he punches my number into his mobile phone. We lay in companionable silence as the sun rises over the sea, I can still hear the waves lapping at the sand, we haven't moved, but my hip is aching, my thigh has gone numb and I know we will have to move soon. None of us wants to be the one to break away, we are both looking a bit crumpled now, Caleb has white linen trousers and a matching linen shirt on, he looked so clean and smart when we set out, now he is all dishevelled and creased, but he doesn't seem to care, we continue to just lie there silently, I know he is awake as he strokes my shoulder gently, we watch as a stray dog comes near us, I am not frightened, we don't move, the dog sniffs about for a while and then before we can react the dog lifts his leg and pees on Caleb's ankle, it takes a few seconds for Caleb to register what has happened when he does he jumps up outraged and shouts at the animal who runs off down the beach, I cannot move, I am paralysed with laughter. He is livid and screams at the departing dog, he stomps off towards the sea to wash his trousers, I am still laughing so much my eyes water, when I finally calm down he is stood over me, his trousers are soaked up to the knees, he manages a smile as he reaches for my hand and pulls me up into his arms, he kisses me gently on the cheek then pulls me against him and hugs me like he never wants to let go.

We arrive back at the hotel to knowing nods and smiles from the family who are sitting down to breakfast, we both look very dishevelled and covered with sand, Caleb has very wet trousers, at first he just washed the bottoms but they got covered in sand as we walked back so he washed them off in the sea before we reached the hotel, they hang off his narrow hips. Both Marcia and Hasani are still missing and the father is sat at the breakfast table a huge knowing smile on his face, sat with his arms folded looking very proud. He winks knowingly at Caleb and says something in Egyptian that I do not understand, Caleb raises his eyes as if in despair, he reaches over kisses my cheek and grabs a pastry and disappears down behind the bar, I don't say anything, I help myself to a juice and a pastry and head for my room. There is evidence that Marcia and Hasani have not been home either, the bed is made and everything is as we left it, I shower quickly and then sit on the balcony in my towel drinking my juice. The weather today is already showing signs it is going to be beautiful and hot but I must think about packing soon.

Marcia comes in about an hour later, she is looking very tousled, her hair is all over the place and her dress is all creased but she has a big smile on her face and she flops on the bed she is exhausted, she lays there silently with a big smile on her face for several minutes before the door knocks and she gets up to open it, Caleb is there with a tray of breakfast for both of us, she takes the tray and I go out, I close the door gently behind me.

"It is better no one knows about last night, if you don't mind," he is watching me and I frown at him, "you know, like nothing happened," he says quietly. "My father is happy now, he thinks I have gotten over Marla, there is no point in him knowing okay."

I take his hand and smile at him, "That is fine, let them think what they like, but you know something, Caleb, another time, another world you would be my Mike and would be perfect for me," I say, he smiles back, but his eyes are dark.

"I know, I know, but you are not Marla and I am not Nike, but I feel closer to you than I ever have anyone else, except my Marla, and one day I might regret not making the love to you last night," he smiles, kisses my cheek and then he disappears, I smile after him, I think to myself, you are so lovely, but you are not Mike.

Marcia is still laid on the bed when I go in. "Mmm good night then?" I smile at her.

"I could ask you the same question," she laughs. "Mine was great, he is a bit moody and I cannot understand most of what he says, oh but wow that man can make my body sing, I am exhausted, I haven't slept all night," she laughs, "how about yours?"

I grab the case, "Come on, you dirty stop out, we need to pack."

She pulls herself up on the bed, "Mmm just two more minutes, then I will be ready," I watch as she falls back on the bed, I pack around her then when everything is done I dig her in the ribs telling her we have to be going.

There is nobody around when we leave, I am pleased as I don't want to see the fathers gloating expression on his face. We go downstairs, Caleb is waiting in the jeep, there is no sign of Hasani despite Marcia looking round for him. "We can wait no more," Caleb advises her gently, "he not come,"

She shakes her head, "I know, he told me he cannot bear to say goodbye," she sniffs, I take her hand and squeeze it gently. I have had a lovely time but now I just want to be home.

Chapter Thirty-Two

There is nothing so wonderful as your own bed, although the flight is on time and we collect our cases very quickly, by the time I get home, it is quite late and I am tired, so I make myself a hot drink then just lie in my bed and just think of everything that has happened over the last week. The wardrobe door is slightly ajar, it is then as I am laying in my bed I remember Sean has been round, I get up and walk to the wardrobe, it is totally empty, everything has gone, I pull out the bedside drawer and all that remains is the book that Jason was reading, still with the marker in its place, it was a library book, I hold the cold hardback cover against my cheek welcoming the coolness, I pull out the drawer below, it is empty, I pull every drawer out, even though I know Sean has been round, it was prearranged, I agreed to it, but the emptiness is still a shock. I still check every drawer, there is nothing left in them, as agreed it has all gone to Ma's, I sit on the bed just holding his book in my hand. The last few months have been a rollercoaster of emotions for me, his parents and Sean have been so supportive, Phil has been a diamond too, I don't know what I would have done without them all. I lay on the bed holding the book against my chest, I run over so many things in my mind and want to laugh and cry at the craziness of my life, my mind drifts to the wonderful holiday, my lovely friend Caleb who was just what I needed. I smile as I think of Marcia, how she is head over heels in lust with her Egyptian holiday romance, we both discussed it on the plane, well she did most of the talking, I just listened, she says she knows how it is, what happens in Egypt stays in Egypt she told me firmly on the plane, almost begging for my silence, but she doesn't need to I totally agree. I think it is more for her benefit than mine having spent most of her holiday in Hasani's room. I am happy with this arrangement; I don't want to be the topic of anyone's gossip or discussions. I lay back on the bed and think about the incident with the dog on the beach and I laugh out loud again. I am so tired, I should get up and shower but I cannot keep my eyes open, I lay on the bed stroking the page where Jason's bookmark is, I fall asleep with Jason's book in my arms.

It is now nearly the middle of February, Valentines happened whilst we were away and I am pleased about that, never my favourite time of year.

There are a few items of mail for me, nothing urgent and no cards or huge bouquets of red roses blocking my entrance into my house. I put all the mail unread on the table, it can wait, nothing looks particularly urgent. There are a few messages on the answer phone, the latest message is from Ruth saying she doesn't know what she has done that I am ignoring her, there are a few more from other people and then the first message from Ruth asking me to call her, urgently, ah she obviously doesn't know I have been away and that explains the other message. Not sure why she didn't text my mobile though.

I am on late shift today, so I have time to sort everything out, put things away and even manage a bit of shopping, I pop to the library to return Jason's book, it is well overdue but they completely understand the situation. I get back home, make a light snack and a drink then I return a few calls, at three thirty I head out of the door ready for my four o'clock start. I get to work in plenty of time, as I pull into the car park I see a familiar face, Mike is leaning against the outside wall speaking to someone, I smile as I see him then the smile dies on my face, I recognise her, it is the blonde girl from the nightclub, she is wearing hipster jeans and a short jumper showing off her flat stomach, they are just stood chatting, I watch as she throws her head back laughing then walks off across the car park, she turns as Mike calls her back and she walks back to him, they chat for a little while longer, I sit paralysed in my seat, she laughs again and this time she leans in closer to him kissing him quickly on the lips before walking away. When she heads to her car, she calls out to him, he waves at her then turns and goes back in. So many thoughts are racing through my head, is it his girlfriend, are they serious, what was she doing here, I never give a thought to him seeing anyone, I don't know why but my stomach jolts, I shake my head, I glance at the clock, I have to go into work.

I just get out of my car when Phil walks across the car park, he has a big welcoming smile on his face and I smile back at him, he picks me up and swings me round, he holds me in his arms. "Did you have a great time, want to show me your white bits?" he asks.

"Perfect thanks and no," I reply, I pull myself away, we laugh together then walk towards the station. He kisses me on the head.

"Catch you later," he calls cheerfully, I go to my locker, hang my coat up then check my mail, there are various news bulletins, some old flyers then I notice a light blue envelope in amongst them. It is hand written with my name on the front, I tuck it in my handbag to open later. The first part of my shift is quiet so I can catch up on gossip, people ask about the holiday remarking how rested and healthy I look, something that everyone finds very hilarious has happened to Mike but before anyone can tell me Steve sees him coming in, so calls out quickly to tell everyone to be quiet. Mike wanders over to me, my stomach does a flip and I feel myself going red, why does he have that effect on me?

"Good holiday?" he asks, he perches on the side of my desk.

"Great holiday you mean, don't you?" Steve interjects.

"Just ignore him," I say. "Yes, I had a lovely rest thank you," I shoot Steve a look, he takes the hint and shuts up. A call comes in and he takes it, he is now listening to the caller so he cannot interrupt, I look at Mike and smile, "how was your hangover after the party, still getting over it are you?" Mike laughs, I do love his laugh, and his twinkly eyes.

"It was the worse hangover ever, I couldn't function for about two days, just sat on my mum's sofa feeling like my head was exploding," I laugh out loud, Mike looks around to see if anyone is listening, when he sees they are all busy he pulls me by the cuff of my jumper, motioning with his head for me to follow him, I get to my feet and I follow him into the admin room. Once there he reaches for my hand, he brings it to his lips, "Thank you for my gift, it was the best ever, I couldn't believe it when I saw it," he looks straight at me, his face serious. "It took me a few days to get round to opening my gifts and I must admit I never realised the watch had disappeared from the desk, I am not sure how you did it, or who you got to fix it but it was a very special thing you did, the book and the wine was lovely too, but the watch was incredible," then he looks towards the door quickly and seeing no one is there he leans in and kisses me very gently on the lips, my stomach does a somersault, I go hot all over, he pulls away. Holding my gaze for several seconds, it seems like an eternity, we don't move, he just looks straight into my eyes, none of us say a word, my heart is beating out of my chest, my face is flushed.

"Sorry, Angie, I shouldn't have done that, very inappropriate of me," he looks nervous, he clears his throat, "but, I wanted, well you know," he seems nervous, but continues, "what I mean is, I just wanted to thank you for the gift." Mike lifts my hand up to his lips again, he kisses the back of it, "You put so much thought into my gift, you know, you are one special lady," he says.

We hear the footsteps of someone approaching, Craig comes in, he looks at us both. "Problem?" he asks, I shake my head.

"Just catching up on his party gossip."

Craig frowns, he looks directly at me, his voice harsh, "Well, can I have you back in the control room, like now," he looks at Mike and then turns and walks back into the control room. I stand for just a few moments, Mike smiles and walks out too, I fetch myself a glass of water and return too, my face has calmed down a bit but my heart is still beating hard in my chest, how can I face him now, how I can carry on as normal knowing that my lips are still feeling the warmth of his, and that I want more, so much more. Then the image of the blonde girl comes into my head, I shake my head, I don't want to think about her now, I take a deep breath and push the door open, I glance over to see that he is now sat back with Craig, they are discussing something, then without warning their voices get louder and Mike stands up.

"Do you want to take this somewhere private?" he asks, Craig nods and gets up and they both walk out, we all look at each other, I have no idea what is going on, they normally get on really well, we all watch silently as they both go into the small meeting room and close the door. We work quietly, there is not much going on but still we are kept busy, Mike and Craig stay in the room for quite some time, then they both come out and return to Craig's desk, within minutes they are back discussing cover for an event coming up. They have their heads buried deep in their paperwork, the mutterings of work going on around them. I have no idea what is going on. Steve is in a very annoying mood today, he is throwing paper at me and I know he is trying to tease me to get a reaction, but so far he hasn't.

"So, Angie, that chap you were snogging at Mike's party, what was his name again?" he continues without waiting for a reply, "ah yes, Dean well he phoned several times, whilst you were away, it seems he has lost something, wanted us to check lost property," he pauses, then smiles a big beam on his face, "he wants to know if he can have his tonsils back," he laughs out loud at his own joke, before continuing, "are you seeing him again?" he winks at me.

I cannot help colouring up, "Shut up, Steve," is all I can reply, I look over to Mike and Craig, I am not sure if they have heard or not. Craig glances up and smiles intimating that he has but Mike keeps his head down, the truth is, I have had text messages from Dean but just funny jokes, nothing else.

"So," Steve persists, "is that a yes, you have heard from him, or yes he can have his tonsils back," I glare at him, it has no effect he persists, "are you going to see him again, he seemed a decent lad."

I mouth to Steve to shut up and he raises his hands in a what have I done gesture. I ignore him, I get up and collect the cups to make a drink, I have to get away from him before I want to throttle him, I approach the main console, both of them have their heads down, but Craig looks up.

"Yes please," he says smiling, "you are a diamond."

"Yes," I reply cheekily, "and you are a creep."

I look to Mike, he is looking up at me, I raise my eyebrows at him questioningly, "Ah that includes me too does it, that makes a change from me having to wait on you downstairs," he raises one eyebrow at me, behind me there is a series of moans and cheeky comments, I raise my eyes at them both.

"Don't start them all off, they don't need any encouragement from you," I tell him, "I will make you one but just to keep everyone from going on at me." I pick up the cups, and walk to the kitchen. I have a wonderful warm feeling all over my body and my lips are still remembering his kiss. Whatever issue Mike and Craig have, they must have sorted it out now.

Helen comes up within minutes of me being out there, my hands are in the bowl full of washing bubbles, I feel all warm inside, I like the way that

Mike smiled at me. I liked his kiss, I love the fact he liked his gift, I am so proud of my dad, he is so clever. Then my heart sinks again as I remember the blonde girl, they must be going out together, they must be, why else would she be here at his work. Helen stands and watches me.

"Any gossip?" I ask her, she shakes her head.

"Nothing exciting." My heart is beating hard in my chest, I have to ask her, I have to know.

"I saw Mike with that blonde woman as I was coming in," I blurt out, Helen frowns.

"Blonde woman, who?" she asks.

"You know the one from the nightclub, very blonde short hair, they were chatting when I arrived, are they going out?" I try and keep my voice light.

She shrugs, "News to me," I wipe the cups. "How was the holiday then come on tell me?" she asks, I tell her it was really relaxing and I had a lovely time, but she is fishing about something, she keeps looking at me, so I turn to her.

"What?" I ask.

"Nothing," she replies but she is laughing, I turn to face her.

"Okay, what has that bloody Marcia said?" it comes out much louder than I intended, Helen at least looks embarrassed.

"Nothing much really, she said you had a holiday romance with a hunky waiter chap in the hotel, who couldn't keep his eyes or his hands off you and that you disappeared one night and didn't come back until the morning," she pauses and then continues, "I am so pleased for you, fair play, honey, what was he like, totally gorgeous I bet." She looks up, "You were at it all night eh," she looks behind her, and before I look at who she has seen I know who is stood behind and must have heard every word, I am right, Mike pauses, he doesn't say a word, just stands there. Before I can stop her Helen blurts out, "What was blondie doing here earlier then, Mike, you know the woman you were talking to," he frowns at her.

"Woman, what woman, where was that then?" Helen looks at me and I blush a deep red, she cannot answer because I didn't tell her all the details, Mike smiles, "You cannot answer that, Helen, because you don't know, you must have been told by someone else," he looks directly at me, then he turns back to her, "and the reason you wouldn't know is that you were six minutes late this afternoon and you thought I wouldn't notice and you clearly were not going to tell me, and you know what that means don't you?"

She nods her head, her face is now unsmiling, "Maybe if you used your interrogation techniques on that shoplifter he wouldn't have got away with it, and maybe your informer." He looks at me. "Should ask me any questions she has about my personal life." He walks off down the corridor, I look at Helen, she pokes her tongue out at his departing back, without turning he calls out, "That is attractive, Helen, very attractive, now put it back in your mouth and get back down to custody," we hear him laughing.

We hear the door close as he goes downstairs. I slam my hands back into the bubbles, Helen gives a shrug, she doesn't seem bothered by him having a go at her, but I am so embarrassed, embarrassed that he knows I told Helen about the blonde girl and so mortified that people know about the holiday; that bloody Marcia, I think to myself, I could kill her, so much for what happens in Egypt stays in Egypt. Before I know it the whole of the shift seems to know that I had some kind of holiday romance, just what I didn't want to happen stupid little comments are made, conversations stop as I walk in to the room with knowing little smiles, I have just had enough, good job she isn't in today I think I might just have killed her. Oh bloody hell, I plunge my hands back into the water, Helen is stood watching me, she looks at Mike's retreating back.

"Oh Christ something has upset him, I guess he will be in a bad mood for the rest of the shift now, and I have to make up double time tomorrow," she looks to make sure he is out of earshot. "Anyway, don't worry about him, he will be over it by the time I get downstairs, he isn't one to hold a grudge, but I am sorry shouldn't I have said anything, I didn't realise it was a secret, I was just so pleased that you, well you know, had some fun," she leans in to look at my face. "Has something happened to upset Mike?" before I get to answer she carries on, "Nothing to do with you is it?"

I shake my head, I look straight into her eyes, then I turn slowly wiping my hands on the cloth, we are stood very close, I keep my voice low, "No, I don't know what his problem is, he seemed fine earlier, so it is not to do with me, as far as I know there is nothing going on, not with Mike or anyone else, chance would be a fine thing for me to have anything going on with anyone, and even if I did, everyone would know before I would," I smile, "Come on, give me a hand with these cups."

We walk back to the control room together, she puts the cups down and leaves giving me a wave as she departs. I can hear Helen and Mike chatting just outside but I cannot hear what is being said. Mike returns to the control room some ten minutes later, his tea is probably luke warm but he looks over and raises it as in a toast, "thanks," he says brightly and downs the whole cup of tea in a few mouthfuls then disappears back out of the room.

Craig looks at his watch, "Angie, time for you to go to CID to type up their reports if you don't mind, only for an hour or so, can you finish what you are doing and go now if you don't mind please." I look to the heavens as I know I am going to get harassed by most of them.

"Gee thanks, Craig, can't you send Steve, he deserves, it, he has been a pain all shift – send him, I am going to get so much stick," Craig shakes his head, "you know you are just sending me to the lion's den don't you," he smiles and I smile back at him, I get my things together, I am not bothered in fact I am prepared for it. I have decided not to defend myself, not to argue, I am just not going to say anything. Let them think what they like.

I am surprised that although Phil is the first person I see, he doesn't look at me, he is looking at some paperwork, studying it intently, I walk up to him, I know he knows I am there, I flick his ear but he ignores me, that is fine, he can sulk if he wants to. I go to the desk and sit with my iPod on whilst sorting the papers into order. I see him approaching but I continue to sift the papers, he stands by me, he flicks the earpiece out of my ear, "Is it true then?" he looks straight at me, I look him straight in the face putting the earpiece back in, I know exactly what he is referring to, I cannot be bothered to face the interrogation, so I don't reply, instead I shake my head at him.

He flicks the earpiece out of my ear again and I look at him, shaking my head, "What do you think, Phil, come on you are the person that always says that they know me best, what do you think," I reply and I smile at him, he smiles back.

"I knew it was bullshit, I bloody knew it," he says, "you are just not that type of girl, you may like to think you are, but you are not," he sits next to me and relaxes in the chair, crossing his leg up on his knee. "So tell me what happened then," and so I do, I tell him about Marcia and he isn't shocked at all by her behaviour he thinks it is hilarious about the stray dog and is throwing his head back with laughter, I laugh with him. I look up and watch as Mike comes in, Phil calls him over, "Mike, Mike, come and listen to this, it is priceless." Mike looks over at us, he frowns then without saying a word he continues down the office.

I grab Phil's arm, whispering fiercely, "No, shhhh shut up, I don't want everyone knowing, please, Phil no," but it is okay, Mike ignores us both and answers the phone that has just started ringing, he holds the receiver out and motions to Phil.

"For you, sorry it is work related," he says, his voice is flat, there is no smile on his face, I grimace at Phil and watch as Mike puts the phone on the side and walks towards the notice board, pinning something up, he doesn't look at either of us, he is such a miserable looking man. For the hundredth time that day I want to kill Marcia.

Phil saunters down the office takes the phone and speaks for a minute or so, when he hangs up he speaks quietly to Mike and they both leave the room together, I finish with the statements and put them all away, then return to the control room. I check the logs, pleased that it is nearly shift end time, the logs show Mike and Phil both attending the town centre to arrest someone who Phil has wanted for a long time, he has received a tip off and the person is known to be violent and aggressive. I know they will be gone for a long time and although Phil will be pleased to have got his man he won't be pleased to be working late, I just want the shift to end, I am exhausted, really exhausted, I just need my bed, I think the holiday has finally caught up with me. I have a quick chat to Gavin as I pack my things away, I pull my coat on, as I reach into my handbag for my keys my hand hits against an envelope, knocking it out of my handbag it falls onto the floor, I had totally forgotten it was there. I look around quickly to see if anyone has noticed and hastily put it back into my bag. I walk down the stairs and to the car park with Gavin who seems unusually chatty today or maybe it is because I am impatient. I cannot wait to get to my car to open it. I slide my finger on the closed part of the envelope, I want to open it carefully, I want to keep it as intact as I can, I cannot make out the writing on the front of the envelope, it is too dark but I can see it is writing in capital letters, but very neatly printed, I switch on the internal light in the car for a better look, on the outside there is a teddy sat on a swing, he has the words "be my valentine" across his chest, I open the card and inside are the words "to the world's most beautiful girl" with a squiggle underneath. I hold the card to my chest, my heart is pounding, my mouth goes dry and I swallow hard, I need to get home, I am suddenly taken back many years, when I lifted the lid of my desk to see my very first valentine card, the feeling that my whole heart was going to explode, now here I am many years later and having the exact same feelings. Suddenly I have an urgent need to look at the other card, I am certain, almost positive that the words are the same. I cannot remember the drive home, couldn't tell you if the roads were busy or not, I almost run up my path and frantically get my key in the lock, I throw my handbag at the bottom on the stairs and race up two at a time, my heart thudding hard in my chest, I know that my special things box is tucked at the back of the shelf in the cupboard in the spare room, it is choc a block with loads of teenage memories, it weighs so heavy, but after some considerable effort I manage to drag it out from the shelf, balance it on my head and tip the entire contents out over the carpet, photos, concert tickets and other memorabilia spill out until finally I find it, there right at the bottom is the card from when I was a teenager, my heart skips a beat as I hold it in my hands again. The lovely picture with its glitter almost gone, the dog-eared envelope a bit worn on the edges, I open it, the written words are the same. I hold the cards side by side, the signature is the same, it is not a squiggle it is a signature, why didn't I see it all those years ago, it is so obvious, there is a first initial and then a surname and I know now exactly who the card is from, at least I am 99% sure, I just don't know what I am going to do about it.

I go to sleep with a smile on my face and both cards on the pillow next to me.

Next morning there is a text message, it must have come in after I had gone to bed, it is predictably from Marcia, but I don't reply, she is not going to get out of it that easily, oh no, I read her text and she has sent one word "sorry" but I am too cross with her to let her off by text message. I sit at the dining table and pull the small pile of mail to me, I am still in my pyjamas, the first mail looks interesting, looks like an invite, it is, Frank and Annabelle are having their twins christened in just a few weeks' time, I am pleased to be invited and relieved not to be asked to be a godmother, I am rubbish at remembering important dates, also I don't really understand the role, what is it the person is supposed to do, so I note the date on the calendar. I am not working that day it falls very neatly into my weekend off before night shift so that is perfect, yes it will be nice to go, the weather might be better by then. I have a flash of an image come into my head of Frank with the stable lad in the bedroom but I banish it immediately. For Annabelle's sake I will definitely go.

Chapter Thirty-Three

Because I have got up early I have achieved a lot of things I wanted to get done, I am all up together with the washing and other domestic chores, I keep looking at the two valentines cards, I cannot help smiling when I see them. I want to tell someone, anyone, but I also want to keep it to myself, there is no one really who would understand, well maybe Judy, but is it all so secretive, I want to just keep it to myself for as long as I can. I read through the other mail there are a few things that need my attention and I sort them out straight away. There is confirmation of the details for the hearing of the life assurance claim and even though it is in a few days after my final late shift, I am not bothered about the outcome now as whatever is decided is not going to change my life drastically. Sean is coming with me, we know we have no control over what happens, if Jason did know about his illness he certainly didn't share it with me, a bit embarrassing to have to admit but it is the truth. I have had to fill in a statement about the wedding as they challenged that, as it all seemed a bit unbelievable, I can understand all that too, when I look back it all seems very surreal to me, so I have told them all I know. I don't know many of Jason's friends from University, I never met them, I answered the phone once or twice and passed them over to Jason, but he mainly communicated with them on his mobile or by email. Even to me our marriage seemed weird, a bit disjointed so I can completely understand everyone else struggling with understanding us. I must have seemed like a terrible wife, I didn't know a lot of information about him when he left his education, I think if Sean hadn't have been there to provide them with all the information they needed they would have certainly written the claim off as dishonest immediately. I must admit that I am nervous over the fact that I have no control over the decision, if found guilty through no fault of my own it might affect my job, what if they think it is fraudulent, I don't know if they will, if things happen that way, will they take things further. I have explained all this to Sean, he totally understands how I feel. I know he wishes that we never had to go through this, yes the money would be nice, he doesn't deny that but we have lived without it, we are both comfortable financially anyway. So we will go and listen to the verdict and take it from there.

My stomach is doing flips all the way to work, as I get closer my heart in hammering, what do I say to Mike, what will it be like when I see him as I now know both cards are from him, well as I said I am ninety-nine per cent sure but I will just need to double check before I make a fool of myself. There should be paperwork with his signature on, it should be easy to check without getting caught. I have both cards in my handbag, wrapped in a protective clear file. I wonder if he thought I had seen the card when I was sat with Phil, is that why he looked so annoyed, because I didn't acknowledge it then, maybe he thought I would have thrown it away, not be interested, I don't know what I will say when I see him, or where we will be, I won't say anything in the control room, too public, why did he not send it to my home address, why would he put it in my cubby hole at work, anyone could have seen it. I go over and over the questions in my head, every time I think of the cards I smile, I cannot help grinning as I get into my car.

The wonderful world of the musicals accompanies me on the way to work, I turn up the volume, I sing very loudly, to the music, I am in very happy mood, I park my car and walk towards the parade room, still walking on cloud nine. I know he is always there well before the shift is due to start, I hope to catch him before I am on shift, but I am quite surprised to see that the day shift sergeant is still there talking on the phone, he doesn't look up as I walk in, he is talking quietly into the phone there is no sign of Mike or anyone else. There is only ten minutes to go before the late shift takes over, this is really odd, there is no one about from my shift. It is all so strangely quiet, I walk up to the control room, even before I get there I can hear the noise of a lot of people speaking, there is something going on in the main meeting room, we also use this as a temporary control room for incidents, I walk towards the control room, Craig is heading towards the meeting room, he looks frazzled.

"Catch you later, grab a drink before you start you might not get the chance later," he says without stopping, he is walking but almost running.

I make my way into the control room, the changeover is taking place, it is normally quite quiet but today everyone is talking, it is very busy, half are packing up and half are preparing to sit down. I go to my normal desk and sit down, Paul the person I am taking over from is packing up his things, he pulls his sweater over his head as I wait for him to vacate the seat.

"What's going on?" I ask, he looks at me incredulously.

"You haven't heard?" I shake my head, he continues, "it has been on the news all morning – we have had a siege incident in the town, we have been rushed off our feet all morning, all the senior officers are here, it started off as a bank job that went wrong and now it is an armed siege with hostages."

"Bloody hell," I reply astounded, "I cannot believe it, I have not had the radio or television on this morning, listened to music in the car on the way to work so I haven't heard anything, is anyone hurt?" I ask.

"Yes," Paul runs his hands through his hair, "one fatal shooting so far, we think from someone on the inside that it is definitely the bank manager, we have someone on the inside who is managing to get text messages out, god knows how they have done that, it is being kept really hush hush, that is all we know so far, and I think someone said one of our officers is now in there, or something like that but I cannot be certain. I haven't read the details it has been too busy, I think it is something to do with the sergeant from the shift just coming on duty, as I said, I am not sure who, we haven't been that involved, but he is doing a good job apparently, I have no idea who or how, but he got in somehow, we have the emergency control room set up to manage it, I am surprised you didn't notice the press parked outside there are loads of them." He rubs his hands over his face, "At one point we had a helicopter up there, though what they thought they would see I don't know," he picks up his bag, "here you go, all yours."

I sink into the seat, I must admit I didn't even look in the car park, I swung my car to the staff car park in the normal way, my music blaring, not looking around me, I was obviously distracted by my thoughts of Mike and the valentines card.

The control room is indeed very busy, we don't see Craig or many of the other officers for several hours, Steve has been taken to man the other incident control room and so we are now running two down, we are quite busy with the regular jobs coming in and needing to be allocated to the reduced staff we have to respond, plus we have to answer all the calls from the concerned members of public, it all takes time and we know like it or not some of the jobs will have to be delayed for the next shift coming in, there will be a snowball effect now on the jobs which will probably go on for days now.

In the other room there are various senior officers milling around, Steve is kept very busy, food and drink is taken in at regular intervals, we are kept totally separate from the main room I only see bits of what is going on when going for a smoke break or coffee breaks. The siege continues for another few hours, then suddenly it is all over, it ends in two further people being injured as the building is stormed by armed officers, although more shots are fired, there are no further fatalities, arrests are made, now the press officer is outside dealing with the hundreds of press swarming the building, there is a helicopter flying back over the station, hoping to get a glimpse of the arrested suspects, the press remain outside and the senior officers remain on site.

By early evening I still haven't seen many of our normal shift. It has been a very busy shift, there is a buzz about with everyone rushing about everywhere but eventually it all calms down and we are allowed to take a lunch break. I make my way to the rest room to eat my sandwiches. The room is empty as I expected and hoped it would be, I am tired, I relax back in the chair enjoying the silence for a while, I close my eyes for a few minutes, the door opens and Steve from my shift is there, I smile at him. "Hi, stranger, you still skiving?"

I sit up and say brightly to him, "don't."

He replies, "It has been bloody chaos up there from the start, I just came here as I thought I would find you," he says, "sorry to disturb your break but you are needed downstairs to start to type up the statements for this afternoons incident. Craig says all breaks are cancelled as they want you straight away as nearly all the statements have been taken verbally and they need them typing up, it is bedlam."

I sigh, "No peace for the wicked eh, Steve," I smile. I don't mind really, I can eat my sandwiches in-between the typing.

I walk down the corridor I head towards the CID office. The whole station seems strangely quiet, normally there is someone in the side offices interviewing or completing paperwork, but it is eerily quiet, I push open the door, Nick is there and waiting for me, I can see him at the end of the office so I make my way towards him, he makes no jokey remark as I approach, he is quiet, he says nothing at all, so unlike him, not even his normal jokes with sexual innuendos. He doesn't even make eye contact, I sense something is wrong, no matter what the situation is, Nick always cracks a joke, whether it be a murder or train crash he has this sick sense of humour that helps him deal with the horrors that his job presents. I know he has been heavily involved in the incident at the bank, but I am not sure how much. There is no one else in the office, I place my jumper and bag on the desk and sit down.

"You okay, Nick?" I ask him, he seems really stressed, he jumps when I speak.

"No, not really," his voice struggles to make the sentence. I get up from the desk and go to him, I can see he is really not himself, his cockiness has gone, I touch him on the shoulder. He is shaking I am really shocked at the sight of him.

"Nick, what is wrong?" I look round to see if anyone can help me, Nick is really shaking now, he cannot speak, he is sweating, I sit him in a chair, he puts his head in his hands.

"Oh, Angie, I don't know what to do, help me please I don't know what to do."

I think he is crying now but I cannot see his face, so I stroke his head and get down to his level, looking up at him I can now see he is crying, unchecked tears rolling down his cheeks, I don't know what to say, I hold him for a second. "Nick, what is it, nothing is that bad what is it, is it work or home or are you ill?" I question him, I have no idea what to do, I have heard of a situation like this before, where senior officers go through a major incident then when it is over they have what could be a minor breakdown or an anxiety attack. I look over to see how far my handbag is away from me, I need to get some help, maybe I can reach my mobile phone to text someone without him knowing, but it is too far away so I sit there, just stroking his head, I cannot deal with this on my own. Nick has now put his head on my shoulder, I am kneeling on the floor between his knees, with his head on my shoulder, he is openly sobbing now, I just do not know what to do, I feel so helpless. So I just sit with my arms around him and one hand stroking his head. With a huge sigh of relief I look up to see the main door opening, I see Helen coming in, I put my finger to my lips to tell her to be quiet, she nods okay and goes back out, I am not sure what she thinks, I really hope she realises I need help.

Minutes go by, it seems like forever, Nick is still sobbing, I haven't moved I still have his head in my arms holding him close to me. My knees have gone numb and my back is aching but I don't feel I can move away. I am going through possible options and doubting if Helen had read my situation correctly when Mike walks in, I have to do a double take, as he is in normal everyday clothes, not his uniform, he looks amazing in light blue jeans with a round neck navy blue jumper, he has trainers on his feet, he looks gorgeous, he comes straight up to me, he puts his hands under Nick's arms and pulls him to his feet. I move away quickly scared that he might trample on me, he is stern when he speaks his voice very authoritative.

"Come on, mate, no more of that, let's get you out of here," he places his arm around Nick supporting him with his hand on his chest, I am still kneeling on the floor, he looks straight at me. "It might be a good idea for you to come too, we're taking him home, do you want to grab his jacket."

I don't argue, I pick up my things and Nick's jacket and follow them both, Mike leads the way as we leave the station, we leave via a side door, there is a police car waiting outside. Nick is still crying quietly, his head held down in his hands, I still have absolutely no idea what has gone on, now is not the time to ask. I send a quick text message to Craig to let him know where I am; I haven't got time to give him a full explanation so I tell him I will text him later. Mike opens the back door of the car and guides Nick into it, he holds the door open for me and indicates that I should get in the back too. Mike doesn't speak at all, his face is hard and emotionless as we head through the traffic, towards the outer part of town, Nick is sat forward with his hands over his face, I just sit with my hand on his back, just occasionally stroking his back, I just look out of the window small talk does not seem appropriate so I say nothing, I don't know what I am supposed to do, I wish I had some idea of what it was all about. It seems that within minutes we are parked outside a neat block of apartments.

"Is this where he lives?" I ask quietly, I have to ask because I expected him to live in a house with his wife and children.

"No," Mike replies, "this is where I live, he needs to get his head down for a few hours, he needs to get his head together, I don't think going home is the best thing for him right now."

I look at Nick, he offers no resistance, "Mike," I say keeping my voice quiet, "should he not be with his wife at a time like this?"

Mike ignores me, he opens the car door to let us out and we follow him silently up a flight of stairs, Mike is at the top unlocking the door he stands back and lets Nick go first and Nick heads straight for the sofa and sits down.

"Not there mate," Mike indicates the bedroom, "spare room through there get your head down." Nick doesn't argue, he walks with his head down towards the bedroom. I look at Mike.

"Mike, do you not think that…" the words are lost as Mike punches a number on his mobile, ignoring me he goes into the hall, he closes the door so I cannot hear what he is saying. Nick has closed the bedroom door halfway but I can see he has collapsed on the bed, I go in remove his shoes pull him further up on the bed and I pull the cover over him, he doesn't look at me just closes his eyes and sinks his head gratefully into the pillow.

I am not sure what to do now, not sure what my role is so I return to the lounge, it is not particularly warm so I pull my jumper on over my head then have a good look around, it is a bright room but has paint samples over one side of the room, there is a step ladder by the window, it is clearly being decorated. There are no curtains or curtain poles at the window, just vertical blinds, there are a few personal items and some boxes stacked in the corner, a large lamp has been covered with a dust sheet, there is a large leather suite and a glass coffee table which is partially uncovered, so I sit there for a few minutes, I look around me, there are marks on the wall where pictures have been, I can hear the murmur of Mike's voice in the hall but even though I strain to listen I cannot make out what is being said. Unsure of what to do next I stand and look out of the window down to an immaculately kept communal garden. I turn, I lean on the window ledge with my back to the window and survey the rest of the room. The room has a large breakfast bar which has a few stools sat against it, the kitchen is the other side of the bar, it is quite large with empty surfaces, with just one coffee maker in the corner on the side, it is one of the really trendy ones and looks expensive. In the other corner there is a huge American style fridge, I wander over to the breakfast bar, there is a large pile of unopened mail on the counter, most of it is circulars, pizza menus and there is a few magazine subscriptions, next to them is a large pile of birthday cards. I pick a few up, there are the usual very rude cards, I flick through automatically looking for mine, but it isn't there, there is a pile of bills on the side, attached to each of them are neatly written signed cheques, I pick up one of the cheques and look carefully at the signature. The account is in the name of M Simms and the cheques are all signed, but the signature doesn't look like the signature on the card I have, I recognise this is my opportunity, probably the only one I will get, I have something that I can use as a comparison for the cards so I can double check it.

I look quickly to the hall, Mike is still on the phone, he has his back to me, I can see his reflection in the glass door, I reach into my handbag, I pull out the two envelopes, I gently remove the cards from their envelopes I hold the bill up next to the card to compare the signature, it doesn't match, so I pick another one up to compare. I didn't hear the door open, I nearly jump out of my skin when I hear Mike's voice, "I think you will find that is private mail, please put it down," his voice is hard and formal, it frightens me, I drop the bill onto the counter, the cheque flutters to the floor.

"Sorry," I say nervously, my heart is beating in my chest, god knows what he must be thinking. I bend down to pick it back up, my face is bright red, I am so embarrassed but I know I have just this one chance to explain so when I stand up I manage to find my voice. "I wasn't prying, I wasn't reading it honestly." I look up at him, he does not look happy, he crosses his arms across his chest, his height makes him look so intimidating, I can understand what his staff means when they say he takes no nonsense from anyone, his eyes are dark, he is frowning.

"Well, it looked that way to me," his voice is flat, I look back at him, his gaze is hard, he doesn't smile, I cannot read his expression. I don't know what to say, then he looks down at my hands with the cards in. "What is that you have there?" he asks, I am caught, I don't know what to say, my mouth goes dry, so I say nothing.

He moves towards me and I back away until I am perched on the stool I take a deep breath, he looks so angry, he frightens me a little bit, I know I need to explain, finally I manage to speak, I clear my throat, "I wasn't prying, honestly I wasn't, I was just trying to look at your signature, I wanted to see if it matched these, but clearly it doesn't, " I shrug, I am so disappointed, I hold up the cards in defeat, I have been so stupid, I really thought it was him that sent them, now I am back to square one. I can feel my cheeks burning with embarrassment, now I have no idea what to say or to do, I have no choice but to hand them to him, he doesn't even look, he doesn't take them, I want him to recognise the card, then I will know it is him but he doesn't give them a glance.

"Oh," he says, just the one word, his brow furrows as if he is concentrating, I can see now he thinks they are his birthday cards. My heart is pounding, I want him to realise without me telling him, but I wait.

There is a long silence before I manage to stammer, "They are not birthday cards," I say it quietly, I am really embarrassed now, surely if he sent them he would recognise them, my face is bright red, I need an excuse to get away, I just need to get out of there, I want to be anywhere than where I am right now, I feel like a little child caught stealing sweets, not knowing what to do I lay them on the breakfast bar I speak quickly, "I'll just check on Nick." I get down from the stool and walk the short way to the spare bedroom.

Nick is still fast asleep, his breathing is quiet and gentle. I stand in the bedroom uncertain of what to do now, I look around me, there is a small chest of drawers with a pile of ironed and folded uniform shirts just under the window, but the window is too small to even think of climbing out, I don't know what to do, my heart is hammering hard in my chest, I lean against the wall and take deep breaths to calm myself but it isn't helping, I look towards the front door, my impulse is just to run, to get out of there, my heart is hammering hard, I turn back to look at Mike, then again at the door, if I can make my way quietly out I can be gone before he realises, but my bag is in the lounge where he is, it has my keys and my purse in there, I know if I can get out the door I can ring a taxi and go home, or just make a run for it. I feel hot all over, my face is still burning, I just need to get out of there, I look to the window again hopefully, maybe I could squeeze out, but I know it is hopeless, it is a second floor flat, I desperately need my bag, but it is the other side of him, so I now don't know what to do, I am stuck. I look over to Nick again, he is snoring gently, I wish he would wake up to create some kind of diversion, I glance at his jacket, I have no idea what that could do to help me, I don't want to be caught going through Nick's jacket after being caught looking through Mike's paperwork, so I just stand there watching Mike, I am unsure what he is doing, he still has his back to me, I can only see the back of his head, I wish I could see his face, to know what he was thinking, I am not sure he believes me, I cannot see if he has picked up the cards, I want to be anywhere but where I am now, I just want to go home. I take a deep breath, I walk slowly back towards the kitchen, my intention is to grab my bag and get out of there. I look towards him, he has the two cards in his hands, I reach out for my handbag, it is just a few feet away, but as I do he holds up the older of the two, very dog-eared and faded.

"I cannot believe you kept this," his voice is low, I hardly hear what he says, it takes a few seconds to register what he has said. My heart hammers hard in my chest. He recognises it, that means he must have sent it, or he knows who sent it. He shakes his head again, "I cannot believe it," his voice is still very quiet and very soft, I struggle to hear him.

I wait a few seconds then I reply quietly, "Of course I did, I treasured it," I move towards him to take it back he holds it away out of my reach, I don't want to snatch it from him, I am scared he will damage it. "Please let me have it back, please don't damage it, it means a lot to me you see, it was my first ever valentines card and I thought I knew today who sent it to me," my voice falters, I have to clear my throat, "you see I thought it was you." I take a huge breath before I continue, "I was trying to confirm it, that is what I was trying to do when you come in, I wasn't prying, I was just trying to match them up, but the signatures don't match at all, and now I just feel very stupid, I am sorry, I should go."

I reach for my handbag but he reaches out to stop me and he smiles, his whole face changes, when he smiles, his eyes twinkle, he nods his head. "Oh right, so you were comparing the signatures, okay, that makes sense I guess," he laughs, and I look at him in surprise. "The reason they don't match is that those cheques are written by my dad Martin Simms, he is paying for the work going on here as I don't have a chequebook, but yes." He smiles a lovely twinkly eyed smile, "You are not stupid, not at all, it was me, I am guilty as charged, both cards are from me."

My stomach does a somersault. He hands them back to me, his fingers meet mine, he doesn't move them away, I feel a thudding in my chest, and finally find my voice, "I don't know why you sent them, but thank you for the first one and thank you for this one." I look up nervously, unsure of what to do, he is smiling at me.

When he speaks his voice is very gentle. "Why do people normally send valentine cards?" he asks, he smiles again then he leans in towards me I don't know what he is going to do, but he moves closer, he is so near to me now, he moves his hand to my chin and tilts it up to face him, his thumb strokes my cheek, he is going to kiss me, I know he is, and I want him to kiss me so much. I gulp nervously, my whole body is wanting him, the doorbell rings and I jump away from him he frowns and bends down kissing my cheek gently, he walks past me towards the front door, he stops and looks back. "Sorry, bad timing, looks like the suits have arrived." Mike turns and goes into the hall, I shove the cards and envelopes into my handbag and straighten my tie down.

I don't know either of the senior officers who come into the room one of them is in uniform the other is in a plain suit. They nod their head in my direction as they walk into the lounge, the suited one of them shakes Mike by the hand, "You did good back there, you kept your cool, well done, good decision to bring him here too."

Mike nods his head, "Thank you, sir." They walk further into the room they look around. "I'm decorating," Mike offers by way of explanation for the boxes and lack of furnishings.

The superintendent who I only recognise from the photograph on the wall in the station looks over to me. "Hi," he says pleasantly.

Mike walks right into the room now he introduces me his hand in the small of my back, "This is Angie Staddon she is from the control room, she is a friend of Nick, she is the one who found him, he is in there," Mike indicates the bedroom, "I think he is sleeping."

The Superintendent pushes the door open and Nick is indeed still fast asleep, he is laid in the foetal position. "Okay, let's leave him there for a while, he needs to be kept safe till we can sort out somewhere for him, who else knows about this, is anyone aware he has left the building," he addresses Mike directly, Mike looks at me.

"Actually I don't think anyone does, Angie was the one who called me, she found him upset in the office and needed help."

I look at Mike, that was not strictly true, I saw Helen, but I wasn't about to argue the Superintendent continues, "Okay great, that is great, let's leave it as that okay, I will get some units here for you, get the car taken away, we won't use your staff, makes things complicated, is he okay to stay or do you want him moved?"

Mike shakes his head, "No, he is okay to stay." The superintendent nods his head, he pulls out his mobile phone.

"Actually," I speak out, "I have sent a text message to my Sergeant, umm Craig McDonald to say I was with Mike helping him but I didn't say with what, I mean I couldn't just leave work without someone knowing where I was, I was supposed to be with Nick typing statements."

The Superintendent sighs and speaks directly to Mike, totally ignoring me. "Okay, clear it with McDonald, strictly confidential this is, keep directly in touch with me," he turns away and speaks into his mobile phone, I don't hear what he says, then he hangs up abruptly, he looks to me. "You staying or do you need a ride home?"

I nod at him, "Yes, I need a lift home please that would be great." My phone bleeps to indicate the arrival of a text message.

The Superintendent looks at me and taps his nose. "Nothing to anyone about this okay."

I nod, but actually I think to myself, I really have no idea what has actually happened. Mike sees us both to the door, the Superintendent walks on down the stairs with the other chap who has not been introduced, throughout the visit he has not said a word. Mike says quietly, "Thanks for your help today, Angie, you have been great." I look back to him. "Oh and don't forget," he adds, "we have unfinished business." He strokes my cheek with his finger, I smile at him, I walk down the stairs towards the very sleek black jaguar that is parked waiting to take me home. As we pull away I notice a marked police car pulling up outside Mike's, this time two senior uniformed officers get out, they head towards Mike's apartment. It is very late, I am very tired, it certainly has been a very busy and exhausting day, I have no idea what is going on and I try hard to look serious, but I am smiling inside.

When I finally get home I sit back with a hot cup of tea in my hand and run the whole events of the day over in my head over and over again, my fingers trace my cheek where Mike had touched me. I lay the cards out in front of me, he sent them, he sent them both, I don't know what to think, but he likes me, he liked me years ago and he likes me now, despite his moody expression and him frowning all the time, he likes me, my face is smiling, then I think of the tall woman with the great body and I think of them together, I wonder if she got one too, the smile leaves my face, why am I so stupid, no matter how much I like him, I cannot be getting myself into difficult situations, he is not a free agent and I am not up for playing games. I cannot cope with complications.

Both Phil and Helen have text me, but it is way past midnight, I am shattered, really tired but a happy tired, so I don't send responses, I put my phone on silent and put it back into my handbag. I think back over the events of the evening, the more I looked at Mike today the more I thought what a gorgeous man he was, so caring as he took total control over the Nick situation. I shower and fall into bed totally shattered, I wake to my home phone ringing, it is Phil but from the way he is speaking he is not aware I know anything about the events of yesterday, he fills me in on the foiled bank raid and the subsequent events that followed, it appears that Nick totally lost control of the situation outside of the bank, he had what everyone thought was a breakdown. Phil doesn't know any more details, he said Nick had disappeared, no one knows where, I don't add anything to his story, we chat for a while, it dawns on me I need a lift to work but cannot explain to Phil why my car is still at work, so I say nothing, I will text Craig later. Helen also calls, she has left messages on my mobile phone but as it is still on silent I haven't heard any. She pretty much repeats the same story as Phil does, everyone is drawing their own conclusions, I call her back, she casually asks me what happened when Mike came in, I cross my fingers and lie to her saying I don't know as I left them to it, she doesn't question me further, I am relieved about that. I hate lying but I know how much trouble I could get into if I told her the truth. However, she is happy to change the subject to non-work, she has really bad toothache and I am trying to persuade her to go to the dentist, we argue good-naturedly for a while then we have to get ready to go to work.

I spend the rest of my morning checking emails and popping to the shops to pick up a few bits, I pop in and see Little Ma I notice that Pa is looking very tired and old, he hasn't been well so he is pleased to see me, I sit for a while chatting, although I am running out of time, when Ma asks me to stay with them for lunch, I don't have the heart to say no, so I stay. We have a nice cooked meal. The hearing is tomorrow but I don't tell them anything, Sean will only tell them if it successful. I totally forget to text Craig, with just twenty minutes to get to work I decide to call a taxi; I know Craig will be already there as he always gets in much earlier than he needs to so he can have a proper handover. The taxi man is chatty and I get there with ten minutes to spare.

As I am walking in I see Mike straight away, "Didn't you get a lift in?"

He indicates the departing taxi, I shrug, "Well I forgot to text Craig, by the time I thought about it I had left it too late to ask anyone else, then I would have to explain my car being here, so I didn't bother, totally my own fault," I shrug.

"You should have called me, I would have picked you up, you didn't need to pay for a taxi, make sure Craig sorts out the repayment," he chides.

I check my watch. "Really it was no bother, I have to go, I don't want to be late," as I walk down the corridor I can feel his eyes watching me and a warm feeling appears in my stomach.

Inspector Wallis is in the control room, I wish I could remember his first name, I think it is Kevin, but it doesn't sound right, that is the trouble with protocol, I have to call him sir at work, I need to check on the system if I have time. He holds out his hand to me as I walk in, in it is a white envelope.

"It is an invitation to our twenty-fifth wedding anniversary party next Friday night," he explains, "no excuses okay."

I smile at him, "Okay, as if I would miss it." Hopefully it has both their names in so I can remember his.

"Well, aren't you the special one," Steve jokes, "the rest of us minions just get a verbal invite." I slit open the envelope, the invitation is handwritten, I cannot help but frown as I see the venue, great, it is being held at the police bar, how classy. Not!

I set up my workstation and accept a cup of tea that is put in front of me, I look around the room. "Who else is going?" I call out to the others, there is a general murmur of yes's and one or two no's, okay that is good I think to myself, should be a good night. The jobs start to come in and I get my head down and get stuck in. Phil pops in a bit later to say hello, but it is too busy to chat so we rope him in to making us all a drink which he does good-naturedly and then disappears.

Craig comes into the control room he is with a chap in normal clothes; he calls Steve out of the room, grabs his tea as he leaves with a wave. I don't see them for the rest of the shift, none of us question what is going on, we know that it isn't worth it, we will be told when and if it is relevant. We run without a sergeant for most of the time with Craig popping in to check the logs then disappearing again, we don't see Steve for the rest of the shift either. I phone Phil on my break, his advice to me is to keep out of it, there is something not very nice going on, the less I know the better. He says Mike is behaving strange too, senior officers keep coming to see him and he keeps disappearing to make calls, he tells me that there is some bad business going on so I need to keep my head down, for Phil to take things this way I know it must be serious, I know Phil will always look out for me so I don't ask any more questions, he hangs up. At the end of the shift I pack Steve's things up, putting them away in his locker, I have no idea where he is, I send him a quick text to tell him I hope things are okay and to let him know where his things are, I add a few kisses and tell him his chocolate bar has mysteriously gone missing, he will like that joke, I am always stealing his food.

Chapter Thirty-Four

Tonight I am out with Phil anyway, it was planned ages ago as we have not caught up with each other for ages, I dress in black trousers and a long jumper, nothing too fancy, just before he arrives the phone rings, it is Ruth, I was half tempted to ignore the phone and let the machine pick it up, but stupidly I picked it up, I heard her sob, immediately I think to myself "here we go again" I take a deep breath, "Hi, Ruth," I say sinking into my chair. Twenty minutes later, I am cross that Phil is late as I am still listening to her tales of woe, then she says something that makes my heart go cold.

"Angie, everything has gone wrong, you have to help me, I know you and I have not been the best of friends lately but I don't know where else to turn, you see I am pregnant, I am not sure who is the father, you have got to help me please."

I freeze, I don't know what to say, I bite my lip almost making it bleed, I say, "Who are the options?" under my breath I say to myself over and over, please not Sean, please not Sean, please not Sean.

"Marcus or Sean," she says, my mind wanders. Sean as a father, I never thought of Sean as being with someone serious, well serious enough to have a child with, never in my mind would it be Ruth. She is still speaking, I try to catch up with what she is saying. "Marcus is living in a bedsit in town, his wife is being dreadful, she has kicked him out, his parents are really angry with him, so are mine, so I have nowhere for him to stay either, she won't let him see the children, it is awful; she has cleared out his bank, the situation is terrible, he doesn't deserve this." I stay silent she goes on. "Now he is only surviving by borrowing off me," she gives a huge wail, "I don't know if I want to be with him on a full-time basis, I am so confused, I liked things the way they were, and I know that I really like Sean but not enough to have a child with him," she sniffs and blows her nose. "I just don't know what to do, the first person I thought of was you, can you help me please, Angie, please you have room in your house, you have money."

My mind is racing, I am not sure what makes me say it but the lie is out before I know it, "I am sorry I have no room, Phil is staying here at the moment, as for money what do you need money for?" I question, I can feel the anger rising in me, she seems to recover herself, her waling voice stops.

She replies quickly, "Phil is there, with you, why is he there, have you two finally got it together, does..." she pauses, "does Sean know, my god, how long has it been with Phil, I cannot believe it, Sean will be very cross you know," she fires the questions at me without answering mine.

I take in the last statement and repeat it out loud, "Sean will be cross, why should Sean be cross?"

Ruth laughs, I can hear the bitterness in her voice, all traces of her earlier upset have gone, she practically spits into the phone. "Oh for goodness sake, Angie, grow up, don't be naïve, you must know, he has liked you for a long time, even before you and Jason, he used to parade girls in front of you trying to get your attention, but you never noticed him, you never notice anything do you, you have everything, you married the one you wanted, the one with the money didn't you, then there is Phil, he cannot keep away from you either, walks round like a puppy dog with his tongue out whenever you are near, it is like you have them on this invisible rope, you just reign them in, don't say you don't notice, of course you do. You really have it all don't you– the guys chasing you, the job, the money, you lap it all up, and all the time you play the part of the grieving widow so well."

I can hear the anger rising in her voice as she continues bitterly, "I knew you couldn't wait to tell Sean about me and Marcus, you had to make sure that no one took your place in his heart didn't you, well I did, for a while we had something good going...."

She is breathing heavily now, her tirade obviously taking it out of her, I cannot take it anymore, I take a big breath, I know I am possibly going to regret it but I cannot stop myself, I just lose it completely. "Hold on just one minute, lady, you knew Marcus was married when you first started with him, you knew, you were the other woman, breaking up his family, you knew what the score was, how did you think his wife felt, did you ever think of her, and did you ever stop seeing Marcus during that time you were seeing Sean, no don't answer that, I know the answer, probably not I am thinking, which means the whole thing was a lie wasn't it. Now Sean might have to pay for your lies, if that isn't enough some poor child is going to be dragged into your hopeless mess, I sincerely hope you are happy, please do not call me again, you are a vile despicable woman," then for no other reason than I have nothing more to say I hang up and burst into tears.

I cannot believe my friend Ruth has spewed such hatred at me, I never once did anything against her, even when I couldn't stand to see her with a married man, I kept quiet, how dare she, I clench my fists, I could punch someone, I am so angry, and what she said about Sean and Phil, I have never encouraged them or egged them on, and Jason, I stop, I cannot think about this anymore, if I do my head will explode. She is evil, pure evil. My chest is heaving as I try and get my breath back, my heart is thudding hard, I feel all hot and so I sit there in my chair breathing deeply.

When Phil comes round I am still so upset we don't go out, we call for a take away, I replay the whole conversation back from memory, Phil just swigs his beer from his bottle, he nods every now and then. He doesn't comment until I get to the point where I tell him I hung up to which he adds, "Well she deserved it didn't she, she had it coming, I am surprised that you lost it though, Angie, not like you babe, not like you at all. Poor Sean, getting caught up with her, I did tell him she was a bunny boiler."

"Ah yes," I challenge him, "thanks for not telling me you had told Sean about Ruth, I went ahead and told him and I could have saved myself the embarrassment," I punch at his arm.

"Ah yes," he replies ducking out of the way, "but can you not see, Angie, how it works, you see, Sean like me, has always wondered about our relationship with you, do you trust us, can we trust you, all these questions go unanswered until one day something happens to make us either hide under a bushel or stand up and be counted, that is what has happened here, it is a trust thing, sometimes the trust has to be tested."

I look directly at Phil. "What about what she said about Sean and me, that cannot be true."

Phil shakes his head, "I don't know, Angie, I think both Sean and Jason, and me all had a soft spot for you at one point, it is just because we have grown up in the same area, it just happens, you were always around, you were a scruffy little kid one minute always following Judy and your brothers around then we go away and when we come back there you are, all pretty and grown up with breasts and stuff."

I punch him on the arm again, "Shut up."

He laughs gently then continues, "Angie, it is true, we watched you grow up, it happens, you were right under our noses," he pauses, takes a sip of his drink then continues, "I know I don't go to bed at night wishing we were together, I am pretty sure Sean doesn't either, however, I think maybe Jason did know he wasn't going to live a long life and that is probably why he needed to get married, as if that made him something, you were there and like us, he liked you, obviously enough to want to marry you, I don't know if he knew you were not totally happy but I guess if he was honest he couldn't miss the signs, maybe it didn't bother him." Phil puts his bottle down, he leans forward and runs his hands over his face and over his head, he continues, "We are a fine lot aren't we, I don't know how Sean will be if he is the father, he will be gutted, so will his parents, how far gone is she, twelve weeks yet?"

I shake my head, " I don't know, I didn't really ask, I would assume so, if she is telling people but I didn't know they had been going out that long, there is just so much crap going on lately, on top of this I have the hearing tomorrow, will you stay tonight?" I ask Phil, he nods his head.

"Yes, of course, if you want me to," and I do want him to, I want to talk to him until I am tired enough to fall asleep, I know I will toss and turn if I don't. Phil goes to the kitchen, he comes back with a fresh bottle of beer and tops my wine up, it is nearly ten o'clock, the doorbell goes, Phil looks at me questioningly, I shrug and watch as he disappears to the hallway.

It is Ruth, she is drunk and in tears, she falls into the lounge, Phil sits her in the chair, she is crying and slurring, I have never seen her so bad, I don't know what to say, I still feel angry with her, those things she said cannot be taken back. She sits there sobbing into a tissue, I want to feel compassion, but I am so angry with her, we have been trying to tell her for years that what she is doing is wrong, she chose to see a married man, she chose to break up a family, she knew what she was doing, part of me hates her for that, she looks up at me as if reading my thoughts.

"You hate me don't you," she sniffs and continues, "I don't blame you, I said some terrible things, I didn't mean them I promise you, I am so sorry," she sniffs again. Phil has been in the kitchen. As he walks in, he puts his arm round her, she turns in to him and continues to sob quietly. The doorbell goes, I look straight at Phil. I hold my hands as if to ask who, he mouths back at me – Sean. I walk to open the door and sure enough even before I have the door completely open Sean walks straight in, straight past me, I cannot read his face, he says nothing to either of us, he kicks off his shoes and strides into the lounge, he takes hold of Ruth by the arm, he practically drags her to the kitchen, I can hear him talking to her, the door is half closed but we can tell his voice is angry, I have never seen Sean angry or even annoyed, he doesn't let things get to him.

Phil walks and totally closes the door that separates the lounge from the kitchen, "Let's leave them to sort it out," I nod in agreement, it is obvious to me that Phil has text Sean to get him round here, so we sit down in the lounge, Phil puts the television on, but I cannot concentrate what is on, so we just sit and try not to listen to the low voices in argument in the kitchen.

It is getting late now, really late, Sean and Ruth are still speaking in the kitchen, they have been there for an hour now, I am really tired, Phil keeps nodding off on the sofa I keep prodding him to wake up, I really want to go to bed. I am just whispering to Phil if he thinks it will be okay for me to go up. When there is a knock at the window, it makes me jump, Phil gets up to answer, at the same time Sean opens the door.

"That'll be the taxi," he offers.

Ruth walks into the room, she comes over to me, hugs me and whispers again, "I am so sorry, please forgive me, I am so sorry." I say nothing I remain motionless not returning her hug, I am really shocked at what has happened tonight, Sean takes her shoulder, he guides her to the door, he spends a few minutes at the taxi then comes back in, when he is out of the room I use the opportunity to grab a glass of water, then return back into the lounge.

"She has gone home to sort herself out now," Sean offers by way of explanation.

I look at him, "So is that what you couldn't tell me the other day, Sean?"

He looks down, "No, it is a bit more than that," he sits down, "Firstly you have to know, there is no baby, not mine or Marcus, she isn't pregnant, she is very sad, very lonely she has been very stupid." He sits down and continues, Phil pushes a beer into his hand, he takes a swig, "You know I met Ruth when I was sorting out Jason's estate for you, she works in the legal office, well it seems she and her fella, this Marcus bloke, have got themselves in a bit of a financial mess, he somehow convinced her to try and get together with me, I think they had plans to somehow get Jason's money, not sure how they thought they would swindle the policy from us, but they didn't realise until very recently that the money is not all mine it is both of ours, then I made it more difficult for them as I told them that once I knew their company fees and there would be a hearing, that I had decided to handle the claim myself, they had no way of knowing how the policy was progressing, I guess she thought I had been paid out," he shrugs. "There was me thinking it was my good looks and charm she was interested in," he laughs but it is a hollow laugh. I yawn, I am very tired, I decide to go to bed, I kiss them both goodnight, they both settle down to watch a movie that is just starting, it is bound to be filled with blood and bullets so I climb the stairs, get undressed and crawl into bed, I don't know if I will be able to sleep but amazingly as soon as I pull the duvet over my head I fall asleep straight away.

Chapter Thirty-Five

I have decided I am not going to dress up for today's hearing, Sean has a nice pair of trousers on with a shirt and jacket, but not a tie, I settle for a neat pair of black trousers, a black polo neck jumper and black low heel leather boots, Sean laughs and says I look like a grieving widow so I add a pretty gold and black scarf around my neck, team it with a nice large black and gold handbag. We catch the train, I am shocked to see Sean has booked us in first class, I have never sat in first class ever on any service, so I sit back and enjoy the experience, I don't ask him how much the tickets are, I offered to pay my share before we go to the station but he said it was all taken care of, he shows no sign of nerves in fact quite the opposite, Sean is not a cocky man, but he seems very confident. There are no delays so we arrive in plenty of time, I am feeling a little bit apprehensive, I am not sure why we have to be there in person, they could just make their decision then just write and let us know, it is baffling. Sean did tell me we could have sent along a representative but he was very interested to see the process, as we have done nothing wrong, we are the benefactors of a policy there was no conspiracy to defraud, we have looked at the legal implications, our consciences are clear.

We arrive at the legal offices of the Assurance Company. It is a very imposing tall glass-fronted building, we are greeted by a very efficient lady who directs us to the oversized couches in reception, Sean plays around with the coffee machine, when he bores of that he stands and flirts with the receptionist, she is quite a mature lady, I can tell she loves the attention. A tall chap comes into the reception area, he comes straight over to me and shakes my hand, "When you are ready," he addresses Sean, with no apparent hurry Sean finishes his conversation with the receptionist, pushes himself away from the reception desk, he walks towards the man holding out his hand to shake it. Sean walks confidently into the meeting room looks around him. He chooses the big chair at the end of the table patting the one next to him indicating I should sit there; he helps himself to water without being invited. I want to laugh out loud at his behaviour, this is so unlike him, the chap sat in the room with us is evidently not a senior person but even so, Sean is not going to be intimidated by anyone. The man shuffles his paperwork, he reads out everything that we have been sent, even though there is no need to, it takes ages, there are pages of it, but I just sit and listen, we haven't rehearsed anything so I leave everything to Sean. Sean stands up and goes to the window, clearly ignoring the chap who is still reading from the paperwork, I watch him, he briefly looks at Sean who is stood with his back to him still looking out of the window, he pauses, Sean turns around.

"You are wasting your time, mate," he says looking directly at the chap, "you are just reading to us what we have received in the post, we are not stupid, we can read, to prove that, we signed the documents and returned them to you, the documents we signed stated that we had read the papers which indeed we have, so do you want to stop wasting time and move on as you have another thirty pages to go and unless you have ordered lunch I am keen to get out of here."

I look at Sean, he is so self-assured, no cockiness, but clearly in charge of the meeting, the other chap is sweating slightly, he sorts through his paperwork shuffling them into piles, he places his hands together, he is trying, and failing to intimidate us.

"I feel the need to remind you both that this is a serious matter, I have to ensure you are fully informed and that you know what you may be getting yourself into, we need you to be aware of the penalty for fraudulent claims and the fact that it could lead to prison sentences," he looks very grave at both of us "we always prosecute."

I feel faint, I told Phil we could be in serious trouble, I wish we never had the insurance policy, I just want to go home, I look at Sean, he is stood leaning against the window ledge with his arms folded across his chest, he is so laid back, the chap is still speaking, I look down at my hands, "I have to remind you that the insured may have deliberately misled the insurers on the state of his health, therefore we may go through the judicial system to challenge this claim." I look at him, he looks out of place, his ill-fitting suit, his whole manner is wrong, he continues, "Of course, I also have to warn you that, if challenged, this may cost you more in legal fees than you may be hoping to claim, to put it in plain words for you," he sighs, "you may lose out substantially financially and," he looks at me then to Sean, I look at Sean, he is now sat back down, he leans back in the chair, he puts his hands behind his head, he interrupts the chap who is in mid-sentence.

"Can I just point out to you," his voice is very serious now, the expression on his face is set, my heart is pounding in my chest, I cannot move, I just stare at Sean as he speaks, "we are the benefactors, we did not know of the existence of the policy until my brother Jason, who you refer to as the insured, died, but you did not ask the insured Jason to have a full medical and you did not add any exclusions, you were happy to take the premium payments from the start of the premium and therefore you have a duty to pay this policy to the benefactors swiftly and if you fail to do so we will be putting in a subsequent claim for the interest on the policy, I believe you are delaying this case deliberately." Sean leans forward leaning on the desk, "Also, quoting case law, we cannot be charged with claiming fraudulently as we didn't know there was a policy in existence, therefore we cannot be accessories, can we, so prison sentences and fraudulence does not come into it, does it," he doesn't wait for a reply, "therefore your threats are empty."

Sean stands up, he walks to the other side of the table, he places his hands flat down in front of the man and leans forward he speaks slowly, "Now before we leave please can you direct me to the department where I claim our out of pocket expenses, we travelled first class as you would if you were visiting us and we were paying, I trust that is in order," he stands up, "I believe our business with you is concluded, I will wait in reception," with confidence and poise Sean walks towards the door, "Angie," he says to me, "would you care to follow me."

I stand up, my knees are shaking as I walk across the room, I feel sick and as I walk past Sean he winks at me, I look back at the man but he says nothing nonetheless he looks shaken, he stands up and shakes Sean's hand, he ignores me completely. We leave the room and go back to reception, I have to use the ladies room and when I come back Sean points to a piece of paper I need to counter sign for the expenses claim. I look at him and smile, he is unbelievable. He winks at the receptionist as we leave.

"What was that all about?" I ask him as we walk to the station.

"I have been very busy you know," he looks at me, "whilst you have been sunning yourself in Spain and Egypt I have been swatting up on the law, Phil has helped me and I knew they were just trying it on, and I also knew..." he puts his fingers on my lips to stop me interrupting, "That you would be nervous but appropriate, you played your part wonderfully, I think we will see the pay-out of the policy quite soon, lets grab a coffee at the station, come on my treat, now what do you think you will do with your share?"

I must admit, I haven't thought about it really, my mortgage has already been paid off, I have a lovely car, I am better off than most, but the one thing I am missing is a man to share it with. I could offer Mum and Dad the money back they have given me both for the initial deposit on my house and for my car but I know they would be offended, so I will give it some thought and put it away somewhere safe. I ask Sean what he would be doing with his, he has it all worked out in his head. "Well, sort out a few debts, invest some and then if my parents are up to it I would like to send them away, there is a little place in Italy my parents went on honeymoon many moons ago, I checked online, it is still a hotel, so I would want to send them back there, before my dad gets too poorly."

I look up at him, "What a wonderful idea, you are such a softie," and I hug his arm closer to mine, we walk onto the platform to get the train home. The sparkling rosé wine in first class is perfectly chilled and as we clink the glasses together both of us have a huge smile on our faces.

I have one more day off then night shift, I am not looking forward to nights, normally this is the time we get to see each other and chat properly, especially in the early hours when not much is going on but for some reason I think there will be a funny atmosphere this set of night shift. Steve has not been in touch like I thought he would, he sometimes sends me silly text messages, but I have received nothing at all, even when his football team lost I sent him a message but he did not respond, I am a bit worried. There are others on the shift I could ask, I get on with them all really well, but I don't like to, maybe if something is going on, they might not know either it will just start all the tongues wagging, but the silence is spooky, I suppose I could give him a call but I talk myself out of it. It is strange that there has been very little by way of new news on the robbery, the same old information is printed every day in the press, two were arrested they are being detained but I haven't seen anything of Nick or Simon, it is really strange. I pick up my phone to send a text to my sister, I see a missed call from Craig, I didn't hear the phone ringing earlier so I dial his number straight back.

"Hi," Craig answers cheerfully, he doesn't wait for me to reply he speaks very quickly, "look I cannot talk for long, I will speak to you about how the hearing went later but I just have a minute to just put you in the picture. Steve has been suspended pending an investigation I cannot tell you more than that but Steve has been told he is not to communicate with anyone on the force but he has let me know you have been trying to contact him, you are okay, I know you are not prying, but we are hoping to have this sorted in the next day or so, please don't worry, the rest of the shift will be told tomorrow, I am just giving you a heads up as he asked me to, no more messages okay." I don't get a chance to respond, Craig has hung up. I am speechless, Steve suspended, why on earth, what could he have done to get suspended?

Chapter Thirty-Six

In my four days off I am going to spend a few days with my sister, I have neglected her lately, I know she is busy with the children but she is always asking me to come and stay with her. My brother Stuart has not confirmed his visit yet so I might have to save a few days for him, but I am ringing my parents later to let them know of the party, they probably won't attend but they will want to send a gift and a card, I am glad I have a written invitation for the party as I just could not remember Inspector Wallis's first name, a bit embarrassing I know. I remember his wife's name is Barb I did think his name was Clive, but I couldn't for the life of me remember, I thought I might have had to ask Phil or text Craig as I could not go to a party and not know their names. I am glad that I didn't have to ask anyone, they would never let me forget it, and Mum was rubbish as when I asked her she thought his name was Cliff.

I have not heard anything from Ruth, I did think of her earlier today as I am going shopping for a new outfit for the christening on one of my days off, I would always go girlie shopping with Ruth, but I am going with Helen and possibly Marcia, yes I have forgiven her, although she knows any further holidays she will be taking on her own. I know what I want, I am looking for a nice dress and I need to buy a christening present. Phil has offered to be my significant other, in fact he wants to go but I think he just wants to have a pop at Frank so I think I will be okay going on my own, even though Frank is a patronising swine at the best of times, he likes to refer to me as the little lady who is fighting crime over the telephone, he laughs at this joke, I would probably laugh too if I hadn't heard it about fifty times. Another one of his favourite tricks is to order a round of drinks at the bar when he knows someone else is coming in, he will offer them to order theirs and then walk away so they get to pay the bill. Jason got caught like that just once the bar bill was over forty pounds, he is a heel, Jason was so cross he wanted to confront him about it but I wouldn't let him, I didn't want to embarrass Annabelle. I really am not sure what she sees in him, she is so down to earth and lovely and he is so pretentious and patronising, I wonder if she ever thought about mine and Jason's marriage.

Shopping with the girls is great fun, both are on good form, I find a lovely dress almost straight away and a suitable gift for the two boys, so I can just relax and chill out, I am enjoying the time with both the girls. We all find what we want and make our purchases then spend some time just wandering about. We find a nice restaurant and sit and order lunch. Helen wants to know what happened on holiday so I tell Marcia she is not to interrupt, I sit back and I tell her from start to finish, to clarify my story I show her a text message from Caleb that confirms we slept under the stars but nothing happened. Helen is too quick for me she reads the last part of the message out loud.

"What does, hope all goes well with Nike and that you finally get together with the man of your dreams mean?" she questions, I blush deeply I forgot he added that bit on the bottom, Helen adds two and two together she gets too many. "Oh my god, he doesn't mean Nick does he, oh, Angie please no, there is nothing going on between you two, oh my god, you are not having an affair with Nick are you."

Helen looks at me with horror on her face, I don't know what to say, if I tell her it is not Nick then I have to tell her who it is, so I think I am being clever, I tap my nose and say, "No it is not Nick, credit me with some sense, Nick is a married man, but I cannot tell you who it is, please can we change the subject."

Marcia's face is a picture finally she blurts out, "I cannot believe that nothing happened, I cannot believe you spent the whole night on the beach and didn't do anything more than cuddle, that man was pure lust."

I pass the phone to her, "The evidence is there," I smile at her "you have to except it, that is exactly what happened and as far as I am concerned the matter is closed." I sit back smiling and sip my water before continuing, "I also have news about Ruth," I put my water down and explain what has gone on with her and Sean. Helen is very cross with her we discuss it at length and fill Marcia in on the few details she needs to know. I explain to them both that I was not happy about the way I spoke to Ruth, it is not like me to be rude and hurtful and I feel terrible about it. Our lunch arrives and we sit eating and drinking. Helen is telling Marcia about the time we all had our tarot cards read.

Marcia is really interested in all things like that. Helen explained that no one knew the lady and it wasn't until Ruth went in and saw all the photographs on the wall of her chap called Marcus with the wife and children, the penny had dropped. It was Ruth's boyfriend's wife reading the cards; what's more she knew about Ruth, it was horrendous. Helen then goes on to tell Marcia about her reading and how she is still waiting for the man of her dreams. Marcia puts down her coffee cup and looks straight at me; I know what she is going to ask, without her saying a word I just know.

"So," she says, "what did she tell you then, Angie, did she say you would meet your prince, did any of what she said come true?"

I must admit I have not thought about that reading for a long time, it seems like years since I sat in the room with the strange cat ornaments. I start to recall what the lady had said, some of it I can recall from memory, the marriage, the nursing bit of it, I feel a cold chill go down my back.

"I cannot remember," I say dismissively, "it was a long time ago, but I am not going to be let off so lightly."

Helen interrupts, "No, you had it recorded remember, she had a CD type machine that she recorded it on for all of us, I still have mine somewhere, you must have yours too, let's see if we can find them, we can have a girls' night in and listen to them together." She looks at Marcia, "Wouldn't it be fun to listen to it, to see if anything has come true."

I look down at my food, suddenly I am not that hungry, I feel a bit sick actually, I take a sip of my water, I don't need to listen to the CD, I think to myself, I don't need to think about what is in the CD and whether it will come true, I know most of it has. Helen tells us about her reading, some of it has come true, she has had an operation, well she had her wisdom teeth out, that counts, also the lady predicted that she would move house, this has happened, but it is all very general. I am trying of think where I would have put the CD, maybe I need to get it out and listen to it again.

Marcia is pressing me, she pushes and pushes, "You must remember something surely, has anything come true, at all?"

I look at her, I give a big sigh, "She said I would have a red car, a brand new red car, I ordered a blue one, but the paperwork got mixed up so I ended up with a red one, that bit came true, then she said I would nurse someone, there would be flowers that bit came true," my heart lurches, I cannot speak, I suddenly feel so emotional, she said I would be married twice," I stop I don't want to speak about it anymore, "I cannot remember much else," I add.

Luckily the waitress arrives to clear our plates and we are distracted by the dessert menu. I look at Marcia quickly, she has a questioning look on her face but I look away, I don't want to answer any more questions.

Night shift and it is all very speculative, lots of gossip but no one really knows where Steve is, but someone on the evening shift that was going off duty said that he was there that afternoon in one of the meeting rooms. Nick has also not been seen, I say nothing, I have nothing to add to the speculation, everyone thinks they have both been suspended but there is no proof. Craig is keeping tight lipped about it, it is in the early hours when it eventually calms down a bit and we are able to take a break that Craig asks for our attention.

"Okay, guys, I guess you are owed an explanation, so here it is, to be kept within this shift please. Yes, it is true, both Steve and Nick have been suspended, there was some confusion over whether the permission was given to storm the building at the siege incident, Nick is saying categorically that he heard the order, that he acted on that order, however, Steve is saying he did not receive the order from senior officers, therefore he did not give the order for the building to be entered thus endangering lives. There are no tapes to use as the main control room is the only one with tape facility," he pauses, before continuing. "Unfortunately, the incident had happened so quickly no link was made to the tape recording facility therefore it is one word against the other." There are a few murmurs around control room, murmurings about Nick being impetuous and Steve being a good officer, Craig puts his hands in the air to silence us all, "Look I appreciate how you are all feeling and I must admit it is a horrible situation, I am asking for you to cooperate in keeping it between us, I am pushing for the situation to be resolved as soon as possible; It must be affecting Steve and Nick in a very negative way." Rob and Max start chatting but Craig calls out again, "Also can I have your attention for a while longer, as you may know we have some new probationers starting tomorrow, they have done their induction at the main training site and will be joining shifts tomorrow night, it was the intention to join them on a day shift but the timing was not right, so we have a man and a woman joining the shift, the chap will be in the control room tomorrow night," he laughs to himself. "Oh and I have assigned his trainer," he looks round all of us but I know it will be me. I just know it and he knows how I feel, he laughs, "Yes, it is you Angie, and I know you don't like it but Max is on holiday then and it is your turn."

I scrunch up my nose, showing my annoyance, I like to come in, just do my job, but I have always said I will support the shift in any way, but I don't like training people, I like to just get on with my job. Craig looks at me and smiles, "Go on poke your tongue out, Angie, I know that is what you want to do." I laugh out loud as do the others, I poke my tongue out to him. "Feel better now?" he asks, we all laugh and I sit down as the phone starts to ring, I listen in as Gavin takes the call but it is nothing urgent so I come out of the call and pick up a new call coming in.

Simon wanders in to the control room, normally both he and Nick are joined at the hip, but today he pulls his chair up to my desk. I finish the call I am on and he moves very close to me.

"Take off your headset," he whispers, I pull it from my head, I look over to Craig but he is busy, Simon's face is very close to mine.

"Where is Nick?" he asks in an urgent whisper.

I shake my head, "I have no idea, I don't know," I answer in my normal tone.

He shakes his head, "Please, Angie, I need to speak to him, I need to, it is very urgent, he isn't at home, his mobile is answered by the admin team, and I need to speak to him."

I pull my headset towards me, as I pull it back over my head, Simon looks at me, "Angie, please, I just need a few minutes," his voice is a whisper but very serious, he is worrying me now, I look over to Craig, he is still engrossed in a telephone call.

Simon tugs my arm, "Spare me a minute," he inclines his head towards the admin room, "please Angie," he gets up and leaves the room, I look at Gavin, shaking my head.

"Did you hear that?" I ask but he shrugs and shakes his head.

"Is he okay?" he asks.

I shake my head again, "I haven't a clue but I have got a bad feeling that he isn't, be back in a minute, please tell Craig to come out." I walk into the admin room, Simon immediately closes the door behind me, he makes me jump, when he speaks his voice is threatening and aggressive, he takes hold of my arm his grip is strong, I try to wriggle free but he holds firm.

"Angie, where did they take Nick, I have to know, I have to speak to him for just a second or two, it is really important, I cannot tell you anymore but please tell me," I look at him, then down at my arm, he looks frightened, he drops my arm but he continues to question me, "where did they take Nick after the bank job, someone said you might know."

I shake my head, "Who told you that?" I ask, he shakes his head, his voice is very urgent now, he is frightening me.

"Angie, that doesn't matter, please just give me the address."

We don't hear the door opening, Craig's voice makes me jump, people ought to stop creeping up on me. "She knows nothing, if you want to know you can ask Sergeant Mike Simms, or me, but she knows nothing and can tell you nothing," Simon turns to Craig, his face is flushed, "I know what this is about, Simon, you won't find the answer to your question here." Craig turns to me, "Thanks, Angie, you can go back now," he smiles and I leave quickly. Craig closes the door behind me, I have no idea what is going on, for someone who likes to keep their head down and not get involved I seem to be right in the middle of something nasty.

As I take my seat I hear raised voices, I look at Gavin, he shrugs. "Let's keep out of it, Angie, the less we know the better okay," I nod my head in agreement. I fully intend to.

Mike doesn't come in until the shift is nearly over, it has been stupidly demanding, lots of domestics and fights in the town centre, I look at the logs and can see that Mike and Phil are dealing with a big fight, custody is hectic and hardly any of the uniform shift get to come and see us, the radios are very busy, the jobs are piling up for tomorrow, the guys are coping so Craig and I stop for a while and have a chat whilst putting the duties on the computer, when I look up Mike is stood by the main door, I don't see him at first, I can just make out the back of someone so I continue chatting. I ask Craig about Simon, but he will not elaborate, but it is to do with the bank incident, that is all he will say, other people have been implicated and it now is looking like it could have been an inside job, someone certainly knew a large amount of money was being held there overnight, maybe someone here was involved, they have no idea. He sits back and relaxes in the chair as I tell him about the recent hearing, he thinks Sean is hilarious.

"Fair play to him, putting them in their place," he laughs, "probably give them a bit of a shock, him knowing what he is talking about," he pauses, looking out the door.

"What is it?" I ask.

"Nothing, I just thought Mike wanted me, never mind probably nothing, he is talking to Max now, he will sort him out, you carry on."

But I have finished what I needed to tell him, I stand up, "Is Mike okay?" I ask, Craig looks at me, he shakes his head.

"Not sure really, he keeps his cards close to his chest even with me, but I know either he was, or someone he knows somehow got quite involved with the bank job and he has," he stops, "well I guess you know that he has Nick at his house still, the force thought it would be good to keep him there, he is not doing so well, they think he is at risk of topping himself, it seems he has problems at home too so his wife has gone off to her parents for a while. Nick has an officer with him all the time, but that is between you and me, luckily Mike has his parent's house he can stay at, the force will compensate him using his house but it is not a very nice situation," he gives a big sigh. "I am not in possession of all the facts so I am not sure what is happening though, Mike is dealing with everything very well, I think he is well regarded by those higher up."

I smile, I wish I didn't know that Nick was at Mike's, I didn't need to know, it is just something else I will worry about, I stand up, "I had better get back anyway, I am glad we had a chat."

Craig laughs as he goes out the door. "Me too, Angie, anytime, chatting to you makes the night go quicker," he laughs again, "now get back and do some work," he says good-naturedly.

As we walk out of the meeting room Mike looks up, when he is sure no one is looking, he smiles and winks at me, I smile back at him. I keep remembering what his last words to me were, he said we have unfinished business. I keep sneaking glances at him, but he is now leant back in his chair and chatting to Craig about general stuff, his shirt has come out and I can see just a small bit of his stomach, I cannot help but stare. My text message goes, I look at it my lap so no one can see, we are not allowed phone calls or text whilst on duty but at night the rules are relaxed a bit. It is Steve, I am a bit shocked. He is asking if Craig has told us about his situation, he wants me to meet him for breakfast before I go home, he mentions a supermarket café a few miles away. I don't know what to do. I go over to Craig and ask him if I can see him privately. Mike gets up as if to go, "no it is okay."

I say to him, "You stay, I just need to borrow Craig."

We go into the kitchen, I show him the text, he groans out loud, "Oh god what is he playing at, he can get into serious trouble, you both can."

Craig runs his hands through his hair he looks at me and says, "Angie, I seriously do not know what to do, he is being very stupid."

We hear footsteps of someone approaching, it is Mike, he puts his thumbs up to Craig through the window he calls out, "I am going back downstairs, you okay, mate?" he looks at Craig, then to me, he frowns then says, "problems."

Craig opens the door lets him in, he pulls a face and replies, "Yes, you could say that," he passes my phone to him, Mike reads the message and looks at Craig.

"Oh for Christ sake, what is he playing at, he knows the no contact rules."

Craig pulls a face, "My words exactly, mate."

Mike looks to me, "What do you think then, are you going to go?"

I look at Craig, I reply, "I don't know, I really don't know, that is why I am asking for help, whatever you think is best."

Craig gives me back my phone. "Leave it to me, don't reply I will sort it out."

He walks back into the control room leaving Mike and I just standing there. "So how have you been?" he asks.

"Well, yes, I am fine, I am okay," I reply.

There is an awkwardness between us, as if reading my thoughts he speaks out, "Is there an awkwardness about us?" he asks.

"I don't know," I reply.

"I kind of think so," he smiles. "Well, there shouldn't be," he continues, "you know you were great with Nick, really nice to him and the way you just held him in your arms, made me wish I was him for a while," I look at him and see he is laughing, he is teasing me.

I swat my hand at his arm, "Stop teasing."

He laughs, "Cannot help it, I love to see you blush." I push him away.

"Can I ask you a question?" I ask him direct.

"Go for it," he replies.

Without waiting I blurt out, "How many Valentine's Day cards did you send and how many did you receive?"

His brow furrows as if trying to work out the question, "Strange question," he replies. "I sent one and received none – why do you ask?"

"Well, you sent one to me, but I was told," I pause, "well I thought you were seeing someone, you know the woman from the party."

Mike laughs out loud, "No, I am definitely not seeing anyone and definitely not the woman from my party. I sent one card only and I am very relieved that the woman from the party didn't send one to me," he pauses. "Don't you have another question to ask me?" I look at him and frown he adds, "The blonde girl." I smile, I can feel my cheeks going red. "It was obvious to me you were the one that told Helen that you saw us together, which makes me wonder, why would you want to know about her, why would you be interested in my private life eh," I blush even deeper red, he laughs, "sorry I am being terrible to you, come on tell me, what about you, how many did you receive and send, am I allowed to ask."

I smile at him, "Sent none, received one."

He laughs gently, "That surprises me, thought you would have a pile of them, I felt sorry for your postman," he laughs again then his face is serious, he continues, "I thought you were seeing Dean, he said he was going to call you, I think you made an impact there."

I shake my head, "No, not at all, lovely chap, in fact there were some very cute guys at your party, but he wasn't the cutest."

I look straight into his eyes, then I smile at him. I walk away a big smile on my face. I have surprised myself, I can flirt. I am still very intrigued about the blonde girl though, and the tall girl; why didn't they send him a card and why would he only send me a card and not them?

I walk back into the control room Craig immediately comes over, "Check your phone messages," he says quietly. I check, there is nothing, but within a few minutes there is, it is from Steve, it is cancelling our breakfast date, he says he has something else he needs to be doing, I smile gratefully at Craig, I don't know what he said, but whatever it was, it worked, I totally understand what they are telling me, I cannot be involved in this mess. It is the rules, when someone is suspended all communication is stopped, no visits or communication of any kind is allowed until the matter is sorted.

When I wake up the next day it is around lunchtime, it is to the sound of the doorbell being pressed over and over again, it is the postman with a recorded delivery letter for me, it is an official letter, inside is a cheque for fifty-eight thousand pounds. I am astounded, I reach for my phone, there is only one person I want to speak to. I ring Sean. He hasn't seen his post yet but says he will call me as soon as he is back home, but we are both sure he will have the same as me, I am shocked they have sent a cheque, it is such a lot of money. I shower and dress quickly, I want to put it in the bank before I lose it, I search around for the paying in book, I am so excited, I finally find it in an old handbag, along with the long lost CD of the tarot reader. I tuck both into my handbag and set off for the bank.

Sean is at my house when I get back, he is sat outside in his car waiting for me, he cannot quite believe it, he has got his through the post too, he shows me his cheque which is exactly the same as mine, we high-five then dance around the room. Sean has agreed that I can contribute half towards the trip to Italy for his parents, he is going to book it soon, I know Jason would want this, I now need to try and think of other areas Jason would want his money spent.

I make a prohibited bacon sandwich for Sean and I, then I send Phil a text to let him know about the cheques, he is really pleased as he rings me immediately, he asks if I have any bacon and I say yes, and he says he is on his way. Whilst we are waiting for Phil, Sean asks me if I would think about giving Phil some of the money as a deposit for a house, I am more than happy to do this, but I am not sure he will accept it, we try to think how we can do this without embarrassing him. Sean says he will think of something and we agree on an amount that we want him to have. Phil arrives and I end up cooking us all a huge fried breakfast, we sit and put the world to rights, Phil is really pleased for us regarding the settlement, I look at them both, they are so dear to me, so protective, I don't know what I would do without them.

Sean says he now needs to tell me something that has been on his mind a long time, he clears his throat, "Even before Jason died, I knew that one of Jason's friends from University was a senior radiographer, he was originally based in London, he had an excellent job, he wasn't at university with Jason, he was in the year above him but they met through their love of quizzing and they did keep in touch when Jason left University. There was a small group of them, all very interested in patents and all very educated, I know they all kept in touch for a while but not sure for how long, they only met up two or three times a year, I don't know where they were all based, I had tried looking him up online but couldn't find him, I think he might be working overseas now."

I look at him, "What do you mean, what are you saying?"

Sean sighs, "What I am saying is that I am not sure if somehow Jason would have approached his friend and whether or not his friend would have actually agreed to scan Jason and give him the result."

Phil shakes his head, "No way."

I cannot believe it either, "That is against medical principles isn't it, don't they sign some kind of oath or something?" I ask.

Sean shakes his head. "I don't know, I mean I have rolled it around my head for so long, even if he did scan him, it doesn't mean he could interpret the scan and tell Jason."

I decide it is all too unbelievable, not medically ethical I decide. Although I cannot help thinking of the trips he took to London on his own and I never thought at the time to question it, it seems we really did live separate lives. So we all talk until it is mid-afternoon. There is a cheesy movie on the television we sit down to watch it, I can hardly keep my eyes open, all I really want to do is go back to bed.

I do manage to snooze during the film, I wake up, the credits are rolling, Sean has gone, Phil is still there, slouched on the sofa, he looks so at home, he has sweatshirt and jogging bottoms on and looks totally relaxed, I watch him for a while, just sleeping, not a care in the world. I really wish he would meet someone and settle down, I am not sure what is going on with him and Jo, I am not certain that it has finished, Helen thinks it has, but Jo still has this smug look on her face when she sees me, as if she is having something I want. Phil changes position to make himself more comfortable, I wonder what it would have been like if we had got together. Without realising I sit and stare at him, I don't realise he is awake until he makes me jump by speaking.

"What you staring at me for?"

"Nothing," I reply, "I was just thinking," he sits up looking at me.

"About what?" he questions.

"Well, you know, loads of things, I was thinking of Jason and then you and just looking at you so peaceful and comfortable, not a care in the world, you are a lucky man, Phil," I pause, then ask, "Phil, are you happy with your life?"

Phil sits up in his chair, "Bloody hell, Angie, that is a bit of a deep question isn't it, what has brought all this on then, was it something Sean said earlier?" I nod to him and he shakes his head.

"And how long have you been thinking about me and Jason then, what is all this about?"

I sigh deeply, "I don't know, I think I am just tired, I just don't know, I have a very happy life and I am very comfortable, but I do miss having someone, you know, in my life, as in physically. I must seem so ungrateful because I know I am lucky to have great friends, a lovely family and a great job, but look at you, you have someone physically but you don't have anyone emotionally – you are so relaxed about life, do you understand what I am saying, do you not miss that?"

Phil leans forward, he rests his elbows on his knees his head on his hands.

"I am a totally different kettle of fish, Angie, I don't think I would cope very well having someone there all the time when I am home, I like the detachment, but when I look at you sometimes I see such a lonely face looking back at me, I think that maybe you are ready for a relationship with someone, maybe you need to let someone into your life, it has been a while now since Jason died, maybe it is time for you to let someone get close to you again, what do you think?" I don't say anything, he continues, "I saw the way you were with that chap at the party, your eyes were sparkly, you looked so happy, what about him?"

I look down at my hands and reply, "I know you are right, Phil, sometimes I do lay in bed at night, I think what it would be like to have someone next to me, to wake up, reach out and touch someone else, someone to laugh and joke with but to share all the crap too. Yes, Dean was a nice distraction, but no, I won't see him again, I must admit I am a bit scared, there are just so many crazy people out there, maybe you do have the right idea, just keep relationships physical, not emotional."

Phil laughs, "Who are you kidding, you forget I know you too well, your marriage was neither physical or emotional, it was a…" he falters, "what is the word I am looking for?"

I look him straight in the eye. "A lie," I reply.

Phil groans, "No, that is not what I was saying, yes, you were more like brother and sister, it was a friendship, I never saw any intimate signals between you in your marriage, only maybe in the last few months, you showed just how much you really cared for him, I know you were more like companions," he shrugs. "It worked for you I guess."

I cannot look at him when I reply, I look down at my hands, "No, it didn't work for me, and I think if you are honest you know that, you are one of the people that knew that," I reply bitterly. "I felt suffocated, Jason began to irritate me, within weeks of him moving in, I suspect I irritated him too, if we loved each other that wouldn't have happened would it? I think if he had not become ill, I would have sought comfort somewhere else, with someone else, I don't think I would have been faithful, I don't think our marriage would have lasted," I look at him. "That is a terrible thing to admit isn't it."

Phil looks up sharply, "Knowing what I know about you and Jason as in what he did, I wouldn't have blamed you, I watched you say your vows with tears in your eyes, but it wasn't tears of happiness, I know, but then I watched you support Jason through his illness, the love you showed his family and him at times. Well, it showed me what a loyal person you are, so you wouldn't have been unfaithful, least I don't think you would, I think I know you very well, I know that, you wouldn't have cheated on him you would have sacrificed your own right to happiness because that is the person you are, that is why I love you, for that reason." I cannot help but smile, he is so lovely sometimes.

"What a lovely thing to say, Phil, yes, you do know me very well, but I still allowed you to kiss me, and to hold me, and we had moments of intimacy together when Jason and I never had anything like that did we..." I don't give him chance to respond I let out a big sigh, "I wish I could be like Marcia, she falls in and out of love but always has a smile on her face."

"Yes, she does," Phil nods his head in agreement, "but she has never settled with anyone longer than a few months, she has never lived with anyone because I don't think anyone can tolerate her mood swings, her need to control and her jealousy. She has two sides to her, one is bright and bubbly but the other is very dark, sometimes she is not a nice person at all."

I smile at him, I know I am being naughty but I cannot resist asking him, "So who is your ideal woman, if you had to pick from say... our shift?"

Phil laughs, he scratches his head, "Well, obviously not you, as you are already crazy about someone but just won't admit it, so I will say..." he pauses, "this is not to go anywhere else okay, I would say Helen, she is cute, smart and has an amazing body, but the sad thing is she doesn't know I exist, not in that way, she is just a mate."

I don't know what to say, it is madness that she likes him and he likes her and I cannot say a word about it, I have promised her and now promised him, what a crazy situation.

275

"Hold on a minute," I protest, "what do you mean, I am crazy about someone and won't admit it, who are you talking about?"

Phil takes my hand, he holds it, he rubs the back of my hand, he looks at my hand, "Angie, my lovely Angie, I know you like someone and I am pretty sure that he likes you, I am not mentioning any names, but I see you look up and your face light up when he comes in the room, he does the same, he asks what he thinks are subtle questions about you, just the odd one so as not to raise suspicion; no one else knows but I notice these things, whenever someone mentions your name my radar goes up, I don't know why for some reason you obviously are fighting how you feel because you haven't mentioned a word to me about him, or do you think I might disapprove," he pauses, he looks at me, "I am right aren't I?"

I don't say anything, my heart hammers in my chest, I don't want to admit I like anyone, I am not sure if he is right or not, we have never been seen together, there isn't anything going on, a few hugs here, a quick birthday kiss, but no one could have seen us, he is just fishing, or maybe he is thinking of someone else or maybe he is putting two and two together and making too many.

I pull my hand away sharply and retort back to him, "I have no idea what you are talking about, you are talking rubbish," he raises his eyebrows and I add quietly, "you are wrong, Phil, you really are wrong, there is no one, no matter what anyone else says or thinks, it is too soon for me, far too soon."

"Okay," Phil stands up, "have it your own way, but I think I am right, the business over the concert ticket, why would he do that?" Phil looks at me, I shake my head.

"You have it wrong there too, Phil I paid for my ticket, I gave the cash to Mike, and whilst we are on the subject, I wasn't impressed at being treated like a charity case, not by him or anyone else," I look at him, "and just whose idea was that, Phil," I pause before adding, "yours." Phil's holds his hands up in defence.

"Hey no, where did that come from? I had no involvement, I bought two tickets, so did he, I was going to ask Gemma, I know she is a huge fan, but I didn't in the end. I didn't know at the time who he was taking, probably big bird, I don't know, but regardless, I wasn't involved and I am not about to blab who was, their intentions were good, leave it at that," he sits down and picks up the newspaper. He doesn't look at me. "And you know what, whatever you decide to do, with whoever and whenever, you don't always need my blessing, or Sean's either, you might think it is too soon but I disagree, I think the time is right for you, I won't see you with a crazy guy, or someone like Simon, don't worry about that," he folds the paper in two, I can see he is looking at the football scores, but he continues, "I know what I see, if it makes it easier for you, he is a great guy, one of the best, I think a lot of him, when you are ready to tell me I will make it easy for you, you take me out, buy me a pint or maybe get him to buy me a pint, then you can say, you were right Phil, okay."

I don't reply, I don't know what to say. My home phone rings, I walk over to answer it, I look back at him, my heart is beating hard in my chest.

"You are so wrong, Phil, so wrong, there is no one and I am not ready for anyone." I pick up the phone but it is just someone selling something, I hang up and look at Phil, but he has his head in the paper. Obviously the subject is closed; I give out a sigh of relief.

Chapter Thirty-Seven

I shower and head off to work. We have had such a deep conversation this afternoon, it wasn't intended but I cannot believe that Phil likes Helen, he has no idea she feels the same, I wish I could play cupid but I am rubbish at things like that, I must think of some way I can make those two get together. The new chap is waiting for me as I go into the control room, he is very keen but he will have to wait a while, I have admin things I need to do, so I put him with my colleague Gavin to watch the jobs coming in, Helen calls up to see me, I have to bite my lip to stop myself from smiling.

"Hey, want to come to Starbucks in the break, I know you don't normally have a break on nights but I have a voucher for buy one get one free on coffee and cake, it runs out tonight, shall we say eleven?"

I nod my head, giving her a thumbs up but as I am listening to someone talking on the other end of the radio, I cannot reply back. When I finish speaking on the radio I log the detail then I check with Craig, he says it is alright to go off site, his parting word to me is, "just make sure you are not late back you have a trainee to think of, it won't set a good example". I nod my head in agreement and return to my seat.

The trainee is a nice enough chap, his name is Bradley, he is very earnest, a bit, well very full of himself, so over confident for someone in a new job. He is young, maybe early twenties, very tall and slim with very blonde hair which he has gel on to make it spiked up, he is all kitted out in his new uniform. He has a funny briefcase with him which looks odd as everyone else just uses a pocket book, but he has a huge spiral bound notebook, he writes everything down, very slowly, maddeningly slow, I have to wait for him to finish writing, I take him through the current jobs, allocate a few via the radio for the officers. Mike comes in, I call him over to sign some jobs off and ask him to take some notifications to the parade room for officers not on duty, I introduce them, they shake hands, Mike walks over to Craig and I turn back to Brad. He is very interested, he asks lots of questions, then when I answer he writes it verbatim, he writes everything down, I try and tell him it is not necessary but he ignores me and writes that down too, I just throw him a look, shake my head and continue. I struggle with him as he challenges everything I do, although I try and tell him we are governed by the police force procedures which is why we have to work a certain way he still argues, I look at Gavin, he smiles and raises his eyes to heaven.

Mike is sat with Craig, they are both sat back in their chairs chatting, I watch them, whatever they are talking about they are not agreeing, I look at Gavin and shrug, it is none of our business. I take a call from a resident who is complaining about an alarm going off at a neighbouring property, it has been going for several hours so I take the details, create a new job and I explain to the caller that I will see if we have key holder details, there is nothing suspicions, it is quite windy out, sometimes this makes alarms go off. There is no alarm company to notify so I explain all this to Brad, I get out of my seat to go and check the address listings, luckily there is a key holder, as I return to my seat Brad remarks, "Didn't notice what a nice pair of legs you have," I ignore him, I call the key holder, they are happy to go and sort the alarm out, so I close the log, explaining the procedure to him, then I get up to return the card and sit back down.

Brad remarks again, "Of course I couldn't see your lovely legs under the desk, I was too busy looking at your chest,"

I turn to him in total disbelief at what he has just said, I am shocked at his comments, I keep my voice quiet, "Hey look," I say, "you cannot be making remarks like that to people you have just met, you are going to get yourself in a lot of trouble very quickly," he shrugs.

"I was just paying you a compliment, don't get excited, love, you are not my type," he taps his pen continually on the top of his notebook.

I hate being called love, it makes me cross, and the tapping is driving me nuts too, everything about him is irritating, I try and keep my voice calm, I reply in a hushed tone, "And please don't call me love, okay, it is rude and demeaning, your remarks are too personal. I am just trying to help you, before you make comments to people, get to know them and their sense of humour, you can get in serious trouble by making sexual comments and calling people inappropriate names," I turn to look at him, I breathe deeply to calm my tone down. I lean in closer to him and speak quietly so as not to be overheard I relax a bit, "Look, I am sure you mean well, and I hope it was just a joke, but you are new, just calm down a bit and you will be fine," he doesn't appear to be listening, he is reaching into his wallet, he pulls out a picture, he passes it to me.

"See, told you, you are not my type, this is what does it for me, this is my girlfriend."

I take the photo, the lady in the photo is enormous, really huge, she is laying on a bed with just a bikini on, her voluptuous body spilling over the bikini leaving little to the imagination.

"You're shocked, aren't you?" he asks.

"No," I reply, keeping my voice calm, "she is a very pretty lady." I pass the photo back to him, "But it doesn't excuse you, you still cannot be making sexist remarks to people, some will take it okay and some will get offended, just be careful," I warn him, he shrugs.

"Nah, I will be okay, you just got a bit of a problem I can tell you are a bit highly strung, you need to get a sense of humour that is all, lighten up a bit, darling. I mean you are pretty enough with a good enough body but too tense really, it puts blokes off, lighten up," he goes back to tapping his pen on the pad.

I dig my nails into my palm, he has really goaded me now and I am trying very hard to keep my temper, he is so arrogant.

"Trust me," I say through gritted teeth , "I have got a good sense of humour, but even I would be careful with some people as they might have an off day I am certain you wouldn't want to offend anyone being so new," he is clicking his pen on and off rapidly now, not taking any notice.

"You seeing anyone?" he asks looking pointedly at my bare hand, I take a deep breath, I turn my chair back to the screen.

"Let's concentrate on the logs again shall we, I will show you the resources we have available," he shrugs.

"I thought not, like I said pretty though you are, nice tidy body but, well you seem a bit cold, a bit detached, if you know what I mean," before waiting for me to reply he continues, "like I said that puts blokes off, maybe you should work on that, make a bit of effort sometimes, waste time having a flash chassis when the engine is a bit dry and crusty isn't it," he replies cockily he continues clicking his pen on and off.

I am not sure how I don't punch him, but I check the time, it is nearly eleven, I look over to Gavin I speak with my teeth clenched, "You are a very rude man, don't say I didn't try to warn you, your mouth will get you in trouble." I flinch as his next words hit me.

"My mouth could get you in trouble, honey, if you would just let me," he lets out a loud laugh, I look at Gavin,

"Your turn now again I think, Gavin," I get up pick up my handbag, "I am off to my break," I call to Craig.

As I walk away Brad calls to me, "Hey, Angie," I stop and look back.

"Think on what I said yeah," I look at him murderously, Craig looks over giving me the thumbs up indicating Brad, I give him the sign for cutting the throat.

At eleven I meet Helen downstairs, it is a general rule that on a night shift breaks are not taken off station, most of the shift have a break in the early hours but we decide to go anyway. The cake is delicious we have a long catch up, she chats about everyone on her shift, she doesn't mention Mike, I am waiting to hear if she has any gossip about him but nothing, she says nothing at all about him, she chats about Phil, she openly tells me how she thinks he is the ideal man for her and he doesn't even know she exists, I have to sit and say nothing, a promise is a promise.

We chat about lots of things then out of the blue she asks, "Has Simon ever been to your house?"

I am shocked, "What?" I ask her.

"Well he was asking about your house, you know, how many bedrooms you had, I thought it was a strange question, but he said he was just interested, I think he likes you, more than just as a colleague," I shake my head.

"I am not interested in Simon, not interested at all, but," suddenly it occurs to me, "Helen, did you tell Simon I was with Nick the day of the bank job?" she nods her head.

"Yes, he was asking, I didn't see the harm in telling him, he seemed okay with it."

I frown, I don't know what is going on, but I don't like that Simon is asking so many questions about me, I take a sip of my coffee and look at Helen, "What is the time, Helen?" I ask her.

She makes me jump by saying, "Bloody hell, it is ten to twelve we are going to be late."

I grab my coffee in its take away cup, I grab hers too, we run to the car. She drives fast so we get to the station at two minutes to twelve, I run up the stairs with her just behind me, on the last but two steps I catch my handbag in my foot I trip, the half-drunk coffees shoot out of my hand, hits into the door in front, it splashes up the walls and down the door.

"Shit," I say loudly. Helen overtakes me and opens the door.

"I will cover for you whilst you clean it up, I will tell Craig you are in the loo okay."

"Thanks, mate," I say gratefully, not sure why she didn't stop to clean it up.

I mutter under my breath, I grab some wet wipes from my handbag wipe the wall and door clean, the carpet is a bit wet so I dab it with some more wet wipes then I pile the huge sodden heap of wet wipes up together. When I finish I pick the pile of wet wipes up, carry them into the small kitchen area. Just inside the door is a flip top bin, I push the top and push them down to the bottom, my hands are sticky from the coffee, I turn to the sink I notice the new chap Bradley is sat on the floor, he looks like he has fallen, he is about to get up, there is another chap stood by him and someone else who I can hear on the phone round the corner but I cannot see them, I say quickly "you okay" when he nods yes I shrug, wash my hands and without drying them I return back to the control room. I slide in my seat and sneak my headset discreetly on my head, Craig has not noticed I am late back.

The rest of the night shift goes quietly, Brad is nowhere to be seen, Phil comes in for a chat he asks what I think of the new chap, but a call is coming in so I answer it and give Phil a thumbs down, when I come off the phone he is speaking to Gavin and I know they are discussing Brad. I watch the clock hoping that I might get lucky and get sent home early but the names go in a hat and it is Max that is the lucky one.

Chapter Thirty-Eight

Looking forward to the party tonight, most of my shift is going, I am dressed and ready to go, Marcia is picking me up in the taxi on the way so we can both have a drink, then we are picking up Helen. I am having my hair trimmed tomorrow, so tonight I am pleased as it goes well first time and I don't have to fight with it. My dress is a short navy blue shift dress but with short sleeves, it has a double layer effect at the bottom, the dress has a lace overlay; it cost a lot more than I normally spend on clothes, but I love it and it fits perfectly, it feels lovely, I wear lace hold ups and finish it off with nude colour high shoes. Helen and Marcia are both dressed up too, they both look stunning – Helen in a fitted red dress with high black patent shoes and Marcia in a green jumpsuit and flat gold sandals, both are looking very glamorous.

We arrive at the party in good time, the celebration is going in full swing, there is the main hall which has the disco then the quiet area where the bar is, this is where the main shift are. As we join them Barbara calls me over to join her in a glass of champagne, I attempt to sit on the bar stool but don't quite manage it so I half sit on the barstool, half leaning, I take the glass politely but I know I cannot drink it or I will be throwing it up later, we chat for a good half an hour. I dutifully pay an interest as she shows me the pictures of her grandchildren and asks about the family. I see Phil approaching me with a glass of rosé in his hand, Barbara turns away to answer someone who is calling her, Phil hands the glass to me, as he does he leans over whispering in my ear, "Do you know your dress has caught on the barstool and we have all had a lovely view of your fancy lacy stocking tops for the last half an hour," he throws his head back and laughs and I want to kill him. I jump off the stool quickly pulling my dress down, there is a round of applause accompanied by boo's and spoilsport remarks.

"Thanks a lot," I glare at Phil, he laughs, he picks up my glass of champagne and downs it in one gulp.

"Don't thank me, I made sure we all had a good look first before telling you," he laughs again and I push him away good-naturedly, he walks off towards the bar.

I look back at Barbara but she has been called away and gratefully I return to the table where the entire shift is sat, I take all the humorous remarks and poke my tongue out to them all. Helen comes and sits with me.

"What do you think of the new chap then?" she ask.

"He seems okay" I reply keeping my voice as flat as I can.

"What about you?" I look at her.

"He is a total dickhead," she spits out, "totally off his head, I think he is on something, heaven knows what they were thinking taking him on."

I laugh out loud, "What did he do to upset you?" I ask.

She shakes her head, "He is mental, he asked me if I ever got sexually excited when arresting someone, then asked if I ever fancied someone I arrested, I mean," she pauses, "what the hell is that all about." I shake my head.

"What did you say to him?" I ask.

She snorts, "I told him not to be so bloody ridiculous." I cannot help it, I laugh, she looks at me, "Was he okay with you?"

I nod my head, "Not the most pleasant person," I don't say anymore, maybe I am a bit of a cold fish, maybe I do need to lighten up, maybe he hit a nerve, that's why I didn't like it.

The buffet is announced we all trudge off to join the line, Mike is stood behind me in the queue, Helen is in front of me, she turns to me, "Who are the cute guys over in the corner there?" she asks.

"Which cute guys?" I reply. "There are so many here tonight."

I cannot help but steal a quick look at Mike, I am not sure if he heard or not, but he doesn't say anything. He is looking lovely tonight, he has on a grey and white stripe shirt with a white collar with black jeans, I can smell his musky aftershave from where I am standing. Phil comes up to the queue pushes in between me and Helen, he is scoffing food as he is loading his plate.

"Hey, you, have you not eaten today?" I protest.

"No," he responds spitting bits of food out, "not since the breakfast you cooked me this morning and that barely touched the sides," he laughs out loud, fills his face with a whole spring roll, turns and tries to kiss me, I push him away, he taps Helen on the shoulder and does the same, she just laughs at him pushing him away playfully. I hope Mike doesn't think we got up this morning together and had breakfast, I glance quickly at Mike but he is talking to someone behind him, he doesn't appear to have noticed.

Everyone is getting merrier. We return to the table and chat noisily as we eat, the food is delicious, I look around the room, there has been a good turnout for them both, I am really pleased. I return to the buffet table, there is no queue so I help myself to cake then I turn round and watch the dancing.

The dance floor is full, everyone is having a good time, I can feel myself getting tipsy, I decide to go onto soft drinks now, I grab a glass of water, taking a long drink I look around the room, I see the admin girls are there,

Sue and the stunningly slim Dee are stood by the edge of the dance floor , I cannot believe she went out with Mike and they are not still an item, they would make an amazing couple – he is so tall and handsome and she is in the supermodel range, tall slim and willowy. I watch her, she is so elegant, so beautiful, her long dress is moulded to her body, she is impossibly skinny, I look down at my cake, suddenly I don't want it anymore, I look back at her, she is stunning, she has no breasts, very flat chested but she is still striking, she has long hair to her waist, worn in a silky long curtain she is just so darn lovely. She is stood talking to Simon, I watch as Mike walks past and she smiles at him, he smiles back but he doesn't stop, I watch her to see if her gaze follows him, but she is giving Simon her full attention. I wonder what went wrong with her and Mike, there is no indication between them that they were a couple, I wonder to myself, why are they not together now. They would make a striking couple.

I look around at everyone having a good time, there has been a really good turn out and I am pleased for them, I stand on my own just watching everyone for some time, my head is beginning to clear, the food and water have helped. For the first time in a long while I am having a great time. Clive and Barbara get up and say a nice speech then they disappear leaving the youngsters to carry on into the early hours. One of Clive's sons come over to me, he introduces himself, his name is Carl, but I cannot remember him from when I was young, I think he went away to school, but he clearly remembers me and my family, he has fond memories of Judy and admits to having a crush on her, then he tells me about how he used to follow the boys around for a few days in the summer holidays. Then he was sent off to stay with relatives, Jason and Sean were his heroes, he is upset to hear about Jason. We talk about him for some time, I feel comfortable telling him about Jason, he seems to know so much about my family, but he cannot remember Phil, even when I point him out, he still cannot recall him. He is chatty, very entertaining, he remembers so many funny stories about our families: when my brothers used to go out with him, shooting rats and scrumping apples. We speak for quite some time about growing up, then he tells me about his work in the armed forces and being away from home for long periods of time. He is very easy to listen to.

I look around the room, there is a group of our shift stood by the bar chatting, all laughing and joking good-naturedly, I look over and at the same time Mike looks up and smiles at me, I cannot help it, I can feel myself blushing, he has such an effect on me, he looks so gorgeous tonight, I lose myself just watching him as he is talking, his hand gestures make me smile, he gets very animated when he speaks, I forget to listen to Carl, who is still speaking, I cannot stop staring at Mike. Carl asks me a question and I jump, I nod yes and he seems happy with this answer, I turn away from looking at Mike so I can listen properly again.

After quite some time Helen comes and drags me away saying we need to dance, I roll my eyes at Carl and smile apologetically as we go onto the dance floor, I look around and Carl is right behind me, he joins us as we dance, he seems to be on his own and the three of us dance together. The night is getting on and the DJ plays some lively tunes, we dance for quite a while then go and sit back down, the shift are all sat down, I watch as Carl leaves us and he returns to the bar.

Phil speaks quite loudly making himself heard, "Who was that you were speaking to over there?" he asks, I shake my head.

"Clive and Barbara's son, you must know him, Phil, I couldn't remember him but his name is Carl, he knows Sean and Jason, he lived in our area, don't you remember him?"

Phil shakes his head as I continue, Helen leans in to listen. "He doesn't remember you either, which is strange, he is a lovely bloke, and he is single and quite dishy."

Helen smiles, "Go for it, girl, what have you got to lose," she laughs out loud as I shake my head at her. The DJ starts playing the grease medley, Helen and Marcia jump up.

"Come on everyone, let's dance."

One by one they pull everyone on to the dance floor, until the whole of the shift have taken over the dance floor. As the lads dance the traditional moves of the greased lightning track I move to the outside of the dance floor.

"Are you scared of getting trampled too?" Mike smiles at me.

"Yes, something like that," I reply.

We watch as the dancing gets more raucous until the big finale, the medley finishes, the strains of hopelessly devoted to you comes out of the speakers, I move to walk back towards the table.

"Yey, where are you going?" Mike catches my hand. "You don't get away that easily, I was about to ask you to dance."

I smile, I walk back to him, my feet are killing me, but I am not about to refuse, I have waited for this moment for so long, my heart is thudding hard, as he holds me in his arms, pulling me close to him. I look around I can see others getting together for the slow dances, Jo and Julian are holding hands on the dance floor they are holding each other very close, I catch Julian's eye and I smile, he smiles back and then looks away, maybe they will be okay after all. I hold my hand on the top of Mike's shoulder I lay my head on his chest, my other hand he is holding close to him, next to his chest. We move round to the music, my heart is hammering so hard in my chest I am sure he will be able to feel it, I want the song to go on forever, it feels so right to be next to him, we don't speak we just move round and round. I can feel his cheek pressing gently on my head. The song finishes, I pull apart for just a second, the new song starts, the strains of Boris Gardiner's 'I want to wake up with you' comes through the speakers, Mike makes no move to let me go, he pulls me very close, I look up to him, he looks down at me and smiles.

"Perfect choice of song," he whispers to me, my stomach does a somersault, my heart is hammering hard in my chest. I look up, Barbara's son Carl is stood watching just a few feet away, I know he is going to ask me to dance, but I just want to stay in Mike's arms, so I close my eyes and snuggle deeper into his chest. We have been interrupted so many times but this time I just want to enjoy this moment.

I wish it didn't but the song finishes, we stand for just a second as he looks down to me he looks into my eyes, I think he is going to kiss me, I look up as someone calls his name, I smile as the flash of the camera startles me, Mike laughs and pulls me close to him. My whole insides are doing a somersault, I so want that kiss, we break the stare as someone bumps into us, reluctantly he pulls away and we go back to the table. Mike holds my hand on the way back to the table but I pull it away as we reach the table, he looks at me a slight frown creases his brow, but I look away, everyone is sat back down apart from a few stragglers still dancing. Mike returns to his seat, I sit opposite, I take a sip of my water, I want to look at him but I cannot do it, I am so embarrassed I can feel my cheeks burning and the hammering in my chest has not gone away, just the smell of his aftershave makes my head spin. I check my watch it is getting late, much as I don't want the evening to end, I have booked a taxi home with Helen it should be here soon, I feel so very jumpy and nervous, my throat feels dry, still I cannot look at him, I gulp down some more of my water before I jump off my stool volunteering to go to see if the taxi is outside. Helen shrugs, she is very tipsy, clearly she is not bothered, she keeps looking around. I guess she is trying to see where Phil has disappeared to. I look round, Julian is sat hunched over, nursing his whisky, looking deep into the bottom of the glass, he sways from side to side, in danger of falling over, I look around quickly, Jo is nowhere to be seen. I cannot be bothered with long goodbyes so I lean over to let Helen know I am going, she looks at me, her big eyes filled with tears.

"I am going to stay a bit longer if you don't mind," she states, I shake my head, I lean in and give her a hug.

"You take care okay," I whisper to her, I cannot believe Phil is behaving like he is.

I look round for Marcia but she is happily chatting with one of the cute guys in the corner, I sneak a quick peep at Mike, he is leaned forward in his chair listening intently to what the chap next to him is saying, he doesn't look up, much as I try and will him to look at me, I place my glass on the table, pick up my handbag and make my way towards the exit.

As I walk down the corridor, Simon catches up with me, "Hey, Angie, Wait up."

I look at him, he takes my arm stopping me, "Look, I am sorry about all the questions about Nick the other day, he is going through loads of shit and I just want to help him, we have some outstanding cases we are working on and I needed just a few minutes of his time, just to tie up loose ends," he pauses before continuing, "I didn't mean to upset you."

I shrug, "It is okay I wasn't upset, I just don't know anything, I cannot tell you anything other than I saw him crying, I gave him a hug and then Mike took over," I smile at him, just a small smile, Simon frowns.

"You see, Angie, he isn't at home still and it has been a while that is all, his wife is not answering my calls, I just don't understand it."

Simon does seem genuinely concerned, I wish I could help but I just don't want to get involved, so I shake my head, "Sorry I cannot help you."

He shocks me by pulling me close in a hug, he whispers into my hair, "Thank you for helping him, Angie, you are a diamond," I pull away just to see a head popping back into the main function room, I don't know who it was but it must have looked like Simon and I were cuddling, maybe he intended it to look that way. I stand away from him, I pat Simon's shoulder.

"I have to go, Simon."

I can see the yellow light of a cab through the window, I walk down the corridor towards the exit, I pass the dark offices and in the silence I can hear Jo and Phil in the dark room where they were before, I know it is them, it is so obvious, I can hear the noises of their intimate coupling, she is giggling and it annoys me. None of them are even bothering to keep quiet, I don't know why I get so angry, but I see red, I just do, I pound on the door saying loudly.

"You are both pathetic you should get a life or at the very least, a room."

I hear the desk scrape, I hear Phil swearing loudly then the sound of hushed voices but I walk out the door into the car park, I laugh out loud to myself at the shock it must have given them, I wonder at what stage of coupling they were at. The door opens behind me but I don't look back. I regret banging on the door and now I don't want a confrontation with Phil and the last thing I want to see is her face. I am cross that ten minutes ago she was dancing close to her lovely husband and now he is sat upstairs nursing his drink knowing exactly where she is and what she is doing with Phil. I push the large exit door open and head towards the taxi reaching it at the same time another couple do, "Angie", I hear my name being called, I groan to myself, I don't want any confrontation with Phil, I shouldn't have banged on the door it was childish, I just want to go home, my feet are killing me. I look around, there is Mike stood watching me he is half in the doorway holding it open.

"Hi," I say in reply.

"Angie," he walks a few feet towards me letting the door drop closed behind him, "have you got a minute?"

I look at the cab and at the other couple looking hopefully. "Sure," I reply I walk back towards him.

He holds out his hand, I take it, not sure why I am going back in, he slides his pass through the security swipe and leads me back into the station.

He opens the door of the lost property office, he pulls me inside, there is a lamppost just outside the window so the room is not in darkness, I can see his face, he doesn't let go of my hand, he seems completely sober, he speaks quietly his eyes looking into mine, he seems nervous.

"Did you have a good time tonight?" he asks, I frown at him, confused at his question, I look at him, I don't reply, I have no idea why he is asking that. My feet are screaming to be released from my high shoes and I have let my taxi go, but I know I don't want to leave. I look at him, I can see that he looks uncomfortable he frowns before he carries on, "Okay, Angie, can I ask you something?"

I frown at him, "Look if it is about Nick or Simon, I don't know what is going on, and I have just told him that."

Mike looks at me. "Oh okay, that is weird him asking you questions, but that wasn't what I wanted to ask you,"

I look up at him this time it is my time to frown. "Okay, what do you want to ask me?"

I try and keep my voice flat hoping that he didn't hear me shout at Phil and Jo, I look up at him, I could just drown in his eyes, if he asked me to strip naked I don't think I would refuse him, he just doesn't know the effect he has on me, my stomach does a flip and my heart starts pounding in my chest, he is stood so close now, he smiles again.

"Well, a few things really?" he asks, I look at him puzzled, I cannot think what questions he has so I shrug at him I frown again.

"Yes, of course," he looks at me.

He looks so totally gorgeous, I want to pull him close and kiss him. I don't want to be answering questions, I want to feel his lips on mine, why doesn't he realise that I want to lose myself in the gentle kisses, instead I watch him as he runs his free hand through his hair, it all seems so theatrical, I want to laugh, I bite my lip to stop myself giggling. We are standing so closely I can hear him breathing, he clears his throat, he seems nervous.

"Look, I don't want to appear arrogant or conceited but you know before when you said there were cute guys at my birthday party," he pauses, "well, would that have included me at all"?

I say nothing, I just look at him, my heart is hammering in my chest, I raise one eyebrow, a slight smile on my face, he is nervous, I can tell, but he goes on. "And tonight when you said there were cute guys here, would I be conceited to hope that there is any possibility you might have meant me in that too?"

I still say nothing I just continue to look at him, still biting my lip, his face is so serious, his dark eyes so solemn, he pauses.

"Is there a final question, or is that it?" I ask him.

"Oh right, okay, you want all of them, well I have one last one, so here I go," he moves closer, we are practically inches away, his breath is light on my face as he leans down to me, his voice is low. " Well, earlier when we danced upstairs, I held you close and I really wanted to kiss you, well not just then I have wanted to kiss you for some time now, but we always seem to be interrupted, and even tonight, well there was so many people around, I didn't want to embarrass you, it didn't seem appropriate so I didn't, I missed my opportunity, and then just now when I came after you but you were," he pauses, "with Simon, I wish I seized the opportunity earlier," he runs his hands through his hair, he looks at me. "Jesus, you must think I am such an idiot."

I cannot help it, I cannot suppress the giggle, I move towards him, "I don't think you are an idiot at all, I think you are very charming, and very sweet when you are babbling," Mike looks at me, his beautiful dark eyes shining, and I am lost, those lovely eyes, the wonderful smell of him, "so" I address him, "are there any further questions, Mr Simms?"

I giggle again, I am loving it, but he is back in his comfort zone now, his uneasiness has gone, he pauses for just a minute before asking, "Okay, Ms Staddon, would you have any objections if I was to kiss you, right now,?" he pauses, moves back a few inches then laughs out loud. "Obviously I want to avoid the risk of getting head butted, so I am giving you notice and as you know, we do have unfinished business, it wouldn't be right to leave it unfinished would it?"

I look into his eyes, they are twinkling and there is a smile playing on his lips, I laugh at his comment, my heart is hammering harder, my stomach is turning somersaults.

"You are so not funny," I whisper, but I smile, "yes," I reply, "to all your questions, Yes, yes, and yes."

Without waiting he moves forward, there is just a seconds pause as he holds my chin up with his finger and gently his soft lips meet mine he drops my chin and holds me round the waist pulling me to him, his tongue meets mine, our teeth crash together, our tongues entwine, my hand is on the back of his neck I never want this to end, he pulls me very close to him, our bodies are so close together I am sure I can feel his heart beating, my head is full of explosions, his lips move from mine, his kisses now running across my cheek, my neck.

We stay like that for quite some time before he pulls away he whispers, "Oh my god, Angie, I have wanted to do that since, it seems forever, you are so beautiful," I push him away gently and look up into those dark eyes.

"Mike," I whisper, he looks into my eyes, my stomach flips over.

"Mmm," he murmurs in response, I move closer to him.

"You should have asked question number three first," I giggle.

Then I am immediately silenced as his lips meet mine again, this time all gentleness gone, I drown in his kisses, a door slams nearby and we pull apart, Mike looks at me.

"Shall we get out of here?" I nod, I cannot speak, my lips are bruised from his kisses, my whole body is on fire, wanting more, so much more.

He opens the door looking both ways, we run giggling out of the station as fast as my high shoes will allow, my sore feet forgotten as I run with him, it feels like I am skipping on clouds, I just cling on to his arm as we head towards the main road. He holds his arm up as vehicles go by.

"Where are we going – your place or mine?" he asks, he laughs mischievously, I cannot answer my head is still reeling from his kisses.

Luckily for us a cab stops, we fall gratefully in the back still holding hands. "Where to?" the driver asks. I give the name of my road I sit back and look out of the window.

"You okay?" Mike asks, he is holding my hand in his lap our fingers are entwined, I nod, but I am not okay. Suddenly the reality of what has happened has hit me, we have kissed and we are in the cab heading to my house, I don't know what to do, my nerves have kicked in, questions are flying around my head: what if I invite him back, what will his expectations be, will he expect to stay over, am I ready, is it too soon.

My heart is hammering hard in my chest but now for other reasons, I am so nervous, we get nearer my house, I speak to the driver, "Just here will do thanks," as he pulls over and stops I open the door quickly. I get out, I just stand there whilst Mike pays then he gets out, stands on the kerb next to me.

"Angie, are you okay?" he looks around. "You were very quiet in the car," he looks around. "I don't think you actually live here, you live the next street along."

He reaches for my hand, he puts it in his, we walk slowly down the road towards my house, I know that I have to explain to him, but how can I? so we walk in silence, the only noise is the clatter of my heels on the pavement, I glance at him and he is looking at me his face frowning slightly, I know I have to explain, so I clear my throat, I cannot look at him, I concentrate on the pavement ahead.

"Mike," I am aware my voice is shaking but I have to ask him, I have to know. "If we do go to mine, what will happen when we go in to my house?"

I glance up quickly at him, and then get brave, I look up at him, he smiles at me and my heart melts a little bit, he takes my hand and we walk towards my house.

"Okay, mmm yes, maybe we should have thought about that," he pauses, we are just a few hundred yards away from my front door, he stops and turns to face me. "Okay, maybe we should have gone to mine instead, but as we are here, how about this," he pauses. "How about, we will go in, you can get me a beer maybe, if not a coffee, if that doesn't sound too cliché then hopefully I can have more of those wonderful kisses, maybe we can just talk, just chill out and talk, how is that, is that okay." I nod my head, he pulls me to him. "Angie, nothing is going to happen that you don't want to happen okay. If you want me to go home now I will do, there is no pressure I promise you, I will be a perfect gentleman."

I hug him to me, "You must think I am a bit crazy," I say. "

Not at all, I think you are lovely, it is very sweet," he replies. He kisses the top of my head. "Come on, you can make me a coffee, you need the practice." I smile and he takes my hand, I follow him the short distance to my front door.

As we enter my house I feel all my nerves disappear, I am in my own home, he is relaxed, he copies me as I take my shoes off, I like that, I like that he is respecting my home. When I am barefoot he looks even taller and I dwarf at the side of him, he looks so at home as he follows me into the kitchen, I flick the kettle on, he leans down and nuzzles my neck.

"Is this okay?" he asks.

I hold him close to me his lips move from my neck to meet my lips, he runs his hands up and down my body I feel myself trembling, I want more, I want this man so very much, it has been so long. The kettle flicks off but we continue kissing. We stay like that for some time, when I pull away, he opens his eyes.

"You do not know how long I have wanted to do that," he whispers, I smile at him, my heart flips, I feel tears prick at my eyelids and I blink them away, I turn back to the coffee making.

"Tell me then," I whisper, he stands behind me, his body is close to mine. He is kissing the back of my neck, then my shoulders, I pour the hot water into the cups add the coffee and milk, he doesn't stop, his hands are on my waist I turn round gently.

"Your coffee, sir," I hand him his cup, I take his free hand leading him into the lounge.

We sit on the sofa, at opposite ends, I am a lot more relaxed now I smile at him, "So how long then?"

He cocks his head to one side laughing, I love his laugh, "You are terrible, fishing for compliments, young lady, but if you want to know it has been since we were in class together, you came back after having your tonsils out, I missed you, you were away all over Christmas."

I laugh out loud, "Wow, I cannot believe you remember that, I had my tonsils out when l was fifteen years old or thereabouts, I had a thoroughly miserable Christmas that year."

"Well, me too," he says laughing. "I had it all planned as that is when I thought I would pluck up courage to ask for a Christmas dance, at the Christmas disco but you were not there, I only found out where you were when I overheard your friends talking, I was gutted, seriously gutted." I kick him gently with my bare foot.

"Shut up," I laugh embarrassed,

"It's true," he moves my feet, he sits up closer, I now have my thighs across his lap. "I told my dad, I thought he would laugh, but he could see I was deadly serious about you, he suggested the next opportunity would be a Valentine's card I thought you would recognise the signature but when I saw it the other week, I can see it just looked like a squiggle. I was gutted when you didn't even look my way, I watched as you put it in your schoolbag, you looked around to see if you had been spotted but you didn't look at the tall dark-haired, spotty geek sat several rows behind you to the right wearing his heart on his sleeve."

I put my empty cup down on the floor I take his from him, I move my leg to one side of his so I am sat straddling his lap, my dress has risen up but I ignore it, I hold his face in my hands.

"Well, we have had the dance and now here it is, your Christmas kiss," I kiss his eyes, his cheek, his chin and then very gently I kiss his lips.

We sit just holding each other, his hands resting on my hips, we sit just kissing, it feels wonderful, his face is shaven and soft, "Was it worth waiting for, Mike?" I breathe deeply, I love his aftershave, he moves underneath me.

"Yes, definitely worth waiting for, but, Angie, my darling, much as I am enjoying this, you will have to move, honey, or I will have to break my promise earlier that I would be a perfect gentleman in that nothing will happen."

I laugh out loud, I kiss him once more then move away back to the end of the sofa, I look at him, cocking my head to one side. "Do you think I am being silly?" I ask him, I watch his face as he replies, he is shaking his head.

"No, not at all, it is a big step and you need to do things when you feel comfortable, in your own time, I appreciate that." He is so lovely, so understanding, I feel completely at ease with him.

"Thanks, I appreciate that too, it is just I have not been with anyone since Jason, it isn't a big thing for me but when I do, I don't want the first time to be here, in my home, it might be a bit weird, I don't know, but I want it to be something special, somewhere special with someone special, do you understand that?" He smiles reassuringly.

"Yes, yes, I do, absolutely understand, but..." he frowns, there is a long pause before he speaks again. "I thought you had met someone on holiday, everyone was talking about your big holiday romance where you were seduced by a handsome Egyptian. I must admit when I heard Marcia telling everyone about your night of passion on the beach I did feel bit pig sick, especially after my birthday kiss from you," he pauses, "you kissed me then left me, the last thing I wanted to hear was the details of your exotic lover, but I found myself unable to walk away, so I sat and listened to how the chap you met was irresistible – he was handsome, he swept you off your feet and how you were gone all night, she told us you were keeping in touch."

I smile at him, I don't say a word, I get up from the sofa, I look in my handbag for my phone, I sit back down scrolling through my messages looking for a specific one.

"Well, you can hear the correct version from me."

I tell him all about Caleb about our night on the beach, he laughs out loud when I tell him about the dog, then I show him the text, when he reads it he looks at me. "Who is Nike?" he asks laughing.

"You are Nike," I look at him, before I continue, "there was something about that night, I cannot explain it, we both felt so comfortable talking to each other, he told me about the love of his life and for some reason I talked to him about Jason, then for some reason I found myself telling him all about you. I listened to him, he listened to me, it was a special night, the best therapy for both of us, but he misunderstood your name, you are Nike," I reply.

"I am so glad to hear it," he replies, he pulls me close to him. I sit up.

"Phil tried to tell you about the dog incident but you were not in a good frame of mind, you ignored him and stomped back to your desk,"

Mike smiles, "I didn't want Phil telling me more details of your holiday, I had heard enough, no matter how hilarious he thought it was."

We talk into the early hours, we cover everything from school to our likes and dislikes, we laugh as we both discover we like a lot of the same foods, we go to the same gym but have never seen each other there, then we talk about the evening, the dance.

Mike frowns, "The chap you were taking to tonight, who is he?" he asks, I shake my head.

"His name is Carl, he is Barbara's son, he lived in the same area as us and knows my family and Jason's but I don't know him at all really. I think he spent the holidays away with family so I never saw him at all, why do you ask?" I frown, Mike smiles.

"When we were dancing he was hovering on the edge of the dance floor."

I nod, "Yes, I saw him too."

Mike smiles, "I am glad I got you on to the dance floor first, I think he was waiting to ask you,"

I nod, "I think you are right, and I am pleased you got there first too," I relax back onto the cushion, stroking my fingers on the back of his hand. "What made you join the police force?" I ask him.

He doesn't have to think about the answer. "It is all I ever wanted to do, I knew when I left school it was what I wanted to do, so I applied when I left college and they weren't recruiting so I went to university then went off travelling for a bit, then my dad told me that they were taking on – I applied and was lucky I got in straight away. I love my job, I love it even more now I get to see you every day." I laugh at him, he pulls me in to his arms, "I remember when I first saw you in the CID office, I think you were working an extra shift, I couldn't believe it was you, I just kept staring, you looked a bit different from school, well a lot different really, but I was sure it was you, then when I made you the cup of tea it was my intention to try and make conversation, but you were too engrossed in your work, never even looked at me once. I used to see you drive in the car park sometimes and I wanted to speak to you but the chance never presented itself, then when the shifts were all changing I saw our shifts would be in line," he frowns, "I

294

didn't know about Jason, I didn't know anything about you at all really, I asked my shift if they knew anything about the people on your shift hoping someone might mention you, but they never said anything, even though it was obvious that Helen and Phil knew you really well they were not forthcoming with any details, they seemed very protective for some reason, and I notice your shift is like that too where you are concerned. It took a lot of effort on my part to find out anything about you, even Craig wouldn't discuss you, I walked in the control room when he was letting people know about you having some time off but he cut the conversation short, I saw on the list that your surname hadn't change, I saw your hand and there was no wedding band, although there was when I saw you another time, I was a bit confused I must admit, then someone, I cannot remember who, told me you were married, and that you were quite recently married. I listened to the talking about a wedding in a castle somewhere, I was gutted. I only found out about Jason when I was out on a job with Phil, Phil asked if it would be okay to pop in as Jason needed something, I cannot remember what it was, but someone had called Phil on his mobile. When we arrived outside the house I asked what we were doing and Phil told me it was your house and that it was your husband he was going to see. I was shocked, really shocked, he thought I knew, for some reason he thought someone would have told me, so he explained everything – he told me then how poorly your husband was, I didn't intend to come right in to your house," he explains. "Well, actually it was the same night we shared our meal, you know the chips and roll." I nod and smile at him, he goes on, "I loved that short time we were together, but then it all seemed to go wrong, you took a call and it was obviously private, so I left you to it, Phil then took a call on his mobile and asked if we could pop in as there was a problem. I don't know why I even got out of the car, but I did for some reason, then I just stood near the bottom of the stairs, just in the hall. It was hammering with rain, Phil was only a few minutes, but once in there, it felt awkward, I could see the picture of the two of you on the mantelpiece. I must admit it was a stark reminder for me that you were actually married to someone else, no matter what my thoughts and feelings were about you, you were married, I shouldn't have gone into your home that night, I was so cross with myself, it didn't seem right for me to be there," he pauses again. "I never actually met him to speak to, I heard him and Phil chatting and Phil quickly sorted the problem out, although I saw him again at the Italian restaurant at Phil's engagement but didn't actually get to meet him properly." Mike frowns, "That was the night he took really poorly wasn't it, the night of the Italian meal, wasn't he taken by ambulance?" he asks, I nod, as he continues, "I must admit, we knew nothing, you all disappeared with Phil and never came back," he looks at me. "It must have been hell for you," I nod my head but I don't respond, I don't really know how to. Mike smiles, "After that I decided that if being your friend was the best I could have, I would settle for that, but your smile still melted my heart and I still couldn't stop myself from wanting to be with you."

I don't want to talk about Jason, I don't want to have to admit to anyone, not least to Mike, that my marriage was a sham. I feel ashamed that I played the part of the grieving widow and the thought of telling anyone the truth about me is something I could not comprehend, as if sensing my discomfort he changes the subject.

"So what made you join the force?" he asks.

I shake my head, "It happened by accident really, I was made redundant from Challis Financial and I saw the job advertised," Mike frowns. "Challis on the high street?" he asks, I nod my head.

"Yes, I worked there almost straight from school," he nods again.

"I know that building, I attended a burglary there a few years ago." I smile at him.

"Yes, I was there then I remember it, they made a terrible mess, that was just before I left."

Mike looks at me he holds his fingers up, "You mean that I would have been this close to you at the time of the burglary, why didn't I see you?"

I shrug, "I don't know, I was interviewed by a plain-clothed officer, I didn't see anyone in uniform."

Mike sighs, "I don't believe it, I could have met you again years ago and I interviewed the wrong members of staff, how crazy is that."

I move close to him, "Well, maybe we need to make up time now," I move close to him, our lips meeting again.

When we pull apart Mike looks down at me, "You have a beautiful home, it is so, so," he pauses, "so calm and comforting, have you lived here long?"

I smile at him, "I am glad you like it, my parents helped me with the deposit, I decorated it myself. Well okay, not actually painted the walls myself but I chose everything; I like soft neutral colours, when I come home I just like to relax and my home is just how I want it to be, I hate clutter," Mike frowns slightly.

"So you didn't buy this with Jason?"

I shake my head, "No, this is my house, Jason moved in here, he never owned his house he preferred to rent." Mike looks around.

"You have done it out really well it is really lovely." I tuck my legs under me.

"Your place is nice too, have you finished decorating yet?" He pulls a face.

"Dad is just finishing off painting then I guess I need to look at furniture, I have a new suite and lounge furniture but just curtains and stuff for the bedroom I guess, oh and a bed, I am hopeless at that sort of thing, I might get you to give me some ideas."

I don't want to talk decorating, I want him to hold me in his arms again, I want to drown in his kisses, as if sensing my need Mike moves his body to face me.

"So when can I see you again?" he asks, I look at him, I cannot resist his dark eyes.

I reply, "Well, I am at work in a few days," he digs me in the ribs making me squeal out loud.

"You think you are so funny don't you. I cannot wait that long, I won't wait that long, so when?" he asks again.

"When do you want to?"

He doesn't hesitate, "Tomorrow, the next day, the day after that." I laugh, he is so adorable.

"Well I have appointments in..." I look at my watch, "a few hours then I am all yours."

He smiles and raises his eyebrows, "Really, you mean that, you are all mine, be careful, honey, perfect gentleman I may be but I might hold you to that," he reaches down lifting my chin to his face.

"Please do," I whisper.

I see him to the front door, we kiss some more, I whisper that I don't want him to go, but I don't want him to stay the night either, not tonight, so we both giggle, he comes back in to the lounge, we sit, we drink more coffee, we chat more, we exchange mobile phone numbers, he won't show me what he lists me under so I don't show him mine either, we cannot stop touching each other I think I am going to drown in his kisses. Before we know it is four o'clock in the morning, he says he will grab a cab from the main road.

"So when then?" he asks. "And what would you like to do?" I smile and raise my eyebrows to him.

"Really," he replies.

"Yes, really," I whisper, "I said I didn't want it to be here, but I didn't say I wasn't ready, and I think with you, Mike, I am ready."

He groans, "Oh baby, what are you doing to me," he looks me up and down, his eyes taking in my whole body, I tremble as he leans over, he traces his finger down my chin and lower to my neck then lower, he stops between my breasts, my heart is hammering, all the nerve endings in my body are suddenly on high alert.

"I promise you I will make it very special."

This time when we go to the front door, I let him leave, I go upstairs, I lay on my bed I cannot stop hugging myself, my text message bleeps, it is a message from him it simply says "goodnight beautiful" with a few kisses, my heart leaps.

Chapter Thirty-Nine

I wake with the alarm and prise myself out of bed, I have to recheck my message to believe it actually happened. I send a text message back to him just one word "morning" it says. Within seconds there is a reply, "morning beautiful what time is your last appointment today." I text back to let him know I will be all done by midday, he asks if he can pick me up at one, that if it is not too soon for me he would like to take me away to a nice romantic hotel for the night, somewhere special but he warns that he cannot promise to be a perfect gentleman. He puts several exclamation marks making my tummy flip. I am so excited; I let out a yelp and jump out of bed.

My whole body has a ripple going through it as I read it again and again, I text back just a kiss and an exclamation mark. I need to get moving, I need to drag my overnight bag out to start putting things in, I reach for the beautiful silky negligee that I had for Christmas from Annabelle, I place it in the bag, I gather a few toiletries, within half an hour I am all packed. I keep checking and rechecking my phone in case he cancels, my heart is hammering in my chest I am so nervous but also very excited. I check my overnight bag again, then go back to check it again. I have a lovely dark green dress to wear tonight with lace hold ups and high black patent shoes; I choose my underwear carefully, matching lace bra and briefs.

I pack my light perfume. I decide to wear my black jeans with low heeled boots and a nice cotton long sleeve black top with a V- neck and pretty false button detail to the front. I put it all out ready on the bed; I add some lovely matching underwear and leave it ready for my return. I drag on a pair of tracksuit bottoms with a matching sweatshirt. I leave in good time for my appointments, I am really early as it is only a short drive, I practically dance into the beauticians and they are there waiting for me when I arrive, within two and half hours I am back with beautifully painted finger and toenails, my personal waxing has been done, my eyebrows are a perfect arch, my eyelashes a deep black, my hair neatly trimmed. I feel great I cannot take the smile off my face, I want to shout out to the world to tell them how happy I am, even when the beautician asks if I am doing anything special, a lovely shudder goes down my spine but I don't want to share my secret, so I reply "nothing much". I pay her, leaving a very generous tip, I feel fabulous, I get home with half an hour to spare, I shower quickly then change into my smart outfit. I try to watch some television, but I cannot concentrate, I am jittery my tummy does somersaults every time I think of being alone with him overnight. I am half excited and half terrified.

Phil has sent a text, he asks if I think I was funny last night, I text back just one word, "Yes". He doesn't reply. He is probably annoyed with me but I don't care, no one can upset me today, he doesn't ask me what I am doing tonight even if he did I would have to lie, as I can hardly say I am having a night away with Mike, if I am honest with myself I have dreamed about this for so long, I hoped he liked me but never dreamed this would happen. I want to tell someone, I want to shout to everyone, I really want to tell Phil but I know I can't, I want to tell Helen but not her either, not yet. I am going to explode if I don't tell someone, so I ring my sister, for the next five minutes I don't let her say a word, I blurt out everything, at the end I ask her what she thinks, there is a silence before she says, "Wow, great, about bloody time."

I ask her, "Do you think it is too fast, I mean overnight with him in a hotel," I go on to tell her that I am frightened at the speed everything has happened.

"Don't be silly" she retorts, "if you are honest it seems that you have fancied him for a long time, just didn't have the bottle to do anything about it, and neither did he , all that skating round each other, well now just enjoy yourself let yourself go, life is too short, sod anyone who says otherwise, how long should people wait, there is no defined time, you wore that black arm band to make Jason's mum feel better, to fill her need, so no there isn't a defined mourning time," she pauses, "and if there is, there shouldn't be, it is how you feel and not anyone else's business," she laughs out loud, "bloody hell he must think all his Christmas's have come at once," she pauses and then adds, "does Phil know?"

I immediately go on the defence, "Why should he know?"

But Judy doesn't bite, she answers calmly, "Because you two share everything, you tell him everything about your life, so if you haven't told him this it is probably because you worry he will be upset, but you shouldn't be, you two would have got it together by now if it was meant to be," she pauses, there is a silence at the end of the phone, "you haven't, have you?"

I don't know how to answer this so I don't say anything, Judy carries on her voice very quiet now, "Oh, Angie, your silence speaks volumes, seriously have you and Phil ever got it together?" she pauses again, "you know what I am saying as in, you know, done anything. "

I eventually find my voice, "No, no, Judy, we very nearly did, but no we never, I think we both got caught up in the moment, and it was all over before it began," There is silence at the end of the phone, "Judy are you still there?" I can hear her breathing.

"Yes, yes, I am still here, Angie, I cannot believe it, that would be Mum's idea of heaven, did you actually, you know..." she trails off, but I don't want to think about it, I don't want to focus on Phil I want to think of Mike. She is relentless, "How, where and when, come on, Angie, this is me you are talking to, how far did it go and why the hell have you never told me?"

So I tell her, about the kiss, she just listens with the occasional "oh, wow and no, really."

"Thank god you both come to your senses, you and Phil would not be a good idea, just like you and Sean, it should never happen, it would have been Jason all over again, oh, honey, you do get yourself in some tangles, don't you?" I nod in agreement even though she cannot see me. Her voice is quiet, "Angie, this Mike guy, well he has liked you when you had fuzzy hair and braces, so just go with it, do this for you, put all that has happened in the past and go and be with Mike, have a good time, no scratch that, have a bloody great time, you both have waited too long."

I put the phone down, I think of the intimate moment Sean and I had, whilst Jason laid downstairs, I vow I will never tell a living soul what happened between us, not even Judy, and definitely not Phil, no one would ever understand. Ever.

Chapter Forty

I don't know what car he drives, how can I know, I have never seen him driving his car, I see him in the police cars all the time but never in his own car, I rack my brain trying to think, but I cannot recall at all. I can hardly ask anyone anyway so I keep checking the clock I am nervously pacing up and down the lounge, I keep looking out of the window and then back at my bag, I look at myself in the mirror, I add a touch more lipstick. "Tonight is the night girlfriend," I speak out loud to myself. My hands are clammy and I am a nervous wreck, I feel sick but I know I am not going to be sick, it is just nerves, what will he do when he sees me, do I kiss him hello, will he come to the door or do I go out to him, what is the protocol?

I sit down, I look around the room, then at the clock, there is just ten minutes to go, I look at our picture on the mantelpiece half covered by a postcard, I move the postcard and look at the picture I speak aloud, "Jason, I hope you are happy for me, I hope I made you happy in the last few months of your life, I tried to carry out all your wishes, I did love you, Jason, but with a different love, a brotherly love, I hope you are happy for me today, I gave you what you wanted, I kept my promise to you and now I have to live my life." The silent picture stares back at me, I stare at it for a minute, looking at the two of us, the emptiness in my smile, I tuck it back behind the postcard, I am nervous now, I sit down then stand up, sit down again, then stand up and move to the window.

I should have asked Judy what to do, she would know. Should I be ready or make him wait, should I be nonchalant when he arrives, what actually is nonchalant. I have never been good at this type of thing. I look out of the window one last time. It is five minutes to one, what if he doesn't turn up, bloody hell I didn't think of that. I shudder, oh my god, I will feel so stupid, I could never face him again. What if he is late, oh no, is it acceptable for him to be late, having been treated so crap by dates in the past I am not having high hopes for this one, but this is more than a date, I really like him, I really hope he likes me too. My stomach is churning, my palms are clammy.

I walk to check the back door, get myself a glass of water, then rinse the glass out in the kitchen, I wash my hands, the doorbell rings, making me jump, my heart starts pounding. I want to look out of the window but it is too late, I know he will see me so I go straight to open the door, he is smiling at me, he comes straight in without being asked, he closes the door, pulls me into his arms and kisses me very gently, he smells of soap and aftershave.

"Hello, gorgeous, how are you?" Without waiting for a reply, he holds my face in his hands. "I have been wanting to do that all morning, he pulls away and looks at me, "your hair looks lovely," he whispers.

I pull him closer to me and kiss him right back, I pull away and look at him, I don't know what to say so I just reply, "Hello you."

I thought I would be nervous and shy but he is so lovely and natural, he just keeps smiling, he walks into the lounge, he looks at me and says, "You look beautiful," he walks over to my overnight bag, "is this it?" he asks.

"Yes," I reply shyly.

"Come on then, let's get going," he takes my hand, we walk out the front door. Parked in front of the house is the beautiful blue Maserati.

"Wow?" I exclaim, I cannot believe it, "that car is beautiful is it yours?" I look at him in surprise.

"Yes, it is, I thought you knew, I thought everyone knew, although I didn't actually buy it, far too much for my meagre salary, but my uncle left it to me when he died last year, he also left me the pocket watch, I treasure both, I would never normally be able to own something as amazing as this, it is one of my four loves in life."

He pushes a button on his key ring, the boot opens, he stores my bag in there next to his, he walks back to me and opens the passenger door, he kisses my head as I get in, he is not embarrassed about the fact we are stood in the street. The inside of the car is all cream leather with walnut trim, it is truly striking, he starts the engine it roars into life. I am not a car enthusiast but anyone can tell this car screams quality and class, even the windows are slightly tinted. The radio bursts into life filling the car with Madness singing "it must be love" Mike looks at me and laughs, he turns it down just a bit, I look at him as he pulls his seatbelt on.

"Cannot argue with that," he smiles again, he is so relaxed where my stomach is doing somersaults.

"What are your other loves?" I ask him, he grins.

"Rugby, my job and beautiful women, not necessarily in that order," he grins at me again and I laugh, just being in his company I am feeling more relaxed now. I lean back in my seat, Madness are still singing, we both join in with the lyrics, then he winks at me and I go all shy.

As he pulls out from my road he looks at me, he smiles, I just love that smile. "Can you tell me where we are going?" I ask.

"It's a surprise," he laughs gently.

My stomach flips, I feel all hot, suddenly I am transported back to another trip and the hair on the back of my neck stand up and my body shudders involuntarily, I am not sure if he hears me but I say quietly, "I hate surprises," if he does hear, he doesn't respond, but the traffic is really busy and he has to concentrate. My hands feel clammy and I clutch hold of the side of the seat, I need to calm down, that was all in the past, it is ridiculous to think this date is the same, I convince myself in my head, I breathe slowly trying to calm my beating heart. I look at Mike, he is still concentrating on the busy traffic, but he glances over and smiles.

We drive for about ten minutes, aiming for the countryside we talk mainly about his uncle and his love of cars, he had two cars when he died, he left this one to Mike the other classic Austin Healy he left to Mike's brother Steven. His uncle, who is his dad's brother was quite young, he died very suddenly they were all very shocked, he was only in his fifties.

Mike looks at me, "I am sorry, am I being tactless?"

"No, no not at all," I reply, I feel a jolt of unease, I have not given one thought about Jason.

Mike changes the subject, his voice is light. "Okay, Mrs I hate surprises, shall I tell you where we are going?"

"Yes please," I reply a little too quickly, "that would be nice," I add.

Mike continues, "We are going to a hotel which used to be owned as a normal family house by my great grandfather, on my mother's side, it was huge, it is now a hotel. I used to spend every school holiday there with my brother and my cousins, my cousin Peter and his wife are now the current owners but my Auntie Sylvie and Uncle Dennis have lived there all of their married life, they were the one who converted it to an hotel, they both still live in a separate wing of the hotel. It has changed almost beyond recognition from when we first used to visit when I was very young. Sylvie is my mum's sister and even now, when the hotel needs extra staff both of them will offer to help. I don't think they are really needed but it makes them feel good and my cousin panders to their need to be wanted." Mike looks at me again with that lovely smile, he continues, "We are staying in the old part of the building, it used to be our playroom, well the boys' room, I love the room, it is now a very classy part of the hotel, so befitting for you, my special guest," he looks at me and winks, my stomach turns a somersault.

Just a few minutes later he pulls off the main road through a huge set of iron gates into a large gravel drive, the hotel is stunning, the afternoon sun is hitting the front windows making them dazzle, Mike leaves the car at the front, he walks round to open my door, he takes my hand and helps me out of the car, I look up to see an older man walking towards us, he is wearing a long tailed evening suit.

"Good afternoon, sir," the chap stretches out his hand to greet Mike formally, then pulls him into a hug, Mike laughs.

"They got you working then, Uncle Dennis." Dennis throws back his head and laughs too.

"Yes, never a day off, you know how it is, lovely to see you, Mike, I will get your bags." Mike takes my hand.

"This, Uncle Dennis," he addresses Dennis direct, "this is Angie, a very good friend of mine," Dennis takes my hand from Mikes, he tucks it under his arm.

"You are very welcome to our hotel, Angie, tell me, how did he manage to catch a beauty like you?" he laughs and hands my arm back to Mike. "I will take your bags to your room, I will leave the car here for now and park it later, looks good for business," he laughs, "I am sure you will want to show her round the gardens and the lake, but don't worry." He taps his nose. "Peter has warned me, I am the sole of discretion," he hands a room key to Mike.

"Thanks, Dennis," Mike shakes his hand again, he turns to me, he takes my hand, he pulls me towards the side of the house.

"What was all that about?" I ask him as we walk along.

"Ah that is because if my Auntie Sylvie knows we are here, she will ring my mum then they will never get my mum off the phone trying to find out all about you, as it was I phoned Peter, asked him to keep it quiet, I can trust Peter and Dennis," he pauses and turns to face me. "I really wanted to show you this house, the gardens, the lake, it has been in my life since I was a baby, I used to know every tree, every bush that grows here, hide and seek was fabulous when I was a child." He reaches forward and kisses me gently on the lips then takes my hand and we walk toward the lake.

There is a wedding reception happening so we sit and watch as the bride and groom have their photographs taken with all their guests by the lake then the bride sits on the swing as the groom pushes her, it is all so very romantic, they look totally happy, it was a truly lovely place to be getting married. As the wedding guests move back towards the hotel I laugh out loud and pull him to his feet, the bride is stood with the groom having a photo taken by Mike's lovely car, Mike shakes his head but he smiles and I know he is secretly pleased. As the wedding party disappear inside leaving the bride and groom having more pictures taken, we sit by the lake watching them, the swans swim up with their young cygnets, Mike puts his arm around my shoulder, he is kissing my head and squeezing me close to him.

"I cannot believe I am here with you," he speaks into my hair.

"Me neither," I reply.

We sit for a long time in silence just holding hands and just watching the swans until the bride and groom make their way back in, then we walk back to the hotel, Mike leads me up the side staircase used mostly by the staff and bypassing the reception. The hotel is beautifully furnished, even the hallways have lovely paintings on the walls. When we reach our room, Mike stands at the door, the key is hovering by the lock, Mike takes my hand.

"You okay?" he whispers, I look up at him and smile.

"Yes, perfectly okay thanks."

He pushes open the door. Immediately the room has the wow factor, I am totally blown away as the room is stunning, it is massive, lovely and light, it has three floor to ceiling windows with gold and cream swags and tails decorating them, in the centre of the middle window is a very large Jacuzzi bath, with a view looking for miles right out onto the countryside. I cannot believe there is a bath right in front of the window, but it is just beautiful, something pops into my head about a bath in an odd location I have a weird sense of knowing the bath would be there, but I cannot recall the relevance. The bed is a huge four-poster decorated in the same gold and cream swags as the window, with beautiful matching cushions in front of the pillows. There is a large table with four chairs, centre table is a fabulous floral display which must be two foot in height, in the corner there is a writing desk in old mahogany. The television shows a welcome screen that says Mr & Mrs Simms, I look at him and raise my eyebrows, but he just shrugs, raises his eyes and smiles. There is a door leading to what I assume is the en suite bathroom. It is not just a hotel room it is a beautiful suite, it is luxuriously furnished, no expense has been spared, it is just stunning, there is an ice bucket on a stand by the two chairs by the window with two glasses with gold ribbons on them, the attention to detail is fabulous, I look at the bottle in the ice bucket. My heart sinks, I think to myself please don't let it be champagne. As if reading my thoughts Mike walks over to the window he pulls the bottle from the ice, it is sparkling rosé.

"You are wondering if I remember that you don't like champagne, well of course I did," he offers me the bottle to look at, I smile at him. "Care for a drink?" he asks.

"Oh yes please, although it is not I don't like champagne, it just doesn't seem to like me," I reply.

He pops the cork, even though I am watching him it still makes me jump, I am still so nervous, he pours two glasses, he hands one to me, I note his hand is shaking, he is obviously very nervous too. I watch as he walks to the other window, he leans on the side of the window looking out.

"Sometimes you can see there are deer in the fields," he explains, "I used to stay in this room with my brother and Peter," he points towards the gardens, "we built a tree house over there by the lake, we could climb out of the window, shimmy down the tree and we would stay out all night during the summer," he doesn't look at me, he just continues to look out of the window.

I sense that Mike is a bit anxious, he coughs nervously, he takes a sip of his wine, he puts his other hand in his pocket, I know how nervous he feels, my heart is hammering, my stomach is doing back flips and somersaults, I look at him, he takes his hand from his pocket and holds it out to me, I go over, he puts his arm around my shoulders and pulls me close to him, we look out of the window for a while in silence. I drain my glass, I place it on the side, I want him to know it is okay, everything is okay, I am ready to take things further, I want him so much, my body is trembling with anticipation, I want to feel what I haven't felt in such a long time, the physical touch of a man, the closeness and intimacy that two bodies can share, so I gently undo the second button on his shirt, then the third until the shirt is undone to his waist, I run my hands through the hair on his chest, he doesn't move, he just watches me, I stroke his chest, I kiss the hair, I smile up at him then kiss him again gently, I get braver, I circle his nipple with my finger tracing the area, he has a beautiful toned chest and a smattering of hair down to his navel.

"You have a beautiful tan," I whisper to him, "when did you get that?" he looks at me, his dark eyes drawing me to him.

"Two weeks in Greece just before the shifts changed, and I don't want to talk about that right now," he brings my face up to his, kissing me, very lightly at first, then he gets more urgent, his hands travel down my back and then to my sides and over my breasts, he runs his hands under my cotton top he lifts it up, one hand stays on my breast whilst the other fiddles with the buttons on the front.

"They are not real," I whisper, he looks at me.

"Seriously," he replies, he looks shocked, I cannot help it, I get the giggles, I know he thinks I mean my breasts are not real, but I meant the buttons.

"The buttons are not real, the breasts are," I giggle, we both dissolve into laughter, the tension is lifted.

In one movement he lifts my cotton top over my head, he looks down at me, "You are totally gorgeous, do you know that," he kisses my neck, he moves his hands to my back, with one flick he has released my breasts from the confines of my underwear, he holds me away, he gazes at my breasts. "Great stack, Ms Staddon," he laughs.

I push him away, scolding him, "You, sir, are very rude." He pulls me back close to him.

"Oh no, rude is what I intend to be right now and I don't think you are going to be able to stop me," he holds me away and gazes at my breasts. "Beautiful, and definitely real," he whispers, he kisses them one at a time, swirling his tongue over my nipples, so very slowly.

I cannot move, I tremble as he touches me, I cannot do anything, my palms are all clammy, I swear my ears are popping. He moves his hands down towards my jeans, still kissing my breasts he undoes my button and zip on my jeans, he pulls them over my hips, "You still okay?" he whispers, I nod to him, "not too fast for you?" he asks.

I cannot speak, I pull his shirt from his jeans, I move it down over his shoulders, trapping his arms but with one shrug from him it falls silently to the carpet to meet my top. I struggle with his jeans, so we move as one towards the huge bed, he lies me down, he shuffles my jeans down my legs, he buries his head in my breasts, he lies down on his side next to me. My heart is hammering, every muscle in my body is fluttering, clamouring for attention, he is so slow and gentle, he is in no hurry but my body is screaming for him to take me, but he takes his time, with excruciating slowness he kisses my face then my neck then back to my breasts, his hands travel lower, I give out a groan with pleasure, this encourages him, he lifts my bottom up, he slowly takes my briefs over my hips and down my thighs, I cannot control the heat that is flowing all over my body, he strokes my stomach gently, trailing his fingers around to my hips.

"What is this?" he traces my tiny appendix scar with his finger.

"Appendix scar," I breathe the words to him, he kisses it gently, I writhe and whimper with his every touch, I need this so much, I need him now, but he is agonisingly slow, he sits back and looks at me from head to toe, his eyes drinking in every detail of my naked body, I squirm and turn into his body but he pushes me away gently, he kisses me on my navel and heads downwards, I hold onto his head. I never want this to end. My whole body is on fire. When I think that I cannot take any more pleasure, Mike pulls himself on top of me, he kisses me deep and fervently, stroking my body all the time, his fingers trailing over the tops of my thighs, before finding my secret place, he kisses me gently before his fingers and tongue stroke me, sending me to heaven, I cannot help it I moan out loud, it feels so wonderful, he pauses.

"You sure you are okay?" he whispers to me.

"Oh so much more than okay" I whisper, he stops and looks at me.

"I can stop if you want me to," he breathes at me.

"Don't you dare," I reply into his chest.

I moan out loud again as his lips kiss me gently, his tongue stroking me, taking me higher and higher towards my orgasm, my whole body is tingling with desire, he raises my leg up towards him and kisses my thigh and then to the back of my knee, I have never been kissed there, it is so erotic. I lay back as he continues down to my feet then back up again, kissing every inch of my body and biting me gently, sending ripples up and down my whole body, I pull him up towards me to kiss him again. Mike reaches over to his jeans, I hear the sound of the condom packet tearing, I stroke his back, when he turns to me he holds me very close, he kisses me, he nuzzles my neck.

"I cannot wait any longer," he whispers.

"Neither can I," I whisper back.

I grab onto his hips as he enters me, I sense his urgency as he thrusts again and again and I scream out as I am transported to heaven. Behind my eyes an explosion of light is happening, I open my eyes, I look into the dark pools of his eyes, he is holding me so tightly as his need takes over, he groans loudly, his tongue pressing into my mouth, my head explodes with longing for him, lights flash in my eyes, my whole body feels totally fulfilled and wonderful.

A wonderful heat takes over my body and my heart beats almost out of my chest. I am exhausted. We lie together holding each other very close just looking into each other's eyes.

"That was wonderful," I say to him gently, he leans closer to kiss me, his hands travel down my back we lay there just stroking each other, my legs wrapped into his.

He kisses my neck and murmurs into my ear, "I have waited so long to make love to you, so long I began to give up hope it would ever happen, and now it has, it was everything I thought it would be and more, you are a very beautiful woman, Angie, very sexy and very beautiful."

He bends his head and takes my nipple into his mouth, he pulls me close to him, I feel his arousal again, I reach down and stroke him, he groans and within minutes he is back on top of me, he reaches for his jeans but I pull his hand back to me.

"It's okay, no need, I want to feel you totally," I whisper.

He is not so gentle this time, I sense his need, this time it is all about him and his needs, I wrap my legs around his hips to pull his body tight to mine, we kiss passionately, his teeth bite into my lip, I move my head away and cannot control the urge to bite into his shoulder, he cries out both with passion and pain, then slumps on top of me.

"Oh, you amazing, beautiful woman," he whispers.

I pull his head to mine, I kiss him. Everything feels just so natural with him. My whole body is shuddering as he lays me back on the bed, his head resting on my breasts. My whole body is glowing with heat and I can feel a film of perspiration between us. We lay that way for quite some time, just lying there in silence, I can feel his heart beating against mine. Eventually we sit up, he holds me close to his chest, I look up at him I cannot help smiling, I indicate the centre of the room.

"Who puts a Jacuzzi bath right in the middle of a window as the focus of a room?" I ask.

He laughs, "Yes we thought that was odd when the designer suggested it, the whole family was called to give their opinion, but it is very popular. Once you are in it no one can see you as the window doesn't look out onto anything but fields."

"Oh," I tease him, "so you have tried it already?"

"No," he smiles back, "but I intend to tonight."

He rolls off the bed he reaches for the ice bucket. I laugh as I notice his beautiful brown tanned body with white marks where his shorts have been.

He looks at me, "What are you laughing about?" I smile at him.

"Your tan lines," I reply, he looks down and smiles.

"I know," he pulls a face then looks at me, "yours are far more attractive." I pull the cover over me, covering my naked body, he laughs again, "That won't protect you, honey, nothing will, when I see something I like I take it."

I giggle, I pull the covers back, and blow him a kiss, "Help yourself," I say fluttering my eyelashes.

He throws back his head and laughs, he just stands there, he is not embarrassed about being naked, he has a superb well contoured body, he retrieves the glasses refilling them.

"I am impressed you remembered about the champagne," I say.

"I make it my business to retain all information about things that matter, I am looking forward to finding out a lot more," he hands the glass to me, we chink glasses and drink, he pulls the bedcover over both of us, we half lay half sit facing each other.

"So what else is it you want to know?" I smile at him.

"Well," he sits up and winks at me, "let's get the bath running, take our wine in there and get to know each other a whole lot better shall we," he bends down, he kisses my stomach.

My whole body is doing somersaults. I watch as he busies himself filling the bath, fetching the large towels from the bathroom and adding bath foam, I slip to the bathroom, when I come out he holds his hand out he helps me to climb into the huge scented bubble bath.

The bubble bath is luxurious, it is very deep, really lovely and hot, I sink into the bubbles I take a sip of my wine, I watch as Mike refills the glasses, climbs into the bath, he sinks up to his chest then he just looks at me.

"Shall we?" he asks smiling.

"Oh yes please." He hits the buttons, immediately the jets come to life, the whole bath is transformed into one massage function.

"Like it?" he asks.

"Oh love it," I reply, I sink further down into the bubbles, "it is truly wonderful, the jets are caressing my back, my thighs and oh," I smile at him, "my bottom too."

He laughs out loud he slides over to my half of the bath, he takes my glass he puts them both on the side of the bath in the glass holders, so cute.

"I think that massaging your bottom, is my job," he runs his hands over my thighs, round the back to my bottom, he kisses my ears, he nuzzles my neck.

It feels so natural to be with him, I move, I kneel in the bath, the water is still so nice and hot, our skin has turned pink, I straddle him so that our chests are touching, I run my hands through his hair, I kiss his face I slip my hands down his back. He is stroking my back gently, his other hand is rubbing me very gently between my thighs. I move my hands to under his buttocks I lift gently, as his buttocks leave the bath we both slip under the water; we both disappear under the foamy suds. With a great deal of splashing we both surface but as Mike reaches out to get his balance he slips, then it seems everything happens so fast, he disappears under the water, he flicks out his hand to try and save himself, in doing so, he hits the glasses, which sends them both toppling into the water, his head is covered with bubbles, I cannot help it, it is so ridiculous I laugh, he sits up, wipes the bubbles from his face and hair then steadies himself, I laugh at him, he reaches for the towel he wipes my eyes and nose gently, then he wipes his own again, I fumble for both the glasses bringing them to the surface, luckily they are not broken.

"It was totally my fault," I offer, "I didn't realise you would slip, sorry."

Mike kisses my cheek, "I am fine, honest but are you okay?"

I move my hand back down to his buttocks, "I am positive I am okay, but you might need to check," I bring his hands up to my breasts, "now where were we," I say quietly. He groans and pulls me on top of him again, he is hard and ready he enters me quickly making me cry out loud.

"I think we were about here," he whispers.

We stay in the bath for so long we are wrinkled, we cannot keep our hands off each other, finally, when my stomach starts groaning I ask what time the table is booked for in the restaurant.

"I think it is seven thirty," Mike checks his watch, "which gives us forty-five minutes, will that be okay for you?"

I laugh, "Only if you keep your hands to yourself," I scold playfully.

"I cannot guarantee that I am afraid," his voice goes quiet, "you are remarkable, truly remarkable," he kisses my shoulder, "but I am also starving, so I will have a shower, get dressed, I will go down to the bar, give you a bit of peace to get ready, how does that sound?"

I cannot resist his smile, I kiss him and reply, "Perfect."

I watch as he climbs out of the bath and pads towards the en suite, the bubbles sticking to him, he has such a fabulous body, his broad shoulder muscles and solid thighs make me want him again.

Mike showers and dresses in the small room next to the en suite. When he comes out he is wearing a pale blue shirt with black jeans and a navy jumper round his shoulders, he looks so handsome, I cannot believe that he likes me as much as I like him. He leans over the edge of the bath to kiss me, I hold on to him tempted to pull him back into the bath with me but he laughs and pulls away. I wait for him to leave then I get out of the bath, I am very pink and very hot, too hot, I feel a bit giddy, but I feel better after I have a nice cool shower. I dress quickly, I wear pale pink lace matching underwear with nude-coloured lacy hold ups with the off the shoulder dress in dark green, I slip on my high patent stilettos, I apply light make-up, with a quick spray of perfume, I grab my patent handbag. Just before I leave I pull the plug on the bath, check my reflection in the mirror and walk out of the door towards the lift. There is a huge mirror in the elevator, when I look at myself I don't recognise the woman in front of me, her eyes are bright, her face is radiant.

Mike is at the bar chatting to the chap serving, he has a pint in front of him, there is a chilled rosé for me, as I approach he smiles broadly he gives a low whistle. I give a cheeky curtsey, then I smile back at him, my stomach is turning somersaults; my body is remembering him from earlier.

"You look beautiful," he announces, "shall we?" He takes my hand guiding me to an empty table in the bar. In the distance I can hear the sounds of laughter and music, Mike explains, "The wedding we saw earlier today is having the party here tonight, but they are in the other side of the hotel so we won't be disturbed."

I don't know what to say in reply, so I just nod, I suddenly feel very shy, I don't know why, this is crazy – I have been naked with this man for the best part of the afternoon now I am tongue-tied. Mike immediately senses something is wrong, he leans in close to me and speaks softly, "You okay, honey?" I nod, he continues, "I think you are feeling a bit overwhelmed maybe, because you know what, if you are, I know how you feel I must admit I am too, you see I have dreamed of being with you for so long, and then, last night everything happened so fast and now I am here with you," he pauses, "and this afternoon, well, it was incredible, and it seems a bit dreamlike, I want to take you upstairs and lock you in the room so this day never ends," I nod in agreement, I cannot trust my voice, he takes my hand he holds it between both of his. "You know, I kept waiting this morning for you to text me to cancel, I don't know why, I just thought you might have second thoughts."

I shake my head, I clear my throat before I speak, "I also had a bit of a panic just before you turned up, I had a horrible thought you might stand me up and I would have to face you at work and I would be a laughing stock, that would be horrible," he smiles.

"Never, I never would do that to you, I have liked you for so long, and you are every bit as perfect as I knew you would be, I watch you at work and I want to do this," he brings my hand up to his lips he kisses it gently, "I listen to you on the radio, your voice makes me melt, I spend far too much time with Craig just so I can look at you, sad case aren't I," he smiles, I shake my head at him, he hands me my wine. "You hungry?" he asks, I nod, I cannot find my voice, I cannot believe that he likes me as much as he says he does, he speaks quietly. "I am famished shall we go in?"

I nod, I cannot think of what to say so we stand, he puts both our glasses down he takes my hand, he leads me through to the restaurant. The maitre'd greets Mike by name shaking his hand and patting his shoulder, it is obvious he knows him, he guides us to the table in the very corner by the window, looking directly out onto the lake. He sits us both down then returns with our drinks from the bar, he hands us both the menu, there is a bottle of sparkling rosé in the ice bucket on our table and I smile at his thoughtfulness. I feel a bit more relaxed now, I look around, the room is beautiful, tiny fountains of light are being thrown from the huge chandelier in the centre of the room, there are only about twenty tables, each set in such a way as to give diners privacy, there are several other diners sat away from us. I turn my attention back to Mike, we discuss the menu in detail and my stomach growls as I read the mouth-watering descriptions. I choose quickly, the waiter arrives and we place our order. Mike waits for the waiter to disappear then rearranges the table, moving his chair round to be nearer to mine. He holds my hand on top of the table, we have our back to the room, we can see the moon reflecting on the huge lake, it is a perfect place. We talk about everything family related, we don't mention work at all, I tell him all about my parents I explain about them living in Spain, he tells me about his family especially his sister's daughter Hannah who has totally changed their family.

"She was very poorly recently," he explains, "hence the extra ticket for the concert, I bought the ticket for my sister, for her birthday, but Hannah got very sick and was admitted to hospital so she couldn't go," I nod, I look down at my lap.

"I behaved horribly to you over that didn't I?" I admit, he shakes his head.

"No, I don't think so, you were entitled to be angry, but Marcia was just trying to be kind."

I nod in agreement I don't want to talk about that, I was petulant and childish, I change the subject.

"How is Hannah now?" I ask.

He nods, "Yes, she is good and back to her old tricks, that little girl has all of us eating out of her hand." He obviously has a very close family he thinks the world of his brother and sister. He is very close with his parents; he is currently half living back home due to the decorating.

"Are you moving back in to the flat soon?"

I ask, the starters arrive, he waits for the waiter to disappear before answering, "Not sure really, Mum wants me to stay at home but that definitely won't happen and although I love her cooking, I like my independence, there is still the lounge to finish then I will decide."

I look to my plate, the food looks delicious, we eat enthusiastically, I am so hungry I have to slow down so I don't clear my plate before him, Mike tops the glasses up and we clink the glasses together, he leans in to kiss me and I close my eyes as my lips melt with his. The main meal arrives, I have ordered lamb, it is soft and melt in the mouth delicious, when the waiter comes back to check if everything is okay we both say yes in unison then laugh. I cannot help but keep glancing at Mike under my lashes, he is just so handsome, so solid, his hands are long and his fingernails are perfectly short and unbitten, he catches me and laughs.

"I cannot help but stare at you," he says taking my hand, "you are so stunning." I blush this makes him laugh, "When you blush you are even more so," he pauses and looks at me. "Remember the training course we were both on, back a while ago?" I nod, he continues, "I saw your name on the list, after we had all sat down there was one spare chair next to me, I was like a kid at Christmas thinking you would be sat by me all day, then when she began the course and you didn't turn up, I was so fed up, I really couldn't be bothered," I shake my head, "I wanted to cry when she was so

312

rude to me, I especially made a point of getting there early, only to find she had changed the time, I just wanted to go home, good job the inspector spoke up for me."

I frown, "What did he say when I was out of the room?"

Mike shakes his head, "I don't know for sure, I only heard a few words," I grimace, "well whatever he said she changed her tune quickly," he smiles, "and I was so glad, I got to not only sit with you but work with you all day, but it saddened me that you looked so tired in fact you seemed exhausted, I just wanted to hold you and take all your stress away." I shake my head.

"I just needed normality, that is what the course gave me, the chance to get back to a bit of normality, and of course darling Martin, I am sure he put roast lamb on the menu just for me."

Mike laughs, "Yes, those two seem to have a soft spot where you are concerned, I see them moving your car on late shift, and de- icing it in winter, it is lovely the way they look after you, but it is my turn now."

I look at him, "You really think after what I have experienced in the last few hours that you have any competitors, because if you need clarification, take it from me, you certainly don't."

I finish the last morsel of my meal I put my cutlery together, I look at him straight in the eyes my face serious. "Mmm okay sorry, I might have to take that back, you do actually have a competitor." His eyebrows raise up in surprise, I smile at him. "That was so delicious, and although you are totally scrumptious and I want so much to forgo my dessert and have more of you instead, but I am afraid that I am being pulled by the raspberry Pavlova I saw on the trolley earlier, I know you are a dead cert for later but the Pavlova might not be," I pause, "tough decision but you lose I am sorry."

He smiles at me, "I love a woman who likes her food, and knows what she wants, I don't mind being second best to a pudding," he replies, "it's any others I have a problem with."

I chuckle to myself as I cannot believe I am flirting with him. I smile at him, the waiter arrives to clear the plates and with a big smile I order my dessert, as the waiter departs I turn to Mike, "Tell me about before your joined the force, what did you do?" He smiles, he places his napkin on the table and leans back.

"Well, I went to college, then university, I had this big idea that I was going to take a year or so out and go travelling with a friend, we did a lot of Europe, worked in bars and stayed in cheap hotels then when we got as far as Cambodia, we were on a boat and he got chatting to his young girl, she was also travelling, before we got off the boat, he was smitten, he didn't want to leave her and I fell in love with the place," he drinks his wine, "it is an amazing place, so there I was playing gooseberry when I got chatting to a woman who worked in the school, next thing I know she has persuaded us to stay, so we did, I taught English to schoolchildren and he and his new love

313

stayed for a month then they both wanted to go back home, but I liked it, it was good fun, so I had decided to give it a year."

I look at him, "You stayed on your own out there," I frown, but he shakes his head.

"No, there were four others, one chap and three girls, he was from Oz and they were from Spain and Italy, we were all supposed to be travelling but we all stayed, it was great, we had a good time," he smiles again and lift my eyebrows questioningly, he just laughs, "come on, you cannot blame me, I was young, they were young, yes, we had a good time, I even learned some Spanish and Italian."

"So what made you come back?" Mike looks up and waits for the waiter to disappear, I look at my dessert, it is huge, "go on," I prompt him.

"Well I stayed for about ten months then my dad phoned to say the force was recruiting, I always knew I wanted to be in the police force, so I applied and got an interview, so I came home and then was offered the job; as soon as I put the uniform on I knew I never wanted to do anything else," he pauses. "How did you know about Cambodia?" he asks.

I take a spoonful of my Pavlova closing my eyes as the taste wraps around my tongue, it is delicious, really light and creamy, I put the spoon back in my mouth for a second taste, he nudges me, I open my eyes, he pulls the spoon from my lips and his lips meet mine.

"Okay, I changed my mind, I won't come second to a pudding," he murmurs as his lips press against mine.

I smile at him, he holds my head gently, his hands caressing through my hair gently, his lips stroking mine. As he moves away he repeats the question.

"Phil told me, when he was telling me about you guys on the shift, I think I said you looked miserable and he put me right, he told me you were not miserable then he went on to tell me you had taught English abroad, he said that you had said you thought you knew me, but I didn't admit I knew you from school, I am not sure why I didn't, you do know he holds you in very high regard." Mike smiles. "I know, he is a good bloke underneath all his bravado."

His lips meet mine gently as he pulls away he whispers, "You were so lovely at school, so gawky, so beautiful, I just wanted you to notice me, but you were totally oblivious to anything and everything around you."

I laugh, "You would never have got past Scott or Stuart anyway."

Forty-One

I have never felt for someone the way I feel when I look at Mike, my whole body longs for him, my heart pounds when he looks at me. I cannot keep my hands off him. We move into the drawing room for our coffee, there is no one else in there, we are in a far corner of the room, I am sitting on very large leather chair with a very high back. Our coffee arrives, I watch as the waiter departs, I take a sip from the oversized cups, it tastes delicious. Mike stands leaning up at the large window looking out, I sit back in the chair crossing my legs, I know he can see the tops of my lacy hold ups, I am being brazen, but I feel brazen. When I glance up he is stood just watching me, I take another sip of my coffee looking up at him.

"How is your coffee?" I ask him sweetly, he doesn't answer, his eyes twinkle he looks from my face to my stocking tops.

"What are you trying to do to me?" he whispers.

I smile innocently then I take another sip of my coffee, "I don't know what you mean," I whisper smiling at him.

I lean forward and I place the coffee on the table and then stand up, I walk the few feet towards him, we are hidden by the back of the chair. I undo the zip of his jeans I slip my hand in, Mike groans, he puts his head on my shoulder, I massage gently, he doesn't move, he doesn't touch me, I can feel him growing in my hand.

"We need to go," he whispers.

"What about my delicious coffee?" I whisper back, he smiles.

"We need to go now," his voice is urgent, I nod my head.

He kisses me deeply and passionately, his tongue mingling with mine, he tastes of strong coffee, his lips bruising mine in a deep kiss. We move quickly to the lift, once the door closes he pushes the button for our floor, I reach for him again, he undoes the zip on the back of my dress, he slides the dress up over my thighs exposing the tops of my hold ups, he slides his hands over the delicate lace, he lets out a groan as I put my hand over his groin, the lift draws to a halt we fall out of it still holding on to each other, we half walk half run the short distance to the room, thankfully there is no one around. Mike opens the door quickly, we step inside still attached to each other as he kicks the door closed, we fall to the floor, sinking into the huge pile of the carpet. Mike fumbles with his jeans then pulls my dress down to my waist he pushes my lacy bra up over my breasts, he kisses each of my breasts in turn and sucks greedily at my nipples. All I can do is groan as he raises the bottom of my dress up over my thighs then without removing my briefs he pushes them to one side and enters me, I squeal with both surprise and shock as he takes me so roughly and quickly. I claw at his shirt until I expose his chest, I bite at him, he groans out loud. This is exactly as I knew it should be as Mike totally consumes me in our lovemaking, my whole body is singing, fireworks exploding in my head, I cannot breathe as he pounds into me, it is over in a matter of minutes, I cry out with compete abandonment, he presses his face into my hair, he murmurs something I can barely make out, we lay there in each other's arms, I am glowing with sweat. My dress is round my waist my bra is hanging around my neck, one of my hold ups is down to my knee and one of my shoes has shot across the floor.

Mike opens his eyes he looks at me, "That was bloody amazing, that was so totally your fault, you little minx, you drive me to distraction," he kisses me and looks over at the lovely grand four- poster bed, "next time maybe," he laughs.

He kneels up he offers me his hand, I pull my dress up, I stand on one foot, pull my hold up down to my ankle, Mike kneels down, he pulls the other one down very slowly.

"You know," he says quietly, "these are very sexy items indeed," he kisses the top of my thigh.

"Oh no," I laugh, "you just wait and see what I have for you for later, a very nice surprise," a frown goes quickly across his face. Immediately I see his eyes darken, his smile leaves his face, he looks at me seriously.

"What sort of surprise?" he asks.

"Well, it wouldn't be a surprise if I told you," I say cheekily and I giggle, I skip away, Mike grabs my wrist gently, pulling me back towards him, he looks so serious.

"I don't like surprises, Angie, sorry like you, I don't like them, in my experience they never come out as intended."

He stands up, he takes my hand. "Sorry just a bad experience that is all." I hug him, I know exactly what he means.

"Okay, no surprises," I whisper.

I drape my dress over the back of the chair, I pop to the bathroom to tidy myself, I have the negligee in with me, I peep through the door. Mike is lying on the bed with the bedcovers covering the lower half of his naked body, his hands are behind his head, his eyes are closed. I shower quickly then put on the negligee and matching knickers, I clean my teeth, I spray perfume on lightly, I pull the light cord and go into the bedroom. As I approach the bed Mike opens his eyes and smiles, there is only the lamplight as I get closer he lets out a low whistle.

"Okay, I lied, but I hope you like it, this is your surprise, sir," I curtsey, Mike sits up quickly, the bedcovers fall down revealing his whole naked body, I slip under the covers, I cuddle up to him. "Nice or nasty surprise?" I whisper.

"Oh definitely nice, I think I might change my mind where you and surprises are concerned," he whispers back.

We snuggle down under the sheets, we just lay kissing for a long while, he strokes my arm and my back with his hand, and we balance on our elbows to face each other. I smile at him, he just stares at me.

"What?" he asks.

"Nothing," I reply, he takes a deep breath he pulls me closer to him.

"Come on, ask me if you have a question, you can ask me anything."

"Okay," I say slowly, "tell me what was your nasty surprise."

Mike sits up, he faces me, he lets out a groan, "Oh no anything but that, I am not telling you that, besides, I thought you knew already, it was all round the shift once one person found out, I am sure I was the laughing stock of the police force for a while, actually I probably still am," he pauses and looks at me.

I raise my eyebrows at him. "Are you kidding me?"

He looks me straight in the eyes, "Are you sure you don't know, it was after my birthday party."

I shake my head, "No, I went off on holiday the day after, so I must have missed it."

"Okay," Mike continues, "Bloody hell, I don't know why I am doing this, but you are not to think badly of me okay, I am not proud of what happened, but if you are going to know I want you to hear it from me," Mike explains, he covers himself up with the bed sheet he speaks slowly. "I was very drunk when I first met Nancy, that's her name, the leather clad girl from my birthday party, I initially met her in town when I was with a group of friends, the rugby lot. I am not sure how it happened, but she came home with me, I was drunk, very drunk, so was she, I woke up in the morning to find her lying next to me and I couldn't remember who the hell she was. Then we went out a few times, well twice, but it was clear to me that she wasn't my type, she was loud and crude, whenever we got back to my flat she thought my lack of sexual advances was down to me being drunk," he looks at me, he picks up my hand, "but the real truth was, I wasn't drunk all the time, not even tipsy, even when I was sober, I just didn't fancy her, I cannot just do it, believe me, I have to fancy the person," he clears his throat. "Anyway the next time I saw her was Phil's engagement party, bloody Phil and his big mouth invited her when he saw her in town," he stops, his voice lowers, "that was the first and only time I saw you with Jason, I couldn't believe you were there, I didn't want to be seen by you with her, you see, I didn't know you were going to be there," he stops and looks at me. "That night was horrendous for both of us for different reasons."

317

I look down at the bedcover, I don't want to think about that night now, I look up at him. "I don't want to think about that night," I admit. "Come on keep going," I chide him he pulls a face.

"Well, Phil thinks she is great, thinks the whole situation is hilarious, sure she is okay company but even that night when I wasn't drunk, still when we got back to my place I couldn't do anything to her, I know now that it was never going to happen, but she persisted, she bought adult magazines, films, books around she tried very hard, but she just didn't turn me on, in any way, I even lied to her about my shifts," he looks up and blows out a sigh, "well, she always seemed to know where I was," he runs his hands over his face. "Anyway, the night after the birthday party was the decider for both of us I guess, I had enough of her, then when she turned up and introduced herself to my parents as my girlfriend I was mortified, my poor granddad nearly had a coronary, my sister couldn't stop laughing, she thought it was a great laugh, I mean did you see what she was wearing." Mike laughs at the memory and continues, "Then, she interrupted us, you know, when I kissed you, that was unforgiveable, when you arrived and we kissed, I would have been happy if everyone else disappeared and it could have been just you and me, but no, there she was dressed as, well I have no idea what the outfit was about, anyway, I knew I had to get through the evening somehow, so I got very drunk as you know and woke up the next morning with her next to me. I didn't know what to do, I just closed my eyes and hoped if I stayed that way long enough she would disappear, but no such luck, I heard her get up, seriously I had the hangover from hell, I am not that great with drink and that night, well, I have never been so drunk in my life and believe me I have been very drunk, it felt like my head was exploding and my eyes didn't belong to me." Mike stops and runs his hands through his hair, "Bloody hell," he continues, "I cannot believe I am telling you this." I sit up, I stroke his bare back, he turns to face me, "You are so incredible," he whispers he pushes me back onto the pillow he kisses me deeply, I wriggle away moving to the bottom of the bed.

"Oh no you don't," I tease him, "there is more to your story and I want to hear it."

Mike groans, "Oh Christ, really, oh well, okay, here goes, well she goes out into the lounge I hear her banging about, so I just lay there, I might have dropped back off to sleep, I don't know, I don't move for a while, I know I have to get my head moving first then hopefully the rest of my body will follow, I have not been that drunk in a long time, everything is very painful I don't know if she has gone or still there, not sure what was going on, my head was pounding, then I hear her she is calling me, she is in the spare room, I don't know how I did it but I managed to stagger in there at first not believing what I am seeing. She has on, this strange black rubber all in one suit with zips in various access areas, the suit is complete with a hood, it looks like something from a horror movie, honestly, she has on these heels that you see girls wear in a dance club, kind of see through plastic with massive heels, it was seriously mental," he pauses and runs his hand through his hair. "The hood has zips across the eyes and mouth, it makes me shudder to look at it, just when I think things cannot get any worse I notice these fluffy things on her wrists she has handcuffed herself to the bed." Mike looks at me and stops, stares at me for a while, he runs his hands over his face.

"Come on, there is more, there must be," I urge him to continue. He stands up, he is still naked, he walks over to the mini bar, he gets two bottles of water out, he opens one and hands it to me, I take a sip from the bottle, he unscrews his bottle and takes a really large drink, glugging almost half the bottle down. "Go on, stop delaying," I prompt him again, he groans, he smiles at me.

"Seriously, must I."

I laugh out loud, "Oh come on, it cannot be that bad, can it?"

"Worse," he says pulling a face, "okay well you asked for it." He sits in the chair opposite me, still totally naked and looking gorgeous. "Okay, well she is laid there, some of the zips are undone, you know, in certain places, so I do what any man would do," he smiles mischievously.

My heart is hammering, I am not sure I want to hear any more, I find my voice, I hold my hands up in front of me, I stammer, "Okay, okay, enough, I have heard enough, stop now, I am not sure I want to know any more, Mike, I am not sure I am going to like this."

Mike smiles, he stands up, he comes over to the bed, he points to his genitals, "Just talking about her has this effect on me," his male member is quiet and very withdrawn, He sits on the bed he pulls the cover over his bottom half of his body, only his chest is still showing. "I went over to her and unzipped the mouth part so she could breathe then I got dressed, I didn't bother washing, shaving or cleaning my teeth, I had to get out, I felt really bad physically and I didn't need that on top of my hangover. I grabbed my keys and just walked out of the flat, I knew I couldn't drive, I was still so hung over, so I walked round to see my parents, I cannot remember walking there at all, I knew I threw up in someone's garden on the way. I must have looked a right state, but eventually I got there, and whilst my mum was cooking me a very large breakfast I asked my dad to go to the flat to remove a nuisance that was there. I didn't tell him what sort of nuisance it was, he never asked, I know I told him to take his bolt cutters, I don't know what he thought but he disappeared and when he came back about half hour later I could tell by the look on his face that he had never seen anything like it in his life." Mike looks at me, he holds his hands up, "I know, I know, it was a cruel and cowardly way to deal with it, my dad was brilliant, I am not sure what he told my mum, or even if he did tell her, we have never mentioned it since, I haven't seen her since either." Mike looks at me, "In my defence it was my birthday I had a headache from hell, and it was your fault in a way."

I look up quickly, "My fault, how do you work that out then?" I question him.

"Okay, well not really your fault, but I tried so many ways to get you to notice me, but you never did, I wasn't sure you knew of my existence, you never even looked up when I walked in the room, you seemed totally oblivious of me, you would laugh and joke it seemed with everyone but me, then on my party night you kissed me, well we kissed, it was amazing, I thought I might have a chance, then every time I saw you, you were laughing or dancing with someone, I just drunk more and more, and all I could see was you dancing and smooching with Dean. Next thing you were in the car park with him, kissing him, I thought you were going home with him, I was gutted, truly gutted, I mean, I have dreamed about kissing you for so long and then he muscles in and in one night he gets to be closer to you than I could have dreamed," he pauses, then continues. "You know, I even dated a girl that smoked to see if I could stomach it, you know the blonde girl, she was a lovely girl but I only took her out because she smoked and I thought you did too, it was horrible it was disgusting, I couldn't believe you would actually have such a bad habit, then I found out you don't anyway, so I blame you for everything, it is all totally your fault."

I laugh out loud, he joins me up on the bed, we fall back together, "So totally not my fault," I laugh at him, I sit up and stroke his chest with my hand, "I cannot be held responsible because you dated a crazy lady, a very attractive but crazy lady and even left the party with her, and she is very attractive, I will give her credit for that, as for Dean, well Dean was to distract me from the fact your stunning but crazy lady was hanging on to you all night, it was killing me, you kissed me, then she pulled you away like she owned you then to make matters worse you then went home with her, the boys were all joking about your birthday night and I was pleased you were so drunk you probably couldn't have done anything even though she is pretty stunning."

Mike laughs, he pulls me on top of him, "Nobody will ever be as stunning as you."

I sit up, "What about that stunning woman you dated from the admin office?" I ask him, immediately the words are out, I regret saying anything, I sound needy, he looks at me then frowns.

"Stunning woman, who?"

I laugh, "Well there are not that many in there are there?" I question.

He shakes his head, "There are none," he pauses, as if thinking he shakes his head, "no, none that I know of."

I poke him in the ribs, "I was told you dated Dee from admin, you went on a few dates, and you cannot deny that she is stunning."

He laughs out loud, "Who told you that?"

I shake my head, "Is it not true then?" I ask.

He looks at me, "which bit, me dating her or her being stunning," he doesn't wait for a reply, "definitely not true and she is not stunning, she is far too skinny and self-absorbed, I cannot believe you were told I dated her, where did they get that from?" he looks up, as if the penny has dropped, "Oh right, I get it now, I gave her a lift home a few times so we must be dating," he laughs, then continues, "her boyfriend lives in the same block as me, well I think he used to, not sure lately, I haven't seen them there recently, but before I saw her there a few times, she asked me if I could give her a lift, I think on three occasions when she had car trouble, it was only ever when we were on late shift, bloody hell, the gossips get it all wrong don't they," he kisses me, we lay very close. "I only have eyes for you my darling, I don't see any other women at the station, don't even look at them, you brighten the room just by being in it."

I just lay there listening to his heartbeat. Mike clears his throat, "So come on then, you have to tell me one of your secrets, it's only fair, I have made myself look a total fool now you go."

I stiffen, I sit up looking him in the face I know my face has gone all serious, my mouth has gone dry.

"What do you mean, secrets, what do you want to know?" my voice comes out too loud, too harsh.

Mike strokes my face he speaks gently, "It's okay, calm down, I was only joking, unless of course," he pauses. "You do have a secret to tell me, maybe you can start with why you don't like surprises either, I heard you whisper as we were getting in the car," he explains.

I need my water, I look around, the mood has changed, I feel heady, my heart beats fast in my chest, I reach for the bottle of water that is on the side of the bed, I cannot look at him, I unscrew the cap then take a huge gulp and sit facing away from him. What will he think of me if he knew I married a man I didn't love and that my marriage and everything about it was a lie, that the sadness over the death of Jason was in a way, not sadness, but for me, a big relief, an escape from an awful situation. I couldn't tell him, I cannot tell anyone ever. I turn to face him, he is smiling, my eyes fill with tears, I don't know why, I cannot stop them, they fall unchecked down my cheeks. Mike doesn't say anything he just pulls me into his arms, then holds me, he strokes my hair, he kisses my head he holds me so close.

"It's okay, it's okay, baby, you don't have to tell me anything, lets both start a new page," he whispers into my hair. We sit and he holds me close until I start to feel okay. I move back to just look at him, I want so much to be able to take this burden of guilt I just want to be rid of it.

Mike stands up, he is so funny, he stands totally naked, yet he seems comfortable in his own skin, he reaches for my hand, "Come here with me, have a look at this," he whispers gently to me he pulls me towards him, he pulls the sheet from the bed and wraps it round us both. I can feel him soft against me, we stand in front of the window as he pulls back the voile curtain, I can see there outside is the brightest fullest moon I have ever seen. "I ordered that just for you," he speaks so tenderly I turn and put my arms around him, he tilts my head up he kisses me gently on the lips. We stay that way until Mike whispers he needs the bathroom. He leaves me still wrapped in the sheet, looking out at the moon.

When he comes back I am sat at the small chaise lounge with my legs lounged out the full length, the sheet is still wrapped around me, he raises my legs and sits with my thighs over his, he is still completely naked, he strokes the side of my arm, he pulls the sheet open, running his fingers through the silk of the negligee.

"This is really beautiful," he comments, I look at him.

"Better than rubber and zips," I reply cheekily.

"Oh definitely," he buries his head in between my breasts he pulls me down on to the carpet with him. "Now," he breathes to me, "I am going to prove to you once again, I don't need adult films or magazines."

His mouth meets my stomach, I moan as his tongue explores my navel, then moves lower, he is slow and deliberate, he tugs at the silky panties.

"I think you are overdressed, but it is okay I can deal with it," he breathes the words. I can feel his warm breath on my thighs, he slowly edges them down and I raise my hips to him, he pushes my legs open, he kisses my thighs, the backs of my knees, he is so slow, my body is crying out for him, his tongue reaches back to my stomach, then he goes down even lower still, I cannot help it, I moan louder, and within seconds I am groaning at him never to stop. He moves up to kiss my lips. "I don't ever want to stop, baby, ever." I drown in the pool of his dark eyes, my heart and body are totally given to this wonderful man.

I wake up in the early hours of the morning, I reach out and feel his body close to mine, I stroke his arm and he turns over to face me, he opens his eyes, he holds me very close, we snuggle up drifting back off to sleep in each other's arms.

When I wake up we are still entwined, I want to stay like this forever, but I need the bathroom, I move my leg and arm, I think I have successfully manoeuvred my way out of the bed without waking him, but as I move off the bed he reaches out pulling me back to him by my wrist.

"I need the bathroom," I whisper.

"I need you," he pulls me to him, he throws the bedcovers back and reveals that he is swollen and waiting for me.

"Really," I look at him in astonishment, "you have just woken up."

"Actually," he grins, "I have been awake for an hour or more, I have been watching you sleep you are so peaceful when you sleep, you look like an angel, it was all I could do not to make love to you."

I laugh and struggle away from him laughing, "You watched me sleeping you weird man," I tease him, "so you waited then now you need to be patient a little longer." I walk the short distance to the bathroom I wiggle my naked bottom at him. "After all, you have waited all these years haven't you," I blow him a kiss.

I wash my face, clean my teeth and return to him, he has made us both a cup of tea I take it gratefully from him I join him back in the bed.

I gaze at him for a few minutes, "So tell me," I ask coyly, "who taught you to make love like that?"

Mike laughs, "Oh okay, you want to do the whole sex history talk now do you." I smile nodding as I sip my tea. "Okay, but I think you will be disappointed," then he stops. "No, no, I got caught last time," he laughs, "you go first."

I drink from my cup then put it on the side, "Okay, okay, fairs fair, I will go first but very boring so please try to stay awake." Mike is playing with the hem of my negligee, "No distracting me," I scold.

So I tell him about my first time, how I waited and waited because I thought it would be wonderful, it so wasn't what I expected. He just sits listening, he cannot recall Gary from school and I am relieved, I tell him about the holiday romance with an older man, he smiles then says quietly, "Lucky bastard."

I am shocked at his language, it doesn't seem right coming from his lips, but he smiles, "Carry on," he urges me, then I tell him about my five or maybe six one-night stands.

Mike frowns, "Really, that shocks me."

I look at him, "Why would that shock you, Mike?"

He looks at me, "Well, I don't know, it just doesn't seem to be like you that is all," he pauses, there is a long silence, "Angie," he asks, "you do know what a one-night stand is, don't you?"

I laugh, "Of course I do."

He raises his eyebrows questioningly, "Well?"

Then I am embarrassed, my cheeks go bright red, I feel very naïve and silly, I am sure I have got it right but I plough on regardless, "One date, you know, just one date then they never contact you again, no reason given." Mike laughs and pulls me to him.

"Angie, you are priceless, you are adorable," I frown at him.

"If I walk away right now, and never contact you again, that is a one-night stand, a one-night stand involves one night of sex, not just a date, honey, I think you mean you have had several blind dates."

I go bright red, how stupid am I, I cannot believe I mixed the two up, of course I knew what a one-night stand is, immediately I feel cross with myself but Mike puts his lips to mine.

"You are just so funny and so delightful, come on tell me more about the lucky men who have shared your life, and the crazy ones who just thought one date was enough."

So I do, I look straight into his face and I tell him the one other man in my life, I tell him about Jason, before I know it everything spills out, everything, about the initial shock of Jason making a pass at me then about the living together about the wedding about our charade of a marriage, I don't look at him, I can't, I play with the frill on the bedspread silently, I know he is trying to take all the information in, he sits quietly, I don't want to see his expression, I continue until I am all talked out, then I look at him, I feel drained, he doesn't say a word, no comment at all, he just nods. When I finished, I am exhausted, I lie back on the pillow not looking at him I talk to the room not addressing him directly, not looking at him.

"My last lover, was a man who makes love to me like I have always dreamt it should be, I feel totally completely blown away by the intensity of how he makes my body feel," I turn and look him straight in the eye. "By the way," I say not breaking his gaze, "that's you," I lean forward, I kiss him.

He pulls me close, he lays me down gently, he makes love to me as he did the first time, he is so tender so unhurried, he takes me to the dizzy heights, leaving me totally fulfilled. We lay there afterwards our legs and arms entwined, we doze for a short while, then when we wake up he places his face very close to mine, he kisses my nose, then he lays back on the pillow just looking at me.

"Can I ask a question?" he speaks quietly, I nod at him, "Well it is just, I always thought you and Phil kind of, you know."

I smile at him nodding my head, "No, never, I realise that people might think that, I think also that Phil almost gives that impression too, but no, we shared a passionate clinch once but we both realised we don't feel that way about each other."

Mike smiles, "I am so pleased to hear that," he says. "Phil is very protective over you, almost too protective," he adds.

"I know," I reply but I don't elaborate.

Mike's phone bleeps to indicate a message he rolls over to check it, he puts his phone back down, he gets out of bed walks into the bathroom.

Whilst he is gone I quickly check my text messages, there is three from Phil asking where I am, two were yesterday, the one sent this morning, I wonder what he would say if he knew. The last text he has sent is to remind me that he is popping around later this afternoon, I have asked him to take some rubbish to the local rubbish dump, he is going to get that done, I will text him later.

We have a long leisurely breakfast, I eat loads as I am hungry, Mike laughs as I eat almost as much as him, we are the only ones in the dining room as the wedding party are next door having breakfast together. I look out of the window, it is a beautiful sunny day, I look at Mike, he looks so relaxed and happy, I stroke the back of his hand and he is just looking at me, I look up to him, those gorgeous dark eyes just twinkle at me.

"Tell me about your holiday, you know Greece wasn't it," he leans back in his chair.

"Nothing special to tell, I went with my brother and two mates, it wasn't a drinking holiday, we did a bit of water sports, nothing exciting. Steven is really into diving, so are the others, but it is not something I like so I stayed on the boat, we had a good time," he looks at me and smiles. "It wasn't a boys' holiday in that sense, there were no late night drinking games and getting in at some stupid hour in the morning, there were no girls pouring out of our apartment, just four lads taking a holiday," he looks at me. "Why, have you been told differently?" he asks.

I shake my head, "No, I haven't heard anything, I just knew you were on holiday just before the shifts changed, no one has said anything, and it wouldn't be a problem if you did have a boys' holiday, I wouldn't blame you, after all, you are young, free and single." He picks up my hand.

"Oh no, not any more I am not, as from last night, I am yours, just yours." I smile at him, he moves his chair closer to mine, "I am really quite an old-fashioned person, Angie, I know people say I am old before my time, maybe I am, I mean, I do go out, but I just don't like going out drinking, getting drunk and pulling women, it isn't my style, not me at all, we did have a really good time though, I think I am like my dad in that way, he doesn't hold his drink very well but he can still have a really good night out," he pauses, "no romantic nights on the beach for me though," he smiles, I pull him close and kiss him gently on the lips. "Well I am sure we can arrange that sometime in the future," he groans as I kiss him again. "Oh yes, I am certain of that," he pauses then adds, "we will keep away from stray dogs though eh." We both laugh and he pulls me to my feet. "Come on we had better be going."

We walk out hand in hand past the drawing room. Mike pulls me in whispering, "Shall we repeat last night!"

I laugh out loud but push him away, "I am far too full for anything more than I cuddle," I reply.

Mike stops at reception and signs some paperwork, I wait for him at the bottom of the stairs, I guess I should offer to pay something towards the room, but there are several people stood around, I don't want to embarrass him, I will ask him later.

When we return to the room I pull Mike to me, "I have a question for you." I look up at him, he frowns. "When you thanked me for the birthday gift, we were in the admin room alone then Craig came in, it was obvious that you and Craig had words afterwards, was that about me?" I ask.

Mike smiles, he walks to the bed and sits on the edge, he leans back crossing his ankles casually, "Yes, it was, he was playing the protective father I think, he wanted to find out what we were talking about and I must admit I tried to lie and not convincingly, so he kind of warned me that he would not look kindly on anyone messing with his staff, particularly if that member of staff was you."

I smile, "And how did it get sorted?" I ask.

Mike smiles, "I told him that he should know me better than that, I told him I had to thank you personally for something and I left it very vague, when he tried to push the issue I told him to back off it was none of his business, but I did tell him that he wasn't to worry."

I walk towards him, he pulls me close, he sits up, kisses me gently, then disappears into the bathroom. I send a quick text to Phil that I am with a friend but I will be home later I know he will assume it is Annabelle I won't correct him, I have decided I will not lie to him if he asks who I was with, instead I will be vague, but if he does ask who I was with, oh well, I will have to cross that bridge when I come to it. Mike has told me the text was to remind him about his match today, he is playing rugby later in the afternoon, so we have to be making tracks; we set about collecting our things and packing them. As Mike is packing up his clothes, we both look as the packet of condoms fall out.

"Hey, looks like we should have maybe been a bit more careful last night, we only used one, probably your fault again," he calls to me, I look at him.

"Not sure how it is my fault, Mr Simms, as I recall, you were unstoppable," I reply cheekily, "but don't worry, I think we should be ok, I took precautions of my own I am sure that will protect us." Mike frowns, "What are you saying?" he asks.

I laugh at his serious face, I know I have to explain, "I have an injection in my arm, we will be okay, no mini Mike's for us this time," I laugh again.

"Now what makes you think that I would have minded," he remarks back, a warm feeling goes through me, I walk back into the bathroom I smile back at the woman in the mirror.

Chapter Forty-Two

The car is parked right outside the hotel reception, Mike carries my small case and loads it into the boot, I watch as he arranges everything tidily, I look up at the hotel and there is a lady stood on the balcony of one of the rooms, she waves and automatically I wave back.

Mike looks up and laughs, he waves and calls out, "You never saw me, Sylvie, okay."

She puts her finger to her lips, then smiles and blows a kiss, he laughs and takes my hand leading me to the passenger door, he opens it and again, kisses my head as I bend down. He stands at the front of the car, I can hear she is asking him something; he calls back to her and then gets in the car.

"Is she okay?" I ask.

"Yes, she is more than okay, I have never brought anyone here, she is made up, look at her, despite what she has just said I know she will be straight on the phone to mum, she is itching for us to drive away so she can hit that dial, " he laughs.

"Does that bother you?" I ask.

He looks at me. "Angie, I have fancied you since we were at school, I look at you at work and think improper thoughts, even when I knew you were married, I still wanted you. I have never had an affair, I don't believe in infidelity but when I found out you were married, then later that you were not happily married, it did cross my mind, I give no thought to your husband at all, so no, I have no problem with anyone knowing about you, I just would have liked to have told mum myself in my own time."

I laugh, "And what do you think she will say?"

He frowns. "I am not sure really, I have taken girlfriends home but nothing serious, she knows we work together, I told Dad, but I also told him you were married, Mum would never approve of anything disreputable like an affair though, so she might get the wrong end of the stick, but she will be careful this time, she has overstepped the mark before she won't do it again, at least I hope she won't," he laughs, "we shall see."

I look at him, his lovely face smiling and relaxed, "Mike, can I at least pay something towards the..." I don't get to finish, his lips are on mine, kissing me, as he breaks away, he smiles at me.

"That is what is going to happen if you ask any more stupid questions, my woman does not pay, not for meals, or drinks or hotel rooms, no negotiation okay."

I smile at him, I pull his face close to me, I bite his bottom lip gently. "Okay, I might have to find some other way to repay you, bake you a cake maybe." I laugh out loud at my own joke, "But I have to warn you, I am no good at cooking."

He turns the key and the engine roars into life. "So," Mike looks at me, "is it too presumptuous of me to ask if I can see you tonight, after the rugby." I frown, I don't mean to but Phil is coming round, I have nothing else happening but I am on early shift the next day.

"Is that wise?" I ask, "we are both on early shift, and besides," I pause, unsure what to say, "well, Phil is coming round to clear some rubbish for me, he should be gone by the time you finish though," I watch his face, his jaw tenses, he drives for a while not speaking, he fiddles with the radio and I can detect slight tension between us, I stroke his shoulder, I look ahead, there is a queue, we are stuck in traffic.

"You okay?" I ask, I know the answer before he says anything but I have to ask anyway there is a long pause before he answers, when he finally does my heart sinks, his voice is low.

"I don't know, I don't know if I am okay," he shakes his head, "I have just had the most wonderful night with you, and now you tell me he will be in your house later, I want to be so okay with you and Phil, and, Angie, please trust me when I say that I do believe you when you say nothing has happened, but you seem to have this closeness that no one but you two can understand, no one else can penetrate this couple thing that you two have, if you are going to ask me if I am jealous, then yes I guess I am." He looks directly at me, "Sad case aren't I," he adds before continuing. "I know I have no right to dictate to you, I have spent one wonderful night with you," he pauses, "it is just sometimes when I listen to him at work going on to you about making mistakes, then I hear you almost begging for his permission for you to be able to go to a bloody concert." He glances at me, "I'm sorry I guess I don't understand it and it just gets to me, that is all."

We move a bit in the traffic, we travel a few miles in silence, I am unsure what to say, there is so much I need him to know, but is now the right time, is it too soon, I look at him but he is just concentrating on the road ahead. I give a huge sigh, I know what I need to do, I notice a parking sign in half a mile.

"Can you pull into the parking lay by for me please?" I ask him he looks at me confused.

"Are you okay, Angie, look I am sorry I didn't mean to upset you, I didn't mean to swear," he frowns at me, I smile at him, but I know it is a weak smile, my stomach churns.

"I am perfectly okay, you haven't upset me, but I would like you to pull over anyway," I reply.

"Look," he runs his hands through his hair, "I am sorry I went on a bit, it was stupid of me, why do we need to pull over, I need to get back and so do you, you can talk to me now if you need to, Angie, seriously you can."

I sit quiet, not looking at him, I wait patiently, when the traffic moves, he gives out a huge sigh, he indicates then pulls in to the lay by, he switches the engine off. He looks straight ahead.

I remove my seat belt, I turn to face him, I feel sick, my head is beginning to throb, my palms are sweaty, I am glad he is staring ahead, I cannot look him in the eye so I fiddle with my watchstrap, I take a deep breath before speaking, when I do I keep my voice as light as I can.

"Mike, I need to tell you something and I need you to listen, please don't interrupt, just listen, I want," my voices catches in my throat, I clear it gently, before I can continue, "no I need to tell you something, something very private, something that I am not proud of, something that I don't want anyone else to know, I don't know what you will think of me after I tell you but you have to know, this isn't light-hearted like leaving someone in a bedroom handcuffed to a bed, it is so much worse than that." I cannot help it, I give out a huge sigh, here goes nothing, "I told you about my wedding," I explain. "But what I didn't tell you, and what I think you need to know, is why Phil is the way he is, I guess after what we have both shared over the last twelve hours, I kind of owe it to you to explain, but you have to know right from the start, there is no romance or any hint of romance between Phil and I, there never will be, but we will always have a past, that in some ways is my fault."

I still cannot look at him, he faces me, twisting in his seat, he is frowning, I glance up and my eyes meet with his chest, I can see the hair poking through the gap in his shirt, I stretch my hands out, I look down at my fingernails.

"As I told you I didn't know about the surprise wedding, but I did know Jason was taking me away, I saw the confirmation just a week or so before we were due to go away, I decided that the perfect opportunity had presented itself, we would be away from everyone, I could end the relationship, then we could come home, we could sort all the domestics of him moving out and my life would be mine again. I wasn't going to tell anyone, but I was at work, not with my shift though, I think I was working an extra shift on your shift, I cannot remember, but I was outside," I smile at him. "Having a fake cigarette break, everything was churning round in my head, I got really upset, Phil was there out by the smoking area, in a moment of desperation I confided in him, I told him everything, I told him that I was going to finish with Jason, I had enough I wanted out, I told him the timing was perfect, that I had found out about the weekend I saw it as an opportunity to be alone with Jason to explain to him, to finish it, I told him I didn't love Jason like I should that I saw him as a brother, an irritating brother at that, I told him I wanted to be on my own, living with Jason was not working for me, also it wasn't fair to Jason either." I glance at Mike quickly, I could tell he was listening intently, so I continue, "Phil listened, but all the time he listened to me, going on and on, pouring out my heart, he knew what was being planned, but you know what, he never said a word, he was the one person who had the chance to stop me making the worst mistake of my life, just a few words from him and my life would have been so different, but he said nothing, I could have, if I was warned, feigned illness."

I can feel a knot forming in my throat, I cannot continue, I look out the window, Mike leans over and takes my hand.

"It's okay, honey, you don't have to go on, really you don't," but I shake my head I have to, I cannot look at him I clear my throat. "If I had known, I could have done something to make it not happen, I know if my sister knew how I felt she would have helped me, but she thought it was what I wanted, Jason had told her as much, I thought I was a failure not making the relationship with Jason work so I told no one, it was my own fault, I had no idea what he was planning."

There is still that big lump in my throat, I try to clear it again, I lay my head back against the headrest and close my eyes, I don't want to continue but I have come this far so I go on, "So on my wedding day I had to paste on a smile for my family, I couldn't hurt my mum and dad by telling them the truth, I felt such a fraud, and afterwards, well afterwards, when the vows were all said, we smiled for the cameras, when Phil came over to congratulate us, apparently he tells me that he shook Jason's hand but he said that as he leaned in to give me a kiss, I pulled him close, I whispered to him so that no one else could hear, I whispered to him that I also made a vow to him on this day, that I would never forgive him for what he had done, I told him I hated him, that I blamed him for everything, he has never forgotten that." I take a huge breath in. "I cannot believe I said that to him, Mike, to be honest, I didn't mean to hurt him, I was so upset, I wish I could have taken back the words but he left shortly afterwards." I pause and look out of the window, then I look back to Mike, I try to smile but it comes out all wonky, so I continue, "He and Sean were my solid support when Jason took poorly, but I can never take back what I said in anger, so here we are, he now says until I tell him to his face that I am happy with the man of my dreams he will look after me and protect me, he says he will never settle until I am settled, I have tried so hard to tell him it was my fault, I am a grown woman, but he won't have it, I have tried to talk to him, reason with him but he just won't listen."

I stop talking and look at Mike, I wish I could read his expression, but he has his head down so I pick the skin on my thumb and after a few moments of silence I add, "Not a very nice story is it, makes yours look like you were an angel?"

I look at Mike, he is staring at me now. "Bloody hell," he swears, "you poor darling, you poor, poor darling," he pulls me to him, he kisses my head, "it all makes complete sense to me now, the way Phil is so controlling over you, the way he acts as if he owns you," he moves away, he looks me straight in the face. "Angie, darling, thank you for telling me, thank you for your honesty, that must have been a very difficult, painful thing for you to tell me that, I want you and respect you even more for it, Angie darling, I promise I will never tell another living soul."

I look at him, I can feel the tears in my eyes, I am so relieved that it is out, I have finally told someone.

"Mike, do you know what my husband said to me on our wedding night, when we went back to the room, when we were on our own."

He shakes his head, "I cannot begin to think, he must have been so relieved that you went through with it, that you thought enough of him, I guess."

I frown, "he asked me if I hated him."

Mike looks at me, "Shit, Angie, what did you say to that, no please, don't tell me, I don't need to know, come here, baby," he draws me into his chest, suddenly I feel relaxed, I have told Mike the biggest secret and he is still here, not running down the road at an incredible speed.

I smile at him, "You want and respect me," I repeat, he smiles, his beautiful smile, his lovely face lights up as he looks at me.

"Seems to me, in some way I always have done, frizzy hair, braces, the lot," he shrugs, he is stroking my hand. "You got under my skin at aged sixteen, you haven't left, despite the fact I have tried and failed to get you out of my system, I don't know what I would have done if I had known you were not happily married, beat your door down maybe," he smiles, "come on," he says, he pulls his seatbelt across him, "let's get you home and get Phil working on your garden rubbish, he deserves it." I laugh out loud, I pull my seatbelt, I feel so much better, a whole weight has lifted from my shoulders.

"Hold on, Mr Simms, don't be in so much of a hurry," I whisper quietly to him, I put my hand on his groin, "there is no hurry is there, Mike," I slowly undo the zip on his trousers, I look at him and smile then move my head downwards, "we have plenty of time, tell me, have you christened this car yet." He groans whist he is undoing his seatbelt and pulling me to him.

"No, but I know it is about to happen very soon."

As the Maserati pulls outside my house, Mike says, "So what about tonight, have you had enough of me or can I see you again?"

I try to contain myself, my whole insides are bubbling with excitement, I try to appear casual. "If you like," I reply.

"Oh I like," he smiles, I just melt.

He carries my bag to the door but I push him away when he tries to come in, "You are going to be late," I scold him.

"I think I would rather stay with you rather than run round a field with sweaty men," he murmurs into my neck, nibbling me and kissing gently.

"Ooh that sounds quite exciting, I like the idea of that, maybe I can come and watch you one day," I tease him, but I push him away "I will text you later okay." I drag my bag into the lounge and go to the window, I stand waving, I am not sure if he waved back as the windows are tinted.

Chapter Forty-Three

I unpack my case, make myself a drink, Phil turns up within about an hour, he gets busy on the garden, he is talking to the neighbour over the wall when I pop out with a cold drink for Phil.

"That was a nice car your friend has," the neighbour remarks to me, my heart sinks, I totally forgot that he spends all his time with one eye to the window. "Yes, it is," I confirm I walk back to the patio door, I listen to see if Phil asks anything but he doesn't, he is talking about sport so I know I am safe. If only for a while!

We tidy the garden, we fill the bags in quiet companionship, he keeps looking over to me but not saying anything, I catch him looking and challenge him with a single word "what", but he smiles, replying "nothing", I cannot judge his mood he seems quiet but is still being the same old Phil I know, he throws snails at me he flicks dirt into my wellies, but he keeps checking his phone every few minutes, he seems in a real hurry to get the garden cleared.

"Are you expecting a call?" I ask him.

He looks at me and shakes his head, "No, just having problems with my phone keep switching off." But I know he is lying, he won't look at me.

"Are you waiting for a call from a woman?" I stand up facing him, his neck goes red, I know he is lying as he always goes red when he is embarrassed. "Who is it?" I ask, I still stand just looking at him.

"Just let it go," he says impatiently, "I told you my phone is playing up," but I know him better than that. This must be someone new as I know he would make some crude remark if it was one of his regular women.

Then I work it out for myself, Phil definitely has a date, and not just one of his one-night stands, if he doesn't want me to know then it must mean he likes her, likes her a lot, he is probably waiting to hear from her, in fact the more I think of it the more I convince myself I am right. I know Phil so well, so even if I press him he won't say who with, he is being very cagey. I hear the text message bleep, I watch him read it, he goes all red again, he punches a reply, I move quickly to him, snatch his phone and hold it up high, his face is all serious.

"Can I have it back," he holds out his hand, he is not smiling.

"Who is the text from?" I tease him.

"Can I have my phone back," his voice is flat.

I sigh and hand it to him I say teasingly, "Thought we had no secrets."

He looks at me, he puts his phone in his pocket he replies very quietly, "Apparently now we do," he walks back to the sack of rubbish, he swings it over his shoulder, walks off towards his car where he loads the rest of the rubbish into the boot of his car. "I am going home straight after I have been to the tip okay?" he calls out, his head half in the boot, he comes back, kisses my cheek. "See you in the morning," he walks back down the path, waves his hand and I wave back, he is gone, I stand watching as his car pulls away. What did he mean apparently we do, oh no maybe he knows about last night, maybe he is cross with me, I know Phil so well I know he knows something.

I text Mike to say Phil has left, Mike texts me back straight away, "I can be there in half an hour, okay, do I bring an overnight bag?"

I have to think for a minute, will it be okay, I don't know, I fight with myself, I really don't know, will it be weird in my home, I argue with myself for a few minutes, my text goes off again, "no pressure, my overnight bag can stay another time, see you in a little while", I smile, I cannot stop tears pricking my eyelids, he is just so thoughtful, just so perfect.

He arrives within ten minutes, he is dressed in a smart rugby shirt with dark jeans, his hair is still wet and he draws me into his arms at the door, his lips press gently against mine then as he pulls me closer to him his kisses are more urgent his lips press harder as his tongue pushes against mine, I feel dizzy, my whole body pushes against him wanting him so much. Eventually we pull apart, he looks into my eyes smiling at me.

"I missed you," he whispers, I snuggle back in to him.

"You should have let me come to watch."

He pulls apart from me and laughs, "No way. You would be too much of a distraction, besides Dean would be fighting for your attention," he laughs again, pulling me close, "maybe one day though eh," I nod my head.

"What position do you play?" I ask.

"Forward, I am a forward, which, if you don't know rugby, means I try and get the ball close to the goal line, it is because I am tall and a big bugger, I don't take any nonsense, it was a good game today."

"What does Dean play?" I ask.

He looks at me, grins then answers, "Left back."

I frown. "Left back?" I question.

"Yes, left back in the changing room if he looks at my woman," he laughs and pulls me close. "No, he is a forward too, there are eight of us, qualities are you have to be tall, strong and willing to take a good kicking, I will take you to watch a game one day if you like." I nod my head.

"That would be good, but I don't know if I want to watch you play if it is really rough."

Mike smiles, "It is really rough, great fun, we lost today which doesn't happen often, might be because I was really exhausted, wonder why that was," he raises his eyebrows at me and I giggle, he continues, "We are all pussy cats really, we had a good game but I did miss a few good chances which is unusual." He pulls my hand, "Come on," we move into the lounge, he has bought a bottle of sparking pink rosé wine and I pour us both a glass then we snuggle down to watch television, there is a romantic comedy on the television and we laugh together, before I realise it the credits are rolling, it is really late when he stands up to leave, he pulls me towards him I nuzzle into his neck and kiss him gently making him groan lightly.

"I don't know how I am going to face you at work tomorrow," he says quietly, "I don't think I will be able to keep my eyes or my hands or my lips off you."

I laugh, kissing him on the lips feeling his tongue push against mine, I totally adore this man I move away from him gently.

"You will just have to try, really hard," I reply, "getting caught is not an option."

He stands up and pulls me up with him, I follow him to the door, when he pulls me into his arms I cannot resist and when he leaves, I lean against the door with my arms around me in a hug, I go to bed with a smile on my face.

Chapter Forty-Four

I wake early, I check my phone, there is a message from him simply saying "morning gorgeous" with a few kisses, I reply with just a kiss, I shower with a grin on my face, even as I eat breakfast I smile, I cannot help it I hug myself, I am so happy, I cannot stop grinning, even the sun is shining. When I arrive at work I see his car in the car park with a space next to it, I cannot resist pulling next to it even though there are other spaces nearer the entrance, it will confuse Rex, he will try and move it for me later. I look back at our cars parked next to each other; I cannot help it I giggle to myself as I head into the station. I resist walking through the parade room I am not feeling that brave, in fact I am feeling a bit nervous to see him. Night shift have been busy which in turn makes us very busy, I don't check my mail tray until much later. There is a plain white envelope with my name written on the front, I recognise the handwriting this time, I tear it open to see one love heart sweet attached to a piece of paper, with the words "be mine" on it, I cannot help but smile as I tuck it into my handbag, I will have to think of something similar to come up with. Craig is sifting through the photographs from the party, I go and stand next to him, making the odd comment about people, his phone rings and he turns away to answer it, I continue to flick through, there is one of Mike and I facing the camera and smiling, it was when we had just finished dancing, we both look relaxed and happy, my whole face is smiling, without being seen I slip the photograph up my sleeve and continue looking through the rest, I return to my desk and hide the photograph in my diary, I cannot help but keep looking at it, it is just a head and shoulders shot but we are both smiling happily. I can hear calls coming in so I slide the photograph out of sight and get back to work, we all work steadily for an hour or so, the mail arrives and the admin office girl hands a huge pile to Craig, I smile at her as she leaves, I look at Craig, she is right, he would have no idea who has given him the mail, he doesn't pay any attention at all, he doesn't even look up when he says thank you, I just keep my head down, I listen to Gavin taking a call but he needs no assistance so I continue allocating officers to jobs, most of the officers are out already and we are kept busy updating and closing the jobs. Strangely I haven't heard Mike's voice on the radio and he hasn't popped up as he usually does, I convince myself it isn't about me, he must just be very busy. I keep working and don't look up until Craig calls me over, he still has a stack of memos and internal mail in front of him which he is working through slowly.

"Look at this lot," he points to the pile, "three days off and I come back to this." I smile at him.

"That is the price for being popular I guess," I go to walk away but he calls me back.

"Angie, wait, do you have any idea what this is about?"

I glance at the paper, "What is it?" I ask.

He shrugs, "Well it seems, you have to go to an investigation meeting downstairs," he advises me.

"Me, what for?" I question, Craig looks nonplussed, he puts his hands up in the air.

"I really have no idea, Angie, I thought you would know, I received a note in my pile today, and it is arranged for today," he looks at his watch, "in just ten minutes time, bloody admin office, cannot get anything right." I look at the paper but I don't touch it, he passes it to me. "Take a proper look," he holds a piece of paper up higher. "I don't know anything more, sorry," he looks at me, his face looks confused, I take the note and read it, it doesn't give any more information than what he has told me, I look at him, "honestly, Angie, that's all it says, really I don't know anything, I cannot give you a heads up, you know I would if I could, but there is just so much going on here lately that I don't know about, I really have no idea, probably just a questionnaire or some rubbish like that all I know is it is in meeting room four at eleven o'clock okay." I shrug and walk away, he calls after me, "Any problems just call me okay, I can be there in a minute or so."

I pull a face but nod at him, Gavin looks up at me as I pass, "let's have a quick look, Angie," I pass it to him and he studies it before handing it back.

"It cannot be that bad, Angie, they have to give you lots of notice if it a disciplinary, and you have certain rights, Craig is right, don't worry, one of us can be with you in seconds if you need us, probably just human resources rubbish."

I smile at him gratefully, I grab my notebook, I have no idea even where meeting room four is, or why I am going but I do as I am told. I pop into the ladies toilet to make sure my uniform is all straight, add a bit of lipstick and then head downstairs, I find the room straight away, it says meeting in progress so I knock, I hear a male voice call out, "Come in," I push the door open. The room is just big enough to accommodate one table and four chairs. Sat the other side of the table is an inspector who I know but cannot recall his name, sat next to him, to my amazement, is Mike, my heart starts to pound hard in my chest, I look at both of them, I just stand waiting, my mouth goes dry.

"Ah, Ms Staddon, thank you for being prompt, please take a seat," the Inspector offers, indicating with his hand one of the vacant chairs.

He is an older man, maybe in his middle fifties, grey-haired with enormous bushy eyebrows, silver rimmed glasses and a severe look on his face. My heart starts beating even faster, Mike doesn't look up, I sit down, he introduces himself as Inspector Morgan, he indicates Mike, "This, as you may know, if Sergeant Simms, he will be the note taker today, he will play no other part in the proceedings."

Mike looks up, he nods, raises his eyebrows but his face tells me nothing, I smile weakly, I have a terrible feeling this is not something good.

The inspector starts to explain, "Ms Staddon, I am sure you are aware that recruitment and training are an enormous drain on the resources of the constabulary, we take great steps to ensure that none of the resources are wasted, we go through a lot of man hours ensuring that we recruit the right people for the very vital job of policing our county," his voice in monotone, I sit and listen, totally unaware of what he is going on about, I chew my bottom lip nervously, he doesn't look at me he looks at something over my head, I don't know what to do or say so I look down at my pad and stay silent, he monotone continues, "Ms Staddon, I am sure you are also aware of how vitally important good working relationships are, in fact, they are absolutely crucial to a police force, it is imperative," he continues, "that we have a solid united relationship with the shifts and that should start with new recruits, and then must be carried on up through the ranks, would you agree?"

I have no idea where he is going with this, I must look a bit nonplussed but I manage to nod my head in agreement, I look to Mike but he is still looking down at his notes, I clear my throat, "I am sorry," I interrupt "I have no idea what this has to do with me, have you got the right person?"

The Inspector smiles, He continues, "Yes, we have the right person, Ms Staddon, we are absolutely certain about that, perhaps I should explain." I nod and look to Mike again, he is busy scribbling, he doesn't look up, the inspector goes on, "We are investigating an internal complaint, you are aware there are lots of policies within the force, with your length of service you should also be aware there is a specific policy relating to grievance, the grievance policy is where people can challenge unacceptable behaviour," he pushes some paperwork across the table to me, I look down, I don't touch it, I don't read it, I don't need to, I know there are such documents but I have no idea what he is talking about, I have never put a grievance in about anyone in my life, and to date no one has ever complained about me.

I look at him and give a weak smile, "I am sorry, sir, I have no idea what you are referring to, yes I know such policies exist, I am not stupid but I still don't think you have the right person."

The Inspector clears his throat, "Ms Staddon," he seems a bit tempered now, as if I was trying his patience, he moves his glasses down his nose and looks at me over them, "no one is saying you are stupid, and I have already clarified we have the right person, so I wonder," he pauses and his eyebrows shoot up and down then he continues, "can you talk me through the events of the last night shift you worked please."

I frown at him, I clear my throat, "Events," I finally manage to say, he frowns.

"Yes, events, Ms Staddon, did anything happen during the last night shift that you want to share with us?"

I look quickly at Mike, he is still writing, his head is down, I will him to look up but his head remains down, there is a long pause then I realise he expects me to say something but words fail me.

"Sorry," I say, "I am not being obstructive, but what part of night shift are you referring."

My heart is beating really fast, does he know that Mike kissed me, oh god, my mouth goes dry, but I am sure no one would have seen that, it cannot be that, surely not, I wrack my brains trying to think of what else they might be referring to.

"Your rest break," he interrupts my thoughts, he speaks quickly almost impatiently.

Mike looks up at me, he doesn't say anything, I shake my head, suddenly I realise what he is referring to, my trip out with Helen, okay it all makes sense now, but it seems a bit over the top, I clear my throat nervously, "Is it because I went off site, is this what this is about, we had a voucher so I went out for a coffee with," I stop quickly, I don't want to get Helen in trouble, even though we are allowed to go out, it is frowned upon due to safety, I take a deep breath, I look to Mike, his expression is still blank, why doesn't he say something, the Inspector looks at me.

"Ms Staddon, we are not interested in your actual rest break, what you did in your rest break is of no interest to us," he looks at Mike, then back to me, "what happened at the end of your rest break."

I look at him then the penny drops, the coffee spill, it must be about the bloody coffee spill, I cannot believe someone has reported me for spilling coffee, how bloody childish and pathetic.

"Ms Staddon," the inspector urges. Then before I can stop it, everything comes out, I am jabbering on about the spilling of the coffee up the walls and doors and over the carpet. "But I cleared it all up," I explain, "I even emailed Rex the caretaker to tell him about the carpet, I said I would pay for the cleaning, I can show you the email if you want me to," I pause, I look down at my hands, trying but failing to keep my temper, "this is pathetic." I am getting cross now, "Surely no one has complained, I cleaned it up the best I could, and if someone has reported me, have they nothing better to do or to complain about?" I question.

The inspector looks at Mike, Mike glances at the inspector, then slowly shakes his head. I push the paperwork away from me, the inspector continues, "When you cleared up the mess, what did you do then?"

So I explain about the big wet wodge of sodden wet wipes that I took to put in the bin. "Tell me about the wet wipes, where exactly did you put the wet wipes?" he asks. "Tell me about that."

My face must have shown confusion, but I continue, "In the bin in the small kitchen, you cannot flush wet wipes, you know, they have to go in the bin, well some you can I guess, but not the ones I had on me," I am babbling now, I have no idea where this crazy questioning is going, "there is a small flip top bin just inside the door," I explain.

"Was anyone else in there?" he asks.

I nod my head whilst speaking, "Yes, the new chap Bradley, with a sergeant, I cannot remember his name, I think he is on the shift that comes on before ours or just after ours, but I don't know for sure," I pause, "oh and there was another chap the other side of the partition, I could hear his voice but I could not see who it was, I think he was on the phone, but I was in a rush, I was late, I put the wipes in the bin washed my hands then left."

Mike is still writing all this down, he doesn't look up. "Tell me about the new chap Bradley, what was he doing?" the inspector asks.

"Well," I start, then I pause, my throat goes dry, I clear it then look at the inspector, I clear my throat again nervously, before I carry on, "it was a bit strange, he was sat on the floor, the Sergeant, Sergeant Boon, yes that is his name, well he was stood over him, I asked if he was okay, one of them said yes, I didn't look at any of them so I didn't know who replied, they seemed okay, I was late so I left them to it."

"Did it strike you as strange that he was sat on the floor?" he continues to question me, I nod my head.

"To be honest," I reply, "yes, I just said it did, but just for a split second, as I explained, I was late, I hate letting Craig, um Sergeant MacDonald down so I was in a hurry, I didn't really think anything."

The inspector crosses his fingers he relaxes back in his chair, his voice is less formal now, more casual, "Thank you, Ms Staddon, we are now getting somewhere," he looks at Mike and gives a shake of his head before he continues, "now perhaps you would like to tell me," he smiles at me, a kind of smug smile, "what do you think of the new recruit PC Bradley Owens?" he asks.

I shrug, "I don't really know him that well, sir," I say honestly, he frowns.

"Really, that surprises me, I thought you spent some time together in training," he pauses, "in fact he was assigned to you specifically and sat with you for a while, well quite some time really and during that time didn't you have cause to have words with him before your rest break," he pauses and I can feel my cheeks going red, he continues, "on the night in question, wasn't he sat with you observing, didn't you have reason to have to speak to him when he was sat with you," he probes deeper, I know what he is referring to, but I am not going to be baited.

I reply honestly, "No, he was observing me working, maybe we might have had a conversation, maybe you could call it a discussion, I just gave him a bit of guidance that is all, it was a training session after all."

Inspector Morgan places his fingertips together slowly, I watch him slowly pushing them together to make them into a point, he is looking down, there is a long silence, there is no way I am going to admit what he said to me, then he looks up then tilts his head.

"Just a bit of guidance, doesn't seem to be the case to us, Ms Staddon, we have a copy of the tape transcript," he indicates some paperwork in front of Mike, my heart sinks, then he continues, "it seems that it was more than guidance to me, in fact were you not trying to stop him being sexually inappropriate towards you in both his manner and verbally, wasn't you trying and failing to tell him he was being inappropriate, and did he not disregard your advice and continue, even going so far as to show you something that could be interpreted as sexually inappropriate." The inspector indicates the tape with a pile of papers underneath, I glance at Mike, who is looking at me, then I look back to the Inspector, I know my face has gone even redder.

"Well, sir," I keep my voice calm, "if you know, all of this and you have evidence, then why are you asking me?" I question, I look him straight in the face I continue, "but as it is me you are asking, I will tell you," my voice is clipped and controlled, my hands are shaking and I put them on my lap out of sight, "no, I didn't think it was a big issue, he is a rookie, he will learn, he was just showing off, we have friendly jokes all the time on the shift, he just took it a bit too far, went too personal in my opinion so I felt I needed to warn him that if he did something similar again then someone might complain about him, as he is new."

I look at them both, Mike is still looking at me, I smile weakly at both of them, I am so embarrassed that Mike has read what that chap has said about me, but I take a breath and speak, my voice is a lot more in control now, "You know if someone is not in a receptive mood or if they didn't find his jokes funny, he might get into trouble, but I haven't complained, I didn't tell anyone."

The inspector smiles, he knots his fingers together then places them flat on the table in front of him. "Ms Staddon, we know exactly what he said to you, his comments, in the force's opinion were both vulgar and crude, they were deeply personal and therefore very unacceptable, also we know you didn't complain, although you have every right to, in fact you handled yourself very well under the circumstances, but it is simply not acceptable, I would like to apologise on the forces behalf that you were subjected to that sort of abuse, however, we cannot and will not tolerate that sort of behaviour from any officer, new or otherwise," he looks at Mike, Mike nods his head in agreement. "Furthermore, we intend to take this matter further, the notes taken today and this statement will be put forward as evidence, we would like you to sign the prepared statement that we have here, the statement is you uphold the complaint and that you are agreeing that you found his behaviour unacceptable and it has caused you great distress."

I don't know why but I just see red, I can feel myself getting hot, I look at the Inspector sat there so pompous, so very far removed from reality, I can feel the anger boiling inside of me, I stand up pushing my chair back noisily, I push the statement away then blurt out, "No, I won't sign anything of that nature, this is ridiculous," I look at both of them, Mike is looking at me, his face is blank, there is absolutely no expression, absolutely nothing, I continue, "look he crossed the line I told him so, he was showing off, but we are both adults, end of, if anyone else has a problem they need to take it up with him personally like I did. I will not be signing anything, if you are trying to drive him out, you are not using our pathetic exchange of words to add clout to your case, find another scapegoat." I look at both of them, "Yes, he was personal, yes it was hurtful but I dealt with it at the time and I will not have his personal remarks about me dragged through any other procedure, I refuse to sign the statement, I trust that is all and I can go now and do what I am paid to do."

I don't wait to hear their response, I get up and leave. I cannot catch my breath, I take huge lungfuls of air trying to calm down. I am so angry, so very angry, my text message bleeps, I take it out of my pocket savagely, it is dear Martin, lovely innocent Martin, with just two words that make me smile, makes me calm down a bit, not much but a bit, "roast lamb". I make my way to the control room, it is nearly lunchtime, my whole morning has been wasted, although the others ask if I am okay I don't respond, but Gavin stands up "Angie, you okay, mate?" he asks.

I look at him I am so cross, "Just petty bloody police politics, Gavin, it is ridiculous, I will tell you later okay, but right now I am going to lunch, I am starving okay." He smiles and sits back down. "Okay, catch you later," I pick up my handbag, I check with Craig it is okay if I go for my lunch but he is busy on the phone so he gives me a thumbs up.

Chapter Forty-Five

I pop to the rest room, I look at my reflection in the mirror, my cheeks are red, I splash cold water on then add a swipe of lipstick across my lips and head for the restaurant, it is quite full of officers collecting lunch to take out, I spot Rex at an empty table, he motions he has saved me a seat, I carry my tray and sit with Rex after having a chat with Martin at the counter, I can feel my blood pressure returning to normal, the food is delicious, Martin brings over a cup of coffee, the three of us sit chatting whilst I eat my lunch, as usual it is far too much for me and too delicious to leave, I am famished and polish it off far too quickly. I look around, the restaurant is now almost empty, too early for some people, both Rex and Martin are very easy going uncomplicated people, they are entertaining me with stories of their pets, I can feel myself getting more relaxed, I banish the recent events from my head. I finish my lunch, pushing my plate away, I look around, the restaurant is getting a bit busier but they are on the other side, just a few people in the far corner eating their home bought lunches meals, I lay back in my chair stretching my legs out in front of me and rubbing my stomach, I am so full. Rex is showing me his new mobile phone, he is so pleased with it, I am showing him how to put in a new contact. The restaurant door opens, I glance up to see both Craig and Mike walk in, I check my watch, I groan inwardly I know they are heading in my direction but I have ten or so minutes still to go, I continue to show Rex his contact list, I watch as both Mike and Craig sit down at the vacant table next to me, they watch for a second or two before Craig turns his body to face me and then speaks first, "Can we have a moment to speak with Angie please, guys," he addresses Martin and Rex.

Both get up as if to leave, but I interrupt, "No, don't, please stay, you don't have to go, I am still on my rest break," I turn to face Craig.

"Whatever you have to say will have to wait," but both Rex and Martin are not the type for confrontation, Martin picks up my plate, mumbles about having to get back anyway and Rex being very old school, respecting the uniform, stands up, picks up his new phone, he faces them and casually saluting both of them.

"On my way, say no more," he says to them. I watch as Rex walks away, I don't want to look at them, I watch Rex walk out of the door then I look down at my hands, I don't face them, I refuse to look at them. I wish Mike wasn't involved, I hate that he has seen those words written down, I cringe inwardly, I wait, saying nothing.

Craig speaks first, "Angie, come on please, we need to talk about this, somewhere private, there is so much crap going on at the moment on our shift, just one thing after another," he pauses but I say nothing I don't even look at him, I am aware Mike is sat so close to me, but I cannot look at him either.

Craig leans forward, he keeps his voice low, "I had no idea what happened on night shift, you never told me anything, I don't know why you didn't," he pauses and I know he is looking at me, I stare at the table as he continues, "you should have told me, Angie, we don't need this rubbish not on our shift, come on, Angie, this is not like you."

I turn slowly, I look him straight in the eye totally ignoring Mike, I keep my voice low, "You know what, Craig, no this might not be like me, I have always conformed to the company line, I have never acted in a way that the force would be unhappy with, never made a complaint about anyone or had a complaint made about me, I have never put a step out of line, you know that, I never told you because I didn't think it was that important; it was a private conversation I had with that chap, no one would have overheard, no one but me could have been offended, I didn't want to complain, I don't know how it has come to this." I look down at my hands, before continuing I speak quietly, "I didn't want what he said to be public knowledge, he was out of order, I know that, it was very personal."

I can feel my face reddening, I am mortified that Mike has read what was said about me. Craig leans over, he puts his hand over mine he speaks quietly, "He was very much out of order, Angie, like you say it was personal, he had no right to say those things and especially not to you, you must be able to see that it cannot go unchallenged."

I look at him I nod my head, "Yes, I do but I don't see how it has to be public knowledge, why should everyone know, why should I have to accept worse things being said to me in jokes, worse than what Bradley said, then, because his face doesn't fit we all gang up on him, that is not fair, is it?"

The restaurant door opens, two office workers come in and head for the counter, Mike looks at Craig, he says quietly, "I think we now need to take this somewhere private."

Craig nods in agreement, he looks at me, "Can we go down and speak privately back in the meeting room?"

I don't know what to say so I just nod my head, it is pointless me arguing, they will just wait till after my rest break anyway, I look at Mike, as Craig walks ahead I say quietly, "Did you know about this last week?"

Mike looks to check Craig is far enough away, he stops walking then turns to me, "No, no of course I didn't." We walk out into the corridor, at the top of the stairs he turns to face me looking me straight in the eyes, "I honestly didn't, I was pulled in this morning and told I was to be involved in a meeting but as a note taker only, I was given specific instructions that I was to play no other part or contribute to the meeting, I had no prior knowledge of who was involved. I turned up at the meeting room just ten minutes before the meeting started, I was told to read the statement so I could make reference to it in my notes then I had to listen to the tape before you came down."

He reaches out and touches my arm, I look at him I can see concern in his face but I cannot see reason, I am beyond that, my fiery temper is surfacing again his next words make me even more cross. "I was shocked when I read what that chap said to you, I was also very angry, how dare he talk to you like that, as you said, he was too personal, he had no right, you could have told me, I would have dealt with it."

I can feel my anger bubbling, ready to explode, I cannot look at him, I walk on down the stairs, I spit my words out, "Oh you would have would you, so if I would have come to you when it happened you would have had a chat in his ear, on the quiet, well Mr Big shot, that is exactly what I did myself, I am a big girl, I can look after myself, I don't know who has complained but they have no right."

I turn to face him looking straight up at him, my stomach is churning, I clench my fists trying to control my temper but I cannot do it I lose it completely, spitting my words at him, "You know what I think," I don't wait for him to reply, I storm on, "I think the only reason you are annoyed is because of what has happened between us since that incident, if any uniform girl on your shift come up and told you what he said to them I don't think you would have said a word, you would have told them it is the nature of the role, get a backbone, comes with the job, wouldn't you, like when the CID chaps commented on my chest, you said nothing," I am breathless, I take in a huge lungful of air, I don't wait for his answer his face looks shocked, "you are such a bloody hypocrite," I manage to choke out.

I don't give him chance to reply, I stomp off down the last few steps pushing open the door and into the corridor. I stamp straight into the meeting room, I push the door open with force, more than I intended, it slams against the wooden frame. I know my face is bright red, I can feel my cheeks burning, I try hard to hold back the tears of anger, without looking or saying a word to Craig who is sat the other side of the desk, I grab the statement lying on the desk, I turn to the back page, sign my name on the statement in big angry letters, throwing the pen down I don't wait for any further discussions, I don't say a word, Craig is just sat there dumbfounded. I walk straight back out, storm up the corridor, narrowly avoiding crashing into Mike coming the other way.

"Hey, Angie," he calls out, "wait up." I storm on down the corridor.

"Drop dead you bloody hypocrite!" I shout back at him.

I return to the control room, I sit back down and start looking through the logs, I try to calm myself, but it is hopeless, I cannot stop shaking. Gavin comes over, he strokes my shoulder, I drop my hands down onto the desk and rest my head on them, he stands at the side of me.

"Do you want to talk about it?" he asks, I shake my head, he strokes my head gently. "Whatever it is, Angie, like you said it is just petty politics, love."

I can feel the hot tears pricking the back of my eyes, I choke them back, I don't know why I am so angry, practices like this go on all the time, but I go on oblivious as I am not generally involved.

Gavin squats down at the side of me, "Just take some time out, honey, it's not busy, I will make you a cup of tea okay." l nod my head, he disappears and after a few minutes I feel him at the side of me, he places my tea down then walks back to his chair, I sit for a while with my head resting on my forearms. Eventually I can feel myself calming down, I hear calls coming in so with a sigh I pick up my headset, Gavin looks at me, I look over the control room, the boys are looking at me, I give them a false smile and call out, "I will be fine, guys honest, I am fine, they just got to me and I lost my temper that is all," they smile back at me, they know me very well. Gavin walks back over to me and pats me on the shoulder, he stands for a while watching me as I listen to the caller reporting a theft, I slowly relax, I look up to him and smile, he nods and walks back to his desk. I will be okay, I just need to be left alone. I need to lose myself in work, I log the call and as another call comes in I hit to receive it, my rage has gone, I take a sip of my tea and listen, I am back to being the controller. Craig doesn't return, the shift works without him. In a way I am relieved, I really don't want any more confrontation. I check my mobile but there is no message from Mike, not sure why I expected one really, I have no doubt that both he and Craig are tucked in an office somewhere trying to decide how they are going to deal with my heated exchange with them and also how they will explain my angry signature to the powers that be.

About forty-five minutes before the evening shift is due, Steve walks in, he give a cheery wave to the other guys, he is in his uniform I am pleased to see him so I give him a wave, he beckons me over to him, he motions with his head I should follow him, we disappear into the admin room.

"How are you?" I say immediately, the door closes, he shrugs, he tries to smile but fails, he shakes his head.

"I guess I am okay, I am back now, that is good, hated being at home, there is just rubbish on TV, nothing to do, drove the wife mad," he pauses, "obviously they have put me on another shift, I am glad to be back but it's not the same though."

"But why?" I interrupt him. "I haven't any idea what has gone on, what has happened?"

Steve sits at the desk. "Okay well I guess it is okay to tell you, it was all over that bloody bank incident, I shouldn't have even been here but I got in early and got dragged into being the controller, it all went wrong very quickly," he looks around to check we are not being overheard, then continues, "it seems that during the incident Nick thought I gave the command to use weapons and storm the building which I bloody categorically didn't, there were all these uniform big bods behind me, but not one of them will collaborate my side of the story, I know they heard, they must have but then everything went wrong – one of the robbers got trigger happy, there was a fatal and they all got nervous," he shrugs. "Well you know what they are like, slopey shoulders where there is accountability." I nod at him as he continues, "It is pretty obvious they would have heard me say it, but you know white shirts stick together, it is fine, I am okay now, I need to forget it," he pauses and looks at me, "if I am honest, looking back, there was so much going on, so much noise, the press outside, the helicopter above, I think maybe Nick's adrenalin was pumping, maybe he misheard, there is no tape to clarify the story so as a result two members of the public were injured, the bank manager died but Nick was clever, he went off on stress leave and I was suspended, not sure what has happened to him, or where he is now."

I touch his arm gently, "Are you okay now to be back here?" Steve laughs, "Christ yes, definitely, it was driving me nuts being at home, not able to text or phone anyone, not allowed to have any contact at all. When you kept sending messages I kind of knew no one had told you, which I can understand, you have had so much on your plate," he stands up and hugs me. "I will be okay on the new shift, I am a big boy, I will cope, it is a fair enough punishment, I don't get to run any big incidents, but you know what, who needs the hassle anyway," he laughs again. "So," he continues, "all excitement for you then."

I look at him, "What, I wasn't aware anyone knew about it, I wouldn't call it excitement though, it is all a bit stupid really, things get blown out of all proportion don't they."

Steve looks at me quizzically, "Do they, how come?" he frowns then breaks into a grin.

"Well," I continue, "the rookie was stupid, he run his mouth off, now he stands to lose his job, it is a shame that all the world has to know about it, it is a bit embarrassing really, well very embarrassing when you see it in black and white, I was really cross but I am getting over it," I slump in the chair, "you coming in here has calmed me down a bit, well a lot really, you have that effect on me, I am going to miss not having you on our shift," I add.

Steve's face is registering confusion, "What are you talking about, Angie."

Steve looks at me, the phone rings he leans across to answer it, before he does he winks saying, "I was talking about you and Mike."

Immediately my heart is hammering in my chest, I can feel my face going red with embarrassment, how does he know? He cannot know, surely not, he is bluffing. His phone call seems to take forever, he is writing information down, then spelling out his name and reiterating it again, I just stare at him, after what seems like an eternity he eventually finishes, he turns to me, "The wedding on Saturday, at the hotel, I was there, it was my cousin's wedding," he laughs, "the first I knew Mike was there was when I saw his car in the car park, that car is unique around here, the bride and groom loved it even had their photo taken by it, although don't tell Mike that, then I saw you both by the lake, I couldn't believe it, but of course you never saw me, you only had eyes for each other."

Oh my god, oh my god, I feel sick, my palms are clammy. "Don't worry," he put his face very close to mine, he whispers, "I think it is about time you both got together, I have seen you looking up when he comes in the control room, and clearly he cannot keep away from you, he spends more time in the control room than he does at his desk, I always thought it was me he fancied," he laughs then his face is serious again, "but don't worry, Angie, of all the people here you must know that your secret is very safe with me."

I stand up and he does the same, pull him close, I drop my head on his shoulder, I whisper back, "Thank you, Steve, I am so glad to hear that."

The door opens, Craig walks in, "Is this a private party or can anyone come in?" Steve and I jump apart, Craig looks at me. "You okay?" he asks.

"Yes, fine now thanks," I answer curtly.

He puts his hand out to shake Steve's. "Glad to see you back, mate," he says.

"Great to be back," Steve replies.

I listen as Steve reiterates the message he has taken for Craig, I am tired now, it has been a long and emotional day, I can feel a headache coming on, I check the clock, just half an hour to go.

Chapter Forty-Six

My mobile phone goes off in my pocket, I see on the screen it is my brother Scott, it must be important, Scott never even rings at home and he never calls my mobile. I look at them both then answer it, I listen for a moment, I stand in the admin office all the room seems to spin, I feel faint, I sit down handing my phone to Craig, I just sit there numb, I wait as Craig listens for a while then hangs up. He turns to Steve. "We need to get her home, you okay to follow me in a police car, I will drive hers, come on," he takes my arm leading me to the control room, "pack up your stuff and lets go." Craig walks over and speaks quickly to the team then takes my arm leading me out of the room.

Scott has phoned, Dad had a heart attack this morning, he is critical, through his various contacts Scott has booked flights, we need to be ready to leave for the airport within half an hour. In the car on the way home I answer my phone, it is Judy she calls to say she is all packed up and ready, she will be at mine in ten to fifteen minutes, I need to be very organised and quick, Scott is meeting us at the airport. Craig drops me off, pats my shoulder. "Keep me updated," he says. I nod, get out of the car and rush into the house, I pack very quickly, I know where everything is what I will need, I can sort cash out at the airport, I am ready when Judy arrives, and within a few minutes the car is there to take us to the airport. Scott has sent a further text that he has sorted everything out for us, we shouldn't worry as he is in constant contact with Mum. Judy goes on ahead in front of me, as I lift my suitcase over the front step, I throw my handbag over my shoulder, not noticing my mobile phone that falls with a quiet thump onto the carpeted floor in the hall.

It is only when we are halfway to the airport that I search for my phone, I search quietly so as not to annoy Judy then I get more worried, I frantically go through my pockets and my handbag, in the end I get Judy to call it, but it isn't there, I could cry with frustration. I lay my head back on the back of the chair, I close my eyes, this is a nightmare, I haven't even told Phil or Sean where I am, the last words I said to Mike was to call him a horrible name and tell him to drop dead. I so desperately need my mobile phone; I have no numbers for any of them, how stupid am I. I could cry with frustration. Judy doesn't seem to think it is a huge problem, little does she know. We check in, meet up with Scott and head for a coffee, I spot an internet café I am so tempted to pop over to shoot off a few emails to explain everything but I cannot do that, Scott would go nuts at me. He would give me such a hard time, go on and on about priorities, I know it really isn't worth it.

So I sit on the flight, I have so many thoughts going through my head, what about my dad, I hope he is okay, mum will be beside herself, what about Mike, I should have spoken to him before I left. My sister interrupts my thoughts, "Looks like we are going to be on time," she looks about the cabin, "they are closing the doors, Angie, we are just about to take off." I don't respond, she continues, "You are quiet, you worried about Dad too, try not to, Angie, he is a tough old bird, he will be fine." I smile at her taking her hand, I don't speak I just nod yes. I cannot tell her can I? I cannot tell her that my silence is not just about Dad, it is about my fight with Mike, obviously she has forgotten about my night away in the hotel, I must not be selfish, this is not about me. I blink back my tears I close my eyes saying nothing.

Customs is uneventful, thankfully there are no queues, there is a car that meets us at the airport to whisk us straight to the hospital, we drag our suitcases through the corridors looking for the cardiac unit. When we arrive I am quite shocked, Dad is all connected up to heart monitors, he is asleep, but looks very grey and older than when I saw him last. After our initial hugs and kisses with Mum we all sit round the bed willing him to get better, the gentle sounds of the equipment reminds me of Jason, I dab at my eyes to stop the tears. We stay for a few hours, then the consultant comes around, he checks everything with the nurse, we all sit and watch as they write everything down, he turns to Mum, in surprisingly good English he says Dad is stable, just resting, he says we must leave him to sleep, just two of us are permitted at the bedside, everyone else must leave, mum nods in agreement, she looks exhausted. After whispered discussions it is decided that Judy and I will go home to Mum's to drop the cases off we will go back up later. It is getting really late but the hospital is happy for us to come and go to spend time with Dad.

Judy is popping to the late night shops to get provisions, I tag along with her, she is happy driving Dad's car so after we get home we unload the shopping she goes off for a shower, I log on to Mum's computer, I feel a huge sense of relief as I log on to my private email account sending emails to Craig, Phil, Sean and Helen, letting them know we have arrived and I have seen Dad, I add at the bottom that I have left my mobile phone somewhere at home, but will be checking my emails as often as I can, with a touch of genius I send one to Steve, I don't know Mike's email, there are several M Simms at the police force so I am unsure what format his email is in, it is strange that I hit send on many emails every day but unless it is in my private email account I don't know any off by heart, so I just have to hope

Steve might just have the idea to forward it to Mike on my behalf. I close the computer with a sigh of relief.

Back at the hospital Dad is awake, he looks so vulnerable tied up to the machines but he can remove his oxygen mask so he manages a weak smile, his face is still very grey, but the consultants say he is going to be okay, it is Mum we are worried about too, she just keeps crying, dabbing her eyes with a tissue saying she wants him home. It is getting really late, we are told by the nurses that we all have to leave, Dad needs to rest, we all trudged down to the car park agreeing to go to a local restaurant for something to eat, we know it will be open until the early hours but none of us are in the mood to eat but we sit chatting and drinking coffee. It is nearly midnight when we get back to Mum's, it is dark, there is a strange car in her drive, from the few feet away we can see a man sat on her chair on the balcony, we all stand back, not daring to go near, we cannot make out who it is, then we hear a voice, "well that is a fine bloody welcome isn't it," we all run at the same time. Stuart looks tired, jet lagged but has made it in record time, he has been to the hospital, with his smooth talking he managed to speak to Dad for about half an hour, he couldn't contact any of us as his Dubai mobile phone won't work in Spain. Scott is so impressed to see he has made it, he interrogates him but Stuart just smiles saying "a friend I know has access to his company jet, when I explained the circumstances to them they let me on board the flight bound for Madrid with just half an hour to spare, then the last internal flight and boom here I am." We are all so pleased to see him, it has been so long, we spend the next few hours sat on the back patio catching up, it is the early hours of the morning, we have drunk several bottle of wine, Mum is overwhelmed with us all being there and with the stress of the situation with Dad she goes off to bed, leaving the four of us to catch up properly. It is fabulous to see Stuart again, both Judy and I sit close to him we cannot stop hugging him, he is here for two or three days only then has to head back.

We have to change the rota system to include Stuart, that way we all get quality time with Dad but also we get to spend time with Stuart, it is decided that Judy and Stuart spend the first hour or so in the morning with Dad then Scott and Mum go in with me. We are all relieved Dad is stable, Judy is concerned that some of the monitors have been removed, she thinks it is too soon because he still looks pale and exhausted, but the nurses make her feel a lot better explaining that the main machine monitoring his heart will remain in place, the nurses are so dedicated, Dad wants for nothing, the consultant comes and checks him regularly, Scott is cynical saying it is because of the extortionate private medical fees but nevertheless we are confident Dad is in capable hands. Dad is now able to sit up and is very pleased to see us all, but we notice he wants Stuart with him a lot, when Stuart is there Dad holds on to his hand, he never does this with the rest of us, but none of us mind really, we all realise how much we have missed him.

Stuart and I have to take our turn to go shopping, we have to get a few provisions, mainly to restock the wine we consumed last night at Mum's. On the way we stop at a small beach, there is a little café where we buy coffees and pastries, we walk a short way down the beach then lay with our toes in the sand, he turns to look at me, "So, come on, little sis, bring me up to date with what is happening with you then."

I look at him, I shrug, "Yes, I am okay," he takes a swig of his coffee.

"I didn't ask if you were okay, I asked what is happening, I mean," he takes another swig, "Phil and Sean keep me up-to-date with most things going on with the birds they are seeing and the football and rugby, you know, stuff like that, but not the private stuff, is there any private stuff you want to tell me?" I shake my head then promptly burst into tears. "Ah," he pulls me to him, "thought there might be, little sis, I can see in your eyes when you are not happy," he makes himself comfortable on the sand, he rests on one elbow then lays out, "come on then, I am all ears, tell me everything."

I look out over the ocean, it is not fair to burden him, he has Mum and Dad to worry about, but I look to him he raises his eyebrows, I copy his pose, laying facing him, running my fingers through the sand, I tell him about Mike, about the concert tickets and the valentine card the initial night we got together, the wonderful night away, the rubbish going on at work then finish by telling him about the horrible scene with Mike and how it ended up with me calling him names then the last straw was losing my mobile phone and not being able to contact him or anyone else.

Stuart reaches over and pinches me, "Ow," I cry out, "what was that for?" I rub my arm.

"You are an idiot, Angie, a real idiot sometimes, this guy clearly thinks the world of you, he doesn't want some jerk who thinks he is a hotshot making personal remarks about you, whether you are an item or not, why shouldn't he defend you, I bloody well would if it was my girl being spoken to like that, or even a female colleague, I would have gone up and punched him one, even if it was my sister, what a bloody cheek," he pauses, he looks out at the ocean for a while then he turns to me, "this Mike, well he clearly likes you a lot, apparently has done for a long time, sounds like a decent bloke to me."

I know he is right, that is what is so stupid, I look at Stuart, "So what do I do now then?"

Stuart gives a big sigh, "Simple, why don't you call him, speak to him."

I pull a face, "Did you not hear me, I left my mobile at home, I cannot call him or text him, stupid," he pulls a similar face back at me.

"How do you think we communicated before mobiles, stupid, you find a phone, you know a common street phone that normal people use, then ring work and ask to be put through to him," he makes it sound so simple, he continues, "no one need to know it is you, dummo, we can do it now if you like, there is no time difference is there." I shake my head, "If you were on days then he will be on day shift, yes?

I look at him nodding my head, "So come on," Stuart gets to his feet and offers me his hand, he pulls me up, he looks around, "now where do we find a payphone round here," he goes off sauntering to the promenade looking around, I have to put my sandals back on so I run after him. "Found one," he shouts pointing excitedly to the phone, "come on, slowcoach."

My heart is hammering, we haven't thought this through, "What do I say if he answers?" I look at Stuart, he passes me some coins.

"That, my darling sis, is down to you," he sits on the bench just a few feet away as I dial the number. I hear the international connection going through then I hear the sound of it ringing, I feel sick, my heart is hammering in my chest, the phone is answered very quickly, I don't recognise the voice so I put on the best foreign accent I can asking for Sergeant Simms. The voice says he has just stepped out but should be back soon, he offers to take a message but I panic hanging up.

Stuart is doubled over with laughter, "That was the worst accent I have ever heard, was it Welsh, Scottish or Irish?"

I go to kick him but he moves away quickly. "Shut up," I say, my face colouring, he stands up walking towards me.

"Ah bless you, you have got it bad haven't you, is my little sis in love," he laughs out loud, "come on we can always try later."

We get in the car returning to Mum's villa, we start the meal then sit on the patio talking some more. He settles in his deckchair, I look at him, he is looking older, but is really well tanned, he catches me looking.

"So," he faces me "what is this Mike like then?"

I smile at him. "He is lovely, Stuart, really lovely, very tall, plays rugby so is very fit, and he has dark hair and darkest eyes," I smile at him.

Stuart leans over, he messes my hair, "You know what, sis, your whole face has just lit up whilst you were speaking about him, sounds like he might be the one." I laugh out loud at his choice words, I close my eyes and think of Mike, I remember his strong arms around me, his lovely soft lips on mine.

We don't get another opportunity until the following day, Stuart stands over me as I dial, as it rings I lose my nerve and hang up, he takes the phone receiver and bangs it against my head as he presses redial and hands the phone over, "Don't hang up," he orders me. I ring through, I am informed that he is out at a job, I hang up redialling the control room number, Craig answers immediately he is really pleased to hear Dad is better, we have a nice chat, he promises to update Phil then the whole shift patch in to the conversation, I come off the phone feeling much brighter and happier.

Chapter Forty-Seven

We have been here three days, today is my 30th birthday, Mum has put banners up around the villa trying to make it all special, we all have a nice breakfast and I sit and open my cards; without my mobile phone there is no messages from anyone back home, I wonder if Mike knows it is my birthday or not, there is no way of me knowing. My family make a nice fuss of me and we have a cake with our lunch, it is all very lovely. Stuart is going home today, we are all going to the airport to see him off, he will be flying for the best part of two days to get him back to Dubai, no company jet on the way home, just normal economy flight for him, we all agree it has been great catching up, I love my brother so much he is a tower of support for all of us, I notice that both he and Scott disappear for a long walk, Scott is very private but I know he opens up to Stuart, all his life he has done what suited him, he stands up to Mum and Dad, even when she kicked up a fuss about him moving to Dubai he stood his ground, when Mum is giving Judy a hard time about her love life he argues back in Judy's defence, Judy doesn't have to say anything, then Mum moans on at me about the state of my life he tells her to leave us all alone, she listens to him where she won't listen to us. I hug him tight at the airport and promise him an update on the Mike situation he says he wants to know regardless of whether it is good or bad news, he hugs me close holding my chin, my eyes fill with tears. "Come on, sis, be brave, let me know if anything happens okay." I smile, a very watery smile. I watch as he motions for Judy to go with him and I know she has something on her mind. Stuart is wonderful, we all seem to go to him with our problems, but actually we don't know of his home life, he never really opens up to us if there is anyone special, we are all too self-absorbed to ask him, and to be honest, he would be very vague with his answers anyway.

Dad is due out tomorrow, he has made great progress. He has been moved onto the main ward, he is sitting up chatting happily when we go to visit him, and the Spanish nurses love him and make a huge fuss of him. Mum wants to make arrangements for him to come home to the UK to recuperate there properly but she has been told that he will not be able to fly for some while yet, my Uncle Clive is flying out to be with her when we leave so she won't be on her own, then when he leaves to go home Judy is coming back out with the children. I have had too much leave already so I know I cannot afford to take any more time out, Mum understands that. Scott has us booked on the late afternoon flight tomorrow, we will land about eight thirty in the evening, my shift are now on evenings, so I use Mum's phone to ring quickly telling Craig my flight details, I let him know when I will be back in, he is fine he wishes me a safe journey, in the background I can hear the comforting noises of the control room, suddenly it is where I want to be, I cannot wait for the journey to begin so that I can get home.

The flight is uneventful, we collect our cases, go through customs with minimal fuss, Jude and I say goodbye to Scott. We have a private car taking us home courtesy of Scott. The roads are fairly empty; we make good time, stopping at my house first. Judy comes to the door with me, she pulls me close to her and we hug, I put my case down, opening the door turning to wave at her as the car pulls off.

I am so pleased to be home, the house is in darkness, I switch the light on immediately seeing my mobile phone tucked under the radiator in the hall, I squeal out loud, I am so happy that I haven't lost it, the battery is dead, I plug it in to charge then dragging my case into the lounge, I collapse onto the chair, the answer phone on my home phone is blinking with several messages, but I ignore it, I kneel down to try to switch on my mobile, I am desperate to check for messages, I just want to hear one from Mike, just one will make everything all right, I want to send him a message, I am desperate to see if he has sent me one, it takes an agonisingly long while to come to life so I tap in my code and leave it plugged in. The doorbell rings making me jump, it must be Judy forgotten something, I walk to the door almost in a daze to open it. There stood in front of me is a very large bouquet of flowers, I cannot see the person behind it but I just know who it is. "Hello you," I say quietly, I reach across and grab his sleeve I pull him in across the doorstep.

Mike kicks his boots off and walks into the lounge, he has a bag of shopping which he places on the floor, he puts the flowers on the arm of the sofa, he indicates the bag. "I thought you might need provisions," he says by way of explanation.

"Thanks," I reply. Suddenly I feel really awkward, I cannot meet his eyes, I try and keep my voice casual, "How did you know what time I would be home?"

He shrugs, "I was in the control room when you called to speak to Craig, I worked out how long it would take for you to get home, I was out and about on enquiries, but I have been parked up waiting for I guess about ten minutes, I saw you being dropped off."

"Oh right," I reply, I don't know what else to say.

There is a sense of awkwardness about us, I want to so much just make it all better, I so want him to kiss me, but he just stands there, it seems like forever but eventually he speaks. "Sorry to hear about your dad," he offers.

"Thanks, it was a shock, he is out of intensive care now, he is going to be okay" I reply.

Why is it so strained between us, it is horrible, really uncomfortable, I can hear the messages coming in to my mobile phone it is bleeping continuous. "Sounds like you are in demand," he says, I nod, "I had better let you get on then," he walks towards the door, I don't know what to say, I want to say so many things but I cannot make the words happen.

"Thanks," I say quietly, he frowns, I point to the shopping.

"Oh that, you are welcome."

He walks to the hall, bends down to put his boots on, I just watch him, he moves towards the front door his hand is on the door handle, I want him to stay, in just a matter of moments he will be the other side of the door, it will be too late, I struggle with the words I want to say, my heart is pounding hard in my chest, I cannot just let him go, but I don't know what to say, what words to use, my mind is blank.

"Mike," I say it so quietly I don't know if he has heard or not," but he stops, turning to face me, I look up at him, there is a questioning look on his face, without saying a word I move the few feet between us straight into his arms, he envelopes me, his strong arms holding me tight. I lift my face to his, he looks deeply into my eyes before his lips meet mine. We stay there, just stood in the darkness just kissing, he doesn't move at all. His lips start off ever so gently over mine then become more urgent. I press my body into his, breathing in the wonderful fresh smell of him. I want to cry with relief that he is holding me in his arms and kissing me.

His radio crackles into life, that bloody radio, how I hate it sometimes, I recognise Gavin's voice on the other end, we stand still as he answers his call sign, he responds, he has a job he needs to attend, he speaks quickly into his radio saying he will call for details in a while. I move away from him walking back into the lounge but he catches my hand, he holds it tight. So very tight.

When he finishes speaking into the radio he releases my hand then follows me back into the lounge. "Oh, Angie, what have you done to me?" he pulls me back to him, he props on to the arm of the chair pulling me between his legs, I look up to him, he takes my face in his hands as he continues, "I have missed you so much this week, I was beside myself with worry as I didn't know where you were, it seemed that no one did, Craig had disappeared your shift had no idea, or wouldn't say anything until Craig got back, then he explained what had happened. I text, I called your phone so many times to try and speak with you," he pauses and pulls me close to him, "it must have been such a shock for you to get the call, to have to leave like that," he pulls away and looks at me, his face is so full of concern.

I find my voice, "Yes, it was a shock, but everything is okay now, Dad is going to be fine, he should be home tomorrow, well back at his villa," I look up at him, "Mike, I am so sorry for the way I behaved, I am so very sorry, I shouldn't have lost my temper and I should never have called you such a terrible name, I felt awful afterwards and just wanted to ring you to apologise, but everything went wrong, in my rush to get to my dad, I got myself all in a state." I realise I am jabbering but I cannot stop, " I didn't realise I dropped my mobile in the hall on the way out, I was desperate to call you or text but I had no numbers, I did try to call you in your office from Spain, but someone picked up and said you were out of the room."

Mike laughs, I love his laugh. "Ah that was you, part of me was hoping it might be, but they said it was an international call from a chap with a bad Scottish accent, they thought I had an informer who was protecting their identity. I stayed in the office waiting for you to call again but you didn't."

I lay my head on his shoulder, "Oh I did try again but you were out so I phoned Craig instead," I explain.

"Ah right," he pulls me close to him. "Okay, I was sat next to him when you phoned but he didn't tell me it was you until after, I think I would have snatched the phone from him if I had known, your shift are quite protective as I could hear them all chatting away and patching in to the call but no one said it was you, although I should have guessed," he lifts my face up to his. "You do have one hell of a short temper and you are quite scary when you are angry, I find it quite sexy really," he pauses to look straight into my eyes. "Angie baby, I have missed you so very much." He kisses me again his hands run up my body over my breasts, where he stops, he massages them gently, he sighs, "So very much."

I want him to just hold me, but I pull away from him. "Don't you have to call the station?" I remind him.

He laughs, "Always the controller baby, aren't you."

He is on his radio taking the details of the job then comes in to join me in the kitchen, I have made tea but he says he has to go. "Can I come back later?" he asks. "It will be after midnight," I nod my head.

"I don't care how late it is." I smile at him. "I cannot go another night without you."

He comes over to me, takes me in his arms again. "Do you mean that?" he whispers kissing my neck.

"Yes I do, I have missed you so much," I pause, "but what will you do about your car?" I ask, "People might see it," he holds me away from him, I see the frown on his face.

"Is that such a big problem, Angie, I mean, so what if people see us, I don't care if the world knows about us, what's the harm?"

I drop my hands from him, I turn to pick up my tea, welcoming the heat scalding my hands, I cannot look at him. "Not yet, Mike, I am not ready yet."

Mike runs his hands through his hair, I can tell he is frustrated and annoyed with me. His radio bursts into life again, within seconds his mobile phone is ringing too, he looks at me exasperated. "Look I have to go, can we speak about this later, meanwhile your car is parked out the front, shall I put mine in your garage so no one can see it, would that make it better?" I look at him trying to give him a smile, but he is not smiling back, so I just nod my head yes.

"Okay," he kisses me again, "see you later."

Then he is gone, I shower then get into my night clothes, I drag my case upstairs and unpack, I send a quick email to Stuart thanking him for being there for us all, adding a little footnote that Mike was waiting with a bouquet for me and I add several exclamation marks. I put my clothes away noticing my negligee lying there, I am so tempted to put it on but I decide on long pyjama bottoms with a vest top. I am so very tired, I feel as if I have been up for hours. I check my answer phone message but it is just the doctors reminding me of an appointment for my contraceptive injection then there is another from Annabelle reminding me of the Christening on Sunday.

I pick up my mobile phone, it is still not charged so I squat on the floor, I scroll through the text messages then the voice messages, there are not that many, there is one from Mike, asking me to please call him so we can talk, then one from Phil, wishing me well asking me to pass on his regards to my parents then another one from Mike, his voice sounding very strained asking me to please call him or text as soon as I can. I check my text messages, there are quite a few from Mike all sent on the day of the argument, one says he has been to the control room but I am not there, another saying "please call", as he is worried, another one asking me "please text me back", then another one sent about quarter of an hour later saying, he cannot believe I am ignoring him over something so stupid. The last one says "hope your dad is okay, hope to see you when you get back, please call me if you can but only if you want to."

I reply to a few of the other messages, Phil sends a response almost immediately, he says he will catch up tomorrow as he is out on the motorway at an incident he cannot see him getting away for quite a while. Sean replies it is short and sweet "speak soon, glad all is okay night night."

I give in to the tiredness, I lay on the sofa, the television is on but I cannot be bothered to watch it so I just lay there listening to some murder mystery on the television, but I have no idea what I am watching, I am thinking about Mike, I cannot bear to be apart from him, I so want him to stay tonight, tomorrow night, forever. I fall asleep but it seems like just minutes later I am woken by my doorbell, I peep out of the curtains there he is, looking so totally gorgeous, I let him in and we kiss at the door, I move to go into the lounge but he remains where he is.

"Are you okay?" I look at him.

"Not really," he says pointing to his trousers, "I have had this since I left you." I laugh, I try to pull him by the hand towards the lounge but we never make it, he makes love to me at the bottom of the stairs, pulling my top over my head he kisses my breasts, then his lips move to mine, he pulls away and I can feel him undoing his trousers. There is no gentleness with his love making, it is swift and urgent, it is all about his needs, my body responds to him immediately, my head is pounding, I shriek as he grabs my breasts squeezing them together as he climaxes, then as he lays on top of me he kisses me gently. "Happy belated birthday, darling," he whispers to me.

"It is now," I whisper back pulling him closer to me. I giggle, "You still have your boots on," I tell him.

He leans back and looks at me, "I think I have told you before, when I see something I want..." he doesn't finish his sentence, his lips are back on mine.

We move up to the bedroom, Mike is not tired, so I lay in his arms. "The last few days have been a nightmare for me, Angie, I know it hasn't been a picnic for you, but all I could think of was the lovely night at the hotel, our lovely breakfast, then everything going wrong and you shouting at me and telling me to drop dead, I didn't even want to be involved with taking any notes at any meeting, I was ordered to," he moves to face me, "but I know it sounds strange, I am glad it was me, I would hate for anyone else to have read those remarks, especially any of our shift, I don't know what that chap thought he was trying to achieve with his comments, but it was way out of order." I nod my head at him, he continues, "I was so shocked when you shouted at me, I have never seen you cross, I had no idea what to think when you disappeared, everything went wrong very quickly, I didn't know what to think," I nod my head, I know how he feels, he continues, "the shift has been a nightmare, really busy, people off sick, no time to catch up, lots of difficult arrests, I have been like a bear with a sore head, and I missed you so much," then his face drops, he frowns, I know it is going to be serious he pulls me close to him then pushes me away gently and looks me straight in the face. "What is all this secrecy about, Angie, I don't understand it, I want to be with you, I certainly hope you want to be with me, why can we not be like any regular couple?" I sit up, I turn to face him, his face is so serious.

"Mike I know what you are saying, part of me wants to tell the world we are together but I don't want any knowing looks or whispers, I don't want to be the subject of people conversations, I had enough of that when Jason was poorly, and again when he died, I just want to enjoy our time, just the two of us, just for a while." I stop and look at him, his beautiful dark eyes are looking so solemn at me, but I have to tell him how I feel, I move away and look at him, "Mike, when we are ready, of course we will tell people, but I need to let people know gently, I have to consider their feelings, especially the feelings of Jason's family for one, the first anniversary of his death is coming up soon, I don't want to be marching round, grinning like a Cheshire cat, saying how happy I am and declaring my love for you when they are mourning their son, you do understand don't you?" I look him straight in the face, "Please say you do."

Mike smiles, "Declaring your love for me eh," he laughs, "so you love me then do you," he tickles my sides, "go on say it again, I want to hear you say it."

I look him straight in the face, "You know what I mean, Mike, but if you are asking me then yes I think you are lovely." We fall together on the bed, "Now you say it back," I tease him.

"No way," he laughs "I am not saying it."

I grab hold of his arm, "Say it," I demand playfully but he pushes me away teasingly.

"No way, I'm just here for great sex." He gets up to go to the en suite he is singing, "She loves me, she loves me, she said it first, she loves me."

I throw a pillow at him but he catches it, throws it back then he laughs out loud. He disappears into the en suite, I lay back on the bed and smile, I am just so happy, as he comes back to the bed I pull him down to me.

"You said it first anyway," I tell him, he half sits up and frowns at me, "When?" he asks.

"In the hotel room, when we got back after the coffee, you made love to me then you whispered it into my ear as we lay on the carpet."

He smiles, "You must have misheard."

I nuzzle my nose into him. "No I never, I heard it clearly, I will never forget one minute of that night, everything was so very special." Mike kisses me on the nose.

"Yes that hotel is good, I always take girls there, I get a discount."

I dig him in the ribs. "Say what you like I am not buying it, you said it, I heard it, and you have never taken anyone there before, you admitted as much." I reach my hand down to his stomach and stroke him gently, looking straight into his eyes I move my hand lower and squeeze. "Say it," I demand.

"Or what?" he asks, my hands moves lower and he lets out a groan. "I like you very much Angela Staddon," he whispers, I giggle, I don't care anyway, because I really do think that I love that man. We make love quickly then I lay in the crook of his arm, I feel him move as he flicks the television on and I snuggle right into him, he feels so warm. I fall into a delicious sleep and when I wake up, he is next to me, I cannot believe that this totally wonderful man is laid next to me, I snuggle back in to him for a while, I look up at him, I watch him breathing gently, he is still fast asleep.

When I wake up a short while later I go downstairs quietly to make breakfast, my text message goes off, I read it quickly; it is Phil, he wants to pop round now to collect his wheelbarrow for a friend. I don't know what to do, I panic a bit, Mike is still in bed, I think he is still fast asleep, I text back it should be okay, I look up the garden, the wheelbarrow is by the back gate which is right next to the garage, where Mike's car is hiding. I hear Mike get up and go to the bathroom, in a panic I run up the stairs quickly I explain to him that Phil is on his way, he laughs, "Well well, you do have a problem don't you," he laughs. "One man in your bed and the other on his way round."

I must have looked a bit panic stricken as he laughs again then says, "Calm down, it is fine, I will stay up here hiding away like some sordid secret whilst you get rid of your other man, he won't even know." I push him playfully but he grabs my arm pulling me back onto the bed.

"Stop it, stop it, we haven't got time, he will be here in a minute," I panic, but Mike is laughing.

"I can do so much in just a minute," he whispers reaching in to my pyjama top.

I struggle to my feet. "Stop it, stop it," I move quickly to the bedroom door just managing to escape his grasp.

I get downstairs to see Phil is walking up the back path, I meet him halfway, he greets me with a big hug planting a kiss on my head, I am embarrassed as I am aware that Mike might be looking out of the window, I am also embarrassed that I am wearing my pyjama top with no bra on underneath. Phil looks me up and down, I knew he would notice, nothing escapes him, I cross my arms across my chest. "You can hang coats on those hooks," he jokes, I poke my tongue out at him. "You okay?" Phil asks, I nod. "Glad to see you got back okay, your dad is okay then. Stuart emailed me, that is good news, see you got a bit of a tan."

I nod again, we stand for what seems like forever in silence which is finally broken by Phil, "Okay well must get on I suppose, you up for going out for a bite to eat on Friday, maybe lunch?" he asks, just you and me?"

I nod again, "Yes, sounds great, Friday it is then, see you later," I walk back in, as I look back to wave Phil hasn't moved he is just stood watching me.

Mike is back in bed, he has the television on low watching sport. "Has he gone?" he asks whispering, hiding under the covers. I swipe at the duvet but miss him.

"Shut up, you are not funny," I reply getting into bed next to him. "Now where was we when I left?" I ask cheekily.

Mike rolls over to face me, his face is very close to mine, "Mmm well I think that you were going to treat me like a sordid secret."

I move my hand lower down his body. "What like this?" I ask.

"Oh yes, so like that." I disappear under the bedclothes, in just a short time he is groaning as I bring him to his orgasm.

We have the rest of the morning together but Mike is still late leaving, I offer to get his car out of the garage but he declines.

"Why won't you let me drive it?" I ask him. "Don't you trust me?" Mike smiles.

"I trust you with most things but not my car."

I don't push it, I am not that bothered. Mike has to go home to get fresh uniform but even though I get to the station with just minutes to spare I notice his car is not there yet, I walk across the car park, I hear running, look behind to see Steve joining me.

"What are you doing here?" I ask.

"Ah you haven't heard then have you, Nick has been transferred to the metropolitan, I don't know all the details but apparently it was his choice, happened two days ago, very quick, very hushed. I should be placed on another shift but they cannot do that because the other shift would be overstaffed and as your shift are short, I got a call," he holds his arms out, and proclaims dramatically, "prepare the fatted calf for the prodigal son has returned," we both laugh, we hug, we are stood in the middle of the car park hugging when a car horn makes us both jump, the driver of the Maserati laughs, reversing into the vacant space. Steve gives a cheery wave then we walk in to the station together, he doesn't mention Mike, neither do I. The control room is busy, everyone is pleased to have Steve back, they shake his hand and pat him on the back, he beams with all the attention until we all pick on him to make the tea, he walks out to the kitchen, a huge smile on his face, everyone settles down to get on with the logs. Craig is in a great mood, everyone seems really happy. When Mike comes in the control room later Steve keeps winking at me whilst nodding his head in Mike's direction then smiling. I keep shaking my head and throwing him dagger looks back, but he doesn't care, he is loving my embarrassment, there is a large abnormal load working its way through our town so we have to keep everyone up to date with its location, we work quickly and keep up with the calls coming in. Mike is sat next to Craig, they both have their heads down looking at some paperwork but I see him keep glancing over, I cannot help but smile. Phil comes in to speak about a few jobs he has been allocated, he drags a chair up and sits by me we chat about my dad and Stuart.

Craig calls over, "The chap from the enquiry office is on his way up, Angie, apparently there is a delivery for you, watch out for him won't you," I nod my head, I have no idea what he is talking about. I pick up a call which turns out to be a long one. When I look around Steve is stood by me, a lovely bouquet of flowers in his arms, he lays them down and looks over to the main control desk.

"Looks like she has an admirer," he says out loud, "and a rich one, this wasn't nicked off a headstone, I know, this bunch cost a lot."

I frown, I have no idea who has sent them, I continue to take the details of the call, I pull the addressed card from the bouquet, I look up, everyone is watching me, including Mike, I turn away. I know my face is red, I tuck the card into my bag, Phil walks round to have a look, he is stood at the side of me, I wish the call would go on and on, I don't know who the flowers are from, I am sure Mike wouldn't send them knowing what we spoke about recently and my need to keep our relationship private, also my birthday bouquet is still as fresh as the day he brought it round, I want to be able to find out by myself. A radio message comes in, Phil moves over to speak to

Steve. I finish the call and drag the small white envelope from my bag, it is typed out, it simply says, "thank you for everything you did for me, you are an angel" and is signed Nick. I don't know what to say, it is so thoughtful, but if I tell anyone they will know I was involved. I look to Mike, I frown and he frowns tilting his head questioningly, I get up and take the bouquet through to the kitchen. Bloody Nick, he is so thoughtful but so thoughtless, how am I going to explain them, what would Steve think, he would be so upset, he would think that I had supported Nick and not him, everything is always so complicated, then Helen comes in, she is my saviour, I explain quickly about the flowers. "Say your mum sent them," she says shrugging, I could kiss her, it is a brilliant lie. I walk back into the control room.

"So who are they from then?" Craig asks.

Helen is behind me, I stop for a second but Helen jumps in, "They are from her mystery lover, he is a millionaire and plans to take her away from all this, very soon," she laughs out loud, "or maybe from her mum and dad, because they love her."

Craig laughs and everyone joins in, no one challenges her lie, I breathe a sigh of relief. The control room is back to normal and I notice that nothing has been mentioned about the business with the new recruit either, I haven't seen him at all, I am happy that the matter has been dealt with.

I receive a text message from Mike, it always makes me smile when I see the name I have him saved on my phone secretly so no one will know it is him, he is still sat with Craig, "you look gorgeous, xx". I blush a deep red slipping lower in my seat so no one can see. Another text comes in, "even more so when you blush". Simon from CID comes into the control room he makes a beeline for my desk, sitting on the edge, blocking my view of Mike and his view of me.

"How's your dad?" he asks me.

"Fine thanks, making a good recovery."

He smiles, "Glad to hear it," there is no mockery in his voice, he seems genuinely interested. "So how is everything else going with you then?" I look at him, he has never asked me questions like this before, I am aware that both Mike and Phil could be watching me. Why can't the shift be busier I think to myself.

"Oh you know, busy as ever."

Simon laughs. "Too busy to come out for a drink with me then?" he asks.

"Far too busy I am afraid." I look up at him frowning. "Haven't we discussed this before?" I ask him. "Wouldn't the mother of your child object?"

Simon turns his body to face me. "No, I am certain that she wouldn't, you see she moved out two weeks ago and is living with her new lover, so," he holds his arms open, "here I am, all for you, just say the word."

A call comes in, thankfully, I hit the accept button shaking my head smiling at Simon. It is a road accident, the control room suddenly comes to life as units are allocated to attend, the other services are tasked to attend. When I look around later Mike, Phil and Simon have left the control room.

Chapter Forty-Eight

Mike is at a performance review meeting immediately after work, he calls me to let me know, I tell him about the bouquet, he laughs. "I did wonder who would be brave enough to send you flowers, who I had to put I my hit list, but it is very thoughtful of him I guess but I can see where you are coming from, Steve might struggle with it," he goes on to explain he is not coming home to mine as he is not sure how late it will finish, so when the night shift come in to take over I pick up my bouquet and walk with Steve to the car park, he is about to ask me something when Phil runs up behind us, we walk the short way to the car.

"What was Simon going on about earlier?" he asks.

"Oh I don't know, you know just Simon being Simon," I try to laugh it off casually. "He was winding me up as usual you know Simon."

Steve stops me, "I don't think he was winding you up, Angie, I think he likes you, really likes you, when he asked you out earlier, he was serious, and I know he has definitely split with his girlfriend recently."

Phil looks at me. "Seriously, he was asking you out again, will he never learn," he shakes his head. "What did you say, please don't tell me you said yes?"

I look at him and smile. "As if," then I look at Steve, "thanks, Steve," Steve shrugs and walks to his car, but Phil pulls my sleeve and I stop.

"What did he want then, Angie, what did you say, you didn't say yes did you?"

I sigh, before responding, "No, Phil, I didn't say anything, I didn't need to, I was saved when a call came in, we got busy, but can you not see that someone we know not too far away from you is winding you up, aren't you, Steve."

Steve walks back he laughs he puts his arm round Phil's shoulder drawing him close to him. "Sorry, mate, it is too easy to wind you up where this one is concerned, you need to lighten up mate, either lighten up or marry her, see you in a few days, have a nice break," he throws his head back and laughs at his own joke, then he heads to his car. Phil stands there then breaks into a smile.

"Bloody wind up merchant," he calls after Steve but Steve is out of earshot and the remark is wasted on him.

I head towards my car and wave as Phil pulls out in front of me, we have Friday, Saturday off then we start night shift on Sunday, the christening is Sunday I still haven't invited Mike yet; I will let him know tomorrow. I get home, shower then crawl into bed, I am so tired.

I wake up with the sun streaming into my room, it is a nice bright day so I put washing in then do a few chores around the house, Mike calls, he is not on night shift next week he has been selected to go on a hostage negotiation course for a week, he is really pleased to be selected, if he does well they keep him for a second week he thinks he can only come home weekends, but he will need to check. I am pleased for him, really I am, but I am so going to miss him. I make a cup of tea then ring my mum and dad for a catch up, Uncle Clive is still there and driving Dad crazy but he is looking forward to Judy arriving tomorrow and creating a distraction. He is getting on really well the doctors are pleased with his progress. I ring Judy to wish her a happy holiday, I finally get to tell her all about Mike. She is really pleased but I swear her to secrecy, we chat about the children and other general things, then I don't know why but I ask her how her love life is she almost bites my head off.

"Why do you have to know every detail," she barks at me.

"I only asked," I reply.

"Well don't," she barks again, "you sound like Mum with your interrogating," she doesn't exactly hang up on me but she says she has to go, promising she will catch up with me later, she then hangs up.

I come off the phone I sit for a minute quite shocked, she is never nasty to me, we have always shared stories of how our lives are going, well okay not always, but she is never horrible to me. I send her a quick text to say sorry if I have upset her then I pick up the phone to Sean. He is on his mobile at his parents, he invites me round, as I am all up together with everything I agree saying I will walk round as it is nice out. Mike is at rugby training this morning and so won't see him until tonight, but I send him a quick hello text, he doesn't reply. Sean is in a good mood as is both Little ma and Pa, she pulls me into the kitchen whispering excitedly in my ear, trouble is she is so excited she is mixing Hebrew with English – I haven't a clue what she is saying.

Sean calls from the lounge, "Mum, I can hear you from here, you said you wouldn't say anything, remember," but Little ma is too excited, I have no idea what she is saying so I give her a hug, pick up my drink then go into the lounge, Sean is sat on the sofa.

"Did you get any of that?" he asks.

"Not a word, I need an interpreter please," I reply smiling at him. "That's if you know what she was saying."

Sean looks at me. "Yes, I know," he takes a drink of his tea, "I wish I didn't, but as you have asked," he puts his tea down and sits back. "Mum let herself into my place the other morning to collect my laundry, she thought I was at work, well I was supposed to be but I was taking some time out, you know," he pauses, "entertaining."

"Entertaining?" I ask him my eyebrows shooting up.

"Yes, you know, entertaining, I was with a lady friend, or as Phil would coarsely put it," he pauses, "shagging."

I nearly spit my tea out, I wipe my chin and look at him. "Oh my, I didn't even know you were seeing someone, who is she, what did you do when she came in the room, what did she see?" I laugh out loud, "this is priceless, come on, Sean, tell me," I urge him.

He continues, "Well, I am not sure how long she was there, but we were both naked, in very compromising position, she came barging in with clean sheets in her arms singing away in her own world."

I laugh out loud, very loud. "Oh no," I manage, Pa looks over at us but he cannot hear very well. "What did you say?" I ask. Sean leans closer so his dad cannot hear.

"What could I say, I threw the pillow at her, told her to get out, trouble is, now she thinks I am engaged, I guess sex to her means engagement, marriage maybe the possibility of grandchildren."

I cannot help it, I laugh so much my eyes water. Sean joins the laughter adding, "My own fault really, I am old enough to change my own bedding, but no matter how many times I try and tell her she won't have it, she happily lets herself in, I haven't the heart to take the keys off her."

I am still laughing as I walk into the pub to meet Phil, we always meet at the same pub, he likes the beer and the food is good, he kisses me when I arrive then moves away.

"No hug?" I ask him, he stands up giving me a big bear hug. We order food then sit with our drinks, "Did you hear about Sean?" I ask him.

"Yes, he told me the day it happened, he was mortified, but I thought it was hysterical."

"Yes, I thought it very funny too," I add.

"Funny that," Phil says as he takes a swig of his drink. The woman arrives with our starter, he waits for her to move away before he continues, "I didn't think you would approve."

I don't say anything, I just shrug, it doesn't bother me who Sean is sleeping with, I never think to ask him about his relationships really. I am starving, so I tuck into my starter we eat in companionable silence for a while, when I finish I look at Phil, "So what have you been up to then, whose garden was you clearing the other day?" I ask him, he shrugs.

"No one in particular, just helping a mate that is all," he is non-committal.

"Well, who is the mate then?" I ask looking up at him.

"Well, if you are asking it is Helen, she wanted some bricks moved and I helped her to move them, well actually she stood watching whilst I did all the work, bit like you do," he mops up the last of his starter and doesn't look at me.

I want to punch the sky, wow, I am so pleased, I try to keep the smile from my face as I know Phil will get all funny if I make a big deal of it so I just say, "That was nice of you."

Phil looks at me. "Don't make a big deal out of it, Angie, it was just a favour, and whilst we are talking about 'friends'," he holds his hands up making inverted commas with his fingers, "can I ask you a question, Angie," he looks me straight in the face, "was Dean round your house the other morning when I came round for the wheelbarrow, or had he been round at any point?"

I look at him confused. "Dean who?" I ask.

"Oh very funny," he scoffs at me, "you know very well who I mean, the chap from Mike's party who nearly sucked your face off."

I laugh, "Oh yes, that Dean, you know I had almost forgotten about him, so no, he wasn't at my house, he has never been at my house."

Phil leans over and mops the last of my starter from my plate, I watch him without speaking, he carries on, "Oh right, it's just unusual for you to walk around with your tits hanging out," he looks at me, "not that I am complaining, thought you had just got out of bed, it was just that I was talking to Mike the other day at work, I mentioned that you were a bit quiet of late and I thought you were seeing Dean secretly, Mike says he hasn't seen him at Rugby for a while, I said maybe you had knackered him out." Phil smiles at me, he winks, I cannot believe he said that to Mike, I glare at him.

"You never said that to Mike surely,"

Phil holds out his hands. "What, yes I did, Mike has been in a right bloody mood for the past week, don't know what is wrong with him but there is definitely something, he is barking out orders, pulling us up on our pocket books, right miserable sod he has been so serves him right if he thinks his mate is getting something he isn't." He stands up. "Another drink?" he asks so casually then trots to the bar. I so want to kill him, poor Mike, he had a fall out with me then had to listen to Phil teasing him about Dean.

When he returns to the table, we change the subject, Phil asks me about the statement I signed, I shrug, "I don't know, I don't really care, haven't heard anything," I tell him, he frowns.

"Bit weird really, all that business, there is something not right there, that bloke was just a bit too sure of himself, he was funny with Helen too, asking her mental questions, and then apparently he tried to pick a fight with Sergeant Boon, but he was having none of it," he shakes his head, "that is just not right for a rooky is it," I shake my head as Phil continues, "there is definitely something not right but I cannot put my finger on it, my gut feeling is that something is going on, I am not sure if Mike is involved or not though, he is a bit of a dark horse sometimes, bit of a forces man, I am sure he knows something but he isn't saying if he does."

Our meals arrive so we tuck in, Phil's text message bleeps, "Ah," he says, "speak of the devil, it is Mike, says he is popping in for a pint."

I look at Phil. "You are so not funny, Phil," he looks wounded.

"What have I said, it's okay he won't bring Dean with him, there will be no reunion," he passes his phone to me showing me the message.

"But he doesn't normally come in here does he?" I ask, he nods his head.

"Yes, he has done, not very often though, all the lads generally come in around 2 o'clock, but you have normally gone home by then, we play pool for the rest of the afternoon, maybe some of us go into town, then maybe later we go for a Chinese meal or a curry, we always meet up on the first day off after day shift sometimes before night shift I thought you knew." I shake my head, he goes on, "That is why I always suggest us meeting here, the food is good and I only have to stroll over to the pool table."

I shake my head again. There is so much going on around me that I just don't know about, I don't know where my head is sometimes. We eat silently, it is not an awkward silence, we make small talk mainly about the meal. Within twenty minutes, and as Phil predicted at least eight of the shift are here, Phil has finished his meal and I have just a little bit left so they go over to set the pool table up, my text goes off it is Sean asking if Phil and I are in the pub, I text him back confirming we are, he says he is on his way.

Phil returns and sits back down with me, we are just chatting about my mum and dad, I have finished my meal, everyone else on the shift are stood around the pool table, I look over at the shift, they all seem to get on really well, Mike is at the bar getting drinks, he brings a pint over to Phil places it in front of him, Phil looks up, "Cheers, mate," Mike winks at me then wanders over towards the pool table, I watch as he walks away, his lovely body dressed casually in blue jeans and a grey jumper. "Told you he sometimes turns up, but I don't know what that was all about, we normally buy our own drinks," Phil looks at me, "maybe because he was such a bastard last week," he adds.

I shrug my shoulders then pick up my drink. "No idea," is all I can offer. Sean comes in. he comes straight to our table to offer us a drink, we both decline so he goes off to the bar, I lower my voice towards Phil. "I cannot believe he got caught by his mum naked in bed with a woman, can you, I mean if it was me I would be mortified?" I ask him.

Phil looks at me, "Well I cannot believe that he doesn't change his own bed, he is not five years old anymore, and more importantly I cannot believe you are taking this so well," he looks at me, "you do know who he was shagging don't you?"

I look at Phil, "Yes of course, I do, well, okay I don't know her name but I assume of course it was his girlfriend."

Phil looks at me, he shakes his head, "Sometimes I don't know what planet you are on, you have no idea do you, things go on all around you and you are totally oblivious, caught up in your own little world, I mean, don't get me wrong I like Sean a lot, but I am not sure I would be happy if it was my sister he was shagging," shaking his head, he picks up his pint, I look at his departing back his words sinking into my head, I shake my head.

"Phil," I call out to him but he doesn't look back, he heads to the pool table.

I stare at his departing back, his words are still registering on my brain when Sean approaches the table, "You are late today aren't you," he says casually "you have normally gone before that lot arrive," he says, I just nod, I cannot say anything, "you okay" Sean takes a mouthful of his pint I decide to confront him straight away.

"Are you sleeping with my sister?" I ask him directly, his mouthful of beer is spat across the table, he chokes noisily then he wipes his nose and mouth with the old napkin on the table.

"Bloody hell, Angie, choose your timing better next time will you," he looks at me but I don't drop my gaze.

"Are you sleeping with my sister?" I repeat. He looks over to the pool table calling, "Cheers, Phil," he raises his glass. Phil just waves back without looking, Sean sits down, he plays with his glass for what seems like ages, I stare at him, he glances up.

"Okay yes, Angie, don't look at me like that, yes I am, yes we are." I don't know what to say, so I say nothing, a million thoughts and questions are running though my head.

I blurt out the first one that comes to my head, "How long?" I ask.

"That's a bit personal," Sean laughs nervously, "bout ten inches I think." I look at him but I don't smile, he places his pint on the table, he holds his hands out defensively. "Oh come on, Angie, don't go all judgemental on me, she is a big girl now, we are both adults." He runs his hands through his hair, just like Jason, it makes me smile I reach across and run my hand over his.

"So tell me then, when and how?"

Sean gives a smile, he is so like Jason in his looks and mannerisms, he pulls his hand from mine and takes a swig of his drink. "We got chatting at your wedding then again at Jason's funeral, nothing major, just small talk really, then I bumped into her a few months ago, started chatting and again we kind of hit it off." Sean takes my hand across the table, he leans in closer to me. "I really care about her, Angie, I love you like I love a sister but that is not the way I feel about her, this isn't a fling, I really do like her," he reaches over, he kisses me on the forehead, I glance up to see Mike is looking over, he does not look happy.

Then I know I have to be the bigger person, I don't own Sean or Phil, I have my Mike, I would be so mortified if Mike had relationships with women as close as I have to both Sean and Phil, so I push him away laughing. "It's okay, I am okay with it, Judy is a big girl now and seriously I think you will be great together, I just don't know why she hasn't told me, we always tell each other things like that, she knows I would be happy for you both, you will both be great together," somehow I know they will be.

Sean takes my hand. "Thanks, Angie, it means a lot to me, I know you are going to struggle to understand this, you have always had your relationships out in the open, you always ask people what they think before you so much as talk to a stranger, but we needed to keep this to ourselves, to just enjoy each other before we get into the whole family scene, she has the children to think of, we want to date each other, you know make sure it is right for us, we don't want to announce it to the world until we are ready, please say you understand, Angie," he looks at me I know exactly what he is saying more than he will ever know.

"Oh, Sean," I smile at him, I echo my thoughts to him, "I do so understand, more than you will ever know," I pick up my drink, "come on, let's join the others shall we." He smiles and we go over to the pool table, when I think no one is looking I tickle Mike's hand, he is leaning with his back against the window, resting on the window ledge, he tickles my hand back, making me smile, Phil is playing pool, waiting to take his shot, he looks over to where we are standing just a few feet away, he is the centre of attention, and he knows it. "Hey, Mike," he stands up and chalks his cue, "I was at the hospital the other day, taking that chap from custody who hit his head, that pretty nurse you fancy was there, think she likes you too mate," he places the chalk down then looks directly at Mike, "looks like you might be in there, she asked after you, must be missing you," his face is impassive, he faces the table and leans ready to take his shot, I cannot help it, I go bright red, Phil looks over again, he looks up at me.

"You hot, Angie, you have gone all red." I shake my head, my heart is beating fast in my chest, Phil knows something, he must do, I feel lightheaded, Mike laughs.

"Ah yes, the nurse, the blonde one, I remember," he squeezes my hand. "Think I might pop up there next time I am on duty, you know, just to say hello, show her the old Mike charm, would be rude not to don't you think," he pauses then adds, "missing me eh."

Phil looks at him, this time his face confused, he looks at both of us, frowns then looks back to the table. I wait a few minutes, watching as he takes his shot, then I finish my drink then say my goodbyes. I think Phil was just fishing, I don't think he knows anything and I think maybe Mike's reply has thrown him off the scent, at least I hope so. "Angie," I look back to see Phil coming after me, "you okay?" he asks, I nod my head.

"Why shouldn't I be," I turn to face him, he looks guilty.

"Sorry about that back there, but I wanted to wind Mike up, I shouldn't have picked on you as well," he musses my hair. "Are you okay with Sean and Judy, you know," he pauses.

371

I reply quickly, "Yes, of course I am, would have been nice for you to give me a heads up though, Phil, and quit messing with my hair." He musses my hair again, I scowl at him but he laughs.

"We are cool though, yes?"

I raise my eyebrows at him, "Yes, you are okay, we are cool, see you later." I leave the pub, I sit in the car park, I text Mike, he says he will be finished in around half an hour so will get a cab to mine. I do offer to pick him up using his car but he declines.

Chapter Forty-Nine

He is at my house within twenty minutes I open the door I pull him inside, I kiss him very softly, he smells of beer and aftershave, he is warm, I hold him very close, I don't want to let him go. Eventually when we do part I ask him what he wants to do for the afternoon, he has been training this morning so he is tired and so we decide to just chill out in front of the television. I tell him about Sean and Judy, I repeat the conversation I had with Phil about Dean, Mike laughs, "Yes, I was a bit of a bastard last week, I deserved to be wound up, Phil knew what buttons to push, but unfortunately for him, I sent him on the worst jobs to get my own back, and the lost property cupboard has never looked so tidy so serves him right." I laugh out loud, Phil would have hated that.

"What was that business with the pint at the pub, you put a pint down in front of him then walked off explain that, Phil says you just buy your own drinks normally," I ask.

Mike looks at me, "You said that Phil won't accept that you forgive him until you tell him you are happy, also I think I recall you said Phil told you that your man has to put a pint down in front of him, so I did." I look at him, "You are amazing you remember everything don't you," he smiles, "not everything, as I told you before, just the important stuff." I snuggle into him,

"Do you think Phil suspects something?"

Mike laughs, "Yes, probably he did, but he doesn't now, he asked me again about the nurse after you left, I said I might pay her a visit, he is happy that he thinks he has embarrassed me and the attention has been taken from you," I look at him, a smile on my face.

"So you like nurses then?" I ask, he pulls me onto the sofa next to him, his hand on my bare stomach and travelling up to my breasts, "oh no, they do nothing for me, you know me, fuzzy hair and braces man, that is me," I push him away playfully but his face is serious.

"You never have to be jealous of anyone, I am definitely a one woman man," I pull his head towards mine.

"Glad to hear that," I whisper.

Mike wants to come to the christening, he is looking forward to it, also he has invited me to his parents for lunch on the Sunday afternoon, I am really nervous but also excited, normally his mum makes lunch late when he is due to go on night shift, so he can have lunch then a sleep ready for night shift, but as he is not on night shift she was going to do it normal time, he gives her a call asking for it to be late again then he tells her to set an extra place as he is bringing a guest, before she has the chance to reply he hangs up. He looks at me smiling. "That was very mean," I say.

"I know," he replies, "but I am not ready for an interrogation, not just yet," he takes my hand leading me to the bottom of the stairs, "now that sordid secret thing you did the other day," he smiles, "I think I might need you to do that again, I am not sure it was done completely right, and as you know, I am a perfectionist," we both laugh and head upstairs.

I am really looking forward to the christening, the day is bright and sunny, it will be wonderful to be able to be with Mike without anyone knowing us, I have to send Mike downstairs as he won't leave me alone, he won't let me get dressed, I am wearing the same blue dress I wore to the bar, but he keeps pulling my dress up, stroking my legs, we start off by having plenty of time, the journey is just an hour away, we lay in bed, we make love, then shower and make love, then I get dressed go downstairs put my patent heels on. I turn to look at him, the look on his face tells me it is going to be another twenty minutes before we get out of the door, he is insatiable and I love it.

We arrive in the car park of the church with just a few minutes to spare, he keeps stroking my thigh, I keep slapping his hand away playfully, in the church we sit at the back, it is a very small church there is only a handful of people, it is a lovely service but the boys are little monsters they go tearing off between the pews, Frank keeps checking his phone, Annabelle looks totally stunning in a white trousers suit, only she could choose white with two tearaway children, she greets everyone then just looks totally vacant throughout the whole ceremony.

The reception is back at the local hotel, I forewarn Mike about Frank and his awful behaviour, I warn him about the bar trick, I also told him about me seeing him with the stable hand, Mike laughed loudly when I told him. "I cannot wait to meet this man," he laughs, "does he know anything about me, have you told him or Annabelle what I do?"

I shake my head, "No, nothing at all."

"Priceless," Mike replies, "let's have some fun with him then yes."

I smile at him. "Oh that would be so great."

"Now remind me, he exports race horses doesn't he?"

"Yes," I reply, "Mike, what are you going to do to him?"

"Do, me do, to him, nothing at all," he laughs innocently, I cannot help it, I join in with him as we pull up outside the hotel and park the car.

The boy's behaviour is worse than terrible, they are tearing round the pub screaming, knocking into everything, the bar staff look at them disapprovingly but neither Annabelle or Frank notice, both seem totally oblivious. I stand watching them for a while before Annabelle pulls me to one side. "What do you think?" she asks.

"Of what," I reply looking around, the bar is decorated with balloons there is a buffet laid out, it all looks very organised and inviting, I am not sure what she is referring to.

"Him," she whispers pointing to the stable hand stood next to Frank at the bar.

"What about him?" I ask, he is about four foot has slicked back hair with far too much gel on it, he looks oily, he is wearing super tight black jeans with a white round neck T-shirt on, again it is very tight, too tight and he looks a bit ridiculous, I cannot help but remember the last time I saw him and what he had been doing.

Annabelle digs me in the side making me jump, "That is our stable hand," she whispers, "isn't he totally gorgeous." Thankfully she doesn't wait for me to reply. "We have been having an affair for the last two months, I cannot resist him, he is so fabulous, rides me like he rides one of his stallions, Frank hasn't got a clue." She giggles, I look around, I feel a little bit sick inside, I need a drink, I need Mike, where the hell is Mike. Then I see him at the bar, he has both our drinks in his hands, he laughs quietly shaking his head as he head towards me.

"Did you get stuck for a round?" I ask him softly.

"No not at all," he replies, "in fact I think you will find our drinks will be free all the time we are here, shame I am driving really, we could really milk the situation," he laughs out loud.

"Oh I could drive for you," I offer hopefully, Mike just smiles and shakes his head.

We stand watching everyone, the children are now stood on the small window ledge wrapping themselves in the curtains, I watch as they hang precariously. "Careful you don't fall," I call gently to them, a huge booming voice drowns me.

"Get down from that window, you little buggers." Annabelle has finally noticed her children and is heading over that way, I look at Mike and we both smile, we watch as she drags them from the curtains and pulls them to the bar area, she turns to pick up her drink and engages in conversation, I look back at the window and am amazed to see that both of the children are back up and happily swinging again. This time I say nothing, we help ourselves to a few nibbles but make our excuses and we leave after about an hour, we need to get home to be in time for lunch. We are halfway across the car park when Frank appears running across to thank Mike for coming he shakes his hand. He doesn't acknowledge my presence at all.

We get in the car. Mike explains that he had decided that when Frank asked Mike what he done for a living he would make something up, purely for devilment he implied that he worked for DEFRA which is the governing body as far as animal welfare is concerned. "He was putty in my hands after that," he adds, "sorry I couldn't resist it, that man is an ass," and I nod in agreement, I tell him about Annabelle with the stable hand, we both laugh.

We are just maybe twenty minutes from home when Mike pulls over in a lay by. "Why are we stopping?" I ask him but he doesn't reply, he gets out, comes round my side and opens my door he offers his hand. I take it and get out somewhat confused, we are in the middle of nowhere, I look about but he just smiles, he seats himself in the passenger seat I just look at him. "Really?" I ask him.

"Really," he replies smiling. I get in, remove my shoes and adjust the seat, it feels so powerful just holding the steering wheel, my stomach turns, nervously I look at him.

"Am I insured to drive this?"

"Yes, of course you are, I added you yesterday, you think I would let my one special baby drive my other special baby if you weren't." I turn the key and cannot help but squeal out loud as the engine roars to life, I look at him and smile.

"Nervous?" I ask him.

"Not at all," he replies.

I press my foot down gently, I can feel the power under the foot pedal, I indicate and pull out, once I get used to the gears it feels like I have been driving it all my life. Even though I take the longest route possible the journey ends too soon I pull up on his parents drive.

"I am quite nervous about this," I look at Mike.

"There is no need to be nervous, Mum is looking forward to meeting you, she has worked out it is not one of the rugby lads, so I think she has gone all out with the best china today," he leans over and kisses me, I look up and push him away gently, the front door is open, his mum is stood there watching as I pull my heels on and get out of the driver's side, she looks with disbelief. "Hi, Mum," Mike walks up kisses her cheek, "this is Angie," he walks in ahead then stands behind her laughing with his mouth open mimicking her.

I reach the door I hold my hand out. "Hello, Mrs Simms," I say a little nervously, she smiles.

"Call me Margaret, dear," she moves aside to let me in, she goes into the lounge, I stand outside, slip my shoes off.

Inside I can see there is a little welcoming committee, a darling little girl comes out to greet me, she is dressed in a lovely fancy dress outfit that I think must be Snow White or something, she has blonde shoulder length hair with darling curls but has no front teeth.

"You must be Hannah," I tell her.

"Yes," she looks surprised, "how did you know that?" she questions.

"Well your uncle Mike told me he had the prettiest niece in the world, from what I can see he wasn't wrong." Hannah runs at Mike he lifts her in the air.

"I never said you was pretty," he teases her, "never ever would I say that," she squeals with laughter as he tickles her, then he puts her back down.

Mike pulls me into the room, the chattering stops, there are three people sat just looking at me, I can feel all the eyes on me at once, he calls out their names and they wave saying Hi, I can only remember his dad and sister Jenny then the chap sitting on his own I cannot recall his name. Margaret has gone back into the kitchen, the smell is delicious my stomach rumbles, as if on cue, "Lunch is ready," Margaret calls out; we all go into the large kitchen diner. It all looks very homely, a very bright and friendly kitchen with a huge wooden table to one end, I stand back as everyone sits down, I can feel Mike's hand in the small of my back I reach behind putting my hand in his, I suddenly feel very shy, but Hannah makes everyone feel comfortable, instructing Mike's dad where he needs to sit then declaring that she wants to sit opposite me, she is bossing everyone about, telling them where they should sit. Eventually everyone gets to sit down I am pleased and relieved that Mike sits to my right, he holds my hand under the table and we wait patiently whilst his mother is dishing up, I watch as the vegetables are loaded onto the plates and my stomach gives out a groan, Hannah looks at me, "Can I ask you a question?" she looks at me directly.

"Of course you can," I reply smiling at her I take a sip of my water and look at her.

"Are you a bloody gold digger?" she asks innocently, I swallowed the water as I choke back a laugh at her question.

"Hannah!" Margaret shouts a little too loudly, closely followed by Jenny who sits there with her face in her hands, Margaret continues, "That is very rude, Hannah, and you are to apologise immediately, I don't know where you get such language." Margaret looks at Jenny as Hannah looks at me, rolls her eyes then she looks at her mother, she is totally unperturbed by being shouted at.

"Oh, Nanny," she says exasperated, "you know mummy said it to you when you said Uncle Mike was bringing a friend, I remember, she said, let's hope it isn't a bloody gold digger like the last one."

I cannot help it but I burst out laughing, I look to Mike he is laughing too, suddenly the whole table is laughing, the ice has been broken, Hannah just looks blank like she doesn't know what all the fuss is about. When the laughter has died down Hannah says to me, "Well, are you?"

I smile at her saying, "No, I am not a gold digger, but my mum asks the same questions about my boyfriends too so don't you worry."

Hannah continues, "What is a gold digger?" she asks.

"Ah well," I say to her, "I can try and explain that to you, if you like," I look at Mike but he smiles and shrugs.

"You are on your own now, honey," he smiles again, then he leans one arm on the table and half turns facing me, he has a big grin on his face, I turn back to Hannah.

"Okay, well if you have sweets and you have a friend who will only play with you for sweets, they can be called a gold digger, they are not real friends, they just want sweets," I look at her, I can see the wheels turning in her head as she is working everything out, I watch as she spears a carrot into her mouth, I wait for her next comment.

"Has Uncle Mike got lots of sweets then?" I feel him squeeze my thigh.

"I don't know, what do you think?" I ask her.

There is a silence around the table, she looks so cute, she is thinking of the answer, eventually she looks at him then answers, "Yes, I think he might have." I cannot help it, I just laugh. I can tell that she is burning with lots more questions, she smiles at me. "Is Uncle Mike your boyfriend?"

Jenny interrupts, "No more questions, Hannah, eat your lunch." Jenny smiles at me. "Sorry she is so grown up at times."

I smile back. "That's okay I don't mind at all."

I obviously said the wrong thing as Hannah pipes up again, "See, mummy, she doesn't mind, anyway," she pauses, "it isn't questions it is conversation." I cannot help it, the little girl is priceless, I look at Mike he smiles but carries on eating.

I look back at her. "Well, let's make a deal, you eat all your lunch up and I will eat all mine then we will have a big conversation afterwards okay."

She seems happy with this she spears another carrot to her mouth, there is a general noise of cutlery meeting plates but other than that the table is quiet. The meal is delicious, the conversation strikes up again when people have finished, Jenny asks me where I met Mike and I look to Mike he answers, "This is Angie Staddon, she was in my class at school, don't you remember?"

Jenny looks at me, I can tell she is struggling to remember but then the penny drops, she exclaims in surprise, "Wow I would never have recognised you, oh god you look so different," she looks at her parents, "how long did he go on about this girl at school?" She looks at me. "Didn't you have your tonsils out at Christmas or something?" she smiles.

I laugh, "Yes, yes, we have discussed that already, that was when he was planning his big move apparently." We all laugh, I look at Mike's dad, "I guess I have you to thank for the Valentine's card idea."

He nods holding his hands up in surrender, "Yes, guilty as charged."

Mike laughs, "You know, Dad, she kept it, all these years and she kept it, I couldn't believe it when she showed me."

His dad laughs, "Women eh, son, they will keep any rubbish." Mike laughs with him.

Hannah has sat very quiet just observing everyone, she looks at Mike, then back to me. "Do you love my Uncle Mike?" she asks, the same expression on her face as if she is asking about the weather, I cannot help but laugh at her.

"Well, I do think he is very nice, but I wanted to hear what you think before I decide, what do you think of your Uncle Mike?" She thinks for a while then she looks at him, as if summing him up, I watch him as he pokes his tongue out at her, she places her head in her hands. "Well he does pull my hair, he tickles me sometimes which I don't like, but he does play with me with my doll's house which I do like."

I look to Mike, "You play with the doll's house do you?" I dig him in the ribs, "something you want to tell me, Mike."

He laughs, "No, I don't play with the doll's house now do I, Hannah, what do we play?"

The darling girl rolls her eyes again. "We play rugby with the dollies and he crashes them together," she demonstrates with her hands, "but," she deliberates for a while, "I think you are pretty and I think my Uncle Mike will be a good boyfriend for you."

Mike slips his arm around my shoulder he pulls me closer to him, he kisses my head. "That is about the best reference you are going to get," he says, "it isn't as bad as what she says about my dad," he laughs.

Mike's dad throws his eyes up to heaven. "Don't get her started on that again, Mike, for heaven's sake," he remarks, but it is too late; Hannah sits up in her chair.

"Yes, I will get started," she leans towards me with her elbows on the table. "Do you know what he did to my doll's house?"

I shake my head, "No, I am afraid I don't, but something tells me I am going to find out."

"Well," she says looking at her granddad, "he broke the dollies head off, and the chimney then he said he would repair it and my chairs only have three legs because he," she points to Mike, "stood on them, when he was drunk, he said he would fix it but they never, they lied to me."

"Okay, Hannah, enough," Jenny speaks firmly. "Sit properly in the chair, Nanny will get your pudding, and the chairs will get fixed," she looks pointedly at Mike and then her dad, "won't they."

Mike laughs, "And I wasn't drunk, little missy, I was tipsy and you had them strewn all over the floor, I couldn't avoid standing on them."

Hannah looks at him, she frowns. "You brought that funny lady round didn't you, the one with the funny foot, she slept in mummy's room."

Mike laughs then groans. "Why does she have to have such a good memory, Jen?" he asks his sister.

She sighs, "I know, tell me about it," Jenny turns to Hannah. "Sit properly in the chair and eat your pudding now, Hannah, no more chatting." She turns to me, "Is it rude to ask if you are still married, Angie, or are you separated?"

I look at her, I can see she is asking genuinely and not to cause offence, I am happy to answer. "I am a widow," I reply quietly, her face drops, she puts her hand to her mouth.

"Oh god, I am so sorry," she looks at Mike, "I thought you said she was married."

Mike shrugs, "I did, she was, she isn't now."

Jenny colours up. "God I am so embarrassed, Angie, sorry, I have got all mixed up," she looks at her mum.

Margaret shrugs, "Don't look at me, dear, Mike told me the girl he liked at school was on the other shift, but that she was now married, that was a while ago."

There is a long uncomfortable silence, which I break, "It's okay really, I was married, for a short time, he fell very ill very quickly and he died almost a year ago, please I don't mind, ask me any questions, I have no problem in discussing him," I pause. "His name was Jason, Mike actually met him, just the once didn't you?"

I look to Mike, he nods his head. "I did, nice chap, he was good friends with Phil, you know, the bloke on my shift." Jenny nods and stands up, she is clearly embarrassed as the others move toward the lounge.

Jenny pulls me by the arm to keep me in the kitchen, she speaks quietly, "I am sorry if I was insensitive back there, I got my wires crossed, I thought you were still married. Mum got a bit mixed up, trouble is with my brother is that he is a man of few words, only says half a story, he plays his cards very close to his chest and she was worried about him getting hurt." I look at her, her face is full of concern.

"Jenny, it is fine, honestly, I really think a lot of your brother, he is the best thing that has happened to me for a long time, I don't intend to hurt him."

She smiles, "Glad to hear that," she pauses, " he just kept going on about you for ages, then when he told Dad he had seen you and that you were working in the control room, but that you were married, I got my wires crossed. Dad told Mum then Mum was really worried he wouldn't be able to keep away from you." I laugh, she continues, "Sorry about Hannah too, she never lets up, Mum and I was chatting and we forget that she listens and takes in everything."

I shake my head, "Seriously please don't worry, my mum is always on at me, especially because of my status," I frown, "the title widow seems to attract the wrong sort, I have to be careful, and I did recognise Mike as soon as I saw him but I couldn't believe it when he showed an interest, although we did skate around each other for a while, I think we were both very nervous."

Jenny grinned, "What is he like, I mean," she pauses, "how long has it taken him, he said you were at his party, but I didn't see you, in fairness you have changed a lot, I would never have recognised you, but at his party he was trying to tell me something but I couldn't hear him properly, one minute he was all happy then that crazy woman turned up and I thought he was pleased that she was there, to be honest, we were all a bit disappointed," she turns to me," why didn't you go to his party?"

I frown at her, "I did go, I came late with my friend, I saw Mike before he got drunk and we shared a moment in the buffet room."

Jenny looks at me, she shakes her head, "No, that cannot be right, I don't understand, Mike said you couldn't make it, then he came out to me and said it was a bloody brilliant night, and that you had turned up, but I never saw you, I thought he was talking drunken rubbish, then at the end of the night, he went home with her, I don't get it."

I laugh out loud, "No, I must admit I was gutted too, we had a brief moment together, I was on cloud nine too, then she came in and dragged him off with her, I must admit I felt very foolish, I thought he was seeing her, playing me for a fool, I don't like that sort of thing, so I just decided to enjoy myself, I drank more than I should have and danced with the rugby lot."

Jenny sits down at the table, "So tell me how you finally got together then."

Mike walks into the kitchen, I open my mouth to reply but Mike beats me to it, "She couldn't resist my boyish charms," he says.

Jenny laughs, "I don't think so, bro, more likely you stalked her until she gave in, or your aftershave acted like chloroform," she laughs at her joke then she turns to me, "Angie, go on, you tell me how did you get together."

Mike is now stood in the doorway, "No, Jenny, not the Spanish inquisition, not now?" he asks, Jenny kicks her foot out but he moves away.

"We are just chatting, Mike, that's all," she says.

He grabs my arm, "Well, I am stealing her back now, I need her for something, you chat another time, right now she is mine," he pulls me into the lounge, he sits me right next to him, I sit with my feet underneath me, it is warm, I am full. I watch television for a short while, but I can feel my eyes closing, Hannah gets up on the couch, I feel her lift my arm and snuggle underneath, I cannot keep my eyes open, I hear the chatting of the people in the room, I cannot help it, much as I try and fight it, my eyes drop and I drift off to sleep.

I wake up, my foot has gone dead underneath me, I look at my watch, I have drifted off for over half an hour. Hannah is still in the crook of my arm. Jenny and her husband Pete are sat watching the television, I can hear raised voices so I sit forward to look out of the window. I look at Jenny and frown, "It is her," Jenny nods her head, "you know the crazy ex-girlfriend from the party, I guess he has told you about her," Jenny offers the information, "you know big hair, mad dress sense, she always turns up when she sees his car here, it is like she has radar."

"What does she want?" I ask frowning.

"Same old," Jenny sighs, "she goes on about them as a couple but he won't just tell her to leave, he tries to be too nice, she turns up at his rugby training regularly, I don't know why he doesn't just tell her he is seeing someone, but typical Mike, he avoids any trouble or confrontation if he can help it."

I can hear the raised voice getting louder, "I know you have got someone else, Mike, why won't you be honest with me," the girl wails, I can hear Mike talking softly a ripple of jealousy shoots through me with a sickening jolt. I lay Hannah gently down I stand up, straighten my dress.

I walk to the door Jenny says quietly, "Be careful she is a feisty one."

I smile at her, "No, she hasn't met feisty yet, and I don't mind trouble or confrontation when it involves me." I open the door into the hall, Mike is holding on to the top of the door he is leaning his body against the open door, his mum is stood just behind him. "Hi," I say brightly I smile at Mike, he frowns but I say cheerfully, "Aren't you going to introduce me?" Mike opens the door a bit wider, there in front of me stands the girl that I once thought was sexy and confident, she is wearing jeans, an old grey sweatshirt and flip flops, no make-up, her hair is tangled, her whole appearance looks sad and neglected.

Mike takes my hand, "Well, Nancy, you wanted to meet her, here she is, Nancy, this is Angie, now you have met her, you can go now, it is time to stop your nonsense," but I know she isn't going to go without an argument, I step out on the porch, my bare feet hit the paving, it is cold, I turn to pull my shoes on, feeling immediately taller, I move closer to her, I actually feel compassion for this woman.

"It's okay, I will deal with this," I smile at Mike and his mum. I pull the door half closed. I know they are still standing the other side. I stand in front of this crazy looking creature. "Hi I am Angie," I put my hand out to her, but she ignores me.

"Why couldn't he tell me to my face he was seeing someone else?" she wails, "why all the secrecy, I cannot understand him, I thought we were good together, why couldn't he tell me?" she blurts out, she slurs her words, she is not drunk but well on the way, she sounds whiny and needy, and the horrible side of me wants to laugh out loud, really I do, I try not to picture her in that strange rubber suit with zips on.

I bite my lip trying not to snigger. "I know, I know," I step closer, I am aware Mike and his mum are just the other side of the door, "but you must have known it was over, honey, you haven't seen him for a month or so now have you," she looks up.

"No, I guess not," she sniffs and wipes her nose on her sleeve.

"Surely you must have realised you two were no longer together, a month is a long time," I pause, just watching her, she is scraping her foot along the ground, scuffing her flip flop, I continue, "if you say he treated you badly, do you really want to be with someone like that, you deserve better," I add, with this, she looks up at me, she looks me up and down.

"You are not so bad," she sniffs, she reaches for her handbag pulls out chewing gum, I notice her nails, before they were perfectly manicured, long painted talons, now replaced with half varnished bitten stumps.

She opens her chewing gum, she offers some to me, but I shake my head, "No I won't, thanks anyway."

She rolls the gum and presses it against her teeth then chews with her mouth open and continues, "You are too good for him, you know, he is a bastard that one, I swear I could tell you a few stories about him, but you seem okay, really nice, you should be warned what he is really like, there is something not right about him, he is as bad as his mate, the both of them, trying to screw around with me, just thinking they can use me and walk away, he did you know, his mate, thought he could have me and then discard me, but I will catch up with him one day, I will show him he cannot treat me like that, I mean, look at me, I can get any man I want but they, they," she pauses, she chews her gum loudly, before continuing, "well they are just pathetic," she stops, there is hesitation in her voice. "Look you are okay, you seem decent enough, I think I should warn you, you ought to know Mike has a problem, you know," she pauses, "we never actually, you know," she pauses, "well, we couldn't, you know, you see he has a problem, he has this dirty little sordid secret, he can't, you know unless…"

I am acutely aware his mum is still on the other side of the door listening, I walk towards her, placing my hand on her arm, "No no, don't upset yourself more, really some blokes are just not worth it, believe me I know." She looks at me surprised as I take her arm guiding her towards the gate. "I am sure I don't need to know, really, I am certain I will find out for myself, I can deal with it, I am a big girl you know."

She turns to look at me, "Thanks," she says, she smiles at me, she looks almost childlike, I look at her, she looks so vulnerable, I do feel compassion for her, I watch as she walks down the street, her mobile phone now attached to her ear, I cannot believe this is the same woman I felt intense jealousy towards. I return to the house, Mike is sat back in the lounge.

"Thanks for doing that," he smiles at me and takes my hand pulling me on to his lap, he is not embarrassed that his parents are there, he kisses me gently on the lips.

"Uncle Mike, that is rude!" Hannah interrupts us and everyone laughs.

"Crazy lady gone now?" Jenny asks.

Mike nods his head, "No she is sat opposite me," he replies then dodges the cushion she aims at his head.

There is a movie on the television, everyone settles down to watch, there is a woman who is crying and Hannah comes over to me.

"Uncle Mike made Mummy cry," she states.

Mike groans, "Hannah, give it a rest," he looks at Jenny.

"Jen, shut her up will you."

She laughs, "Easier said than done, bro, you know that."

Hannah stands in front of me. "And it was her birthday, and he made her cry."

I lean forward and look at her, "Oh dear, that wasn't kind was it."

Hannah shakes her head, "I don't want a brother if he will make me cry," she states.

Jen smiles, "It was happy tears, Hannah, I told you at the time, Uncle Mike bought me a lovely birthday gift and it made mummy cry."

Hannah frowns, "How can a birthday present make you cry, Mummy, presents make me happy."

Jen pulls Hannah towards her, she pulls her onto her lap, "It was because it was a very lovely present and I was very pleased, Uncle Mike is a very lovely brother and you are not to keep on about having a brother."

Mike laughs, "You been talking out loud then, Jen?" he asks.

She pulls a face, "I know, we should have text each other, it is the only way we can communicate in our house without her knowing, and before you ask, no, we are not planning on having another child, not as yet anyway."

Mike looks at me, "It was the concert ticket, I bought it for her, I told you, but Hannah took really poorly."

Jen laughs then she frowns, "Which means you still owe me a birthday present doesn't it."

Mike laughs with her, "Good luck on getting that," he retorts back, he pulls me back into his arms and we watch the rest of the movie. Mike's parents are out in the kitchen they don't come back in. The rest of the afternoon passes quickly, Mike takes me upstairs to show me the rest of the house, as we stand outside his bedroom door the crazy lady's comments come back to me, she said his mate, what mate, I look at Mike, but he is smiling at me, I know what that smile means, I make a mental note to ask him later, he pulls me into his bedroom, the bedroom he had as a child, it still has several items from his childhood there, he lays on the bed, I stand just looking around, he strokes my thigh, his hands go higher, I smack him playfully, "No, Mike, not here," I scold him, but he doesn't take any notice.

"Yes here," he whispers, "it will be a first for me, having someone here in my bed." I just cannot resist him, he pulls me on to bed, he kisses me passionately on the lips at the same time pushing my skirt up to my waist. He kisses my stomach, "We can pretend we are teenagers, sneaking in whilst the parents are busy," he whispers, I cannot help giggling, but he silences me with his tongue, his hand is now inside my bra, I know he won't take no for an answer. "I wish this was us in our teenage years," he whispers, "I would have loved to have laid here with you, to have been your first lover, that would have been incredible, you, laid here with your strange fuzzy hair and your braces."

I push him away playfully, "Okay, Mister, you can tell me now who was your first, and who I need to thank for your skill at making me feel the way I do," Mike moves away, just a few inches.

"Ah well, I don't think you will be impressed by my initiation."

I sit up, "But I want to know anyway," he laughs.

"Okay, have it your own way." I pull my dress down to a decent level, but his hand stays on the top of my thigh, he props himself up on one arm, "remember a chap in our class Paul Parker,"

My eyes widen, "Really!" I exclaim, "He was your first." I feel the slap on my bottom, I squeal.

"That is what you get for being cheeky," he laughs.

"I must be cheeky more often," I tease, his eyebrows shoot up.

"Mmm like that do you?"

I smile again, "I am not sure, you might have to do it again, but not before you spill the beans, Mr Simms." I watch as his eyebrows shoot up in surprise, I realise how he has interpreted my choice of words, "I mean carry on with your story."

I push him playfully, he pulls me close to him, "Okay, well Paul was involved in a really bad car accident just two weeks after we left school, he was one of my best friends so I was up the hospital most days, his mum would take me, she is divorced, not sure where his dad went, he disappeared years ago. Anyway Paul was in a bad way, in hospital for nearly two months, she would drop me off at her house which is just over there," he points over to the other side of the street, "one evening she invited me in for a beer, I think she was just very lonely, and the rest is history, we had eight weeks whilst Paul was in hospital, I was the student, she was the teacher, I think I got an A," he smiles and winks, "then when he came home I was off to college."

"Did Paul ever find out?" I ask.

Mike shakes his head, "No, no not at all, there was no reason for him or anyone else to find out, I have never told anyone until today; it wasn't like it was a big deal, I went to college and started dating a girl there, it wasn't a romance I had with his mum, she was lonely, that is all, she is remarried now. Paul has just moved back home after his marriage collapsed, I see him occasionally, he has a son called Parker."

"Parker Parker," I look at Mike, "seriously, he called his son Parker Parker."

Mike laughs, "Yes, I know, parents can be cruel can't they, I won't do that to my children I can tell you that." His face becomes all serious.

"You intend having children then?" I ask, I stroke his cheek, his hands roam up my back pulling my dress with it, I moan gently, his hand massages my bottom.

"Oh yes."

I push my bottom away from him, "And how many do you intend to have?"

He looks at me, his gorgeous dark eyes just making me want to melt, "Well I am one of three and that seemed to work well, I don't think I would just want one, doesn't seem fair to the child really, what do you think?"

I just smile at him, "I have another question," I whisper, his hand rests gently on my hip, "so how many lovers have you had?" I ask,

He groans into my neck, "Really, Angie, now, you want to know, right now?" he moves his hand away, "Okay, have it your way, I have had more than ten but less than twenty, okay, that is enough detail." I pull him closer, kissing his lips gently I suck on his bottom lip, he groans gently, "Oh yes, baby, I love that, do that again."

"You do what you did to me again," I cannot believe I am being so blatant, Mike looks at me, his jaw drops, I feel his hand move from my bottom, I tense waiting for his palm to make contact, when it does I moan loudly, he groans into my hair, "I have to have you, right here, right now, in my childhood bed," he kisses me, "any objections?" I giggle, but don't reply, "I take that as a no then," he pulls me close, his lips meet mine tenderly as his hands push my dress right up, he rolls over on top of me and I moan loudly as he pushes himself into me, silencing my moans with his mouth. I can hear the movement of people downstairs, but I am past caring, I just need this man right now, I wrap my legs around him and give in to the wonderful feeling sweeping over my body. I watch as the expression on his face shows complete abandonment as his body takes pleasure from mine. It lasts just a matter of minutes but my whole body is on fire from his touch. We lay on the bed afterwards, just cuddling; we whisper then giggle as we tiptoe to the bathroom to tidy ourselves up.

When I come back I sit on the side of the bed waiting for him. I really do feel like I am a naughty schoolgirl being sneaked into the boys' bedroom, there are car pictures all over the walls, a signed rugby ball, a few old school photos of him in the sports teams, I pull one of his books down and start reading, the bedroom door is pushed open and instead of Mike it is Hannah.

"Will you play doll houses with me?" she asks.

I look up, Mike is just behind her, "I am not really dressed for squatting on the floor," I look at him, "have you got anything I can put on?" he laughs and passes me a pair of tracksuit bottoms which are several sizes too big, they will have to do, as we leave the bedroom Mike pulls me back towards him his kiss is gentle.

"That was wonderful, and I have to admit that I lied to you earlier, I think you are number 21 which incidentally is my favourite number," he whispers. I pull him to me and bite his bottom lip gently making him groan.

We go downstairs, Jenny and Pete are now cuddled up together asleep on the sofa. Jenny opens her eyes as we enter the room, she looks at Mike, "Your bed squeaks, bro," I blush a deep red, but she smiles, "don't worry, Angie, that would be the least of your problems, could you imagine explaining to madam," she indicates Hannah. "What you were up to, she has been plaguing me for the last half an hour to go up and see you both, it was all I could do to keep her down here," Mike laughs, he is not embarrassed at all, "Mum and Dad have gone for a nap too," she explains, "but no bed squeaking there thank goodness," she laughs and snuggles back down.

I sit cross legged on the carpet, Mike has disappeared somewhere, Hannah and I get everything out of the doll's house, for the next twenty minutes I lose myself in arranging the tiny furniture, setting everything out, there is a lot of items need repairing so we sort them into a pile, I hear Mike's mum and dad come back down and are talking in the kitchen with Mike, I have a plan, I whisper to Hannah that we are going to ask Uncle Mike and Granddad if they will play dolls houses but if they don't want to, can they mend the furniture instead and she nods excitedly. We find Mike with his dad in the garden, Mike's dad is smoking his pipe Mike is sitting on the swing, both chatting away happily, they both look up and smile as we approach, Hannah goes to her granddad, I go to Mike, he pulls me close to him, but I push him away, I look over to Hannah, we smile at each other then we both whisper in their ears and they both laugh out loud together, Mike looks at his dad, "Think we are being railroaded, Dad," he laughs.

"Seems that way to me, son, come on, no sense in arguing with women."

We follow them to the garage they route around then come back with the items they need – sandpaper and glue. Whilst Hannah and I put all the other toys away we sit and watch as the tiny items of furniture are restored to their former glory. Jenny sits and watches, her face registering disbelief. "Bloody hell, Angie, you will have to come round more often," she says laughing.

I want to stay longer, I feel so relaxed, I love their family, but I have to have a proper sleep for tonight's night shift so I thank everyone for a lovely day, Hannah cries because I am leaving. She makes me promise I will visit again. Mike drives me home, outside he turns to me, "How did today go for you?" he asks.

I smile at him, "They are lovely, Mike, really lovely, and Hannah is a darling." He frowns, he looks out of the front window and taps his fingers on the steering wheel, "Mike," I pause, there is something on his mind I just know there is, "Mike," I try again.

He turns and faces me, "You have been so totally honest with me, Angie, and I need to tell you something."

My heart is thudding in my chest, I look at him but he looks away, I know it is serious but I attempt a joke, "Okay I am not your number 21 then," I quip.

He smiles, "Angie, you are my number one, but Hannah mentioned a woman she met with a bad foot, do you remember?" I nod my head, he gives a half smile, "I was kind of engaged to her, well engaged isn't probably the best way to describe it, her name is Carrie and we went out for a while, she proposed to me, yes she actually proposed marriage and I said yes," I look at him, my eyebrows shooting up in surprise, he continues, "it was quite a public proposal, well at a family barbecue actually, I was embarrassed but I couldn't humiliate her by turning her down, but we never took it any further, Hannah met her when she was having an operation on her foot."

I look at him, "Why are you telling me this now?" I ask.

He shakes his head, "I want to be completely honest with you, that is the only kind of serious relationship I have had, and although it is in the past, I hadn't given her a thought until Hannah mentioned her today, I thought you needed to know okay," I nod my head, he smiles, "you have a question, come on, I know that look, what do you want to know?"

I smile at him, "Where is she now?" I ask.

He frowns, "She went back to Italy, I saw her a while ago, she was at a friend's wedding back here in the UK and she popped to see me, she is now back living in Italy, she was one of the girls I met when travelling, she came back here for a while, but I was obsessed with my new job and had no time for her, well not just her, any relationship really, she lived in a shared house in town and worked locally, but when she had an operation on her foot Mum invited her to stay at ours for a few days."

"In your bed," I interrupt him, the question is out before I can stop it, I put my hand to my mouth but he is smiling.

"No, not in my bed, in my sister's old room, the relationship was kind of over by then and when she was well enough to travel her parents came over to collect her, it was all very embarrassing and it caused a big fall out between me and Mum, I wasn't happy with her interfering, she took it upon herself to invite her to stay, she didn't ask me, I was very unhappy to say the least," he pauses, "she was here for just a week or so but that was bad enough, then it was just a short time after she left that I bought the flat and moved out, Mum was really upset thinking I wanted to leave home because of what she did, we are okay now though, well more than okay, but she did learn a lesson about interfering on things that doesn't concern her," I nod my head.

"And what about the girl, this Carrie, where is she now?" I ask, he shrugs.

"Still in Italy, she emailed me a while ago to say she has just had her first child," he looks at me, "so there you go, all my cards on the table, no skeletons in the closet for me," I move closer to him.

"Who knows about her?" I ask.

He shrugs, "No one but my family," is his immediate response, "I had literally just started at the force, I didn't know many people and I don't tell people my business, I think Mum was a bit relieved today that you didn't have two heads or something, they have seen me date a few crazies, then that Nancy came on the scene, and, well, the least said about her the better, and Carrie, well she had a very fiery temper, which she couldn't control. Dad was on the receiving end several times in the short time she stayed with us." I glance at the clock, I really have got to go, but I don't want to leave him, he pulls me close to him and kisses me. "Shall I come in for a cuddle?" he whispers.

"Definitely not," I reply gently pushing him away. "I have to sleep and you are a distraction."

Chapter Fifty

Night shift is horrible, I miss him, it is crazy, up to about eleven thirty he is sending me text messages but then he has to sleep, he has a long journey in the morning, although Craig is very lenient with the odd text message he doesn't look too kindly on overuse of the phone so as I am in danger of being caught, I text this to Mike then put my phone away concentrating on the work coming in.

Phil comes up, he is in a jaunty mood, "How was the Christening?" he asks, I tell him the children were very naughty then I tell him about Annabelle's affair with the stable hand.

"Bloody hell," Phil blurts out, "wasn't Frank shagging him too?" I laugh out loud because it is so ludicrous, a man and wife having an affair with the same person, that is priceless, really priceless. "How did you get there?" Phil asks, he is multi-tasking by completing his pocket book as he speaks, he doesn't notice me colouring up.

"My friend came with me," I am not lying to Phil.

"Oh," he says distractedly, "I thought I saw your car outside your house all day yesterday." Phil stands up and I really think I have gotten away with it. "What friend was that then?"

I don't know what to say, I doodle on my pad, I pray for an incident to come in so I don't have to answer, but the damn phone stays silent, there is nothing, Phil looks at me, "Well?" he asks.

"I don't know," I say because I don't know what else to say.

Steve shouts over, "Hey, Phil, come and have a look at this, mate." Phil looks at me he shakes his head, he wanders over to Steve.

I feel awful, I have lied to Phil, I don't lie to him, I call him back over but he holds his hand up as if to tell me to wait, both he and Steve are engrossed watching something on the screen. A call comes in and I grab it thankfully. By the time I get off the call he has disappeared back on patrol, we don't get a chance to catch up again as the shift is busy.

Helen is off tonight, finally after months and months of complaining about the pain and filling herself with painkillers finally she has given in and is having her tooth out, she is dreading it, but is being brave and has to have a sedative prior to having the tooth out so won't be back in until tomorrow, but in the early hours she calls in on the phone, she cannot sleep as she is waiting for her painkillers to work and so we chat, I ask her about her weekend, she says that Phil has finished the garden for her on the Sunday and she cooked him a meal then he left to get some sleep, I ask her if anything happened but she just laughed and said yes, her garden got tidied. I want to carry on chatting but she says she is tired and I let her go, we chat in the control room, just general chit chat, I log on to my emails but there is nothing of interest there, Marcia is away at the moment, her whole family have gone on holiday for a few weeks, she normally sends me chatty emails that keep me entertained, night shift will be very quiet.

I wander down to the parade room later, Phil and a few others are sat looking through some property, I perch on the edge of his desk. "What did you do yesterday then?" I ask him, he finishes counting.

Without looking up he says, "Nothing much, watched a bit of sport," he shrugs his shoulders.

"Oh, right," I reply, "didn't you go out then," I push him.

"No, I had stuff to do at home instead."

I push a bit further, "What you stayed in all day yesterday, you stayed in on a Sunday, that's unusual for you, you hate being at home," he looks up at me then looks around to see who is listening, he opens his mouth to speak, but changes his mind, even though there is no one about, he looks up to me but says nothing, I shake my head at him and walk out, Touché I think.

It is Wednesday, just only one more night shift to go, I miss Mike so much but all we have managed is text message due to him being on the course all day and then out in the evening with the group, I don't want to come across as needy or call him at an inopportune moment, so I leave it to him to contact me. I get settled in for the night shift when Phil wanders in, he props himself on my desk waiting for me to finish speaking on the radio, he calls over to Craig, "Hey have you heard about Mike?" Craig shakes his head, my heart is pounding, I am trying to listen to the radio but also to hear what Phil is saying, I cannot do both, the radio wins, I listen as the message is relayed and I update the log, I can only watch as Phil walks over and squats down in front of Craig so they are both at the same height, I cannot hear what he is saying and I am desperate to know what is going on, the last I heard from Mike is that they were having theory and practical exams but I haven't heard any more. It is an agonisingly long wait for Phil to finish speaking, but then he raises his voice and talks about the football, I am not sure, I know Phil pretty well if I didn't know him better I would think he is doing this deliberately. On the way out he waves his hand shouting, "See you later," very cheerfully. Too cheerfully.

I try to wait as long as I can trying to think of a way to mention Mike's name without it being obvious, I want to kiss Gavin when he asks Craig,

"What was Phil on about, what is going on with Mike then, are we allowed to know," he adds.

Craig takes his headset off, he lays back in his chair and nods his head, "Well, it is good news for Mike but not for us long-term I don't think, apparently he scored the highest ever for his practical and theory exams today, so he has been selected to go on the senior officers' negotiation course which runs next week, that means they are keeping him there, not even letting him come home the weekend," I feel sick, I am so proud of him, but he hasn't told me, not even by text but Craig speaks again, "apparently he doesn't know it yet, they phoned down to Inspector Wallis to tell them to cover his shift next week, he is being told tomorrow, great news for him but bad news for us, that man is definitely going places, somehow, we will have to cover him," he sighs and reaches for his tea, "which means more work for us, ah well, couldn't happen to a nicer bloke."

There are general noises of approval, Gavin speaks up again, "Is he married?"

Craig shakes his head, "Don't even think he is seeing anyone, at least nothing serious that I know of," Steve looks over to me but I will not meet his eyes. "Ah well," Gavin continues, "that is good for him then, no complications with women."

Craig nods his head in agreement, then Steve pipes up, "Well there might be, do you remember there was a bit of a crazy lady at his party, then some kind of scandal afterwards, cannot remember what it was though, can anyone else?" he looks around at everyone and then he looks over at me and smiles, I so want to kill him, to wring his neck and kill him. To make it worse, Simon and a few other officers come wandering in, we really should lock that door, they join in with their over exaggerated comments and they all have something to say about the crazy lady from his party but they all cannot be more pleased for Mike I am really glad he is well liked and respected.

I cannot tell Mike how well he has done, it is not my place, I don't want to spoil his surprise so I wait for him to text me, but to my surprise just after lunch my house phone rings, no one ever rings my house phone, most people know I work night shift so they text my mobile so it doesn't disturb me, I leave it on silent for night shift it is still that way now. I am lying in bed, just dozing I am jolted awake by the answer phone kicking in, I reach over and answer it, I hear his voice and I lie back on the pillow, I have missed him so much. He is so excited, he tells me everything I know already but I listen, my heart swells with pride, he is such a dedicated officer I knew he would do well, but, not so good for me, I have to wait another whole week before I get to see him again. I am not tired now, Mike has to go, he has to go back into the training room so we say our goodbyes. I lay there trying to get back to sleep, but it is no use, I am not tired, I am going to go for a nice run I think. I get up and pull on my tracksuit and trainers, it is a nice clear dry day and so I run the short distance to the end of my road and head to the park area. I run for some twenty minutes, my chest is burning so I have to slow down and walk, there is hardly a soul in the large open country park. I stop for a while under the shade of the trees; my heart is hammering in my chest I take a small swig of water then squat down to recover a bit. Walking towards me is a young couple, they are holding hands, he is looking at her and talking, they are oblivious to anyone that might be around, he puts his arm round her shoulders and draws her closer to him, she throws her head back laughing I watch as they pass me unnoticed, my heart drops to my stomach when I realise it is Phil and Helen.

I stay in the squatting position until my leg goes dead, I have to stand up, they are way out of sight now, I try and run it through my head, I am sure I am happy, I have wanted them to get together for so long, now it seems they have, I don't know how I feel. I should be pleased, I know they would be good together, but something in me won't let me be happy. He has always been my Phil, he swore he would be mine until I found someone, well I have found someone else, but he doesn't know that, at least I don't think he does, but he made a vow, I find myself having a huge argument with myself. I know, if he is dating her it will be serious, especially with Helen, she wouldn't have any nonsense from him, she would want him to be totally hers, but what about me, what if I needed him, would he come, or would he stay with her, before I can talk myself out of it I am punching the keys on my mobile phone. Within minutes I hear the bleep of a message, Phil, he has responded, yes he would love a late lunch with me, he will see me in twenty minutes to half an hour. I punch back a kiss, I put the phone in my pocket, a self-satisfied smile on my face, he must still be with Helen, but he is still willing to leave her to be with me, the smile on my face stays there, he is still mine. Then the argumentative side of my brain takes over, I feel guilty, I feel quite ashamed of what I have done, but I justify it in my head saying if he wanted to, he could have made an excuse, after all, he doesn't know I know he is with Helen. I give myself a self- satisfied smile, then a pang of remorse sets in and I feel horrible, she is my friend after all.

I half walk, half run home, I shower quickly then start to get the lunch prepared. Right on time Phil arrives, he kisses me, he is jovial as ever, he watches me as I make a snack, helping himself to most of it before I have finished, we are like an old married couple, I watch him as we sit at the dining table to eat, I ask him what time he slept till he answers he hasn't managed to sleep well on this set of nights, so he is permanently knackered. We seem to be skirting round each other, normally the conversation flows, but I think I am on edge because I want him to be honest with me about Helen, I think he cannot be honest with me as he will feel he is letting me down, it is a catch 22 situation. I am not ready to tell him about Mike, not yet. So we chill out and watch daytime television, mid-afternoon he leaves to get ready for our night shift, I doze on the couch for an hour or so but I still wake up tired.

Last night shift, Thursday can be a mixed night, the nightclubs are a bit busier but once the people have dispersed home it quietens down. I have nothing much to do by way of admin so I just sit updating the logs, preparing everything for the day shift, we are all sat chatting, we discuss our plans for the weekend, I don't have much planned but will try and catch up with Judy at some point. The time is dragging, I am due to work until seven in the morning but at five Craig pulls my name out of the hat I am the lucky one, he sends me home. I have three whole days off to do nothing, usually I would love this but I have no Mike, I wave a cheery goodbye to everyone, throw my bag over my shoulder and head for the door.

I am about to get into my car when Phil jogs across the car park. "Sneaking off early are you?" he calls out.

"My lucky day, I got to go early," I explain, he walks with me to the car.

"What you doing on your days off then?" he asks.

"Nothing exciting planned, what about you?" I answer back.

"Nothing at all," Phil looks at me, "fancy going away somewhere?" he asks.

"What with you?" I reply, I am confused now; surely he would want to go with Helen.

"Yes, with me, just me, we could go to my mate's caravan in the new forest, there is an eighties night planned for tonight then a barbecue for Saturday if you fancy it, we could leave at say, midday, be there for three o'clock, come back on Sunday, we can have a kip this morning, it will be a good laugh, come on, we haven't done that for ages," I laugh I don't see the harm, it will be good fun, I look at him.

"Sounds brilliant, who can resist the eighties," he laugh.

"Pick you up later then, bring nibbles for the journey," as I walk away, he calls me back, "you won't have to worry about what you wear, you have been trapped in the eighties fashion for years," I laugh out loud, he is so cheeky and such good fun, suddenly I am pleased that my three days of nothing has been filled.

I pack quickly then climb into bed, I send Mike a quick text to say I am away the weekend on a eighties weekend in the new forest then put my phone on silent so I can sleep for a few hours. When I wake up I check my phone, there are two missed calls from Mike but no message, I look at the time, I cannot call him now he will be in the classroom. I will call him later.

Phil picks me up, we load the car, we eat snacks all the way there and play stupid travelling games, the radio is playing good music so we sing along, I am so relaxed and happy, we get there in good time, unload everything into the caravan, shower, change then traipse off to the clubhouse, I keep checking my mobile phone but the signal is rubbish I cannot get a call to connect through. We have a nice meal, we start drinking too early, we sit back to watch the eighties tribute band, it is hilarious; most people are in fancy dress. We dance ourselves silly and even join in with the cheesy dances, the people on the next table win a bottle of tequila, they invite us to join them, we are knocking them back and getting more raucous, everything is hilarious. The evening finishes too soon, although way past being tipsy we decide it is a good idea to get more, so we grab a bottle of wine from the bar and head back to the caravan, we support each other on the short walk, Phil keeps falling over, as he falls on to the grass we giggle loudly then in loud whispers we tell each other to be quiet it is the early hours of the morning, it seems to take us ages to get to the caravan, they all look the same and we go round and round the park until we spot Phil's car, after manoeuvring up the small set of stairs laughing hysterically and with a lot of fumbling we manage to get the key into the lock of the caravan, we fall inside, everything is super funny to us, Phil opens the wine, finally after discussing the tribute band and singing songs finally we settle on the sofa under the blanket, we get slowly more tipsy, beyond tipsy, almost too soon the wine is gone Phil finds some brandy in a cupboard, we relax back sipping our drinks, I know I am drunk, I left tipsy long ago, my sight is blurred, my body seems to have a will of its own, I take a swig of the brandy, it burns the back of my throat, I am unused to the taste I can feel it burning as it hits my stomach. We flick through the channels with the remote control. There is a film just starting so we snuggle down to watch, I lay with my head on his chest, it is warm, very comforting, my head is spinning I cannot feel my legs, I whisper to Phil, "I cannot feel my legs."

He reaches down and stroked my knees. "It's okay," he whispers back, "I have found them," we both screech with laughter, I fall off the sofa and he pulls me back up, everything is so hilarious, my eyes are rolling in my head with the brandy and the wine mixing together, we both concentrate on the film but it has a weird plot line which we are struggling to follow, I watch as the films gets a bit heated in places, there is a tall dark man speaking to a woman, I have no idea what he is saying but I am reminded of Mike, the woman is undressing on the screen the man is watching her intently, oh how I am missing Mike, my whole body feels like it is on fire, my lips feel numb, my cheeks are burning, I cannot keep my eyes from dropping, the alcohol is numbing my senses. I look to Phil, he is watching the film intently now, the woman is undressed, totally naked she is approaching the man on the bed seductively, Phil reaches for the brandy bottle he tips it to top my glass up, as he does so he spills it on my hand, he bends down to lick it off, I watch as his tongue gently licks my wrist, it is like I am watching from afar, he turns my wrist over, he licks to my elbow, he looks up to me, I giggle, I slur at him. " I have spilt my brandy," he laughs, I laugh, everything is so comical, I can see two of him, my head swims, the effects of the brandy, wine and tequila are sloshing around in my head, I feel his breath on my face, I feel his lips on my chin. I look to the television, the couple are now making love, both are very vocal, I watch the screen for a second, I look at Phil, he is watching too, the woman is now straddling the man I watch as her huge breasts are bouncing up and down as she screams out with pleasure, I suddenly feel very hot, my brain is whirling, I cannot think straight, I know am very drunk, my body is covered with tiny beads of sweat, I close my eyes, I feel his tongue mingling with mine. Oh it feels good, it feels so right, his hands stroke across my breasts gently, so very gently, I groan loudly, I open my eyes, I see he is watching me, his face is going in and out of focus, I smile at him, this is my Phil, not Helen's, not Jo's he is mine, no one else's, he is mine, he puts his hand up my jumper he squeezes my breasts I push them into his hands, encouraging him, I arch my back, I stroke his back, I rub my hand round his neck, he feels wonderful, I run my hands down to his buttocks and squeeze, his tongue is deep in my mouth, he pulls away and gently tugs my jumper over my head, pulling my lacy bra out of the way his lips immediately on my breast, teasing my nipple with his tongue, he is not gentle now, he kisses me again, our teeth crash.

"Your breasts are amazing," he whispers, dragging his teeth over them and making me groan out loud, he reaches behind and releases my breasts from the bra, his hands and lips caressing them. "I have to have you," he breathes, "only you" then his hands are on my jeans, then they are in my jeans, he pulls the zip down, I wiggle, I help him move them over my hips, the voice in my head just keeps saying, feels so good, feels so good, I need him, he moves his head up to meet mine. "Say you want me, Angie, say you want this as much as I do," his face is so close to mine, I pull him close to me, my lips meeting his again, I cannot form the words in my mouth, all I can manage is a soft moan, I want him, this is my Phil, my head is spinning, my ears are pounding in my head, his hand is in my lacy briefs, I hear him moan out loud he is whispering, I can hear him whispering, I look at him, "just beautiful, you are just so beautiful," he whispers to me, he puts his fingers on my secret place, going lower, I arch to him, I can hear the moan coming from my mouth, his lips are on my breasts, then on my mouth, my tongue meeting with his, I arch my back pushing myself into him, the brandy is making me lose all my inhibitions, the tequila and the wine is swimming in my head. I feel for his groin and he groans, he moves his mouth from one breast to the other, I can hear him speaking softly, he sucks my nipples gently, I moan uncontrollably, this is fabulous, I push my jeans lower I slip one leg out, he has better access now, he pushes my legs wider, his fingers go lower, he strokes me oh so gently, with his fingers, I cry out very loud, he silences me with his tongue. "You are so beautiful, Angie, and so mine," he breathes to me, "no one else's just mine, I have wanted to make love to you for so long baby." I pull him up to me, our tongues dance together, my head is throbbing my eyes are floating round my head, I cannot focus, everything just feels so wonderful, I want more, so much more, I move my hand to his zipper but my fingers won't cooperate with my brain, so I just stroke the outside of his jeans, there is nothing happening, I stroke him very gently but nothing moves, I slip my hands down the front of his jeans, but I cannot move them any lower than the waistband, I lay back, as he moves his mouth down to my stomach, he kisses my stomach, then he moves lower, I am powerless to stop him, I can feel his fingers and his hot breath on my secret place and I open my legs wider I want him I want him never to stop, I hold on to his head, this just feels so right, I moan out loud, lifting my hips higher, I am in heaven, I feel a pounding in my head, I scream out as his tongue sends me to heaven, I never want it to stop, I groan out loud, my whole body is overtaken by the wonderful feeling he is creating, my legs feel numb, my eyes are heavy, I raise my leg to wrap it over his shoulder, feels so good. I hear another scream and I know it is mine, the whole world is spinning so fast, everything goes black, I think I pass out.

Chapter Fifty-One

The sun is streaming through the curtains when I wake up, my jeans are folded on the chair and I have my top and bra and briefs on, Phil is nowhere to be seen, I have flashbacks of last night, I can recall his hands on me, his kisses bruising my lips, his lips on my, I go hot all over, I shudder with cold but I am not cold. I feel so sick, I look around I can still see the evidence, the empty wine bottle on the side alongside the brandy bottle and the glasses. I groan, I close my eyes and lean back against the sofa, what have I done, what about my Mike, my lovely, strong sexy Mike, the love of my life, what possessed me to do what we done last night, I have a flashback of Phil kissing my breasts, I push the thought from my head, but his face comes swimming back, I am so stupid, I have ruined everything. I sit up, immediately I regret it, my head is throbbing, my neck aches, I feel sick, I know I am going to throw up, but I cannot move, I retch and hold my hand to my mouth, I hold my head back I feel so ill, I lay down again, my head is running through the events of last night, why did I drink so much, how did we get back to the caravan, who got me undressed, did I actually get undressed, another flashback comes into my head of Phil kissing my stomach, my bare stomach, oh god, I push my head into my hands, I want to cry, my head is banging I cannot focus properly, I don't know why we did it, just how far did we go, more importantly why did I do it, was it because I was jealous when I saw him with Helen, my head is a jumble of thoughts and emotions, I don't know, maybe it was meant to be, perhaps when I was looking for the man of my dreams he was right by me. Possibly, just possibly it has always been Phil all along.

My text message bleeps, I reach for the phone, it is Mike, my heart leaps in my mouth, he says they are just having a briefing but he will call me in about twenty minutes, I don't know what to reply, so I don't send anything. My arm flops back onto the sofa, my mobile phone drops to the floor, I feel so guilty, I feel so ill. My stomach is churning, I retch again, oh god, poor Mike, what do I tell him, he will be devastated?

The caravan door opens, the stream of sunlight hurts my eyes and I put my hand up to shield them, Phil comes in, he is very cheerful, he holds up a bag of provisions, "Morning, gorgeous, how's your head?" I groan "Ah that good eh, well don't worry I am going to make us a big fry that will make it all be better." I groan again, he is too damn cheerful, I roll over on the sofa pulling the blanket over my head. I can hear Phil banging about in the kitchen I just lay there, I wish he would stop, my head is throbbing, how do I broach the subject, what do I say, what can I say? Without looking at him, I wrap the blanket round me, grab my jeans and head for the bathroom, only just making the bowl I throw up until I think my stomach has come out as well, my head is throbbing, my nose is running, my eyes are watering, my throat feels like razorblades, I just lay there with my head on the side of the toilet throwing up until I have nothing left and eventually, I close my eyes, the world around me is still spinning.

I don't know how long I lay there with my head on the toilet seat, but eventually I start to feel a bit better, I stand up very gently, a wave of dizziness runs over me, my body is hot, I am sweating, I stand holding onto the wall getting my balance, I just manage to undress, I take a look at myself in the mirror, a sorry sight looks back at me, my eyes have huge dark rings under them, my skin looks yellow and my hair has vomit stuck on the ends, I groan out loud, I look and I feel really bad. I pull myself into the shower, the water pounds my head and my body unmercifully, at first it is painful but I stand under the jets until I start to feel human, I hear Phil banging on the door, "You okay in there?" he calls.

Eventually I switch the shower off, clean my teeth then wrap myself in a towel, I sit on the lid of the toilet, I don't know what the protocol is for meeting your best friend and now lover after you have spent one drunken night together.

"Your phone has been ringing!" Phil shouts as I move to the bedroom and pull some clothes from the case, the loudness of his voice makes me wince in pain, I fight with my jeans and eventually win, I really don't have any energy so I lay back on the bed until I hear Phil shout again, "I didn't get to it in time to answer it though, so you might have a message," I sit up and groan as I open the door to face him.

He is sat happily munching toast whilst reading the paper, the wine and brandy bottles have gone, my breakfast is there on the table. "Good night last night wasn't it," he says cheerfully not looking up from his paper.

I shake my head, "Exactly what bit was good for you?" I ask gingerly but do I really want to know the answer, I sit down at the table, I cannot look at him. Despite being poorly I am ravenous, I tuck into my breakfast, mopping every little bit up with my final piece of toast, I don't look at Phil, I make no attempt at conversation, everything still hurts, my head still feels like it is going to explode. I slurp down my orange juice and then my tea. I just sit there silently for what seems like ages; eventually I start to feel a bit better.

Phil puts down his paper, "Thought we could have a walk this morning if you like the barbecue is around lunchtime, what do you think?" He looks at me directly, he seems his normal self.

"Phil," I say his name quietly, "last night," I cannot put the words I want to say into the right context, the words won't form in my mouth.

"Yes," he replies. "Sorry about that, I was pissed I think I made a pass at you, we had a fumble, nothing more, nothing less, I was so drunk I don't think I was capable of anything anyway, can't remember much really, we kissed, I grab your tits, then I think you passed out, that brandy was strong, I think it was cooking brandy, I cannot remember much else, boy did we drink though, I woke up about three then went to bed." I look at him, he isn't looking at me, he is reading the paper again, I don't know what to think, is he telling the truth, can he really not remember.

"I think we did more than a little fumble, Phil" I look at him, I have to know the truth. "Seriously you cannot remember."

Phil looks at me, he looks confused, "No, nothing much after a bit of kissing, which, I might add was very nice, but not much after that, you see, Angie, sexy bird that you are, I don't really feel that way about you anymore, few years ago yes, but now," he punches my arm, "nah nothing," he picks up the dirty plates moving to the kitchen.

My phone rings it makes me jump up, I can see by the name it is Mike,, I move out of the caravan, I close the door walking a few feet away out of earshot of Phil, I put the phone to my ear pushing accept, as soon as I hear his voice my heart is pounding. "Hi, honey," he says, "how are you?" he sounds tired.

"Yes, I am fine, how about you?"

"Well," he replies, "it is really tiring, but very interesting."

"Yes, I bet it is," I reply brightly.

"Where are you, I can hardly hear you, the signal is rubbish?" he asks, so I explain about the eighties night and the caravan, the barbecue, the line is very quiet, he doesn't say a word.

"Mike, are you okay, are you still there?" I ask, but I know he is as I can hear his gently breathing, "Mike, hello, hello," I push the phone against my ear so I can hear him.

He speaks very quietly, "Yes I am still here, Angie, and no I don't think I am okay, not okay at all," my stomach flips over.

"What is it?" I whisper, but I know what he is going to say even before he says anything. "Angie, I thought we were a couple, just us, but there always seems to be this third person, always there in the background, whispering and giggling with you, touching you as if they own you, if it isn't Phil it is the other chap," there is a long pause, so long I have to look at my phone, but he is still there, eventually he continues, I hold my breath, not daring to breathe. "All these hugs and kisses and whispering, although I said I understood your relationship with Phil in that he is just a friend, you know what, I don't think I do, I don't understand it, I don't understand you, I don't like it, but I cannot do anything about it and you don't seem to want to either," there is a pause again, I don't know what to say, but I don't need to say anything as he continues, "is that the real reason why we have to be such a big secret, Angie, so we don't upset Phil?" there is another pause then he goes on. "Well what about me, Angie, do my feelings count at all, what about what I want?" My eyes fill with tears, he continues, "How would you feel if I went away with a female friend and stayed in a caravan, how would you feel if I shared so much of my life with another woman, how would you explain that to your friends, I cannot tell a soul about you because you don't want me to, but what about what I want, Angie, what about me?"

There is a silence, I hear someone in the background calling him, "I have to go, Angie, I am really struggling with this, I think the world of you, Angie, I wish you would think of my feelings sometimes," there is a pause, "Angie, I could really do without this now, I really could," there is another pause, I press the phone hard against my ear so I can hear him breathing, then he continues and my heart pounds hard in my chest, "you know what, Angie, I am sorry but you cannot have your cake and eat it, it doesn't work that way, I hope you enjoy the rest of your weekend, say hello to Phil for me," he pauses again, when he speaks his voice is calm and controlled, "Oh no you can't can you," the phone goes dead.

Chapter Fifty-Two

I just stand there, just staring at the phone, I don't know what to say, he is right, but I think I love them both, I cannot imagine my life without Phil, he is my rock, I don't want Phil to have anyone else, I want him to be mine, I don't want Sean to be with Judy, I want to be the centre of their attention, but I want Mike too, I want everything. I sit on the small deckchair outside. I am not aware of Phil until he is squatting next to me. "Problems?" he asks, I nod my head, "want to share them?" he continues, I shake my head. I don't know how I would even begin to explain to him, I would sound petty, controlling and needy, because that is exactly what I am being. "I cannot help you then, instead I will do the washing up."

Phil stands up and walks back into the caravan. I just sit there, not moving. I hear Phil banging about, I hear the television on, I must have sat there for at least half an hour, I keep churning things over in my mind, I have been guilty over the last year of playing a game, a game with Sean and Phil, we have shared moments of intense closeness that could have moved on to something serious, but I played games with them. Now I have lost Sean to my sister, now I might stand to lose Phil to Helen and even worse, I have even upset Mike, my heart flips as I think of him.

Phil comes out of the caravan he squats down next to me, he puts his arm around me. "Angie," he speaks so quietly, "what are we going to do?" I look up at him, he moves and sits in the chair opposite me, he leans forward, "Angie, I know what happened last night, I know everything," he shakes his head, he looks down at the grass, then he leans forward and takes my hand, "Angie, I am so sorry, I don't know what to say, but I need to tell you, you need to know," he rubs the back of my hand he drops it gently and places his hands together, before continuing, "it was all kind of planned, you see, I am a conceited, arrogant man."

I look up at him, "No you're not," I reply, but he puts his hand up.

"Angie, listen to me, let me speak, please, I have to tell you something," he pauses, " I planned last night, I planned it because I was resentful and angry, I love you, Angie, believe me when I say that, I love you from the bottom of my heart I would never hurt you, but I feel excluded from your life because for the last few weeks you have been distant with me and I know the reason is that you have met someone, I can see in your face, whoever he is clearly lights up your life, I don't know who he is, and you must know, that deep down I know I am very happy for you," he stops and looks away from me, not looking at anything specific, just looking away, then he looks back at me. "I was cross and resentful because you wouldn't tell me about it, you tell me everything normally so I know this is serious, and, I felt excluded," I look up at Phil, he is holding his hands together in front of him, he is still speaking. "So I planned to bring you away, I thought if I made something happen between us it would make everything okay, it would make everything go back as it was before, when you needed just me, but when I woke up this morning I felt so disgusted with myself, I cannot believe how I treated you, I got you drunk and," he stops, he drops my hand, he looks away, "I was going to make love to you last night, just to prove that I could have you, that if, even though you were with someone else, if I really wanted you, I could snap my fingers and have you, just so I could gain points against the man who you are seeing, Christ," he runs his hands over his face, "what sort of heel am I, I got you so drunk, you were so vulnerable, I took advantage, I know what I did to you, I know everything we did." He looks at me, "What does that make me?" he asks.

I look at him, I don't know what to say, I feel sick to my stomach, my beloved Phil had let me down, he had planned it all, he encouraged me to drink then he had taken advantage of me in my drunken state, my heart pounds hard in my chest, I feel tears in the back of my eyelids, but I close my eyes tight quickly to make them go away. I look at Phil, I have to know something, something I can recall from last night and I need to know, so I look at him, "Let's walk, Phil, let's walk, please I think we both need to talk," he nods in agreement, so we leave the caravan unlocked, we take nothing with us, we leave everything, we just stroll off, we don't hold hands, I shove my hands deep into my jeans pocket.

I need to start the conversation back up, there is so much I need to know, we walk, we are totally oblivious of anyone around us or where we are going, we stroll slowly and keep to the forest path, we just walk. I manage to find my voice, struggling with the words, "Phil, last night, we didn't make love," my words fumble, "we didn't have sex, not totally, I know that we fumbled around just as you said, but we didn't make love, I know we didn't, at least not fully," I stop, my voice is shaking, but I know I have to tell him what I know, "I think maybe we were very intimate, but I would have known, certain things need to happen for us to have made love but you couldn't, I know, I do remember some of it, I have flashbacks, I remember that you just couldn't, you know." I pause and look at him, "Maybe the drink affected you, maybe it was because it was me, but I think we got very close but then I cannot remember much else, I keep having these flashbacks though," I stop, I touch his arm turning him to face me. "Phil, a woman knows if she has had sex, I know we didn't, so although you are beating yourself up for what might have happened, actually you don't need to, I am as guilty as you, I got drunk, I accepted the drink I should have stopped, but I never, I let it happen, I am an adult, I could have pushed you away, but I guess maybe, I wanted it to happen too," I struggle to find my words, "you see, Phil, I was scared that I wasn't your number one any more."

I stop and lean over a fence, I look out over a field, Phil stands beside me, "Oh, Angie, you are always my number one, and last night, you were beautiful, laying there in front of me, giving yourself to me, so trusting, I wanted to have you so very much, but my body," he chokes , I watch as he pushes his fingers into his eyes and I know he is close to tears, "I couldn't do it, Angie, I just couldn't, not all the way," he looks at me, "I looked at you almost naked in front of me, your wonderful kisses, your beautiful body, I watched your body shudder as your orgasm took over, you were totally exquisite, then I looked at you, your eyes looking at me so expectantly, so trusting, I love you, Angie, I love you so much, but for some reason my body wouldn't respond to you, and I guess you didn't get fireworks either, or if you did, you cannot remember," he attempts a smile but I frown and then shake my head at him, he continues, "so what are we going to do?" I turn to face him, but I cannot look up at him, I cannot meet his eye. "So you were feeling like you wasn't my number one, I guess you saw me with Helen then," I nod to him, I cannot speak, I cannot trust my voice, he continues, "and I know you were away for the weekend, you know when I come to do your garden, I think probably the chap was still there when I came round, I just know he was, I was so angry, I thought I was okay with it, but clearly I wasn't." Phil moves back to lean on the fence, he looks out over the fields, "Can I ask?" he says, "no actually don't answer that."

I smile, "You haven't asked me anything yet."

He shrugs, "Okay I wanted to ask, but I am not sure I want to know, so here goes," he pauses and looks away, he finally blurts out, "is it Dean?"

I shake my head, "No, not Dean."

Phil glances at me, he smiles, "Thank god for that, he was so full of himself, don't tell me who it is, Angie, not today, not now, I don't think I want to know, I did see a name pop up on your phone, I promise you I wasn't prying I was going to answer it for you, I just saw a name, I thought it might be his surname." I nod then walk on a bit and look back, Phil is still leaning on the fence, he doesn't move, I stop and wait for him to join me, we walk on for a short time.

"So," I say nervously, "where do we go from here?"

Phil doesn't look at me, "Was that your chap on the phone earlier?" he asks.

"Yes," I reply, I feel my eyes fill with tears again.

"Everything okay with you both?" he asks, I wipe my eyes with my sleeve.

"Not really, he is struggling to understand us, as in me and you, he is struggling to understand me being here with you, why I came here when I am in a relationship with him, it has only made things worse."

I cannot help it, the sob that have been holding back just erupts from me, Phil puts his arm around me, he nods in agreement, I lay against his chest, I let the sobs just come out, Phil speaks into my hair, "I cannot blame him, Angie, I mean look at us, no one really understands us, we get flack for it all the time, I tell you all my secrets and until recently," he pushes me away gently, "you told me yours."

I look at him, "Do you, Phil, do you tell me your secrets?"

He looks at me, "Yes, most of them, well," he hesitates, "yes, I do, Angie, why do you ask?"

I remember the comment made by Nancy, I know if it was anyone that she was talking about it would be Phil but do I dare to ask him, do I really want to know. Phil is watching me.

"Come on then ask, whatever it is you are mulling over in your head, ask me, now is the time for no secrets."

I sigh, "I don't know if I want to know the answer really, Phil, but I heard a rumour that you had a," I cannot do it, I falter, I cannot ask him, "it doesn't matter," I say, "really it doesn't."

Phil looks at me, "I know you too well, Angie, it does matter, go on ask, I have nothing to hide, until last night I had nothing to be ashamed off, yes I shag women, lots of women, some married some not, if you are wondering about one of them, if it is rumoured I have, then it is probably true," I don't look at him.

"Nancy," I blurt out, Phil looks at me in surprise.

"Jesus, well okay, well I never expected that, but," he pauses, "okay, caught me off guard there, didn't ever think anyone would know," he runs his hands over his face, "oh Christ, Angie, how do you know, who told you?"

I realise then I have been very stupid, I have nothing to say that wouldn't direct it back to me and Mike, I look at him, he screws his face up, "Ah I get it, Simon put two and two together."

I smile at him, Phil looks away from me, "Trust him and his big mouth, well, I guess he couldn't wait to tell someone, and especially you," he pauses, "shit, I wonder who else he has told, Christ I hope he hasn't told Mike," he walks on a bit then turns to face me "probably with the exception of last night it was the biggest mistake of my life, she is bad business," he pauses, then rubs his head with his hand and continues, "I, well we went out for a curry, just a few lads, Simon was with us, I was drunk, not totally off my head, then I looked up and she was there, she was with a couple of girls and she came over asking loads of questions about Mike, where was he, was he seeing anyone, on and on, we both went outside for a cigarette, well she smoked I just stood there listening to her going on and on, then she got upset, she was going on and on about him, how great he is, she got on my nerves. Mike has really pissed me off lately at work so I thought why not, why not shag his bird, I don't know why, maybe to get back at him, but I was stupid, it was all too easy, I used the Phil charm and it all happened very quickly in the car park, it was dark, not that great and over very quickly, not one of my best moments I have to admit, I don't think Mike knows, well I hope he doesn't." I look at him, I am so shocked, he smiles, "Don't look at me like that, I now know why Mike needed to get away from her, she is a bunny boiler that one, she is obsessed with him, I think she is scared of being left on the shelf, that what I reckon," he looks at me, "I expect Simon told you, it was obvious to the lads what I was up to, and Simon would have told you in the hope he would discredit me." Phil looks at me, "You know what, Angie, Simon really likes you, finds any opportunity to talk about you, drives me nuts, if you ever wanted to break me emotionally all you would need to do is tell me the chap you are seeing is him."

I shake my head, here is the opportunity I have been waiting for, I take a deep breath, but Phil turns to look at me, "no one understands our relationship, Angie, not even me sometimes, so I can see how your fella struggles, it must be strange to someone who doesn't understand us, to be on the outside, to be honest if it was my bird I would have none of it."

Chapter Fifty-Three

That very moment, that is when I realise, when it hits me and I really realise that I am clinging on to Phil and Sean because I am scared of having no one, scared of being on my own, I spent all my time waiting for the right man to come along, then when he does, I forsake him for what is comfortable, what is secure.

I look at Phil, "I'm sorry Phil, I don't think I should be here with you for another night, even though I know we will be okay, I don't think we should, I think I need to go home," he smiles at me.

"Yes, I think you are right, I don't think another night in the caravan is a good idea, and certainly no more drink, I think we both need to go home, but" he looks around, "do you have any bloody idea where we are?" We both laugh, he takes my hand, then drops it quickly, I look up to him he explains, "Angie, when I said I loved you, I wasn't lying, I know I do, I have done for a long while, well for always really, but we," he pauses, "it cannot be, I don't think we are what we need," he looks me direct in the face I see his lovely eyes staring back at me. "New rules I think, Angie, if we are to make it work with anyone else, we need new rules," I nod in agreement because I don't think I trust my voice. He turns to me, "I have a question for you, you don't have to answer but I am going to ask anyway," I look at him, my heart thumps in my chest, if he asks about Mike I will tell him, I have to. "Why did Nick send you flowers?" I look in surprise. "You know the bloody great bouquet that came to work, he isn't the chap you are seeing is he, he is married, Angie, I would be shocked if it was him, but the flowers, I cannot work it out," he stops and looks, "no, he isn't the one, I know he isn't, I don't know why I even asked, don't bother to answer that."

I smile at him, "No, it isn't Nick, and yes, I know he is married, and you are right, I would never, but he was very upset over the incident and I was the person who found him crying, I called someone to help and they sorted him out."

I hope he believes me, he looks at me, "Yes that was a real shitty business wasn't it, I felt really sorry for Steve, he didn't deserve what he got," I breathe deeply, I know Phil, he has accepted my explanation with no further questions, I look at him, "do you want me to tell you who I am seeing, Phil?"

My heart is hammering in my chest but Phil shakes his head, "Not today, Angie, I have got too much running through this head of mine to take that in as well, when the time is right you will know, you tell me then okay."

I smile at him, "Okay." We look up, the caravan is in sight.

We pack up in silence, but it is companionable silence, we listen to the radio and clean up behind us, we both know our relationship with each other needs to change, if we are to move on with our lives to give each other a chance to move on, like it or not I have no choice but to change. Mike is right, I would hate it if he had a relationship with a woman as close as mine is with Phil. As we pack the final items into the boot of the car Phil grabs hold of my hand, he pulls me close to him and holds me tight, I feel his lips on my forehead and we stand for a few minutes just holding each other, he pulls his head away and looks at me, "I am going to miss our nights in together, Angie, our take away meals, our pizza evenings, I am so going to miss everything about you." I smile at him, I feel my eyes fill with tears again, then he pushes me away. "Well apart from your temper that is," he laughs and then he pulls me close once more, I look up at him and as he looks down at me he moves his head to mine, he kisses me gently on the lips, "Goodbye, my lovely Angie, it has been fun," he whispers.

The return journey goes quickly, we talk about nondescript stuff; sing along to cheesy songs on the radio. We pull up outside my house, I get out, go straight to the front door, Phil remains in the car for a minute, I cannot see what he is doing, I turn and wait for him he gets out opens the boot, carries my small case in.

We stand in the lounge, we both just stand there uncertain of what to say or do, Phil speaks first, "Angie, can we pretend last night didn't happen?" his voice is quiet and nervous, I look at him, he is standing just a few feet away from me.

I just stare at him I nod my head, "I think that would be a very good idea," then because I need to lighten the mood I add, "seriously, you brag all the time but you really aren't that good," I push him away, he smiles.

"You are a liar, Staddon, you were loving it, I think we both know that." We both laugh, but it is a false empty laugh, he reaches over, he places my house keys on the side. "I think it is for the best that I ring the doorbell from now on don't you," he smiles again, a better smile, the nervousness has gone, "thanks" is all I can reply. I watch as he gets back in the car, he gives a cheery wave, I wave back but my heart feels heavy and I feel like I have said goodbye to my best friend.

I unpack then put some washing in, I need to keep myself busy, I cannot be thinking of Mike it is too depressing, I ring my mum I have a chat with her, she asks me if I am seeing anyone and I am honest, I tell her yes, but nothing serious, after just another small lecture on gold diggers she lets me speak to Dad. He is getting on really well, he is working on a huge cuckoo clock that someone has sent him from America, he is taking it slowly, just one job at a time so he doesn't get stressed and let people down, he is chatty, he sounds upbeat and pleased, I come off the phone I smile whilst dialling another number. Judy answers on the second ring, her voice sounds very cheerful, we chat for a while, then I ask if I can pop over for a coffee which she extends to inviting to spend the night, the children are away at a sleepover so she is on her own, I drag my overnight bag out again, within just a short while I am in the car driving the short distance to her house. I think a heart to heart is what we both need, it is well overdue. I reach for my mobile phone, I punch out a quick message to Mike, just that I hope he is okay, I add a few kisses, I don't know what else to send, my heart beats faster as I hit send, I don't know if he will want to see me, I have no idea what I will do if he says he doesn't. The phone delivers a message back to me, *message not sent at this time*, I swallow hard, a lump is in my throat and once again, before I can stop them the tears flow.

Chapter Fifty-Four

We have a fantastic night, really great, I have needed this for a long time, Judy is good company, she orders a take away, we settle down to chat, we leave the television off we just put music on, she offers wine but I shake my head, I have had enough of alcohol, just the thought of it makes my stomach churn, so we have tea, we make ourselves comfortable and then just sit and we catch up, we cover everything – she tells me about Sean, she explains how she liked him even as a girl she had a crush on him, but he spent all his time with the boys so their paths never really crossed. She never told a soul, she knew Mum and everyone else always thought she preferred Phil, Judy saw no need to change that, then things changed when I got with Jason, she saw Sean a bit more, decided she still liked him but the timing was wrong. She had met Michael her husband and in the space of a year she had married him had her first child and then Juliette came along, Michael lost his job and then had the affair and left her for the other woman and from there it seemed everything went wrong, she had lots of domestic nonsense to deal with, the divorce, then the wrong one came along causing her grief and debt and heartache, so she just got on with life, then she saw him at the wedding but he was with someone else, then again at the funeral she thought how lovely he was but it was inappropriate timing. They had literally bumped into each other at the local shopping mall, got chatting, he was funny and interesting, so when he invited her for a coffee, she saw no reason to decline, they sat in the café until the owner kicked them out, she knew she was smitten.

"Why couldn't you tell me?" I asked her, she looked at me puzzled.

"You don't get it do you, you had Jason, you had Phil, Sean too, all in this bubble, at your beck and call, just the four of you, very cosy. When you were nursing Jason it was like no one else existed, none of your family were included, you spoke to none of us about Jason, you never asked us for help, although we offered to help you, you pushed us away, we felt like we were not even allowed to visit, or we felt like we shouldn't, we were excluded, no one else could get a look in, everything was about you, what you wanted, even now, you and Phil have this cosiness which is nice," she puts her hands up, "don't get me wrong, but just so very weird, very controlling from any outsider."

I nod my head in agreement, then I cannot help it I burst into tears, she pulls me into a hug, she just lets me cry, until the tears stop, then I tell her everything, well not everything I tell her about the caravan, about the eighties night I tell her about us getting drunk, about me and Phil kissing, but I don't elaborate more than that, I cannot do that to Phil, no one needs to know, I owe him that much. Then I tell her about Mike about our phone call, she totally agrees with Mike, "Of course he is annoyed and upset about you going away, why wouldn't he be. He works with Phil, that makes it worse, he knows Phil, he knows him too well as both a womaniser and a big mouth, so people will automatically think you and Phil are an item, you have never really dated anyone else since Jason, well one blind date hardly counts does it, and I bet Phil was not impressed with that either was he," I shake my head as she continues, "all your time is spent with Phil so why wouldn't people assume that you are a couple," she takes a drink from her tea, she reaches over and strokes my hand. "What sort of message are you giving to Mike, it seems like you want to keep him a secret, is it because you think he is not as good as Phil, are you ashamed of him, or are you keeping your options open?"

I look at her, "Options open, that is a horrible thing to say."

But Judy is no fool, "Really, do you think so," she moves to make herself more comfortable in her seat, "this Mike, he is good- looking yes," I nod as she continues, "he obviously likes you," I nod again, "and yet you think it is okay to go away with Phil, to spend a night with Phil I don't understand it, do you like this Mike or don't you?" she looks at me.

I shake my head, "I do, Judy, I really do, in fact, I know it is early days but I think I love Mike, I cannot wait to be with him, I miss him when he isn't with me, I have never felt this way about anyone, and certainly not Phil." I look at her, she looks so serious.

"Then what is it, Angie, as I said are you keeping your options open, is that it, in case it doesn't work out with Mike?"

I shake my head, "I don't know, Judy, I really don't know, I have been so stupid, Judy, I have been so worried about everyone else, what they think of me, then there is Jason's family, I was so busy thinking about me and how I feel and how Phil feels in fact worrying about everyone else so much that I totally forgot about Mike," I look at her, "help me, Judy, what am I going to do?"

And my darling older sister puts it all into perspective for me, "Okay," she says, "here is what you need to do, firstly and most importantly you have agreed with Phil on the new boundaries for your relationship, no matter what, you must stick to them, don't worry about what Phil is doing and with who, why do you care, it is his business now, not yours, he will never stay with one woman anyway, we all know that, but who cares; it is you I am worried about, you need to make sure everything is right with Mike, I am not sure how, but you will know what works best." She laughs, "Get the negligee out, it worked last time didn't it," she smiles, then her expression changes, she becomes serious. "Then you are to tell Jason's parents that you have met someone, don't tell them all the details, they don't need to know, but it must be face-to-face as that is only fair, they shouldn't hear it from anyone else, believe me if you leave it too long someone will tell them and it is not right for them to hear that way. I will come with you if you like," she laughs again, "that might be a bit weird for me but I will come if you need me too, I might have to show my naked bum so his mum recognises me." We both laugh out loud, then she stops, her face is serious again, "Seriously, Angie, I would come with you if need be," she offers, I shake my head.

"Thanks for the offer, but I have to do this on my own," she nods her head in agreement, then stands up, we collect the plates and move into the kitchen, I watch as she fills the dishwasher. "Judy, what if it is too late?" my voice is shaky and I know it, "with Mike I mean," she stands up slowly, she turns to look at me.

"I don't know, Angie, I just don't know." She pulls me to her she hugs me tight, she releases me and strokes my hair, "But he has liked you for so many years, Angie, he liked you as a gawky schoolgirl with fuzzy hair and braces, he surely isn't going to give up on you now is he." I close my eyes and pray, no please not.

I don't think I will sleep very well in Juliet's bed, surrounded by hundreds of teddies with their weird glass eyes staring at me but surprisingly my head hits the pillow and I am asleep. When I wake up I hear the movement of someone downstairs, I go down, Judy is busy in the kitchen she asks if I mind if Sean comes over for breakfast, I smile and say it would be great, I know I am going to be okay with it, we chat about non-event things and when he arrives, it is like he is coming home, he lets himself in the back door immediately he kisses Judy pulling her close to him, then he comes over, kisses me on the forehead, there is no awkwardness about it, he seems relaxed and happy, he tucks in to his bacon sandwich, his prohibited bacon sandwich, his mother would never allow. I try to examine my feelings as Sean is very tactile with Judy, he strokes her arm when she is sat next to him at the table, he listens intently when she speaks, when the phone rings and she goes off to answer it he turns to me, "You okay, Angie?" I smile my brightest smile, my eyes filling with tears.

"I have been a very stupid woman, Sean, I am fortunate to have friends like you and Phil, so very lucky to have a sister like Judy."

I drink my orange juice and watch as Sean frowns, "You are not stupid, at all, you have been through an awful lot you know," he runs his hands through his hair, so very much like Jason, "you know, with Jason, him moving in, the marriage, the funeral, then your dad being ill, we are all here for you, you know that don't you?" I nod my head, "we always will be," he adds, Judy comes back into the room, she stands next to him, he puts his arm around her waist, Sean continues to speak, "by the way, Phil won't accept any money from Jason's estate, despite me insisting, he says he doesn't want to buy a house yet and would only squander it on cheap women and booze, well something like that," Sean throws back his head and laughs at his own joke.

I look at them both, Sean is so very different from Jason, he is very tactile, very comfortable being intimate, I know both he and Judy are going to be great together. She is very lucky and I know she knows it, I just have to find my perfect happiness and I cross my fingers that everything will be okay.

Chapter Fifty-Five

Monday, I am back at work, late shift, I hate it, really hate it, the control room is busy, I am feeling really low, I haven't heard from Mike since I sent the text. I am struggling to concentrate if I hear anything remotely emotional I can feel the tears pricking my eyelids, when the door bangs I look up hopefully, but it is never who I want it to be. Gavin senses something is wrong, when Phil comes in he calls him over and they chat for a while, I know they are talking about me, normally the boys can lift me out of any bad mood, but today I just feel so low, Phil comes and sits by me.

"You okay?" he asks quietly I shake my head, "anything I can do?" he offers, I shake my head again, "Have you spoke to him yet?"

I shake my head before replying, "I haven't heard from him at all since Saturday, I think it might be over." I cannot help it, the tears fall down my cheek. Phil hands me his tissue, it is a bit dog-eared but I take it gratefully dabbing at my eyes, willing the tears to stop.

"Would you like me to meet with him to try to explain?" he offers, I shake my head, I look around but no one has noticed they are just getting on with work as usual, "Look," Phil continues keeping his voice low, "I don't know who this chap is, but surely if you explain that we went out had a drink watched the show came back to the caravan, watched television then went to bed, separately, say it won't happen again, he should be fine," he looks at me, he lowers his voice to a whisper, "he doesn't need to know anything else, no one does," he puts his face up close to mine, he places his hand over the mouthpiece of my headset, I can hear him breathing he is so close. "Listen to me, Angie, whatever you do, don't have any half- baked idea in your head of telling him anything else, that would make it not fine okay, that would make it never fine, he would never trust you again, we could never be friends, where he is concerned, you know that don't you?"

I look at him I just nod in agreement. I am not that stupid, Phil moves away a bit and moves his hand from my headset, he looks at me straight in the face, "Can I just ask, I know I said I didn't want to know, but I kind of need to ask, is he a foreigner?" Phil asks.

I look at him a bit confused, "No, no, not at all." I ask, "Why do you ask?"

"Well," Phil explains, "when I picked up your phone it looked like a foreign name to me, that's all." I smile to myself, he hasn't worked it out, Mike is not in my phone as a name, it is a description.

Craig calls over to me, "You okay, Angie," I look up and nod yes, Craig comes over, he looks at us both, I know he has noticed my red eyes. "Come on, Phil on your way, we are getting busy here." Phil doesn't argue, although there are no calls coming in, he just gets up and leaves, Craig leans over. "You okay, was he bothering you?"

I look up, "No, I just got myself upset over something stupid, I am okay now, sorry," he pats my shoulder.

"Okay, when you are ready, you are needed downstairs," I stand up.

"I am okay, I will go now," I respond, I walk out, Phil is waiting for me.

"I will walk with you."

I push open the door, there are people coming up the stairs, we wait for them to pass, Phil pulls me back by the arm, his grip is vice like, his tone has changed, it sounds like a warning, "Don't forget what I said, Angie will you," I shake my head, I am so upset, I cannot answer, I just want to get home and close the world out from me.

I wait for my break to ring Little Ma, I arrange to go to their house for lunch the following day, they are really pleased to hear from me, then I ring Judy to say I have not only done this but also spoken to Phil and we are okay, I don't go into details but she agrees with him that we should never mention the kissing at the caravan. When I tell her I called Mum too she is impressed. "Oh wow, well done you," she congratulates me, "everyone will be fine, it will all work out, Sean's parents are understanding people and besides, now she knows that Sean is seeing someone, they will be pleased for you both, any news from Mike?" she asks.

"No nothing," I reply, "I think I have made a terrible mistake there, Judy, I think I have let the love of my life slip out of my hands," her silence speaks volumes, I feel so down, I cannot help it I just want to cry all over again. I cannot wait to get home and crawl into my bed and hide under my duvet.

Little Ma and Pa are fine, looking so much older lately, it has been too long since my last visit to them and I feel so guilty, Pa is suffering with his arthritis, Little Ma is fussing over him, we eat a nice lunch of stew served with potato pancakes as she knows they are my favourite. I am not sure how I am going to broach the subject so I ask her how is Sean, she smiles, she puts down her napkin, "Oh he is a good boy, he has a good girl, she is pretty," she puts her hand on top of mine, "she is not as pretty as you but she is smart too, she keeps my Sean in order, she has no messing about." I laugh at her funny little accent and her description of Sean and Judy, I must remember to tell Judy what she said, Little Ma looks at Pa, he nods, she speaks slowly, "What about you?" she says.

"I am okay," I reply brightly.

"No," she nods, "you have maybe found a new boy for you yet," she nods then continues, "yes, I think so, I see that your heart is smiling again," she gives a little clap then asks, "is he a nice Jewish boy yes, you bring him here to meet us yes?" and I nod yes, because I know Sean has made it all okay for me, even though he is with Judy, he has paved the way to telling them both I am seeing someone.

Little Ma's eyes are bright with tears, she takes my hand, leads me over to the sofa, she scampers off and rifles through the cupboards looking for something, eventually she brings down the wedding album, mine and Jason's wedding album I have never seen it before, I didn't know she even had one, but it is all wrapped up in protective tissue paper, she unfolds it carefully, then she places it on her lap, "We have one last look together," she explains, "and then I put it away here," she taps her heart, she turns the first page and there is Jason's smiling face looking at me, I cannot help it, I lean against her shoulder and cry with her. She holds me close to her, as I sob and sob into her shoulder, she closes the album and just holds me, I am sure she thinks I am crying for Jason, she has no idea of the real reason I am sobbing, she just holds me close. I love this woman, with her strange little ways; I love her so very much.

Chapter Fifty-Six

Last late shift, I still have not heard from Mike, I check my phone ever and over again staring at the blank screen praying for a message, I turn it off and on and then call the mobile myself making sure it is working, but I know deep down there is nothing wrong with the phone, he just hasn't called or text me. I don't send him any more text messages, there is nothing else I can say, the ball is in his court now, I don't try to ring him either, but my heart aches for him. I listen as Craig is speaking to the sergeant going off shift, he says that Mike is doing really well on the course and everyone is impressed with him. When I am down in the main office I catch Simon, he is waiting to use the photocopier after me, I try to keep my voice light, I ask if everyone is going to the pub tomorrow lunchtime as usual, he shrugs, he says maybe but says there is never any definite arrangement; people just tend to turn up if they want to. We chat for a while and for once he is talking normally and is professional, I text Phil to see if he is going and he confirms he is, he asks if I want to have lunch beforehand, I text back yes please I will meet him at twelve noon, I see no reason not to, I have to eat and if Mike and I are over then I need to drown my sorrows too.

The shift is busy, too busy, it is manic, I get my head down and we all work really hard, the weather is awful so there are more road accidents than normal, I get up to make a drink for everyone. I still have to check my phone continually to see if I have a missed call or a text, I don't care if I get caught, all I want is one message, just one small message from him to tell me I am in his thoughts, but nothing, the screen stays blank, my mood with my heart sinks lower. I pop to the ladies then returning to the coffee area I pick up the tray and go into the control room, I hand around the teas, there stood in front of me is Bradley, the new recruit, he is the last person I would want to see, but he looks different, he is not in uniform, he has a casual suit on and is happily chatting to everyone, I smile politely at him then go and sit down. I feel so low, I know that he will blame me for his being sacked, but I don't care, I feel so rock bottom anyway so him adding to it cannot make me feel worse, it just isn't possible. I am not even sure why he is here, once someone is dismissed it is all very quick and almost never do they get to come back in again. I look over at him, he seems to be quite relaxed and chatty, maybe he didn't lose his job, I sigh and look through the new logs that have come in.

Gavin takes an emergency call and I listen in to see if he needs assistance, I watch as Craig and Bradley stand up and walk towards the exit, Craig calls me over, asks me to join him in the office, I motion to him that I am on a call and he gives the thumbs up, the call is not urgent so

I pick up my tea, I look at Max questioningly, but when he shrugs I walk into the meeting room and close the door. Bradley and Craig are sat together on one side, leaving me to sit on the other side, Craig asks if I remember who Bradley is and I nod yes, "He is a new recruit," I reply flatly.

"Well, yes okay, not exactly," Craig responds, "unbeknown to us, Bradley here was put in amongst our shift to monitor our personal working environment."

Bradley raises his hand, "Guilty as charged," he smiles, "let me introduce myself, I am the force psychologist, I was asked to write a paper on working relationships in the force, specifically those who work shifts, this was in order to promote best working practices and positive working environments."

"So," I interrupt, "it was a set up then," I frown at them both.

Bradley holds his hands up again, "Well, yes, you can call it that if you want, but we prefer to call it silent observation, in that, we can join your shift just as any new recruit would and not be treated any differently."

I interrupt him, "But you goaded me to get a reaction." I am being defensive and I know it, "That is not normal practice at work is it?" I continue.

"Ah," Bradley nods his head in agreement, he smiles, a self- satisfied smile, "I can see your point, but in order to ensure the correct processes were followed I had to ensure I had a series of complaints against me, unfortunately in order to do that, I had to" he raises his fingers in inverted commas "goad you."

"Yes," I continue, "but I never made a complaint though did I?" Bradley smiles, "No actually you didn't, I didn't realise what a," he pauses, "may I use the word, feisty character you were and the senior officers did struggle to get that complaint signed, we even had to, at that point call in your immediate superiors," he looks at Craig, "we needed that complaint, all credit to you, I am not sure how they persuaded you, and judging by the signature you still were not happy, but what you should understand," he pauses, "what you need to understand is that, we have learnt a lot of valuable information about respect and how in house issues are dealt with," he smiles, "even on a one-to-one basis you tried to guide me appropriately when you had every right to just report me, my behaviour was not acceptable, I apologise that I had to get personal but you handled it perfectly, the force thinks very highly of that behaviour," Bradley stands up, "thank you so much for your time, Ms Staddon, and thank you for being involved in our operation," he smiles again, this time it looks more genuine, "albeit unwittingly," he adds shaking his head, he shakes my hand, I put my hand on the door then I turn back.

"One question please," he looks up at me.

"Of course," he smiles.

"Was Sergeant Simms or my sergeant aware of this whole," I put my fingers up to show inverted commas "set up".

Bradley laughs, "No, I am afraid, much to their chagrin, they were not involved initially, it was only this morning I advised Sergeant McDonald about the true reason for the complaint, I know I can speak for him when I say he was not impressed to say the least." I look at Craig and he pulls a face, Bradley continues, "Sergeant Simms is apparently away on a course but I can confirm he had no prior knowledge that this operation was taking place, although I think he was only involved to take notes, I am not sure if he will be made aware of the full circumstances." I raise my eyes, and then turn to the door, as I walk back to my desk, the next person I see to go in is Sergeant Boon, I hope he fares as well as I did.

Just twenty minutes to go, the jobs are dying off now, what cannot be sorted by the night shift we delay to the morning, I print everything off, I head to the copier to make several duplicates of everything. I am really tired now, I can hear voices coming up the stairs and I can hear Inspector Wallis congratulating someone, I cannot see who it is as I am in the other office. I walk back to the control room I can now see Inspector Wallis and another person with their back to me, they are stood in front of Craig's desk, I can see the hairline and the shoulders of the second person, I know those shoulders so well, my heart starts thudding hard in my chest. My knees don't belong to me, my mouth goes dry, I walk slowly to my desk, I put the pile of paperwork down and glance over, Craig is pumping Mike's hand in congratulations, Steve is patting Mike on the back, Craig spots me and calls me over. "Ah there she is," they all look over. "Come over here, Angie, come and congratulate this clever bugger, he not only passed the course with flying colours but he got the highest mark ever recorded."

I don't know what to do, I cannot move, my feet seem to be glued to the ground, I wish I had never come back in, I know I have to do something, everyone is looking at me, Mike looks round at me and I look straight back at him, my heart beats hard in my chest, his expression is hard and cold, but then I guess so is mine, his dark eyes just stare at me, as if penetrating right to my very soul, he still looks so gorgeous, so bloody handsome, he has on his full uniform complete with tunic and outdoor coat, even as I walk nearer to him, I can smell his aftershave. I don't know what the code of behaviour is, so I reach out and put my hand out for him to shake, he doesn't move and I pull it back towards me.

"Give him a kiss, you miserable bugger," Steve chides me, but I shake my head.

I don't know what to say or do so I let out a weak, "Well done."

He doesn't move, not a smile not anything, just a blank look, if anyone notices the tension between us, then no one comments. Thankfully the phone rings and I nod my head, "I had better get that," no one argues and as I walk away.

I look back and Steve is looking at me questioningly, Craig is frowning at me, but I slip into my chair and answer the call, I watch as Inspector Wallis puts his arm around Mike, his voice booming, "You know, only a few officers get selected for this type of work, we are very privileged, come on, Mike, they are waiting for us downstairs, I know it is late but we need to take official photos whilst we have everyone here." They disappear out of the control room, he doesn't look back. Steve tries to catch my eye but I ignore him, I create a new log for the call that has come in, it is not urgent, I note all the details and then sit back in my chair, my heart feels heavy, I cannot speak, I know I will cry if I do, I let out a huge sigh of relief as the new shift arrive. I am tired, I want to be anywhere but here, I pack up quickly and leave on my own, almost running to the car park without waiting for Steve. I cannot bear it, the look on his face when he turned and saw me make me want to cry all over again. Mike's car is still in the car park, I sit in my car, I think about him and how much I have missed him. I pick up my phone, I punch a quick message of congratulations before I change my mind I hit send. I look up to see Steve waving to me, I know he wants me to stop and chat but I wave back quickly and drive out of the car park, I cannot answer questions about us, I know I would just break down in tears.

I cannot sleep, I toss and turn, I get back up, I watch a bit of television, I make myself a milky drink, it is the early hours when my phone bleeps, my heart jumps in my mouth, I practically leap on the phone, but it is only Phil asking where I have disappeared to, it is a drunken message but I manage to work out, it is to find out where I am and have I heard about Mike. Everyone is really pleased they are all with him at the police bar, lots to celebrate so going to be a long night he texts, I am glad I am not there, I am really pleased for him but it would break my heart to watch him, knowing that I might never be with him again, never feel those wonderful soft lips on mine or his body close to me, I can feel the tears welling up, I feel so sorry for myself, I give out a huge sigh, Phil is right, it is going to be one hell of a long night. I have my phone at the side of me but it stays silent, as if mocking me, I keep picking it up, keep checking it. Eventually I fall asleep through exhaustion.

My mood is not brighter when I get up. I am angry and tired, there are dark rings under my eyes, I drag the bedding from the bed and throw it all in the washing machine then I pull on my trainers and go for a run, that generally clears my mind and makes me feel better but after twenty minutes I am still upset and angry with myself, and even worse I am now hot and sweaty, and starving. I get back home, looking in the cupboards, I have nothing by way of food in the house so I eat the last of the biscuits. Without bothering to shower or change I scrape my hair back in a ponytail, grab my purse and I drive to the supermarket. As if on autopilot I throw items into the small trolley, I know I look an absolute mess but I don't care, luckily the store is not busy and I get through the tills quickly. Walking back to my car I bump into an old friend of Judy's, she knows the family, I know hers, I feel rubbish and know I must look a sight and I tell her so, but she has issues too so isn't looking so great either, I don't care enough to argue when she invites me for a coffee. I store all my shopping in the boot and as we take our seats in the small café I check my phone again, still nothing, my heart sinks further, we sit for a long while and have a good chat, none of us are in any particular hurry. The coffee tastes too strong and too bitter but I sip it gratefully, she is going through her own personal drama and I listen, it is a diversion I need from my unhappy thoughts, we have another coffee and I add croissants and cake for both of us, by the time I leave her and get home it is late morning, I am not feeling any better, but I pack the shopping away then drag myself into the shower, I let the hot jets hit my sorry sad body, as the water flows I burst into tears, I wrap myself in a towel and dry my hair. I am not due to go out for a while so I pull my dressing gown on and continue to do chores. I text Phil to see if we are still on for lunch, he texts back a short reply yes still midday, he texts that he has yet another hangover adding that he didn't get in until the early hours so I am to be nice to him. I laugh to myself, I can imagine the state he will be in later. The doorbell rings and my heart races, I run to the door hoping that it might just be him, but it is a religious group trying to talk to me about crime in the area, I am very short with them and stomp back to the kitchen, I sort the rest of the shopping and put it away, I am trying so hard to keep busy and banish Mike from my thoughts, it is too painful to think about it. I don't know how I am ever going to face him at work, my heart feels like it is breaking in my chest, I feel sick when I think of work, just facing him is going to be very painful, hearing his name and seeing him, speaking to him on the phone and knowing what we had together. I cannot believe how stupid I have been, I know I feel the same about him as I did before he went away. I miss him so much I wish I could have the chance to tell him, just a chance to give my side of the story. I might try to be subtle and ask Phil how he thinks Mike was last night. I cannot help it the tears flow down my cheeks again as I think of him, I sit at my table and sob until my throat is raw, my heart aches, I can still see the expression on his face in the control room when he looked at me, so empty, so cold, so expressionless. I blow my nose and look in the mirror, a tired, red-eyed sorrowful state looks back at me.

Chapter Fifty-Seven

I fill the kettle for a coffee then go out into the garden, I have a fight with the washing on the line, everything is conspiring against me today, even the washing, I am desperately losing the battle in trying to get the double duvet cover to go over the rotary line, it is very windy, the rotary line swings round clumping me across the head, I cry out in pain, my eyes sting with tears of frustration, everything is just going wrong for me, I just about manage to hold back the tears, I hear the doorbell ring again, I throw the duvet cover over the whole line in frustration then watch it fall straight to the floor, I kick it angrily, the doorbell rings again, whoever it is they are not going to get a good welcome, I stomp through the house to the front door swearing loudly to myself, my face red, still in a temper, I fling the door open, and there he is, stood there, in front of me, looking tall and handsome, in his jeans and a navy polo shirt he looks cool and gorgeous, stood just staring at me. "Bad timing," he says softly.

"Fight with a duvet cover," I sniff then reply weakly in explanation, "I am losing, in fact, I have lost, I gave up," I add, I shrug at him.

"So might you have a need for a fully trained negotiator?" he asks raising one eyebrow.

My tummy flips, my heart pounds in my chest, "I think I definitely might," I reply with a slight smile, I step back wiping my face on the sleeve of my dressing gown, I watch as he kicks off his shoes then he walks into the lounge, he turns to me.

"I came round earlier, but there was no reply," he says.

I shrug then reply, "Yes, I went for a run and then food shopping, I had nothing in the house, then bumped into a friend and we got chatting, a friend of Judy's," I add quickly.

"Oh I see," there is no tone to his reply, I cannot read his expression, there is no smile or half smile, I sniff again then wipe my runny nose with the back of my hand, I know I must look an absolute wreck, he just stands there.

"Coffee?" I ask for want of something to say.

"Yes please," he responds, we walk in to the kitchen together, like two strangers, he stands and watches me silently as I make the two mugs of coffee, it takes seconds as the kettle is boiled, I hand him the mug, I know I must look a terrible state, we stand and look out of the window silently, eventually he speaks, "I didn't know you went running," it is more a statement than a question.

I shrug, "Yes, generally when I am upset or stressed, or both." He doesn't look at me.

"Which one was it this morning?" he asks, his voice is gentle.

"Both," I reply.

"With me?" he asks immediately.

I shake my head, "No, not with you, with me." He nods his head, then without saying anything he puts his coffee down and walks to the back door then out in the garden in just his socks, I watch as he picks up the duvet cover and in a few short moves he has it neatly hanging from the washing line, he walks confidently back in.

"All negotiated," he smiles at me. Without thinking I look at the clock, I should be meeting Phil in twenty minutes, "You need to be somewhere?" he asks quietly.

"Nowhere important," I reply.

"Ah," he says, "I remember now, don't you meet with Phil today for lunch, isn't that the regular arrangement, what time is that?"

I shrug, "I don't have to go, I don't have to meet Phil, if I am not there he won't mind, I am sure of it."

Mike looks at me, "But do you want to go?" he asks gently, he is staring at me, his eyebrows go up as if waiting for the answer.

"No," my voice comes out in a whisper, "no, I don't," I feel like a small child, he moves towards me.

"What do you want, Angie, tell me?"

I cannot help it I sniff again and wipe my runny nose on my sleeve, my throat is closed with tears when I speak it comes out strangled whisper, "I just want to be with you," in just two paces he is by me, his lips meet mine and my whole body turns to jelly, his kiss is urgent and passionate, his hands are on my face holding me in place so I cannot move, but I wouldn't want to move anyway, I cannot help it, my eyes fill with tears, but I know they are tears of happiness.

When we pull away from each other he wipes the tears away with his thumbs then pulls me into a tight hug, he whispers, "Please don't cry, Angie, I hate to see you upset." I sniff again, as he continues, "Oh, Angie what have you done to me, I have missed you so much, darling, you make me so crazy, I wanted to call you, or text you, but I couldn't do it, in case you might tell me it was all over, I couldn't bear that," he whispers, he clears his throat, "so I threw myself into my course and every time I thought of you, I banished it from my head, I couldn't bear to think of you in that caravan with Phil, or Sean or anyone, I got so angry, I was too far away to do anything, so I had to shut it from my mind and got through the course the best I could." I hold him tightly, I never want him to go away, he pulls away and looks at me stroking my cheek with his finger. "I thought we were over before we had really began, I was so angry, but as it happened getting angry was good for me, it worked out well for the course results, but last night, I missed you so much, there was everyone there at the bar, but not the person I wanted to have there, I wanted so much for you to turn up," he pauses to look at me, "I kept looking at the door expecting you to be there, why didn't you come, Angie, why were you not there?"

I shake my head, "I have been so stupid, Mike, I was so scared to face you, your face in the control room was so, so," I cannot help it I sob into his chest.

"Hey hey, none of that, honey, come on," he kisses my lips gently, "I have missed you so much, baby, please don't cry, last night was horrible without you."

I put my arms around his waist, pulling him close to me, "Well, if it is any consolation, I had a pretty horrible night too, I couldn't sleep a wink." I pull away and look up at him. "Mike, I need you to know, that we didn't stay in the caravan for a second night, Phil overheard me on the phone, he asked me and I said you were not happy he said he wouldn't be either."

"So he knows about me then?" Mike looks at me.

I shake my head, "No, he knows I am seeing someone but not who."

"Ah right," Mike says resignedly, "still your guilty secret."

"Afraid so," I reply I kiss him but I have an idea, "you hungry?" I ask Mike.

"Why?" he asks.

"Thought I might treat you to lunch that is all, give me five minutes and I will get dressed."

Mike laughs, he eyes me up and down and my tummy flips over, "Don't get dressed on my account," he tugs at the belt on my dressing gown.

"Do you need a hand?" I look at him, his boyishly good looks looking back at me. "No," I say firmly, I laugh, I playfully slap his hand and I skip up the stairs with a huge smile on my face I pull my clothes on, apply some make- up which makes my red eyes look a bit better. Within just a few minutes I am back downstairs, Mike has finished hanging out my bedding. "Domesticated too," I smile at him.

He laughs, "Oh yes, there are a lot of hidden talents I have, if you are lucky I will show them to you one day." I smile at him as I take his hand.

"Yes please do," I reply.

As we go to the front door he pulls me back towards him, "Where are we going?" he asks I tap my nose.

"You'll see."

"Okay," he smiles at me, "but one thing before we go," he pulls me close and presses his lips against mine, his hands travelling over my body.

I look at him, I have to tell him how I feel, "Mike, I was so scared it was over between us, I just kept thinking how unbearable it would be at work to see you and not be with you, I couldn't sleep or think straight."

He pulls away and looks into my eyes, "Times that by ten and that is how I felt too, when I was on the course I spent nearly every night in the gym pounding the treadmill or rowing just to work out the frustration I was feeling, this morning I drove round here three times before I had the guts to knock on the door, I thought you might tell me it was over, then when I did pluck up courage, you were out, I was gutted." We hold each other very close, very tight, neither of us wanting to let go.

We go in my car, I insist, it feels really strange to be driving with him in the passenger seat, I cannot help but keep glancing over at him, he catches me and puts his hand over mine, we approach the pub which is well known to both of us.

"I need the cash point before I go in," Mike says so I drop him off at the corner.

"Meet you inside," I smile as he gets out. It is probably a good idea that we arrive separately, I know what I need to do, and I know that the timing is right.

Phil is already there when I go in, he is sat reading his paper, but he looks up as I approach the table, he passes me the menu, "Phil," I don't sit down I stand and look at him, he looks up at me frowning. "I think I would like you to meet the man in my life, I think I am ready," my heart is pounding, "ok."

Phil folds his paper, then takes a sip of his pint, "when?"

I reply immediately, "Soon," I say then quieter, "very soon." Phil stands up, "Okay cool, what you drinking, and choose your food quickly, I am starving," he walks to the bar.

"Phil," I call him back, "come here for a minute," he turns and walks back to me his face frowning, "you sure you are okay with meeting him?"

Phil looks at me, "Yes, of course I am sure, you name the day and the place I will be there," he looks at me, "and if I don't like him I will report him to the authorities and have him deported."

I shake my head, "I told you he is not a foreigner, I don't know why you think he is."

Phil frowns, "I told you I saw his name on the phone, it looked foreign."

I shake my head, "Okay, I understand, well I think that you need to meet him, sooner rather than later, but there will be no deporting necessary."

I see Mike walking though the bar, I turn to Phil I try to pull him back to the table, but it is too late, he has seen Mike, he ignores me, shrugging off my arm and leaving me with my mouth half open, he walks over, puts his arm round his shoulder. "Hi ya, mate, how's your head?" he says in greeting he looks back at me, "I will be with you in a minute, Angie, but first let me buy this clever bastard a drink," he says.

425

Phil saunters to the bar and looks at me, I just stand there, I don't know why but I am so nervous I am shaking, I am so uneasy I feel sick, I am now not so sure this is a good idea, but I look at Mike and he smiles and that is all the encouragement I need, I walk over to Mike, I take his hand, Mike smiles at me again, he raises his eyebrows questioningly, but I just smile back as we both turn and head towards Phil, Phil looks at Mike's hand, then at me, his mouth opens and closes, I clear my throat then say, "Phil, I would like you to meet Mike, Mike this is my good friend Phil."

Mike puts out his hand and Phil shakes it, he seems a bit shaken but if he is then he recovers well and claps Mike on the back again. "You sneaky buggers," he exclaims, if he is shocked then he covers it well, he narrows his eyes, "I must admit, at one point I had my suspicions, but I am really surprised," he looks at Mike, "you asked too many questions, but you covered it well, fair play to both of you, I couldn't wish for a better bloke for her, mate," he says, he turns to me, "and you, sneaky, very sneaky, how did you snare a good one like this, he obviously hasn't tasted your cooking," he pushes me playfully.

He turns to the bar, but I interrupt him, "My round I think," I hand over a note.

Phil laughs, "Bloody hell, Angie, calm down, love, there is only so much shock I can take on in one day."

We sit and eat together, everything feels right, Mike is very chilled out, very chatty they talk about rugby, I sit back and watch them both, Phil seems very laid back and comfortable with us being a couple.

"So how long have you two been an item then?" he asks. "And how did you eventually get together?" Mike and I look at each other, but before we can answer Phil looks at Mike, "And more importantly how did you get rid of the bunny boiler?"

Mike looks at him and smiles, "You have such a way with words, Phil."

Phil frowns, "Mmm that means you haven't then, oh well," he takes a drink of his pint, "good luck with that then."

Mike tilts his head towards Phil, "I don't really think the bunny boiler as you so eloquently call her is too bothered about me anymore, she knows I am seeing someone, and apparently she is now chasing some chap she met at a curry house, trying to hunt him down, so seems the pressure is off me," I watch as the colour seems to drain from Phil's face, Mike pauses and I practically hold my breath, but Mike is not to be silenced, he continues, "you eat a lot of curry, Phil, maybe you know him," without another word Mike stands up, he is stood behind Phil. "Another drink anyone?" he asks lightly, I shake my head.

Phil doesn't say a word, he waits for Mike to be out of earshot before letting out one word, "Shit", he looks at me, "shit, Angie, he must know, how the hell would he know, you didn't tell him did you?"

I shake my head, "No of course not."

426

I pull a face at him, I can only assume that he must have overheard her when she told me, but I say nothing to Phil, he pulls out his phone and checks his messages, then slots it back into his pocket, I watch as Mike turns back towards us, he has a pint in his hand for Phil and some kind of soft drink for himself, I smile brightly, "Anyway, Phil, to get back to what I was saying, I have told Little Ma and my parents," he looks at me nonplussed, I don't know if he is still trying to absorb the comment from Mike or at my news, but he manages to speak.

"Bloody hell you have been busy."

"But, Phil," I look at Mike, he nods, "we didn't want to lie anymore, we wanted you to know, but we don't want the whole shift knowing until we are ready, okay."

Phil shrugs, "No worries, I get it, no problem, my lips are sealed."

I feel so relieved, Phil waits for Mike to sit down, he leans back and puts his hands on his head, "So how did it happen then, you know, you two?"

I smile and look at Mike, he sits back in his chair, but the waitress arrives with the meal so he doesn't respond, Phil's text goes off and he pulls his phone out of his pocket again, his face is serious. "Problems?" I ask.

He shakes his head, "Where me and women are concerned, Angie, it is always problems," he puts the phone back without replying to the text, he continues to eat in silence, his text goes off a few more times but he ignores it. Mike raises his eyebrows to me and pulls a face; Mike's phone is ringing he frowns when he looks at who is calling.

"I better get this," he stands up and walks away.

Phil leans in, "So what is the situation with the bunny boiler then?" he asks.

I smile at him, "The bunny boiler has gone, yes," I reply.

He nods his head, "You might have to tell me how he got rid of her, it seems some joker has given her my mobile number, bloody woman won't leave me alone, calls and texts all the time."

I snigger at him, "Well, it is your own fault, Phil, you thought it was hysterical when Mike had to deal with her and now the shoe is on the other foot."

I leave my words unfinished as Mike comes back to the table, he gives no indication of who was calling he just sits down and continues to eat. I sit back and eat my meal listening to them both chatting about football and rugby, when Phil asks again how we got together I tell him, he looks at Mike, "Ah that explains it then." Mike frowns at him but smiles as Phil continues, "Well I thought there must be some bird, I told you at the time you looked knackered all the time, mate," Phil laughs at his own joke and we both join in, it all seems so natural.

In the next hour the rest of the shift arrives, it becomes very noisy in the pub and the pool tournament begins, Mike doesn't play, he prefers to watch. We stand next to each other he keeps stroking my back. Surprisingly Helen turns up and although I am pleased to see her and even though I give her plenty of opportunity she doesn't confide in me about Phil. When Mike discretely touches my elbow, he motions for me to finish my drink, he nods his head towards the door, I understand. I say my goodbyes just as I am leaving Mike calls out to me to ask if he can have a lift, "sure" I say brightly then my heart sinks as another officer asks if I can drop him off too, I cannot refuse, Mike sits in the back and keeps blowing kisses to me in the mirror, the conversation on the journey in the car is mostly about work, I drop the chap off at his house and finally we are alone. "Any plans for tonight?" I ask as I look at Mike, he looks me up and down.

"Oh yes," he replies, "plenty." My heart flips.

We have all night tonight then the morning together, we spend the evening just talking, none of us mention the Phil comment about the bunny boiler, we are just content with each other. I have no idea how Mike would know about Phil and Nancy, or why he didn't mention to me, but I don't care, I am just happy that Phil knows about us and I don't have to lie to him. Mike and I just chill out, with the music playing softly in the background, we order a take away but just before it arrives we are busy in the kitchen putting out trays, being very domesticated, making drinks. I catch him looking at me, he smiles pulling me towards him, I know that smile, he kisses me so passionately, he pulls me onto the cold tiles in the kitchen and still fully dressed we make love quickly and urgently, there is no gentle foreplay. I groan loudly as he climaxes, we just lay there as one. I feel completely content. I kiss his chin, his cheek then his neck then lower; we just lay there just stroking each other. The doorbell rings, we both giggle as one of us has to go to the door to collect and pay for the food. He loses. I grab the opportunity to tidy myself and adjust my clothes quickly before he gets back.

We don't need to see or speak with anyone, I don't check my phone, his is just lying there on the table ignored, I hear it bleep and I tell him but he shrugs and doesn't look at it.

"What if it is urgent?" I ask.

But he just shrugs, "They will ring if it is urgent, by the way, that was my sister who called earlier, something about a family meal, wanted me to check when we were both free."

I nod my head, "Okay, what date is it then?"

But he shrugs again, "She isn't sure, Mum is organising it, not sure what the occasion is, Jenny will find out and ring me again, she doesn't do texting."

He pulls me close to him, I snuggle in to him, I just want to be with him. We chat about lots of things, but nothing about work, his phone continues to bleep indicating messages coming in but still he ignores it, I don't know how he can, it would drive me nuts, I would have to know, but it just lays there on the table. We continue talking, I tell him about my mum and dad, I update him on Judy and Sean, he is really pleased. I tell him about seeing Phil and Helen together in the park; he says he suspected it for a while but as Phil is always Jack the lad he never thought Helen would put up with it. I wait for him to mention about Phil and Nancy again, but he cuts the conversation short and I know he has no interest in anyone else's relationship but ours.

When we finish our food and we retire upstairs, he looks into my eyes, "I like you very much, Ms Staddon, very, very much, is there a word for how I feel about you," he whispers, he makes me giggle.

"I like you very much too, Mr Simms, and I cannot think of the expression I have heard other people use, I think it might be I heart you or something similar." We both laugh then we reach for each other, this time he leisurely undresses me so agonisingly slowly making me wait until he is ready, and then when I whisper to him I cannot wait any more, he enters me and we reach our climax together.

Chapter Fifty-Eight

Jenny has called him back and it seems that Mike's parents have arranged a celebratory meal for his success, he doesn't want the fuss but they are insisting. I think it is wonderful, this is planned at the same hotel we stayed in, there is a party of ten of us, just close family so we are staying over, it is in two days' time, we are on day shift so I book the day off as holiday so we can leave shortly after we get home from work then we will have the next day off. No one puts two and two together that we are both off on the same day, I am very excited, Mike is a bit overwhelmed with all the attention, he is pleased he done well on the course, there was even a snippet in the local paper about him gaining the highest mark ever achieved – I am so proud of him. Day shift is harder than I thought it would be, I keep seeing him about the building and wanting to touch him, to kiss him. I sit in the restaurant with Rex having our roast lunch. Mike comes in with a senior officer and they sit on the table just a few down from where I am sat, as he sits down he winks at me. A warm feeling comes all over me I cannot help but watch him as he is talking very seriously about something. I watch as they both stand up, they shake hands and both walk out in different directions.

Later by the photocopier he waltzes past he picks me up, spins me round and kisses me full on the lips, "Mike," I say very surprised "I thought we were being discreet, someone might see," but he just laughs, he kisses me again.

"Guess what?" he asks.

"I don't know, but whatever it is it must be exciting, so tell me."

"I was speaking to Chief Inspector Drummond they want to fast track me to Inspector, can you believe it."

I jump up and down, "Oh wow that is incredible, I hold on to his arms. "Inspector Simms, that sounds wonderful, you so deserve it."

He kisses me again he whispers, "So, I get to choose my prize tonight then do I?"

I smile at him and his eyebrows shoot up, "You know what my prize will be don't you," I laugh and push him away.

"You are so rude soon to be Inspector Simms." He turns and walks off down the corridor and I can hear him laughing.

Phil is being a star, he is so discreet. In fact he doesn't say a word to me at all, there is no discussion, he doesn't refer to Mike and I as a couple so I don't really know how he feels, but I am really happy that I have told him about Mike. I am feeling really good today, everything just makes me smile, I am sat in the control room just checking through the logs, it is not busy, we are keeping up with everything.

Craig wanders over to me, "You okay?" he asks.

"Yes," I smile at him, "why do you ask?"

He sits on the side if my desk. "Because you look positively radiant," he moves closer, he looks around quickly but seeing the others are busy chatting he leans over towards me, his hand reaching out and covering the mouthpiece of the headset so we cannot be overheard, our heads are almost touching, "it wouldn't have anything to do with a certain clever chap in uniform would it?" he whispers, I hear someone walking up behind but Craig is blocking my view.

"I don't know what you mean," I whisper back at him very coyly, Mike is stood behind Craig.

"What's going on here then, mate?" he asks, Craig jumps.

"Bloody hell, don't go creeping up on me like that, you'll give me a heart attack," he moves away, I touch Craig's arm and pull him back down.

"Is it that particular clever chap in uniform you are talking about?" I ask smiling at him, Craig looks at me. Then back to Mike.

"I knew I was right, I bloody knew it." He walks back over to his desk shaking his head and smiling.

"What was that about?" Mike asks.

"He was practising his interrogation techniques, but he is not as good as you," I reply, I stroke his hand so no one can see. I love that I can touch him subtly when no one is watching. Mike is more demonstrative he takes more chances, if I am making tea he will put his hand in my blouse, he will sneak up behind me at the copier, I love it. I smack his hand I tell him to behave but I still love it. I am looking forward to the dinner tonight I have decided to wear the same outfit as the first time I was there with him.

We arrive in good time, we check in, I am pleased to see we have the same room we giggle as we run the bath, then we jump in together. We have a leisurely bath then I lay on his chest, we just cuddle and kiss until it is time for us to get ready. I cannot believe I am with this totally amazing man; he is the world to me.

The private dining room looks wonderful, beautifully ornate chandeliers hang from the ceiling, there are soft candles flickering around the room, the table is decorated with navy tablecloths and matching napkins in blue and gold, the silverware looks sparking the wine decanters have been highly polished. I can see there are people already in the room, milling about sipping their drinks and chatting so I head as if to join them but Mike pulls me away from the room taking me by the hand, heading towards the exit, we head out of the door towards the lake, I am in heels so I tiptoe unsteadily across the lawn until we meet the gravel path, we walk without speaking. It is a lovely clear evening, Mike pulls me to the swing where we sat before, he looks me in the eyes, his face is very serious, he sits me on the swing and drops to his knee, my heart is pounding, his face is so serious he looks me straight in the eyes, his hands holding mine.

"Angie, this might be a bit soon for you, and I appreciate that, but I thought my life was good until I met you, now suddenly my life is fantastic, I wake up every day feeling great, I cannot stop smiling, I know it is all because of you. I knew I wanted to be with you when we shared a classroom all those years ago, I know I want to share the rest of my life with you, I want to tell you, Angie, that I," he pauses, giving a little laugh, "I like you, I like you very much indeed, what was the expression you used the other night, I heart you," he smiles as I raise my eyes at him. "I want to ask you, Angie, to be my wife, but I want it to be when you want to, planned how you want it to be, with no surprises, no regrets, no secrets," he pauses and looks up at me, I can see the love in his eyes, those beautiful dark eyes .

My heart is beating hard in my chest, my eyes fill with tears, I know what I want to say, I wanted to hear those words all my life, and I want to throw my arms around him and say yes, but he said no secrets, and I do have a secret, a big one, big enough to destroy us both, I have the caravan secret, it still haunts me sometimes when I am in Mike's arms after we have made love, or when I remember how Phil is when he is drunk really drunk and spouting off his big mouth, not caring what he says and who he says it to, what if one drunken night Phil blurts out the truth about what really happened. Mike would call me a liar and a cheat, because I was a liar for not telling him, he would never trust me again, I cannot live with lies or deceit. But what if I tell him, what if Mike doesn't believe me that we never actually had sex and that we were too drunk to go all the way, will he believe me, my tears spill onto my cheeks, that one night might have cost me my lifetimes happiness.

Mike pulls me to him, he kisses me gently on my lips. "Oh, my darling Angie, is that a yes?" I nod my head; I cannot speak as he kisses my tears. We stand together he holds me close, so close, I don't ever want to leave his arms, he pulls away and looks at me, he doesn't say a word, he doesn't need to, I see the total love he has for me, it shows in his eyes. What I wanted, what I have been looking for all my life is stood right in front of me and saying the words I have always wanted to hear. Eventually we pull apart, he takes my hand up to his lips and kisses it gently, we walk hand in hand slowly back to the hotel and I glance back at the swing, no matter what happens in my life, I know, I will never forget this very special moment.

The meal is delicious, Mike has such a lovely family, it is relaxed and informal, I sit back and listen to them chatting, Jenny is talking to her mum about a lady at work I lean forward to listen, she includes me in her conversation. "Do you believe in the tarot cards, Angie?" she asks.

I take a sip of my coffee, not sure how to answer, I don't need to Mike's brother speaks up, "Bloody waste of money," he scoffs, "hocus pocus the lot of it, you will buy a red car, oh maybe a green car, you will marry and have two children, give me the twenty quid, Jen, I will tell your fortune, you will be twenty quid poorer," he laughs as she pokes her tongue out to him.

"I haven't said I am having it done, I said I am thinking about it," she replies haughtily, "but now you have made my mind up for me, I am definitely having it done."

He shakes his head and laughs at her, but she turns away, I sit back, I think back to my reading, the confusion over the car I originally ordered a blue car but due to a mix up at the dealership I ended up with a red one, just like she said I would have, sometimes I have strange feelings like I have been told something before by the tarot reader and it scares me a bit that everything else seems to be coming true, one by one.

Mike takes my hand, "Penny for them?" he asks, I look at Jenny, she is still talking about the tarot card lady.

"Just listening to Jenny," I reply honestly.

"And do you think it is all nonsense?" he asks.

I shake my head, "Not necessarily, I am still keeping an open mind," I look at him and he frowns, but I don't explain, maybe one day I will explain I look at Mike, "what about you, do you believe in it?" he nods his head but I don't get to hear his answer as Mike's dad asks Mike about his training course, he sits back and I listen as they are discussing it, his parents are clearly very proud of him and every so often Mike will take my hand on top of the table and give it a squeeze. My heart keeps hammering in my chest, I so want to be married to this man, I know he is the one, the key to my future happiness, I love him so very much, I have never felt for anyone the way I feel about him, I know we are good together, I know what I have with him is real, I want to spend the rest of my life with him, but I cannot accept his proposal with this secret. And I don't know what to do. I wish someone would help me sort this mess out, please I silently pray, please someone help me. Please make it all better; I pray that someone is listening.

Chapter Fifty-Nine

The last of the evening visitors have gone, Mike is sat with his dad and brother having a brandy in the drawing room, Mike's mum has retired and gone to bed, I am also very tired, so I go over, I lean and kiss Mike on the cheek, "I am going up now okay," I speak into his hair, he reaches for my hand, he kisses it.

"Okay, see you shortly," he says. I say goodnight to everyone else and head up the stairs, I check my mobile phone I have a missed call from Judy, I look at the clock, it is very late, past midnight, far too late to be calling anyone but this is Judy, she won't mind me calling, so I undress, get ready for bed then I get comfortable in bed, I punch her number in and wait for the connection, she answers immediately.

"You okay, Judy?"

I say as soon as she answers, "Yes, I am fine, just fancied a chat earlier, the kids were tired, Juliette isn't very well, she has a cold so they went to bed early, where are you?" she asks. I explain about the celebratory meal and the training course Mike was on and how well he had done, I lay back on the bed, she waits for me to finish, "Oh right," she says casually then adds, "so what is wrong then, Angie?"

"Nothing," I reply a little bit too quickly.

She gives a sigh, "Come on, Angie, this is me, Judy, I know when something is wrong, come on just tell me."

I cannot help it, I blurt out, "Judy, Mike has proposed to me, tonight before the meal, in the gardens here," there is silence at the other end, she is waiting for me to speak again, I take a deep breath, "Judy, there is something I need to tell you, something I need to tell someone."

I know she can tell by my voice it is serious, I sit up, I take another deep breath then I tell her the truth about the caravan, I tell her everything, I tell her just how far Phil and I went that night, when she finally speaks I can tell she is very angry with me, she interrupts me, "For god's sake, Angie, stop it, stop doing what you always do, stop making a big issue of it all, it is in the past, Phil will not say a word, even when he is drunk, why would he, what has he got to gain from it, he will come out the worst if he told anyone, I mean he took you away, he plied you with drink, he took advantage, what does that make him, Angie, let it go for goodness sake, Phil doesn't have the problem here, it is you that has the problem, if you need to, then tell Mike but you will be throwing away a good relationship, he is not going to understand is he, I mean would you? If he told you he went away on the course and nearly shagged someone but actually never, but was very intimate, it is just as bad really, why does Mike need to know, be real here, Angie, you are going to sabotage probably the best man you will ever meet over something that happened ages ago, you need to get over it, forget it, everyone else has, it was something that meant nothing, it probably needed to happen for you two to come to your senses."

"But, Judy," I protest, my voice getting louder, "it wasn't ages ago and Mike has the right to know, I know both him and Phil are okay, they are fine with each other, good mates even, Mike is cool with Phil and I, he is okay with the fact that we are friends, but if I am to be married to Mike I have to know we have no secrets, the fact Phil and I were very intimate, so intimate that we very nearly had sex in the caravan is a secret that if I don't tell Mike about, he will find out someday, somehow, I just know he will, things have a habit of coming out, they just do, and that will make it worse. To me it doesn't matter that we didn't have sex but just fumbled, the fact that I don't tell Mike I was intimate with someone else while we were going out, it just makes it worse, I cannot have a secret with Phil that Mike doesn't know about, I owe him more than that, it just isn't fair. Can you not see that our marriage will be based on lies, so if I tell him and I lose him because of it then I only have myself to blame, I am the one who has to live with it, but if I tell him and he can forgive and forget then at least I will not be worrying that someone will find out and tell him."

Judy wails at me, "For Christ sake, Angie, you are inviting trouble, you always do."

I interrupt her, "No, Judy, I am not inviting trouble, I love Mike unconditionally, I need to know he loves me that way too, I cannot lie next to him knowing I have a secret, it is not fair, my first marriage was a lie and I cannot and will not do it to Mike."

"Well you are a fool," Judy scoffs, "don't say I didn't try to warn you, remember how bad you felt when you two split up the last time, you were heartbroken, you are inviting trouble, Angie, mark my words, don't do it, girl, you will regret it," she pauses, "look I have to go, I can hear one of the kids, please, Angie, think this through, speak tomorrow okay." I put down the phone, I sit quietly just turning it over in my head. I walk to the bed, I sit on the edge, I feel sick, I look at my watch, Mike has been gone for forty-five minutes, I wonder what is keeping him.

When the hour has gone I slip my shoes back on, I pull my dress over my short nightdress and head downstairs. Mike is sat in the drawing room alone, he has an empty brandy glass in his hand he has his head bowed, I go and sit by him, I take his hand, he looks up, his eyes are red, it almost looks like he has been crying.

"Oh, Mike," I drop his hand and put my arm around him "whatever is the matter, what is it?"

Mike says nothing he shakes his head, he picks up my hand and holds it in his, he looks at me, "I came up over twenty minutes ago," he chokes out, "you didn't close the door properly, I stood and listened, I know I shouldn't have, and god how I wish I had walked away, but I didn't, Angie, I stood there, I heard everything, well almost everything," he looks up to me his face is full of anguish. "Why, Angie, Why, him, why anyone but for god's sake why Phil?" he drops his head before continuing, "wasn't I enough for you, didn't I make you feel special enough, didn't I please you in the bedroom, what did I do so wrong, please you have to tell me Angie because I am struggling here, struggling to understand when we had everything, everything going for us, why would you do that, why would you let that happen and of all people why with him, answer me, Angie, why wasn't I enough for you?"

He drops my hand, he places the glass on the floor between his feet and puts his head in his hands rubbing his face, I feel sick, I go and stand by the window, my head is hurting, my chest is painful, I have an indescribable pain in my heart, I stand silent for some time just staring out of the window trying to find my voice, I try to hold back the tears, then trying to find the words I need to say, I clear my throat, "Mike, please listen to me," I look over to him but he doesn't move, he doesn't look my way, his hands are covering his face, so I continue, "Mike, I am not proud of myself or my actions, but I was drunk, very drunk, drunker than I have ever been, so drunk I actually passed out. I could blame it all on Phil as he was the one filling my glass but I was the one who chose to drink it, I didn't want it to happen, it wasn't planned, at least not on my part, it just did, Phil was dressed the whole time, we never actually, you know," my voice catches in my throat, I cannot continue, I can hear how it sounds coming from my voice, I am so scared I have lost him, I cannot answer his question as to why, why when I had everything I have ever wanted I risked it all and lost. My heart sinks, I have been so stupid, I don't know what to do now, I lean my head against the cold of the window pane. Tears prick my eyelids, I cannot hold them back. I know I have two choices – to fight for this relationship or to walk away, I stand up and walk in front of him, my voice is shaking, I cannot stop sniffing, but I manage to clear my throat and speak, " Mike," I take several deep breaths until my voice is calm and steady, "Mike, you have to know that you are the best thing that has ever happened to me in my life, I need you to know that," I pause, he doesn't move, I continue, "in a way I am kind of glad it happened."

He looks up at me his dark eyes staring at me, "Yeah right, thanks for that, Angie, it explains everything and that makes it better," he scoffs.

I move quickly and sit in the chair opposite him, I am scared but I have to tell him how I feel so I continue, my heart thudding hard in my chest, "no,

I am glad it happened, okay maybe glad is not the right word, but I am struggling to find the right one, but maybe it was meant to happen, maybe it had to because it finally put any feelings I might have had for Phil to rest and he for me, we could have stayed the whole weekend in that bloody caravan and got up to all manner of things, but we didn't, because we didn't want it to happen." I pause, he still isn't looking at me I go on, "We got up in the morning, it was horrible, both of us realised how badly we cling to each other and exclude everyone else. That morning we realised we are not good for each other, we are controlling and we are too needy, unhealthily so, none of us want that, so even if you and I didn't get together," I stop, I cannot breathe, I pause for a while. "If you and I didn't get back together then Phil and I never would be together, as in a couple, you have to believe me. Phil and I made a pact that we wouldn't be so needy with each other, the relationship is not healthy, not good for either of us, so when we got to my house he gave me my key, we decided we had to have new rules, to be friends, that is all and friends with boundaries," I pause to catch my breath, still he doesn't look at me. "I am glad that you know, because I could never have a marriage with secrets," I sniff noisily, I cannot speak as my tears flow, I cannot stop them my voice is choked but I continue, not realising my voice getting louder and louder. "My whole relationship with Jason was a lie from start to finish, no one ever knew because I didn't tell them anything, I lived with that for too long, Mike, and I would rather be on my own than live one again."

I take a huge breath in, I am exhausted, my head is throbbing now, he doesn't move, I stand up in front of him, still he doesn't look at me.

"Do you want me to go? I could get a taxi home," I wait for him to respond, it seems like forever, but eventually he shakes his head, I take a deep breath, "then I am going up to bed, I would like it rather a lot if you came with me."

I stand for a minute or so, my hand outstretched, it seems like forever, but I cannot drop my hand for fear he will let me walk away, but still he doesn't move, he shakes his head, "I have one question, I don't want to know the answer but I have to know." I drop my hand, he chokes the words out, "Did you......., did you and Phil."

His voice cracks with emotion, he cannot go on, I kneel down in front of him, I know what he is going to ask, I know because it is such an intimate thing. I cradle his face in my hands looking direct into his eyes, then I place my hand on his shoulder, "No, Mike, I know what you are asking, and the answer is no, I never touched Phil at all, not in any way sexually, please believe me." I stop and look at him. "I will never lie to you, so if you want me to tell you what happened in detail then I will, if it will help you understand but I never did what I know you are asking, as I said I passed out and I might not remember much but I know he was fully dressed." I hold my hand out to him, "Please, Mike, come upstairs with me."

I pray so hard to whoever might be listening; I pray that he will take my hand and when he does, he reaches for me, pulling me down to him, he kisses me gently on the lips, but it is a very quick kiss, not the kiss I am used to from him, he stands and pulls me behind him as we head up the stairs. We walk to the room in silence, still holding hands, my stomach is churning. It is a victory that I am holding his hand and going upstairs with him, but I feel so utterly deflated. We stand silently in the lift and say nothing as we walk to the room.

We undress in silence and lay next to each other in bed, not touching but just facing each other in the darkness.

"I do like you so very much," he whispers, it is more a statement than a declaration, but it is what I need to hear.

"I like you very much too," I whisper back. I smile to myself that he has used our secret way of saying I love you. He moves and lays on his back, one arm is back behind his head. "Mike" I whisper, "I can never tell you enough how much I regret what has happened, I will regret it forever, I want you to know that I would never intentionally hurt you."

He doesn't move, he doesn't say anything, I look at him, he is laid with his eyes closed but I know he is not asleep.

I close my eyes, but I cannot sleep, thoughts are churning through my head, over and over, Phil and the caravan, Phil touching me, me touching Phil, I remember he didn't respond to me touching him, was it the drink or something else, I don't know, I remember Phil admitting he had planned it all, I feel sick. I listen to Mike breathing gently next to me, I so hope we are going to be okay, I really hope so. I feel a huge sense of relief that I have told him, whatever he is thinking or feeling now I know I did the right thing. When he turns over I turn towards him and wrap my arm around his chest, I can feel his heartbeat, I snuggle close to him. Eventually I fall asleep.

When I wake up Mike is turned towards me just watching me, as I open my eyes he leans forward and kisses me. "Hello you," I whisper.

"Hello you," he whispers back, "did you sleep well?" I ask him.

His reply is instant, "Not at all, I was up most of the night looking out of the window, then I went for a walk around the lake," he pauses, he sits on the edge of the bed, he pulls on his boxer shorts and stands up, he walks to the window and looks out, there is something he is not telling me, I can tell, I feel slightly lightheaded, he looks at me then goes on, "and I made a phone call," the words hit me and I sit bolt upright, I don't like the sound of that."

"You made a phone call?" I question, I am almost afraid to ask but I have to know. "What time was that, and who did you call?" I ask, but I already know the answer, my heart sinks.

"I phoned Phil," Mike looks at me, he looks directly at me, my heart is thumping in my chest.

"Why on earth did you ring Phil, didn't you believe what I told you?"

I pull the covers over me, when he replies his voice is flat, "Yes, I did believe you, but there was one comment you made that I couldn't get out of my head; I knew only one person could answer it, so I asked him."

I slip out of bed I pull the sheet around me, I don't like where this is heading. Mike glances at me, then looks away, he flicks the kettle on and busies himself getting the cups ready, the silence seems to go on forever, but I don't know what to say to fill the silence, I want to ask him but the words won't form in my head.

"Do you want to know what I asked him?" I nod my head yes, but I am not sure I do, Mike continues, "I asked him if he planned it, if he planned to seduce you, to prove a point, and do you know what he said?" I shake my head. "He said yes he did, he said he admitted it as much to you to, but it wasn't to get at me, he said that at that point he didn't know it was me you were seeing, he thought you were seeing a foreign chap, he was angry for being excluded in a part of your life, he thought you were making a big mistake and had got yourself into something you would regret."

I shake my head again, I don't know what to say, there is a long silence again, I look up to Mike, "What time did you call him?" I ask.

Mike makes a face, he shrugs, "Not sure really, two, maybe three o'clock, might have been later, I didn't care, you see, I laid there for a long while just going over what you told me, and I knew when you said it wasn't planned at least not on your part, I knew that you and Phil must have spoken about it afterwards, and that although you wanted me to know the truth, you didn't want to betray Phil to reveal him to be the scheming, manipulating bastard that he was, did you?"

I shake my head, but I have to be honest, "But, Mike, there were two of us in that caravan and no one forced me to drink did they, I have to be responsible and accountable for my actions and take the consequence that come from those actions."

Mike looks at me, he brings my tea and hands it to me, sitting on the edge of the bed he turns to me, "How many times have you got drunk or tipsy with Sean or Phil, once, twice, maybe more, how many times have they tried it on, once, twice, never? But that weekend, that night, Phil went out with the sole intention of getting you so drunk and then having sex with you, the fact that you passed out before anything could really happen is beside the point the intent was there."

I nod my head, I can see he is right but it is in the past now, I put my hands around the mug, it is hot, too hot but I welcome the pain, I just want it all to go away, I just want it all to be right again, as if reading my thoughts Mike comes over and takes my hand from my mug and holds it up to his lips.

"But it is me that has to forget it, it is in the past now and you are right, if we have no secrets then no one can hold it over our heads as a threat, you are right, there is no room in our marriage for secrets or lies." I cannot help it,

439

tears of relief spill down my cheeks, Mike takes my mug and places it on the bedside cabinet, he pulls me close to him pulling my head to rest on his chest, "Angie, my darling Angie, please do not cry, don't cry I cannot bear it when you are upset."

I pull him close, "Mike," I look up and smile at him, "these are my happy tears."

We go down to breakfast, I wanted him to pull me back to the bed and make gentle love to me, but there is nothing, he dresses and stands looking out of the window waiting for me as I shower and get dressed, he looks at me as I walk from the shower room and I see in his eyes that he loves me.

I feel a totally different woman; a huge burden has been removed from my shoulders. As we walk to the elevator I keep looking at Mike, I cannot stop smiling, he holds my hand as we walk to the restaurant, in a total contrast to how I felt last night. I have this lovely buzz about me and when we are all sat around having breakfast Mike taps his juice glass asking for everyone's attention. There are just eight of us round the table – Mike, his parents, his sister and her husband, his brother and his girlfriend, Hannah is not here she is being looked after by her other grandparents, Jenny and Peter look relaxed and happy, everyone is chatting and there is a general hum of conversation across the dining room. I feel my eyes prick with tears at how happy I feel, relief flows out of every pore that we are going to be okay, everyone looks at Mike and he begins, "I won't stand up," he says, "but I wanted to finish the celebrations with an announcement."

My stomach flips over, I don't know what he is going to say, I am not expecting him to tell everyone, we haven't really discussed it, then I take a deep breath and calm myself, it might be that he is telling them about his work news, I look to him and smile encouragingly.

"I know," Mike continues, "that it may seem very soon, but I have known for many years that I had found the woman I want to spend the rest of my life with, and after a few stumbles I am pleased to say," he clears his throat, "I asked Angie yesterday, if she will marry me, and," he pauses and looks at me, he winks and smiles, and I smile back at him, "after much negotiation." He laughs, then looks around at everyone, "she has agreed to be my wife" he looks at his mum, he holds his hands up, "but not immediately, Mum, okay, we are in no hurry, are we, honey?"

I look at him and smile, I know that whatever is thrown at us, we will cope together. Mike's dad reaches over, he claps Mike on the shoulder, "Well done, my son," he stands up and kisses me on the cheek, the others make similar comments and everyone seems genuinely happy, I look over to Margaret, she is wiping her eyes with the napkin, I just hope they are happy tears.

When we stand up to leave she comes over to me, "I have an apology to make," she says quietly, I frown, I have no idea what she is talking about, "I misjudged you, I thought you were married, well separated, I thought you were," she pauses, "well, you know, and I was worried about Mike getting involved in unpleasant business," she smiles, "I know I am too protective with my children, Mike has probably told you that we have fallen out in the past over it, but when he told me you were working with him but you were married, I could tell by his voice that he still liked you a lot, he kept talking about you all the time but in true Mike fashion, he didn't tell us that your husband had died, I am so sorry."

I move closer to her and pull her into a hug. "It is okay, really it is, I would never have betrayed Jason with Mike, I couldn't do that to him." We hug and I watch as Jenny comes over towards us.

"Can anyone join in," she calls happily, we separate and she joins us. "Well, Angie, welcome to the family, Hannah is going to love having you as an auntie," she laughs.

As Mike and I take the lift up to our room he takes his phone from his pocket, "Would you like to see what your name is listed as?" he asks.

I smile at him, "Okay." He holds the phone then tips it away so I cannot see it.

"Show me yours too," he laughs.

I grab his phone and look at the listing then look up and smile at him, "Bit presumptuous of you wasn't it?"

He shakes his head, "Not at all, Mrs Simms, not at all." Then he pulls me close and I feel the zip of my dress undoing, he kisses my bare shoulder. "I told you, I knew years ago." I take my mobile from my handbag and search for his name, as I turn the phone towards him, he reads his listing and pulls me close to him. "That is just so lovely," he whispers into my hair. We nearly never make it to the room as he pushes his hands into my dress and releases my breasts from my underwear.

Chapter Sixty

Back to work after a very eventful few days, I haven't heard a word from Phil and I am very surprised he hasn't been in touch, not even a text message, nothing, at all which is really surprising but I don't care. I don't know how him and Mike will cope working with each other and I try not to think about it, whatever happens they will have to deal with it. I waltz around floating with happiness, we have decided that we are going to wait a while more before announcing our engagement to everyone; we want to wait for a year or so before we tie the knot. I want Mike to meet my parents in person so we are looking at booking flights when we next have time off after night shift. We are going to see Judy tonight, I really want her to meet him, I know they will get on well, as he will with the children, it seems that everything is happening at break neck speed, but I want everything to just calm down so we can just enjoy dating – enjoy getting to know each other better; so does Mike.

I drive to work with a big smile on my face, I park up, I am in a great mood, I have spent the last few days walking on air. When he is with me I am totally happy and when he isn't I miss him so much it is ridiculous. There is no one in the car park, it is a bit early, I grab my bag and I hear a loud bang, as I get out of the car the main reception door crashes open. I look up to see Phil storming towards, me, I stand with my door open, he looks like he is about to explode, for one second I think he is after someone, then as he gets nearer I realise, it is me.

"Get in the car!" he shouts, his face is red with anger, my heart starts to pound in my chest, I hesitate with my car door open, he stands at my bonnet. "I said get in the fucking car," he roars at me.

There is a white line around his lips, I have never seen Phil so angry, even when he is dealing with an abusive or aggressive person he has arrested, he is in control, I don't think about arguing, I sink into the car seat and close the door. He pulls open the passenger door with such force I think he is going to rip it off, he gets in and slams the door behind him making me jump. He turns to me, his eyes are blazing with anger, I look around the car park, it is still deserted, I am frightened, genuinely frightened, he turns to look at me, "What the fucking hell were you thinking, you stupid thoughtless selfish bitch."

I can feel the tears in my eyes, Phil has never ever raised his voice to me and never called me names, I feel sick in my stomach, my face goes bright red, he is so much more than angry. I look at him, I cannot stop them, the tears form in my eyes and then fall down my cheeks, I am not sure yet why he is so angry, I wipe my tears with the back of my hand, I reach out to touch his arm, he shakes it off, he is shaking with anger, his voice is shaking as he speaks.

"Fucking hell, Angie,", his words spit out, "you are fucking priceless, what the fuck were you thinking, you could have warned me that you told Mike," he slams his clenched fist down on the dashboard, I jump. I must admit I am really scared of him right now, I think he might hit me, my palms are wet with sweat, I cannot catch my breath, I can see the vein pulsing in his neck as he goes on he is looking straight ahead.

"Seriously, what the hell were you thinking, if you were thinking at all," he turns to face me. His face is contorted with anger, he spits his words out. "I thought we agreed, I thought we said that we wouldn't tell anyone, I told you no one would understand, we agreed that didn't we?" he doesn't wait for me to speak before he continues, his voice getting louder, "And then what do you do, tell him everything," he wipes his mouth, I turn to look at him, I wipe my eyes, then I clear my throat as I know if I don't everything I want to say will come out croaky.

"Oh my god, Phil, I am so sorry, I really am, but I didn't plan it." He shakes his head but says nothing so I continue, "Phil, you have to believe me, I had to tell him about the weekend, I had to, Mike has asked me to marry him." I look at Phil's face, I can tell he is shocked and angry, he is clenching and unclenching his fists, but I continue, "I couldn't accept his proposal with this hanging over me."

Phil interrupts, "With what, Angie, big fucking deal, we made out, it was once and no one needed to know, but you, well you have made it into this big thing, this big fucking deal, you have made me look a real asshole, thanks, Angie," he is facing the front again now, not looking at me, he is pounding his fist into his hand, I know he does this when he is trying to calm down.

I try to breathe deeply to try and keep my temper, but I cannot do it, I can feel it bubbling, the rage inside of me, why can he not see it from my point of view, I storm back at him, "You know me better than anyone ,Phil, I am sorry you feel that way, the fact we had been intimate, and that I had been unfaithful and betrayed him with you, it is a big deal to me and I couldn't do it, I just couldn't, so I told him the complete truth, I told him that you were not responsible," I stop, I cannot get my breath, there is a long silence, I run my hands over my face, I calm my voice a bit but it still comes out too loud. "We were both responsible, Phil, we both were, there were two of us, Phil, and I told him that, I told him that it wasn't planned." I stop, my heart is hammering so hard in my chest as I remember I told Mike that it wasn't planned, well not on my part. I turn to face Phil, my heart is thudding so hard, my chest is hurting, I lower my voice, "Phil, look at me," he immediately looks out of the window, so I ask him again, "Phil, please look at me," this time slowly he faces me, his face is expressionless, his lips are pursed hard, so hard the skin around the edge is white. I look him straight in the eyes before I continue, I know that by explaining to him I might lose him as I friend, but I have to. "Phil, listen to me please, I had to tell him, Phil, you must understand that, no matter what he thinks of you, or of me, I had to tell him because somehow, sometime in the future, this would have come out, I don't know how or when but I know it just would, then he would always wonder why I didn't tell him, what I was hiding, it wasn't just a fumble, Phil, we didn't just make out, we were far more intimate than that, we were." I hold my fingers apart a few inches. "This close to going all the way, you were there, you know that, if I hadn't of passed out, this might have been a different conversation, but, Phil," I choke on my words and clear my throat, "I have to be truthful or I would have a marriage full of lies, where we hid things from each other." I look away as Jason's face comes to me, "I cannot have that, Phil, not again, surely you of all people must understand that." I look at him, "Phil, I love Mike, this is the real deal for me."

Phil is rubbing his chin now and nodding, I can see he is calming down, he looks at me, "Christ, Angie, I just wish I could have been forewarned, I look a right bastard now don't I, I look like some kind of sexual fucking predator, I admitted to you that I planned it, I admitted that to you, Angie, not so you could share it with him, not to share it with anyone, I am not some kind sexual stalker that goes out to pray on vulnerable women, Angie, I am not that kind of person, you know that, I really truly love you, in a strange way I know I always will, but I don't take advantage of people."

I look at my hands, that is exactly what he did I think to myself, I was that drunken vulnerable woman, but I don't say anything, I am as much to blame, I have been stupid and naïve, but I don't regret telling Mike.

Phil looks at me, "Do you think if I would have known it was him you were seeing I would have taken you away, of course I wouldn't, but you kept it secret from me, I was angry with you, this isn't about him, it is about me and you," he pauses, he looks out of the window then looks back at me, "you know when he called, it was the early hours of the morning, I saw his name on my phone, I thought something serious had happened, and there he was interrogating me, going on and on at me, banging on asking questions one after the other, barely giving me time to collect my thoughts, let alone answer him, he went on and on, where, what, why, I was in bed for Christ sakes," he looks at me, "and not alone," he smiles then his face is serious again. "Then I have him on the phone and I am answering questions that I really could have done without," I smile at him, a very weak smile, he continues, "then she starts, who is it, why are they ringing so late, what have

I been doing, both of them, him shouting; her yipping in my ear, I could have done without it, seriously I could."

I cannot help it, I smile at him, I want to lighten the situation. "So who was the lucky lady then?"

Immediately I want to bite back my choice of words as Phil smiles, "Lucky lady," he raises one eyebrow, his voice has the old Phil cockiness about him. "Ah so now you are remembering eh, the old grey cells are working, well, Angie, maybe you wanted more than a fumble, maybe you wanted more of the old Phil charm, by my memory, you certainly was enjoying it, bit of the old green eye monster there, eh just maybe," he laughs scornfully.

I reach for the door handle, I feel so stupid, again he has made me so mad, I half turn to face him, "You know, Phil, you know what you are, you are exactly what you said people would say you are and add to that you are a calculating manipulative bastard, so just," I pause not knowing what to say, words fail me so I finish with, "just fuck off, okay." I am so immediately angry, angry with myself for lowering myself to his level with foul language and angry with his casual remark about what happened between us. I thought we had moved on, but he has just confirmed what I knew deep down, at some point in the future Phil would have not been able to resist teasing me about our encounter either privately or publicly he would have made reference to it thinking he had the upper hand.

"Hey, hey okay," Phil puts his hand up in surrender, the old Phil has returned. "I was only joking, okay sorry not funny, thank you for asking, the lucky lady," he smirks, "was Jo, yes I know, don't give me a hard time, I know how you feel about her, but I don't care, she was available, I was available, she wanted it, so did I. We are both grown-ups here, Angie, she knows the score, for her it is just sex, I know that, I give her what she doesn't get at home, it's just two bodies meeting, it is only you that seems to have a problem with it."

He smiles but it doesn't meet his eyes, I shake my head, "I don't have a problem at all, Phil, it is your business, but do you really think you two will ever have something more than sex, in fact, do you ever think you could have a relationship with anyone that ever gets past the bedroom?" Then because he is smiling that stupid smirk I add spitefully, "Or the office or the car park of some sleazy curry house, well anywhere really suits you doesn't it, Phil?" I ask him, I cannot keep the disgust out of my voice, but he cuts me dead.

"Or caravan, don't forget caravan, Angie."

I am lost for words, there is a silent pause between us before I speak again, "And that is exactly why I had to tell Mike, Phil, because of your big mouth, you could never have kept it to yourself, always thinking you had the upper hand, the silent joke that only you and I would understand, I mean look at you now, take a good hard look at yourself, Phil, do you think Jo would leave Julian to be with you?" I question, "because you know what, Phil, I don't think she would, in fact I know she wouldn't, she is playing you both for fools and you think you are the winner, all the time you are with her you will never have the decent, committed and exclusive relationship that I know that deep down you want, whether you admit it or not," I am exhausted, my breathing is hard, I stop and look at him, I am almost panting for breath, he hasn't moved, still sat in the passenger seat, whilst I am stood outside holding the door open, I shake my head at him. "How the hell do you think Helen feels, or Julian for that matter?" I ask him. He shakes his head, the smile has totally gone from his face, I take a quick look at my watch, I have a bit more time but I am aware we can be seen, I have to think of Mike's feelings, me sitting in a car with Phil in sight of everyone is not good, especially in light of what we have just been through.

"You know what, Phil, do what the hell you want, you always do," I say reaching for my handbag, "but you put it to the test, I think you will find I am right."

I shut the car door harder than I intend to, and I stand and watch as Phil opens the passenger door and gets out too, we walk without speaking to the parade room, he is just a few feet behind me. As I reach to open the door Phil pushes his hand up holding the door closed. "You are wrong," he says facing me, "I would never have betrayed our secret, I would have taken it to the grave." I look at him, he holds my chin up with the crook of his finger, his voice is barely more than a whisper. "That night in the caravan was the first time I have ever totally connected with anyone emotionally and physically in my life and I will never forget how beautiful you looked, how amazing your body felt, but I will also always remember it was the night I betrayed you, my best friend, and I will never forget that either, for me it was the best and worst night of my life, worse than watching you get married."

He pulls the door open and I walk ahead of him, he calls my name and I look back at him he speaks quietly, "No one needs to know that part, Angie, and I mean no one." I nod my head, I walk to the end of the parade room. Mike is there with another officer, I know he has seen us in the car, he must have heard the shouting, Phil strides off towards the other end of the office he doesn't acknowledge Mike at all. As I watch his departing back my heart sinks as I see Simon walking towards me.

"Oh dear, fight with lover boy eh, what happened, did you burn his breakfast, or was the bed not warmed enough," he looks at me and laughs, "don't worry," he continues, "I am sure there is someone around here who can make him feel better," he throws back his head and laughs at his own joke, I shake my head at him, aware that Mike has heard every word, I walk towards Simon, he is now sat at his desk.

"Grow up, Simon," I whisper to him, "just fucking grow up." I don't give him a chance to respond, I glance back at Mike, he briefly looks up from the paperwork he is holding, he gives me a weak smile, but it is still a smile. As I walk out of the door I pause and look back again, Mike is still watching me; I silently blow him a kiss. This time his face lights up and his smile is real and genuine as he shakes his head then looks back at his paperwork grinning to himself.

I am walking up the stairs when my mobile bleeps it is from Mike: "Hope all is sorted now, certainly seemed that way, see you later," it reads, "I bought your favourite wine, looking forward to opening it with you" he adds kisses. A warm feeling shoots all through my body, I cannot help it, I smile. In the last ten minutes I have gone through so many emotions, I feel dizzy and exhausted from it all, I cannot resist sending him a text back, "explain everything later and I want those kisses soon." I walk into the control room.

"Someone looks happy," Craig greets me and I cannot help it I go up to him I give him a hug.

"Yes," I reply, "I am very happy, in fact couldn't be happier, so happy I am going to make everyone a cup of tea." I smile as I listen to the cheeky comments they all call back at me.

I am in great mood, the incident between Phil and I had to happen, I know that, the air had to be cleared and although the location was not great at least we have both said what we needed to say, and maybe a few things that shouldn't have been said but it is over now and I feel much calmer. As I sit looking through the logs, I play Phil's words over in my head, I know he meant what he said but I don't feel anything towards him, he is a friend, that is all he can ever be. I pull my headset on and sit down, I don't even mind that there is a lot going on and it is quite busy but I soon get my head down with the rest of the group and within a short while everything is looking organised and controlled. Helen pops in to see me, I am busy but she sits and waits, she sits close by me, I know she has something on her mind, but the call goes on and on, I look up, Mike comes into the control room, he frowns, he looks over at us both, even though I smile at him I can tell he does not look happy, he puts the duty sheets in the tray then he comes over to us, he speaks quietly to Helen but as I have a headset on I don't hear what he says but she immediately gets up. Without saying a word or looking back she leaves, I am still in the middle of a call so I cannot say anything but I do look at him, I give a frown, something has clearly upset her and I am not sure what, I am very confused. He smiles at me then goes to sit with Craig, they are discussing the events coming up in the next few weeks, I can hear them in a friendly argument over who to send, their voices get louder as they argue, but Craig clearly wins and Mike laughs out loud. I hear the control room door open, it slams against the wood, Phil storms into the control room for the second time today his face is red with anger, luckily this time it is not directed at me, I am waiting for my caller to go and get some information for me, all I can do is sit and watch, I look around the control room, there is silence, everyone is just watching. Phil is obviously another one who is not happy, he practically storms up to Mike, his hands are on his hips, he leans over and speaks to him, pointing his finger aggressively. Mike says something I cannot hear then pushes his chair back and stands quickly, they both walk swiftly to the exit, the door slams again in the admin office and we can all hear raised voices next door in the admin room. I come off the phone, we all sit and listen at the argument between them, we hear another door close loudly and within a few minutes Mike walks back in he says nothing, he sits back down, he chats quietly with Craig, they then both stand and move to the farthest part of the control room and continue talking quietly. Mike has his back to us all, the mood has changed, I can tell he is definitely not happy, my silent mobile phone flashes indicating a message, it is Helen she is in the ladies bathroom she is asking me if I can go to her. I tell Steve quietly where I am going and get up to leave, as I walk down the corridor I hear footsteps behind me, I look back, it is Mike.

"So?" he asks flatly "has he called you to go and see him?"

I shake my head, "I don't know what you are talking about, Mike, honestly I don't – I am off to see someone else," I explain, I watch as he frowns so I pull my phone out of my pocket to show him the text from Helen.

He reads it quickly and then sighs, handing it back to me he says, "They are like bloody children the both of them," he pauses, "well, I cannot tell you not to get involved as clearly she has asked to see you, but I can warn you, I would rather she did not involve you, it is not going to be pleasant, see you later okay," he rolls his eyes back and I smile at him and he smiles back. He looks tired. "You okay?"

I touch his arm, "Yes, I am ok, just tired that's all, but I am okay, what about you?"

I smile and nod my head, he looks at me, "Even after this morning?" he questions, we walk down the corridor.

"Yes, even after this morning. Phil was very angry, but then so was I, we both said some things that needed to be said," I pause, "and also some things that didn't need to be said, but the air is a bit clearer between us," I look at Mike, I lower my voice, "I thought at one point he was going to hit me, seriously I did."

Mike stops by the door, "Yes, I must admit I did keep one eye on the situation, but I know Phil, he would never do that, Phil is many things to many people but he would never physically hurt anyone, and certainly not you, he is not in a good place at the moment, there are a few of us like that," he touches my shoulder as I turn to walk in the opposite direction. "Hey," he calls out, I look back at him, "that doesn't include me and you though okay" he winks at me, a grin on his face, I smile back. That man is so gorgeous.

I push open the door to the ladies changing room, I can hear sobbing even before I see her, I rush over and squat down to speak to her, she is sat on the wooden bench, her make-up is streamed down her face.

"He is a real bastard," she sobs.

I pull her hair back and lift her face up, I agree with her, "I know, I know he is, tell me what he has done, tell me what happened." I pass her a tissue and she blows her nose noisily, I pass her a drink of water, she drinks it in one gulp. "He is a real bastard, just because his heart is stone cold and no one will ever love him, he treats everyone the same, so devoid of emotion, I hate him, he is a pompous ass."

"I know, I know," I am still agreeing with her.

I cannot believe Phil has upset her so badly, I have to know what it is he has done, but I struggle to find the words, but I don't need to she continues without me prompting her, "He has put me and Phil together on patrol and he knows we have had a falling out, and all over that stupid bitch Jo, Phil cannot or will not leave her alone," she looks at me, "he cannot say no to her, I don't know why."

I don't know what to say, I am not sure who she is talking about, I just stand looking at her, the tears spilling down her cheeks as she speaks. "Can you believe she snuck out after she had gone to bed with Julian. Phil had been at mine," she sniffs, "I thought he might stay but he didn't, we watched a film then had a take-away," she pauses, dabbing her nose with the tissue. "We had a really lovely evening then he goes off home, I found out she snuck out and went to Phil's, what a total bitch, and he is being such a cocky bastard, he spent the evening with me then went to bed with her. We had words this morning, I told him what I thought of him, he didn't even bother to deny it, he thought it was quite funny," she sniffs again, "now I have to face him at work, so when I come in, I asked to speak to Mike privately, he could tell I was upset, I asked him to swap me with someone else, so I didn't have to put up with Phil's crap all day, but he refused, he asked me why and I told him, I wish I hadn't now, but I thought he would be supportive, he was anything but, he was quite nasty really, he said that if we cannot control ourselves at work then we shouldn't engage in personal relationships at work, he prattled on about being committed whilst on duty, honestly, Angie he was quite nasty about it he is not normally like that." She blows her nose on the tissue then continues, "Now we have a sudden death to attend and I am going to be sat in a room with Phil and a bloody dead body for god knows how long before the doctor and undertaker gets there, we are not even speaking, all because I thought we were kind of going out, you know as in, exclusive, just the two of us, then I find out I got it totally wrong, he is still shagging that little tramp Jo," she looks at me. "You know what, the thing I don't understand is that we had a great night, a real laugh, you know we kissed and that and then he tried it on but I pushed him away, but I thought he was okay, he said he understood it was too soon for me to be jumping into

449

bed with him," she shakes her head, "I mean for Christ's sake, Angie, I cannot believe it, it is just so unfair of Mike, he is being a real bastard," she sniffs again she blows her nose.

She goes to the mirror, cleans up her face a bit, I just stand and watch her. I don't know what to say, I mean I can kind of see both sides, she has a job to do she is expected to be professional but we all have our fall outs with people – maybe Mike could have been a bit more tolerant, but I don't know what I can do, Mike has said he would prefer me not to be involved, but unfortunately I am. There is a tap at the door Helen immediately stands up and goes into the adjoining locker room as I go and open the door, Mike is stood there, well it is not my Mike, his face tells me he is very much in work mode and he is not amused, I can see by the expression on his face.

"Is she in there?" he asks curtly, I nod and he walks in, Helen is now stood over by the sinks, Mike approaches her, he doesn't look at me, but I can see both of their reflections in the mirror, he speaks in a very clipped and controlled manner, his voice is low, "I have asked you to attend a job that has now been waiting fifteen minutes, if you are not sick then I suggest you get your act together and get yourself out to the car park where PC Foster is waiting for you, are you sick WPC Judd?" his voice stays very calm, Helen looks at him and shakes her head, Mike clicks his radio on and calls Phil's collar number, when he responds he advises Phil that WPC Judd will be down shortly and he is to wait for her, he adds that on no account is he to leave without her, he looks at Helen coldly then at me and walks out.

Helen picks up her bag, she grabs another tissue, "See what I mean," she says "Coldhearted bastard."

She gives me a hug then moves towards the door. I go up to the control room as I walk past one of the empty offices I am pulled in very quickly by my hand. I cannot help it I shriek out loud.

"Ssshhhh," Mike whispers, and the next second he is kissing me very passionately on the lips, his wonderful musky aftershave makes me go weak at the knees, his tongue meeting with mine, he runs his hands up my back, then to my breasts, he holds me close against him, pressing our bodies together, then almost as quickly he lets me go. "Mmm, you said you wanted those kisses and soon, and I so needed that, see you later," he whispers and strides off down the corridor. I watch his departing back and cannot help smiling, I take my mobile out of my pocket and send him a quick text, saying "Good job I didn't say I wanted you to make love to me" and several exclamation marks. My body is wanting him so much, my lips bruised by his, I adjust my uniform and I almost skip back to the control room and when I sit back down I check the logs, there is a sudden death and I can see that both Phil and Helen are both booked as arriving. Craig comes over and asks where I have been, he sits on the desk beside me as I explain quickly to him keeping my voice quiet, stupidly I think Craig is going to be supportive of Helen and Phil but he so isn't.

"We are paid to do a job, those two really push it as far as I am concerned," he says firmly. "Mike is making sure that whatever happens in their private lives, stays that way, they won't get the better of him, I know the way he works, he is very strict like that, when they are at work they should make sure they are totally professional, it is the only way to behave, and I wish they wouldn't involve you," he speaks gravely and shakes his head, he stands up and walks back to his desk, I nod in agreement yes I think to myself, two minutes ago Mike was being very professional with me, dragging me into an empty room, my cheeks blush as I think of his soft lips on mine. I check the logs over the next few hours and Mike continually puts Helen and Phil together. I would smile if it wasn't so tragic.

Chapter Sixty-One

I finish on time and head for home, I let myself in and start to prepare my evening meal, Mike is playing rugby then going straight to the gym for a sauna, he says he may be coming round later, depends how tired he is, I really want him to but I don't want to be needy. I change into sweatpants, oversized tracksuit top with big fluffy socks, I flick through all my scheduled saved favourite programmes then settle to watch with my food on my lap, my text message bleeps and it is Helen asking if she can call me. I finish my meal then text back and within seconds my phone rings, at first she is really cross about having to sit for two hours with a dead body, and to make matters worse Mike had turned up to sign the paperwork and had asked them both lots of questions to make sure their pocket notebooks matched, she was so annoyed, how dare he challenge them like they were rookies she seethes, I don't get a word in as she rants on about the fact they were sent immediately afterwards to make enquiries for Mike on a burglary which Mike should have done himself, and again Phil virtually ignored her, they went to a domestic where the wife had found her husband had been cheating, she had destroyed all his clothes by setting fire to them and when we arrived the fire brigade was hosing down the heap of suits and shirts that were piled in the garden, he wanted her arrested for malicious damage, there was a huge row which turned into a fight, both had to be separated. Helen goes on to explain that once the fire brigade had left that she had sat in the kitchen with the wife whilst Phil spoke to the husband, between them they had managed to sort the situation out but Phil was with the man for ages and they had both had to work on late, Mike has told us it is not paid overtime she grumbled. She goes quiet for a while.

"Sorry, Angie, I didn't mean to spout off at you, but I have never seen Mike behave like this, it seems we have really pushed him to his limit, he seems really cross with us all the time, it seems he doesn't even like us anymore. The atmosphere is terrible and it is all our fault, I feel really awful and I know Phil is not happy about how we have behaved, I guess we need to give it time and hope he trusts us again, what do you think?" I don't get a chance to answer as my doorbell rings making me jump, I am not expecting anyone so I peer out of the curtains it is Stuart, my brother Stuart stood on my doorstep, I let out a yelp, I tell Helen I have to go and we will catch up soon. I rush to open the door throwing myself into his arms, he would be the last person I would expect at my door, so I drag him and his flight bag through the door excitedly. We go to the kitchen to make drinks.

"Can I crash here for a few days?" he asks.

I reply immediately nodding my head, "Yes, of course that will be fabulous." I put the kettle on, make us coffee, then we take our mugs through into the lounge I sit and face him. "So what is with the surprise visit?" I ask, he sinks back into his chair, he lets out a large groan and rubs his face with his hands.

"Oh, Angie, I am knackered, can I first grab a shower then relax and have a beer, then we will catch up properly okay."

He stands up, even though his coffee must be scalding hot, he drinks it down, puts his cup on the floor, grabs his bag then disappears upstairs. I take the cups to the kitchen, I am so pleased to see Stuart, I pop down to the garage to check on my beer supply, as I suspected there is nothing there so I grab my trainers, fetch my purse and start off on the short walk to the local shop. It is only on my return as I am putting my key in the lock that I realise that the garage light is on, that must mean that Mike is here, he obviously changed his mind and he would have parked his car in my garage as we had planned. I walk quickly in, then when I hear raised voices I run up the stairs two at a time. Mike is stood in his gym stuff just a few feet from Stuart who is just stood soaking wet with just a towel around his waist. As I walk in, both look round at the same time I look at their faces I cannot help it, I burst out laughing.

Breathlessly I manage to speak, "Stuart, I had hoped you would get to meet him, and I know the timing is not great, but I would like to introduce you to Mike," I turn to face Mike. "Mike, this is my older brother who lives in Dubai, this is Stuart, I had no idea he was visiting, he knows all about you," Mike laughs, I think it is with relief he puts his hand out to shake Stuarts. The towel drops and Stuart grabs it unsuccessfully, it hits the carpet leaving Stuart stood naked for just a second, I shriek out loud and turn quickly away, both Mike and Stuart laugh.

"Nice to see you, mate," Stuart replies.

"Nice to see you too," Mike laughs back, "although to see less of you would be nice too." Mike shakes his head and turns to the door. I shake my head at both of them before speaking to Stuart who now has covered himself.

"I got you some beers, bro, I will see you downstairs."

I follow Mike as we both walk downstairs, I walk into the kitchen, he stops in the lounge then follows me, he takes me in his arms he pulls me close, "Please don't give me a hard time," he says.

I push him away gently and look at him, "Why should I give you a hard time?" I question, Mike walks away to the window he runs his hand through his hair, looking out before he speaks. "Because I have to be honest, I came in, I could hear a man whistling, the shower was going I automatically and very wrongly assumed it was Phil – I don't even know why I thought it was him, I was stupid, I just saw red, I went up to confront him to ask what the bloody hell he was playing at, but now I realise what a bloody fool I am," he turns to face me, "I apologise, Angie, I am so sorry, I am such an idiot, " he stands looking at me.

I don't know what to do, or to say, so I walk to the fridge with the beers I store them on the shelf, taking my time, just thinking, I wipe the side and just stand there, Mike comes towards me, "I know what you are thinking and you are wrong," he covers the short distance he puts his hands on my shoulders, "Angie, please."

I turn to face him, "Please what?" I look into his face, his eyes are serious, "I am sorry okay", I shrug, I am not sure what to say or what to think, I am not upset, more disappointed, but I look up to him, his face is so serious, his face frowning, "Mike, why would you think I would allow Phil to shower at my house, even if he had the world's best reason to be showering here, he never has in the past, there is no reason for him to, he has no reason to come here, we have established that, Mike," my voice cracks, I don't want to cry, but I can feel the tears forming under my eyelids, I look at him, my voice comes out all croaky, "Mike, I cannot bear the thought of you not trusting me, but you don't do you, you don't trust me, after all that I have told you, I have told you everything about me, I have told you things I have never shared with anyone, but you still cannot trust me."

Mike puts his head on the top of my shoulder, he pulls me close to him, I can feel the warmth of his skin against mine, I see the hairs on his arms and I want to stay like this forever.

"Oh, Angie baby, I do so trust you so very much, I totally trust you," he places a kiss on my head, his face buried in my hair, "I have tried so hard to get the image of you and Phil together out of my head, but it is so bloody difficult, it is him I don't trust, I bloody hate him sometimes, really hate him for what he has done to us."

I hear Stuart's footsteps on the stairs, Mike and I pull apart. When Stuart walks into the kitchen, he looks at us both questioningly, but I smile brightly at him and reach for a glass, I plaster on a smile and pass him a beer from the fridge, Mike gets a bottle of water, and we all go back into the lounge.

Mike and Stuart hit it off immediately, they have a lot in common, Stuart used to play rugby and is interested in having a work out or going for a run whilst he is here, so Mike disappears into the kitchen to make a phone call so Stuart can use his gym membership for a few days, on his return.

Stuart looks at me, "Everything okay, Angie?" he asks, I nod my head.

"We will be, Stuart, just have to sort things out," he nods his head.

"No relationship is going to run smoothly, Angie, you have to accept that there are going to be some rocky times so you appreciate each other more," I look at him.

"What made you so wise, Stuart?"

He laughs, "Not wise, Angie, not wise at all," he takes a swig of his beer, "but Mike is a good bloke and obviously thinks the world of you, I did hear a bit of what you two were discussing and I heard Phil's name mentioned, my advice to you, Angie, is forget Phil, whatever you think of him and your relationship, you deserve better, so don't blow it, sis, don't blow it." I nod my head in agreement, I have nearly lost Mike once, I do not intend to let it happen again.

Stuart looks up as Mike comes in, he smiles, "So you never got to hear my sister's Scottish accent then?"

Mike frowns but I know immediately what he means I turn to Mike, "When I called you from Spain, Stuart was with me, it was his idea to call you, I tried to disguise my voice."

"Ah," Mike laughs, "right, no I never got to hear it myself, someone thought it was a male informer."

Stuart laughs, "Yes, my sister does tend to overcomplicate matters, especially those of the heart," he looks at me and winks.

Mike takes a swig of his water, he nods in agreement "She certainly does."

I stand up, I am not going to listen to them tease me, I walk out to the kitchen, I grab a few more beers from the fridge then return, handing one to each of them, I flick through the television channels and we settle down to watch a film. Mike sits next to me he continually touches me on my thigh and then my arm, just stroking gently, I have no idea what the film is about, I have missed half of it by thinking of Mike's words from earlier. The credits roll on the film, I look over to Stuart and he has fallen asleep, I reach over to nudge him to wake him up.

"Where is he staying tonight?" Mike asks.

"He is staying here," I reply without looking at him, I don't know why but I feel annoyed with him.

"Does that mean I should go home?" he says quietly, I am shaking Stuart's leg, but I turn my head to look at Mike.

"Do what you want to do, Mike, if you want to go home then go," I look at him, I cannot read his expression. "Do you want to go home?" I say very quietly.

And he replies just as quietly, "No."

My heart leaps just a little bit, Stuart wakes and we help him with the rest of his bags from his hire car and he goes into the larger of the spare rooms I hear him speaking on the phone, I shower, clean my teeth and pull my short nightdress over my head. When I come out Mike is in bed and he pulls the bedcovers back for me, I snuggle in against him and I wait, he makes no move to make love to me, I stroke his thigh, there is no response from him, I want to stroke his chest and lay my head in the crook of his arm but I turn and I look at him, he is laying on his back with his eyes closed but

I know he is not asleep, I let out a deep sigh then turn over and lay with my eyes closed, maybe he is just tired, but I was very troubled when he said he couldn't get the image of me and Phil out of his head. Eventually I fall asleep.

Chapter Sixty-Two

The alarm goes off at five a.m. I reach out to switch it off, Mike is already up I know he has to go home to get fresh uniform before he can go to work, but I was hoping for at least a quick cuddle, I give out a huge sigh as I pull my dressing gown on and sneak past Stuart's room so I don't wake him. I am surprised to see that Mike is sat at the dining room table reading yesterday's paper and listening to the television, he still has his sports clothes on, he has his back to the television so I know he isn't watching it, "Morning," he smiles as I walk towards him I go to pass he grabs my waist, he pulls my housecoat open, pushes up my short nightdress and he kisses my bare stomach.

"Mike, no," I push him away, "Stuart might come down."

Mike doesn't stop, his tongue teasing my navel, "Stuart got up and went to the gym half an hour ago," he laughs he pulls my hand and guides me down on to the kitchen floor. "Although I was too tired to make love to you last night, I have just enough time to prove to you that this is the best way to start the day, especially as this is our three month anniversary." I smile at him, three months of being with this wonderful man, suddenly all of my worries about Mike having the image of Phil and I in his head disappears, as he kisses the tops of my thighs he reaches his hands up to my breasts, within minutes he has me begging him to slow down, to stop, but his tongue is making my whole body flutter with longing, I need him so much, I pull his head up to meet mine, wrapping my legs around his waist I guide him to me, I surrender to his wonderful lovemaking.

Afterwards we lay on the kitchen floor. I kiss his chest I run my hands up and down his torso. Mike pulls me up so I am facing him, he kisses my face then my lips then he looks me in the eyes, "Tell me honestly, did you remember it was our anniversary today, three months since the party?"

I shake my head, "No I didn't," I reply honestly, "I am truly rubbish at dates and things, but I am glad you did," then as his kisses get more passionate, I can feel his hardness as he holds me close to him, I have to push him away, "you have to go home and get fresh uniform and I have to go to work," I remind him.

"Oh bloody hell yes," he responds and immediately sits up, the kitchen floor is uncomfortable, I stand and reach into the small drawer in the kitchen.

Mike turns to face me, I hold out my clenched hand, "What it is?" he frowns, he looks at my hand.

"Call it an anniversary gift," I say with a smile, he slowly turns my hand over and opens my fingers, there on my palm is two keys, Mike looks at me quizzically.

"What is this?" he asks.

"The keys to my house," I reply, my voice is shaking with nerves, "I thought maybe you might like a set," I smile at him he holds them in his hand, he pauses, it seems like the pause is forever.

"Thank," the pause again, "that is great, might be useful if I need to let myself in and you are not here," he pauses, a long pause, far too long I didn't know what I expected but the silence is horrible. I want him to show some emotion, some pleasure in what the gift means, but there is nothing, we have gone from intimate lovemaking to awkwardness in just a few minutes, he is just looking at the keys in the palm of his hand frowning at them, I feel very childlike I want to run away, I don't know what I have done, is it too soon? He looks at me, then back at his hand uncertainly before repeating, "Thanks, honey, that is great," he kisses my nose, my nose, not my lips but my nose, it seems like everything is happening in slow motion, I don't think he understands what I am trying to say.

"Mike," I look at him and my voice comes out all strangled, I don't know why I am so nervous, I clear my throat, "Mike, what if you didn't have to go home for uniform?" I look at him, my heart is pounding, but I continue, "what if you had all of your uniform here."

Mike looks at me, "I don't understand, what?" he hesitates, he frowns, he sounds confused, I am now sure he doesn't realise what I am trying to say and to be honest I am not making a great job of it.

I take a deep breath, my heart is pounding in my chest. "What if, you kept all of your clothes here," I look at him through my eyelashes, I cannot meet his gaze, my head is buzzing, with the words over and over again, is it too soon, am I making a huge mistake, but I look at his face he smiles, his whole face lights up.

"You mean," he moves towards me and nuzzles his lips into my neck, "that you want me to move in here?" he asks, he adds, "both of us, together?" I just nod my head as I cannot answer because his lips meet mine and we sink back on to the kitchen floor. I think he has just said yes. And we are definitely going to be late for work.

Thankfully I am not late, just in time, as I drive into work I cannot help but think about my gift to Mike, I have an argument with myself – what if it is too soon, what will people think, what will Phil think, should I tell him today, then another thought crosses my mind, oh god, my parents, they will have kittens, I have been going out with him for just twelve weeks, and I have asked him to move in, I know I want him next to me every day, I know in my heart he is the one, since his proposal it is the natural next step but oh no, my mum will die on the spot, I can hear her sermon already, about how Judy lost everything and how I am being irrational, too hasty, how it will end in tears, I can hear her voice droning on and on, I shake my head to rid the words, I park the car, I glance at the clock, I have just a few minutes to spare, I race across the car park and up the stairs arriving breathless but on time. As I walk into the control room Steve tells me and everyone else straight away that Mike is going to be delayed, he has called in and he will be an hour or so late, he didn't give any explanation he adds but I cannot help but smile to myself, he is obviously very keen. Craig has gone down to allocate the shifts jobs for the morning, when I look at the allocated jobs, I am not sure if it is deliberate but Craig has put Phil and Helen together all day again.

It is quiet in the control room thankfully, although I know it will be very busy later, I am only sat down for a few minutes when Steve brings my tea over to me, "How are things going then?" he asks perching on my desk, "you look bloody glowing, so someone is obviously making you happy, is it our favourite boy in blue?"

I smile at him, "Might be," I grin but push him away.

"Gad to hear it," he says, his face changes he is serious, "maybe it is not my place to mention it, and I don't want to upset you, but it must be coming up to the anniversary of Jason's death mustn't it," he pauses, "do they do anything to mark the anniversaries in Jewish religion?" he asks, I automatically smile, nod, then shake my head.

My heart stops for a beat, the smile freezes on my face, bloody hell, yes it is, I check the date, I then double check. I cannot believe how self-absorbed I am in two days' time it will be a year since he died, my face must register upset as Steve puts his arm around me, "The first year is always the worst, honey, always the worst."

I smile at him, a weak smile, I have been so totally absorbed in my own life, my own happiness that I have totally forgotten, Oh my god and I have asked Mike to move in, oh no, I cannot believe it, the timing is terrible, what if Little Ma and Pa come round and Mike is there, I feel sick to my stomach, I am so cross with myself, what will people think of me, they will think I am such a thoughtless bitch, and I am. I quickly send Sean a text asking him if he has any plans, if not can we meet for something to eat tonight, within minutes he responds, yes pick me up tonight at seven, we will catch a bite to eat, go out and catch up properly he replies, I want him to know that I have remembered the anniversary so I send a reply confirming the time and ask him if there are plans to mark the anniversary in any way, he sends a quick one back saying he is useless he had totally forgot, he adds a few kisses, thanking me for reminding him, he says we will discuss tonight. I heave a sigh of relief, I look over to Steve, that man is my saviour and he doesn't even know it. I know I need to include Phil somehow but I am not sure how,

459

so I do nothing I will wait until I speak to Sean later. He will know what to do.

As predicted the shift gets busier as the day goes on, which I am pleased about there are a lot of new uniformed officers starting, they have all been on the initial training and now they are being shown around, they all look so fresh faced and keen, and although I don't get to actually have a long chat with them they are all nice and friendly, we don't have time to chat as the calls and radios are really busy, there is a huge gala day with an open-air concert planned later in the town so all resources are being stretched to the limit. I still manage to negotiate with Craig popping out for a short while, I need to pop and collect a retirement gift for one of the ladies in the offices, the traffic is really busy, when I get back to the station there is a woman struggling to park her vehicle, I sit there unable to get past her, feeling very frustrated at the time wasting, I look up and see Mike stood outside leaning against the wall, his arm up supporting him, he has on his short sleeve shirt that I ironed for him last week, it makes me smile, then I look as the woman he is speaking to reaches up and strokes his cheek, it is so intimate, my stomach turns, I watch as she stretches up and kisses him on his cheek, first one side then the other, she is slender and has long jet black hair piled up on her head, I cannot see her face, whatever she is saying is making Mike laugh, I watch as he throws back his head and laughs out loud, she laughs too, he has no idea that I am sat watching him. I clench my fists, I feel all hot with jealous rage, I don't know who she is but she is too tactile with him, and he is putting up no objection, she is obviously very entertaining, his face is lit up with laughter and I hate it, I really hate it, I haven't heard from him all morning and the first thing I see is him being intimate with someone else, my heart beats hard in my chest. Eventually the car in front manoeuvres into a space, I stare at Mike, just this morning we were making love and making plans and now I am watching him with another woman, my heart pounds hard in my chest, then he looks up, I am just about to turn in my space and he waves at me, she looks over and smiles, and I don't know what to do, I cannot ignore him, I give out a huge sigh, I park the car and get out, I grab my bag and head for the door, he looks at me as I walk towards them I give him a tight-lipped smile, but I have to pass them both. As I get closer he moves away from the wall immediately he pulls me to him and with a smile he introduces me to the woman but before he can say her name I know who it is.

"Carrie, this is Angie," he announces, I look around quickly, not sure if anyone has seen this open display of affection.

I smile at her, "Nice to meet you," I say graciously.

She smiles, "Mike has told me all about you, I came over here for my friend's wedding, thought I would just pop and say hello to Mike, it is nice to meet you."

I nod my head, she is so friendly, and so very beautiful, I would like to stay and talk a while but I really have to go, I look at my watch, "Sorry I have to be going, I just popped out, but it is lovely to meet you," she is looking back up at Mike and smiling, I feel so angry with her, I don't know why, just the thought she has been intimate with him, I am not sure how I keep calm, but I somehow do, I look at her and smile back, she leans forwards and kisses me on both cheeks before turning back to Mike. I make my way back upstairs, glancing out of the window I see she has walked back to her car and Mike has obviously come back in too, I race up the stairs and settle back into work. Helen comes up to the control room, she is not in a great mood, she has to spend the day with Phil, things between them have not improved, it seems to be affecting the shift as we hear other officers mumbling about them both, it is just one of those horrible days for us in the control room and Helen is feeling it too, so far all the jobs her and Phil has been given have been a nightmare with lots of paperwork, she has been sent out on enquiries for Mike again which she is seething about and to make matters worse the new girl on their shift has been put in the car with them, she swears Mike has done it deliberately. I try to point out to her that Mike didn't come in until late this morning but it falls on deaf ears. The new girl, in Helens words is a man eater, she wears too much make-up, even though Helen has told her to tone it down, she speaks like a little girl, has an irritating laugh and has no time at all for women or her fellow female colleagues, I look at Helen and laugh.

"You like her then?" I ask.

Helen shakes her head, "As if I don't have enough to put up with already." I smile I am surprised as Helen is usually really supportive of all new arrivals so I know this one must have started off on the wrong foot and annoyed her big style, so far all I know is her name is Amanda.

Helen is just about to tell me more about her when I see this young girl stride confidently into the room, she is tall, well as tall as Helen, she has blonde hair worn loose which is unusual for a police officer due to the nature of the job, she is very slender, her new uniform blouse is worn quite tight showing off her curves, she would be quite pretty but she is a little over made up for the daytime, I have to do a double take as I think she is wearing false eyelashes, if she is she will definitely be told to remove them and the make-up is definitely too much, she will probably be told by someone more senior to remove some, her whole attitude seems to scream look at me.

She looks around then comes over to where Helen is sat next to me, "Hi," she breezes looking me up and down, "I am Amanda," she puts her hand out in a handshake.

I put mine out to meet it, I smile at her as I reply, "Hi, I am Angie, nice to meet you," but her attention has gone, she looks over to Steve and Gavin, without giving me a backward glance she breezes over to them with the same confident air, I watch her as she sits on the desk next to Gavin, throwing back her blonde hair she leans in to speak to him, I have to admire her confidence, but she has got it so wrong with Gavin, who is happily married to Tony, although he never discusses his private life, it is only a handful of people that know he is gay, and to look at him you would never ever know it, there is nothing effeminate about our Gavin, she has totally got him wrong. I watch her as she strokes his arm playfully, he raises his eyebrows at her, then turns to answer a call shrugging her hand from his arm.

"Lovely isn't she?" Helen says through gritted teeth, I try to disguise my smile, Helen is not in a good place, I try to sound friendly.

"She is okay, give her a chance I am sure once she has calmed down she will be fine."

I look at Helen, she pulls a face, "Really, you think so, you haven't seen her in action, three days she has been in service, two days as an onlooker in admin and today, already she has put herself around a bit," she lowers her voice, "seriously she has already been on a date with Simon, last night apparently," she whispers, "he was crowing about it this morning, she seems to be a sure thing, a bit like Jo," she raises her eyebrows, "like we need another one of those, like I said I have already had a word with her about her excess make-up, and the false eyelashes I have advised her to wear her hair up, but hey who am I, she has totally ignored me, Mike will not be pleased, I just know he won't beat around the bush, he will tell her straight," she adds confidently.

I smile at her, but she doesn't smile back I lean forward speaking quietly, "Hey you know what it is like, first few days, all exciting, I am sure she will calm down when she realises that coppers are just like any other blokes without the uniform on, just give her time."

Helen shakes her head, "No she won't, I know her type, but she isn't interested in just the common old coppers. Oh no, she was asking lots of questions this morning, you see she isn't as clever as she thinks, she obviously didn't listen at training school, she thought as Simon was in plain clothes he was something higher than a normal regular PC, she didn't realise a DC is a PC attached to CID so they just don't wear the uniform, so she lost interest in him quite quickly," she stops as the part-time person Mark goes past, she waits until he is too far to hear, "now it seems she has worked out the hierarchy and she has her sights set higher," Helen looks over to make sure we are not being overheard before she leans in and whispers, "it is Mike she is interested in, we all think it is hilarious, the way she fawns over him and he has no idea, you know what he is like, work is work and as for Mike, well you know what he is like, he is totally unaware of it," she fiddles with her hair putting on a baby voice, fluttering her eyelashes. "Yesterday she was all like, would you like a cup of tea, Mike, is it okay, is it too strong, Mike, then later, Mike, can you check my pocket book can you check this report to see if it is okay?" She stops and looks at me, "But you know what, in my opinion, he deserves it, he is completely oblivious, it is hilarious, and as he has been a complete git lately they deserve each other, after all, she fits the bill," I frown at her she shakes her head, "you know, he likes them trashy doesn't he, remember her?" she pauses "you know, remember the girl from his party – loads of make-up, tight clothes, impossibly high shoes, really full of herself, and her from the club, again trashy, dyed blonde hair big chest, " she adds spitefully.

I don't know what to say, I stare at her then hearing a squeal of laughter we both look over, Amanda is sat on the edge of Gavin's desk, she is twiddling her hair, exactly as Helen mimicked her, she is leaning forward, listening intently as he speaks, then she throws her head back, laughs a very silly girlie laugh. Gavin looks a bit bemused by it all; as she struts away he shakes his head. Helen raises her eyebrows, "Gotta go, duty calls," she follows Amanda then turns to me, "Hey," she calls to me, "you free for lunch today? Would be nice to catch up properly, not just you listening to me moaning, just in the restaurant here though as I am skint okay."

I smile, show her the thumbs up as I hit the button to take a call. When I finish the call I call to Gavin, "So what do you think then," he frowns, "of the new girl," I explain.

He laughs out loud, "Apparently she has earned the nickname Amanda the man eater, which I initially thought was quite cruel, however, having met her, I now think it is very apt and would be a good description of her, she is very," he pauses, "full on, don't you think?" I laugh, nodding my head in agreement.

Steve joins in, "You know who she would be good with," he pauses for just a second before he adds, "Phil," we all nod in agreement, "do you think there is enough room on their shift for two egos the size of theirs?" we all laugh, Gavin adds, "or a big enough mirror." I can actually imagine her and Phil clashing quite badly once he had got what he wanted from her, and I know Amanda and Jo are going to hate each other on sight. Oh dear, there is going to be eruptions, this should be fun to watch.

Craig is back within an hour or so we all work quietly, I check with him it is okay to also have a lunch, he gives me a hard time but I know he doesn't mean it, I don't often ask to pop out and it was work related so he is cool. Gavin and Craig are looking at a huge map on the wall when Mike walks in, Steve is on a call, the other two staff are sat over the other side of the room, Mike walks up to me, "All done?" I ask him, he looks a bit confused.

"What, is all done?" he asks.

"I thought you were moving your stuff, I thought that is why you were late."

Mike laughs out loud, attracting attention, everyone looks over, but he ignores them, he sits down on the chair next to mine.

"No, I was busy doing other stuff," he smiles, "you okay?" he asks.

"I wasn't but I am now," I whisper to him.

He frowns, "Why wasn't you okay then?"

I smile at him, "I saw you as I came in the car park, I didn't know who the woman was, and I didn't like what I saw."

He smiles, "And are you okay now?" I nod my head he stands up and whispers, "Times that feeling by ten, honey, and that was my world before you were mine," he winks at me.

A call comes in, I have to take it, I stroke his hand as I listen to the caller. Mike has lovely long fingers with a smattering of hair on the back, I love his hands, his beautifully cut nails, I could hold his hands all day, but I need to type so I squeeze his hand and then move my hand away to the keyboard, I spend a few minutes speaking to the caller, creating a new job log, I watch as Mike wanders over to Craig and Gavin, I look at the back of his head, his beautiful solid shoulders, a tremor runs through my body as I remember our lovemaking earlier, how could I ever doubt him, I watch them all over the other side of the room, they are all stood discussing the upcoming event and the resources needed, we will be off shift by then so I will not be involved. The control room door opens, I look up, and watch as Amanda comes in, she has so much confidence for such a young new recruit, too much really, she will need to be careful she doesn't alienate people as she ignores everyone else, tossing her hair back she almost swaggers straight up to Mike. As she waits for him to finish speaking she puts her hand on his arm, he turns around to face her, she pulls him away gently. For the second time today a pang of jealousy shoots through me as I watch them from across the room, he has to lean down to her to hear what she is saying, her head is close to his, whatever she says he is not happy, I can see by his face, I catch a small bit of the conversation she says, "I don't like to say anything but I feel you need to know what is going on, Mike," I look at her, I don't like it that she still has her hand on his arm.

I don't like it at all, I feel a second wave of jealousy run through me, in that split second I fully understand what Mike feels when he sees me with either Phil or Sean. I felt the same this morning and am feeling the same now, I feel a sickening in my stomach, I have to look away I cannot watch them together.

Mike walks as if to leave the control room with her, but he stops, he comes over to me, she waits but he turns towards her, in a few short words he instructs her to go downstairs he will be there shortly, I do not imagine it, she shoots me a really dirty look, and I know what that dirty look means, it is true what Helen said about her, Amanda likes him, she likes him a lot and I know her sort she will do what she can to get him, I watch as she throws back her hair and flounces off.

Mike leans over to me, "You ok?" I question, frowning.

He replies straight away, "Yes, I am," he says but his face is set, I can see he is not okay, he seems to be very cross, "but when I get downstairs there are going to be a few that are not going to be okay, not okay at all, I am sick of babysitting children and there will be some heads rolling, I can tell you," I pull a grimacing face at him he walks away then walks back he lowers his voice, "hey, just wanted to check, don't suppose you are free for lunch?"

I shake my head, "Sorry, I have already said I will meet Helen."

He nods his head, "Okay, no problem, just thought we might pop home for lunch, you know... round two maybe." I blush deep red, he raises his eyebrows and laughs gently before adding, "So my guess would be it is roast lamb today then is it?" he smiles, as I nod, he knows me so well, "see you tonight then."

I can see Steve watching us, so I stand up, I tug Mike by the cuff of his jumper, "Come with me," I walk to the admin room where we cannot be heard, I tell him about me forgetting the anniversary, then I tell him about my arrangement to meet Sean this evening. "Do you think I should include Phil?" I ask.

He looks at me, he holds my shoulders, "Ask Sean, he will be the best to advise you, if he thinks Phil should be there, and wants him there then you invite him but if he says no, there is your answer, but you know, if he says yes," he pauses, "I really won't have a problem with it, I appreciate that Jason was not just a part of your life but also a part of Phil's too, I promise you I am cool with that," he pauses, "listen," he looks at his watch, " I really have to go before they kill each other down there, speak to you later okay," he kisses my lips gently before disappearing out of the room.

I return to the control room, Craig is on a call, when he finishes he stands up, "For the next half hour to an hour let me know of any urgent calls, Mike is tied up with something, I think it is serious as he has asked not to be disturbed, no radio, mobile or tannoys please, run anything by me first please," he sits back down and looks back at his screen, Steve looks at me and I shrug, I look at the screen, Craig has put both Helen and Phil as unavailable for jobs, I look up at him but before I can speak he calls out again, "oh and there are some officers I have put as unavailable, please leave them at that status." I have no idea what is going on, I look at Max but he just pulls a face, Craig would normally tell us so it must be serious, I am soon to find out.

I meet Helen for lunch in the restaurant, she really is not happy, I can see by her face she is ready to explode, we find a quiet table and eat our meals as she explains that Mike has read both her and Phil the riot act, she looks me straight in the face, "Honestly, I have never seen him so cross," she explains, "I know things between me and Phil are not great, in fact that is an understatement, things are really bad, we basically just ignore each other as much as we can. Anyway, we went out on a job earlier together and we were okay, okay not chatty and we were both silent in the car but I don't have to make small talk with him that is not my job, anyway I didn't think it was that noticeable, well he dropped me off at the leisure centre as I had to take a statement there and he had some other stuff to do, then when I came back here I could tell that Mike was not happy, I put my stuff away, and was completing my pocket book when he asked me to join him in the office, I was with him on my own, he asked me to sit and wait then he went off and came back a short while later, I was really shocked when he brought Phil in, he told us to switch our radios off and then he said that the conversation we were about to have was between just the three of us but if any of us wanted to stop the meeting and make it formal he was happy to do that, I had no idea what he was talking about but then he explained that Amanda had complained to him that the atmosphere in the car first thing this morning was making her uncomfortable. Apparently she has asked to be transferred to another shift, two days she has been on shift, she is a bloody troublemaker, blowing things out of all proportion, I bet she loved it, taking all her little problems for Mike to sort out." She takes a drink then continues, "Bloody hell, Angie, when he came in with Phil he was so angry," she smiles at me, "honestly, I wanted to laugh at first, I thought he was joking, because I have never seen him cross, his eyes were blazing, he did look a bit you know… sexy, and a bit Mills and boonish, " she laughs out loud, then she looks around, to make sure no one has heard, she goes on. "The funny thing is, people think he is older than he is because he acts it, but he is in fact, younger than most of his shift, but he is just so mature all the time, and this morning oh my god, honestly, Angie, I know I joke but it was not a joking matter, I have never let Mike down, I think he is a great boss, I think a lot of him as all the shift does, I was near to tears, seriously, Angie, he was mad as hell with both of us, some of the things he said were really personal; he said that he has never had any member of staff ask to leave his shift and he wasn't going to have one now, he said it reflected very badly on him, he ranted on that he didn't know or care what was going on in our personal lives but we were to sort it out and fast, he said the way we were carrying on was pathetic, he said we were both acting like adolescents," she pauses, "he actually called us adolescents, he went on and on, at one point banging his fist on the table, we were both too scared to interrupt, he told us that he was going to make sure we work together every day on every job until he is happy that we have sorted it out."

I look at her, "Really, Mike said that, what did Phil say?" I ask, she looks around then lowers her voice even further.

"Well, it was really strange, you know what Phil is like, he was really cocky at first, when he first came in the room he leaned up against the wall until Mike told him to sit down, he didn't at first he just stood there, then after a short stand-off," she pauses, "Mike and Phil just stood facing each other, but Mike looked at Phil, he told him to sit down and said he wasn't going to ask him again, so Phil did, but when he did sit down he was sat back with his hands behind his head, tipping his chair, you know, typical I am in charge Phil, but Mike was having none of it, he was actually really quite rude to Phil, well very rude really, he told him that if he put as much energy in to his work as he did in chasing unavailable women and womanising he would make a very good officer, or words like that," Helen pauses to catch her breath. "Bloody hell, Angie, I couldn't believe it, he actually said that, I could see Phil wasn't happy, the vein in his neck was practically popping out, he kept clenching and unclenching his fists, you know the way he does," I nod my head. "At one point I thought he was going to punch Mike but he didn't, he stood up and went to leave the room but Mike told him to sit back down and stop acting like a bloody child, you know what, Phil did," she looks at me and I shake my head, she continues, "well, he stood there a while then he sat back down, not a word, just sat there," she pauses again to take a drink, she looks around making sure we are not overheard, "I could see he was really angry, I thought he was going to punch Mike, he was really red in the face and his hands were shaking, but if we were angry then Mike was bloody livid, I have never ever seen him like that, well not to us, I have seen him deal with idiots on the street and he takes no messing from them, but even when I went to speak he put his hand up to stop me, he basically told me to shut up, I couldn't believe it, he told us he didn't want to hear our version of events, he wasn't interested," she takes a sip of her drink. "He is so laid back generally, lets us just get on with things, we do sometimes push the boundaries but I think we both knew on this occasion we were not going to win, he did stop at one point to ask if any one of us wanted to make this formal but neither of us said a word, I was too scared, I don't know about Phil. Mike then calmed down a bit. He got up and said he would be back in a minute, we both just sat there in silence, we didn't even look at each other, when he returned he was really quite calm, well quite a lot really, he said to Phil that he was giving him the task to allocate all the jobs for the shift over the next few days and Phil is to ensure that he and I will be working together and attending our jobs together, he said Phil is to come in half an hour early unpaid on every shift to ensure the jobs are ready for officers to attend almost immediately, that is when I thought things were going to get out of hand as Phil said he wouldn't do it, and Mike told him he would, he had no choice, it wasn't his decision to make and that the matter was not for further discussion, and what is more, he said Amanda is to come with us whether we like it or not, she has to attend the jobs with us," she shrugs. "In fairness he knows we would never make something like that formal, it would be professional suicide, that is about it, Mike then asked if we had any comments but before we could reply he said good because he wasn't interested in hearing them anyway and the subject was closed. He then brought out lots of jobs that needed allocating immediately then he went on to explain about the non-urgent routine remaining jobs that we have to get organised, that did pretty much calm things down, when we left Phil was different, not happy, but certainly he had calmed his temper, he even stuck his hand out to Mike and they shook hands then Mike stopped us at the door he said that in his opinion we were great officers, he was proud to have us on his shift and we were to put our differences behind us and move on, then Phil and I left." Helen looked at me, "You know what the first thing that Phil did when we left?" I shake my head, "He asked me to print off another copy of all the jobs and we sat down and got on with them, we had most of them sorted in an hour and we picked out the ones we were doing, not once did Phil say anything to me about the conversation though, he was really quiet for a while. When Mike came back in he asked Phil how it was going and he just said fine, they seemed to be okay." Helen smiles, "Mike is not stupid, he must have known what Phil was thinking as his parting shot was that he wanted to see copies of our pocket note books for every job we attend to make sure they match." Helen laughs out loud, "Phil's face was a picture, he isn't stupid, Mike knew what Phil intended to do, he was going to pick out jobs for me to go off and do and he would do the others but pretend we were together, Mike was making sure Phil knew it too, there is no way we can get away with it, our pocketbooks have to match," she smiles, "but Mike hadn't finished, he leaned over to me and told me I was to have a quiet word with Amanda, he wants to see her make-up drastically reduced, she is to go easy on the perfume and her hair is to be up when she is on duty." Helen looks at me, "I told him I have told her off the record and all he said was well then now tell her on the record," she rolls her eyes, "as if that girl doesn't hate me enough as it is."

I look at Helen, she is so lovely and sweet, she hates any sort of confrontation, she must be hating this, "Have you told her yet then, about the make-up etc?" I ask.

Helen shakes her head, "I have tried and I have told Mike I have tried, I have also noted it in my pocket book, but it is water off a duck's back, she takes no notice of me whatsoever."

Helens phone rings and she smiles at me as she answers it, it seems like it is going to be a long call, I take our plates to the counter. I place the plates on the rack and return; I sit and wait for her to finish her call. I think about what she has just told me.

Wow, I don't know what to say, Mike is certainly not to be messed with, poor Phil, I am not sure how Phil would be feeling, he always has to be top dog, always having the last word, normally I would seek him out to discuss it but I just don't want to, I am not interested. Helen finishes her call.

"Anyway," Helen continues, "just before I came to lunch Phil called me into the private office, he told me that he is sorry for the way he treated me, he has told me that he has already called it off with Jo, he said it happened last night, not because anyone told him to but because he knew he deserved better." I cannot help it, I smile but Helen doesn't notice, she goes on, "But you know what, Angie, I am through with chasing him – fed up with trying to get him to notice me, I really am, I will always like him, but I know I am worth better than him. I am seeing this chap tonight, nothing serious but he works at the gym, you know him the one with the long blonde hair to his shoulder, wears it in a ponytail."

I nod, "Yes, I do know him, he is lovely looking and so friendly."

Helen smiles, "I know, and he has been asking me out for a while so I thought why not."

I reach over and squeeze her arm, "Why not indeed, you are right – you are worth someone much better than Phil so good luck, tell me tomorrow how it goes won't you." I look at my watch, my break is nearly over, I have to go, I pick up my drink drain my cup, take it to the server area and we walk out together.

As we are walking down the corridor Phil is walking towards us, "Hi," he says to me, he doesn't acknowledge Helen, doesn't even look at her, I smile and say hi back, but he stops.

"Have you got a minute, Angie?" he asks, Helen shrugs and walks on.

Phil leans against the wall, "You okay?" he asks.

"Yes, I am fine, how about you?" I lean against the opposite wall facing him.

"So, I suppose he has told you then?" he asks.

I shake my head, "Not sure what you are talking about, Phil, who, told me what?"

He looks directly at me, "Well you must know about Mike, the fact that he gave me and Helen a right dressing down this morning."

I laugh, "No, he hasn't told me anything, but Helen did mention it just now, how are you now, you okay?"

Phil shrugs but a smile appears at the corner of his lips, "It has been a crap day from start to finish, and that this morning, seriously I could have done without that," he pauses, "bloody hell, Angie, Mike went bloody mental, I have never seen him like that, I have been out on patrol with him loads of times, been to fights and domestic disputes and there is no messing with him but this morning well seriously he flipped, he had us both in the room, give us the biggest bollocking. Honestly at one point, I was going to walk out, seriously I was just going to tell him to shove it but I tell you, he was having none of it, he actually told me to sit down and shut up, I was going to smack him, speaking to me like that, but when I looked at his face, just one look I knew I wasn't going to argue with him, I mean he is a big bastard but that doesn't scare me, but his whole face told me not to mess with him. Helen tried to speak at one point but he wasn't having it, he told her he wasn't interested in anything she had to say, she was shocked too, she was near to tears; at one point he even slammed his fist on the table, Jesus, Angie, he doesn't mess about. Luckily it is all off the record but I am not going to mess with that big bastard, no wonder he scored high in that course he went to. I have only ever seen the nice friendly side of him, shit." he runs

469

his hands over his face. "I have seriously got to sort myself out, Angie, I am a total asshole aren't I?"

I smile at him, then I cannot help it I laugh, "No, you are not a total asshole, Phil," I laugh out loud pushing him, "just an asshole."

He raises his eyes, "Thanks for the vote of confidence there, mate, just make sure you don't upset him, or if you do, run very fast, very fast indeed, and don't call me for backup, I will be running the other way, you might have a bit of a temper on you but bloody hell, nothing like him."

We both laugh out loud, we walk on, he comes into the control room with me, Mike is there with an inspector and they call me over. Mike asks if I am available for an hour this afternoon to help them type up seized property, I look round for Craig but I cannot see him, so I shrug, "I am happy to do it, but Craig has the final say."

They both nod in agreement so I return to my desk to look at the job logs, I can see Phil and Helen have been allocated to attend a missing person enquiry, I check the other jobs, I can see the jobs that are allocated to them later, every single job has been marked that no officer is to be substituted, Mike certainly is not having any nonsense from them two.

Chapter Sixty-Three

When Craig comes back he asks for a bit of quiet, he basically tells me what I know already, but the shift are told about Phil and Helen and they are to be sent to jobs together and not substituted unless either Mike or Craig says so, all the team nod their head.

"About bloody time those two were taken into line," Gavin retorts, and judging by the nodding of heads everyone agrees, he continues, "Mike has quite a long tolerance but they must have seriously pushed his buttons for this to happen, fair play to him." I don't say anything but the comments continue, Craig comes over to me, he stands and listens to the comments then turns to me, "I know you probably know this already but you are needed downstairs, something a bit different this time I think, something about missing and seized property reports not the normal statements for CID, you need to speak to Mike," he advises me, "he knows exactly what he wants doing okay." I nod yes, smile, I grab my bag and my pad, as I walk out he calls out to me, "Keep your head down and don't get involved in any of the nonsense down there will you?"

I shake my head, I head downstairs. Mike is in the office on his own on the phone, I stand by him and watch him scribbling notes down, waiting for him to finish. When he does he directs me to an empty desk, he is explaining what he needs me to do, pointing at the screen which is loading up, he is so close, I want to pull him close to me and kiss those wonderfully soft lips, I watch him speak as he explains how he wants it done in a particular way I look up at him.

"Okay," he says looking down at me.

"Yes," I reply, "but even if it wasn't I think I would be too scared to argue," I add.

"Ah," he smiles, "so you have spoken to Phil then and he has told you about our exchange this morning."

I shake my head, "No, I heard it from Helen first then as we left the canteen we bumped into Phil so he added his bit, I think you shook them both up," I add.

"Good," he says, "I am glad, that was my intention, I am totally fed up with the both of them, they both had it coming, that is a strong message for anyone else who tries my patience."

I nod to him, "Okay, I will bear that in mind, Sergeant Simms."

He groans, he leans in to me, "I don't think you will ever try my patience, I am not sure this was a good idea having you here, I am not sure I will be able to control myself having you so close for the rest of the day, I should have asked for Steve, he isn't half as pretty as you, and although he has a tidy body his beard puts me off kissing him, it tickles too much," I laugh out loud at his joke. "I might have to call on all my powers of self-control," he leans in to me, I know he is going to kiss me but I also see someone approaching the office so I move out of reach. Mike straightens up as Amanda enters the room, I see a flash of annoyance on his face.

"Hi, Mike," she smiles brightly at him but totally ignores me, "can you help me with this?" she indicates some paperwork she is working on, Mike takes the paperwork, glances quickly through it then hands it back and pulls a chair forwards sitting down next to me.

"I am a bit busy at the moment, take it upstairs, the main admin office will help you, that is what they are there for." I see by her face she isn't happy but she puts on her bright smile.

"Oh, but it would only take you a second."

Without looking at her Mike says coldly, "And I have told you to take it upstairs where it needs to be dealt with," he doesn't look at her, he watches the screen as it bring ups the new spreadsheet.

I watch as she frowns then recovers quickly and with a, "Okay, Sarge, see you later."

She turns to leave but he calls her back. "Amanda," she turns and smiles her big girlie smile at him but it disappears in his next sentence, "I know that Helen has advised you and I thought I told you to tone down that make-up, and put your hair up, you shouldn't need to be told twice, now go and do it now please, I don't want to have to mention it again."

I watch as her face drops, then she recovers and smiles again before she breezes out of the door. "Not sure she liked that," I remark.

"Couldn't care less what she likes," he replies.

We sit waiting for the system to load all the data, I turn to Mike, "So what was you up to this morning then, when you were late, I thought you might be moving your stuff in, or is that very needy of me?"

Mike smiles, "Well actually, no, I was busy, but not moving in," he pauses, he looks away from me before continuing, "I had to do something, I was," he seems to be struggling for an explanation, he pauses again before saying, "I was helping a friend," he pauses again before continuing, "and you know, honey, I kind of hoped that we would move my things in together, is that okay?"

I smirk at him, "Oh yes, more than okay, I cannot wait, because I don't need all your things there, just you being there and I have everything I need at my house."

Without realising it my eyes drop down so I am looking at his crotch area but he just laughs, he reaches out touching my thigh, "You are so bad."

I turn to the screen and input my log on details, I feel his hand on my thigh and I push it away, but immediately it is back there, I look at him, "Don't, please don't," I whisper "because once you start I won't be able to say no to you," he laughs, I love his laugh. I push his chair away, I continue in a hushed whisper, "I think we need to maintain an appropriate distance, Sergeant Simms, so we are not tempted." He doesn't move the chair back.

"Too late for that," he whispers back.

My whole body is doing somersaults. I pull the paperwork towards me, he leans back in his chair and points out what he needs me to do, I look up to see Simon storming down the office towards us, Mike has his back to him so he doesn't see him but the roar of Simon's voice has Mike turning quickly.

"You couldn't bloody help yourself could you," Simon is stood over Mike aggressively pointing his finger at his chest, Mike remains seated. "You cocky shit, you blocked my promotion, I know you did, don't deny it, I know it was you," Simon is roaring now, spittle coming from his lips, his face red with rage.

Mike looks at me, "Angie, could you please excuse us for a minute I believe DC Windsor has something to say."

I look at Simon who is blocking my path, "Excuse me," I say quietly, Simon doesn't move, I look to Mike, his face is set hard.

"The lady asked you to move, I suggest you move," he says. Simon takes one step back and I duck past quickly, I have nowhere to go so I just wait outside, no sooner have I moved away Simon is shouting again, "I bloody know it was you, all because you got knocked over by a dog, for Christ's sake, I thought you would have got over it by now."

Mike voice when he replies is very calm and controlled, "You put two officers in danger, not just from the police dog, but from the occupants of that house, you had no idea if they were armed, you didn't do your homework properly and you took chances. You let your adrenalin take over and you lost focus, you forgot the most important commodities when carrying out any incident – the welfare of your team, you compromised our safety," he pauses, "that is the way I saw things, you might have a different version of events, but if you lost a chance of promotion and it was because of that incident, you only have yourself to blame, however," I peer through the door, Mike has sat back down, he crosses his foot up onto his knee, he is calm and controlled as he looks up at Simon, "I was not asked to give feedback on your performance, positive or otherwise, so you need to look elsewhere if you are trying to apportion blame," he looks at the computer. "Now I am busy, so if you don't have any other business," he leaves the question hanging. I look through the door, Simon is just stood there, I hear Mike call my name and I go back in, Mike is all business like. "Can you create a new property sheet, I want specific headers over each column?" he asks me, I glance at Simon, he is still stood just watching us both, he is still seething, I give him a half smile and he walks away, he is about ten feet away when Mike turns in his chair. "Simon," he calls, Simon half turns, "thank you for asking, the shoulder is okay now," Mike turns back to the computer screen and when I glance back the room is empty. I look at Mike, I cannot believe what I have just witnessed, he can go from formidable to loving in such a quick time, he smiles at me. "What?" he asks, I smile at him, he puts his foot down and sits facing me, "Angie, two things you need to know about me, the first is, I don't like being messed about, as you have seen already with Phil and Helen, and that exchange there, I am very serious about my work, I give 100% and god help anyone who tries to stop me, crossing me is not a good idea, not a good idea at all."

I look at him, "And the second thing?" I ask, I raise my eyebrows at him.

"I want you so bad it hurts," he smiles, he leans forward and with a quick glance behind him, kisses me gently on the lips.

I finish on time; I walk through the office downstairs. Mike is now with the late shift sergeant busy with the handover, so I don't stop, I will text him instead.

Stuart is home when I get in so I tell him of my plans tonight. "What will you do?" I ask him.

He is very cheerful. "Oh Mike and I are going to the gym then we might go for a pint, he is a decent bloke, Angie, you have a good one there."

I smile, but I am confused, "When did you get so friendly with him?" I ask.

Stuart smiles and then follows me into the kitchen. "Angie, you haven't asked me why I am here yet, surely you must know it isn't a social visit."

I must admit, it had crossed my mind that he asked me not to tell Judy or Scott but I didn't pay much attention, I turn to him now, "You obviously didn't want to tell me then, do you want to tell me now?" Stuart sits down, I look at the clock, I have plenty of time, I sit down at the dining table taking a sip of my tea. This doesn't sound great. Stuart explains, "Well, as you know, I work for the middle east business side of the company, which means for me being based in Dubai is perfect, however, not so at the moment because they are reviewing everyone's contract. The bad news is, that there is every chance mine might not be renewed, things work much differently over there in that immediately there is a problem the company notify the banks who then freeze your accounts, you cannot pay your bills and until your company sort everything out, worst case scenario, you could find yourself in prison; I didn't want to risk that so I flew home. I didn't tell anyone I was going, I just booked a flight and came home, I thought I would sort things out from here," Stuart looks at me, "I needed a witness to certain documents, I don't know if he has told you but Mike helped me this morning, he came with me to the solicitor, helped me out at the bank, I needed to transfer funds so I can go back and sort the matter out with no risk to me. I needed access to a scanner and a fax machine, I have spoken to the people in the UK office, they are helping me, it is all very complicated as I work as a consultant, the contract doesn't offer me much protection, but I think I might come back to the UK, I think it is time, things are not as rosy in Dubai as people like you to think." He stands up and goes to the sink, pouring himself a drink of water he drinks it down then turns to face me, "Can I crash here still?"

I nod my head, "Yes, no problem, although I have asked Mike to move in, so if you don't have a problem with that, it will be fine," I pause, "Mike is pretty special though isn't he," I pause, then turn to him. "Oh and, Stuart, you will have to tell the family what is happening in Dubai, or they will be cross with me."

He nods, "I know, I will get everything sorted tomorrow, and yes Mike seems a great bloke, glad you have got that bloody Phil out of your system, he was like a limpet hanging round your neck – he is bad news," he shakes his head, "definitely bad news." He laughs again, "Has Mike found out about your fiery temper yet or is that something he is yet to meet with?"

I poke my tongue out, "Unfortunately yes, he has been on the receiving end but it was his fault, and I have not got a fiery temper, I just get cross quickly."

He turns to the television. "Same thing, Angie, same thing."

Sean is in great form, he is really happy, he bounces into the car kissing me on the cheek. I smile as I notice immediately he is wearing one of Jason's shirts. "Sorry," he says looking down at his shirt, "I totally forgot, is it a bit insensitive."

I shake my head, "Not at all, in fact." I lean in closer to him and take a deep breath, "I recognise that aftershave, you both had good taste, and it is lovely to see you wearing his shirt, he would have liked that." Sean nods his head and I look at him again, "Sometimes, Sean, when I look at you, it is like he is back, your mannerisms are so alike." I lean in and kiss him on the cheek, "Obviously, he was the better looking of the two," I laugh out loud and Sean joins in. Then I realise I totally forgot to ask him about inviting Phil, it is too late now, so I drive towards the pub.

Sean frowns looking at me, "You not invited Phil then?" he asks.

I shake my head, "No, just you, if you want to text him you can but I haven't invited him this evening, no."

I can tell Sean is surprised, "Bloody hell," he says quietly, "I thought you two were joined at the hip." I pinch his leg he shouts out in pain. "Oi you," but he laughs adding, "it is lovely though, to have an evening with you, just the two of us, eh." I pull the car into the traffic and smile, Sean is so easy to be with.

The evening goes really well, I do admit to Sean that I also forgot the anniversary – I tell him that I was mortified when Steve reminded me, I am bloody useless with dates, then I tell him about Mike about how happy I am, how happy Mike makes me. Sean admits he has been aware of Mike through Judy but didn't know how serious it was. "Have you got fireworks?" he asks teasingly.

I look him straight in the face, "Yes, definitely I have."

His eyebrows shoot up in surprise, "Bloody hell, Angie, eventually you got your fireworks, I am very pleased for you," he replies, "in fact scratch that," he adds, "I am over the moon for you."

I smile at him, "And what about you?" I ask, "How are you and Judy?"

"Ah well," he leans back in his chair, the waitress arrives with cutlery he waits for her to leave, "I thought you would ask me that, and you know what, Angie, she is everything I was not looking for, after the Ruth nightmare, and believe me it was a bloody nightmare, I thought I was in love with Ruth, I really did, maybe because I haven't really dated anyone properly for a while, I was flattered by her constant attention, but then Judy comes along and anything I felt for Ruth just pales in comparison, I am totally blown away by her, she is totally unexpected for me, we are complete opposites, I mean she has baggage, as you know, I always said I wouldn't date a woman with children and crazy ex partners, and she has both. She is messy, she is indecisive, she has the most annoying habits, she is not like you at all, I don't believe you are sisters, you are so neat, so tidy and organised, she drives me nuts with her haphazard lack of organisation but," he looks at me, "I am so totally in love with her that I cannot imagine what life was like before her or the children, it is like it was meant to be. I love the children and for some strange reason they seem not to be repulsed or repelled by me as most kids are."

I feel myself well up, I cannot stop the tears pricking my eyelids, I am so totally over the moon with happiness for both of them, Sean continues, "Obviously with our little indiscretion she has met Ma once but I think I would like her to meet them both properly," he smiles, "with our clothes on." We both laugh out loud. "Also I want them both to meet the children, I think Ma would love the children don't you?"

I smile nodding because I feel so choked up. Ma would be in heaven with the two children, having been desperate for grandchildren for years, she would love Judy too. I am so pleased for him, I love him like a brother, I am having a really lovely evening, I forgot how entertaining he can be, then he gets serious, the plates have been cleared he reaches over stroking the back of my hand. "Can I say something, Angie, something that you might think is out of order, but please hear me out before you get all cross and shout at me and storm out eh," he smiles and I nod my head, I think I know what is coming, but I let him continue, "I am really glad you have met someone, seriously I am, I was beginning to get concerned about you, especially the way that you became very dependent on Phil after Jason died, he seemed to dominate your world, your life, everyone and everything in it, I told Phil I had given my key back to you, he was there when I left it on the table but for some reason he didn't do the same, even though I expected him to, I had to get it off him when I sorted your post and Jason's stuff, but he insisted on having it back, I was worried that he thought he could slip in to the role that Jason left, as your partner, lover, husband, whatever you want to call it, and that concerned me, I didn't know how you felt about him. Sometimes, I felt there were just the two of you; it really wasn't a healthy mix, he seemed to be very controlling, you didn't seem to be able to make any decision without the thumbs up from either Phil or me," he looks at me, "am I being insensitive?" I shake my head, he is totally right I know that, obviously Judy has not told him about the caravan incident. "I am so pleased you didn't invite him tonight," he adds, I cannot speak, so again I just nod my head. "I am going to be totally honest with you, Angie, some small part of me always had a bit of a mistrust of Phil, you know, his motives, I don't know why, don't get me wrong, he is a great bloke, great company and I trust him with my life, but not yours, where you are concerned I don't think it was totally healthy in that he looked on you like a possession."

My throat is tight and I cannot say anything, I just nod, Sean is so right, in fairness he has not said anything that I don't already know or have suspected in the past. I smile at him, I clear my throat, "Well all that has definitely changed now I have my Mike," I inform him then I add, "I have asked Mike to move in with me, Sean, we have been together for three months, do you think it is too soon?"

Sean runs his hands through his hair, he looks at me, for a moment I am transported back years as he looks exactly like Jason, for a second my eyes fill with tears, but I blink them away, Sean leans forward in his seat, "Why are you always seeking approval, why does it matter so much to you what everyone else thinks? It is how you feel that matters, it is totally your business but if you have to know what I think then no I don't think it is too soon, no not at all. Jason has gone now, you are a young woman, you don't want to live your life hesitating or not doing things because of what other people think, so do it, why not?" He adds, "What is the point in waiting, although," he stops, "you might want to get your Uncle Clive to write a pre-nuptial to satisfy your mother," he laughs, he knows my family so well.

"My mother is going to have kittens when she finds out about you and Judy," I laugh, "I think she always thought it was Phil Judy liked."

Sean smiles back, "So did I, Angie, so did I."

I lean back and stretch then look at him, "So tell me," I smile at him, "how did it happen that you got together, and if you are going to say it is a long story then we have all night, tell me." I relax forward in my chair and rest my chin on my hands, "I am all ears."

Sean sits back in his chair, "Well, after that Ruth incident, and by the way, despite what Ruth said I have never wished for us, as in me and you to be a couple, that was just her jealousy talking. If I am honest I have always kind of liked Judy, she was feisty as a girl and I liked her a bit then, but I went off to University and never saw her after that, we obviously saw each other at the wedding, then the funeral, but I never really spoke to her, I wanted to but it didn't seem the right moment, then I saw her in the shopping centre and I asked how her parents were and that was it, we went for a coffee and I was totally smitten, I couldn't believe it when I offered her back to mine for more coffee, she said yes, the children were at their dads and she didn't go home that night, hence Ma catching us the next day. I couldn't believe how bloody lucky I was, she is a wonderful person and a great mum to those children." Sean reaches his hands behind his head, "Looks like we have both found our life partners eh, and you get to keep me as a brother-in-law."

I laugh then realise what he has said. "What you?"

I sit with my mouth open but no words come out. "Oh yes," Sean smiles, "keep it to yourself for a while, but I intend to marry that crazy disorganised sister of yours."

Chapter Sixty-Four

The traditional Jewish anniversary is very quiet and respectful, a candle is lit in the family home which burns for twenty-four hours, Sean and I stop and purchase them on the way home at his mum's local Synagogue, we stop in at Ma's on the way home, she doesn't care it is getting late, she is delighted to see us both, we show her our purchases, she is very pleased that we are marking the event following the correct tradition. Sean promises he will light one in his home, I make the same promise. Little Ma calls me into the kitchen.

"You bring your new man to see me soon?" she asks. "You promised me remember?" I nod my head, I cannot remember making such a promise but I will bring Mike round one day, but I make no commitment, she pulls me closer to her. "I see my Sean with his new lady, still the same one," she whispers, "maybe I get to meet her too," she smiles.

I look back to the lounge I look at Pa in his chair, he never changes in that his clothes, always the same, black trousers with grey shirt and waistcoat, but I realise that he looks so old, so very old, very frail, he smiles back at me, I take Little Ma's hand, "You take care of Pa for us won't you," she nods yes and we go back into the lounge I give Pa a huge hug, he pulls me to him,

"You are a good girl," he whispers, his voice is old and gravelly. I fill up with tears again. It is getting very late so we say our goodbyes, I drop Sean off, we promise to keep in touch then I drive off, I am so tired, I get in but there is no one home, I shower, then crawl into bed. I am not sure what time it is when I hear Mike moving about in my en suite, then I feel him getting in bed beside me, I snuggle into him running my hand across his chest and breathing in the delicious smell of his aftershave mixed with the slight aroma of beer and toothpaste. I have one more day shift then a few days off, it feels like just an hour later the alarm goes off, Mike ignores it so I lean over to switch it off, he doesn't move, I look at him, he is sleeping soundly.

I try to shake him awake, after several attempts he opens his eyes, groaning, "What time is it?" he asks.

"Time to be getting up," I reply, he looks over at the clock groaning again. "I am going to kill that bloody brother of yours," he pulls the duvet over his head rolling over to my side.

I shower, I bang about noisily. When I come back out of the en suite Mike is sat up in bed, he has tea by the side but is rubbing his head, he is naked, I look around to see what he wore downstairs, there isn't anything obvious so I lift the duvet, studying his naked body. "What did you wear downstairs to make the tea?" I ask him.

"Nothing, I couldn't find anything," he groans back at me.

I raise my eyebrows in surprise, "What if Stuart would have seen you?"

He groans again, "I don't care, it would serve him right," I laugh and reach for my tea, I sit on the side of the bed and look at him, he looks terrible, but at least he is talking now, he sits up gingerly holding his head.

"How was last night then?" I venture.

He groans again, "Christ your brother can drink, we got in just after midnight, I am knackered and could barely walk and he drunk twice as much as I did and practically skipped home." I laugh, my brother has always had a reputation for being able to handle his drink.

"Come on, honey," I put my cup on the side and lean down to kiss his cheek, "I shouldn't have let you out to play with the big boys should I." He pulls me down on the bed, his breath smells dreadful, I turn away from him.

"Do I smell that bad?" he asks.

"No, much worse," I reply.

I move out of his way, I dress quickly and turn to the bed, he has fallen asleep again, I pull his arm out of the duvet and then I realise he is only pretending, he pulls me close, his hands making their way inside my blouse, with expert precision he releases my breasts from my underwear and pulls me towards him, much as my body reacts to his touch, I pull away, "I have to go to work and so do you," I scold him. He pulls back the duvet to show me how much he wants me, but I just laugh at him, "Cold shower for you I think." I pull away and skip downstairs a huge smile on my face.

I light my candle, placing it in the glass hurricane lamp so it is safe; I leave a note for Stuart to explain what it is and why it must burn for twenty-four hours. I leave it on the dining room table. I can hear the shower upstairs running and I assume it is Mike trying to clear his head. I know he will see the note to Stuart so I won't have to explain again. I drive to work thinking of my delicious man laid naked in my bed, I switch on the radio and sing along to Madness 'It must be love', I cannot help but smile. I have plenty of time so I stop at the 24 hour supermarket to pick up a few provisions for work then I park up still smiling, Helen knocks on the window.

"What are you so happy about?" she asks. "I don't reply but get out and lock the door, I stand waiting for her as she gets her bag out of the car, I watch as Mike's car pulls into the car park, he parks just a few spaces down, Helen gets to me first and she is chatting on about nothing in particular, Mike walks past both of us.

"Morning," he says without stopping. We both reply back; Helen looks at his departing body.

"Christ he looks like shit, he looks like he been up all night or has the flu or something doesn't he?" I don't comment, she adds, "And he is normally in way before us, I hope he doesn't take it out on us, hey do you want to hear about my date?"

I put my arm through hers, "Do I, go on," we walk toward the entrance together.

"Well, it went really well, we are seeing each other again, he was the perfect gentleman, so funny and interesting, I really like him."

She is on a high, her face is radiant, there is a bounce in her step as we walk in together. Within twenty minutes she is back up in the control room, her face has changed she drags a chair over sitting down next to me with a thump, she has to wait for me to finish speaking on the radio but then she launches into a whispered tirade, "That bloody woman downstairs, I could kill her, she has one hell of a big mouth, apparently she saw me on my date, she saw us going in to the pub, so she had to say something, we were in the locker room getting changed and she didn't say a word, not one word to me but waited until we were all downstairs waiting for Mike then in front of everyone in the office she mentioned about my date, she said her mate used to date him and he cheated on her," she adds, "then she says she wants me to know for my own good, she makes sure she says everything so sickly sweet so everyone thinks she is being lovely, everyone heard her, I just had to sit there and listen as she simpered away, I mean she had to say it in front of Phil and Mike didn't she, oh god I am so embarrassed," she pauses for breath, there is silence for a minute, but she is still so very angry. "I could kill her, she is still so bloody creep arse around Mike but he is a bloke, he cannot see what she is really like, she makes his tea and simpers on, hope it isn't too strong, Mike, do you take sugar, Mike, can you check this for me, Mike, I don't want it to be wrong," actually Helen does a pretty good impression of her, I laugh out loud, Helen stops. "That isn't the worst of it," she pauses, "you will never guess what Mike has done." She stops to take another much needed breath, "He has told me and Phil that we have to organise a social event for all the shift on Friday to boost morale on the shift, bloody cheek of it, on our night off too, I nearly told him where he could go, but he didn't actually ask us, he told us." I smile at her. "What is so funny?" she asks.

"You are," I reply, "before you two fell out that would have been your idea of heaven, you know, spending time with Phil, now look at you."

She sighs, "I know, bloody ridiculous isn't it."

The control room is busy, we all work hard keeping everything up to date, it is a crazy day, the fire alarms keep going off for no reason and there is a fight in custody, Craig is called down to give assistance to the custody sergeant as two of his staff are injured, we just mange to keep up, Craig comes back after an hour or so, most of the units are out on patrol or attending jobs. I make everyone a cup of tea but no sooner have I set all the

481

teas down and return to my seat then I hear calls are coming in reporting an accident. On first report it seems to be a serious road traffic accident on a major road, the accident requires all the services to attend, the control room comes to life as we all work together. Gavin takes the initial call and remains taking all the details, Steve calls the ambulance and I radio a unit to attend, Mike responds he is in the area, within minutes he lets us know he is the first officer at the scene, he calls through the details on the radio, within minutes other officers book at scene, Mike radios in the update, that it is a taxi driver with injuries, it seems he has crashed his car into the central road barrier after having what is thought to be a suspected heart attack, he has hit the central barrier but was not travelling at speed, he is with the ambulance staff now and is going off to hospital. Mike requests a second ambulance is called for the other passengers, also he advises that short-term the road needs to be closed, the control room leap into action, we are all ready, we know what we have to do, I radio all the units to ensure they are in the right areas to set up temporary diversions. Max deals with notifying the council and other authorities of the diversions and Craig is monitoring everything, my shift work really well together at times like this, the part-time person is left to monitor the other jobs for a while whilst we sort everything out, dealing with the other services, directing them to the correct area. The whole shift is busy working as a team, there are other cars involved but nothing more than minor scratches, I hear Mike telling Steve over the radio that one lane of the road has to be closed, the three services work together, we send other offices and recovery to take over to ensure the scene is cleared and the lane is opened soon as it is a major route so there needs to be the least amount of inconvenience to the road users as possible. It is so busy, there is no time for breaks or anything else, the roads must be opened as soon as possible, it will be rush hour soon and that will just cause more chaos, the time goes really quickly.

Mike leaves officers at the scene to deal with the vehicle removal. I monitor the log for an update, he radios in to Steve that he is dropping the taxi passengers to their destination which is local but he will call in with a full update later. Within an hour the whole road is opened again, the incident is closed and we go back to reallocating the jobs back to the officers. I don't actually get to see him but he sends me a text to say all is okay, he will be home late as he wants to go and check on the taxi driver, he says that I am not to worry he will grab something to eat later. Craig is really pleased with how everyone has worked today, we have a quick debrief, we appreciate that he takes the time to let us know we are appreciated. We are all relieved when the next shift come in to take over, they have a lot of logs to deal with and will be very busy but that is the nature of the beast.

Chapter Sixty-Five

When I get home from work my candle is still burning, it throws a lovely warm glow around the room, Stuart is working on his laptop in the dining room, the phone rings, it is Mum, she says to put the kettle on she will be there in twenty minutes, then she hangs up, I am stumped, I had no idea she was here, I tell Stuart but he just as stumped as I am, he says he spoke to her yesterday she was in Spain, she never mentioned it. Flights are so regular from Spain that within a few hours she can be home. I ring Judy quickly and she says the same, she didn't know she was coming either, she only spoke to Mum last night on skype there was nothing mentioned, Judy asks to speak to Stuart, they talk for a few minutes, when he comes off the phone, "Judy says she will be here in a short while okay" he says to me, I nod my head at him. "Seems like we are going to have quite a few visitors so I best get some provisions then, I will be back soon."

I pop to the shops for extra milk and other bits and pieces, I generally only keep in the house what I am going to eat, never any extras but I feel a bit of a get together coming up so I grab biscuits and cakes too, when I get back I grab a quick shower.

It is only when I am in the shower that I realise, I have totally forgotten Mike, I was so blown away by my parents coming over here, I forgot to tell him not to come over, I need to send him a quick text, tell him to come over much later, or maybe delay seeing him until tomorrow. I don't really want him barging in and having to explain to everyone, it is too soon, and not today of all days, not on Jason's anniversary. I dry my hair vigorously, then dress quickly, applying light make-up, texting him goes right out of my head. As I make my way downstairs it is just in time to see Stuart opening the front door to my parents, everything happens very quickly after that, everyone is so busy saying hello and catching up and getting comfortable, there is a lovely buzz of conversation as we all sit about chatting. Judy arrives with the two children, they are over excited to see everyone then the door goes again, it is Sean, he has popped in to bring me some mail but we don't get to open it as Mum wants to catch up with Sean, she wants to know what he is up to, and to find out how his parents are, then Judy decides she is going to introduce him as her new partner, there is so much noise, Mum is totally overwhelmed and seems a bit speechless but Dad is brilliant, Sean takes it all in his stride, Stuart shakes his hand I don't think I have ever seen Sean smile so much, I look at Stuart as he watches Sean with Judy, then he looks up and smiles at me, I frown and he says quietly, "He is so different from Jason isn't he?"

I nod my head, "Yes, he is, Judy is very lucky," and I mean it. I watch Sean, he is so good with the children, Juliet just wants to sit on his lap, the children are so comfortable with him, he is just so chilled out. Judy suggests we phone out for pizza, she takes control asking everyone what they want then we place the order, we all sit around chatting and catching up, there are so many conversations going on at one time, it is noisy and happy. Stuart is due to return to Dubai in a few days but he is happier that he will be okay, Dad asks him lots of questions and Stuart tells him that he will be moving back to the UK. Mum knows a bit about these things, she tells him what he needs to do to register back so everything is above board. "Mum, it is okay," he reassures her, "Mike helped me sort it all out when I first got here."

Mum looks confused, she looks around us. "Mike," she looks puzzled, "who is Mike?" she asks, I shoot an 'I am going to kill you' look at him, which silences him.

The question lies heavily in the air unanswered. Judy looks at me and smiles. "Yes, Angie, who is Mike?"

I shoot her a look but she just laughs, there is a ring on the doorbell, I heave a sigh of relief, "Pizza I think," I state to no one in particular, Stuart grabs cash and escapes to the front door with me chasing on his tail, we both escape the interrogation. As I come back in with my hands full of pizza boxes I glance at the back door to see Mike as he opens it and comes casually striding in, everyone looks at him, he looks totally gorgeous still in his uniform, my mum's jaw drops open, Dad looks at Mike then back to Mum.

"Hello, officer," he pauses, "nice to see you again."

I look at Mike, he is stooping down to remove his shoes, I walk slowly back into the room my hands still clutching at the pizza boxes, he frowns as he looks at everyone in the lounge in turn.

"Mike," I suddenly feel very unsteady on my feet, as I walk towards him, "meet my family," I pass the boxes to Sean then turn to face my parents, both are looking dumbstruck, I take his hand, "Everyone, this is Mike," everyone seems to start talking at once.

Dad goes over and shakes his hand, "We met already once today, son," he says, "thanks so much for looking after us, great job you boys do."

I look at Mike confused but he smiles. "The road accident with the taxi driver, seems your folks were the passengers, I took them home, didn't know it was your folks though." Everyone laughs at the coincidence of it all, the pizza boxes are opened and everyone dives in, Mike sits on the arm of the chair helping himself to pizza, he seems so relaxed.

I move to the kitchen to get drinks, Mum follows me, I brace myself – here comes the interrogation I think to myself.

"Isn't he lovely?" she starts "So handsome, you know he really looked after us today, he was in charge you know, he was telling everyone what to do, and you know what, no one argued with him, he was so concerned that we might be injured, he made the ambulance people check us all over before he took us home, he was ever so worried about your dad, I was too as he was as white as a sheet, but we are okay, he is so charming," she pauses. "You know he even took us home in the police car, he wouldn't take any money for petrol, and he carried our cases right up to the apartment, that was so kind of him, wasn't it?" I want to laugh out loud, she is so funny sometimes, she fills the kettle. "How long have you been seeing each other then?"

I smile, no interrogation from her this time as she has already formed an opinion of him, "Just three months," I reply.

She shakes her head, "I had visions of both you and Judy ending up on the shelf," this time I shake my head at her, but she pulls me into a hug, she holds me close stroking my hair, my eyes fill up with the closeness I feel towards her, then we pull apart, she looks me in the face, "we are very proud of you, you know that don't you," I nod, unable to speak, "you have been through so much in the past few years, don't think we didn't know, and now, well now you need some happiness," she holds me close for a few seconds then she lets me go and we return to the lounge.

I listen as dad is asking Mike about the new police response vehicles when Juliet interrupts my thoughts, "Auntie, Angie, what is that funny candle burning for?"

There is a silence, I look at Sean, he smiles back at me, it has been burning quietly in the background, but it has obviously got the attention of Juliet.

"It is to remember Uncle Jason," I tell her direct, "it is the one year anniversary today since he died."

She shrugs then turns to Judy, "Mum, can we watch television if we have it on low?" she asks, she has been told what it was for now she is happy, Judy nods yes, Juliet skips over to the television flicking it on.

"Is it really a year?" Mum asks, I nod to her, "such a shame," the room goes quiet.

My phone bleeps, I reach to check it, it is a message from Phil, he is in the pub if I fancy a drink.

I text back a quick message to say that I am sorry, but I am busy with the family. I add some other time maybe. Judy stands up she goes to the kitchen, Sean follows her, we can hear them mumbling quietly, they come back in, even though we are all sat quietly Judy asks for our attention, I look at her, she smiles at me, Sean is stood behind her, she reaches out to take his hand. "Well, as we are all together it seems to be a good time to announce that Sean has proposed to me and I have accepted, we have spoken to the children and his parents as we thought they needed to know first, that we are going to be married," she smiles; we all clap and cheer but she holds up her hand. "Oh, one other thing, he is moving in with me and the children," she looks at Mum as if challenging her to argue, but Mum is so happy her eyes are filling up, I hand her a tissue.

"I am so happy for you, my lovely," she says, she looks at Sean, "you are such a lovely boy, she is so lucky."

I reach over I whisper to Mike, "Is that sparkling wine you bought still in the fridge in the garage?" I ask, he nods, we get up, he goes to find it whilst I sort out glasses, I look up and watch as Judy follows Mike into the garage, I wonder for a second what she is doing but I put all the glasses on the tray then go back in the lounge, everyone is congratulating Sean, Judy comes back in to the lounge, she stands by Sean, Mike pops the cork, he starts pouring, then Judy asks for silence when everyone is stood waiting patiently, she looks around to ensure she has everyone's attention, she takes the bottle from Mike.

"Haven't you got something to announce too, Mike?"

I look at her, then at him, he doesn't seem perturbed at all, he smiles as he reaches for my hand, "Well, okay, I was going to ask for her father's permission first but," he takes a deep breath, "seems I am on the spot here," he looks at Judy, "thank you, Judy," she laughs at him as he goes on. "I will just say that when she is ready, and," he looks at me, "only when she is ready, I intend to make this beautiful woman my wife." He leans forward and kisses me on the lips, I blush with embarrassment, I don't think my parents are used to seeing loving gestures in front of everyone, but Mike doesn't seem to notice or care, he pulls me into his arms. "Oh and," he adds quickly, "it seems that I too am moving in here with her."

We all raise our glasses, my heart is soaring, I glance quickly at my mum and she has a huge beam on her face, Juliet shouts out, "Look at the candle, everyone."

We all look at the table, I swear the flame has doubled in size it seems to be dancing happily. Sean comes over to me, he pulls me away from Mike. "Can I borrow her for a minute, mate?" he asks, he wraps me in his arms, "I think Jason has just given his approval." I hold him close in a bear hug, I cannot help it my eyes fill with tears of happiness. A memory comes into my mind, something the tarot reader said about the brightest candle burns with love, I shake my head, it is all too unreal, too unbelievable.

I am on cloud nine, everything is perfect, and mum and dad are over the moon to have Sean and Mike as family. Everybody is talking, there is a general murmur across the room, later I watch as Stuart is showing Mike and Dad something to do with Dubai on the laptop, with Sean watching over their shoulder, Judy and I just smile at them, the most challenging thing in both our lives has happened so easily – getting mum's approval on a man, we cannot believe how lucky we are. Later Stuart checks his phone, there is an email telling him that he will definitely be coming back to the UK, there are just a few formalities with him but his company are transferring him so he will not be affected by redundancies. We get Scott on the phone, Judy updates him with all our news then Stuart speaks to him and tells him his news too.

Sean calls me to the kitchen, "Sorry to interrupt the celebrations, but I need to speak to you about some mail I have received regarding Jason." I pull the dining room door closed, Sean pulls paperwork from his pocket, "as you know Jason had several patents pending, his old company contacted me a week or so ago, they are asking, as the anniversary of his death was approaching if you would consider selling them, releasing them so they can use the information, they would do all the paperwork, they need that information to be released to them so they can continue to work on Jason's ideas, the patents are worth a lot of money, you would be a rich lady, well we would both be very financially secure because he had them in both our names, for some reason he put them in mum's address, they wrote to me a week or so ago, I guess because I was the executor of his will."

I am astounded when he shows me the figure they are offering. "You are joking me," I manage to splutter.

"No, definitely not," Sean replies, "you would get half that amount, it is split between us they will sort it all out they will even pay the legal admin fees, can you think about it, you need to let me know, if you don't want to do it then let me know and I will notify them."

Sean pushes himself from the unit and walks back towards the lounge. I call him back, "Sean, there is no point in us holding on to them is there, they are no use to us at all."

Sean smiles, "No, they are no use to us, I love the fact that my brother was one hell of a clever bastard, he made sure everything was so secure they cannot do anything without our permission." Sean moves closer to me, he holds my chin with his hand, "Angie, I know we have spoken of this before but can I ask you, honestly, do you regret what he did to you?" Almost immediately he moves away, "Sorry, I shouldn't have asked that question, it isn't right of me, forget it."

I look at him, I watch as the handle turns on the dining room door, I can hear the noise coming from the lounge, but I need more time with Sean, I walk to the door, Judy is waiting, she frowns at me, "What are you both up to?" she asks, I don't look at her, I pull the door closed.

"Five more minutes, Judy, please, just five more minutes." I don't see or hear her reaction, I turn to face Sean, "You have every right to ask, and you are probably the only person that can," I walk to the sink and pour myself a drink of water, I turn to face him, "the honest answer is yes, I did, back then I was very angry, part of me hated what he had done, I hated the wedding, I felt trapped, I didn't understand why he did it, in my mind he trapped me and I hated it, but the feelings I had for Jason changed with the different circumstances. I loved him, I know that, in our own little way, we loved each other, I know he was never demonstrative or tactile in the way I would have wanted, in a way I needed, we did have some good times though, Sean, we did and I know by the way he prepared everything for me, that shows me just how much he loved me, and without him, I wouldn't have your parents or you, so the answer to your question is no, I don't regret it, not at all."

Sean pulls me into his arms, "You were so good to him, Angie, when I think of all the crap you had to deal with, all his funny ways and those mountains of paperwork stacked everywhere, it would have driven me crazy, then the illness, you were a star, your whole lounge almost taken over by that huge mechanical bed, and all those carers trotting in and out, seriously I don't know how you coped," he pauses, "he was lucky, very lucky," he laughs out loud. "Do you remember how we came in and caught you two, well you were half undressed, your boobs out and him helping himself to a grope, that made me laugh and made me so happy that there was intimacy between you, thank you."

I pull him back close to me, his arms envelope me, he smells like Jason did, the familiar aftershave wafts in my face and for a moment I am transported back to another time.

"You don't have to thank me, Sean, really you don't." We stand holding each other.

"Mike seems like a really nice bloke, Angie, really nice." I nod my head, I cannot answer as my throat is tight with tears. The dining room door opens, but we don't pull apart, Judy and Mike are stood watching us, I push Sean gently away.

"What are you two up to?" Judy asks.

"Just saying a final goodbye to Jason," Sean replies, he looks me in the eyes for just a short while, then he lets me go and turns to Mike, "Well, mate, my brother asked me to look after her until she found someone else to love her, and I have tried to look after her for the past year, I think I have done a good job, but now I have a challenge all of my own," he looks at Judy then looks back at Mike, "there is only one man for the job now and I think it is you, mate," he laughs, "but watch out she has got a bit of a temper on her."

I look at Sean, we both have tears in our eyes, Mike moves towards me and Sean. "I know about the temper, Sean, I have been on the receiving end more than once, but I take it on with pleasure, mate," he says, "with great pleasure," he pulls Sean into a hug and claps him on his back.

I am exhausted, I can barely keep my eyes open, Mum and Dad leave really late. Sean and Judy allow them to take the children with them. We sit sipping coffee, Judy looks at Mike, "How did you not put two and two together with the surnames, Mike, my parents are Staddon, it is not a common name."

Mike shrugs, "I didn't really deal with your parents at the scene, I dealt with the taxi driver, we had to get him out of his car and into the ambulance, another officer took their details, I told him to call another ambulance as your dad looked quite shaken. Once they were checked out they wanted to go home the officer asked me if he should take them home, but when he said their address it was near to the hospital so I offered to take them, I was heading that way anyway as I had to check on the taxi driver, so I never actually knew their names, I chatted to your dad in the car, but nothing more than about the police cars really," he smiles, "it all seems a bit incredible now though."

Judy nods her head, she looks at me, "Cannot believe we both got away without the normal interrogation from Mum, Angie, but I am sure Clive will have something to say." I laugh out loud and Judy and I cannot help but keep smiling at each other.

I sit by Mike holding his hand, he strokes my wedding finger, he pulls it to his lips, "We must get something on that you know."

I smile at him, "I know."

Judy looks at us both, "You know, we could have a double wedding," she suggests.

Mike looks at me, we both laugh together, but it is Mike that answers, "No, definitely not," he replies, "I am not sharing the most special day of my life with anyone but this woman."

Judy laughs, "Just testing." she says.

Sean pulls Judy close to him, "And I would never agree to that either," he adds. I look at Judy, she looks so happy and relaxed in Sean's company.

"When do you think you will tie the knot?" I ask them both. Sean smiles, "As soon as possible for us, a quiet ceremony we have decided with a low-key honeymoon, as we want to take the children to Disneyland so we might just take a week for just the two of us in the UK somewhere, eh, Judy, what about you two?" he asks, Judy smiles and I smile back at both of them, Mike takes my hand and the smile dies on my face as Sean continues, "Phil's mate has a caravan in the new forest somewhere, might ask him about using that."

My breath catches and I look at Mike, I see a frown flicker across his face but he looks at Sean and it is obvious Sean is totally unaware of what has gone on, the expression on Judy's face is blank. Mike recovers quickly. "Sorry, Sean, I only intend to have one honeymoon so it will be somewhere a bit more memorable than a caravan, regardless of the location."

Sean nods his head, "Yes, you are probably right there, might have to put our heads together and come up with somewhere exotic we can also take the children." Mike pulls me close to him, I look up and see that Judy and Sean are snuggling in together, I stand up.

"More coffee, anyone?"

Judy shakes her head, "We have to be getting off now, it is late." I watch as they gather their coats and make their way to the door, as we wave them off Mike puts his arm around my shoulder.

"He doesn't know does he?" he asks, I know exactly what he is referring to.

"No," I shake my head, "why do you ask?"

Mike sighs, we walk back into the lounge and he pulls me onto the chair to sit on his lap, "Well this must all be a bit strange for him, you know, you, his brother, you and his brother living here, him being Phil's mate and everything, I thought he might be having a dig at me."

I move my head away from Mike, "No, Mike, definitely not, Sean is not like that, not at all, he thinks you are great, I know that, only yesterday he was telling me that he has always had a mistrust of Phil and his intentions. Don't get me wrong, he likes Phil as a mate, he said as much, but he said he thought Phil had ideas of maybe taking Jason's place, as my partner, when I told him all about you he was really pleased for me, for us," I pause, "I think his actual words were 'I am over the moon for you both', and tonight in the kitchen, he asked me if I regretted everything that has happened and I told him honestly, no I don't, I don't regret it because I have him, and little Ma and Pa, the little time we had in the kitchen was enough for us to tell each other how we feel about each other, so I know he likes you." I push him away playfully.

"Likes you enough to hand me over to you like I was a naughty girl," Mike laughs, "come on let's go to bed, show me just how naughty a girl you can be."

I laugh and get up, I leave him to switch the lights off and by the time he is upstairs I have my special nightdress on just for him, he flicks on the light, his eyes light up as he notices, "Oh, baby, what are you doing to me," I cannot reply as his lips meet mine.

The next morning we wake up and face each other, he looks so totally relaxed. "Wasn't yesterday a totally crazy day?" I ask.

He smiles, "Totally," I snuggle into his lovely warm body, my legs crossing over his, we fall asleep again and wake up an hour or so later.

I am so totally comfortable with him, we get up and shower, I am popping in to see little Ma today, I want to see her to make sure everything is okay and that she coped with the anniversary okay. I have bought her a lovely shawl which I know she will love. Mike heads off to the gym. I arrive at little Ma's I am shocked that Phil is there, his car is parked outside, I sit in my car indecisively I am torn between coming back later or going in, I don't want to see Phil today I am not sure why but I want to see Ma today, so I walk up to the door and before I have a chance to ring, he answers.

"Hi," I say brightly. "Surprised to see you here."

He shrugs, "Don't know why, I always pop in to see them, sometimes to have breakfast, I thought you was Sean. Pa isn't very well, we are waiting for the ambulance," he looks up as the ambulance car comes into view, he waves at them, then looks at me. "He had a bad turn in the night, you had better go through."

Phil's phone rings, he answers it on the second ring, I know by the batman tone it is Sean. "Yes, yes, he is okay, the ambulance is here, they have just arrived," I hear him say, I walk past him into the lounge, it is dark, the curtains are closed, he is laid on the sofa, Little Ma is sat by him, holding his hand and praying quietly, I touch her shoulder gently and she stands to hug me to her. The ambulance staff come in, they ask lots of questions and check his heart and blood pressure, they ask Little Ma for his tablets but she is upset and confused, I run to the bathroom to try and find them, Sean finds me searching the bedroom, he joins in to help me, I have never been in their bedroom before, it is nice and bright and there are two large close up pictures on the wall, one of Sean and the other of Jason and I at our wedding, we are both smiling, it is weird to see his smiling face looking back at me, I haven't looked at any of our pictures for a while.

Sean stands and looks at it with me, "It is like it was a lifetime away isn't it." I look at him and nod, he smiles at me, "On another day you should go and see his bedroom, she has it all as if he never left, quite lovely if it wasn't so tragic."

A lump comes into my throat, we hear Phil call out to us so we head downstairs, Phil has found the tablets in his waistcoat pocket, Pa hasn't taken them. With extreme care the ambulance staff sit him up and give him the tablets with a glass of water, they check his blood pressure and put the monitors on his heart, I stand back with Phil, Sean is in the kitchen, with his mum.

"Why didn't you tell me, Phil?" I ask, he looks at me frowning. "About what?" he asks.

I look at Pa, "About Pa," I reply.

He shrugs, "Angie," he takes my arm and moves me away from the ambulance staff, "Angie, I didn't exclude you, I was dealing with a situation, I called the ambulance then Sean, then I was dealing with Ma, I didn't deliberately exclude you, I would never do that, although I noticed you pause when you saw I was here, was you deliberating whether or not to come in, was that because I was here?" I look at him, he raises his eyebrows questioningly.

"He is improving now," the paramedic interrupts us. We move closer, Ma is right behind us, she pushes past moaning under her breath, Pa sits up he shakes his head at us mumbling apologetically, "I fell asleep, I think I forgot my tablets, I was very scared."

We cannot give him a hard time, he is old and frail and as the ambulance staff pack up we sit round him chatting. Phil is the first to leave, he pulls

Sean into a hug. "Thanks, mate," Sean says quietly to Phil, Phil kisses Ma and leans down to me, but as I look up expecting him to kiss me, he plants his hand on my shoulder and pats it gently, I nod back to him, I know that things are changing, this is just the beginning I have to accept that, but it all feels so removed, so distant and detached, to think I used to look forward to Phil kissing me after quiz night, and now it is like we are becoming strangers.

I follow him to the door, I hold the door open as he walks out, I pull at his sleeve, he turns to me, "Sorry, Phil, yes I did pause outside, so much has gone on in the last few weeks, and I was unsure what to say to you."

He smiles, the old Phil smile, he holds his arms out and pulls me into a hug, "You know, Angie, I know things have to change between us, but we don't have to be strangers okay." I smile at him, he lifts my chin up to his, "I cannot kiss you, as you are another man's woman, not that, that has ever stopped me before but Mike is my mate and he is a big bastard, but I can give you a hug and tell you I still think the world of you, that will never change okay".

I smile at him, "Okay," I watch as he walks to his car and he turns and smiles, as he pulls off he waves and I wave back at him with a smile.

I go back in, Sean has to go too but when Little Ma invites me to stay for something to eat I accept, I text Mike to let him know, Little Ma pulls me to her, "Where is your young man, why haven't you brought him to see us, you said you would, please, Angie, we would like to meet him."

I smile at her, "Okay, I will ask him, see what he says."

She pokes me in my side where she knows my mobile phone is, "Do it now," she insists, I laugh at her.

"Okay, okay, I will call him, but he might be busy," I warn.

"Not too busy for the woman he loves," she replies insistently, she goes into the kitchen, I call him quickly. "Really?" he asks questioningly, "they want to meet me?"

I explain about the ambulance and Pa and then I tell him that Ma has insisted they want to meet him. "Okay, if you are sure, I mean the anniversary was just yesterday, are they going to be okay with it?" I tell him she is insisting and he laughs, "Okay I will be round soon but I just need to shower, are you totally sure?" he checks again.

"I am sure," I reply. I sit with Pa, I hold his hand. "Ma has asked me to invite Mike round to see you, is that okay with you?" I ask.

He takes my hand, the colour has come back into his cheeks, he sits up, "You are like our daughter, we want to see you happy, Angie, we want to see this man for ourselves, make sure he is good enough for you," he smiles, "if not," he makes a motion of a cut throat and I laugh, he laughs too, that is the most I have heard him speak in a long time. Little Ma comes in from the kitchen.

"He coming now?" she asks.

I nod my head, "Yes, he is, he will be here soon," I reply, her whole face lights up with a smile, suddenly I am nervous, this is their son's home, he grew up here, they have so many memories of him and now they are welcoming my new partner in to their lives, they are such wonderful people.

As soon as Mike arrives and meets them I know they are going to get along, Little Ma takes his big frame into her arms and hugs him, with a lot of effort Pa manages to stand up to shake his hand, I am ignored as she pours him a drink and busies herself in the kitchen, within minutes she has a bowl of stew and a large chunk of soda bread which she presents to him, I watch smiling as Mike eats everything she puts in front of him, she stands watching proudly, Mike listens attentively as Pa explains how he came over to the UK with nothing and how he built himself up, got a good job, learned the language, Mike is listening without interrupting, eating and also looking at photos and newspaper clippings, Pa leans forward, "I am very proud of my family," he tells Mike, "I love my two boys, you make me very proud."

Pa's eyes glaze over, I know he is thinking of Jason, I hold his hand gently, Little Ma chides him, "You silly man, this isn't your boy, this is Mike, Angie's new partner." She looks at Mike, "Sometimes he gets confused," she explains.

"That's okay," Mike reassures her, "it's fine really."

She takes his hand, "You will come and see us again, yes?" she asks.

Mike looks at me, "Of course we will," he replies.

She chatters on, "Oh no, not just together, you come on your own, she eats like a bird but you, I will cook for you, you need to eat you are skin and bone."

She takes his tray from him and I laugh out loud, Mike is anything but that, but he nods his head, "Yes, I would like to pop in again, it would be nice to look at more photographs, I enjoyed today." It is getting late, we should go, I tap Mike on the arm, he stands up and shakes Pa's hand, "I have enjoyed meeting you, sir, I would like to call in again soon," he adds, Pa nods his head, his smile tells me he is very happy, we say our goodbyes and leave.

Outside, I pull Mike to me, "Thank you so much, you are the best, the very best."

He smiles at me, "Anyone who is important in your life is important in mine, and they are truly lovely people," he says matter of fact. "Besides that, she is a brilliant cook," I laugh as he pulls me to him, "you know I love you very much don't you?" he asks.

I look up at him, I frown, "Of course I do."

He smiles, "It is just sometimes I forget to tell you that is all," he brings his lips down to mine, kissing me gently, showing me just how much I am loved.

Chapter Sixty-Six

Helen and Phil have organised bowling for the shift, she is sat in the control room making lists. "He is a bastard that Mike," she says, "but a clever one, Phil and I are okay now, we have been working together practically every day for the past week or so, we know we have to get on for the sake of the job, but you know," she pauses, "we get on better now than we ever did, I think there is a mutual respect for each other's private life, none of us cross that line, I prefer it that way," she nods her head. "Mike was right, when we are at work, the job comes first and relationships second, you coming?"

I am deep in thought, she pulls me from my thoughts. "Oh sorry, when is it, Friday, I don't know, can I let you know?"

"Yes, of course," she nods her head.

"Oh you will never guess what, Mike is bringing someone, he says he doesn't know who yet so he cannot give a name but Amanda is so pissed off about it, but I am made up, couldn't be happier, serves her right, but I must admit I didn't know he was seeing anyone, I wonder what she is like, cannot wait to meet her. Hey you don't think it will be that mad girl from his birthday do you, can't see her wearing bowling shoes, can you, or maybe it is blondie, you know the short one, or maybe, it is the tall slim woman someone saw him kissing outside the station, he is a dark horse that one, I wonder who she is." I smile at her, I see a call coming in, I hit the button to accept it, what is he up to now, I wonder.

I catch up with him later, but he just smiles when I ask him, we are in the admin room, he is signing paperwork, I go and stand behind him, stroking his arm gently, he is waiting for documents to print. "What are you up to now?" I ask, he smiles then frowns. "The bowling," I explain, "Helen said you might be taking someone, she thinks it is one of three."

He laughs. "Three?" he questions.

"Yes, Nancy, blondie and also you were spotted by Helen recently, kissing someone outside the station, I guessed when she told me, that it was Carrie," I smile at him.

"Kissing her, I don't think so," he retorts.

I look down, "Yes, you did, remember, well you weren't kissing her, she kissed you, I was stuck in the car park waiting to park, I saw her kiss you on both cheeks. I cannot tell you how intensely jealous I felt," I look at him, "of course I didn't know who she was, but I should have known you only have eyes for me," I flutter my eyelashes at him then smile at him, "then you introduced me to her remember."

He smiles back, "Ah yes I remember." I smile at him again, but his face is serious, he continues, "Look, Angie, the invitation is there for you if you would like it, but I would like you to only come along as my partner, not as control room staff okay, I am not going to make polite conversation with you all night, and I certainly won't be able to keep my hands to myself, those are my terms okay, it is up to you what you want to do."

I smile at him, I run my hands up the side of his body, "I will have to check my calendar, any other terms I should know about?" I skirt past him as he tries to catch me, I walk away laughing. He is playing rugby straight from work tonight, so I am not seeing him, then on Friday he will be going straight to rugby training then coming home changing quickly and then going straight out to the bowling. I will hardly get to spend any time with him.

I leave work and after doing some shopping I head home, but I cannot resist it, I turn the car in the direction of the sports field and head towards where he is playing, I spot him immediately, he is racing down the pitch with three huge men chasing after him, I watch and howl as they take him down, landing on top of him in a heap.

"Big brutes, aren't they?" a friendly voice speaks to me, I look around, it is Dean, dressed in his rugby kit.

"Hello," I exclaim, I smile at him, I am really pleased to see him, he stands next to me and crosses his arms across his chest.

"I would ask if it was me you have come to see but I know now that you only have eyes for him over there," he laughs and points to Mike who is now running down the field again. "How is it going with you two?" he asks, I nod my head.

"Great, really great thank you, he is just perfect."

Dean laughs, "Yes I have always thought that, but only in a rugby sense," he laughs. "Although I also get to shower naked with him," he frowns, "oh dear, I think he has just clocked us chatting," he looks up, he puts his arm around me and shouts to Mike, "just looking after the little lady for you okay" he makes loud kissing noises, I look at Mike as he frowns, I pull away quickly.

"Don't, Dean, please don't."

He laughs, "Just joking with him, Angie, don't worry, he can take a joke."

I look over at Mike and blow him a kiss, he smiles and is distracted enough to allow the chap on the opposing team to pass him with the ball, Dean groans out loud, "That is it, you are banned, off with you," he scolds good-naturedly.

I laugh back and walk away towards my car, I look back to see Mike being dragged down onto the hard pitch again, I cannot bear to watch him, it must hurt and it is freezing cold, I have seen enough, I am going home. When he comes home from rugby surprisingly he has no injuries, he kisses me as he comes in, I watch as he gets changed in my bedroom. "So you told Dean about me then?" I ask smiling.

He shakes his head, "No, it is a small world, he knows my brother Steven, they drink in the same pub, so I guess Steven told him, it isn't a problem is it?" I shake my head he smiles. "Good, I am glad, and much as I loved seeing you there today, you distracted me, and you cost us a try and you will have to pay for that later, you will also receive a match ban, Dean is the captain and he says you are too much of a distraction," he smiles as he pulls on his jeans. "Those are the rules I am afraid."

As he is stood half naked I reach for him, "Well rules are rules I guess," I laugh as I pull him onto the bed. "And I am willing to pay for it now," he groans as I kiss him and reach for his zipper.

The bowling is planned for tonight, Helen is really excited, she is taking her new man from the gym, she still isn't happy with Amanda but they will have to make it work somehow, she chats to me whilst she is waiting for Phil who is booking in a prisoner, Phil has asked why I am not going but I quickly make an excuse that I had a commitment before I knew about the bowling, he doesn't pursue it I don't offer a more full explanation. I cannot say anything as Helen is there, but later Phil catches me on the stairwell, "Strange you are not going to the bowling," he comments as we pass each other on the stairs," I shrug, he tugs at my sleeve, "what does Mike think?" he asks, I shrug again, "Tell me to mind my own business if you want, Angie, I don't mind, but if I know Mike, and I think I do, this must be really difficult for him, liking you for so long then having to sneak about like it is a bad thing," he doesn't wait for a response, he walks on down the stairs, then he stops. "What is the worst that can happen, Angie, with people knowing, it is not a bad thing, you are single, he is single, what are you worried about, are you embarrassed or ashamed of him or something?" he carries on down the stairs and out of the door, not waiting for me to reply, he knows his words would hit home but no matter what he says, I still don't want to go. The truth is, I am just not ready to tell everyone about us, it is too soon for me, I love the fact we have his secret between us, I try to explain to Mike, he seems okay with it, he says he is disappointed, but I am disappointed he hasn't made any plans to move his stuff in with me.

It seems like it has been forever since he has been given the keys but he hasn't made any arrangements, I don't know why. Judy says maybe it is because Jason lived there, but it was my house first, I don't want to sell my house I want him to live with me, for us to live together, I know he is still staying at his mum's as the decorating is still going on, so why doesn't he move in, he hasn't said he would prefer to live at his flat, he hasn't mentioned anything, it is as if he has got the keys to my home and that is enough I cannot see any reason for him delaying. I feel frustrated and angry especially as he knows also that Stuart is moving in to Mum and Dad's apartment when he comes home so there will just be the two of us. It makes me cross that Mike doesn't just use one of his days off to get everything sorted, he seems to have lots of time to play rugby and go to the pub, I feel resentful but I cannot mention it again, I have asked him several times and he obviously has his reasons. Meanwhile he is happy to stay overnight and suffer having to pack and unpack his bag all the time, that is his choice, but it still makes me cross.

Tonight he is at rugby practice then he is getting ready at my house, I sit on the bed and watch him as he pulls his clothes from his holdall, see if he lived here there would be no need for the holdall, but it doesn't seem to bother him at all. I watch him as he dresses, he wears his tight black jeans and casual jumper, it has a V neck and I love the way his chest hairs poke out of the top, it is just so sexy, as he leaves he takes me in his arms. "Still not ready to tell the world yet then?" he questions, I shake my head, he kisses me gently on the lips, "no problem, you know I will wait until you are ready don't you, well I don't have much choice really but until then, I am happy to remain your guilty secret," he pauses "okay not happy but I do understand," I smile, I close the door behind him.

You are a fool I tell myself as I watch him get in the taxi, he looks at me and waves through the windscreen. I look at myself in the hallway mirror I speak aloud to myself, "You are a bloody fool, who are you keeping it a secret from." I go into the lounge, I sit down to watch television, but I fidget I just cannot concentrate, I keep thinking of that Amanda being there tonight with her hand resting on his arm, her stupid silly giggle as she twists her hair, she wouldn't care who knew about it if she was lucky enough to be with him, her stupid false laugh comes into my head, I close my eyes and think of him in his tight black jeans, his wonderful aftershave, I try to read the paper but throw that down in frustration. I pull my phone to me, shall I call him to let him know that I have changed my mind I am going to go. I put my phone back down again; it will be a surprise for him.

Twenty minutes later I am showered, dressed and looking out of the window waiting for my taxi, it is ten minutes late, I keep ringing to chase it up but I keep being told they are just very busy, I have my nose glued to the window. After over half an hour waiting it finally arrives, I tear out of the house and practically pull the car door off I am in such a hurry, but the driver is not local, he goes the wrong way round taking him several miles out of his way along a dual carriageway, despite me giving him instructions, I want to scream but eventually nearly forty-five minutes late I arrive. The impossibly loud music hits me as I go in, I make my way to the busy lanes, I can see the whole group just maybe fifteen feet away, they haven't even started playing yet, some have their bowling shoes on, others haven't got that far they are stood around drinking, Marcia is holding court with a few officers listening to her, Mike is leaning down listening to Amanda, who as I anticipated has her hand possessively on his arm, I stand for a moment, I just look at him, I am so very lucky to have that man love me. As if he senses my presence he looks up, I smile as his eyebrows shoot up, he smiles back at me, walking away from Amanda leaving her in mid- sentence, her mouth open, the track ends on the music, the DJ is announcing something, it is now a bit quieter. Mike walks right up to me, kisses me gently on the lips, whispering, "You came." He smiles at me, his whole face lighting up. "I hoped you would, I kept looking at the door just hoping to see you," he pauses and looks at me, "are you sure you are ready to be fed to the lions?"

I nod my head, I whisper back, "Yes, if you look after me," he holds my hand, we walk towards his group, suddenly I feel very shy, all his staff look over watching us as we approach, he puts his arm round my shoulder pulling me to him. "Add another name to my team," he tells Phil, Mike kisses me on the forehead, he doesn't seem to care who sees us. The shift make various whooping noises, then there is clapping, Mike holds his hands up, "Okay, calm down the lot of you, yes I guess it is official now."

I notice some of them looking at Phil but he is smiling, he walks over, shakes Mikes hand then pulls him into a bear hug, he says something which I cannot quite hear, Mike throws his head back and laughs out loud. "What was that he said?" I ask.

Mike looks at me, "He says you have to be on my team as you suck at bowling," everyone laughs.

I look over, Helen walks over to me, I cannot read the expression on her face, my heart sinks, I hope she isn't going to make a scene, I smile weakly at her, when she gets close I lean towards her. "Are you very cross with me?" I ask her but she shakes her head.

"No, not at all, I totally understand."

She pulls my hand, we move into a quieter area, "Angie, I am so happy for you, my heart sank when I saw him kiss you, but I trust you with my life and I know that you would never have broken the confidence between us," Helen looks at me.

I shake my head, "Of course not, Helen, even though, for my reasons not Mike's I didn't want to tell anyone we were seeing each other you are right, I would never tell him what you said, I couldn't do that, not break a confidence, not to a friend, it wouldn't be fair on anyone, not Mike or me and certainly not you, I would never betray you, even when you did say he looked sexy when he was angry," I smile at her, "and not even when you said mean things about him." I look at her, "I think he deserved it sometimes, he has his own way of dealing with things, sometimes a bit unorthodox but I just leave him to it, where work is concerned I don't get involved, I try and remember work is work and home is home, it works for us," we laugh together, she pulls me into a hug.

"You are a good friend, Angie, one of the best."

I pull away gently. "Ditto, Helen, ditto."

We chat for a little while more and I watch as Mike walks over to join us, "Well, it seems you are next to bowl, come on here are your shoes, Angie," he holds out my shoes and I slip my boots off and push the funny shoes over my socks then he takes my hand. We walk back to the lanes, I pick up my bowling ball I turn to look at him, he smiles, "Don't let the team down now, okay" he winks at me, adding, "no pressure though." I smile, I wink back. I glance to the left Amanda is glaring at me, I cannot resist it I smile and wink at her. I look down the lane then at Phil, he is watching intently.

As my ball knocks six pins down Phil looks at me, "Well I don't believe it," he remarks, "you are good at something."

I ignore him and bowl again, knocking three down, I walk past and dig him in the ribs, far too hard making him cry out, I walk and stand by Mike, he drapes his arm around my shoulder, "Not bad, Angie, not bad at all."

It feels so natural, just standing close to him, being held by him, we watch as Phil bowls, his ball heading straight for the gutter. As he walks back he is shaking his head. "Don't say a word," he warns me, I don't need to, the smug smile on my face says everything. Our team goes on to win, not by a huge amount but enough to make the others shake their heads in defeat. I watch Mike as he mingles with his team, he is very well liked, I can see that, they all take the micky out of his inability to drink a lot of alcohol and he takes it all good naturedly.

Helen and I get to have a quiet chat as we watch Mike she turns to me, "When the shifts changed I thought he liked you then, he asked a lot of questions, but he is so difficult to read sometimes, when we are out on a job he has no nonsense approach when he deals with people who are taking the mickey out of us, but then he can be really gentle and sympathetic with others, then as soon as we are back in the car, he is a different person again, he is a really nice bloke, Angie, one of the best, I am so glad you got together," she pulls me into a hug and as I move away she kisses me on the cheek, Mike looks over and smiles at me, I leave her and stand next to him, I snuggle into his arms, where I belong.

The next morning Mike wakes me, very early, far too early, I cannot even open my eyes I cannot understand him as we don't have work today, I groan pulling the duvet over my head, I peep out, there he is fully dressed and he seems to be very excited about something.

"What's going on?" I mumble, I rub my eyes and look at him.

"Come on, get up quick," he is very eager, "it is moving in day today."

I groan again, pulling the duvet over my head, but he is too quick, he throws it totally off the bed and pulls my arm, this time I am quicker than he is, I grab him and pull him towards me, "We don't have to go right now do we?" I ask.

"There is something that I need first," he scoops me up into his arms and pulls my nightdress over my head leaving me totally naked, he presses his lips to mine, his hands trailing down my body, as I respond to him he pushes me away, reaching for his zipper his eyes never leave mine and still half-dressed within seconds he has me screaming out for him. It takes another hour before we finally get to his apartment.

As we pull up I turn to him, "Why today, Mike, why not a few weeks ago, why didn't you move in when I gave you the key?"

He smiles at me, "I know you wanted me to, I know you were getting cross with me, but I didn't want my moving in to be a secret, I want people to know you are I are a couple, I totally understand how you felt about Jason and his family, I respected that, but once they were told I really could see no reason for us to hide it, I had no intention of skulking in and out of your house like a bad secret but you still seemed uncomfortable with it, with people knowing about us, and last night, well last night for some reason known only to you, you decided that you wanted people to know, the timing was obviously right for you and I am glad I am no longer your sordid little secret."

I smile at him, "I love you," I say gently as he pulls me into his arms.

His flat is amazing, it is beautiful, I cannot believe the transformation, the lovely warm colours in his lounge is just what I would have chosen, lovely warm caramel with magnolia, the leather suite is gorgeous, and all the furnishings are new and compliment the room, he leads me into the bedroom, there is a huge gap where the bed should be, I turn to face Mike, "Where is your bed?"

He frowns, "It should have been here a week ago but it has been delayed, I received a call that it is now ready for delivery, I have been sleeping in the spare room until it is delivered, and when it is here I am sure you will like it, well I hope you will." he moves to the kitchen and pulls out a brochure, there he shows me the most beautiful bed, with a very ornate headboard, at the other end is a built in television which disappears into the bottom of the bed, "it is gorgeous and I love it" I breath at him, I look at the price and have to look twice, it is crazily expensive, but Mike takes the brochure from me, "if I had it here right now I would seduce you on it, I can picture you laid on it, totally naked" I pull him close "shall we have it at our new home" I ask, he pulls away "seriously, you would like it, do you think it will go with your furnishings" I laugh, "if not, we change the furnishings, I love it Mike, I love everything you have done here, it is a shame we cannot live here, but it makes sense to be at mine, it is bigger, and has the garage and garden" I pause and look around "what are you going to do with it", he shrugs, "I don't know, I guess you and I need to discuss that", I walk into the spare room, nothing has changed in there, I look around, "I think, maybe we take the best of your things and take them to my house, our house, and then bring all my old things here and maybe rent it out, what do you think", Mike shrugs "you don't think I should sell it then", I shake my head "no not at all, you can have it as an investment", he nods his head "yes good idea", the rent would easily pay the mortgage". He sits at the breakfast bar he takes my hand, "remember the last time we was here," I nod my head, that seems like forever ago, he pulls me to him "we need to talk about us, so much to sort out, as in bills and things, you know this is all new to me, I have never lived with anyone before, well except my brother when he stayed here, I mean, how do we agree who pays what, I want to pay my way, more than my own way, I will not be kept by you, have you thought about that at all", I shrug, "no not at all, no thought at all, I don't care about all that Mike, I just want you there with me waking up next to me every day, in that wonderful brand new bed I cannot wait Mike, I really cannot wait, so let's get packing"

In just two days my house is transformed, it is chaos to start with but I love it, boxes are piled up everywhere, sports bags occupy the hall, his dad and brother arrive to help him carry everything, then Jenny and Margaret arrive just to be nosy, it is all very busy, but I find I don't mind them coming round, Margaret is in the kitchen making tea for everyone, Hannah is running from room to room very excited, but I don't see it as an intrusion, I love the fact they are all there with us and within a few hours he has totally moved in and my old furniture has gone to his flat. We all sit together eating pizza, I look around at everyone, they are all chatting happily, everything seems to fit, although the new suite is huge, I will get used to it, I don't resent his things taking over. My old sofa had to go to accommodate his huge leather suite, his glass coffee table and lamp are all here, his flat looks a bit weird with the new décor and old furniture, but it will still rent out, his sports equipment takes up most of the spare room and it doesn't bother me, the new bed has just been delivered and I laugh as his brother and dad fight to get it up the stairs, it puts up a huge fight and his dad curses and swears at it but they finally get it all set up and everyone watches television sat on the bare mattress, then everyone says their goodbyes, they are clearly exhausted. We go back upstairs and look at it. It looks huge and dominates the room but I love it, we will just need to buy new bedding, it looks perfect, before we even get to put the sheets on Mike pulls me down on the bare mattress and undresses me very slowly, I try to protest but my words fall on deaf ears, the bed is well and truly christened.

Within days it seems like he has lived there forever, our photograph, taken at the party is on the mantelpiece, pride of place, if anyone was to pull the picture from the frame they would see the picture of Jason and I behind it, I didn't know what to do with it, I didn't want to, well I couldn't bear to throw it away, so I placed our picture over the top it seemed the right thing to do, I didn't tell Mike, I didn't tell anyone, when Mike saw the picture of us both he couldn't stop staring at it, "we look so right together" was all he said, there is a lovely picture of Hannah on the coffee table next to the one of Juliet and Harry, it looks like home, our home. My sky package has now been increased to again include the sports fixtures, every cupboard I open has something of his, I love it, I love his clothes in the laundry, I want to cry with happiness when I see his washing besides mine drying on the line in the garden. His car now occupies my garage and I am relegated to the street for parking, but I find I don't mind it all, I love it, just mundane things like shopping becomes a joy, walking hand in hand in the supermarket I want to pinch myself that I can be this happy.

Mike is attentive and generous, I have yet to find anything nasty about him, despite looking miserable and frowning a lot, he is always happy, people seem to love him when they meet him, when we are out and about he seems to say hello to everyone, I cannot believe when I look at him that he is with me, I watch him reading a magazine at home, just chilling on the sofa, I watch as he falls asleep, magazine in hand, he looks so totally comfortable and at home, I have to pinch myself to believe it is all so real and that he is actually mine, with me, living with me, making love to me. Everything is so different than before, fresh flowers appear for me without me asking, we are like soul mates, I am so happy I could burst.

I get up on the first morning of his officially moving in, I start making breakfast, I hear his footsteps coming down, I busy myself making toast and cooking bacon but within seconds he pulls the silk tie on my dressing gown then as I stand naked he pulls me down onto the kitchen floor, as the cold tiles meet my warm body I cry out, but his kisses silence me as he makes love to me, as he gazes at me he smiles. "We need to rethink the flooring down here," he laughs.

"Or maybe you can just wait a few minutes until I get upstairs," I reply.

"Mmm no, that wouldn't work for me, when I see what I want I have to have it, there and then," I giggle as he snuggles into my neck and bites me gently, we lay on the cold hard floor until I remember the bacon and jump up to rescue it. It is too late breakfast is ruined but Mike just laughs.

He stands up he puts his arms around my waist, "That floor has definitely got to go."

I turn to him, "Well until I met you I didn't have a problem, so I will leave you to choose something more comfortable."

He laughs and nestles into my neck, "Okay, I will make it my first project."

We have our first official party as a couple tonight, an engagement party, it is really weird for me, and we are going into town to choose the gift together and both drinking tonight so we will get a taxi. I am looking forward to being able to dance with him, being held in his arms and no one making comments.

We head off into town, at his insistence, we have to sort finances out, we need to open a joint account, I look at him, as we sit eating a pub lunch, I totally adore that man, I watch as he is writing down numbers frantically working out figures, he is shocked that I don't have a mortgage, really shocked, he was totally unaware that the insurance paid it off, we have a long debate then finally decide on how to split the bills, like two excited children we queue up to open a joint savings account for our holiday savings, everything is so domesticated and we nearly agree on everything. Mike is playing golf with his dad later, he rings him to check the details I drop him off, he admits to not being very good at golf, finds it boring, but his dad and brother enjoy it so he goes along with them.

I pop and see Judy, we chat and catch up, she is as happy as I am, she has spoken to Sean about their wedding and they plan to marry in a very small ceremony, just immediate family and one or two friends, we spend the afternoon just chatting before I head for home, Mike is due in very soon so I begin to prepare our meal, once everything is ready I relax in the lounge watching television, every time I hear him using his new key in the front door I cannot help but smile at the thought of seeing him, but today when he comes in he is quiet, a bit too quiet, I can tell he is deep in thought, I know he has got something on his mind, he normally comes straight in and kisses me, then we talk, I flick the television off and walk out to the kitchen, he is leaning against the unit reading a leaflet. As I walk in he looks at me, he hands me the leaflet, I frown and take it from him.

"My dad gave me this earlier, it seems him and Mum have been talking and he wanted me to consider this."

I look down, the leaflet is about pre-nuptial agreements, I frown whilst reading it, I feel a bit sick, I swallow hard, I thought they liked me, and trusted me I look at Mike, I can feel tears stinging my eyes, "Why, Mike, why do they think you need this, do they not trust me?" I ask, my words come out all choked, "I love you so much I would never cheat you, ever."

Mike pulls me close, "No, honey, no, you have it all wrong, you don't understand, they think that you should have one for me to sign," he pulls me tight against him, looking down at me. "You see Dad was asking what I was going to do with the flat and about finances and things, so I told him today about our plans to rent it out then I told him about your situation," he looks at me, tilting my chin up so he can see my face. "I hope you don't mind, it's just I discuss things like that with my dad, he has a good head for figures and investments," I shake my head, "the thing is, he said he thought as much, he discussed it with mum and the next thing I know he is giving me that leaflet, saying I need to sign something to protect you from me, I did get a bit cross with him, I thought it was a bloody cheek, but he explained it logically, Jason provided for you, and it seems to me he went to great lengths to make sure you were provided for, I respect that, and I have no right to expect anything, should anything happen to us," he pauses. "I can see his point, maybe your Uncle Clive's services will be needed."

I pull his head down to meet mine, my lips meeting his, "You can have everything of mine, Mike, I trust you with my life, I really do, I don't need any pre-nuptial agreement between us, but I love them for feeling protective over me, I really appreciate that, I don't want any agreement." I tear the leaflet into pieces and leave them on the side, for the first time in a long time I have the sense of belonging, I know that the people around me love and care for me.

The engagement party is busy when we arrive, I wear my lace dress with hold ups and high shoes, we take ages getting ready and I love the intimacy of us both getting dressed together, the party is for one of the custody chaps, I don't know him that well but Mike knows him really well and likes him a lot, there are quite a lot of officers there but not that many from our shift, just one or two and no one from my shift in the control room. Mike is a great dancer, he has me spinning round the dance floor and I am exhausted by the time we finally leave. As we are just a street away from home he asks the taxi driver to drop us off, my feet are throbbing but I don't argue, he pays the driver and takes my hand, walking towards home he holds me close.

"Remember this," he whispers, he stops and takes my face between his hands kissing me gently, "this is where it all began," he gives a small smile, "remember how nervous you were about my intentions," he laughs, "if you only know what I wanted to do to you, you would have never let me in the front door."

I smile at him, pulling him close and pressing my body against his. "Are you absolutely certain about that?" I ask.

He smiles at me, his hands wandering over my body, stood in the street he kisses me passionately, "I would never have allowed me and you to be just a one-night stand, I am certain of that," he whispers, his body tells me we need to go home.

I take his hand, "Come on," I pull his hand and walk on, "even though you are not a secret anymore, you can still be my sordid secret," he laughs and follows me, we barely get the front door closed before he has my dress unzipped and is pulling me to the carpet.

People at work are getting used to us, it was a bit weird for me at first, I don't think I will ever get used to him sitting with me at breakfast in his pyjama shorts and then later sat in his uniform, talking seriously with Craig at work. Or like today, arguing heatedly over an incident that I think should be done immediately and Mike thinks should be delayed for the next shift, I win, Craig backs me up and the job is allocated to his shift and he has to sort it out, Mike whispers that he will make me pay for it, and I smile at him, within an hour or so later I trot down to the photocopier and he is there waiting for me, he runs his hands over my body making me long for him, then he leaves me and walks several feet away, "That will teach you to argue to a senior officer," he laughs. No more than an hour or so later we are both snuggling up on the sofa, no mention of the incident, I love just being in the same room, knowing he is mine, my man. He sends me little text messages when he is sat with Craig, just as he did before, I am truly happy. I struggled with the comments from the shift initially, I was paranoid that people were talking about me, about us, and judging us, I was expecting comments from Simon, but he strode into the admin room one day, kissed my cheek and said Mike was a lucky sod but he was pleased for us. Whatever beef he had with Mike he has soon got over, they are okay with each other and work as if nothing had gone on.

Amanda on the other hand, well she has been impossible, she makes me feel really uneasy, the way she looks at me, and when I speak on the radio to her she says she cannot hear me, but seems to hear everyone else; it is frustrating for me, especially when she ignores my instructions on certain incidents. Helen says she does the same to her. Craig pulls me over and asks if there is a problem, but I tell him that personally I cannot see there is one as far as I am concerned , I like her, she is okay, but it seems she has a real issue with me, I tell him that I am certain it will sort itself out, he says he will be monitoring the situation even though I tell him there is no need, personally it does affect me, in the rest room she will try and exclude me in conversations but as I know the jobs they are attending she doesn't succeed, then she gets cross and I am not imagining it, she excludes me by whispering or her favourite is to say to whoever she is speaking to "I will tell you later" then looks pointedly at me, it is very childish and she doesn't often get support from the rest of the group who I get on with. Of course it upsets me a bit as I have never fallen out with her over anything. Helen says it is because she likes Mike and is angry we are together, well there is nothing I can do about her feelings for him, I love him and we are a couple she just needs to get over it. I don't mention anything to Mike; he has this way of cutting any work related conversations short when we are at home.

On our last night shift Craig comes to me at five in the morning and tells me it is my turn to go early, I don't argue, I pack my things up and wish everyone a good break, I pop in to see Mike but he isn't there, I try to ring but he doesn't answer his phone, that is really strange, I will send a text when I get home, there is no traffic so I am home in minutes, I see a suitcase in the hall and recognise it as Mike's, I frown, I don't know what he would be doing with his case out, I look up and he is walking down the stairs fully dressed in normal clothes.

"What are you doing home?" I ask.

He smiles, "Well I sneaked off early and asked Craig to let you go too, the cases are packed and in less than half an hour our car arrives to take us to the airport, we are going to spend the next five days with your brother in Dubai."

My mouth falls open, I am speechless, I throw myself into his arms and hold him so tight. "You are amazing and I love you so much."

I cannot believe that he has organised this trip for us both and without me knowing, he pulls me close into his arms, "I am going to remove your fear of surprises, my darling, I am going to make as much of our time off together very special indeed, although you might want to check I have packed the right items."

I cannot help it I text Craig and Steve to tell them of our plans, but of course they all know already. We have a totally amazing time, Stuart and Mike are like brothers, they get on so well, and Dubai is beautiful, I really love it, I look forward to more surprises with Mike.

When I am back to work Steve teases me about living with Mr Perfect, but I laugh back at him, I have found out something that Mike is not good at, in fact he is hopeless, it is DIY, I tell Steve as much and explain that Mike said he would make his first project to be to change the cold hard tiles in the kitchen, I know Craig and the others are listening so I explain that Mike did his homework, and chose laminate floor, he said with confidence that it looked quite easy and both him and his brother would do it on the next day off, the flooring was delivered and it all looked fairly straightforward, I left them studying the paperwork with a lethal looking cutting saw in their hand and a huge tub of glue, I went off happily to have my hair cut and visit Judy.

On my return the house was in a terrible state, apparently Steven had turned round too quickly holding a large strip of the flooring, he knocked over the lamp that Mike had bought from his flat, causing it to smash on the floor, the fragments seem to have gone everywhere, then things got worse from there on in: the laminate wouldn't lay flat on the old tiles; there was a chunk out of the wall where the long plank had fallen and hit the wall; there was glue up the walls and odd pieces of laminate floor everywhere. Mike had lost his temper after kneeling in the glue and Steven had several plasters on his fingers. I opened the lounge door and surveyed the mess, Mike was in the garden speaking on the phone and Steven was sat on the floor looking defeated eating biscuits from the biscuit tin. I tried so hard not to laugh, but I couldn't hold it back, I laughed until my sides ached, Mike came in and was cross with me for laughing but after a short time he could see the funny side. "It looks so easy," he stated, his brother nodded in agreement, I couldn't be mad at them, they were so dejected. Within half an hour his dad was round sorting out the mess, he arranged to come round when Mike was at work to put right the damaged wall and to lay the flooring properly.

His dad looks at me, "Why did you let him loose on something like this, Angie?" he asks.

I shrug, "He said it was easy," I respond.

He shakes his head again, "Why do you think I was doing his decorating at the flat?" he asks.

I shake my head, "I didn't give it a thought."

He laughs, "I am very proud of my boys but I don't know who they take after, none of them can tell one end of a paintbrush from another and none of them can mend anything, that is what I am useful for."

We all laughed and Mike pulled me into his arms, "I just wanted to have a go, it looked so easy, honey, but I will leave DIY to my dad in future while we still have a solid roof over our heads okay."

I tell the shift the complete story and everyone was laughing, then we got back to our work. When Mike came in later they couldn't resist teasing him about it, but he took it all in good heart, and laughed with them, then he came over to me and when no one is looking he whispers, "You are such a snitch," he slaps me playfully on the bottom. "You are lucky I don't let them know about your one-night stands eh, Angie, what about that then," his dark eyes twinkle and he laughs and I laugh with him.

Mike and I were soon old news as several things happen at once, Amanda disappears, there is lots of speculation but no one really knows for sure where she has gone, there is no mention of a transfer or anything, her name is off the rota, Steve asks Mike when he comes into the control room but he won't be pulled into the conversation so we just speculate, Craig is tightlipped too, we all know that he must know something, Mike and him would definitely have discussed a member of the shift leaving, but he won't be drawn into any conversation about her either.

Steve quips at me, "She never liked you did she, Angie, from day one it seemed to me she had some beef about you."

I shrug, "I don't know either, Steve, she seemed okay to me, I quite liked her."

Gavin laughs out loud. "She was a bit of a one for the chaps through, wasn't she?"

I don't answer, I look at Mike and his face is expressionless, I smile at him and immediately he breaks into a smile, he comes over and stands by me just listening as Steve and Gavin carry on about how useless she was, then before we all have a chance to discuss it further, Max comes in, he has been typing statements downstairs, he sits down and listens to us for a while before suddenly announcing Marcia's pregnancy and even more astonishingly it is with a chap from custody, I look up to see Mike's reaction but he has disappeared. I am absolutely speechless, I know I had been all wrapped up in my own world and haven't spoken to her for a while, but I didn't even know she was seeing anyone, I wasn't the only one, everyone is shocked, no one else even knew they were dating, I certainly didn't, she never said a word. The pregnancy well, it was a shock for everyone, and I think maybe even for her, I am amazed that the person that told us was Max, Max who never gossips about anyone, suddenly spoke out, he plays darts with the chap who works in custody, he is known as Podge, I try to place him and can recall a young round faced portly chap, very friendly, I have spoken to him on the phone many times, Max said he was told but couldn't remember who Marcia was, he didn't know that I knew her, that she was my friend. I cannot believe it, Marcia has said nothing to me at all, I send a text to Helen, being careful not to be caught by Craig, a text comes back almost immediately, she didn't know either, she is very surprised, we decide we need to organise a girlie get together, I tell Helen she needs to make the arrangements as I am in danger of getting caught texting, I warn her it has to be very soon. Within minutes a text is back, booked for tonight, Marcia is on a day off, she admits she has been waiting for our call, half expecting it, so she knows she is in for the interrogation, she will meet us at the restaurant, meanwhile Helen and I will have lunch together, I cannot wait. Mike is playing rugby later, or at training, I cannot remember which so I send him a text message letting him know. I look up and Craig is watching me, I put my phone in my bag away from the temptation to carry on texting Helen, I will see her in an hour or so.

She is waiting for me in the staff restaurant, food is the last thing on our mind, so we just grab a sandwich, we cannot believe it, Helen knows Podge really well, she says he is a really lovely bloke, unfortunately very overweight, hence his nickname but so friendly all the time, she had no idea he liked Marcia and we are both confused as to how they would have got together, Marcia has no need to go to the custody area, she never eats in the restaurant, he would have no reason to go to the main admin office. It is a mystery as to how on earth their paths cross, we try and work it out but we cannot come up with a scenario, but we are both delighted for her, really thrilled, she will be a good mum.

The day drags, I just want to see Marcia and Helen, it seems like forever before I get to go home and shower and change, Mike lays on the bed watching me get ready, I sit on the side of the bed, turning to him, "Am I allowed to ask about Amanda?" I ask.

He shakes his head, "Nothing to tell, the job doesn't suit everyone, Angie, that is all you need to know really, no big mystery."

I nod my head, "And if..." I start to ask but he interrupts me.

"Angie, I don't want our life to be an extension of what happens at work, I want us to be totally separate as much as we can, I don't bring my work home, I don't exclude you, I just don't include you in matters that you can be dragged into, it is not fair to you, I hope you understand, I didn't fall in love with you at work and we will always have more in common with each other outside of work."

I smile, "Okay."

But Mike frowns at me, "What, Angie?"

I shrug. "Well it is just, you know, if you have a bad day I want you to be able to talk to me, to discuss it, like couples do."

Mike lays back on the bed and looks at me, "Okay, Angie, I take your point, but try to see mine, how would you have felt if I had discussed the Phil and Helen situation with you beforehand, would you have tried to advise me on how to deal with it, I don't need that, would you have tried to help Helen and Phil, I don't know, so it was best you were kept out of it. As far as I am concerned I keep family and work separately, well, as separately as I can, the bank incident is proof of that." I frown at him, and he smiles, "Yes, I know there was a lot of speculation at the time, the truth is, that a member of my family was in the bank at the time of the robbery, they were able to report everything to me by text that they were seeing from the safety of an office with no danger of being seen but before I disclosed any information to any senior officer I made absolutely sure their identity would never be revealed, I would never compromise on their safety or anyone I love and that includes you," he smiles at me, pulling me close to him. "Besides if I have a bad day at work, I know someone not too far away who knows exactly how to make it all better," his lips meet mine and he pulls me close to him.

"I have to go," I whisper, he flicks the buttons on my blouse and they immediately ping open, his hands reach in and within seconds my naked breasts are in his hands, he moves his lips towards them. "You might be a bit late," he whispers back.

Mike drops me at the restaurant on his way to training, I am only a little bit late, as he kisses me he whispers, "Be gentle with her, you know, with your interrogation, this motherhood, it is all new to her," I look at him in surprise.

"Did you know?" I ask, but he doesn't reply he leans over and opens the door, I turn to him. "You are full of surprises, Mike, you keep so much in your head, and never tell anyone, not even me," he frowns, "everything we have discussed tonight," I say by way of explanation, he nods his head.

"Ah that, well as I said that is all work rubbish, Angie, just work, and as soon as I take the uniform off I forget about it, it is just you and me, you don't need to know the nonsense that I deal with, or the idle gossip that goes on, now you go and have a good time, see you later," he kisses me again, I watch as he drives off, that man is incredible at keeping secrets.

Marcia is sat there at the table texting on her phone when I arrive, she looks up and smiles, she looks amazing, her skin in glowing and her eyes are bright and there is a huge smile on her face. Helen is just behind me, we exchange hugs and kisses then sit down, the waitress is over immediately, we order quickly desperate to hear her story.

She looks at both of us and puts her hand up in submission. "Okay, I am sorry, I owe you an apology, I know that I should have told you, you should have heard it from me, but I couldn't believe it myself, it all happened so quickly, so quickly that even now I still cannot actually believe I am now

509

with Podge, pregnant with his child and so deliriously happy," she pushes out her little bump proudly, you can hardly notice.

I smile at her, "So come on then out with it, start with how, then when, then how again, details, girl, tell us the details," I urge her, she sits back.

"Well, I will start with how, firstly I have no reason to have any contact with him at work – our paths don't cross, but I have seen him around, you know, about the station, everyone says how friendly he is, but I had never spoke to him, never had any need to really, never really noticed him really, not in that way," she pauses. "The way it happened, well, it is all Phil's fault really," my eyebrows shoot up in surprise, she laughs, "that man is incredible, and I know I am not sat with two of his greatest fans right now but nonetheless Phil is really a lovely bloke." The drinks arrive, she sips at her water before continuing, "Phil was called to custody, as Podge had been hit by a chap who was arrested, not badly injured, it was a genuine accident, the chap fainted and as Podge went to catch him the chaps wristwatch had caught him, Podge in the face and he was bleeding, Phil was called as he is the first aid person, but he came to my office and asked me to go as he was busy," she pauses. "I remember I was really mad at him, as I was busy too, but I went, and I was clearing up the wound which was more of a scratch, and as I leaned towards him, he kissed me."

Helen and I look at each other, Helen is the first to speak, "Seriously?"

Marcia laughs, "Yes seriously, honestly, I couldn't believe it, I was shocked, I mean I didn't know what to say, but he kissed me so gently then pulled away, and just looked at me so I looked at him, as I said I didn't know what to say or do."

Helen responds, "Oh my god that is so inappropriate, what did you do?" she asks, without waiting for a reply she continues, "You should have reported him."

Marcia laughs, "Well, you know me, Helen, I don't have any nonsense and ordinarily I would have slapped his face, the damn cheek of it," but Marcia smiles, "what I did was, I kissed him back," Marcia replies. I look at her, I am speechless, but she sips her drink again then looks at us both, "I know, I cannot believe it, that one kiss, he kissed me like no one ever has, so gentle, so tenderly, I felt it right down to my toes, that one kiss, I was so taken back, so then, when I could finally get my words out, I asked him why he kissed me and he told me it was because he wanted to, so I gave him the Marcia attitude, I told him it wasn't on and he was to explain himself before I called the custody sergeant, he shut me up by kissing me again, I couldn't believe it, his kisses are amazing, he stroked my face so gently, and just stared into my eyes, it was like something from a movie," she pauses, "I am telling you, no one has ever kissed me like that, then he told me that he has liked me for a long time, then he went on to explain that when Phil came in to do first aid, he saw it was Podge and told him he was going to get me and this would be his one and only chance. Apparently they were up the hospital with a prisoner the other week and Podge told Phil he liked me, so when he was called to custody Phil said to Podge that if he didn't make his move on me then Phil would."

I laugh out loud, that is so like Phil, Helen frowns, "What?" she looks confused, "I don't understand, does Phil fancy you then?"

Marcia laughs, "Helen, honey, please try and keep up, no, Phil doesn't fancy me, not at all, I think he was just pushing Podge to make a move, he would have never done it otherwise," she pauses, then laughs gently, "me and Phil, ha, I really don't think so, I know Phil, I know him very well, but not in that way, he is a great bloke, a bit of an enigma, far too complicated for me, there is a woman out there he is destined to be with but it is definitely not me."

I pick up my drink, sipping it slowly I let her words sink in, I don't know what to say, she surely doesn't know about me and Phil, he would never betray our secret, not to Marcia, not to anyone. Our food arrives and it creates a much needed diversion, I tuck in, not daring to look at them, we eat for a short while then it is Helen that breaks the silence, "So where did you go from there then?"

Marcia smiles, "Well, he took my number and asked if he could call me, I saw no reason not to and before I had got back to my desk he had sent me a text saying he wanted to take me out that night, so he did, and we haven't been apart since." She looks at both of us, "Okay, the pregnancy was a bit of a shock to us both, but I guess that is how things happen sometimes, we are both overjoyed and I cannot see my life with anyone but him," she looks at both of us one at a time, "but that is not the question you want to know the answer to is it?" she looks at Helen, "go on, I know you are dying to ask."

Helen looks at her, "Okay I will, just who is this woman that Phil is supposed to love?" she asks, I can see she is trying to sound casual but failing.

Marcia smiles, "Okay, stop right there," she waves her fork around in the air as if making a point, "stop changing my words about, I didn't say love did I?" she smiles at Helen. "The thing you both need to understand is that Phil puts up this barrier, to protect him, the jack the lad image is his defence mechanism, you must both know that, he has been hurt badly in the past by someone he loved very much, he is really a very deep character," she pauses, looking at us both. "Your food okay?" she asks, we both nod, she puts a large forkful of food in her mouth and chews slowly. "You ask me who the woman is that Phil is in love with, but that is a different question, and so that might be a totally different answer, but I will tell you the one he is going to be with," she takes another forkful of food and chews thoughtfully, she wiggles her fork around again in mid-air. "Well at one point in his life he thought it was you," looking at both of us in turn she frowns, "yes, you heard right, both of you, he has loved both of you," she turns to me, "I guess he still does love you in his own way, Angie, you must know, in fact I know you do know, he loved you long ago, he told you as much, a deep unrequited love, that broke his heart, he told me he realised he loved you before you and Jason were an item, even when you were married to Jason and even when Jason died, he still loved you, part of him, I guess always will, but back then he knew it would never be, it couldn't happen, despite being there for you, just waiting for you to hint at something more than friendship, you never did, he told me you were intimate with him, shared so much but not in that way," she looks at me, raising her eyebrows. "Shall I go on, or have I said too much?"

I shake my head, I look at Helen, her face is shocked, I put my hand on hers, "we never did anything, Helen, honestly, I never felt that way about him, Marcia is right, I know he has always had feelings for me, but I never felt the same," I look up to Marcia, "although how she knows all this is beyond me."

I look back at Helen, she is just staring at me, I look back at Marcia, she is eating and takes her time before continuing, "Phil told me all of this, he talks to me, he knows I never judge him, he annoys me, drives me nuts, and I guess I get on his nerves too, I hate him sometimes but I love him too, I mean who am I to judge him, I am the female version of him, well I was before I met Podge," she smiles and places her hand protectively over her tiny bump, then she looks at us. "Phil knows he can tell me anything, so he does," she looks at Helen, she shrugs, "you were too perfect for him, too controlled, too organised, he idolised you, but not in a good way, when you showed him you were interested in more than just a friendship, he got scared, scared of hurting you, that is why he made that big show of making out with Sue on her hen night, yes he told me about that, you both saw him making out with her but you didn't see him put her in a taxi home, he doesn't want people to see he cares but believe me, he does," she pauses. "Phil knows he is a destructive person where relationships are concerned, he wants to own someone, then when he does he cannot cope, he destroys the relationship, he very nearly broke Gemma, emotionally, he knew it, so he was frightened he would do the same to you. He is a very complex person." She pushes her plate away, "Wow, I am so full," she announces, "but I am sure I can manage a dessert." Helen and I just look at her in amazement. "What!" she exclaims, "I am eating for two you know, I am allowed dessert."

Helen almost shouts at her, "Who is she then?" Marcia frowns, Helen continues, "The woman for Phil, surely you are going to tell us, aren't you?"

Marcia pulls the menu towards her, "And if I do, what does it matter to you two, you are obviously happy now," she looks at me, "I wish I had placed a bet that you and Mike would get together, I knew even before you did that he liked you, I think a few people suspected even you, Helen." Helen nods her head Marcia continues, "It was so obvious."

I smile at her, "Not to me it wasn't."

Marcia leans back in her chair and stretches. "No, I know that, Angie, you were caught up in your own emotional situation with Jason, but I watched him sometimes, even when you were married, I caught him so many times watching you when you were working downstairs, you were totally unaware. Before the shifts changed he would look out of the window and I knew he was looking and waiting to see your car arrive, he asked questions about your whole shift but never bothered to listen about the others, and I knew, but I could never tell you; even the business over the concert ticket, Sue in the other office wanted to buy it but he held back saying he might take someone else, then when I said about you going, suddenly it was available again," she laughs out loud. "In some ways he was so obvious, and I am so glad you two are happy, you deserve each other, really you do," she looks at Helen, "and you are too good a police officer to go out with one too, there would always be the element of competition, you are a pretty hard act to follow for most people, that is why Amanda struggles to get on with you, apart from the fact you are too bloody beautiful."

We all laugh, I look at Marcia, I always had her down as an airhead, someone who flitted from relationship to relationship not caring about anyone but herself and her needs, but it is obvious, I had her so wrong, she looks at me, "If I tell you who the woman is that Phil will be with, or who I think it is, will you keep it to yourself and not judge him?" I frown at her, I look at Helen, "No, don't look at her," she chides, "I am asking you."

I look at her, I shrug, "Why do I care, Marcia? Phil and I have moved on in where we were in terms of a relationship, we had to, it wasn't fair on Mike for Phil and I to be so close."

She purses her lips, then shakes her head, "Yes, I know all of that it was not good for either of you, but," she pauses, "Okay, the woman who Phil needs to be with, has had such a horrible time over the last few years, which people won't know, and don't need to know, she is his one and only, and he feels the same, they hide it well, but…"

She doesn't get to finish, my words come out in a whisper I am shocked, "It is Jo, isn't it?"

Marcia looks at me for a second before answering, "What if it is?" she asks.

Helen almost spits her drink out. "You are bloody joking," she scoffs, "you have got to be kidding me."

Marcia tilts her head to one side studying Helen. "Why do you say that?" she asks.

Helen looks at me then at Marcia, "Well she is married for one, she is a slapper for another, she has been shagging him for nearly as long as she has been married, flaunts it in Julian's face, poor bastard, sneaking off for sex, her leaving Julian's bed and going to Phil's," she stops, then looks at both of us before continuing, "well if you are correct then they deserve each other, none of them can stay faithful."

Marcia leans forward, "I think you will find that Phil has always been faithful to Jo, okay, not in that way faithful but faithful in that he never lets her down, he might have spent the evening with you Helen but they were together later, she needed him, he was there for her, as it is meant to be, he is always there when she needs him, and no matter who he dates, or who he has one-night stands with or liaisons in car parks," she looks at me, "he always goes back to her, there is no doubt in my mind he loves her, he really cares about her, she is trapped in a loveless marriage – to an alcoholic who only cares about his next drink, although he did initially cover it well, the cracks are appearing now," she pauses and looks at both of us. "You didn't know did you?" We both shake our heads, she continues, "Oh dear, maybe I have said too much, but she married him out of pity, out of duty, because she was scared of what would happen to him if she didn't, he falls into bed pretty much in a coma and she leaves him to seek a bit of love and affection elsewhere, what is wrong with that, sure she is silly and brazen sometimes, but I know she is frightened to do anything like leave Julian; Phil knows that, he also knows how she really feels about him, how much she loves him, they will be together, I would stake my life on it, and everyone judges them, for what they are doing to Julian, but no one ever sees the complete picture, do they?" she looks at both of us, slowly waiting for her words to sink in.

I open my mouth and close it again. I realise I have been so very mean to Phil, always spouting off about her and her infidelity, and I have totally misunderstood Jo, I can see how difficult it must be for her, I mean Jason was poorly and died leaving me free to love again, but for Jo, she is trapped, the guilt would be so immense, if Julian did something stupid, if what Marcia is saying is true I can see they need each other, they steal time to be with each other to make life more bearable, I suddenly see them both in a whole new light. I look at Marcia then to Helen, I cannot believe it, Phil and Jo are happy in their own way, it works for them, until the solution is found, and who is anyone else to judge.

Helen still looks nonplussed as I nod my head, "I think you are right, Marcia, you are an incredibly insightful person, Phil is lucky to have a friend like you, you see I thought I was his friend, but clearly I wasn't, he was there for me every time I needed him, but I never realised, I never cared about his life outside of me, didn't really care about his needs or wants for the future, I regarded him as just a playboy figure, scared of commitment."

Marcia interrupts, "And to some degree that is what he was, he needed to have some escape from the reality of his relationship with Jo, sometimes I think when things were particularly bad he wanted to try and force her to leave Julian so he would go out with women she knew personally," she looks at Helen, then continues. "He wanted her to find out and react, like the business with Sue, she never got home at three in the morning after her hen night, but it suited Phil to let everyone know he had kissed and made a play for her. Sue played along, to her it was a bit of fun, but to Phil it was in the hope that it would filter back to Jo, which of course it did," she pauses, "I think maybe he wanted her to show some reaction, but it failed, she didn't, she never has, and he would always inevitably go back to her because that is where his heart belongs."

Helen and I sit and take it all in, it all seems to make sense, no matter what I said to him about Jo never leaving Julian, Phil never argued with me, never stood up for himself, because he never wanted anyone to know the real truth about the nightmare that was Jo's life.

I look at Marcia, "Why now, why are you telling us this now, you could have told us before, many times we have been out and you never said a word, we have bitched and moaned about Jo and you never told us the truth, why?"

Marcia looks over and beckons the waitress, she places her order and we add coffees, as she watches the waitress disappear she looks at us one at a time, "Because you are now both in a good place, the right place, you are both in love, happy and you both know how it feels, she needs to feel that too, and she does when she is with Phil; you have to acknowledge that she is entitled to some happiness, however she manages to snatch it."

I nod my head in agreement, I look at Helen, she is crying, I pull her close to me, "I was so horrible to the both of them, I gave them such a hard time, her especially," she wails.

I can only nod my head, "Me too, honey, me too."

When the coffee arrives we turn the conversation back to happier things – Marcia and her new relationship, the baby, she is moving in with Podge soon, she is taking him to meet her parents and she knows her life with him will be perfect. I take her hand across the table and squeeze it, she squeezes it back.

"I think it was important for you to know about Phil and Jo, and all the other stuff, but I don't think anyone else needs to know, I hope you agree, I mean, you both understand how it feels to have your private life made into public ridicule," she looks at Helen, she nods her head, "so I hope you won't say anything."

We both nod our heads in agreement. We finish our coffees, pay the bill and leave. We wave to Helen as she pulls off in her car, Marcia is giving me a lift home, as we walk across the car park Marcia suddenly stops, I look at her.

"You okay?" I ask.

She shakes her head, "I thought Phil was going to hurt you, as in physically hurt you, you know when he got into your car the other week, I was seriously worried for your safety, I was so worried I even thought about ringing Mike for him to go out there, but I didn't. I don't know what you had said or done, but I was very concerned for you that day."

My heart beats hard in my chest, my voice comes out as a whisper, "You know about that?" I ask.

She shakes her head, "No, I only know that Phil was the angriest that I had ever seen him, I don't know why and I don't want to, when I got to work he was in our office looking out of the window, clenching his fists like he does when he is really angry, he couldn't calm himself down, and he wouldn't discuss it, I looked out and at first I couldn't see what he was looking at, so I asked him, but he ignored me, when I asked him again he told me in no uncertain terms to mind my own business. I knew something was really bad, as he never is offensively rude to me, then as I saw your car pull in he went storming out of the office. As I said I don't want to know, I have too much in this head already, but I saw him, nearly wrenching your door off, I heard him shout at you, then I saw you both having what looked like a very heated argument." We get in the car and she starts up the engine before she continues, "I notice a lot of things, and I also notice that since your argument with Phil your relationship with him has changed, changed beyond recognition, and that has to be a good thing for both of you," she smiles, then adds, "and he is totally different now you are together."

I turn to her. "Who are you talking about now?" I ask.

She laughs, "Mike, you know the miserable sod that hardly ever smiles, well now he seems so happy, he never stops smiling, and it is lovely to see, it must have been impossible for him to come to work and see you every day knowing how he felt about you and you having absolutely no idea," she pulls up outside my house she turns to me. "We all deserve to be happy," then she looks serious, "it is a shame about Amanda too, but it is her own fault isn't it, she pushed him to the limit." I frown and immediately she puts her hand to her mouth, "Oh my god, Angie, he really does keep work and home separate doesn't he?"

I nod then turn to face her. "Yes, he really does, we were only talking about that tonight, but now you have started, you need to finish, I need to know."

She shakes her head, "I don't know if I can, Angie, if he hasn't told you it really isn't my place to."

I turn to face her, "Mike is Mike, Sergeant Simms is Sergeant Simms what he chooses to tell me is his business but you are my friend, Marcia, and you cannot stop now, you have to tell me."

She takes a deep breath, "Okay, but you never heard it from me," she looks down at her hands then looks back up, she shrugs, "you know what, I owe her nothing, so I will tell you," she looks me straight in the face. "She, as in Amanda, well she made several complaints to Mike that you were excluding her, making her feel uncomfortable, Mike told her if she wanted him to take her seriously she would need to make the complaint official, then he would take the complaint on board, he said if there was a case, then he would help her with locating tape transcripts that would prove that what she was saying was true, but she was told by him, that she needed to also provide evidence or witnesses, and that he would ensure the matter would be investigated fully, it was all there in the meeting notes, of course she couldn't, because it was absolutely made up rubbish, so her complaint was not upheld, in fact the report that was made found that it was the other way round, there is evidence she ignored your instructions on several occasions causing important information on jobs to be missed and some jobs she ignored had to be reallocated, but apparently you never said anything against her, seemed to me in the notes that you had just cause to raise a grievance but you never did, then when I was doing the rotas for next month Mike came and sat with me, I watched as he deleted her name, told me she was no longer on the shift," she looks at me. "He said that any enquiries with her name is to be directed to him, he said the shift would be told later that day, I asked if I could ask why and he said no, so I didn't ask any questions, but I did sneak a peak in her file before it was sent off, I saw the notes, he left the file in the secure post ready for me to seal and send to personnel, but I couldn't resist having a peek, he would go mental if he knew and he would definitely have no hesitation in having me reprimanded, so please don't say anything." She pauses, "Anyway she has resigned, there it was in black and white, not sacked, but she said she had been offered another position somewhere else and it was an opportunity she couldn't miss, she didn't want to work her notice, it is really odd," she looks at me I raise my eyebrows.

"What is?" I question.

"Mike is, he is willing to investigate a complaint about you, you know, a complaint about the woman he is in a relationship with and he doesn't say a word to you." I shrug, "I guess he would have told me at the relevant time, maybe he knew it was rubbish and it was his way of getting rid of her, maybe he thought I would be different towards her, which in fairness I probably would have."

I sigh, "I wonder if Craig knew."

Marcia looks at me, "Yes, Craig knew, as your sergeant he had to go through the tapes with Mike, they both worked together, they came in one day when they were supposed to be off duty, it was all in the file," her face is so serious, "don't tell anyone, Angie, please don't tell anyone," she urges me.

I shake my head, "No of course I won't, I promise." And I will keep that promise, Mike and Craig, they are certainly a force to be reckoned with, if Craig knew then he would have had his own reasons, same as Mike for dealing with matters in their own way. I cannot believe that Amanda disliked me so much or wanted to be with Mike so much she was willing to risk her own job.

I watch as Marcia drives off giving a cheery wave, my head is reeling with the information. When Mike comes in I relay the information back to him about Jo and Julian, he just nods and says, "That explains a lot."

I frown at him, "Explains what exactly?" I ask.

He shrugs, "Well it is no secret with Julian and his alcohol problem that is probably why he was desk bound and not given anything very challenging, but I wonder why Phil never mentioned anything to you, you seemed to share everything but something that important he never mentioned to you."

I shrug, "I don't know, Mike, Phil knows how I feel about infidelity, you know, you make promises, in sickness and in health, I once told him I felt very lonely and he said himself I was not the sort to have an affair, but he never elaborated," I shrug again, "I guess that is his business, and hers of course."

Mike taps the sofa, "Come here," he says, I move to him, he frowns then speaks, "I don't believe in infidelity either, but I must admit when Phil indicated that your marriage might be less than happy, it did cross my mind to try and seduce you."

I push him playfully, "You are so bad."

He laughs, "I know, it also worries me that my mum knows me so well too, she was so worried that I would get into some sort of trouble, cause a marriage to break up, that, in her opinion is the world's worst sin, she even got Dad to have a word with me," he pulls me close, "how do you feel about Jo and her situation?"

I shake my head, "I don't know, Mike, I really don't know, part of me thinks that it is all wrong, but then I am not in her shoes, she is living with the nightmare, but she also chose to marry him, our scenarios may seem similar but they are very different, I don't see that I had a choice but to marry Jason and part of me always hated him for that, but she chose to marry Julian, she made her vows and now she is cheating on her husband." I take a deep breath, he is just looking at me, his head tilted to one side, I continue, "Whatever reason or however Marcia dresses it up, it isn't right, not right at all, but it is their business, what her and Phil do is their own business not mine, I cannot say what I would have done if I was in the same position, I would hope that I would stick to my vows, but I don't see her situation and mine as being similar, they are not, and dress it up how you like, what she is doing is wrong," I shrug, "but as I said it is their business, it is their lives, they can do what they like."

Mike puts his hand under my chin and tilts my head, he kisses me gently on the lips, "I am so glad to hear that, honey," he pulls me close to him and we snuggle on the sofa together.

Chapter Sixty-Seven

We marry just ten months later; it is a lovely sunny day, I have planned every single detail of my wedding with Mike, we set a budget at his insistence, our obvious choice for the reception is Mike's family hotel, even though the honeymoon suite is fabulous I insist on the original playroom guest room for our first night together as man and wife. My smaller bridesmaids, Hannah and Juliet look so adorable they are in white frilly dresses with light blue sashes and blue ribbons in their hair, they look fabulous, since they have met they are virtually inseparable and they are the greatest of friends, I am in great danger of being upstaged by them, they are just so sweet and so cute. Judy is my maid of honour. I did think of asking Helen but she got to me first, she is on holiday the week before we get married, she only gets back on the day we actually get married, she is gutted but she will be back for the evening party she said she wouldn't miss it for the world. Mike's brother Steven is his best man, Scott, Stuart and Sean are the ushers, although it was never discussed, Phil is just down as an evening guest, when I added his name to the evening list Mike didn't challenge it in any way, I wouldn't have cared if he had, the rest of the shift are just coming to the evening do and just a choice few are invited all day, I don't need Phil there to make my happiness complete. Little Ma and Pa are coming all day, they are over the moon. They absolutely adore Mike as he often pops in to see them when he is out and about on patrol. I always know when he has been there as he never needs feeding, she loves the fact he has a huge appetite. Both Mum and Mike's mum are wearing light blue, they both wanted to tone in with the bridesmaids. When they both come round to ask me if it would be okay, I was fine with it, they seem to be good friends too. I got very emotional when Mum told me that they would very much like it if Little Ma could also wear the same colour as them too. Both of the dads, Pa and all the ushers together with the best man are coordinating in wearing navy suits with a light blue waistcoat and matching ties with not a cravat in sight, I was most insistent of that. My dress is everything I want it to be, simple ivory off-the-shoulder dress with a small train and sequin detail all over it, so very different to the one before, I love it so much I want to keep it on in the shop. I wear lacy hold ups with a blue garter thoughtfully provided by Judy.

My dad is a very proud man he has a huge smile on his face as I hold onto his arm walking towards Mike, I look up, Mike is looking back at me, his face lit up with a huge smile. He half walks up to meet me but his brother takes his arm and gently pulls him back which makes me laugh, I look into his dark eyes, I want to hold the moment forever. The man stood in front of me begins the service and asks if anyone knows of any lawful impediment, I hear the silence in the church, then my vows, I don't need for him to tell me what I need to say, I say them clearly and loudly, I want the whole world to hear me. I don't want to cry, I look at Mike, and he looks me in the eyes as he says his vows back to me. Forsaking all others, I smile at him, in sickness and in health, our eyes meet, none of us blinking, to love and to cherish, we move closer. Even before we are pronounced man and wife Mike leans forwards, he looks up to the vicar and waits for permission then he pulls my face towards him and kisses me, then we turn to the congregation I give a huge curtsey and he gives a deep bow, everyone erupts into applause. Just as I always imagined it would be. The gold band on my left hand fits perfectly and feels like it has been there forever.

The evening reception is busy and exciting as all our family and friends are together in one room, everyone is dancing, having a good time, Hannah and Juliet are tearing around excitedly, Marcia is there with a very slimmed down Podge and their beautiful son Daniel, she looks radiant and oh so happy, I see Phil and Helen stood chatting to each other for a long while, I watch them for a while, she is explaining something and using her hands to gesticulate, I notice the sparkle of the diamond on her left hand, I cannot believe it, she has got engaged, I wave frantically and she comes over, I grab at her hand but she pulls it away, "No, not now, Angie, not today, we got engaged on holiday and I wanted to wear my ring as I cannot bear to take it off but you have your day and then I will have mine," she looks at me and smiles, "I am so very happy, Angie, I love him so much." We both look over to where her fiancé Cole is standing, she turns back to me. "He is everything I want in a man, I even don't mind his ponytail," she laughs. "Looks like we both got what we deserved in the end doesn't it." I smile at her, I pull her close into a hug and notice Phil making his way over, I push her away gently as he approaches.

"Can anyone join in?" he asks jovially, we both laugh, Helen puts her finger to her lips to indicate I should remain silent and walks off, Phil watches her leave. "She seems happy," he comments.

I look at him, "Yes, Phil, I think she finally is," he looks at me, a slight frown on his face, "and what about you, Angie, you got your fireworks then?" he asks.

I nod my head, "Oh yes, Phil, I am so very happy and yes fireworks, every time," we both laugh.

"You are a funny thing, Angie," Phil looks at me, "but you are a lovely funny thing," he pulls me into a hug.

I look over at Mike, he is chatting to little Pa, squatting down so he can hear him, he is listening intently as Pa speaks, then he leans over and helps Pa take a sip of his drink, it is all done so genuinely with love, and as I watch Mike I know that finally I know what true love is, what it really means, I look at Phil and he is watching Mike too, he holds my hand for just a second.

"He is a great bloke, Angie, one of the best, and you two deserve each other," he pauses, "you know, I came to see you at the church today, I wanted to see you make your vows with a smile on your face this time, I am sorry but I had to see it, I understand why I wasn't invited to the whole event, I am fine with that, but can you understand why I needed to be at the church with you?"

I smile and nod my head, "I do, Phil, thank you, I really do."

He holds me close and kisses my head, "I know you are going to be very happy, and if you would allow me to, I would like to continue to be part of that happiness, part of yours and Mike's life, do you think that would be okay?"

I smile at him. "I am sure it will be, Phil," I turn and look around the room then I look up at him, frowning, "bit different to the last time we were in this position isn't it, Phil."

He laughs, "Much nicer dress," and I smile at him.

"Everything is as it should be," I need to let him know all is okay, he is forgiven, he looks at me, I can see Mike walking towards us.

"Forgiven and forgotten now then?" he asks, I take Mike's hand, I lean in and kiss Phil on the cheek.

As I pull away, I look at him and smile. "Forgiven and forgotten, Phil, now you need to find your woman," I pause, "she is out there somewhere and you know it, and whoever it is," I smile at him, "I want you to know, you don't need to seek my approval, you have it already," I laugh as his frown shows his confusion over my remark, then he smiles at me, the same Phil that I know so well, and I know I will be happy for him, and for Jo if that is what he wants.

The DJ announces our first two dances, as Mike takes my hand he guides me to the dance floor, I look at him, "Did you know Phil came to the church today?"

Mike smiles then nods his head, "As I turned to watch you walk down the aisle, I saw him, stood at the very back, and even if I didn't see him, I knew he would be there, I guess he needed to see you take your vows of your own free will," he smiles at me, "and before you ask, no I don't mind he was there, you are mine now, I know that and so does he and everyone else."

I lay my head on his shoulder as I hear the beginning of the music that was playing on the radio in his car on our first date 'It must be love' by Madness, this will be followed by our first romantic dance 'I want to wake up with you', as Mike holds me tight in his arms I look up and see the look of love in his eyes, I am glad we have no secrets, well only one.

The one thing Mike insists on keeping secret is the honeymoon, he won't let me know where we are going, he will only tell me it is hot and sunny, he adds that I will need beach clothes but I will also need a formal dress. I show him the dress I have picked out and he approves, but I am very confused, we go to the airport, we check in, I now know we are going to Egypt, I am a little bit disappointed if I am honest, it certainly would not be my first choice for a honeymoon, a normal holiday would be fine but not my actual honeymoon, but I don't say anything, I don't want to spoil our first real holiday together, so I sit back and enjoy the flight. Mike tells me a little bit about the hotel and the resort but tells me I must wait for the explanation of why I am taking a formal dress. He is being very mysterious.

On arrival I am shocked into silence as we are met by Caleb and a beautiful woman who I assume is Marla, Caleb is very pleased to see us both, kissing me then shaking Mike's hand like they are old friends, Marla and I just stand and watch them. Mike explains that they are also getting married and we are there as guests, Mike admits he heard my phone bleep and saw a text come in on my phone a while ago, he thought it would be from Stuart confirming pick up times for the cars or some other arrangement for the wedding, so he read it, it was Caleb telling me that Marla had made a full recovery and she was out of hospital, they had booked their wedding and Caleb wanted me to be there, Mike saw that the timings were perfect so he called Caleb, introduced himself, Caleb was delighted to hear from him. I am really looking forward to see him marry his sweetheart. Marla knows all about me and despite the fact everyone calls Mike Nike for the time we are there we have a great time I am surprised that we are only here for three days, and we are not staying at Caleb's family hotel but a larger hotel just a short drive away.

Mike pulls me to his arms, "I cannot share my honeymoon with anyone but you, we cruise to Cyprus tomorrow and spend the rest of the time there." I am so happy I think I might explode, he pulls me into his arms, "I remember you saying you had a wonderful experience a long time ago in Cyprus, and I intend to replace that memory with a new one." And he does. The honeymoon is perfect.

One year later

My first scan is due, I am nearly twelve weeks pregnant, I am so proud carrying my small bump, eating really healthily and feeling great. Mike and I are blissfully happy, he is now Inspector Simms, which he loves to remind me when I am on duty as it is protocol for me to address him as sir, he is still very naughty and will behave inappropriately whenever he knows or thinks that he won't get caught. I am still very happy in my job in the control room.

I am really excited for the scan, I have a small bump so some people notice, they are sworn to secrecy, Craig was the first to comment as I was unwell on day shift, but he kept it to himself and others have no idea yet, Mike is sat next to me in the waiting room when my name is called he jumps to his feet, Mrs Angela Simms, I will never tire of hearing that, I hear it called at work and I cannot help smiling, no Ms Staddon for me, Mike was absolutely insistent on that, and I take his name with pride, so when they call it at the hospital I get up, Mike almost runs down the corridor totally forgetting me. He makes me laugh out loud, the scan is very routine for the nurses but not for us, we ask for every scan we can, bless her, the nurse is very patient, it might be because Mike still has his uniform on that we get more time to look at the screen, she leaves the room then comes back with a chap who double checks, he looks at both of us, one at a time, I know what he is going to say, even before he says anything, "It is twins isn't it," I tell him.

Mike looks at me in amazement then at the stenographer who just nods his head, "Yes, definitely twins, I know you have asked to know the sex, it might be too early to tell but we shall see." He moves the screen round so we have a better view he frowns, "Well I am almost certain that even at this stage we can see one is a boy, although we cannot be 100% sure though, and as for the other one, well the other one is laying in a strange position, it is hiding, we cannot tell." Mike and I just look at each other, I can see the look of total amazement in his face, I burst into happy tears.

We get back into the car, Mike turns to me, "Twins," he smiles at me. "How could you possibly have known it was twins?"

I look at him and smile, "Oh, Mike, if I am completely honest, I knew when I met you."

He shakes his head, "Sometimes I have no idea what goes on in that beautiful head of yours," he replies.

He starts the engine. On the journey home we cannot help but keep looking at the scan, we chat excitedly, it is beautiful, we have had lots of copies made to give to the grandparents, one is pinned on the dashboard, I keep stroking my tummy and looking at the scan in absolute wonder, I cannot help but keep smiling. We pull up outside his parent's house, I go to open my door but Mike stops me.

"How did you know it was twins, Angie, there are no twins in our families, how could you possibly know?"

I look at him, "I don't think you will believe me if I told you."

I push the door open but he holds my arm, "I would still like to know."

I close the door, "Well, a few years ago…" but I don't get to finish, Margaret is at the door looking very excited.

"Come on, come on, don't sit there all day, come and tell us how it went."

I look at Mike, "Later, honey, you probably need to hear it when we are alone." I lean over and kiss him, his hand strokes my stomach, "I cannot believe that inside that tiny bump is our children, our two children," I look down, it does seem incredible.

I carry well I am totally enjoying being pregnant. Eventually people find out, but before they do, I take Helen to one side, swear her to secrecy then do the same with Phil, he is over the moon and I think he is happy that he has been told before everyone else, I am sat in the CID office when he comes through, Mike has said he thinks it is a nice idea to let him know before everyone else, his smile is immediate and genuine, "I am made up for your both," he sits down and takes my hand, "I hope I am always part of yours and Mike's life, Angie, I really hope I am."

I smile at him, "Might hold you to that when we need a babysitter."

He leans in closer, "I would consider that to be an honour," and the strange thing is, I know he means it. I tell Mike later and he says the same.

We leave it a few weeks later then when it becomes common knowledge I get spoiled even more at work, I don't have to make the tea so often but I still have to do the statements for CID, but I use this time to catch up with everyone. There is a new sergeant on the shift, Richard is really nice and friendly and will always make me a drink and stop for a chat. Helen is getting married in a few weeks and Mike and I are looking forward to the day. I spend many a lunch time going through books for wedding favours and I am so excited, she did ask me to be matron of honour, but I don't want my bump to take away the attention from her, and I also want to sit on the same table as Mike, I don't really know her family that well, Helen understands, the honour has now gone to her older sister which she is over the moon about, and she doesn't need to know she was second choice.

Marcia is now part-time but she still manages to keep up with all the gossip going on, I cannot wait to be on maternity so I can spend, more time with her, she calls me regularly but most of what she tells me I already know, like Julian, who is now on long-term sick leave, Jo still works and although I hear about her and Phil going out for lunches and being seen together I keep out of it, they seem to be happy to be seen as a couple now, Helen and I sometimes discuss it but both of us decide it is their business. Mike and I sometimes go out for lunch, it is lovely to be able to sit with him in a restaurant and no one knows that he is a police officer, the other uniform was too obvious, I love it when I hear people referring to Inspector Simms, I still get a kick out of hearing him being called that.

Judy cannot wait to be an Auntie, she spends lots of time with me, preparing the nursery and helping me get the house ready, we have really become much closer since we have both got married. I love being pregnant, despite having further scans they still cannot confirm the sex of the other baby, but we don't care. Everyone is overjoyed for us; we scour through baby books thinking of names, we are very happy. Mike is so attentive, he massages my feet and rubs my back, he reads the newspaper and the rugby scores to the bump, I try to tell him they might prefer music but he is adamant, his dad done the same when his mother was carrying him, I just let him get on with it. I work until I am eight months pregnant then I start to struggle, everything is an effort, I get tired so easily, it feels like my bump arrives everywhere several minutes before I do, everyone at work is so supportive and kind, Phil brings in little treats for me, fruit and healthy snacks, he sits with me chatting about the babies and how big they are, he is really interested, we talk about the birth and I admit to him I am really scared, he tells me it will all be okay, then he tells me he is applying to join the traffic division, he is really excited, but it won't be for a few months. Our relationship has changed, it is still a close friendship but much more natural now, when we talk we include the rest of the shift, it is general conversation and I feel so much more relaxed, he rubs my back for me but nothing more, but in fairness I suffer with shoulder pain so try and get anyone willing to massage my shoulders, this is not just kept to Phil, Gavin and Steve both get roped in much to the amusement of Mike, with Phil, I still talk about his plans but keep clear of relationships, I know he is seeing Jo and he doesn't seem to be such a flirt anymore with other women, he seems to have really calmed down, Helen said as much when I remarked to her, but I make no comment to him. Craig is really pleased that I am happy, Steve keeps coming up with crazy baby names and both Rex and Martin make sure I am fed well and that my car is always near to the door for me, Mike finds this very amusing, I think they are so lovely. I still love my job but as the pregnancy progresses I have had to give up night shift but I still am managing to cover shifts, I miss Mike when I am not on nights, that is when I loved it the most, I also miss cuddling up to Mike in bed, I miss our intimacy, although he is an attentive lover and fulfils my needs, it seems to me that I cannot get close enough to him, he is far too gentle with me and I miss the spontaneous physical side of lovemaking, I miss being able to do things I could do before, I cannot get into my car so as Mikes seats go back further I get to use his Maserati, but even then I struggle to reach the pedals and it is only a two-door.

My last day at work is very emotional, my whole desk is decorated with balloons and streamers, when the new shift come in to take over both Mike and I are presented with a huge amount of gifts and flowers, everyone we work with is there, I am very emotional and cannot stop crying. Craig laughs and Mike just shakes his head and smiles at me, everyone promises to keep in touch and say they will pop to see me at home, I am so overwhelmed by everything. Craig does a wonderful speech which makes me laugh until my sides ache, then he pulls me into a hug which makes me cry all over again, he then hands over to Mike.

"It is over to you now, mate," he says, "you need to control her now."

Mike shakes his head, "I would like to think I can, but I don't think it is possible." Everyone laughs and Steve and Phil help me down with all the parcels, unfortunately for Mike my car has been decorated with balloons and good luck banners, I know this has been done by Phil and Steve, everyone laughs out loud as I walk past my car and drive off in Mike's, I look at their surprised faces, laughing out loud with the thought that Mike will have to drive mine home later.

On his next day off Mike disappears with his dad leaving me to relax, I had a restless night so I lay happily on the sofa with a book and drift off to sleep, my ankles are huge, walking hurts, my back aches and I feel very emotional, so when he comes back with a huge smile on his face, I cannot help but smile too, the smile disappears very quickly as he explains, "I have sold the car," he announces proudly, "so now we can go shopping for a new one, when you have rested would you like to go looking."

He is so excited but I cannot believe him, his dad is stood next to him looking equally pleased, I look at Mike then at his dad, I look at his dad accusingly, I am so upset, I know I am going to cry, I cannot hold back my anger. "You let him do this!" I wail at him, "How could you, that car was his pride and joy, how could you make him sell it, why did you let him?"

I try to get up but fail miserably, I slump back in my seat.

Mike's dad holds his hands up, "Hey now, you need to calm down, Angie, no one made him do anything, love, he wanted to, he can hardly swan around in a sports car with two children in the back now can he, be reasonable."

But I don't feel reasonable, I burst into tears, I look at Mike, the tears streaming down my face, they both just stand looking at me, I know I must look a sight, my red face, runny nose, but I don't care, I sob my words out, "We went on our first date in that car," I sob, "you made love to me in that car, now you are getting rid of it."

Mike squats down in front of me, he takes my hand, "Come on, Angie, calm down, be reasonable, honey, Dad will fetch you a drink."

He sits at the side of me on the sofa, he places his hands on my tummy, his dad returns from the kitchen and is stood behind him, he passes me a glass, I ignore it. "Angie, maybe I should have discussed it with you first, but you know why we have to do it, our needs have changed, darling, I knew if I told you beforehand you wouldn't want to get rid of it."

I know I am being silly I sniff and I wipe my eyes, "But I love that car." I cannot help it the tears come again.

Mike speaks quietly, "We can go and buy the new one tomorrow if you want to, Angie, if you feel up to it, we don't have to go today, but I am sorry, it has to go," his voice is patient but firm, he reaches for the glass of water and hands it to me.

I wail back at him, "But we can keep it, Mike, we don't need the money, we have the patent money we can spend that on a new car," I wail again.

He is so patient, his voice very quiet, "I know that, Angie, but it isn't the money." Mike takes my hand, "It is about the car, that car was perfect when I was single, when it was just the two of us, we could swan around in it, it was perfect, but we have two new babies coming very soon, we need to move on, we are the same people, but our needs have changed. I don't need to make love to you in a fancy sports car, I don't want to be a sad old git swanning around in a sports car; I want to be a proud husband and father with twin car seats in the back of a practical car where all my family will be safe, do you understand?"

I know he is right, I drink some of my water then I smile at him through my tears. "Just one more drive, Mike, please just take me for one more drive."

He nods in agreement, looking at his dad he laughs, "I am going to need some help with this, Dad."

So they pull me up and with a lot of help from his dad we both load into the car, Mike stops outside a local shop to buy provisions, we drive out to the country and sit on the top of a hill, we look down on the lights of the town. Mike turns to me, "You know, Angie, I keep thinking about it, but I forget to ask you, you have yet to tell me how you knew it was twins, how could you have known something so incredible," he pulls me close, I lay my head on his shoulder as I explain about the tarot card reader, I tell him everything – the colour of my car, everything about Jason and the illness, the betrayal, the pocket watch, he doesn't say a word.

When I finish, he shakes his head, "And you have this CD at home?" he asks.

I nod, "Somewhere, I am not sure where but it is there."

He blows out a short whistle, "Wow, I would certainly like to hear that one day, that is incredible."

I snuggle back into him, "There was even some mention of a bath, a strange bath, and I remember when we went to the hotel on our first real date and I saw the bath, I felt a chill run down my back, it is incredible how some things she said have come true."

Mike pulls me close, "Let's dig it out and have a listen, sounds very interesting."

We watch the skyline until the day disappears and the black night sky appears, we sit eating our car picnic, the stars shining down on us, I lay in his arms and he holds me close, kissing me gently we say goodbye to his lovely sports car with the walnut trim and the tinted windows. As the night draws in he turns to me, "Okay now?" he asks.

I nod my head, "Yes, I am now, sorry I was so silly, everything just makes me so emotional, say sorry to your dad won't you?"

He nods, "It is okay, he understands." He starts the engine. "So, how do you feel about looking for a new car tomorrow then?" he asks.

I shake my head, "You choose, Mike, whatever you choose I will like, I know I will, I don't need to come with you do I?"

He shakes his head, "No, not if you don't want to, honey."

He drives us home and helps me out of the car, I cannot look back at the beautiful car. I know it has to go, I just hope it goes to someone who enjoys it as much as we did. The next day I have a huge smile on my face as Mike tells me his Uncle Dennis has bought the car, although it is his mum's brother and not his dad's, the car still gets to stay in the family.

The next few weeks drag by, in just a few days the babies are due I seem to be tired all the time, but I am pleased everything is ready. My ankles have totally disappeared and ben replaced by huge swollen ones that mean I am always uncomfortable. I just have the last minute finishing touches to do in the nursery, so before Mike leaves for work he sits with me for a while upstairs in the newly painted babies room, we talk about the twins and how we will be as parents, I tell him how scared I am of the birth and he hugs me and reassures me he will be there with me, holding my hand, when he leaves for work I continue to sit in the nursery, the house is nice and quiet the sun streaming through the window. I look out at the garden and watch the birds for a while, the car has now gone from the drive, every time I look at the garden, I can see into the garage window and it is the first thing I notice. I am so tired, so cranky and everything makes me cry, just stood in the beautiful nursery and the tears fill my eyes, Judy has made a fabulous job, Little Ma has made the curtains and everything is nearly ready, the largest of the spare rooms is now a lovely light yellow with moons and stars, the furniture has been delivered and Mike's dad has put them all together, the cots and pushchair have to stay at Mike's mums house as she is superstitious, both the mums are coming today to help me clear out the large wardrobe in the smaller spare room so all Mike's sports equipment can be stored there leaving the nursery floor clear. Mike is taking two weeks off to be with me after the babies are born then the mothers are coming, my mum coming for a week then Margaret coming to stay for a week after that, I know Little Ma won't be able to keep away, and with the shift all excited to see the new arrivals I know I will have plenty of visitors. Mike has a course coming up where he will be away for a whole week and I don't want to be on my own, so the parents are making all the plans for me, I am so happy and overwhelmed with their love and support, I have no idea how I was going to cope with two babies.

I am folding the tiny outfits in preparation, we still don't know what the sex of the second child is so we have a good mixture of yellow and neutrals just in case, Judy has bought a few pink items as she is convinced it is a girl. I feel huge, my legs are swollen, my stomach feels tight and uncomfortable.

It is warm, too warm, I have done a bit too much, I feel exhausted, I wish Mike was still here with me, I feel overly hot, so I lean against the wall to catch my breath. I look down at the box in front of me, it is my old treasures box ready to go into the attic space, as I lift out a pile of envelopes, old photos and other paperwork, a CD falls out, I immediately recognise it as being my tarot card reading, all those things the woman told me flashes back into my memory, the two marriages, the nursing of someone poorly, the red car, the pocket watch, the bath the flowers, the betrayal, the candle and the twins, I go all hot, I feel very giddy and I feel a strange sensation when I look down, my waters have broken. I stand for a few minutes just leaning against the wall, I call Mike but his phone is engaged, I want to cry with frustration, I send him a text message, I ring my mum first, she is at Judy's, then I ring Margaret, both say they are on their way, I know they will be here within minutes of me calling them, I sit down on the top of the stairs not trusting myself to get down on my own. When they arrive, Margaret is trying to find Mike's number in my phone and failing. Despite being in pain I laugh and tell her to look under Theone. As I am getting into the car Mike calls, he makes me laugh as he is on a blue light run to the hospital and I am travelling in his mum's car at normal speed. He gets there way before me and is waiting impatiently, he nags his mum about her driving and as we enter the hospital he is still giving her a hard time, I hold his hand as we go together to the delivery ward.

Seven hours later our beautiful son Benjamin and our beautiful daughter Ruby enter our lives. Mike and the grandfathers are outside as there are initial complications, Mike doesn't cope too well when he sees me getting distressed so, on his mother's orders he has to wait outside, I prefer it that way, I don't want him to see me in such agony. Both mums are with me, Judy is in the background; they are just wonderful, they know exactly what to do and what to say to help me, they are just what I need, both calm and in control. After initial complications and a lot of gas and air, finally the decision is made that I have to have a caesarean. I am surprisingly calm, I just want my babies safe, my mum holds my hand as the screen is put in place and Margaret goes to let Mike know, I still don't want him with me, he understands and is happy to wait, it might seem selfish but I don't want him to see me all upset and in agony, I just need my mum, Judy and Margaret. The midwife is amazing, as she holds my tiny son to my chest I feel a rush of love for him, I am totally numb and just have to lie there and wait for my darling daughter to be placed next to my son. I just hold them both and cry with absolute joy.

Afterwards, when it is just us together with the babies Mike holds me in his arms, he holds me so close, I take a deep breath and smell his aftershave, the best smell in the world, I love everything about this man.

"You have made me the proudest man in the world," he whispers stroking my head, "I love you so much, I cannot tell you just how much you mean to me, I have everything I will ever want in this room, my darling wife and my beautiful children."

I watch as he takes them from me and lies them both gently in the crib next to me, he turns and faces me, sitting on the bed and half lying next to me, he strokes my cheek gently and whispers, "Probably the timing is not great but I cannot wait to be close to you again, is it wrong for me to say that I have missed your beautiful body so much I long to make love to you," he whispers.

I groan back at him, "Me too, I have missed you so much."

He kisses me passionately his lips entwining with mine, I feel a tremor go through my whole body, the parts of my body that are not numb respond to him, remembering his touch, I close my eyes and see the flash of lights exploding in my head, my heart is hammering, despite just having given birth my aching exhausted body starts to respond to him.

I always wanted fireworks, when I dreamed of love that's how I imagined it should be I always wondered.

Is anyone listening?

And now I think _ Yes I think they probably were.